STEPHEN JONES lives in London [...] [...] [...]ee
World Fantasy Awards, four Horror W[...]
Awards and three International Horror Guild Awards as [...] [...] [...]
eighteen-times recipient of the British Fantasy Award and a Hugo Award
nominee. A former television producer/director and genre movie publicist
and consultant (the first three *Hellraiser* movies, *Night Life, Nightbreed,
Split Second, Mind Ripper, Last Gasp* etc.), he is the co-editor of *Horror:
100 Best Books, Horror: Another 100 Best Books, The Best Horror from
Fantasy Tales, Gaslight & Ghosts, Now We Are Sick, H. P. Lovecraft's
Book of Horror, The Anthology of Fantasy & the Supernatural, Secret
City: Strange Tales of London, Great Ghost Stories, Tales to Freeze the
Blood: More Great Ghost Stories* and the *Dark Terrors, Dark Voices* and
Fantasy Tales series. He has written *Coraline: A Visual Companion,
Stardust: The Visual Companion, Creepshows: The Illustrated Stephen
King Movie Guide, The Essential Monster Movie Guide, The Illustrated
Vampire Movie Guide, The Illustrated Dinosaur Movie Guide, The
Illustrated Frankenstein Movie Guide* and *The Illustrated Werewolf
Movie Guide*, and compiled *The Mammoth Book of Best New Horror*
series, *The Mammoth Book of Terror, The Mammoth Book of Vampires,
The Mammoth Book of Zombies, The Mammoth Book of Werewolves,
The Mammoth Book of Frankenstein, The Mammoth Book of Dracula,
The Mammoth Book of Vampire Stories By Women, The Mammoth
Book of New Terror, The Mammoth Book of Monsters, Shadows Over
Innsmouth, Weird Shadows Over Innsmouth, Dark Detectives, Dancing
with the Dark, Dark of the Night, White of the Moon, Keep Out the
Night, By Moonlight Only, Don't Turn Out the Light, H. P. Lovecraft's
Book of the Supernatural, Travellers in Darkness, Summer Chills,
Exorcisms and Ecstasies* by Karl Edward Wagner, *The Vampire Stories
of R. Chetwynd-Hayes, Phantoms and Fiends and Frights and Fancies* by
R. Chetwynd-Hayes, *James Herbert: By Horror Haunted, Basil Copper:
A Life in Books, Necronomicon: The Best Weird Tales of H. P. Lovecraft,
The Complete Chronicles of Conan* and *Conan's Brethren* by Robert E.
Howard, *The Emperor of Dreams: The Lost Worlds of Clark Ashton
Smith, Sea-Kings of Mars and Otherworldly Stories* by Leigh Brackett,
The Mark of the Beast and Other Fantastical Tales by Rudyard Kipling,
*Clive Barker's A–Z of Horror, Clive Barker's Shadows in Eden, Clive
Barker's The Nightbreed Chronicles* and the *Hellraiser Chronicles*. A
Guest of Honour at the 2002 World Fantasy Convention in Minneapolis,
Minnesota, and the 2004 World Horror Convention in Phoenix, Ar-
izona, he has been a guest lecturer at UCLA in California and London's
Kingston University and St. Mary's University College. You can visit his
website at *www.stephenjoneseditor.com*

The Mammoth Book of

BEST NEW
HORROR

VOLUME TWENTY

Edited and with an Introduction by
STEPHEN JONES

RUNNING PRESS
PHILADELPHIA · LONDON

Constable & Robinson Ltd
3 The Lanchesters
162 Fulham Palace Road
London W6 9ER
www.constablerobinson.com

First published in the UK by Robinson,
an imprint of Constable & Robinson, 2009

A copy of the British Library Cataloguing in Publication
Data is available from the British Library

UK ISBN 978-1-84529-932-3

1 3 5 7 9 10 8 6 4 2

First published in the United States in 2009 by Running Press Book Publishers

9 8 7 6 5 4 3 2 1
Digit on the right indicates the number of this printing

US Library of Congress number: 2008944135
US ISBN 978-0-7624-3727-6

Running Press Book Publishers
2300 Chestnut Street
Philadelphia, PA 19103-4371

Visit us on the web!
www.runningpress.com

Printed and bound in the EU

CONTENTS

ACKNOWLEDGMENTS

I would like to thank David Barraclough, Kim Newman, Mandy Slater, Amanda Foubister, Rodger Turner and Wayne MacLaurin (*www.sfsite.com*), Hugh Lamb, Peter Crowther, Gordon Van Gelder, Barbara Roden, Andrew I. Porter, Johnny Mains, Robert T. Garcia, Mark Samuels, Simon Clark, David J. Schow, Tina Jens and, especially, Duncan Proudfoot, Pete Duncan and Dorothy Lumley for all their help and support. Special thanks are also due to *Locus, Variety, Ansible* and all the other sources that were used for reference in the Introduction and the Necrology.

2008. Originally published in *Shades of Darkness*. Reprinted by permission of the author.

THE LONG WAY copyright © Ramsey Campbell 2008. Originally published in *The Long Way*. Reprinted by permission of the author.

THE PILE copyright © Michael Bishop 2008. Originally published on *Subterranean*, Winter 2008. Reprinted by permission of the author.

UNDER FOG copyright © Tanith Lee 2008. Originally published as "Under Fog (The Wreckers)" in *Subterfuge*. Reprinted by permission of the author.

ARKANGEL copyright © Christopher Fowler 2008. Originally published on *Exotic Gothic 2: New Tales of Taboo*. Reprinted by permission of the author.

THE CAMPING WAINWRIGHTS copyright © Ian R. MacLeod 2008. Originally published in *PostScripts* Number 17, Winter 2008. Reprinted by permission of the author.

A DONKEY AT THE MYSTERIES copyright © Reggie Oliver 2008. Originally published on *Exotic Gothic 2: New Tales of Taboo*. Reprinted by permission of the author.

THE ORAM COUNTY WHOOSIT copyright © Steve Duffy 2008. Originally published in *Shades of Darkness*. Reprinted by permission of the author.

THE *NEW YORK TIMES* AT SPECIAL BARGAIN RATES copyright © Stephen King 2008. Originally published in *The Magazine of Fantasy & Science Fiction*, October/November 2008 and *Just After Sunset: Stories*. Reprinted by permission of the author.

OUR MAN IN THE SUDAN copyright © Sarah Pinborough 2008. Originally published in *The Second Humdrumming Book of Horror Stories*. Reprinted by permission of the author.

"DESTINATION NIHIL" BY EDMUND BERTRAND copyright © Mark Samuels 2008. Originally published in *PS Showcase #4: Glyphotec & Other Macabre Processes*. Reprinted by permission of the author.

THE OVERSEER copyright © Albert E. Cowdrey 2008. Originally published in *The Magazine of Fantasy & Science Fiction*, March 2008. Reprinted by permission of the author.

THE BEGINNINGS OF SORROW copyright © Pinckney Benedict 2008. Originally published in *Sonora Review* No. 54, November 2008. Reprinted by permission of the author.

THE PLACE OF WAITING copyright © Brian Lumley 2008.

In memory of old friends
Forrest J Ackerman
and
Christopher Wicking
plus
Fantasy Centre
London's last genre used bookstore

INTRODUCTION

Horror in 2008

FOLLOWING THE SURPRISE resignation of Jane Friedman, CEO of HarperCollins US, in June, executive editor of Children's Books Ruth Katcher was fired after fifteen years with the company, and children's executive editor Melanie Donovan was also let go in apparent cost-cutting measures. Several other editors and staff also lost their jobs.

Having lost its Arts Council grant in January, British publisher Dedalus Books was in danger of having to close down after twenty-five years. The imprint mostly specialized in translations, including genre fiction.

After twenty-nine years, the British weekly trade magazine *Publishing News* produced its final issue in July. Loss of advertising revenue was blamed.

Bertelsmann sold its struggling North American Direct Group, which included the Science Fiction Book Club, to a private firm, and all the assets of the Greenwood Publishing Group were transferred to a California company. As a result, Greenwood closed its UK office in early December.

With the global economic slowdown starting to bite, December 3 became "Black Wednesday" in the New York publishing industry when the mighty Random House, Houghton Mifflin Harcourt and Simon & Schuster all announced major firings, layoffs and restructuring of staff.

Casualties included Irwyn Applebaum, president and publisher of the Bantam Dell group, who left after twenty-five years with the company.

The following week Macmillan fired sixty-four people (4% of the company's US workforce), while several other imprints announced pay and hiring freezes.

In February, a survey of 3,000 people discovered that more than half of Britons thought that Sherlock Holmes was a real person. Probably even more worryingly, 47% of people believed that Richard the Lionheart was not real, almost 25% didn't believe that Winston Churchill ever existed, and 3% were convinced that Charles Dickens was a fictional character.

This perhaps comes as no surprise when, the previous month, Woolworths announced that it was launching a range of bedroom furniture online for young girls called "Lolita". When it was pointed out that this was maybe not the most appropriate name, a spokesman for the soon-to-be-defunct British retail chain admitted that nobody at the company, or from the website responsible, had actually heard of Vladimir Nabokov's 1955 novel, Stanley Kubrick's 1962 movie adaptation, or even the 1997 remake.

A study in March from the National Foundation for Educational Research discovered that comics and celebrity magazines have overtaken fiction books as children's favourite reading matter in the UK.

It did not help that, from September, English Literature A-level students could study books selected by teachers rather than compulsory set texts. Critics of the move said that it was another example of exams being "dumbed down" in Britain.

That same month, compilers of Collins' English dictionaries announced that they would have to cut certain obscure words for the forthcoming edition because there was not enough space for newer words. With the help of celebrity supporters and a public vote, words could be saved if it could be proved that they were still in popular usage. Among the words threatened with eradication were "Caliginosity" (darkness or dimness), "Exuviate" (to shed, skin or similar outer covering), "Fatidical" (prophetic), "Malison" (a curse), "Olid" (foul-smelling), "Perlapt" (a charm or amulet) and "Vaticinate" (to foretell or prophesize).

When NASA's Phoenix space probe landed on the surface of Mars on May 25, it was carrying a DVD compiled by the Planetary Society of the United States containing "personal messages from visionaries of our own time to future visitors or settlers on Mars". Made from a special form of silica glass designed to last for 500 years, the disc contained messages "from beyond the grave" by Arthur C. Clarke and US astronomer Carl Sagan, along with books and audios that helped shaped mankind's impression of the Red Planet. These included works by Edgar Rice Burroughs and Leigh Brackett, a "Flash Gordon" story, and Orson Welles' 1938 radio broadcast of *War of the Worlds*.

October 26 was designated "World Zombie Day", to commemorate the 40th anniversary of George Romero's *Night of the Living Dead*. People dressed up as the walking dead in cities all over the world, with many using the event to raise money for charity.

In January, the Vatican condemned the *Harry Potter* books in its official newspaper, *L'Osservatore Romano*. The article described the boy wizard as "the wrong kind of hero".

J. K. Rowling appeared in a New York court in April in an attempt to prevent the publication of RDR Books' *The Harry Potter Lexicon*, which the author described as constituting "the wholesale theft of seventeen years of my hard work". She went on to claim that Steve Vander Ark's book of his fan website had "decimated my creative work over the last month".

Five months later, a US judge ruled that the *Lexicon* was banned because of copyright infringement as the book appropriated "too much of Rowling's creative work for its purposes as a reference guide", and that the publisher "had failed to establish an affirmative defence of fair use". Because *The Harry Potter Lexicon* had not yet been published, Warner Bros. (which owns the property rights to the *Potter* books) and Rowling were awarded statutory damages, which amounted to $6,750.

"I don't feel bad about the decision," said Vander Ark, who announced that he was writing a new book, *In Search of Harry Potter*, about real-life inspirations for locations in Rowling's series.

Meanwhile, independent imprint RDR Books announced that, despite the ruling, it was going ahead with plans to publish a rewritten version of Ark's *Lexicon* early in 2009.

Wealthy fans were reportedly rushing to stay in the same suite at Edinburgh's luxurious Balmoral Hotel where J. K. Rowling completed *Harry Potter and the Deathly Hallows*. Renamed in the author's honour and containing a marble bust that she signed, the room cost almost £1,000 per night.

In July, a signed set of all seven first edition *Harry Potter* books sold at auction in the UK for £17,800.

To celebrate National Year of Reading, in August Waterstones issued the postcard collection *What's Your Story?*, which included a 800-word *Harry Potter* prequel by Rowling featuring Harry's father James and Sirius Black in the 1970s. It became the fastest-selling short story collection of all time, with 10,000 copies sold on its first day of release.

Rowling's original hand-written postcard was sold for £25,000

(£31.25 per word) to a mystery bidder at a charity auction to benefit English PEN and Dyslexia Action.

Originally produced as an extremely limited, hand-crafted, illustrated edition of seven copies (one of which sold at Sotheby's in December 2007 for £1.95 million), Rowling's book of spoof fairy tales, *Beedle the Bard*, was issued commercially in time for the Christmas market. With a print run of eight million copies worldwide, the author donated a percentage earned from each copy to her special charity, Children's Voice.

J. K. Rowling topped *Forbes* magazine's list of the world's richest celebrities, with her 2007 earnings estimated at $300 million. Stephen King was at #3 with $45 million and Dean Koontz tied at #6 with $25 million.

Stephen King's *Duma Key* was about a crippled millionaire living in a house situated on a remote Florida island, who discovered that his prognosticate drawings had revived a malignant evil power. The book had a first US printing of 1.5 million copies.

In the UK, publisher Hodder & Stoughton held a competition for the public to design an advertising poster for the film, which the author himself judged.

Just After Sunset: Stories was King's first collection since 2002. It contained thirteen tales, including the previously uncollected "The Cat from Hell" and an original Lovecraftian tale written for the volume, plus an Introduction and story notes by the author. The American "collector's set" included a bound-in DVD of the animated twenty-five episode webseries *N*, which appeared online during the summer.

Thirty-four-year-old Stephenie Meyer, author of the bestselling "Twilight Saga" series was named one of *Time* magazine's "100 Most Influential People of 2008". The author had more than fifty million books in print worldwide, including a new adult SF/horror novel, *The Host*, which went straight to #1 in the US.

Little, Brown announced a 3.7 million-copy first printing for Meyer's *Breaking Dawn*, the fourth and possibly final volume in her young adult vampire series. When an unfinished draft of a fifth novel, *Midnight Sun*, was leaked on the Internet, the author ceased work "indefinitely" on the book.

According to Nielsen Bookscan, Meyer's "Twilight" books took four of the top six slots (including #1 and #2) in the top fifty bestselling books in the US in 2008. Depressingly, the author's titles were also at #13, #15, #24, #30 and #42. By the end of the year there were around thirty million copies of the books in print in the US alone.

Set thirty-five years after *The Witches of Eastwick*, John Updike's belated sequel to his 1984 novel, *The Widows of Eastwick*, found the three ageing witches returning to the eponymous Rhode Island town for the summer and taking stock of their lives.

Dean Koontz's *Odd Hours* was the fourth book in the "Odd Thomas" series. It debuted at #1 on the *Publishers Weekly* bestseller list with 600,000 copies in print. To promote the book online, Bantam Books produced a four-part film about the character, *Odd Passenger*, created by Jack Placione, Jr and Jerry White.

A heart transplant patient was pursued by the organ's original owner in Koontz's *Your Heart Belongs to Me*.

Fifty-nine-year-old Terry Pratchett, who revealed at the end of 2007 that he had a rare form of early-onset Alzheimer's disease, gave £500,000 ($1 million) to the Alzheimer's Research Trust charity in March, as well as taking on the role of a spokesperson for Alzheimer's research. The author's bestselling "Discworld" series celebrated its twenty-fifth anniversary in 2008.

Jim Butcher reached the #1 slot in America for the first time with his tenth "Dresden Files" novel, *Small Favor*, in which wizard Harry Dresden found himself in a supernatural battle, with the fate of the world as the prize.

Supposedly sealed for 125 years, Dan Simmons had fun playing literary games with his hefty novel *Drood*. It was a murder mystery told in the first person, in which writer Wilkie Collins teamed up with his former friend Charles Dickens to pursue the eponymous spectral figure through the slums, sewers and catacombs of Victorian London.

Repairman Jack was on the trail of a legendary Japanese sword in F. Paul Wilson's *By the Sword*. There was also a limited edition from Gauntlet Press.

Inaccurately described as "Lovecraft meets *Blade Runner*", Gene Wolfe's novel *An Evil Guest* was set in the future.

In John Farris' *Avenging Fury*, which concluded the author's epic four-book series that began with *The Fury*, psychic Eden Waring's *doppelgänger* Gwen had to travel back through time to the 1920s to prevent an ancient evil from being resurrected.

Swedish author John Ajvide Lindqvist followed up his acclaimed vampire novel *Let the Right One In* with *Handling the Undead*, in which the dead of Stockholm just wanted to go home.

New York City medical examiner Dr Laurie Montgomery and her husband Dr Jack Stapleton went to the aid of an idealistic medical student who had become aware of a series of unexplained deaths in overseas hospitals in Robin Cook's latest thriller, *Foreign Body*.

Although she died in 1986 at the age of 63, V. C. Andrews had the first in a "new" Gothic series published in 2008. However, *Delia's Crossing* was most probably written by a pseudonymous Andrew Niederman. Also published under the late author's by-line was *Secrets in the Shadows*, a sequel to *Secrets in the Attic*.

Button, Button: Uncanny Stories collected eleven reprint stories and a poem by Richard Matheson. The cover trumpeted a forthcoming movie version of the title story starring Cameron Diaz.

ER doctor Marie Laveau, the descendant of New Orleans' famous voodoo queen Marie Laveau, was on the trail of an African vampire ("wazimamoto") in *Yellow Moon*, the second volume in Jewell Parker Rhodes' trilogy that began with *Voodoo Season*.

In Britain, Virgin Books launched a stylish new horror list with Stephen Gregory's psychological suspense novel, *The Perils & Dangers of This Night*, plus mass-market reprints of *The Grin of the Dark* by Ramsey Campbell, *Teatro Grottesco* by Thomas Ligotti, *The Unblemished* by Conrad Williams and *Banquet for the Damned* by series editor Adam L. G. Nevill.

A Glimpse Into the Abyss was a paperback sampler of Virgin's horror list that included excerpts from the books by Ligotti, Campbell and Williams.

Dorchester's Leisure Books imprint continued to churn out mass-market paperback originals. The demolition of an old church revealed an object of great power in Michael Laimo's *Fires Rising*, while more ancient artefacts unleashed evil on a small Maine town in Sarah Pinborough's *Tower Hill*.

A great evil waited beneath a New York building in Edward Lee's *Brides of the Impaler*.

A woman tried to hide her psychic ability in Deborah LeBlanc's *The Water Witch*, and a girl with telekinetic powers was held prisoner in a research facility in *The Reach* by Nate Kenyon.

Bryan Smith's *Queen of Blood* was a sequel to the author's *House of Blood*, while Mary SanGiovanni's *Found You* was a sequel to *The Hollower*.

Old Flames collected two novellas (one original) by Jack Ketchum, while Gary A. Braunbeck's serial killer novel *Coffin Country* was a prologue to the author's "Cedar Hill" cycle and also reprinted two stories from the same series.

Ghost Walk was a Halloween novel by Brian Keene, in which a rookie reporter and an Amish sorcerer were forced to confront the darkness that existed in LeHorn's Hollow, while a werewolf epidemic menaced a small Californian town in *Ravenous* by Ray Garton.

Reprint titles from Leisure included John Everson's Bram Stoker Award-winning *Covenant*, Brian Keene's *Dark Hollow* (aka *The Rutting Season*), Gord Rollo's *The Jigsaw Man*, a "definitive" edition of Robert Dunbar's *The Pines* and the late Richard Laymon's *Cuts* and *Beware*.

A reissue of Laymon's 1981 novel *The Woods Are Dark* restored almost fifty pages of previously-deleted material, and Thomas Tessier's 1979 werewolf novel *The Nightwalker* included the reprint novella "The Dreams of Dr Ladybank", a new Introduction by Jack Ketchum, and an Afterword by the author.

Strangely credited to "William Heaney" on the UK Gollancz edition entitled *Memoirs of a Master Forger*, Graham Joyce was properly credited as the author on the American Night Shade printing, confusingly retitled *How to Make Friends with Demons*. Whatever the title, the genre-bending novel was about a bookseller of fake first editions who believed he could see demons.

Steve Rasnic Tem and Melanie Tem expanded their World Fantasy Award-winning novella *The Man on the Ceiling* into a novel for Wizards of the Coast's "Discoveries" imprint. However, after publishing only seven titles in 2008, the adult fiction imprint was cancelled when the parent company decided to refocus on core brands.

I, Zombie by Al Ewing was the latest volume in Abaddon Books' *Tomes of the Dead* series.

Unmarked Graves was more grue from Shaun Hutson featuring zombies, and zombies invaded New York in Christopher Golden's *Soulless*.

Following her mother's brutal murder, a woman at the centre of an ancient conspiracy discovered a secret world below London's Underground system in *Mind the Gap*, the first volume in a new supernatural series by Christopher Golden and Tim Lebbon.

Graham Masterton's *The Painted Man* was the author's second novel about "Sissy Sawyer", while music opened up a composer's mind in the same author's *Ghost Music*.

Vincent Van Gogh was among the characters that turned up in Simon Clark's supernatural mystery, *The Midnight Man*. The author's other novel of the year was *Vengeance Child*.

William Hope Hodgson's psychic detective Thomas Carnacki, the

Ghost-Finder, came to the aid of Sherlock Holmes, who was suffering from amnesia, in *The Shadow of Reichenbach Falls* by John R. King (aka J. Robert King).

Author Bram Stoker became a suspect in the Ripper murders in *The Dracula Dossier* by James Reese, while an immortal warrior was sent to Victorian London to stop Jack in *Night Falls Darkly*, the first in the "Shadow Guard" series by Kim Lenox.

Paranormal psychologist Gillian Key encountered Jack the Ripper in *Key to Conspiracy* and the Phantom of the Opera in *Key to Redemption*, the second and third books in the series by Talia Gryphon.

Night Child by newcomer Jes Battis was the first in a series about the OSI – Occult Special Investigations – in which urban forensic investigator Tess Corday became involved with vampires, demons and other supernatural creatures.

Supernatural investigator Quincey Morris and his partner Libby Chastain attempted to banish an ancient curse in *Black Magic Woman*, the first in a series by Justin Gustainis. It was followed by *Evil Ways*, in which the pair investigated the murders of white witches.

The Outlaw Demon Wails (aka *Where Demons Dare*) was the sixth volume in "The Hollows" series by Kim Harrison (Dawn Cook), in which witchy private investigator Rachel Morgan was menaced by an escaped demon at Halloween. Although intended to be the final book in the series, it wasn't.

A man could hear the final thoughts of the dying in Jan Burke's *The Messenger*, while a clairvoyant woman was invited to join a group of demon hunters in *The Exorsistah* by Claudia Mair Burney.

The Unnatural Inquirer was the eighth volume in Simon R. Green's "Nightside" series, in which a tabloid newspaper reporter went looking for proof of life after death.

Solaris reissued more of the author's "Nightside" novels in the omnibus volumes *Into the Nightside*, *Haunting the Nightside* and *The Dark Heart of the Nightside*.

Fleeing for her life, Destiny McCree teamed up with a master thief whose powers matched her own in Keri Arthur's *Destiny Kills*.

A British Civil Service clerk found himself fighting against the forces of evil in *The Domino Men* by Jonathan Barnes, and a group of Texas teens were infected by strange cave water in *River Runs Red* by Jeffrey J. (Jeff) Mariotte.

The Fabric of Sin was the ninth book about Merrily Watkins by Phil Rickman, while *Blood Colony* was the latest entry in the "Black Immortals" series by Tananarive Due.

Psychic twins abducted children for bizarre experiments in Cameron Cruise's paranormal thriller *Dark Matters*, and an unearthed plane from World War II revealed dark secrets in the thriller *Crucified* by Michael Slade (Jay Clarke and Rebecca Clarke).

Visitors to modern-day Greece fell foul of an ancient mythological cult in David Angsten's supernatural thriller *Night of the Furies*, inspired by *The Bacchae* of Euripides.

A Native American spirit menaced Underground Seattle in Kat Richardson's *Underground*, the third book in the "Greywalker" series featuring supernaturally-tinged investigator Harper Blaine.

Neuropath by [R.] Scott Bakker was a high-tech horror thriller about a serial killer scientist who could control human emotions.

A mysterious pathogen transformed people into psychotic killers in *Contagious*, Scott Sigler's sequel to *Infected*, and mutant militia invaded a small town in *Afraid* by Jack Kilborn (J.A. Konrath).

Strange things started happening in a former high school in Bentley Little's *The Academy*, and an office building fed on fear in Gary Frank's *Institutional Memory*.

When offered a deal that seemed too good to be true, a Boston District Attorney uncovered the malignant evil that possessed a hospital treating his young daughter in Alexandra Sokoloff's *The Price*.

In Larissa Ione's *Pleasure Unbound*, a slayer had his life saved in the Underworld General Hospital staffed by demons. It was the first volume in the "Demonica" series.

In the cursed New England town of Raine's Landing, the descendants of the original Salem witches found themselves confronting an ancient god that fed on blood and terror in *Dark Rain* by Tony Richards.

The residents of the small Pennsylvania town of Pine Deep found their Halloween Festival beset by a monstrous evil in *Bad Moon Rising* by Jonathan Maberry.

The Hollow and *The Pagan Stone* were the second and third volumes in Nora Roberts' "The Sign of the Seven" trilogy, in which a blood oath brought evil every seven years to the idyllic town of Hawkins Hollow.

Lilith Saintcrow's *Night Shift* introduced renegade exorcist Jill Kismet, who battled the hellbreed and the humans who worked with them. It was followed by *Hunter's Prayer*.

Half-demon tabloid journalist Hope Adams infiltrated a gang of young supernaturals and investigated a murder with necromancer homicide detective John Findlay in Kelley Armstrong's *Personal*

Demon and *Living with the Dead*, the eighth and ninth books in the "The Otherworld" series. The Canadian author also had a new short story in the second issue of Bantam Dell Publishing's *Spectra Pulse* magazine.

A demon preyed on refugees of Hurricane Katrina in Kassandra Sims' paranormal romance *Hellbent & Heartfirst*.

Ghost of a Chance was the first in a series about ghost-hunter and house exorcist Karma Marx by Kate Marsh (aka Katie MacAlister and Katie Maxwell).

Terri Garey's *A Match Made in Hell* was a humorous sequel to *Dead Girls Are Easy*. It once again featured vintage clothing store owner Nicki Styx, who could see dead people.

Devil May Ride by Wendy Roberts was the second in the "Ghost Dusters" series, about a crime scene cleaner who could see ghosts.

Ghost-hunting psychic M. J. Holliday and her team investigated an attack by the legendary "Hatchet Jack" at an exclusive private school in Victoria Laurie's *Demons Are a Ghoul's Best Friend*, the second in a series.

In the thirteenth volume of Nancy Atherton's cosy mystery series, over-protective mother Lori Shepard and her ghostly aunt uncovered a local scandal in *Aunt Dimity: Vampire Hunter*.

Damien and *Noah* were the fourth and fifth volumes in the "Nightwalkers" series by Jacquelyn Frank.

Jamie Leigh Hansen's *Cursed* was a sequel to *Betrayed* and again featured fallen angels and demonic forces, while *House of Cards*, the second volume in C. E. Murphy's "The Negotiator/Old Races" series, found lawyer Margrit Knight once more involved with vampires, dragons and gargoyles.

Predatory Game was the sixth volume in Christine Feehan's "GhostWalkers" series, while *Dark Curse* was the latest title in the same author's "Carpathian" books.

A housewife discovered that her suburban life was a demonic illusion in *Bedlam, Bath and Beyond* by J. R. Ward (Jessica Bird). *Lover Enshrined* was the sixth volume in the same author's "Black Dagger Brotherhood" vampire romance series.

Laurell K. Hamilton's sixteenth novel in the ridiculously popular "Anita Blake" series, *Blood Noir*, had the vampire-hunter doing a favour for her werewolf lover and ending up involved in a plot to overthrow the vampire hierarchy. After four printings, 246,500 copies were in circulation.

While spying on the court of the Czar in early eighteenth-century

Russia, Chelsea Quinn Yarbro's grand vampire Count Saint-Germain discovered that someone was impersonating him in *A Dangerous Climate*, the twenty-first volume in the series.

From Elder Signs Press, *Saint-Germain: Memoirs* collected five stories (two original) along with an Introduction by Sharon Russell and an Afterword by the author.

Lynsay Sands' *The Accidental Vampire*, *Vampires Are Forever* and *Vampire Interrupted* continued the paranormal comedy/romance series about members of the Argeneau family of vampires, who were actually immortal Atlanteans. The novels were released over three successive months. *The Rogue Hunter* was the first in a new spin-off series from the same author.

L. A. Banks' *The Darkness*, a new novel in the author's "Vampire Huntress Legends" series, included a guide for reading groups. From the same prolific writer (real name Leslie Esdaile Banks), *Bad Blood* and *Bite the Bullet* were the first two volumes in the "Crimson Moon" series, about Special Ops soldier in paranormal activity Sasha Trudeau and her team of werewolf attack survivors.

Mike Resnick's *Stalking the Vampire*, a belated follow-up to his 1987 novel *Stalking the Unicorn*, once again featured private investigator John Justin Mallory.

Written by original "Scream Queen" Adrienne Barbeau (John Carpenter's *The Fog*) and Michael Scott, *Vampires of Hollywood* was a murder mystery set in a studio run by undead producer/actress Ovsanna Moore.

A link between a current series of killings and a murder in the 1860s lead an archaeologist to Dracula himself in Lee Hunt's *The Vampire of New York*. Dracula also turned up in *Midnight's Daughter*, the first in a new paranormal romance series by Karen Chance.

Dark Wars: The Tale of Meiji Dracula was a translation of the 2004 book *Meiji Dorakyura Den* by Hideyuki Kikuchi, which placed Dracula in 1880 Japan.

The Last Vampire and *The Vampire Agent* by Patricia Rosemoor and Marc Paoletti were the first two titles in a new series, "Annals of Alchemy and Blood", involving an escaped vampire and super-soldiers created from the DNA of an ancient mummy.

A woman became involved with a New Orleans vampire musician in *I Want You to Want Me* by Kathy Love, while another fell in love with a New Orleans vampire hunter in Heather Graham's *Blood Red*. From the same author, *Deadly Night* was the first in a new series about a pair of brothers who inherited a haunted New Orleans plantation.

1920s New York was the setting for Susan Krinard's vampire romance *Dark of the Moon*, while *Come the Night* was a werewolf romance from the same author.

Police investigator Laura Caxton confronted her undead mentor in David Wellington's *Vampire Zero*.

A woman became a vampire to battle the undead in *The Chosen Sin* by Anya Bast, a nineteeth-century English witch teamed up with a band of vampire warriors to fight evil in Jenna Maclaine's *Wages of Sin*, and a hunter was after a vampire enforcer in Jocelynn Drake's *Nightwalker*, the first in yet another series.

Sam Stone's first novel, *Gabriele Caccini* was reissued in a revised "author's preferred edition" by The House of Murky Depths under the title *Killing Kiss*.

The Ravening by Dawn Thompson was another volume in the "Blood Moon" historical vampire series, and a telepath fell in love with a vampire prince in the historical vampire romance *Under the Blood Red Moon* by Mina Hepsen (Hande Zapsu).

Book publicist Chris Rountree's *Necking* was about a book publicist whose paranormal authors were really vampires.

A female con artist helped vampires save their radio station in Jeri Smith-Ready's *Wicked Game*, while a woman discovered her date was a vampire in *One Bite with a Stranger* by Christine Warren.

A psychic vampire who was a ghost tour guide was the main protagonist of Nancy Haddock's paranormal mystery *La Vida Vampire*.

Hungers of the Heart was the latest title in Jenna Black's "Guardians of the Night" series, while *The Devil You Know* was the second volume in the author's series featuring exorcist Morgan Kingsley. It was followed by *The Devil's Due*.

The Undead Next Door was part of Kerrelyn Sparks' "Love at Stake" series. A Texas schoolteacher's encounter with an undead Parisian fashion designer put her life in danger. It was followed by *All I Want for Christmas is a Vampire*, in which a woman needed to prove the undead existed.

And still they churned them out. A harpy met the vampire of her dreams in *One Bite Stand* by Nina Bangs, and a witch and a dhampir teamed up to solve a series of murders in Necropolis in *Veiled Truth* by Vivi Anna (Tawny Stokes).

Nina Harper's *Succubus Takes Manhattan* was the second volume in a series featuring succubus Lily and private investigator Nathan Coleman.

Richelle Mead's *Succubus on Top* (aka *Succubus Nights*), the follow-up to *Succubus Blues*, once again featured bookseller succubus Georgina Kincaid and her complicated relationship with her bestselling author boyfriend. It was followed by *Succubus Dreams*, in which something was draining Georgina's energy. Mead was also the author of the young adult vampire novels *Frostbite* and *Shadow Kiss*, the latest volumes in the series that began with *Vampire Academy*.

The Mark of the Vampire Queen was the second in Joey W. Hill's erotic "Vampire Queen" series.

Lynda Hilburn's *Dark Harvest* was a sequel to *The Vampire Shrink*, Sara Reinke's *Dark Hunger* was a sequel to *Dark Thirst*, and Susan Hubbard's *The Year of Disappearances* was a sequel to the author's *The Society of S*.

Hex Appeal was the sequel to *50 Ways to Hex Your Lover* by Linda Wisdom, while *Midnight Reign* was the second volume in Chris Marie Green's "Vampire Babylon" series.

Bond of Fire and *Bond of Darkness* were the second and third volumes in Diane Whiteside's "Texas Vampires" series, and *Lover's Bite* and *Angel's Pain* were the second and third volumes in Maggie Shayne's series about a group of vampires that hunted their own kind.

Mario Acevedo's vampire private eye Felix Gomez investigated apparent alien abductions in *The Undead Kama Sutra*, the third in the mystery series.

The Bride of Casa Dracula was the third in Marta Acosta's humorous vampire romance series, while *One with the Darkness* was the third book in the historical vampire series by Susan Squires.

A female assassin and a vampire were both on the trail of a magical object in *Lady & the Vamp*, the third in the series by Michelle Rowen (Michelle Rouillard).

An amnesiac discovered he was a vampire in Michele Hauf's *His Forgotten Forever*, third in the "Bewitching the Dark" series. *Break of Dawn* was the third book in the "Vampire Babylon" series by Marie Chris Green, and *Romancing the Dead* by Tate Hallaway (Lyda Morehouse) was the third in the "Garnet Lacey" series.

Darkling by Yasmine Galenorn was the final book in the "Sisters of the Moon" trilogy.

Real Vampires Get Lucky, *Real Vampires Live Large* and *Real Vampires Have Curves* were the first three books in Gerry Bartlett's series about vampire entrepreneur Glory St. Claire.

Because Your Vampire Said So and *Wait Till Your Vampire Gets Home* were the third and fourth books in the humorous series by Michela Bardsley.

Colleen Gleason's *The Bleeding Dusk* and *When Twilight Burns* were the third and fourth titles in the historical romance "Gardella Vampire Chronicles" series.

Biting the Bullet and *Bitten to Death* were the third and fourth titles in Jennifer Rardin's series about Jaz Parks, who aided CIA vampire assassin Vayl.

Kimberly Raye's *Just One Bite* was the fourth book about the Dead End Dating agency run by vampire Lil Marchette, while *A Body to Die For* completed the same author's "Love at First Bite" trilogy.

In *Legacy*, the fourth in Jeanne C. Stein's series, vampire Anna Strong was about to inherit a fortune until a werewolf widow showed up.

Raven Hart's *The Vampire's Betrayal* was the fourth book in the "Savannah Vampire Chronicles", and Jennifer Armintrout's *All Souls' Night* was the fourth volume in the author's "Blood Ties" series.

Every Last Drop was the fourth in Charlie Huston's hardboiled series about vampire private investigator Joe Pitt.

Midnight Rising and *Veil of Midnight* were the fourth and fifth volumes in Lara Adrian's "Midnight Breed" series, and *Dark Deeds at Night's Edge* and *Dark Desires After Dusk* were the fourth and fifth volumes in Kresley Cole's "Immortals After Dark" series.

Under Darkness was the fifth book in the "Darkwing Chronicles" by Savannah Russe (Charlee Trantino), while *Dark Night Dark Dreams* was the first in the "Sisterhood of Sight" series from the same author.

The sixth volume in Katie MacAlister's humorous "Dark Ones" series, *Zen and the Art of Vampires*, featured a tourist in Iceland involved with ghosts and vampires.

Undead and Unworthy was the seventh volume in the prolific MaryJanice Davidson's humorous series about "Betsy the Vampire Queen". *Dead Over Heels* contained three novellas based around different series from the same author, including a "Betsy" story and another involving "The Wyndham Werewolves".

From Dead to Worse was the eighth volume in Charlaine Harris' popular series of "Sookie Stackhouse" Southern Vampire mysteries. This time the telepathic waitress had undead boyfriend trouble while trying to deal with warring werewolves and the bombing of the Louisiana vampires in the previous book.

Dream Chaser, *Acheron* and *One Silent Night* were the latest volumes in the long-running "Dark-Hunter" series by Sherrilyn Kenyon (aka Kinley MacGregor).

First Blood contained four vampire romance stories by Susan Sizemore, Erin McCarthy, Chris Marie Green and Meljean Brook.

Scions: Insurrection and *Scions: Revelation* were the second and third books in Patrice Michelle's vampire/werewolf romance trilogy, while a vampire and a werewolf fighting terrorists(!) shared a forbidden passion in Susan Sizemore's *Primal Needs*.

The Wolfman pitted small town werewolf Marlowe Higgins against a fiendish serial killer. It was the first published novel by twenty-eight-year-old Nicholas Pekearo, who was killed in the line of duty in 2007 while serving as a NYPD Auxiliary Police Officer.

Published by Snowbooks, *Maneater* was the first English-language novel by pseudonymous Welsh author "Thomas Emson". It was about a female werewolf.

Having emasculated the vampire genre over the past several years, romcom authors and publishers moved on to werewolves in 2008.

A cosmetics saleswoman was bitten in *The Accidental Werewolf* by Dakota Cassidy, while in the sequel, *Accidentally Dead*, a dental nurse was bitten by a vampire.

A shy schoolteacher turned into a werewolf in Sharie Kohler's *Marked by Moonlight*, and a werewolf was unlucky in love in *Enemy Lover* by Bonnie Vanak.

A psychic and her werewolf boyfriend were stalked by their former partners in *Touch of Darkness* by C. T. Adams and Cathy Clamp.

Devlyn Greystoke protected a shape-changer on the trail of a murderous werewolf in *Heart of the Wolf* by Terry Spear, while *Alpha Wolf* by Linda O. Johnston involved a pack of military werewolves.

A cursed Viking were-creature was the protagonist of Lisa Hendrix's *Immortal Warrior*, and a phantom werewolf turned up in *Ghost Moon* by Rebecca York (Ruth Glick).

Flood was an erotic werewolf novel by Anna Clare, published by Black Lace. Mathilde Madden's *The Silver Crown* and *The Silver Cage*, the second and third volumes in an erotic series about a werewolf and hunter, were available from the same imprint.

Caitlin Kittredge's *Night Life* and *Pure Blood* were the first and second books, respectively, in the "Nocturne City" series featuring werewolf homicide detective Luna Wilder, who came from a family of witches.

Howling at the Moon and *On the Prowl* by Karen Macinerney were the first two volumes in the "Tales of an Urban Werewolf" romance series about Sophie Garou.

Patricia Briggs' *Iron Kissed* was the third in her paranormal romance series about shape-shifting mechanic Mercy Thompson. It went to #1 on the *New York Times* mass-market bestseller list in January. From the same author, *Cry Wolf* introduced werewolf enforcers Charles and Anna in the first of a spin-off series.

Dance of the Wolf was the third book in Karen Whiddon's "The Pack" series.

Last Wolf Standing, *Last Wolf Hunting* and *Last Wolf Watching* by Rhyannon Byrd (Tabitha Bird) comprised the "Bloodrunners" trilogy, about a pack of werewolf "Runners".

Werewolf Kitty finally returned home to Denver to visit her ailing mother and became involved in a vampire turf war in *Kitty and the Silver Bullet*, the fourth in the series by Carrie Vaughn.

Wolf Tales V and *VI* were the latest volumes in Kate Douglas' erotic series about a race of shape-shifters known as the "Chanku".

Three romance stories about werewolves were collected in *Running Wild* by Sarah McCarty.

Having been bought for a reported $1.25 million by Doubleday in the US, Canadian author Andrew Davidson's debut, *The Gargoyle*, opened with its ex-porn star narrator being treated in a burns unit after a drug-fuelled car crash. When a former nun and psychiatric patient informed him that she was his long-lost lover from 700 years ago, the book just got weirder. Perhaps not surprisingly, the much-hyped novel was one of the biggest flops of the year.

Anton Strout's first novel, *Dead to Me*, was about New York's Department of Extraordinary Affairs, and an amnesiac found himself involved in a war between angels and demons in Alex Bell's first novel, *The Ninth Circle*.

A woman returned to her hometown and encountered the supernatural creatures that existed there in Lauren Groff's debut, *The Monsters of Templeton*.

A late night radio show host got caught up in the stories of his call-in listeners in Leopoldo Gout's first book *Ghost Radio*, two northern California cops were convinced that the dead were not at rest in Doug Dorst's *Alive in the Necropolis*, and Zombie teenagers faced prejudice in Daniel Walters' debut novel, *Generation Dead*, aimed at the young adult market.

Kimberly Pauley's *Sucks to Be Me* was intended for the same readership, as teen Mina Hamilton had to choose between her human life and her vampire parents, while J. F. Lewis' debut novel *Staked* involved a vampire suffering from short-term memory loss.

In *The Casebook of Victor Frankenstein*, Peter Ackroyd reset Mary Shelley's classic in nineteenth-century London and added such historical supporting characters as Percy Bysshe Shelley, Lord Byron, Samuel Taylor Coleridge and even Mary herself, along with a surprising twist ending.

The Man in the Picture was a new supernatural novel by Susan Hill, author of *The Woman in Black*.

A female ghost sent to escort a man to Heaven who didn't die at his appointed time found himself stranded on Earth in Jonathan Carroll's *The Ghost in Love*.

Joyce Carol Oates' *Wild Nights!* collected five original stories about the final days of major literary figures, including Edgar Allan Poe and Henry James.

From Barnes & Noble, *H. P. Lovecraft: The Fiction* collected all Lovecraft's fiction in a single hardcover volume, along with his influential essay "Supernatural Horror in Literature". Edited with an Introduction by S. T. Joshi, the texts were the so-called "corrected" versions.

Necronomicon: The Best Weird Tales of H. P. Lovecraft was a leatherbound "Commemorative Edition" published in both hardcover and export softcover editions by Gollancz. Containing thirty-four stories and two poems, it was illustrated by Les Edwards and included an extensive historical Afterword by editor Stephen Jones. The book went through six printings in a year.

Lovecraft was also involved in the writing of at least four of the tales – including the controversial title story – to be found in *The Loved Dead and Other Tales* by C. M. Eddy, Jr. The author's grandson, Jim Dyer, edited the new collection of thirteen stories from Fenham Publishing, as well as supplying the historical Introduction.

The Horror Stories of Robert E. Howard collected thirty-six tales, twenty-one poems and four fragments with an Introduction by editor Rusty Burke discussing Howard's relationship with Lovecraft. Illustrator Greg Staples also contributed a Foreword.

As part of general editor David Stuart Davies' bargain-priced "Tales of Mystery & the Supernatural" paperback series, Wordsworth Editions issued a number of novels and collections by classic authors (not all of whom were in public domain). The attractively designed series also included the anthologies *The Werewolf Pack* (seventeen stories) and *The Black Veil & Other Tales of Supernatural Sleuths* (sixteen stories) both selected and introduced by Mark Valentine. Although these volumes contained original material by Ron Weighell, Steve Duffy, Gail-Nina Anderson, A. F. Kidd (a new "Carnacki" story), R. B. Russell, Rosalie Parker and others, including the editor, they failed to incorporate any copyright information or credit their contributors on the contents pages.

Published in trade paperback by Dover Publications, *Gaslit Horror: Stories by Robert W. Chambers, Lafcadio Hearn, Bernard Capes and Others* was an omnibus anthology of thirteen stories selected by veteran editor Hugh Lamb.

An Itinerant House and Other Ghost Stories collected the surviving thirteen stories by obscure nineteeth-century American author Emma Frances Dawson. First published in 1897 with illustrations by Ernest C. Peixotto, the new edition from Thomas Loring & Co contained three additional stories not found in the original volume along with a lengthy Introduction by co-compiler Robert Eldridge.

Edited with a Foreword and notes by Victorian scholar Leslie S. Klinger and with an Introduction by Neil Gaiman, *The New Annotated Dracula* was a stunning, oversized illustrated edition of Bram Stoker's classic novel (plus "Dracula's Guest") published by W. W. Norton & Company.

From McFarland & Company, *Bram Stoker's Notes for Dracula: A Facsimile Edition*, edited, annotated and transcribed by Robert Eighteen-Bisang and Elizabeth Miller, made an indispensable companion volume. Michael Barsanti supplied the Foreword.

Anne Rice's 1976 novel *Interview with the Vampire* enjoyed its ninetieth paperback printing from Ballantine in 2008.

In October, UK imprint Gollancz reissued eight classic books in uniform trade paperback editions under "The Terror 8" banner. The promotion comprised *Darker Than You Think* by Jack Williamson, *Exquisite Corpse* by Poppy Z. Brite, *Fevre Dream* by George R. R. Martin, *Ghost Story* by Peter Straub, *The Green Mile* by Stephen King, *Something Wicked This Way Comes* by Ray Bradbury, *Song of Kali* by Dan Simmons and *The Tooth Fairy* by Graham Joyce.

Diana Wynne Jones and Philip Pullman were among those authors who objected to an attempt by publishers to label every book that might appeal to children with a recommended reading age sticker.

Neil Gaiman's *The Graveyard Book* contained a series of linked stories about orphaned boy, Nobody Owens ("Bod"), who lived in a graveyard, was raised and educated by ghosts, and had a witch as a friend. It was published in two differently designed editions, one illustrated by the author's regular collaborator Dave McKean, and the other by children's illustrator Chris Riddell.

Jack: Secret Histories was the first in a new young adult trilogy by F. Paul Wilson featuring a fourteen-year-old Repairman Jack.

Death's Shadow was the seventh book in the "Demonata" series by Darren Shan (Darren O'Shaughnessy). The author also reissued a heavily revised edition of his 1999 novel *Procession of the Dead* under the byline "D. B. Shan".

The Shade of Hettie Daynes was a young adult ghost novel by Robert Swindells, and a boy encountered ghostly children in *The Hunt for the Seventh* by Christine Morton-Shaw.

J. P. Hightman's *Spirit* was a Victorian ghost story about two teens who had to quiet the souls of the dead on a carnival-bound train.

The titular schoolboy of Douglas Anthony Cooper's amusing *Milrose Munce* could see ghosts, and a girl had the ability to see dead people in *The Summoning*, the first volume in Kelley Armstrong's "Darkest Powers" series.

After discovering some old letters, two children encountered a phantom postman in Stephen Alter's mystery *Ghost Letters*, while a boy into video games was possessed by his grandfather's spirit in *Slipping* by Cathleen Davitt Bell.

A girl helped the ghost of a young slave on a Louisiana plantation in *The Secret of Laurel Oaks* by Lois Ruby, and another girl was haunted by the spirit of a slave in *Pemba's Song* by Marilyn Nelson and Tonya C. Hegamin.

Wicked Dead: Snared, *Wicked Dead: Crush* and *Wicked Dead: Prey* were the third, fourth and fifth books in a series narrated by the ghosts of dead girls by Stefan Petrucha and Thomas Pendleton (Lee Thomas).

An abused boy discovered he possessed paranormal powers in *Mason*, also by Thomas Pendleton, a girl experienced other people's nightmares in Lisa McMann's *Wake*, and a teenager could see through the eyes of a serial killer in A. M. Vrettos' *Sight*.

Two years after the first book was published, orphan Rossamünd Bookchild discovered hidden secrets surrounding his chosen career in D. M. Cornish's Gothic mystery, *Monster Blood Tattoo Book Two: Lamplighter*, illustrated by the author.

A young girl found herself teaming up with various bizarre monsters that haunted the dreams of her cruel and angry Aunt in Leander Deeny's delightful debut novel *Hazel's Phantasmagoria*, illustrated by David Roberts.

Lauren Myracle's *Bliss* involved a psycho teenager and the Charles Manson trial.

The Last Apprentice: Attack of the Fiend (aka *The Spook's Battle*) and *The Last Apprentice: Wrath of the Bloodeye* (aka *The Spook's Mistake*) were the fourth and fifth books, respectively, in Joseph (Joe) Delaney's series about Thomas Ward, a boy apprenticed to a local Spook.

In Joanne Dahme's *Creepers*, a young girl discovered that her family's new home was haunted by a witch, and a coven of teenage witches battled vampires, werewolves and ghosts in *Revealers* by Amanda Marrone.

The skeleton detective and his teenage helper had to prevent the rise of the evil "Faceless Ones" in Derek Landy's *Skulduggery Pleasant: Playing with Fire*, the second book in the series.

A young girl battled creatures that fed on fear in Simon Holt's *The Devouring*, while *Demon Stalkers: Prey* was the first in a new series by Douglas Hill, who was tragically killed in 2007 after being hit by a bus.

Lost children roamed the world's largest shopping mall after dark in Kit Reed's *The Night Children*, and a girl's friends at a new high school were dead popular in Brian James' *Zombie Blondes*.

A girl lacking the powers of her psychic family suspected that a cheerleader in the Californian town of Nightshade could be a vampire in *Dead is the New Black* by Marlene Perez.

Another young girl found herself at a new boarding school in Claudia Gray's vampire novel *Evernight*, and Nancy A. Collins' *Vamps* was set in the Bathory Academy for privileged undead teenagers.

A vampire showed interest in a twelve-year-old girl's powers of teleportation in Jennifer Anne Kogler's *The Otherworldlies*, while Justin Richards' *The Parliament of Blood* involved vampires in Victorian London.

Vampires were called "hemovores" in A. M. Jenkins' *Night Road*.

A teenager's other split personality was an ancient vampire in *Persistence of Memory* by Amelia Atwater-Rhodes, while another teen was set to be revealed as a vampire in Brian Meehl's *Suck It Up*.

The Chronicles of Vladimir Tod: Ninth Grade Slays was the second book about the half-vampire boy by Heather Brewer.

Chosen and *Untamed* were the third and fourth volumes, respectively, in P. C. Cast and Kristin Cast's "House of Night" vampire series. They were also issued in audiobook format.

Feast of Fools was the fourth book in "The Morganville Vampires" series by Rachel Caine (Roxanne Longstreet Conrad), and Melissa de la Cruz's *Revelations* was the fourth volume in the "Blue Bloods" series.

The Coffin Club was the fifth volume in Ellen Schreiber's series that began with *Vampire Kisses*. The books were also adapted into graphic novel format.

The Ghosts of Kerfol collected five stories by Deborah Noyes, inspired by Edith Wharton's 1916 story "Kerfol", while Kelly Link's *Pretty Monsters* collected nine stories (one original).

Edited by Peter Straub, the anthology *Poe's Children: The New Horror* featured twenty-four reprint stories by Stephen King, Ramsey Campbell, Neil Gaiman, M. John Harrison, Thomas Tessier, Elizabeth Hand, Thomas Ligotti, Glen Hirshberg, John Crowley, David J. Schow, Steve Rasnic Tem & Melanie Tem, Joe Hill, Kelly Link, Graham Joyce, M. Rickert and others.

Published by Down East Books, *Otherworldly Maine* was an excellent cross-genre anthology edited by Noreen Doyle and containing twenty-one stories (eight original) set in the state of Maine by Edgar Pangborn, Elizabeth Hand, Stephen King, Gregory Feeley, Melanie Tem, Gardner Dozois, Mark Twain, Scott Thomas, Jack L. Chalker, Steve Rasnic Tem and others, including the editor.

Edited by Marvin Kaye, *The Ghost Quartet* featured four original novellas by Brian Lumley, Orson Scott Card, Tanith Lee and the editor himself.

Disappointingly trivial for an anthology supposedly presented by the Horror Writers Association, *Blood Lite* edited by Kevin J. Anderson contained twenty-one humorous horror stories by Charlaine Harris, Jim Butcher, Kelley Armstrong and Sherrilyn Kenyon, amongst others.

The Mammoth Book of Vampire Romance edited by Tricia Telep contained twenty-five stories (two reprints) by Nancy Holder, Lilith Saintcrow and others. From Black Lace, the uncredited *Lust at First Bite: Sexy Vampire Short Stories* contained fifteen erotic vampire stories.

As the title suggested, *Wolfsbane and Mistletoe* edited by Charlaine Harris and Toni L. P. Kelner contained fifteen Christmas stories about werewolves.

Edited by Peter Washington, *Ghost Stories* from Everyman's Library contained nineteen reprints by M. R. James, Ray Bradbury, Edith Wharton, L. P. Hartley, Elizabeth Bowen and P. G. Wodehouse, amongst others. The editor contributed his own list of the top ten ghost stories to the Hallowe'en edition of UK newspaper The *Guardian*.

Christopher Golden edited *Hellboy: Oddest Jobs*, an anthology of fourteen original stories based on the comic book character, illustrated by creator Mike Mignola. Authors included Joe R. Lansdale, China Miéville and Garth Nix.

Published by Chaosium and edited by William Jones, *Frontier Cthulhu: Ancient Horrors in the New World* collected fifteen Mythos stories (two reprints). From the same editor, *Horrors Beyond 2: Stories of Strange Creations* from Elder Signs Press contained twenty-one Lovecraftian stories (one reprint) from Richard A. Lupoff, A. A. Attanasio and others.

Hotter Than Hell edited by Kim Harrison and Martin H. Greenberg featured twelve supernatural romance stories by Tanya Huff, Carrie Vaughn and others. Greenberg also teamed up with Daniel M. Hoyt to edit *Better Off Undead*, which contained eighteen afterlife stories by Jay Lake, Nina Kiriki Hoffman, Esther M. Friesner and others.

My Big Fat Supernatural Honeymoon was editor P. N. Elrod's follow-up to the anthology *My Big Fat Supernatural Wedding* and contained stories by Jim Armstrong, Kelley Armstrong, Lilith Saintcrow, Ronda Thompson and the editor, amongst others.

From Barnes & Noble's new imprint Fall River Press, *A Whisper of Blood* was a 600-page omnibus of Ellen Datlow's superior vampire anthologies *Blood is Not Enough* (1989) and *A Whisper of Blood* (1991).

The Year's Best Fantasy and Horror 2008: Twenty-First Annual Collection edited by Datlow and Kelly Link & Gavin J. Grant contained various yearly summations along with thirty-five stories and six poems.

The Mammoth Book of Best New Horror Volume Nineteen edited by Stephen Jones collected twenty-five stories and novellas, plus the annual Introduction and Necrology.

For the first time in a long while there were no stories that appeared in both annual volumes, although British writers Gary McMahon and Reggie Oliver were represented in each book with different contributions.

Edited by Angela Challis and available only from the publisher's website and selected specialty stores, *Australian Dark Fantasy & Horror: Volume Two* from Brimstone Press featured eighteen stories published in 2006 by such Australian writers as Terry Dowling,

Margo Lanagan, Robert Hood, Stephen Dedman and others. A third volume appeared in December.

In potentially the biggest copyright theft in publishing history, electronic search engine Google came to a proposed settlement in lawsuits filed by the Authors Guild and the Association of American Publishers. This allowed the company to digitize the text of every book in the world and offer excerpts from copyright material or the full texts of public domain works under its controversial Book Search program.

What was particularly troubling for authors is that Google was forcing them to formally *opt out* of the program, otherwise it would be assumed that the writer had accepted the settlement's provisions, which involved a small and complicated royalty payment scheme for copyrighted material.

Meanwhile, in September, Google was forced to modify its new multi-million dollar Internet browser, Google Chrome, when it was revealed that users of the program would lose the copyright to their own files. Google claimed that the all-encompassing clause in its licence agreement was an "accident" and deleted the offending terms and conditions, making the changes retrospective.

Launched almost a year after Amazon's Kindle electronic reader debuted in America, Sony's digital Reader had 200 megabytes of memory and could hold up to 160 e-books. The size of an average paperback, a single charge could handle 6,800 page turns. Each unit was sold with a CD containing 100 books, including Bram Stoker's *Dracula*.

From Australia's Brimstone Press, the e-anthology *Black Box* edited by Shane Jiraiya Cummings was a follow-up to *Shadow Box* and contained a mixture of fiction, artwork and music. Authors represented included Stephen Dedman, Jay Caselberg, Robert Hood, Lucy Sussex, Rick Kennett and Jason Sizemore, amongst others, with all profits donated to the Australian Horror Writers Association (AHWA) to help support emerging dark fiction writers.

Posted online daily at NBC.com and SCIFI.com, the fifty-part *Gemini Division* featured Rosario Dawson as an undercover cop who discovered that her boyfriend (Justin Hartley) was really a synthetic supersoldier on the run from his military creators.

Created by *Buffy*'s Joss Whedon in July for the Internet, *Dr Horrible's Sing-Along Blog* featured Neil Patrick Harris as the crazed yet musical mad scientist of the title. Nathan Fillion played the doctor's arch-nemesis, Captain Hammer.

Richard Christian Matheson wrote and directed the pilot episode of *Shockers*, a series of twist-in-tail mini-films available on the Internet.

For Halloween, FEARnet.com's "66.6 Second Film Festival" presented movies such as *Hostel*, *Evil Dead 2* and *Candyman* edited down to just over a minute each.

Available as print-on-demand trade paperbacks, Welsh publisher Mortbury Press issued *The Second Black Book of Horror* and *The Third Black Book of Horror*, both selected by Charles Black. Containing thirteen (two reprints) and seventeen stories, respectively, authors represented included Gary McMahon, David A. Sutton, David A. Riley, Mike Chinn, D. F. Lewis, Eddy C. Bertin, L. H. Maynard and M. P. N. Sims, John Llewellyn Probert, Joel Lane, John Mains, Paul Finch and Gary Fry.

Gary Fry's Gray Friar's Press produced Nicholas Royle's *The Appetite* as the third in its "Gray Matter Novella" series with an Introduction by Michael Marshall Smith. The book was available as a 300-copy on-demand softcover and in a hardcover edition limited to just 100 copies. Tony Richards' collection *Passport to Purgatory* was available as a trade paperback from the same imprint.

Available from Canada's Creative Guy Publishing, *Peripheral Visions* was a collection of twenty-one stories (three original) by up-and-coming British writer Paul Kane. Christopher Fowler supplied the Introduction, and the on-demand trade paperback came with numerous glowing testimonials by an impressive roster of Names.

From Wordcraft of Oregon, *Crazy Love Stories* contained seventeen "gonzo" stories by the incomparable Leslie What, with an Introduction by Kate Wilhelm.

Gerard Houarner explored three wildly different facets of *The Wizard of Oz* (one reprint) in the novella collection *The Oz Suite* from Eibonvale Press.

From on-demand imprint Raw Dog Screaming Press, *Worse Than Myself* was a collection of eleven stories (five original) by Adam Golaski, set in New England, New York and Montana, while *Sheep and Wolves: Collected Stories* spotlighted the fiction of Jeremy C. Shipp with seventeen stories (eight original).

Midnight Call and Other Stories was a collection of twenty-six new or revised stories by Jonathan Thomas, published by Hippocampus Press with a Foreword by S. T. Joshi.

From the same on-demand imprint, *Inconsequential Tales* contained twenty-four previously uncollected stories by Ramsey Campbell (two original), along with an Introduction by the author.

Clockwork Phoenix was the first in an impressive new series of annual anthologies of literary fantasy from Norilana Books, edited and introduced by Mike Allen. It contained eighteen original stories of beauty and strangeness by Tanith Lee, John Grant, Laird Barron, Cat Rambo, Cat Sparks and others.

A group of criminals took refuge in a haunted mine in Lawrence C. Connolly's first novel, *Veins*, illustrated by Star E. Olson.

The Undead: Headshot Quartet contained four original zombie novellas by John Sunseri, Ryan C. Thomas, David Dunwoody and D. L. Snell. It was edited by Christina Biyins and Lane Adamson for Permuted Press.

Available in both PoD hardcover and paperback format from AuthorHouse, the collection *Why You Should Shudder: 27 Tales of Terror* included five previously unpublished stories by author Kent Robinson.

Edited by Aaron Polson and available under his own Strange Publications imprint, *Tainted: Tales of Terror and the Supernatural* was an anthology of thirteen stories (eight original) inspired by the work of Ambrose Bierce, E. F. Benson, Algernon Blackwood, H. G. Wells and Edgar Allan Poe, who were each represented with a reprint story.

John Langan's debut collection, *Mr Gaunt and Other Uneasy Encounters* from Wildside Press/Prime Books, contained five academic horror stories (including an original novella) along with an Introduction by Elizabeth Hand.

Edited by the redoubtable Philip Harbottle, *Fantasy Adventures 13* was the final volume in the pulp-inspired series from Cosmos Books/Wildside Press. The bumper paperback contained twenty-two original short stories by the late Sydney J. Bounds and Philip E. High (seven and four apiece, respectively), Eric Brown, John Glasby, E. C. Tubb, Brian Ball, Tony Glynn and Antonio Bellomi, along with the revised version of a complete novel by John Russell Fearn. The editor also contributed two personal remembrances of Bounds and High.

Translated from the French by Brian Stableford for Black Coat Press, *Vampires of Mars* was an omnibus of Gustave Le Rouge's *Le prisonnier de la planete Mars* (1908) and *La guerre des vampires* (1909).

Charles Derennes' lost race novel from 1907, *The People of the Pole* (*Le peuple du Pole*), about the discovery of a reptilian civilization, was also translated from the French by Stableford.

Stableford's own *The Shadow of Frankenstein* was a sequel to Paul Féval's *John Devil*, set in an alternate world based on literary works, including those by Féval and Mary Shelley. From the same author and on-demand imprint, *Sherlock Holmes and the Vampires of Eternity* was a fix-up pastiche that included revised material from *The Hunger and Ecstasy of Vampires* (1996).

Black Coat Press also published the anthology *Tales of the Shadowmen: Lords of Terror*. The fourth volume in the pulp anthology series edited by Jean-Marc Lofficier and Randy Lofficier, it contained sixteen stories featuring established and obscure fictional characters by Kim Newman, John Shirley, Brian Stableford and others, including the two editors. The book was followed by *Tales of the Shadowmen: The Vampires of Paris*, which contained eighteen stories by Stableford and others.

Although available from Texas imprint Swimming Kangaroo Books, half the contributors to *Killers* edited by Colin Harvey were from the UK. These included Sarah Singleton, Philip Lees, Paul Meloy, Charlie Allery, Gary Fry and the editor.

A sequel to *A World Torn Asunder*, *Vampire Apocalypse: Descent Into Chaos* by Derek Gunn was once again set in a world ruled by vampires and was available through KHP Industries/Black Death Books.

From the same on-demand publisher, Bob Freeman's *Keepers of the Dead* was the second volume in the "Cairnwood Manor" series.

Self-published as a hefty paperback and e-book through iUniverse Inc., *Unnatural Journeys Part One* was the first of a planned four volumes containing two linked novels and sixty-four short stories by Australian writer John Ezzy.

Rio Youers' vampire novel *Everdead* was published by Graveside Tales. It was set on the island of Ibiza.

The undead also turned up in V. M. K. Fewings' *Stone Masters: A Vampire's Reckoning*, from Canadian on-demand imprint Lachesis Publishing.

Quite possibly the most important debut short story collection in the genre since Mark Samuels' *The White Hands and Other Weird Tales* five years earlier, it was only appropriate that that author supplied the Foreword to *Beneath the Surface* by Canadian writer Simon Strantzas. Published as an unjacketed hardcover by Humdrumming Ltd., the book contained twelve superior stories (seven original).

Also from Humdrumming, *The Land at the End of the Working*

Day collected four very different stories by Peter Crowther, all set in the eponymous New York drinking establishment. Ian McDonald, Elizabeth Hand, Joe Hill and Lucius Shepard each contributed an Introduction to a story. It was published in hardcover as a 200-copy numbered edition signed by the author and fifty-two lettered and slipcased copies signed by all the contributors.

Less Lonely Planet (Tales of Here, There & Happenstance) was a hardcover collection of thirty-two stories (nine reprints) by Rhys Hughes, who also supplied the Introduction and Afterword.

Published by Humdrumming in 450 numbered copies signed by the author and a fifty-two copy lettered edition signed by both contributors, Tim Lebbon's novella *The Reach of Children* came with a Foreword by Michael Marshall Smith and an interesting Afterword about how the story came to be written.

Selected by Ian Alexander Martin, *The Second Humdrumming Book of Horror Stories* was (like *The Black Book of Horror* series) inspired by *The Pan Book of Horror Stories*. It contained fifteen previously unpublished tales by such authors as Conrad Williams, Gary McMahon, Simon Strantzas, Tim Lebbon, Rhys Hughes, Christopher Fowler, Gary Fry, Mark Morris, Sarah Pinborough and others. Despite the annoying contributor biographies, this was a far superior collection to the first volume.

Unfortunately, Humdrumming announced in November that it was going out of business. The poor state of the economy and amount of money owed to the company were blamed.

At the end of December, Andrew Hook also announced that he was closing down Elastic Press with immediate effect because the independent British imprint was "becoming a burden rather than a pleasure".

During the year Elastic Press published *Subtle Edens*, editor Allen Ashley's anthology of so-called "slipstream" fiction, containing twenty-one original stories by Mike O'Driscoll, Joel Lane, David A. Sutton, Steve Rasnic Tem, Gary Fry and others, along with an article by Jeff Gardiner that attempted to make a case for labelling the diverse stories in the book such. The editor supplied an Introduction, and there was an uncredited Afterword by Nicholas Royle slipped in to the back of the book.

Continuing its series of classic Ray Bradbury hardcover reprints, Peter Crowther's PS Publishing issued 100 signed and numbered deluxe slipcased sets of the collections *The Day it Rained Forever* plus *A Medicine for Melancholy*, featuring introductions by Caitlín R. Kiernan and Jonathan Eller, respectively. Five hundred unsigned copies and 200 signed slipcased editions of *The Day it Rained Forever* were also available.

Even better, as a Christmas present for Bradbury fans, PS reprinted *The Halloween Tree*, *The October Country* and *Something Wicked This Way Comes* in a special slipcased gift set limited to 274 unsigned copies and twenty-six signed by Bradbury. The deluxe editions featured matching text-free dust-jacket artwork by James Hannah over the original cover illustrations, and were introduced by James Lovegrove, Stephen Jones and Peter Crowther, respectively, with Afterwords by William F. Touponce.

Ramsey Campbell's latest novel, *Thieving Fear*, was about four cousins who were forced to confront an event in their past linked to the home of a Victorian occultist. The PS edition was introduced by Kim Newman and limited to 200 signed and numbered slipcased editions and 500 unjacketed hardcovers signed by the author.

PS Showcase #2: Conscientious Inconsistencies collected five feminist fantasy stories (one reprint) by Nancy Jane Moore with an Introduction by L. Timmel Duchamp, while Robert T. Jeschonek's *Mad Scientist Meets Cannibal* was *PS Showcase #3* and contained five offbeat new stories along with an Introduction by Mike Resnic.

Ramsey Campbell supplied the Introduction to Mark Samuels' latest collection, *Glyphotech and Other Macabre Processes*, which was *PS Showcase #4* and contained eleven stories (two original). *PS Showcase #5: Impossibilia* contained three novellas (one original) by Canadian author Douglas Smith with an Introduction by Chaz Brenchley.

All four books were issued in editions of 300 unjacketed hardcovers signed by the authors and 100 jacketed hardcovers signed by both contributors.

Published in editions of 500 unjacketed hardcovers signed by just the author and 200 jacketed hardcovers signed by all contributors, PS Publishing's welcome novella series continued with Nicholas Royle's Venice-set *The Enigma of Departure* with an Introduction by Robert Erwin; *Living with the Dead*, a surreal story from Darrell Schweitzer with an Introduction by Tim Lebbon; *The Situation* by Jeff VanderMeer, and *The City in These Pages* by John Grant with an Introduction by David Langford.

A retired Nazi hunter contracted a strange disease and travelled into the heart of the Brazilian jungle to find a cure in Jack Dann's hallucinatory novella *The Economy of Light*. It was published by PS in three states, including twenty-six lettered, slipcased hardcovers signed by the author, cover artist Vincent Chong and Michael Swanwick, who contributed the Introduction.

From Earthling Publications, *The Hellbound Heart: 20th Anniversary Edition* contained Clive Barker's original novella (the basis for the *Hellraiser* films), along with a Foreword by actress Ashley Laurence, an Introduction by screenwriter Peter Atkins, a reproduction of the first chapter of the manuscript, and illustrations by the author. It quickly sold out in all three editions, including a $650 signed, lettered and traycased edition that included an original sketch by Barker.

Peter Atkins' own *Moontown* was the fourth volume in Earthling's Halloween Series. Involving an empathic student who went too deep into the dreamscapes of troubled patients, the novel was published in an edition of 500 numbered copies and fifteen lettered copies.

From Cemetery Dance Publications, *The Folks 2: No Place Like Home* was a hardcover novella by Ray Garton issued in a 1,500-copy signed edition and a leatherbound lettered edition of twenty-six copies ($175.00).

Norman Prentiss' *Invisible Fences*, about a man confined by his fears, was the nineteenth volume in Cemetery Dance's Novella Series, published in deluxe hardcover.

Available from Canada's Ash-Tree Press in a limited edition of 400 hardcover copies, *Coffin Nails* was an enjoyable collection of eighteen often amusing horror stories (eight original) by British writer John Llewellyn Probert that owed much of their inspiration to the work of R. Chetwynd-Hayes and the Amicus anthology movies. The author supplied both the Introduction and an interesting Afterword in which he detailed the origins of each tale.

Also from Ash-Tree, *Ghost Realm* contained nine original stories by Paul Finch, based around the myths and legends of Britain, along with an Introduction and story notes by the author.

Rope Trick: Thirteen Strange Stories was the first collection of Mark P. Henderson's "quiet" supernatural tales (ten original).

Shades of Darkness was the fifth in the Ash-Tree series of superior anthologies edited by Barbara and Christopher Roden. Available in both softcover and limited hardcover editions, the book as usual boasted a surreal cover painting by Jason Van Hollander and featured twenty-six stories by Steve Duffy, Paul Finch, Reggie Oliver, Mark Samuels, David A. Riley, Melanie Tem, Christopher Harman, Gary McMahon, Simon Kurt Unsworth, Joel Lane, Michael Cox, Glen Hirshberg and others, including co-editor Barbara Roden.

Not quite as impressive was *Exotic Gothic 2: New Tales of Taboo* edited with a Preface by Danel Olson. Despite the editor's attempts to brand the twenty-four original contributions *nouveau Gothic*, it contained a decidedly mixed bag of horror fiction (and at least one SF story) from, amongst others, Steve Duffy, John Whitbourn, Nicholas Royle, Nancy A. Collins, Christopher Fowler, Reggie Oliver, Steve Rasnic Tem, Elizabeth Massie, Adam Golaski, Terry Dowling, Robert Hood and Barbara Roden. It was published as a 350-copy hardcover and an unlimited softcover.

Published by Centipede Press, *The Autopsy and Other Tales* collected seven stories (one original) by Michael Shea, along with the 1984 Lovecraftian novel *The Color Out of Time*. It was issued in a signed edition limited to 500 copies, with an Introduction by Laird Barron and an Afterword by the author.

Compiled by John Joseph Adams for Night Shade Books, the zombie anthology *The Living Dead* contained one original and thirty-three stories selected from other sources, including no less than six from the anthologies *Book of the Dead* and *Still Dead*. Among the impressive line-up of contributors were Stephen King, Clive Barker, Neil Gaiman, Harlan Ellison and Robert Silverberg, Dan Simmons, Poppy Z. Brite, Joe R. Lansdale, Douglas E. Winter, Joe Hill and Nancy Holder.

From Subterranean Press, *Coraline* was a 1,000-copy limited edition of Neil Gaiman's young adult novel signed by the author and artist Dave McKean. A twenty-six copy deluxe lettered edition was also available for $400.00.

Haggopian and Other Stories collected twenty-four Lovecraftian tales by Brian Lumley in a signed, limited edition of 1,500 copies. A twenty-six copy traycased, leatherbound lettered edition was also available from Subterranean for $200.00.

Edited by Stefan E. Dziemianowicz, *Skeletons in the Closet and Other Stories* contained sixteen tales by the late Robert Bloch.

Those Who Went Remain There Still was a short novel by Cherie Priest involving the extended family of Daniel Boone and a monster that lived in a Kentucky cave.

Backup was a hardcover "Dresden Files" novella by Jim Butcher, featuring Harry's vampire-incubus half-brother Thomas. It was available from Subterranean as a signed leatherbound edition of 500 copies and a lettered, traycased edition of twenty-six copies.

The imprint also continued the Wandering Star series of Robert E. Howard limited editions with *Kull: Exile of Atlantis*, illustrated with colour plates and black and white illustrations by Justin Sweet. It was published as 1,500 slipcased copies signed by the artist, and as a fifty-copy deluxe leatherbound edition ($400.00).

George R. R. Martin's classic vampire novel *Fevre Dream* was a welcome reissue from Subterranean with new illustrations by Justin Sweet. It was available in a signed, slipcased edition of 448 copies, or a fifty-two copy traycased lettered edition for $200.00.

The Shadow of the Wind was the title of a fictional book chosen by the Spanish protagonist of Carlos Ruiz Zafón's literary mystery, also reissued by Subterreanean.

The Golden Apples of the Sun and Other Stories was a reprint of a 1990 compilation of Ray Bradbury's classic stories that included facsimile manuscripts for theatrical versions of "The Fog Horn" and "En la Noche". It was published by Subterranean as a 300-copy limited collector's edition and in twenty-six signed and lettered copies ($750.00).

Published by Comma Press, *The New Uncanny: Tales of Unease* edited by Sarah Eyre and Ra Page challenged fourteen authors to write fresh fictional interpretations of what the uncanny might mean in the twenty-first century. Contributors included A. S. Byatt, Ramsey Campbell, Christopher Priest and Nicholas Royle.

From Tachyon Publications, *The New Weird* edited by Ann VanderMeer and Jeff VanderMeer, with an Introduction by the latter, contained sixteen stories (two original, including a round-robin tale) and nine essays (seven original) supposedly reflecting the spurious literary "movement" first identified by M. John Harrison in a 2003 online discussion. Contributors included Harrison, Clive Barker, Michael Moorcock, Kathe Koja, Thomas Ligotti, China Miéville, Jeffrey Thomas, Jay Lake, K. J. Bishop, Jeffrey Ford, Paul Di Filippo, Sarah Monette, Hal Duncan and Conrad Williams. The oldest story in the book dated back to 1979.

Tachyon also published a newly-revised edition of Tim Powers' 1989 literary vampire novel *The Stress of Her Regard* in a handsome trade paperback edition.

Edited by Mark S. Deniz and Amanda Pillar, *Voices* from Swedish imprint Morrigan Books contained sixteen original linked stories set in the rooms of a haunted hotel. Although strangely not credited on the contents page, contributors included Robert Hood, Paul Kane and the incredibly prolific Gary McMahon.

Also from Morrigan came *How to Make Monsters*, an impressive trade paperback collection of fourteen short stories (half of them original) by McMahon, with story notes and a brief Foreword by the author.

McMahon also contributed an Introduction to *The Exaggerated Man and Other Stories* from The Exaggerated Press, which collected nineteen stories (one original) by Terry Grimwood.

Christopher Teague's Pendragon Press produced a stylish edition of *The Reef* by Mark Charan Newton, about the quest for a fabled lost continent.

From the same imprint, Gary McMahon edited *We Fade to Grey*, an impressive anthology of original novellas by Paul Finch, Stuart Young, Mark West, Simon Bestwick and McMahon himself, with an illuminating Introduction by Mark Morris.

McMahon also supplied the Introduction for *Bull Running for Girls* from Screaming Dreams, which collected twenty-one stories by Allyson Bird.

Issued by Canada's Edge Science Fiction and Fantasy Publishing, *Gaslight Grimoire: Fantastic Tales of Sherlock Holmes* edited by J. R. Campbell and Charles Prepolec contained eleven original stories by Barbara Hambley, Barbara Roden, Chris Roberson, Kim Newman and others (including one of the editors), along with a Foreword by David Stuart Davies.

Published by Dead Letter Press as an 800-page hardcover limited to just 500 copies, *Bound for Evil: Curious Tales of Books Gone Bad* edited by Tom English contained an impressive sixty-six stories (thirty-seven original). Contributors included M.R. James, Simon Strantzas, H. P. Lovecraft, Fred Chappell, Ramsey Campbell, Gary McMahon, John Llewellyn Probert, Gary Fry, Barbara Roden and Rhys Hughes. Allen Koszowski supplied the numerous interior illustrations.

A continuation of the magazine, *Premonitions: Causes for Alarm* was a paperback anthology from Pigasus Press edited by Tony Lee. It contained twenty stories and poems by Cardinal Cox, Andrew Darlington, Cyril Simsa, Steve Sneyd and others.

Boyd E. Harris' Texas-based Cutting Block Press issued *Horror Library Volume 3* in trade paperback. Edited by R. J. Cavender, the anthology featured thirty original stories by Bentley Little, Kealan Patrick Burke, Michael A. Arnzen, John Everson, Jeff Strand, Lisa Morton and others (including a collaboration between the editor and publisher).

Richard Satterlie's *Agnes Hahn* from Medallion Press was about its titular damaged protagonist, while Gregory Lamberson's *Johnny Gruesome* from the same publisher was even more firmly stuck in the world of 1980s slasher films.

From Chaosium, *The Strange Cases of Rudolph Pearson: Horri-*

pilating Tales of the Cthulhu Mythos by William Jones was a linked collection of ten stories (four reprints) featuring the occult investigator of the title.

California's Dark Regions Press continued to keep the horror short story collection alive with a series of handsomely produced, signed trade paperback volumes and limited edition hardcovers that showcased a wide variety of contemporary authors.

Shadows and Other Tales was a major retrospective of twenty-one world-spanning stories (one original) by Tony Richards, who also contributed a Foreword.

Jeffrey Thomas' *Voices from Hades* collected seven stories (two original) and the author's Introduction to the Taiwanese edition of his novel *Letters from Hades*, while *Voices from Punktown* contained ten stories (two original) and a graphic novel script set in the same author's far-future colony.

Meanwhile, Jeffrey's brother Scott Thomas came up with eighteen new Victorian ghost stories set in either England or Massachusetts for *The Garden of Ghosts*.

Dark Regions Press also issued Scott Nicholson's *Scattered Ashes*, which contained twenty-two stories (three original) and an Introduction by Jonathan Mayberry, while J. C. Henderson's *Degrees of Fear and Others* collected twenty mostly Lovecraftian and occult detective stories (two original), illustrated by Ben Fogletto. William Jones supplied the Introduction, and there was an Afterword by Joe Mauceri.

From the same imprint, *Ennui and Other States of Madness* featured seventeen stories (three original) by David Niall Wilson with an Introduction by Brian Hodge, while Stephen Mark Rainey's collection *Other Gods* contained sixteen stories (one original) with an Introduction by Elizabeth Massie.

Simon Clark's *Stone Cold Calling* was the third novella from Australia's Tasmaniac Publications. Published in a 300-copy softcover edition and twenty-six lettered hardcovers, it came with an Introduction by Kealan Patrick Burke.

Tales of the Callano Mountains was a self-published collection of thirteen Western horror stories by playwright and film-maker Larry Blamire, who also contributed the cover painting.

Issued in hardcover by Baysgarth Publications with an Introduction by Garry Killworth, *Fourtold* contained a quartet of novellas (one reprint) by Michael Stone and was the British author's first collection.

Produced by Salt Publishing with financial assistance from the Arts

Council of England, '68: *New Stories from Children of the Revolu-tion* edited by Nicholas Royle contained ten original stories by Toby Litt, Justina Robson, Christopher Kenworthy and others born in the transitional year of 1968.

Joseph D'Lacey's *Meat* was published under the Bloody Books imprint, as was Bill Hussey's *Through a Glass, Darkly* and *Read by Dawn Volume 3*, an original anthology edited by Adèle Hartley containing twenty-eight often short-short stories.

Edited by the busy Ian Whates, *Myth-Understandings* from New-Con Press was an anthology of fifteen dark fantasy stories (one reprint) by female authors, including Pat Cadigan, Gwyneth Jones, Storm Constantine, Liz Williams, Sarah Pinborough and Freda Warrington, amongst others. From the same editor and imprint came two other anthologies, *Subterfuge* and *Celebrations*.

A man teamed up with a woman being pursued by a demon in Peter Mark May's *Demon*, from Vanguard Press.

Keith Gouveia edited *Bits of the Dead* for Coscom Entertainment. The trade paperback anthology contained thirty-eight "flash fiction" zombie stories by Piers Anthony, Simon Strantzas, Nancy Kilpatrick, Michael Laimo, Paul A. Freeman, Tim Waggoner, Adam-Troy Castro, Kurt Newton and Charles A. Gramlich, amongst others, illustrated by Sean Simmans.

Michael A. Arnzen's novella *The Bitchfight* with an Introduction by Brian Hodge was available from California's Bad Moon Books, as was Simon Janus' serial killer novella *The Scrubs*, introduced by Weston Ochse.

Gene O'Neill's post-apocalyptic novella *The Confessions of St Zach* came with an Introduction by Gord Rollo (which compared the author to Joseph Conrad and William Golding!) and a less excitable Afterword by Brian Keene, while Tim Waggoner supplied the Introduction to Steve Vernon's *Plague Monkey Spam*.

All Bad Moon Books editions were available as signed 200-copy trade paperbacks and in twenty-six copy hardcover lettered editions.

Published under Bad Moon's Eclipse imprint as a limited edition hardcover, the dead past returned to haunt a failed farmer in Steven E. Wedel's *Little Graveyard on the Prairie*.

Orgy of Souls was a novella about two brothers by Wrath James White and Maurice Broaddus, published in a print-on-demand edition and as a signed hardcover by Apex Publications.

It was not difficult to see why all the stories in editor Mike Philbin's *Chimeraworld #5: Twenty Three Misfit Tales* had pre-viously been rejected by other markets.

Published by The British Fantasy Society, *Houses on the Borderland* was a trade paperback anthology edited by David A. Sutton. Inspired by William Hope Hodgson's novel, it contained six original novellas about unusual buildings by Allen Ashley, Samantha Lee, Simon Bestwick, Gary Fry, Paul Finch and David A. Riley, with a cover painting by Les Edwards.

Another BFS publication was *A Dick and Jane Primer for Adults*. Edited by Lavie Tidhar, it contained ten stories about the perennially popular children's characters "Dick and Jane" by Liz Williams, Adam Roberts, James Lovegrove, Conrad Williams and others, along with an Introduction by Jeff VanderMeer.

Published in a single hardcover edition by Hippocampus Press, *The Atlantis Fragments: The Trilogy of Songs and Sonnets Atlantean* was an omnibus of the three books of poetry by Donald Sidney-Fryer, with an Introduction by Brian Stableford.

Subscribers to PS Publishing's *PostScripts* were rewarded with a hardcover Holiday Chapbook of Ramsey Campbell's original novella *The Long Way*, the fourth in a continuing series of special publications. As an extra bonus signed copies went to hardcover subscribers of the magazine.

Published to coincide with his Guest of Honour appearance at FantasyCon 2008, Christopher Golden's *The Hiss of Escaping Air* was issued as a chapbook by PS in a signed edition of 300 numbered copies.

Ray Bradbury's *Skeletons* chapbook from Subterranean Press contained two stories entitled "Skeleton", illustrated by Dave McKean. It was limited to 500 copies, while a hand-bound, tray-cased, signed and lettered edition of sixteen copies sold out before publication.

Bev Vincent's *Overtoun Bridge* was a chapbook from Cemetery Dance Publications with cover art by Jill Bauman. It was issued in a signed chapbook edition of 500 numbered copies.

Skullvines Press issued Paul Kane's novella *Red*, a contemporary urban reworking of the Red Riding Hood story, in a handsome softcover edition with an Introduction by Tim Lebbon and cover art by Dave McKean.

Published in an edition of just fifty copies by Screaming Dreams, *Bloodsucking in Berkshire* was a humorous horror story from John Llewellyn Probert, featuring occult investigators Mr Massene Henderson and Miss Samantha Jephcott.

Charles Urban's Brutal Spirits was a chapbook collection of story notes by the "late" horror author Charles Edward Urban, purportedly "edited" by Gary McMahon with illustrations by Meggan Kehrli. It was published in a numbered edition of 150 copies by Ireland's The Swan River Press.

Once again, Peter Atkins and Glen Hirshberg took their Rolling Darkness Revue musical reading tour on the road in October to locations in California and Arizona. Kevin Moffett was the guest. With a format based on a 1930s radio show, *KRDR: Welcome to the Ether* was the tie-in chapbook produced by Earthling Publications.

A survey by the UK's leading wholesaler and distributor of newspapers and magazines warned of a declining market in magazines during the economic downturn.

This was also reflected on the other side of the Atlantic, with *Analog* and *Asimov's* announcing a change of format to a larger size but a drop in the page count of each issue.

Still surviving in a difficult market, it was a pleasure to see more of Gordon Van Gelder's editorials in *The Magazine of Fantasy & Science Fiction*. As usual, the stellar line-up of contributors included John Kessel (with a combination of *Frankenstein* and *Pride and Prejudice*), Ron Goulart, Albert E. Cowdrey, Nancy Springer, Tim Sullivan, Steven Utley, Kate Wilhelm, Rachel Pollack, Robert Reed, M. Rickert, Michael Blumlein, Lisa Goldstein, Marc Laidlaw, Geoff Ryman, Stephen King, Scott Bradfield, Terry Bisson, Carol Emshwiller and Michael Swanwick.

There were the usual reviews by Charles de Lint, Elizabeth Hand, Lucius Shepard (his demolition of J. J. Abrams and his over-hyped *Cloverfield* in the June issue was masterful), Michelle West, James Sallis, Paul Di Filipo, Kathi Maio and Chris Moriarty, while Gwynplaine MacIntyre, Peter Tremayne, Bud Webster, David Langford, Paul Di Filippo, Dave Truesdale, Fred Chappell and Lucy Sussex all contributed fascinating "Curiosities" columns.

The March issue featured a particularly impressive horror cover by Vincent Di Fate illustrating Albert E. Cowdrey's novella, "The Overseer", and to celebrate the magazine's sixtieth year of continual publication, *F&SF* began reprinting stories from its past issues.

As always, Peter Crowther and Nick Gevers' quarterly PostScripts offered an excellent mix of genre fiction by the likes of Sarah Monette, Jeff VanderMeer, Rhys Hughes, Brian Aldiss, Scott Edelman, Garry Kilworth, Steven Utley, Jack Dann, Ray Bradbury, Brian Stableford, Terry Bisson, Stephen Baxter, Paul Di Filippo, Jay Lake, Michael Moorcock, T. M. Wright, Chaz Brenchley, R. B. Russell,

Lisa Tuttle, Ian R. MacLeod and Douglas Smith. Available in both magazine format and as a 200-copy signed and numbered hardcover edition, there were guest editorials by Eric Schaller, the late Arthur C. Clarke (a reprint), Peter Atkins and James Lovegrove.

PostScripts #15 was a "Special Worldcon All-SF Issue" that featured a section devoted to Paul McAuley and (only in the slipcased edition) a colour portfolio of the work of legendary EC Comics illustrator Al Feldstein.

The publishers announced that future *PostScripts* would drop the magazine edition and go to an all-hardcover format, adding up to 25,000 words more fiction per issue.

Following the introduction of a new logo design in 2007, the once-venerable *Weird Tales* should have been re-titled *"New Weird" Tales* as incoming fiction editor Ann VanderMeer took the magazine in a new editorial direction. The five issues published in 2008 were more likely to showcase whimsical fantasy than the weird or unusual, with stories by Darrell Schweitzer, Cat Rambo, Tanith Lee, Sarah Monette, Michael Moorcock (a new "Elric of Melniboné" tale), Nick Mamatas, Norman Spinrad and Zoran Zivkoviá, amongst others. Interviewees included writers James Morrow and China Miéville, artists Mike Mignola and Viktor Koen, and animator Bill Plympton.

Ill-judged attempts to apparently make the magazine more "accessible" to modern readers took the title even further away from its pulp roots, with guest columnists musing upon real-life weirdness, a contentious list of "The 85 Weirdest Storytellers of the Past 85 Years", and Kenneth Hite providing a guided tour of Lovecraftian locations every issue. At least the unwise inclusion of an illustrative narrative was quickly dropped.

Another ill-advised revival was *Startling Stories* from Wildcat Books. The original magazine ran from 1939–55, and although the new print-on-demand version nicely recreated to look and format of the old pulps, the quality of the artwork was appalling. Half the first issue was taken up with a reprint of Ray Cummings' classic 1922 novel "The Girl in the Golden Atom".

As usual, John O'Neill's *Black Gate* did a much better job with the same pulp format. Issue #12 featured a superb reprint cover by UK artist Bruce Pennington.

Issue #58 of Richard Chizmar and Robert Morrish's *Cemetery Dance Magazine* was billed as a "Charles L. Grant Tribute Issue". It featured a reprint story by the late author, along with appreciations by Kealan Patrick Burke, Matthew J. Costello, Craig Shaw Gardner,

Rick Hautala, John Maclay, Thomas F. Monteleone, Bill Pronzini, Al Sarrantonio, David B. Silva, Thomas Smith, Steve Rasnic Tem, Wendy Webb and Chet Williamson. Thomas L. McDonald contributed an overview of Grant's writing career.

This issue of *CD* and the following one featured short fiction by Sarah Monette, Gerard Houarner, Brian Keene, Paul Finch, Eric Brown, Stephen Mark Rainey, Sarah Langan and others. Bev Vincent, Michael Marano and John Pelan contributed their usual regular columns, and there were interviews with the elusive T. E. D. Klein, Stephen Graham Jones, David Morrell, Robert Masello, 1980s author "Daniel Rhodes" (Neil McMahon), Brian Keene, the other Stephen Jones and Steve Vernon.

After an uneven start with its first two issues, Andy Cox's *Black Static* finally began to find its own identity with the six bi-monthly editions published in 2008. Although it still did not reach the standard of *The 3rd Alternative* – the title it replaced – the magazine presented some impressive short fiction by Tony Richards, Cody Goodfellow, Conrad Williams, Nicholas Royle, Steve Nagy, Joel Lane, Gary McMahon, Nina Allan, Bruce Holland Rogers, Lynda E. Rucker, Steve Rasnic Tem, Gary Fry and others. There were also short interviews with Williams, Sarah Langan, Jack Ketchum, Scott Sigler, Tim Lebbon, Simon Clark and Leisure editor Don D'Auria. However, the periodical's best bits remained the regular columns by Christopher Fowler, Stephen Volk, Mike O'Driscoll, Peter Tennant and, especially, Tony Lee's insightful DVD reviews.

Lee also provided DVD reviews to *Black Static*'s attractive sister publication, *Interzone*. Issues included short fiction by Chelsea Quinn Yarbro, Paul McAuley, Lavie Tidhar, Geoff Ryman, Christopher Priest, Greg Egan and Rudy Rucker, plus interviews with Egan, Tim Lebbon, Iain M. Banks, Charles Stross, Mike Carey and Alastair Reynolds. David Langford supplied a regular news column, and Nick Lowe contributed movie reviews. Issue #218 was a Chris Beckett special with three stories and an interview with the writer.

Dell's long-running *Alfred Hitchcock Mystery Magazine* contained a number of borderline short horror stories by James Van Pelt and others, along with an annotated Sherlock Holmes story ("The Adventure of the Red Circle") by Sir Arthur Conan Doyle.

The two always-attractive issues of Patrick Swenson's digest-sized *Talebones* featured stories by James Van Pelt, Dean Wesley Smith, William F. Nolan and others, plus some impressive poetry by Greg Schwartz and Mikal Trimm, and interior artwork from Tom Simonton, Laura Givens and Brad Foster.

The twelfth issue of Jason Sizemore's *Apex Science Fiction and Horror Digest* included fiction by Brian Keene, Cherie Priest and Lavie Tidhar, along with interviews with Jeff VanderMeer and Laura Anne Gilman. In the summer, the magazine went from a quarterly print publication to a monthly e-zine called *Apex Magazine*, doubling its pay rates.

Editor James R. Beach announced that his magazine *Dark Discoveries* was officially going to three-times-a-year publication after eleven issues. In 2008 the title published fiction by Tim Lebbon, Cody Goodfellow, Michael Laimo and others, along with interviews with Joe Hill, Edward Lee and Charlee Jacob.

Christopher M. Cevasco's *Paradox: The Magazine of Historical and Speculative Fiction* included the usual mixture of fiction, poetry and reviews.

The two issues of Ireland's *Albedo One* contained interviews with Ellen Datlow, Raymond E. Feist and the busy Alastair Reynolds, along with fiction by Steve Rasnic Tem, Nina Allan and others.

Issue #10 of the Canadian web spin-off magazine *Dark Recesses Press* featured reprint fiction by Ramsey Campbell and Clive Barker, along with interviews with Barker, Gary Braunbeck and Jack Ketchum.

Canada's *Rue Morgue*, edited by Jovanka Vuckovic, continued to lead the field in glossy horror magazines with eleven issues featuring interviews with the late Maila Nurmi ("Vampira"), José Mojica Marins ("Coffin Joe"), film-makers Tim Burton, George A. Romero, Paul Lynch, Dario Argento and Guillermo del Toro, singer Alice Cooper, writers Brian Keene, Gary A. Braunbeck, Clive Barker, John Ajvide Linqvist and Dennis Etchison, plus artist Bernie Wrightson.

The bumper October issue celebrated fifty years of *Famous Monsters of Filmland* with interviews with Forrest J Ackerman, Basil Gogos (who painted the cover portrait of Forry), John Landis, Joe Dante, Gene Simmons and others.

Subtitled "Australian Dark Culture Magazine" and edited by Angela Challis, *Black* was a glossy publication from Brimstone Press looking at horror books, movies, TV, music and pop culture. Along with stories and reviews, issues included interviews with actors Jensen Ackles and Jared Padalecki from *Supernatural*, George A. Romero, Guillermo del Toro, Alice Cooper, Robert Hood and AHWA founder and president Dr Marty Young. The magazine also published Stephen King's short story "Graduation Afternoon" in its July issue.

Celebrating its second anniversary, editor Joe Vaz's *Something*

Wicked: Science Fiction & Horror Magazine covered much the same ground from South Africa. Along with plenty of short fiction (including contributions from UK writer Ian R. Faulkner and Canadian Douglas Smith), there were interviews with Neil Gaiman, Alastair Reynolds, John Connolly and *X Files* actress Gillian Anderson, plus some interesting articles about the history of science fiction.

Neil Gaiman was also interviewed in the October issue of the UK's useful *Writing Magazine*.

Book and Magazine Collector featured Graham Andrews' article about the Roger Corman/Edgar Allan Poe film tie-in editions. Unfortunately, the piece turned out to be more about the movies than the books.

Despite finally being back on a regular schedule again, a shift in editorial direction for Tim Lucas' *Video Watchdog* meant that the reviews and articles in "The Perfectionist's Guide to Fantastic Cinema" became increasingly self-indulgent and irrelevant. Nobody really needed twenty-two pages devoted to *Sweden Heaven and Hell*, twelve pages about Japanese actress Meiko Kaji, nor a tedious round-robin discussion about *Grindhouse* (twenty pages!).

Interviews with forgotten child actress Ann Carter (*The Curse of the Cat People*) and obscure Euro actor Rodd Dana were way too long, and we certainly could have done without the editor's back-handed "tribute" to the late Forrest J Ackerman. At least an informative discussion between Joe Dante, Roger Corman and Daniel Haller, interviews with veteran producer Richard Gordon and character actor Dabbs Greer, and articles about screenwriter Charles B. Griffith and film pioneer Georges Méliès went some way to restoring the balance.

Aimed at the *Famous Monsters of Filmland* generation, Jim Clatterbaugh's glossy *Monsters from the Vault* featured fascinating interviews with the daughter of Oscar-winning special effects ace John P. Fulton and Mexican monster movie star Germán Robles.

The two issues of Steven Puchalski's excellent *Shock Cinema* included interviews with actors Bo Svenson, Barry Primus, Isela Vega, Sy Richardson, Suzanna Love and Tony Musante, plus reviews of hundreds of obscure movies and DVDs.

Along with lists of his favourite pop songs and the best films and books of 2008, Stephen King's occasional "The Pop of King" columns in *Entertainment Weekly* included the author's thoughts on electronic books (he liked the Kindle), blurb writing, why horror works, movie theatre snacks and "manfiction". In another piece for the magazine, he recalled his favourite year (1999).

Founded in 1968 as a fannish newsletter, Charles N. Brown's monthly *Locus* celebrated its fortieth anniversary starting in the April issue with tributes from Robert Silverberg, Joe Haldeman, Ginjer Buchanan and Brian Aldiss. The magazine also featured interviews with, amongst others, Aldiss, M. Rickert, Lucius Shepard, Terry Pratchett, Jeffrey Ford, Garth Nix, Christopher Barzak, Ursula K. LeGuin, Greg Bear, Caitlín R. Kiernan and Gardner Dozois (who became a new *Locus* reviewer).

Locus celebrated Arthur C. Clarke's 90th birthday with its January issue. Three months later it had to report the author's death, publishing numerous tributes in the May edition. The July issue focussed on young adult fiction, with contributions from Neil Gaiman, Graham Joyce and others.

David Longhorn continued to publish his small press fiction magazine *Supernatural Tales*. Low on design but high on quality, issues #13 and #14 contained stories from Adam Golaski, Tina Rath, Simon Strantzas, William I. I. Read, Michael Chislett and others.

Despite both featuring covers better suited to a science fiction title, the two issues of Trevor Denyer's *Midnight Street: Journeys Into Darkness* included fiction by Joel Lane, Gary McMahon, Allen Ashley, Simon Bestwick, Stephen Gallagher, Nina Allan, Mark Samuels, Peter Tennant, Andrew Hook and others, plus interviews with Gallagher, Samuels, Hook and the inevitable Neil Gaiman.

Printed in colour throughout, the first three issues of Adam Bradley's *Morpheus Tales* contained plenty of short fiction along with interviews with writers Joseph D'Lacey, Michael Laimo and the late Joseph McGee, plus artists Jason Beam and Dave Gentry.

The ninth issue of Heather and Tim Pratt's *Flytrap* was an (almost) all-female edition with fiction and poetry from M. Rickert, Jenn Reese, Sarah Monette, Catherynne M. Valente and others. The next issue was the last.

The four issues of Chris Roberts' *One Eye Grey*, described as "a penny dreadful for the 21st century" contained old folk tales or ghost stories set in another London.

Weighing in at a hefty 200 pages, the thirty-four stories in the third issue of John Bruni's *Tabard Inn: Tales of Questionable Taste* certainly lived up to the magazine's subtitle.

Fans of Harlan Ellison could read his unused 1974 story/treatment for an episode of TV's *Land of the Lost* and a short essay about rejection letters (with examples) in the *Rabbit Hole* newsletter.

Published by the University of Tampa Press, the first issue of

Studies in the Fantastic edited by S. T. Joshi included articles on J. Sheridan Le Fanu, Bram Stoker and Robert Aickman. Meanwhile, the second edition of Joshi's *Lovecraft Annual* from Hippocampus Press contained articles and reviews, along with cover art by Allen Koszowski.

Under editor Lee Harris, The British Fantasy Society's nicely-produced newsletter *Prism* had an erratic publishing schedule. Along with all the usual news and reviews, issues included columns by Ramsey Campbell, Mark Morris, Eric Brown, Conrad Williams and James Barclay.

Peter Coleborn and Jan Edwards gave up their editorship of the BFS' *Dark Horizons* magazine with #52, and Stephen Theaker took over with the following issue. Among those who contributed fiction and poetry were Joel Lane, Jo Fletcher, David A. Riley, Robert Holdstock and Allen Ashley, while Charles de Lint and Lawrence Watt-Evans were both interviewed.

The title was joined by a sister publication, *New Horizons*, edited by Andrew Hook. It was hard to see what the difference was, as the first issue also featured fiction and poetry, along with interviews with independent publisher David Rix and writer Tony Richards.

Handsomely published in hardcover and limited to 250 numbered copies edited by Mark Valentine and Ray Russell, the eighteenth issue of *Faunus: The Journal of The Friends of Arthur Machen* included a 1924 Introduction written by Machen, along with various essays about the author.

The August issue of *The New York Review of Science Fiction* included an article on obscure *Weird Tales* and Arkham House author Greye La Spina.

In his controversial study *The Original Frankenstein*, Charles Robinson, a professor of English at the University of Delaware, claimed that Mary Shelley's husband, the poet Percy Bysshe Shelley, made at least 5,000 changes to the manuscript of her famous novel, many of them significant. Robinson scrutinized the hand-written drafts of the book at the Bodleian Library, Oxford, and concluded that, "The book should now be credited as 'by Mary Shelley and Percy Shelley'."

Peter Ackroyd looked into the manner of Edgar Allan Poe's mysterious death in his fascinating biography *Poe: A Life Cut Short*.

Leslie A. Sconduto explored the werewolf myth in early literature in *Metamorphoses of the Werewolf: A Literary Study from Antiquity Through the Renaissance* from McFarland & Company. From the same imprint and edited by Jason Colavito, *A Hideous Bit of Morbidity: An Anthology of Horror Criticism from the Enlightenment to World War I* collected reviews and essays by Sir Walter Scott, Daniel Defoe, Andrew Lang and others.

Tour de Lovecraft: The Tales by game designer Kenneth Hite was a chronological exploration of all H. P. Lovecraft's stories. It was available in both electronic and print form from Atomic Overmind Press.

Lisa Rogak's biography *Haunted Heart: The Life and Times of Stephen King* included eight pages of black and white photos.

Prince of Stories: The Many Worlds of Neil Gaiman was a substantial guide all things Gaiman by Hank Wagner, Christopher Golden and Stephen R. Bissette, with a "slightly worn" Foreword by Terry Pratchett.

With a Foreword by J. K. Rowling, *Harry, A History: The True Story of a Boy Wizard, His Fans, and Life Inside the Harry Potter Phenomenon* was written by Melissa Anelli, webmistress of The Leaky Cauldron fan site.

Lois Gresh's *The Twilight Companion: The Unauthorized Guide to the Series* was a young adult study of Stephanie Meyer's vampire books.

From PS Publishing, *Basil Copper: A Life in Books* compiled and edited by Stephen Jones was an illustrated hardcover that contained a comprehensive working bibliography of the British author's work, along with a number of short stories, a television script based on M. R. James' "Count Magnus", and an in-depth look at Copper's life and career by Richard Dalby.

Keith Seward's *Horror Panegyric* explored the "Lord Horror" sequence of novels and comics by David Britton. It was published in small hardcover format by Savoy Books.

Edited by Benjamin Szumskyj, *Dissecting Hannibal Lecter: Essays on the Novels of Thomas Harris* collected twelve critical essays with a Foreword by Daniel O'Brien, from McFarland. From the same imprint, *The Great Monster Magazines* by Robert Michael "Bob" Cotter was a guide to the classic black and white monster comics of the 1950s, 1960s and 1970s.

David Hajdu's *The Ten-Cent Plague* looked at the birth of the American comic book up to Fredric Wertham's infamous decency battle in the mid-1950s, which resulted in the self-imposed Comics Code.

Edited by Amy Wallace, Del Howison and Scott Bradley with a brief Introduction by Gahan Wilson, *The Book of Lists: Horror* was an ideal bathroom read featuring peculiarly subjective lists complied by Ramsey Campbell, George Clayton Johnson, Brian W. Aldiss, Michael Marshall Smith, Michael Slade, Poppy Z. Brite, Kim Newman, Lisa Tuttle, Gary Brandner, T. E. D. Klein, Nancy Holder, Thomas Ligotti, Caitlín R. Kiernan, John Skipp, Steve Rasnic Tem, S. P. Somtow, Stephen Volk, Tim Lebbon, Christopher Golden, Bentley Little, Joel Lane, Lisa Morton, Edward Lee, Jack Ketchum, Sarah Langan, Gary A. Braunbeck, Sarah Pinborough, Don D'Auria, Tim Lucas and film directors Eli Roth, Neil Marshall, Jörg Buttgereit and Richard Stanley, amongst numerous others.

Equally disposable was *Zombie CSU: The Forensics of the Living Dead* by Jonathan Maberry. Purportedly employing scientific crime scene methods for investigating and identifying the *walking* dead, it featured commentary by Ramsey Campbell, Brian Keene, Ellen Datlow, Stephen Jones, film-maker Dan O'Bannon, actor Tony Todd and many others, along with some wildly variable zombie fan art.

The big movie novelizations of the year included *Iron Man* and *The Incredible Hulk* both by Peter David, *The Dark Knight* by Dennis O'Neil, *Hellboy II: The Golden Army* by Robert Greenberger, and *The Mummy: Tomb of the Dragon Emperor* and *The X Files: I Want to Believe*, both by Max Allan Collins.

Indiana Jones and the Crystal Skull was written by James Rollins, and the three previous movie tie-ins were reissued in a bumper omnibus edition entitled *The Adventures of Indiana Jones*.

30 Days of Night: Eternal Damnation by Steve Niles and Jeff Mariotte was a spin-off novel from the comic series created by Niles and Ben Templesmith, while S. D. Perry's *Aliens: Criminal Enterprise* was another spin-off novel, this time based on the movie series.

Jack Ketchum's 1989 novel *The Girl Next Door* was reissued as a film tie-in with an added interview about the movie with the author and scriptwriters Daniel Farrands and Philip Nutman. A movie tie-in of Ketchum's 2001 novel *The Lost* was also published by Leisure.

Steven Gould's 1992 novel *Jumper* and the third volume in the series, *Jumper: Griffin's Story*, were both published as movie tie-in editions.

Batman: Gotham Knight by Louise Simonson was based on the animated film of the same title.

TV shows getting the tie-in treatment included *Supernatural: Bone Key* by Keith R. A. DeCandido, *Ghost Whisperer: The Plague Room* by Steven Piziks and *Primeval: The Lost Island* by Paul Kearney.

Diana G. Gallagher's *Charmed: Trickery Treat* was based on the long-ago cancelled series, as was Kenneth Johnson's *V: The Second Generation*, written by the show's creator.

The 4400: The Vesuvius Prophecy by Greg Cox and *The 4400: Wet Work* by Dayton Ward and Kevin Dilmore were both based on the cancelled CBS show.

As always, there was a plethora of *Doctor Who* tie-ins based on the BBC series, including *The Doctor Trap* by Simon Messingham, *Shining Darkness* by Mark Michalowski, *Ghosts of India* by Mark Morris, *Martha in the Mirror* by Justin Richards, *The Many Hands* by Dale Smith and *Snowglobe* by Mike Tucker.

Edited by Cavan Scott and Mark Wright, *Doctor Who: Short Trips: The Ghosts of Christmas* was a shared-world anthology featuring twenty-two stories and a wraparound. *Doctor Who: Short Trips: The Quality of Leadership* was edited by Keith R. A. DeCandido and contained thirteen original stories, while Richard Salter edited *Doctor Who: Short Trips: Transmissions*, featuring seventeen tales.

Torchwood: The Official Magazine Yearbook included five stories based on the *Doctor Who* spin-off series, along with articles.

The second volume in a trilogy, *Hellgate: London: Goetia* by Mel Odom was based on the computer game.

David Pirie's *A New Heritage of Horror: The English Gothic Cinema* was a revised and updated edition of the author/scriptwriter's groundbreaking 1973 study.

In the neatly-designed *Silver Scream: 40 Classic Horror Movies Volume One 1920–1941* from Telos Publishing, American writer Steven Warren Hill (with the help of some friends) looked at key films from the perspective of plot, highlights, lowlights, goofs, versions, trivia and major cast and crew.

Published by MacFarland, Derek Pykett's guide explored *British Horror Film Locations*, while Brian Albright's *Wild Beyond Belief! Interviews with Exploitation Filmmakers of the 1960s and 1970s* had another self-explanatory title.

William Schoell's critical study *Creature Features: Nature Turned Nasty in the Movies* was available from the same imprint.

The Pocket Essential: Vampire Films by Colin Odell and Michelle Le Blanc claimed to contain "almost everything you need to know in one essential guide" about movies featuring the undead.

Tomahawk Press' *Hazel Court: Horror Queen: An Autobiography* appeared a month or so after the death of its subject/author.

The first edition of Robert Sellers' *The Battle for Bond* from

Tomahawk had to be pulped when the estate for Ian Fleming objected to the inclusion of court documents from the *Thunderball* plagiarism court case of 1963, which the James Bond author famously lost. In his new Foreword to the revised edition, thriller writer Len Deighton accused the Fleming family of censorship and demonstrating "bad taste".

To mark the centenary of Fleming's birth, Sebastian Faulks' new James Bond novel, the 1960s-set *Devil May Care*, was published in May.

Quite possibly the biggest art book of the year, if perhaps not the best assembled, was *A Lovecraft Retrospective: Artists Inspired by H. P. L.* edited by Jerad Walters and published by Centipede Press. Weighing in at an impressive 400 pages, the book was available in a bewildering array of different limited editions, ranging from $395 up to $2,495. With a Preface by film director Stuart Gordon, an Introduction by Harlan Ellison, Afterword by Thomas Ligotti, and text by Stefan Dziemianowicz, Robert M. Price and Jane Frank, the beautifully-reproduced plates showcased the work of more than forty artists, including Virgil Finlay, Hannes Bok, Lee Brown Coye, Frank Utpatel, Michael Whelan, Dave Carson, Gahan Wilson, Les Edwards, Bob Eggleton, H. R. Giger, Stephen Fabian, J. K. Potter, Ian Miller, Harry O. Morris, Randy Broecker, John Jude Palencar and John Picacio, amongst many others.

Spectrum 15: The Best in Contemporary Fantastic Art edited by Cathy Fenner and Arnie Fenner featured the work of more than 300 artists, plus a profile of Grand Master Award winner John Jude Palencar.

Edited by Stephen D. Korshak and J. David Spurlock, *The Paintings of J. Allen St. John: Grand Manster of Fantasy* was a combined biography and superb retrospective of the artist's commanding paintings. The book also included appreciations by Jack Williamson, artist Vincent Di Fate and Edgar Rice Burroughs' son Danton, along with an Introduction by Lin Carter and an Afterword by Frank Frazetta. It was published in various states by Vanguard Productions, including a deluxe slipcased hardcover that included a sixteen-page portfolio, and a signed leatherbound edition with an additional tipped-in plate ($250.00).

Mark Evanier's *Kirby: King of the Comics* was a giant-sized look at the career of influential and pioneering illustrator Jack Kirby, who died in 1994.

From Fantagraphics Books, Blake Bell's *Strange and Stranger: The*

World of Steve Ditko was the first critical retrospective of the work of the reclusive co-creator of *The Amazing Spider-Man*, while Bill Schelly's *Man of Rock: A Biography of Joe Kubert* looked at the career of the comic artist most famous for DC's *Sgt. Rock*.

Edited by Jacques Boyreau and published in a "VHS format" by Fantagraphics, *Portable Grindhouse: The Lost Art of the VHS Box, Vol.1* reprinted around 100 examples of the outrageous artwork that used to be featured on video boxes.

Tales from Outer Suburbia combined the short fiction and bizarre sketches of Australian artist Shaun Tan.

Adam Rex's delightful blend of humorous poetry and artwork, *Frankenstein Takes the Cake* was a follow-up to the author's bestselling *Frankenstein Makes a Sandwich*.

The Facts in the Case of the Departure of Miss Finch was written by Neil Gaiman and illustrated in colour by Michael Zulli. It concerned a mysterious adventure beneath the streets of London that involved The Theatre of Night's Dreaming and the Cabinet of Wishes Fulfill'd.

Gaiman also teamed up with artist Gris Grimly for the children's picture book *The Dangerous Alphabet*, a piratical ghost story involving two brave children, a no less courageous gazelle, and various trolls, bugbears and monsters.

The Vampire Hunter's Handbook by "Raphael Van Helsing" (writer Michael Howard and artist Miles Teves) was presented in the form of an illustrated diary with fold-out maps.

In March, a federal court in the US finally decided that Time Warner had to share the rights to Superman with the heirs of co-creator Jerome Siegal. The retroactive "Widows and Orphans" ruling covered copyright in the comic book character from 1999 onwards.

Despite its hefty size, *The Mammoth Book of Best Horror Comics* edited by Peter Normanton was a disappointing black and white collection of almost fifty comic strips dating from the 1940s up to nearly the present day. Although the book included adaptations of works by H. P. Lovecraft and Robert E. Howard, the format did not really support the best presentation of the material.

Joe R. Lansdale teamed up with artists Nathan Fox and Dave Stewart to adapt Robert E. Howard's *Pigeons from Hell* as a four-part series from Dark Horse Comics.

From Marvel, *Stephen King's The Dark Tower: The Long Road Home* was an original five-part series plotted by Robin Furth and scripted by Peter David, with artwork by Jae Lee and Richard Isanove.

P. Craig Russell adapted and illustrated the graphic novel of Neil Gaiman's young adult book, *Coraline*, while *In Odd We Trust* was a graphic novel based on Dean Koontz's "Odd Thomas" series, illustrated by Queenie Chan.

Jim Butcher scripted *The Dresden Files: Welcome to the Jungle*, a graphic novel prequel to the popular book series, illustrated by Ardian Syaf.

Zinescope Entertainment published three issues of *The Straw Men*, based on the novel by Michael Marshall (Smith). Zenescope president Joe Brusha adapted the book, while Brett Weldele contributed the minimalistic artwork and David Seidman supplied the evocative covers.

The same publisher also launched *The Chronicles of Dr. Herbert West*, a re-imagining of the serial by H. P. Lovecraft.

The Nightmare Factory Volume 2 from HarperCollins/Fox Atomic Comics contained illustrated adaptations of four stories by Thomas Ligotti. Scripted by Joe Harris and Stuart Moore, with art by Vasilis Lolos, Bill Sienkiewicz, Toby Cypress and Nick Stakal, each story featured a new Introduction by the author.

The CBS-TV show *Ghost Whisperer* became a five-issue series from IDW, while NBC's *Chuck* got a six-issue limited series from DC's WildStorm imprint.

Joss Whedon brought his character Fray into the sixteenth issue of Dark Horse Comics' *Buffy the Vampire Slayer*.

From Bluewater Productions, *Vincent Price Presents* was an ongoing series adapting some of the late actor's best-known films, along with new stories based around Price's iconic image. Bluewater's companion series of *Ray Harryhausen Presents* titles included *Sinbad Rogue of Mars*, *Flying Saucers vs. the Earth* and *Back to Mysterious Island*.

Although titled *Frank Frazetta's Dracula Meets the Wolf Man*, Image's one-shot comic was actually scripted by Steve Niles with art by Francesco Francavilla.

Niles also wrote Dark Horse's four-part *Criminal Macabre: Cell Block 666*, while writer Mark Verheiden and illustrator John Bolton teamed up to expand Sam Raimi's cult favourite *The Evil Dead*, which collected the four-issue mini-series.

Written by Joe Hill, *Welcome to Lovecraft* from IDW concerned the members of a family trying to rebuild their lives on the eponymous island in Maine. Gabriel Rodriguez supplied the art.

Published by DC Comics in bumper trade paperback format, *Showcase Presents The House of Secrets Volume One* collected in black and white eighteen complete issues of the comic book edited by Joe Orlando. Similar volumes were dedicated to *The House of Mystery*, *The Unknown Soldier*, *The Phantom Stranger* and *Challengers of the Unknown*.

The damaging screenwriters' strike carried into 2008 and resulted in the Hollywood Foreign Press' usually prestigious 65th Golden Globe Awards ceremony being reduced to a dull press conference.

However, 100 days after the strike began, The Writers Guild of America finally reached a settlement just in time for the 80th Academy Awards Ceremony in February, when more than 90% of WGA members agreed to a deal giving them a larger share of profits from the Internet and other new media. The strike reportedly cost Hollywood and the wider Los Angeles economy an estimated $1.6 billion.

Presented at LA's Kodak Theatre on February 24, the lowest-rated Oscars ever threw up few surprises as Best Art Direction went to *Sweeney Todd: The Demon Barber of Fleet Street*, *The Golden Compass* won Best Visual Effects, Disney's *Ratatouille* was voted Best Animated Feature, and the Best Animated Short Film went to the British-Polish co-production *Peter and the Wolf*.

A special honorary Oscar was presented to ninety-seven-year-old art director and production designer Robert F. Boyle, whose credits include *The Wolf Man*, *Flesh and Fantasy*, *It Came from Outer Space*, *The Birds* and *Explorers*.

Less than two months after the studio settled its royalty dispute with *Lord of the Rings* director Peter Jackson, New Line Cinema was sued by the estate of J. R. R. Tolkien. The heirs claimed that the film-makers had failed to pay "a single penny" of the contractual 7.5% of gross receipts from the trilogy of films, which to date are estimated to have grossed around $6 billion. The lawsuit reportedly demanded $150 million in damages and a court order to terminate the studio's rights to Tolkien's works.

In early June, a huge blaze engulfed the *King Kong* exhibit at Universal Studios in Hollywood, causing widespread damage to the five-acre backlot, damaging the *Back to the Future* courthouse square set and destroying the New York street scene. Thousands of videos and reel-to-reel music recordings were also lost in the fire, although duplicates were reportedly stored in another location.

Later that same month Tartan Films, the UK distributors who

imported many Asian horror titles, declared bankruptcy after struggling for several months.

At the beginning of September, the US box-office recorded its lowest gross since 2003, with the top twelve movies taking a combined $50.3 million. That was a 32% drop from the same weekend a year before and 23% lower than the previous weekend.

A group of unsympathetic New Yorkers recorded the destruction of their city by an unexplained CGI monster on a shaky handycam in J. J. Abrams' style-over-substance *Cloverfield*. Despite a record-breaking opening in February, the film took a 72% drop at the box-office in its second week.

Shot for under $4 million in Toronto, George A. Romero employed the same technique with more finesse and logic in *Diary of the Dead*, the fifth film in his masterful zombie series. Stephen King, Wes Craven, Quentin Tarantino, Guillermo del Toro and Simon Pegg could all be heard on the soundtrack. The DVD release included five zombie shorts made by winners of a MySpace contest, including magician Penn Jillette.

Also employing a shot-on-video narrative, *Quarantine* was a US remake of Jaume Balagueró's impressive 2007 Spanish film *[REC]*, about a TV crew trapped in an apartment building where a mysterious virus turned the inhabitants into cannibal zombies.

Obnoxious American tourists found themselves at the mercy of a carnivorous Mayan pyramid in *The Ruins*, scripted by Scott Smith and based on his bestselling 2006 novel.

Made back in 2006, *All the Boys Love Mandy Lane* involved a series of killings centred around Amber Heard's eponymous high school student, while Angela Battis returned to her hometown and was menaced by the serial killer who tortured her years earlier in *Scar*, shown in 3-D.

A bloodless reimagining of a not very good 1980s slasher movie, *Prom Night* opened in the US at #1 with a take of just $20.8 million. Brittany Snow was the unlucky high school student who was the target of a serial killer's obsession.

Aimed at the same teenage audience, a troubled high-schooler (Haley Bennett) couldn't escape her past in the Halloween release *The Haunting of Molly Hartley*.

Promoting its teen abstinence propaganda under the guise of Gothic romance, *Twilight* explored the relationship between seventeen-year-old Bella (Kristen Stewart) and immortal vampire Edward (Robert Pattinson). Based on the first of Stephenie Meyer's bestselling books, the movie debuted at the US box-office at #1 with a gross of $69.6 million. Despite the film's success, it was announced that director Catherine Hardwicke would not be involved with the sequel, *New Moon*.

Liv Tyler starred in the home-invasion chiller *The Strangers*, which grossed a surprise $21 million on its opening weekend, and Josh Randall and Brianna Brown played a city couple hiking in the Virginia woods who were attacked by a family of religious maniacs in *Timber Falls*.

Despite being killed off in the previous entry, Tobin Bell returned as "Jigsaw" in *Saw V*, which was not screened for critics. Neither was the plane-crash mystery *Passengers* starring Anne Hathaway, which is always a bad sign.

After an interesting opening, M. Night Shyamaian's ecological disaster movie *The Happening* quickly fell apart as Marc Wahlberg and Zooey Deschanel wandered around aimlessly while airborne plant toxins caused people to commit suicide. Wahlberg also starred as a glum cop hunting the killers of his wife and infant child in *Max Payne*. Based on a 2001 video game, it opened at #1 in the US in October.

Brendan Fraser starred in both Eric Brevig's digital 3-D remake of *Journey to the Center of the Earth*, which used Jules Verne's source novel as a guide to its dinosaur-filled underworld, and Rob Cohen's *The Mummy: Tomb of the Dragon Emperor*, which moved the action to Asia. The third *Mummy* movie also featured Jet Li as an evil emperor and Michelle Yeoh as an immortal sorceress, along with hairy yetis, an impressive dragon and a terracotta army of the undead.

Another disappointing sequel was Chris Carter's long-awaited *The X Files: I Want to Believe*. Six years after the TV series ended and ten years after the previous movie, there was absolutely no chemistry between David Duchovny's Fox Mulder and Gillian Anderson's Dana Scully, as they investigated a secret Russian experiment in head transplants. The "extended cut" DVD added just four extra minutes.

Former British footballer Vinnie Jones walked through his role as the subway serial killer in Ryuhei Kitamura's unpleasant and pointless expansion of co-producer Clive Barker's story, *The Midnight Meat Train*. When the film was given a delayed and limited theatrical run by distributor Lionsgate, Barker publicly blamed studio politics.

Kiefer Sutherland's troubled nightwatchman discovered that evil demons were reflected in *Mirrors*, a remake of a 2003 South Korean movie, while Jessica Alba could see dead people after a cornea transplant in a remake of the 2002 Hong Kong film *The Eye*.

Shutter was a remake of a 2004 Taiwanese film, as ghosts haunted the photos of a newlywed couple (Joshua Jackson and Rachael Taylor), and people received text messages predicting their deaths in *One Missed Call*, based on a 2003 Japanese original.

An electronic signal sent through televisions and radios on New Year's Eve turned people into angry psychopaths in *The Signal*, a low budget independent feature shot in three sections by different directors.

Alyssa Milano turned up in *Pathology*, in which medical interns planned the perfect murder, and FBI cyber-crime agent Diane Lane hunted a serial killer who used the Internet to stream his victims' deaths in *Untraceable*.

A high school cheerleader (Jess Weixler) discovered she possessed a set of *vagina dentata* in Mitchell Lichtenstein's darkly humorous *Teeth*.

Ricky Gervais' misanthropic dentist could see ghosts in David Koepp's comedy *Ghost Town*. After debuting at #8 in the US, the film was just as dead as Greg Kinnear's self-obsessed spirit.

Eva Longoria Parker starred as a jealous Blithe Spirit who made life hell for her former fiancé's new psychic girlfriend (Lake Bell) in the charmless romcom *Over Her Dead Body*. It might have done better if they had gone with the original title, *Ghost Bitch*.

Anthony Stewart Head's creepy mad scientist harvested body parts for Paul Sorvino's biotech business in the horror musical, *Repo! The Genetic Opera*, which also featured soprano Sarah Brightman and the pointless Paris Hilton. Lloyd Kaufman's *Poultrygeist: Night of the Chicken Dead* was another low-budget musical comedy, this one set in a fried-chicken franchise built over a Native American burial ground.

The British horror film industry made something of a comeback in 2008. Sibling kidnappers (played by Andy Serkis and Reece Shearsmith) were menaced by a psychopathic farmer in Paul Andrew Williams' comedy *The Cottage*, and a team of mercenaries discovered Nazi zombies survived in an abandoned World War II bunker in Steve Barker's *Outpost*, shot in Scotland.

The derivative *Doomsday* from the overrated Neil Marshall had its tough heroine (original "Lara Croft" model Rhona Mitra) heading north of the border to find a cure among the cannibals for a zombie plague that was infecting London.

Filmed on the Isle of Man and based (uncredited) on the role-playing game, *Mutant Chronicles* featured Thomas Jane, Ron Perlman, Sean Pertwee and John Malkovich attempting to survive a zombie apocalypse 700 years into the future.

A tragedy involving the titular sex act led to escalating violence in the deeply unpleasant *Donkey Punch*, and a nursery teacher (Kelly Reilly) and her boyfriend (Michael Fassbender) were menaced by terrifying teenagers in *Eden Lake*.

During the Christmas season a mysterious virus caused youngsters to turn on their parents in Tom Shankland's genuinely unnerving *The Children*. Shankland's other film of the year was *WΔZ*, in which two mis-matched detectives (Melissa George and Stellan Skarsgård) hunted a serial killer who carved an equation into his mutilated victims' flesh.

Directed by Nicholas Roeg and based on a book by Fay Weldon, *Puffball* featured a cast that included Miranda Richardson, Rita Tushingham and Donald Sutherland in a story about a pregnant architect (Kelly Reilly) beset by pagan forces.

Simon Callow's Cambridge don was possessed by the spirit of Aleister Crowley in Julian Doyle's totally bonkers *Chemical Wedding* (aka *Crowley*), co-scripted by Iron Maiden's Bruce Dickinson.

Set in Russia, Stephen Dorff's professional thief found himself trapped by brother-and-sister maniacs in the Irish comedy *Botched*.

In something of an Australian cliché, three tourists were menaced by crocodiles on a swamp river cruise in *Black Water*, and another giant killer croc made life hell for a group of tourists in *Rogue*, Greg McLean's scary follow-up to *Wolf Creek*.

Spanish director J. A. Bayona just about avoided the clichés in *The Orphanage* (*El orfanato*) about an old building haunted by the scary ghosts of abused children. Executive produced by Guillermo del Toro, Geraldine Chaplin turned up as a psychic researcher.

In the French-made *Frontiers*, four criminals encountered a family of neo-Nazi cannibals.

Scripted by John Ajvide Lindqvist and based on his novel, a twelve-year-old Swedish boy discovered that the mysterious young girl who moved in next door was actually an immortal vampire in Thomas Alfredson's atmospheric variation on the traditional mythology, *Let the Right One In* (*Låt den rätte komma in*).

The four Pevensie children were called back from World War II London to the magical world they had left 1,300 years before in Andrew Adamson's improved sequel *The Chronicles of Narnia: Prince Caspian*. In a surprise cameo, Tilda Swinton recreated her role as the seductive White Witch.

Based on the young adult book franchise created by writer Holly Black and illustrator Tony DiTerlizzi, *The Spiderwick Chronicles* condensed the entire series into a stylish and scary children's film, as Freddie Highmore (as twins) and Sarah Bolger investigated their great-great-grandfather's spooky old dark house and discovered a dark world of faeries.

The stories Adam Sandler's hotel handyman told to his niece and nephew came magically true, but with unexpected results, in Disney's children's fantasy *Bedtime Stories*, while Brendan Fraser's book collector had the ability to bring literary characters to life in *Inkheart*, and adaptation of Cornelia Funke's bestselling children's novel.

Based on Steven Gould's YA series, *Jumper* featured Hayden Christensen as a moody teen teleporting around the world, pursued by Samuel L. Jackson's white-haired assassin, and two teens defied Bill Murray's corrupt Mayor in an attempt to save their underground *City of Ember*, based on the 2001 novel by Jeanne DuPrau.

Shot in 2006 and produced by co-star Reese Witherspoon, *Penelope* was a modern fairy tale that starred Christina Ricci as an heiress cursed with the nose of a pig until she met her one true love.

Robert Downey, Jr was perfectly cast as billionaire industrialist and playboy Tony Stark, who became the titular tin-pot hero in Jon Favreau's exhilarating *Iron Man*. Downey also recreated his character for an uncredited cameo in Louis Leterrier's *The Incredible Hulk*. Edward Norton (who re-wrote much of the script and fell out with the studio) starred as a glum Bruce Banner battling Tim Roth's "Abomination".

Although the two films boosted Marvel's licensing profits by 60% in a single quarter, shares still slumped when the company's improved forecasts fell short of market expectations.

Punisher: War Zone was the third attempt to create a franchise based on another Marvel character. Ray Stevenson took over the role of the vengeful killer.

Not to be outdone, *The Dark Knight* – Christopher Nolan's sequel to *Batman Begins* – pitted Christian Bale's morose Batman against the late Heath Ledger's anarchic Joker. The film broke records for the biggest opening day ($67.2 million) and biggest weekend ($158.4 million). After three consecutive weeks at #1 in America, in August the film smashed through the $400 million (£206 million) mark for US earnings after being on release for just eighteen days – half the time it took *Shrek 2*, the previous record holder, to reach the same target.

Guillermo del Toro's overblown sequel *Hellboy II: The Golden Army* relied too much on CGI and not enough on plot, as the horned hero (Ron Perlman) and his cohorts attempted to stop renegade faerie Prince Nuada (an impressive-looking Luke Goss) from declaring war upon mankind.

Based on Will Eisner's classic newspaper strip – through you wouldn't have known it from the ads that promoted writer/director Frank Miller – Gabriel Macht starred as the masked crime-fighter in a highly stylized but ultimately disappointing *The Spirit*.

Will Smith played a drunken deadbeat superhero in *Hancock*, which took more than $100 million in its first week.

The whole genre was sent up in Craig Mazin's lamentable spoof *Superhero Movie*, in which nerdy costumed hero "Dragonfly" (Drake Bell) avenged the death of his beloved uncle (poor old Leslie Nielsen). Even worse was *Disaster Movie*, which spoofed everything from *Cloverfield* to *Enchanted*.

Nineteen years after the previous episode, sixty-four-year-old Harrison Ford returned as the adventuring archaeologist in Steven Spielberg's disappointing fourth instalment, *Indiana Jones and the Kingdom of the Crystal Skull*. Cate Blanchett's Cold War spy was after the eponymous extra-terrestrial artefact, while a returning Karen Allen and the annoying Shia LaBeouf were along for the ride. In the second highest Memorial Day weekend gross ever, it took $152 million in five days at #1.

Despite the film's box-office success, the makers of Comedy Central's *South Park* cartoon were not impressed either, and they took their anger out on Spielberg and George Lucas in an October episode of the TV show.

Meanwhile, Spielberg was named as a defendant when his studio DreamWorks, its parent company Viacom, and Universal Pictures were accused of stealing the plot of the short story that inspired Alfred Hitchcock's 1954 classic *Rear Window* for *Disturbia*, also starring LeBeouf.

A remake of the 1975 *Death Race 2000*, Paul W. S. Anderson's *Death Race* pitted Jason Statham's framed convict against Joan Allen's scheming prison warden. An unlikely Statham also turned up in Uwe Boll's sword & sorcery video game adaptation *In the Name of the King: A Dungeon Siege Tale*, which also included embarrassing turns from John Rhys-Davies, Ron Perlman, Ray Liotta and Burt Reynolds.

As the emotionless "Klaatu", Keanu Reeves was perfectly cast as the alien messenger who arrived in Central Park with his warrior robot Gort in Scott Derrickson's totally pointless remake of the 1951 classic *The Day the Earth Stood Still*.

Vin Diesel's mercenary helped smuggle a mysterious girl (Melanie Thierry) to a dystopian New York City in *Babylon A.D.*, based on a French novel. The studio took the final cut away from director Matthieu Kassovitz, but it still didn't help.

Eddie Murphy played an alien spaceship searching for salt in Brian Robbins' comedy flop *Meet Dave*.

Although it opened at #1 in the US, Roland Emmerich's (pre-) historically inaccurate *10,000 BC* was also not a mammoth hit.

Based on the 1960s Japanese *anime* TV series, the Wachowski Brothers' futuristic *Speed Racer* was all flash and no substance, and was quickly overtaken at the US box-office after grossing just $40 million.

Even Steve Carell couldn't save *Get Smart*, an updated reworking of the 1960s CBS-TV sci-spy series.

Carell and Jim Carrey added their vocal talents to the CGI cartoon *Horton Hears a Who!*, based on the classic 1954 children's book by Theodor Geisel ("Dr Seuss").

Featuring the voices of John Cusack, Steve Buscemi and Eddie Izzard, the Frankenstein-inspired 3-D CGI cartoon *Igor* debuted at #4 in the US.

Christopher Lee voiced his character "Count Dooku" only for the animated movie version of *Star Wars: The Clone Wars*, which was basically an extended trailer for the highly stylized TV cartoon series.

From Pixar/Disney, Andrew Stanton's annoying *Wall.E* featured the eponymous garbage-collecting robot left behind on an abandoned Earth. It took more than $60 million in its first week.

The French-made *Fear(s) of the Dark* was an anthology of disturbing black and white cartoons from six different directors.

In July it was reported that a complete if worn print of Fritz Lang's classic three-and-a-half hour SF movie *Metropolis* was discovered in the archives of the Museo de Cine in Buenos Aires, Argentina. It apparently included reels removed from release prints after the film's 1927 debut. The discovery came less than two weeks after New York's Kino International announced that it had completed a frame-by-frame restoration of the film.

Rouben Mamoulian's 1931 version of *Dr Jekyll and Mr Hyde* starring Fredric March received a welcome theatrical revival in the UK.

Spine Tingler! The William Castle Story looked at the career of the veteran exploitation film producer and director of the 1950s and '60s.

Among those who contributed to Jeffrey Schwartz's documentary were Leonard Maltin, Bob Burns, Stuart Gordon, Fred Olen Ray, Roger Corman, John Landis, Joe Dante and Forrest J Ackerman.

Dreams with Sharp Teeth was a feature-length documentary by Erik Nelson about the often controversial but always entertaining Harlan Ellison. It had its New York premiere in June.

Almost before it had time to get established, Toshiba's HD-DVD format was withdrawn in February and Blu-ray Disc was declared the winner in the format wars.

Meanwhile, as part of the run-up to the controversial 2008 Olympic Games in Beijing, the Chinese government banned videos containing "strange and supernatural storytelling for the sole purpose of seeking terror and horror". The crackdown included depictions of "wronged spirits and violent ghosts, monsters, demons and other inhuman portrayals".

Although it starred the director's daughter Asia, her mother Daria Nicolodi, and genre veteran Udo Kier, the much-anticipated final entry in Dario Argento's "Three Mothers" trilogy, *Mother of Tears* (*La Terza Madre*), was a huge disappointment for fans.

Reeker 2: No Man's Land, David Payne's sequel to his own 2005 film, was this time set around a Death Valley motel menaced by the smelly supernatural serial killer, while the monsters were back to menace a small town in John Gulager's comedy sequel *Feast II: Sloppy Seconds*.

Two years after the events in the first film, C. Thomas Howell's gloomy hero was back battling the blood-drinking Martian invaders in the no-budget sequel *War of the Worlds 2: The Next Wave*, which the actor also directed.

Corey Feldman and Corey Haim returned as vampire-hunters in P. J. Pesce's *Lost Boys: The Tribe*, a late and unnecessary sequel to Joel Schumacher's original 1987 cult favourite. *Lost Boys: Reign of Frogs* was a prequel comic book from DC/Wildstorm that bridged the gap between the two movies.

We also did not need *Creepshow III*, an anthology film produced without the participation of either George A. Romero or Stephen King.

While it seemed equally unlikely that the world was waiting for either Phil Tippet's South African-shot *Starship Troopers 3: Marauder* with Casper Van Dien, or Russell Mulcahy's prequel *The Scorpion King 2: Rise of a Warrior*, one can only wonder what possessed Jeremy Kasten to remake Herschell Gordon Lewis' 1970 cult classic *The Wizard of Gore* with Crispin Glover, Jeffrey Combs and Brad Dourif.

Trailer Park of Terror was loosely based on the Imperium Comics series, as Nichole Hiltz's sexy trailer trash and her redneck zombie companions laid waste to a coach party of troubled teens.

In the near future, dead soldiers were reanimated to fight America's increasing number of wars in the comedy *Zombie Strippers*, featuring adult film star Jenna Jameson. Unfortunately, the virus spread to a pole-dancing club owned by Robert Englund.

Even with a cast that included Mena Suvari, Ving Rhames and Ian McNeice, genre veteran Steve Milner (*House*) couldn't do much with his direct-to-DVD remake of George A. Romero's 1985 *Day of the Dead*, set in a mountain town overrun with zombies.

A mad scientist (Peter Stormare) was turning asylum patients into flesh-eating psychopaths in Jeff Buhler's cleverly-titled *Insanitarium*.

R. Lee Ermey's redneck cameo was the only reason to see *Solstice*, a remake of the 2003 Swedish ghost story *Midsommer*, directed by Daniel Myrick (*The Blair Witch Project*).

Reuniting many of the cast members from the TV series, the direct-to-DVD sequel *Stargate: Continuum* involved the team returning to Earth, only to discover that history had been altered.

The Boneyard Collection was an anthology compilation directed by Edward L. Plumb. Hosted by the late Forrest J Ackerman as "Dr Acula", with soap opera actor Ronn Moss as a long-haired Count Dracula, the real mystery was how they managed to get cameo appearances by such industry veterans as Candy Clark, Brad Dourif, Elvira, Ken Foree, Ray Harryhausen, Tippi Hedren, George Kennedy, Robert Loggia, Kevin McCarthy, poet/songwriter Rod McKuen, the late Bobby "Boris" Pickett, William Smith, Barbara Steele, Brinke Stevens and Susan Tyrrell. Writers Peter Atkins, Donald F. Glut, George Clayton Johnson, C. Courtney Joyner and Brad Linaweaver were also involved in the low-budget madness, along with Dark Delicacies bookstore owner Del Howison.

Larry Blamire's *The Lost Skeleton Returns Again* was a sequel to the writer/director's 2004 spoof on "B" sci-fi horror movies, *The Lost Skeleton of Cadavra*.

The DVD boxed set *Fox Horror Classics Vol. 2* contained *Chandu the Magician* (1932), *Dragonwyck* (1946) and *Dr Renault's Secret* (1942), along with audio commentaries, featurettes, still galleries, an isolated *Dragonwyck* score track and two vintage *Dragonwyck* radio shows performed by Vincent Price.

Legend of Hammer: Vampires was a nicely compiled feature-

length documentary narrated by actor Edward De Souza that looked
at all of Hammer's vampire movies in chronological order, illustrated
with clips, stills, rare behind-the-scenes footage and mostly contemporary interviews with many of those who were involved. Extras
included a brief interview with screenwriter Tudor Gates about an
unproduced "Karnstein" movie and a candid audio interview with
director John Gilling.

Produced by Renegade Arts Entertainment, *Doug Bradley's Spine
Chillers: The Outsider* was the first in a proposed new series of
collector's DVDs. It featured the *Hellraiser* actor (who also produced
and directed) presenting a dramatic reading of H. P. Lovecraft's short
story. Disappointingly, neither the film's graphics nor the packaging
matched the standard of Bradley's bravura performance.

The Sci Fi Channel continued to churn out numerous shot-on-a-
shoestring movies for TV. Soap opera actress Kristen Renton discovered that her family was descended from *Ghouls*, while Antonio
Sabato, Jr was among a group of disparate characters who found
themselves on a mysterious ship bound for Hell in *Ghost Voyage*.

Jeremy London's archaeologist had to stop fellow scientist Scott
Hylands from reviving the titular Sumarian storm god in Paul Ziller's
ludicrous *Ba'al: The Storm God*, which also featured a wasted Lexa
Doig as a radical meteorologist.

Meanwhile, a group of archaeological students in Iraq uncovered
Noah's *other* Ark and the darkness it contained in Declan O'Brien's
Monster Ark, and backpacking college student Chad Collins pulled a
sword from a stone, unleashing the titular *Rock Monster*, also
directed by O'Brien.

Bruce Boxleitner, Gil Gerard, Veronica Hamel, William Katt and
Walter Koenig were among the veteran TV cast battling a giant
Native American skeleton monster in Jim Wynorski's silly *Bone
Eater*.

During the final days of World War II, a band of women fliers on a
top-secret mission found themselves stranded on a remote island full
of flying dinosaurs in *Warbirds*.

Brian Trenchard-Smith's *Aztec Rex* was about a small band of
seventeeth-century conquistadors that encountered a pair of surviving Tyrannosaurus Rex in a lost valley in Mexico.

John Schneider and Daryl Hannah confronted hundreds of mu-
tated sharks in *Shark Swarm*, and Schneider was back as a town
magistrate who sacrificed strangers in return for immortality in
Ogre.

Bio-engineered snakes escaped and started attacking a cast that included Tara Reid, Corbin Bernsen and the late Don S. Davis in *Vipers*, Brad Johnson saved a Western town from poisonous snakes in the surprisingly fun *Copperhead*, and David Hasselhoff and John Rhys-Davies went looking for a giant snake in *Anaconda III: The Offspring*.

Rhys-Davies also played a mysterious survivor rescued by two couples sailing to Fiji in the supernatural thriller *The Ferryman*, filmed in New Zealand.

Grizzled veteran Bruce Dern tracked down a were-tree in the Vermont woods in David Winning's enjoyable *Swamp Devil*, while six teens found themselves trapped in a remote campground in *Flu Bird Horror*.

Aliens were behind global warming in *Heatstroke* starring D. B. Sweeney and former model Danica McKellar.

Purporting to relate a missing chapter from Homer's *The Odyssey*, the Sci Fi Channel's *Odysseus and the Isle of the Mists* set its shipwrecked Greek hero (Arnold Vosloo) against the first vampires.

Noah Wyle returned for the third time as Flynn Carson in Jonathan Frakes' *The Librarian: Curse of the Judas Chalice* from TNT. This time the naive globe-trotting adventurer had to track down the eponymous artefact that had the power to resurrect vampire king Vlad Dracul.

Scottish actor Dougray Scott was the latest actor to portray the kindly doctor and his psychotic alter-ego in a contemporary reworking of *Dr Jekyll and Mr Hyde* for ION Televison.

Peter Fonda and Rick Schroder starred in yet another version of Jules Verne's *Journey to the Center of the Earth*, also on ION.

Adapted by Andrew Davies from the novel by Sarah Walters, *Affinity* was a ghost story set in and around a notorious women's prison in London during the 1870s. Amanda Plummer portrayed a prison warder with an unconvincing British accent.

Sara Rue's writer-turned-teacher encountered a student who seemed to be the reincarnation of a dead classmate in *Nightmare at the End of the Hall* on the Lifetime Movie Network. Also from LMN, *Secrets of the Summer House* starred Lindsay Price as a woman whose family were endangered by a curse, while Amy Acker began seeing ghosts following *A Near Death Experience*.

Small town newcomer Catherine Bell wondered if she had the power to conjure up spells in the Hallmark Channel's original movie, *The Good Witch*.

Soap opera star Justin Bruening portrayed the son of Michael

Knight (a returning David Hasselhoff) in NBC's updated *Knight Rider* pilot, which featured an upgraded KITT (voiced by Will Arnett) that was powered by nanotechnology. In the subsequent TV series, an uncredited Val Kilmer took over as the voice of the car.

Benjamin Pratt and Eric McCormach discovered that the biological plague which had wiped out a small town in Utah was a warning from the future in Mikael Salomon's unnecessary remake of Michael Crichton's *The Andromeda Strain*, shown in two parts on A&E Networks.

Christopher Lee replaced the late Ian Richardson as the voice of Death in Sky's four-hour miniseries *Terry Pratchett's The Colour of Magic*, based on the author's first two "Discworld" novels. David Jason starred as hapless wizard Rincewind, with Tim Curry as the villainous Trymon, who attempted to kill off his fellow wizards.

The BBC's feature-length *Clay* was an adaptation of David Almond's children's novel, about a boy (Ben-Ryan Davies) who created a golem.

Broadcast by the BBC over Christmas, Aardman Animations' half-hour *A Matter of Loaf and Death* involved claymation duo Wallace and Gromit on the trail of a "cereal killer" who was preying on the town's bakers.

Comedian Catherine Tate's "Donna Noble" (from the 2006 Christmas special "The Runaway Bride") joined the BBC's *Doctor Who* as the time-traveller's new companion for thirteen episodes.

Together they encountered the Doctor's possible future wife (Alex Kingston) and his rebellious daughter (Georgia Moffett), and they teamed up with Agatha Christie (Fenella Woolgar) to solve a murder. In the blockbuster two-part season finale, the Doctor and Donna were joined by previous companions Rose Tyler (Billie Piper), Martha Jones (Freema Agyeman), Captain Jack Harkness (John Barrowman) and Sarah Jane Smith (Elisabeth Sladen) to prevent Davros and his Daleks from stealing the Earth. The poignant final episode, "Journey's End", achieved the highest viewing figures for the series with an average 9.4 million/45.9% share of the audience.

For the Christmas special, "The Next Doctor", the Doctor (David Tennant) travelled to Victorian London, where he encountered another man (David Morrissey) claiming to be him. Between them, they stopped the cybermen from controlling a giant CyberKing.

In May, Russell T. Davis announced that, after reviving the show in 2005, he would be standing down as the lead writer and executive producer of *Doctor Who*. He handed over to writer Steven Moffat

("Blink"), who would assume control of the show for the fifth season, to be shown in 2010.

That was followed by a shock announcement live on TV in October, when David Tennant announced that he would also be leaving the show after the next series of specials.

Season two of the BBC's *Torchwood* kicked off with the introduction of villain Captain John Hart (*Buffy*'s James Masters), a rogue bisexual Time Agent who used to be Captain Jack's (John Barrowman) lover. However, the show slowly improved as Freema Agyeman joined the cast for three episodes as Martha Jones (from *Doctor Who*), Owen (Burn Gorman) was killed and resurrected without a soul, and the team found themselves battling a personification of Death. In the season finale, "Exit Wounds", the real villain behind Captain John was revealed and two major characters were surprisingly killed off.

For some inexplicable reason, the BBC moved the show from Wednesday to Friday nights towards the end of its thirteen-episode run.

In the second season of the other *Doctor Who* spin-off, *The Sarah Jane Adventures*, the Doctor's earlier companion (Elisabeth Sladen) and her "son" Luke (Thomas Knight) once again teamed up with teenager Clyde Langer (Daniel Anthony) and new character Rani (Anjili Mohindra) to investigate alien incursions. Guest stars included comedian Russ Abbot, Samantha Bond, and Nicholas Courtney recreating his character "Brigadier Lethbridge-Stewart".

The much-improved second seven-part season of ITV's enjoyable *Primeval* found Douglas Henshall's dour Professor Nick Cutter returning through a time "anomaly" into a subtly-changed world where Claudia Brown (actress Lucy Brown, who turned up in another role) never existed. What had not changed was that prehistoric utahraptors, giant worms, sabre-tooth tigers, Silurian scorpions and other CGI-created creatures were continuing to cause chaos, while Cutter's duplicitous wife Helen (the wonderful Juliet Aubrey) could still not be trusted. Although the multi-monster finale failed to quite live up to expectations, despite the apparent death of he-man Stephen (James Murray), the conspiracy subplot and time-space paradoxes kept the series moving along nicely.

It was certainly livelier than Joe Ahearne's devilishly dull *Apparitions*. Martin Shaw (who was also executive producer) played Catholic exorcist Father Jacob battling demons, Vatican conspiracies, and his own faith. Originally intended to be a two-part special, the BBC inexplicably extended the run to six mind-numbing episodes.

Written by critic Charlie Brooker and obviously made on a shoestring budget, Channel 4's surprisingly effective three-hour limited series *Dead Set* was situated in and around the British *Big Brother* house besieged by flesh-eating zombie hordes (including regular presenter Davina McCall). In the UK it ran over five nights the week before Hallowe'en.

The third season of The CW's *Supernatural* ended with Dean Winchester (Jensen Ackles) fulfilling the deal he had done to save his brother Sam (Jared Padalecki) and going to Hell. The fourth season kicked up a gear (and substantially increased its viewing figures) when it was revealed that Dean had been saved from eternal damnation by a warrior angel named Castiel (Misha Collins). With the Apocalypse fast approaching, the brothers found themselves caught up in the ultimate battle between the forces of Good and Evil, even if they were not sure which side they were on.

In a fun black and white Halloween episode, Dean and Sam found themselves hunting a shape-shifter that took the form of old horror film monsters, including a barely-glimpsed werewolf, an impressive mummy and Count Dracula himself (Todd Stashwick).

With episodes adapted from stories by Del Howison, Peter Crowther and Paul Kane, NBC-TV broadcast just eight of the thirteen episodes of Mick Garris' anthology series *Fear Itself* over the summer.

Originally shown by the BBC in three half-hour episodes in the run-up to Christmas, the derivative *Crooked House* owed far too much to the fiction of R. Chetwynd-Hayes and the old Amicus anthology movies. Writer/producer Mark Gattis played the enigmatic museum curator who revealed three stories centred round a haunted mansion.

In the first season finale of HBO's *True Blood*, based on Charlaine Harris' series of "Southern Vampire" novels, Louisiana waitress Sookie Stackhouse (Anna Paquin) – with a little help from her 175-year-old vampire boyfriend (Stephen Moyer) – discovered the identity of the serial killer who was bumping off her neighbours.

The show was promoted with an innovative mailing campaign in which letters written in dead languages led their recipients to a website that explained the background to the series and why vampires no longer needed to feed on humans.

No sooner had Alex O'Loughlin's undead Mick St. John temporarily regained his mortality on CBS' *Moonlight*, than the lack-lustre vampire detective show was cancelled after just one series.

From the BBC, *Being Human* was an hour-long pilot about a rebellious vampire (Guy Flanagan), an intelligent werewolf (Russell Tovey) and a tea-making ghost (Andrea Riseborough) sharing a house. Thanks to the three leads, the offbeat drama deserved to go to series.

With a complicated back story that involved vampires and a group of *League of Extraordinary Gentlemen*-type immortals, a Mary Poppins-voiced Amanda Tapping played the sexy Dr Helen Magnus, whose team of helpers took care of the misunderstood monsters in the Sci Fi Channel's enjoyable thirteen-part *Sanctuary*.

Slacker Sam (Bret Harrison) dated the mysterious Candy (Jessica Stroup), who might just have been the daughter of Ray Wise's dapper Devil in The CW's *Reaper*.

Melinda (Jennifer Love Hewitt) discovered that Grandview was built over a cursed underground city that had become a repository for all the evil spirits in CBS-TV's *Ghost Whisperer*. Jamie Kennedy joined the cast in Season 4 as a psychiatrist who could hear ghosts, and Melinda's supportive husband Jim (David Conrad) was shot to death.

Following the revelations that turned life upside down for psychic sleuth Allison DuBois (Patricia Arquette) in NBC's *Medium*, the star's sister, Rosanna Arquette, guest-starred as a woman who seduced and killed her partners, while younger brother David directed an episode. Recurring guest star Anjelica Huston joined the fourth season for six episodes as a mysterious private investigator whose daughter had disappeared.

After the departure of producer David E. Kelley and the pilot being almost completely recast and reshot, ABC-TV's remake of the BBC's hit *Life on Mars* eventually debuted in October. Jason O'Mara played modern-day NYPD detective Sam Tyler, who was hit by a car and mysteriously transported back to the Big Apple, circa 1973. Veteran actor Harvey Keitel turned up as craggy ex-marine Lt Gene Hunt.

Back in the UK, *Ashes to Ashes* was the BBC's follow up to *Life on Mars*. Detective Inspector Alex Drake (Keeley Hawes) was thrown back in time to 1981 London, where she had to deal with Chief Inspector Gene Hunt (the wonderful Philip Glenister) and his sexist cronies. Although the show featured a clever connection between DI Drake and the earlier series' Sam Tyler, Alex's increasingly bizarre attempts to save her parents from a car bomb simply did not ring true.

Even more bizarre was *Lost in Austen*, a four-part drama in which twenty-first century bank worker Amanda Price (Jemima Rooper) went through a mysterious door in her bedsit bathroom and found herself in her favourite novel, Jane Austen's *Pride and Prejudice*. But when the plot started to deviate from the story she knew by heart, Amanda was forced to step in and try to control the action, with disastrous results.

However, possibly the year's most bonkers genre show was the six-episode *Bonekickers*. Starring Julie Graham and Hugh Bonneville (who should have known better), it involved a team of unlikely archaeologists investigating an historical conspiracy linked to the legend of Excalibur. After the show lost more than three million viewers in four weeks, the BBC decided not to commission a second season.

Still, Julie Graham quickly joined other BBC "regulars", such as Max Beesley and Freema Agyeman, in *Survivors*. Focusing on the aftermath of a deadly virus that wiped out most of the world's population, it was a six-part reimagining of the late Terry Nation's novelization of an earlier series (1975–77) he created. The 1976 book was reissued with a new cover to tie-in with the remake.

After being saved from cancellation by a write-in campaign by fans, CBS-TV's *Jericho* returned for seven episodes in February with a new federal government taking control of the eponymous post-holocaust town. In the final episode, Skeet Ulrich's character recovered a nuclear bomb from the corrupt government in Cheyenne, Wyoming. When viewing figures dropped to 7.1 million, the network decided not to commission a third season, although the production shot two alternative endings – just in case.

Frances Fisher joined the third season of Sci Fi's *Eureka* (aka *A Town Called Eureka*) as a tough corporate boss brought in to sort out the town filled with scientific geniuses.

Created by J. J. Abrams, Fox's *Fringe* was basically *X Files*-lite as Olivia Dunham's FBI agent brought together cynical genius Peter Bishop (the likeable Joshua Jackson) and his eccentric scientist father Walter (John Noble) to investigate a "Pattern" of bizarre phenomena. It was one of the year's consistently watched shows, possibly due to its shorter ad breaks.

Based on the series of British TV movies created by Stephen Gallagher and starring Patrick Stewart, CBS' *Eleventh Hour* featured

Rufus Sewell as superscientist Dr Jacob Hood and Rachel Young as his FBI handler investigating scientific mysteries.

Having dropped the plotlines from Jeff Lindsay's source novels, the third season of Showtime's sublime *Dexter* concentrated on the sympathetic serial killer's friendship with Miguel Prado (the superb Jimmy Smits), which turned sour when Dexter (Michael C. Hall) discovered that the corrupt Assistant District Attorney was a bigger monster than he was. In the season finale, he finally married his pregnant girlfriend Rita (Julie Benz).

ABC's hugely-hyped *Lost* returned in January for a fourth season with flashbacks and flashforwards revealing which of the "Oceanic 6" got off the island. The dead Charlie (Dominic Monaghan) showed up in the future, a new group of "rescuers" (including a grizzled Jeff Fahey) arrived, and the traitorous Michael (Harold Perrineau) returned before the entire island disappeared. The writers' strike resulted in the planned sixteen episodes being cut to thirteen. The show returned in April before going on hiatus again at the end of May until early 2009.

Set after the events in the second film, there was little point to Fox's *Terminator: The Sarah Connor Chronicles* when fans of the movie series already knew the outcome. Still, British actress Lena Headey made a solid action heroine, trying to keep her gloomy fifteen-year-old son John (Thomas Dekker) safe from killer cyborgs with the help of friendly Terminator Cameron (Summer Glau). Following the highest-rated series debut of the January season, viewing figures dropped 53% in the third week, although they eventually recovered slightly.

The ten-part Season 2 introduced Garbage singer Shirley Manson as a corporate villain and shape-changing "Terminator T-1001".

After a car crash left Jaime Sommers (Brit actress Michelle Ryan) near death, her fiancé rebuilt her faster and stronger in a re-imagining of *The Bionic Woman*. *Battlestar Galactica*'s Katee Sackhoff then turned up as an earlier, discarded model with a homicidal grudge against her replacement. Production stopped after eight episodes because of the writers' strike.

The Sci Fi Channels' *Battlestar Galactica* returned for its fourth and (eventually) final season. The most intelligent and daring science fiction show on TV finally revealed who the hidden human Cylons were, and ended up on a devastated Earth.

Stargate SG-1's Teal'c (Christopher Judge) made a guest appearance on Sci Fi's *Stargate Atlantis*, while actress Rachel Luttrell's pregnancy as warrior woman Teyla was written into the storyline.

The fourth season ended with John Sheppard (Joe Flanigan) arriving back on Atlantis, but 40,000 years in the future.

In The CW's *Smallville*, Lex Luthor (Michael Rosenbaum) discovered the connection behind a secret society called "Veritas" created by his father, Lionel (John Glover), before apparently meeting his end when the Fortress of Solitude imploded. Back in Metropolis for the eighth season, after the Justice League showed up to rescue Clark (Tom Welling) from the Arctic, Justin Hartley's Oliver Queen joined the regular cast, and Sam Witwer showed up as monstrous villain Doomsday. Meanwhile, series creators Al Gough and Miles Millar decided it was time to move on.

Natalie Morales' struggling artist became a superhero after being saved by *The Middleman* (Matt Keeslar) in the ABC Family show based on the graphic novel series. Despite a guest appearance by Kevin Sorbo as a 1960s Middleman and an army of trout-eating zombies, it was cancelled after just twelve episodes.

At least NBC gave Zachary Levi's reluctant sci-spy another chance, after renewing *Chuck* for a second season when it managed to survive its difficult time slots. Guest stars included Nicole Richie, John Larroquette and Michael Clarke Duncan.

The increasingly convoluted and ludicrous third season of NBC's *Heroes* ("Villains") kicked off with a two-hour premiere in which it was revealed who shot politician Nathan Petrelli (Adrian Pasdar) moments before he was going to confirm his superpowers. With ratings plummeting 22% in early November, the show's co-executive producers Jesse Alexander and Jeph Loeb were fired after reportedly refusing to return to the character-driven stories of the popular first season.

Writer Bryan Fuller rejoined *Lost* after ABC cancelled his screwball series *Pushing Daises*. In the second season, pie-maker Ned (Lee Pace) and his resurrected dead girlfriend Chuck (Anna Friel) encountered killer bees, circus clowns, and Fred Willard as a murdered magician.

Brit actor Jonny Lee Miller starred as a lawyer-turned-divine prophet suffering from a brain aneurysm in two seasons of ABC-TV's quirky fantasy, *Eli Stone*. Singer George Michael turned up as God and himself, and other guest stars included Katie Holmes and Sigourney Weaver. After a rocky first season cut short by the writer's strike, the show was abruptly cancelled in November.

Put under a spell by a Native American maiden, Nikolaj Coster-Waldau's 400-year-old detective John Amsterdam was looking for a love worth dying for in Fox's *New Amsterdam*, which was cancelled after just eight episodes.

Also cancelled in 2008 were *The 4400*, Cavemen, *The Dead Zone*, *Flash Gordon* and *Journeyman*.

Filmed on location in France, the BBC's thirteen-part family drama *Merlin* featured younger versions of the legendary characters, as the trainee wizard (Colin Morgan) was forced to keep his powers secret from his friends Arthur (Bradley James), Morgana (Katie McGrath) and Gwen (Angel Coulby). The adult cast included Anthony Head as the inflexible Uther Pendragon, Richard Wilson as the kindly apothecary Gaius, John Hurt as the voice of an impressive CGI dragon, plus Michelle Ryan as recurring villain Nimueh.

Executive producers Sam Raimi and Rob Tapert attempted to recreate the success of their *Hercules* and *Xena* series with the syndicated *Legend of the Seeker*, based on the fantasy novels by Terry Goodkind.

Jonathan Pryce's Dr Victor Blenkinsop's attempts to produce a prototype soldier resulted in the scientist and his naive creation (Stuart McLoughlin) taking refuge in a country village to escape Mark Gatiss' homicidal army colonel in the old-fashioned BBC comedy *Clone*, which ran for six episodes.

Also from the BBC, the one-off drama *A Number* was based on the 2002 stage play by Caryl Churchill, in which a father (Tom Wilkinson) created multiple identical clones of his supposedly dead son (Rhys Ifans).

After an extended hiatus, Kyle (Matt Dallas) finally revealed his bio-engineered origin to his adopted family and tracked down his real mother (1980s actress Ally Sheedy) in Season 2's final ten episodes of *Kyle XY* from ABC Family.

Steven R. McQueen, the nineteen-year-old grandson of the famous movie actor, starred in *Minutemen*, a teen time-travel comedy on the Disney Channel.

Stingray – The Reunion Party was a new half-hour episode of the 1960s puppet series edited together from clips and recently discovered linking material under the supervision of co-creator Gerry Anderson.

Following the success of the 2007 live-action film, *Transformers: Animated* was an update of the original 1980s TV show on Cartoon Network.

Hollywood veteran Lauren Bacall, Hayden Panetiere and Jay Leno were guest voices in *Scooby-Doo and the Goblin King*, the latest Halloween movie featuring the Scooby Gang.

The Cartoon Network's *Batman: The Brave and the Bold* teamed a retro Caped Crusader up with other heroes, including Green Arrow, Aquaman, Atom, the original Blue Beetle and Plastic Man.

The irritating Jar Jar Binks from 1999's *Episode I: The Phantom Menace* returned for an episode of the Cartoon Network's juvenile *Star Wars: The Clone Wars*, in which he helped C-3PO rescue Senator Padmé Amidala. Much more entertaining was the spoof *Robot Chicken: Star Wars Episode II*, which included Billy Dee Williams voicing his "Lando Calrissian" character.

The Simpsons nineteenth *Treehouse of Horror* on Fox Network opened with a timely gag about the Presidential election and then went on to spoof *Transformers: The Movie*, the TV show *Mad Men* and the Halloween classic, *It's the Great Pumpkin Charlie Brown* (and included the original 1966 music score by Vince Guaraldi).

In an October episode of Fox's *Family Guy*, Stewie and Brian travelled back in a time machine to Nazi Germany to rescue Jewish pharmacist Mort from numerous movie spoofs.

To celebrate the 40th Anniversary of ABC's daytime soap opera *One Life to Live*, Viki (Erika Slezak) had *A Matter of Life and Death* moment in which she encountered past characters in Heaven, while Bo (Robert S. Woods) and Rex (John-Paul Lavoisier) were hit by lightning and transported back to 1968 – the year the show made its debut.

Before NBC's supernatural soap *Passions* ended its nine-year run in August, it featured daytime TV's first legal gay wedding between Norma (Marianne Muellerleile) and Edna (Kathleen Noone), while local Lothario Julian Crane (Ben Masters) was castrated by a crazy teenager and then had his penis reattached upside down by a drunken doctor – with potentially fatal results.

Katherine Heigl's Izzie had sex with the ghost of Jeffrey Dean Morgan's Denny in a ludicrous November episode of ABC's morose medical drama *Grey's Anatomy*, while the residents of the small North Carolina town had to deal with Torrey DeVitto's psychotic nanny Carrie in The CW's *One Tree Hill*.

Hallmarks' *Psych* ended its second season with fake psychic detective Shawn Spencer (James Roday) and his reluctant assistant Gus (Dulé Hill) investigating a 3,000-year-old mummy that apparently walked out of a museum. The third season opened with an episode involving a supposedly haunted house.

BBC4's *The Worlds of Fantasy* consisted of three hour-long documentaries exploring fantasy literature from *The Water Babies* to *Harry Potter*. Among those taking part were Philip Pullman, Alan Garner, Lyra Belacqua and Amanda Craig.

Martin Scorsese narrated the original TCM documentary *Val Lewton: The Man in the Shadows*. Kent Jones' feature-length look at the legendary "B" movie producer was subsequently included in a reissue of the DVD boxed set *The Val Lewton Horror Collection*.

H. P. Lovecraft's early story of madness and obsession, *The Tomb*, was read by Ryan McCluskey in a half-hour radio adaptation on BBC7 at the end of March.

BBC Radio 4's *The Saturday Play: The Voyage of the Demeter* was an original hour-long reworking by Robert Forrest of the Dracula story, set aboard the eponymous schooner in 1897.

From the same station in July, Mike Walker's *Afternoon Play: It's Better with Animals* emulated the old Amicus portmanteau films, in which a mysterious New York furrier (Russell Horton) set in motion three macabre stories.

Written by Sebastian Baczkiewicz, *Pilgrim* was a four-part series on Radio 4 about the eponymous book-dealer (Paul Hilton) cursed with immortality in 1185 and compelled to walk between the worlds of faerie and man.

Dramatized by Robin Brooks, *Terry Pratchett's Night Watch* was broadcast on Radio 4 over February and March as five half-hour episodes featuring the voice of Philip Jackson as the time-travelling Commander Sam Vimes of the City Watch.

A two-part, two-hour adaptation of Victor Hugo's *Classic Serial: The Hunchback of Notre Dame* was produced as a collaboration between BBC Radio Drama and the disabled-led theatre company Graeae. Deaf actor David Bower played Quasimodo, who fell in love with Candis Nergaard's gypsy girl, Esmeralda.

To coincide with the £5 billion Large Hadron Collider experiment near Geneva, Switzerland, where scientists attempted to recreate conditions moments after the "Big Bang" by smashing protons together at almost the speed of light, Radio 4 presented a special radio edition of the TV series *Torchwood* on September 10. Written by Joseph Lidster, "Lost Souls" featured the voices of series regulars John Barrowman, Eve Myles, Gareth David-Lloyd and Freema Agyeman as Martha Jones.

Unfortunately, the experiment itself was shut down after less than ten days when a faulty electrical connection resulted in a helium leak.

Based on a short story by Nikolai Gogol, *Christmas Eve* on Radio

4 was about a local witch in league with the Devil who tried to steal the moon and the stars.

In January, Amazon.com reportedly paid $300 million to acquire New Jersey-based website Audible.com, which provides digital downloads of spoken-word material.

From the H. P. Lovecraft Historical Society, *Dark Adventure Radio Theatre Presents H .P. Lovecraft's Dunwich Horror* was a seventy-five minute audio drama with music by Troy Sterling Nies. The CD package included a clipping from a 1917 copy of the *Arkham Advertiser*, a vintage map of Dunwich and the surrounding region, a page from Wilbur Whateley's diary, and a replica of a key page from Whateley's copy of John Dee's *Necronomicon*.

A Message from The Twilight Zone CD featured George Clayton Johnson reading "All of Us Are Dying" and the script for his story "Nothing in the Dark", adapted by Rod Serling for the classic TV show.

Demon Lovers and Other Eroticisms contained seven erotic poems written and recited by Sam Stone, with music composed and performed by Penny Nicholls.

George Langelaan's 1957 *Playboy* story "The Fly" was turned into an opera directed by David Cronenberg (who also directed the 1986 film version). With music composed by Howard Shore and a libretto by David Henry Hwang, the production premiered in Paris, France, in July and opened in Los Angeles in September. Tenor Plácido Domingo conducted the orchestra.

David Lynch's 1997 movie *Lost Highway* also got the opera treatment at London's Young Vic, thanks to the English National Opera company and Austrian composer Olga Neuwirth's score.

With *Matthew Bourne's Dorian Gray*, the London-born choreographer updated Oscar Wilde's story as a modern-day dance-drama. Richard Winsor played eternally young waiter Dorian, whose aftershave poster aged instead of him.

In February, Chicago's WildClaw Theatre company opened its production of Arthur Machen's *The Great God Pan* at the Athenaeum Theatre. It was followed in November by WildClaw's stage production of H. P. Lovecraft's *The Dreams in the Witch House*.

Ten imaginative stories by Edwardian author "Saki" (H. H. Munro) were re-imagined by writer Toby Davies for Thomas Hescott's stage production *Wolves at the Window* at London's Arcola Studio.

The Love&Madness ensemble's touring stage adaptation of Mary Shelley's original *Frankenstein* starred Nathan Brine as Victor and Craig Tonks as his sympathetic Creature.

A victim of falling ticket sales, it was announced that Mel Brooks' Broadway stage musical *Young Frankenstein* would close early in 2009, after fourteen months and 484 performances.

In July, former companions Catherine Tate and Freema Agyeman co-hosted the *Doctor Who Prom* performed by the BBC Phiharmonic Orchestra at London's Royal Albert Hall. David Tennant appeared on-screen via an interactive clip, and various monsters (including Davros and his Daleks) invaded the stage.

Probably the hottest survival horror game of the year was *Dead Space*, a gory and genuinely creepy adventure set aboard the remote mining spacecraft *USG Ishimura*, where the crew had been transformed into monstrous creatures ("necromorphs"). The player took on the role of communications engineer "Isaac Clarke" (a nice homage), who had to battle his way through zero gravity to rescue his girlfriend and escape.

In development from EA Games for three years, there was also a tie-in *Dead Space* comic book, while an animated movie was also in the works.

Almost as impressive was *Left 4 Dead*, in which the player was one of four survivors of a global infection that had turned the rest of the population into fast-moving zombies. Not only could you also play as the living dead, but the game also monitored the player's skill and adapted accordingly.

In *Dracula: Origin*, players took on the identity of "Professor Van Helsing", who attempted to track down Dracula and destroy him in a fairly faithful reworking of Bram Stoker's original novel.

Devil May Cry 4 introduced demi-demon Nero, who teamed up with regular gunslinger hero Dante to travel through the underworld.

Based on the ever-more convoluted TV series, *Lost: The Video Game* might possibly have worked better in game format than it did on the small screen. Unfortunately, as played from the perspective of an amnesiac victim of the Oceanic plane crash, it was just as slow and frustrating at the show itself.

Released just in time for the Christmas market, *Tomb Raider: Underworld* saw the return of heroine Lara Croft as she took her puzzle-solving skills to Mexico, Thailand and the Arctic. Although the Eidos video game did well in Europe, it flopped in the US with sales of just 1.5 million up to the end of the year.

Sculpted by Bryan Moore for Arkham Studios, the twelve-inch "H. P. Lovecraft Bust" was finished in a bronze rub and was limited to just fifty signed and numbered pieces.

A life-sized replica of "The Tingler" from William Castle's 1959 movie came fully assembled and painted from Amok Time.

From EMCE Toys/Fearwerx, the *Night of the Living Dead* eight-inch Mego-style action figures celebrated the 40th anniversary of George Romero's seminal zombie movie. The line was launched with posable dolls of hero "Ben" and the graveyard "Zombie".

A deluxe action figure of "Bub" the zombie from Romero's second sequel *Day of the Dead* came complete with a laboratory diorama and a bucket full of bloody bits.

A twelve-inch statue of Vincent Price's "Don Nicholas Medina" from Roger Corman's *The Pit and the Pendulum* came with a battery-operated light-up cauldron and an additional poker from Amok Time. The same company's deluxe boxed set of "Gort" and "Klaatu" limited edition collectible figures from the original *The Day the Earth Stood Still* featured two interchangeable heads for Klaatu – regular hairstyle and flat hair to use under his helmet!

Mattel produced a Barbie doll that resembled Tippi Hedren being attacked by the feathered fiends from Alfred Hitchcock's *The Birds*.

Britain's Royal Mail issued a set of stamps commemorating Hammer Films and the *Carry On* series. Among the images featured were *The Curse of Frankenstein*, *Dracula*, *The Mummy* and *Carry On Screaming*.

A first edition of *The Hobbit* by J. R. R. Tolkien sold at a London auction house in March for £60,000 ($120,800) – double the estimate, and a world record for a signed edition of the book. Published in 1937 and illustrated by the author, only 1,500 copies were printed.

In May, a copy of *Beeton's Christmas Annual* for 1887, containing Sir Arthur Conan Doyle's first Sherlock Holmes story "A Study in Scarlet", sold at auction for £18,600 ($35,500). It had been discovered in an Oxfam shop by two charity workers.

At the end of the same month, an original poster for the 1933 *King Kong* sold at auction in Calabasas, California, for $345,000 (£180,000). Measuring almost seven-foot square, the poster was one of only three examples of the size known to exist.

*   *   *

The World Horror Convention was held in Salt Lake City, Utah, over 27–30 March. Guests included author Dennis Etchison, artist John Jude Palencar, academic Michael R. Collings, toastmaster Simon Clark (replacing Simon R. Green), serial killer specialist Dr. A. L. Carlisle, special guests Jeff Strand, Mort Castle and Larry Edwards (replacing Dave Dinsmore), and "Ghost of Honor" Edgar Allen [sic] Poe. Robert McCammon was announced as the winner of the WHC Grand Master Award.

The 2007 HWA Bram Stoker Awards were announced at a Banquet on March 29 at World Horror. Sarah Langan's *The Missing* won Novel, while the award for First Novel went to Joe Hill's *Heart-Shaped Box*. The Long Fiction Award winner was "Afterward, There Will Be a Hallway" by Gary Braunbeck (from *Five Strokes to Midnight*), David Niall Wilson's "The Gentle Brush of Wings" (from *Defining Moments*) won Short Fiction. The Collection award was a tie between Peter Straub's *5 Stories* and Michael A. Arnzen's *Proverbs for Monsters*. *Five Strokes to Midnight* edited by Gary Braunbeck and Hank Schwaeble picked up the award for Anthology, while Nonfiction went to *The Cryptopedia: A Dictionary of the Weird, Strange & Downright Bizarre* by Jonathan Maberry and David F. Kramer. There was another tie in the Poetry category, between Linda Addison's *Being Full of Light, Insubstantial* and Charlee Jacob and Marge Simon's *Vectors: A Week in the Death of a Planet*. Life Achievement Awards were previously announced for John Carpenter and Robert Weinberg.

Created "in recognition of the legacy of Shirley Jackson's writing" with permission of the author's estate, and introduced without much fanfare, the inaugural Shirley Jackson Awards were announced by Jonathan Lethem on July 20 at Readercon in Burlington, Massachusetts. Voted upon by a jury of writers, editors, critics and academics, with input from an "Advisory Board" (including Ann VanderMeer, S. T. Joshi, Mike O'Driscoll and Ellen Datlow), the winners were Elizabeth Hand's *Generation Loss* for Novel, Lucius Shepard's "Vacancy" (from *Subterranean* #7, guest-edited by Ellen Datlow) for Novella and Glen Hirshberg's "The Janus Tree" and Nathan Ballingrud's "The Monsters of Heaven" (both from Ellen Datlow's anthology *Inferno*) for Novelette and Short Story, respectively. Laird Barron's *The Imago Sequence and Other Stories* won for Collection, while Datlow's *Inferno* was the inevitable winner of Anthology award.

The 2008 British Fantasy Awards were announced at a banquet at FantasyCon in Nottingham on September 20. The August Derleth

Award for Best Novel went to Ramsey Campbell's *The Grin of the Dark*, and Best Novella was Conrad Williams' *The Scalding Rooms*, both from PS Publishing. Joel Lane's "My Stone Desire" (from *Black Static* #1) won Best Short Fiction, Christopher Fowler's *Old Devil Moon* won Best Collection, and *The Mammoth Book of Best New Horror Volume Eighteen* was voted Best Anthology.

Peter Crowther's PS Publishing won the Best Small Press award, Vincent Chong was voted Best Artist, and Best Non-Fiction was awarded to Peter Tennant for his reviews on the *Whispers of Wickedness* website. The Karl Edward Wagner Award for Special Achievement went to Ray Harryhausen, and Scott Lynch received The Sydney J. Bounds Best Newcomer Award.

Having dropped its presentation ceremony at the World Fantasy Convention, the winners of The International Horror Guild Awards for outstanding achievement in the horror and dark fantasy field were revealed online on Halloween.

Chosen from a list of nominees derived from recommendations made by the public and a panel of judges, Dan Simmons' *The Terror* won for Novel, Lucius Shepard's *Softspoken* won Long Fiction, Lisa Tuttle's "Closet Dreams" (from *PostScripts* #10) won for Mid-Length Fiction, and Nancy Etchemendy's "Honey in the Wound" (from *The Restless Dead*) won for Short Fiction. Shepard's *Dagger Key and Other Stories* picked up the Collection award, while Non-Fiction went to *Mario Bava: All the Colors of Dark* by Tim Lucus. Ellen Datlow's *Inferno* was the winner in the Anthology category, Peter Crowther and Nick Gevers' *PostScripts* won for Periodical, and Thomas Ligotti's *The Nightmare Factory* collected the award for Illustrated Narrative. The Art award went to Elizabeth McGrath for "The Incurable Disorder" (Billy Shire Fine Arts, December 2007).

Peter Straub had previously been revealed as the recipient of the IHG's annual Living Legend Award, and it was announced that 2008 would be the last year that the awards would be presented.

The World Fantasy Awards were presented on the Sunday afternoon banquet at The 2008 World Fantasy Convention, held over October 30 – November 2 in Calgary, Alberta, Canada.

Guy Gavriel Kay's *Ysabel* won the Novel award, Elizabeth Hand's *Illyria* picked up Novella, and the Short Fiction award went to Theodora Goss' "Singing of Mount Abora" (from *Logorrhea*). It was a hat-trick for Ellen Datlow's *Inferno* in the Anthology category, scriptwriter Robert Shearman's debut book *Tiny Deaths* won for Collection, and Edward Miller (Les Edwards) won for Artist. The Special Award – Professional went to Peter Crowther for PS Publishing, and Midori Snyder and Terri Windling won the Special Award – Non-Professional for their Endicott Studios Website. Life Achievement awards went to Patricia A. McKillip and artists Leo and Diane Dillon.

Twenty years is a long time in publishing. In horror publishing it is a *very* long time.

Very few horror anthology series have succeeded in reaching a two-decade milestone – especially with the same editor at the helm.

In the 1920s and '30s Christine Campbell Thomson edited eleven volumes and one omnibus edition of her *Not at Night* series, mostly drawn from the pages of *Weird Tales*.

From the early 1970s onwards, *The Fontana Book of Great Horror Stories* clocked up an impressive seventeen volumes (the first four edited by Christine Bernard and the remainder by the redoubtable Mary Danby), while *The Fontana Book of Great Ghost Stories* did actually make it to volume #20 (the first eight edited by Robert Aickman before R. Chetwynd-Hayes took over for the rest of the run).

From the same publisher, but aimed at a younger readership, Danby succeeded Bernard again after two volumes to edit the remaining thirteen editions of *The Armada Ghost Book*, while Chetwynd-Hayes only managed six volumes of *The Armada Monster Book*.

The late Charles L. Grant produced eleven volumes of new stories in his acclaimed *Shadows* series, plus *The Best of Shadows* in 1988.

When it comes to "Year's Best" compilations, the seminal *Year's Best Horror Stories* made it to twenty-two volumes from DAW Books. Richard Davis edited the first three, Gerald W. Page handled the next four, and the matchless Karl Edward Wagner made the remainder his own.

The Year's Best Fantasy and Horror ran it a close second, with twenty-one volumes. Ellen Datlow compiled the horror content for all of them, while Terri Windling was responsible for the fantasy material up to when Kelly Link and Gavin J. Grant took over from the seventeenth annual collection up until it was abruptly cancelled in early 2009.

Perhaps the most successful anthology series (in terms of durability, if not quality) was the venerable *Pan Book of Horror Stories*, which ran for thirty editions from 1959 until 1989. Herbert van Thal was credited as the editor for the first twenty-five volumes until, following his death in 1983, Clarence Paget replaced him for the final five.

When Ramsey Campbell and I first started editing the *Best New Horror* series back in 1990 the world was a very different place. In our genre we were coming to the end of the unprecedented 1980s boom in horror fiction and the traumatic events of 9/11 – and the ways in which it changed our world forever – were still more than a never-imagined decade away.

Personal computers were just becoming established work tools, but there was no public Internet. E-mail did not exist, and neither did DVDs, print-on-demand publishing or electronic readers.

Since then, we have weathered a couple of recessions and economic recoveries, learned to listen to buzz words such as "global warming", and not to trust others like "war on terror".

In short, the world today is a very different place to what it was two decades ago. Yet here I am, still reading hundreds of short stories every year and being given the wonderful opportunity to present you with a selection of those that I consider to be amongst the best examples published during that particular period.

As history has illustrated, there are never any guarantees as to how long a horror anthology series will last. But as we celebrate this particular landmark, I would like to thank all the authors, editors, publishers and – especially – readers who have helped us to get this far.

Horror fiction – most importantly, *good* horror fiction – will always be with us. New writers are constantly being discovered and published, while established names continue to push the boundaries and hone their craft.

With your continued support, I hope that we shall be around to showcase their talents in these pages for many years to come.

The Editor
May 2009

PETER CROWTHER

Front-Page McGuffin and The Greatest Story Never Told

MORE THAN ANY other comparison, Peter Crowther can best be described as the contemporary August Derleth. A multiple award-winning editor, novelist and now – with the highly respected PS imprint – publisher, Crowther has edited twenty anthologies (plus more than eighteen volumes of the acclaimed *PostScripts*) and is the author of more than 120 stories and novellas.

He has also written the novel *Escardy Gap* (with James Lovegrove) and recently started work on the fourth volume of his *Forever Twilight* SF/horror cycle. His work has been adapted for television in both the UK and the US.

Crowther lives on the Yorkshire coast of England with his wife, Nicky, and an unfeasibly large collection of books, magazines, comics, DVDs and CDs . . .

As he recalls: "When I was working on *Narrow Houses*, my first anthology, and the two subsequent volumes (*Touch Wood* and *Blue Motel*), all of them on the theme of superstition, I desperately wanted to try my hand at a superstition story myself . . .

"Heck, I had plenty of ideas – I had suggested most of them in the anthology's commissioning letter. But, in the end, the idea I *did* decide to work on turned into *Escardy Gap*, and time just kind of ran away from me.

"By the time *Gap* was done, I'd forgotten all about it. Many years later, having created my New York watering hole The Land at the End of the Working Day, I had an idea about a guy who had died but was stuck on Earth . . . desperate to see his departed wife again. And I figured the reason he'd become that way was because the surfeit of talismanic gestures and portents that he had employed while looking after his sick wife. But, despite his ministrations, she had died anyway . . . while, somehow, his karma or id or whatever had been destabilized.

"Like all of the Working Day stories – there are four of them, plus umpteen one-, two- and several-page outlines – it pretty much wrote itself, with me just hanging on there for dear life and hitting the keypad every now and again. It features one of my favourite characters – I'll let you figure out which one it is."

I T'S NOT ALWAYS AS EASY as you'd think to tell dead folks from those that are still alive, and certainly not by where you happen to find them. Or where they happen to find *you*.

Take now, for instance.

And *here*.

It's a Tuesday in The Land at the End of the Working Day, a Tuesday Happy Hour, that no-man's land between afternoon and evening, when the drinks are half the regular price and the conversation is slow. But then the people who come in to the Working Day specifically for Happy Hour, no matter what day of the week it is, don't come in to talk.

The conversationalists of Manhattan (of whom there are many) don't bother with the hard-to-find watering holes tucked into the street corners and tenement walk-downs; they concentrate instead on the gaudily-coloured window-painted bars on the main drags, the bars with the striped awnings and the piped music spilling out past the muscled doormen with their emotionless stares, out onto side-walks littered with people looking in and wondering if – *wishing*, maybe – they could be a part of that scene.

There is no scene in The Land at the End of the Working Day. Not as such, anyways.

And there is no piped music here. Only the soft strains of one of Jack Fedogan's jazz CDs wafting in and out of hearing the way trains and car-horns Doppler in and out of existence as first they approach you and then they pass you by, going on someplace else.

Tuesday, a little after 6:00 pm, and Oliver Nelson's "Stolen Moments" is lazily washing around Jack Fedogan's bar, Freddie Hubbard's lilting trumpet solo making conversation unnecessary even if it were desired. Just a lot of introspective folks nursing Manhattans and Screwdrivers and Harvey Wallbangers and Sours, sitting staring into the mirror behind the bar, occasionally chomping on an olive or pulling on a cigarette, nervously flicking ash into a tray even before it's formed, sometimes going with the music by tapping a foot on the bar-rail or a hand on the bar itself, thinking of the day that's done or maybe the day that's still to come. Another one in an endless parade of days stretching out through the weeks and the months, the seasons and the years.

They look into that mirror like it's the font of all knowledge. Like the silvered glass is going to tell them what's wrong and how to put it right.

Every few minutes, one or another of the guys shucks the shirt-ends free of his jacket sleeves, picks lint-balls from his pants and pulls them up at the knees to keep the creases fresh, occasionally waving to the ever-watchful Jack to pour another whatever, some of these guys lost – or appearing to be lost – in the headlines of the *Times* or *USA Today*, but mostly the headlines on the sports pages.

The women in the booths along the back wall cross their legs first one way and then the other, sometimes checking in their purses for something though these checks always end without their pulling anything out. And then they just sit, staring into space or maybe glancing across at the bar while they light another cigarette, wafting the match out and tossing it in the tray in a kind of subconscious synchronized motion with the music.

For those who don't know it, The Land at the End of the Working Day is a walk-down bar in the greatest city in the world, New York City.

It's a Tuesday and Tuesdays here are quiet.

Most everyone here tonight knows everyone else. Not by name, nor by job nor by relations nor even by what they each like or what they don't like. They know each other by the lines on their faces and the depth of their sighs. These are the irregular regulars or maybe the regular irregulars, exchanging nods and pinched smiles like they were passing out on the street. They know what they're here for and it isn't company.

They're here to drink.

They're here to forget.

And a few are here to remember.

But there's also a nucleus of *regular* regulars, folks who *do* know each other's name. Usually, these guys – they're mostly guys – sit together at one or another end of the bar, clustered around the soda and beer taps and always within reaching distance of one of Jack's bowls of pretzels and nuts. But not in the great misnomer that is Happy Hour.

There's nothing particularly happy about Happy Hour.

Come 7:00, 7:30 pm at the outside, the place will start filling up. Folks will come in as couples, some married and some not but all of them comfortable with each other's company. And, generally speaking, all of them comfortable with life itself. They'll come in before going to a show or before going for a meal. Some of them will even come in to make a night of it, to get lost in conversation. And laughter and talk will fight for position with Jack Fedogan's CDs and the result will be a curious but entirely right amalgam of energy and sound and excitement.

But not now.

Now it's a little before 6:20. The heart of Happy Hour.

At this time, the regular regulars usually sit at the tables between the booths and the bar, conversation low and intense. Like a hospital waiting room.

There's only two tables filled tonight.

The table tucked in behind the bar close to the back wall has one man sitting at it. One man and a pack of playing cards. He's turning the cards over one by one, placing some on one pile and some on another. Every once in a while, he starts another pile by placing a card away from the others and then leaves it alone, putting cards on the other piles. For anyone watching, any casual observer, there wouldn't seem to be any rhyme or reason for the way he's turning those cards. But what do casual observers know about another man's chosen path in life?

This man is dressed in black – shirt, jacket and pants; the shirt buttoned right up to the neck but with no necktie – and he slouches back in his chair, a glass and a pitcher of beer on the table amidst the piles of playing cards. His eyes are hooded, bushy-browed, his face is thin – some might say "gaunt" or "drawn" – and he sports a small, neatly-clipped goatee beard which covers the tip of his chin and not a lot else.

This man is Artie Williams, sometimes known as "Bills" and others as "Dealer". He is something of a communicator, his head filled with numbers and probability percentages and ratios. There are those who say he has a direct line to the world beyond the rain-slicked streets of Manhattan and far away from the leafy thorough-fares of Central Park: the world where the spirits roam. But where this reputation has sprung from nobody knows. Artie Williams keeps himself very much to himself. Like tonight, Happy Hour, turning cards over on the table, drifting with the music, making piles and occasionally smiling to himself. And occasionally frowning.

The table midway between the stairs and the bar has three men sitting at it. One is Edgar Nornhoevan; another is Jim Leafman and the last of the three is McCoy Brewer.

They're talking about the condition of the subways right now. A little while ago, they were discussing the flow of traffic down Fifth. In a while, they may be talking about what kind of winter they're going to have this year. It's the middle of September now and the weather is a big consideration in New York, particularly after the excesses of the previous winter.

These men are what you might call real friends.

They can talk deep-down personal stuff – like Jim's wife Clarice cheating on him or Edgar's prostate problems or McCoy being laid off from his job with the Savings and Loan company – or they can talk controversial stuff like religion or life after death or abortion rights, but that isn't always necessary. Like tonight. And the truth is that only real friends can discuss trivialities with the level of intent and interest that Jim, Edgar and McCoy are displaying right now.

But that conversation about the subways will be interrupted in just a minute. And it won't drift into the weather. At least not tonight.

For tonight, the City will be sending to The Land at the End of the Working Day one of its casualties for healing.

It does that sometimes.

The sound of shoes echoes through the bar, shoes coming down the stairs. One guy at the bar stops tapping his hand for just a couple of seconds, the wink of an eye, and takes in this sudden intrusion. Then he goes back to tapping. An elderly man further down the bar mutters something to himself and then smiles into the mirror, gives a kind of half-chuckle and then reaches for his drink, running a finger down the iced-up side. The man he sees looks right back at him and returns the smile, runs a finger down his own glass.

Over in one of the booths, a woman in a red dress that's so red it looks like she just spilt berry juice all over it – looks like it should be dripping that redness onto Jack Fedogan's polished floor – she looks up for a second, drinking in the sight of the descending feet, then looks back at the glass she's twirling around the coaster on the table in front of her, the glass next to the pack of Marlboro Lights and matchbook, next to the ashtray with a collection of butts sitting in it that she is determined not to count. The feet don't mean anything to her. There's nobody knows she's here tonight. Nobody who even cares where she is, tonight or any night.

The truth is the feet don't mean anything to any of the irregular regulars.

But they mean something to Jim and McCoy and Edgar, and they stare at the line where the ceiling meets the diagonal stairs and watch as the owner of the feet comes fully into view.

As the feet get closer to the floor, walking strangely stiltedly on the stairs like one or both of them is favouring a broken shin-bone or a twisted ankle, these feet grow into legs and the legs grow into a waist and the waist turns into a full body and that, at last, leads into a head. The feet reach the floor and stop. The body sways slightly, like it has already had enough Happy Houring without looking for more, but the face on the head does not appear to be Happy Houred. Not at all.

The eyes are wide, wide but somehow not taking in what they're seeing, and the hair is mussed up and in bad need of a comb not to mention a razor and clippers. The sports coat hangs off of one shoulder, its sleeve obscuring the hand at the end of the arm it contains. The necktie is undone and hangs askew, the thin end flopped out over his sports coat lapel. The pants hang baggy around his crotch, no creases in them at all, the ends sitting crumpled up on mud-caked shoes whose laces are trailing untied on the floor.

"Hey," says Edgar Nornhoevan in a voice little louder than a whisper, "isn't that—"

"Front-Page McGuffin," says Jim Leafman, keeping his own voice low, nodding slowly.

McCoy Brewer keeps the nod going. "Sonofabitch, so it *is*," he says.

It won't surprise anyone to learn that Front-Page McGuffin's first name isn't really Front-Page, so it hardly seems like worth mentioning. But it kind of leads into other things that *are* important, so I will.

Front-Page McGuffin's first name is Archibald and the only other Archibald he ever *heard* of – he has never actually *known* any at all – is Cary Grant. And, as Front-Page is wont to remark at regular intervals – such as when someone introduces him to someone he doesn't already know (though there has never seemed to be many that ever fit *that* particular bill) as Archibald McGuffin, just for a joke kind of – *he* renamed himself. The fact that there are so few Archibalds says it all as far as Front-Page is concerned. And so he changed his name.

But, like it happens so often, the truth is slightly different. Front-Page didn't actually rename him*self*. It was done for him.

When A. D. McGuffin joined the *New York Times* back in the

1940s, he was sixteen – "too young to fight but old enough to cuss and make coffee," is how he usually tells it. The guys in the *Times* newsroom called him Adie, making something almost tuneful out of the acronym of his initials, sometimes putting their hands on their hips in an effeminate manner and shouting across the hubbub clatter of ringing telephones and pounding typewriter keys, "Hey, Adie, howsabouta coffee over here?" And they'd laugh. They'd laugh every time, like it was a new joke that nobody had ever heard before.

Hank Vendermeer, the guy who employed Front-Page, didn't make a big thing out of Front-Page's reluctance to divulge his first name. At that time, Hank had got a boy out in the Pacific, a problem making the payments on his house, a meeting with the Editor in about ten minutes (for which he was decidedly unprepared) and a peptic ulcer that made him wince every time he burped up wind. The fact was, Hank Vendermeer couldn't care diddly about names.

"What's the 'A' for?" Hank Vendermeer asked at the time, suddenly thumping his chest with a hand shaped like a fleshy meathook into which a tiny pencil had been incongruously placed.

"Just 'A'," Front-Page responded.

"Okay." Hank wrote it down. "And the 'D'?"

"Just 'D'," said Front-Page.

Hank Vendermeer shrugged and wrote the 'D' alongside the 'A' on the sheet on the desk in front of him, then made a few ticks here and there. And that was that. "Okay," he said. "You start tomorrow."

Front-Page had a job.

The 'D' in Front-Page's initials actually stood for Donald. But this seemed even worse to Front-Page than Archibald. Hell, the only Donald he'd ever heard of was a grumpy cartoon duck. No Thank You, Ma'am.

A. D. McGuffin worked hard and he learned fast and, pretty soon, he was making less coffee . . . though he was cussing more. At first, his daily routine pretty much consisted of schlepping copy around the various offices, doing a little typing, answering a few telephones, generally pinch-hitting around the floor. Then he got the chance to write up a piece on LaGuardia's speech in Atlantic City, when the Mayor of New York agreed to head up the UN Relief and Reha-bilitation Administration, imploring Americans the country over not to overeat and not to waste. A. D. wrote a nice piece and made it onto page four. His first solo flight in print. "One day," he told Sonny Vocello, "I'm gonna be on the front page."

"Sure," said Sonny, nodding his head. Hell, it was just a filler piece.

"Well, I am," said A. D.

"Sure," said Sonny Vocello. "We gonna have to call you *Front-Page* McGuffin." And he laughed, calling it out to anyone near enough to respond.

A. D. smiled and went along with the gag. But it made him even more determined to succeed.

A. D. didn't officially earn this sobriquet until December 1954 when he reported on the censure of the senator from Wisconsin for what the Senate called "four years of abuse of his colleagues". A week later, albeit in smaller print and in a keylined box in the bottom right corner, A. D. got his second front page story when Papa Hemingway was awarded the Nobel Prize for literature for his sparingly written story of an old fisherman who just refused to give up.

From then on, Front-Page McGuffin got a lot of lead stories and he just stuck with the name.

He retired from the *Times* in 1991 at the not-so-tender age of sixty-five. He was happy to be leaving it all behind, even though he still yearned for those years when newspaper reporting meant something more. But, he still had his wife, Betty, and he intended to write a book, a kind of memoir of the post-war years when everyone had a mental eye on the nuclear clock, watching its hands tick around to Armageddon.

He had his friends, too.

And his favourite watering hole, a two-flight walk-down that had just opened up a couple of years earlier on the corner of 23rd and Fifth, where he had met people who seemed real and where folks off the street just didn't seem to come. He made some *new* friends there, too, at a time of life when a guy couldn't really expect to make new friends but just to sit around and lose the ones he already had.

That last part was true enough for Front-Page McGuffin.

Cancers took a half-dozen of them in only half as many years, cut them down in their prime, wasting them to skin and bones and puckering up their mouths into thin-lipped sad little smiles. Bobby DuBarr, who could make a pool cue ball near on sit up and bark like a dog; Jimmy Frommer, who taught Front-Page all there was to know about subjunctive clauses; even Lester "Dawdle" O'Rourke, Front-Page's friend of friends, who was always late for everything, even the punchline of a joke . . . all of them went that way, eaten up from the inside like wormy apples, their skins yellow-white like old parchment and their ankles blown up over the sides of their house shoes because of all the steroids they were taking.

Heart attacks took another couple – Jack Blonstein, who had a singing voice that the angels would love, and Nick Diamanetti, who knew every joke that had ever existed (or so it seemed) – Front-Page watching them slip away in quiet hospital rooms with a barrage of blipping machines and suspended drips fixed onto scrawny arms.

A traffic accident took one of his best friends, a car crash up in Vermont where Bill Berison and his wife, Jenny had gone to see the fall colours on the trees. It had been something Bill had always planned to do.

Then, on New Year's Eve of 1994, in a lonely hospital ward in the South Bronx, Betty McGuffin gave in to the cancer that roiled inside her, slipping regretfully away from Front-Page into the waiting bedsheets, holding Front-Page's hand so tight he thought it would shatter and biting her lip to try to hold on another few minutes. To stay with him.

Thus, as millions of people celebrated the sudden movement of a clock-hand to midnight, the world ended for Front-Page McGuffin.

It didn't end with the cataclysmic explosion that Front-Page and his friends at the *Times* had been predicting in the 1950s and 60s, but with a sudden rush of silence that accentuated all of the minutiae of sound and colour that surrounded him.

He didn't remember getting home that night. Didn't remember getting into the suddenly wide and empty and lonely bed: it had been wide and empty for all of the nights that Betty had been in hospital but then Front-Page had been praying and hoping she'd come back. Now that he knew she would never be coming back, the bed was the loneliest place in the world.

The next night, he had been gone down to The Land at the End of the Working Day the way he'd gone down there to Jack Fedogan's bar most nights round about 6:30, for just a couple of drinks before going home to Betty and supper. Edgar Nornhoevan had been in that night, just like he was most nights, and Jim Leafman, too. Even McCoy Brewer came in, at around 10:00, armed with a passle of jokes that would have made even Nick Diamanetti smile.

Nobody mentioned Betty even once, but everyone bought Front-Page a drink and everyone gave his shoulder a squeeze. Once or twice, Edgar and Jim and McCoy saw Jack wiping his face with a towel, making out like the heat was getting to him, even though it was the first day of January and cold enough to freeze the spit as you swallowed it. Edgar, Jim and McCoy figured Jack Fedogan was thinking back about his own Phyllis and recognizing Front-Page's grief and his loss.

At a little after midnight, Front-Page made his farewells and stumbled up the stairs and out into the night. They never saw him again.

Not until tonight.

Three years later.

The three men at the table sit and stare.

Jack Fedogan stands and stares, the seemingly ever-present glass that he polishes held limply in one hand and the towel in the other.

Over behind them, Edgar, Jim and McCoy hear the sound of chair legs being pushed roughly across the floor. When they turn around they see Bills Williams standing up at his table and staring across at the new customer.

It's a night for staring, though none of the other patrons – the irregular Regulars – are paying any attention to Front-Page McGuffin.

"Hello," says Front-Page, like he's been here every night for months, but stammering the word and making it come out in a kind of croak.

Jack Fedogan leans on the bar and shakes his head. "Front-Page," he says, "Where you been hiding yourself?"

Front-Page McGuffin looks around like he's seeing the place for the first time, frowning and blinking his eyes. As they watch, Edgar, McCoy and Jim notice one of the eyelids seems to hang down longer, like it's got stuck on the way back. Front-Page lifts his left arm and starts swinging it towards his face, the fingers moving slow and robotic like the pick-up-a-prize machines out on Coney Island. Eventually, the hand gently connects with Front-Page's neck and then crawls – there's no other word for it – crawls its way up onto his chin and then around the cheek up to the eye socket where one of the fingers extends and pushes the lid up. Front-Page rubs at it, blinks a couple more times, and then drops the arm by his side.

"Not . . . well," says Front-Page, leaving a big space between the words. "How you guys?"

Edgar gets to his feet and moves to take Front-Page's hand, having to lift it up from the man's side first, and pumps it furiously but carefully. "Good to see you," he says, "been a long time."

"Long time," Front-Page echoes.

He looks to the other two men at the table and then walks across stiltedly, listing to the left at first until he whacks himself on the hip. This seems to cure the trouble and he makes it all the way to the table without further mishap. His co-ordination seems to have improved a little but it's still shaky, like he's not in control of his movements.

Front-Page takes hold of Jim Leafman's hand, shakes it and says, "Jim." Jim nods, returns the shake.

"How about that?" Edgar is saying to Jack Fedogan.

"Something's wrong," says Jack, keeping his voice low.

Over at the table, McCoy Brewer is reaching his hand across to Front-Page but Front-Page backs away, looking at it in a kind of blank-faced horror . . . a quiet desperation.

McCoy looks across at Jim and then over at Edgar and Jack. "What did I say?" he asks, but Front-Page is already making his way around the table. When he reaches McCoy, he leans forward and takes hold of McCoy's hand in both of his own and shakes it emphatically. "Bad luck," says Front-Page, shaking his head slowly and uncertainly, looking like maybe he's already had a few Happy Hours of his own before hitting the Working Day.

McCoy pulls his hand back from Front-Page, who seems momentarily unable to detach himself, and flexes the fingers and then rubs it in his other hand. "Jeez," says McCoy, "must be cold out there."

Jim moves across and puts an arm around Front-Page's shoulder. "You okay?" He pulls a chair across from a nearby table. "You want to sit down?"

Front-Page moves his head slowly and jerkily to face Jim Leafman. His eyes are all white for a second and then the pupils slide slowly down. "Not well," he says.

Jim helps him to the chair and Front-Page drops onto the seat.

Bills Williams moves over to stand by the table. Jim and McCoy look at him and shrug.

"How you doing, wordsmith?" says Bills.

Front-Page shakes his head. "Not well," he says, the words sticking partway out.

McCoy and Jim take their seats and pull their chairs into the table. Edgar says to Jack Fedogan to bring over a pitcher of beer and four glasses. When he sees Bills Williams pulling another chair across, he tells Jack to make that five glasses.

Over at the table, McCoy asks what was bad luck.

"Bad luck," Front-Page agrees enthusiastically.

"No," McCoy says, raising his voice like he's talking to someone who speaks a different language to the one *he* uses, separating out the words. "What. Did. You. Mean. About. Bad. Luck. When. You. Shook. My. Hand?"

Front-Page nods. "Bad luck." And then he leans forward, raps the table with his knuckles, puts his head on his arm and commences to let out the most fearful noise.

"He's really lost the plot," McCoy Brewer observes.

Edgar Nornhoevan looks down at his hands and notes, with some surprise, that they're shaking. "I'm not even sure he recognized me . . . or any of us," he says, more to himself than to anyone else.

Jim Leafman taps Edgar on the shoulder and nods in the direction of Front-Page McGuffin. "He having some kind of attack?"

"He's crying," Bills Williams says quietly.

"Crying?" says McCoy. "That's *crying*?"

The sound that the one-time star reporter of the New York *Times* is making is a noise that's a little bit like nails being dragged across a blackboard, a little bit like the busted air conditioning in Edgar's apartment, and a little bit like the whine of the loose fan-belt on Jim Leafman's aged Plymouth. And with every new expulsion, Front-Page's back arches like a mad cat.

Bills reaches across and takes hold of Front-Page's hand, raises his eyebrows. Then he shifts his hold to the wrist.

"He's cold isn't he?" says McCoy. "He's one sick man."

"He's worse than that," says Bills.

Edgar frowns. "What's worse than being sick?" he asks.

Front-Page lifts his head and that eyelid has stuck down again. He lifts his hand and adjusts it, this time a little easier. "I do . . . I do remember you guys," he says, the words sticking here and there, coming out croaked, and then raps the table with his knuckles.

"You eating, Front-Page? You gotta eat you know," says Edgar, sounding like he's talking to a child. "Keeps your strength up."

"Not hungry," says Front-Page, rapping his knuckles on the table again.

"Ask him when he last ate something?" Jim whispers to Edgar.

"Two weeks, maybe three," says Front-Page without waiting for Edgar to pass on the question. He raps his knuckles again. "Don't remember. Just remember the pain."

Edgar says, "Pain?"

Front-Page slaps a hand heavily against his chest. "Pain," he says, "right here. Fell over in the street . . . down near Battery Park. Late night. Nobody around." He pauses and makes a wheezing sound. When he speaks again, the lips barely come apart, cracked and discoloured. "Just lay there for a time. Thinking of Betty."

"Oh God," Edgar says, hanging his head.

"Then what happened?" asks Bills.

"Pain went away. Got up . . . went somewhere."

"Where'd you go, Front-Page? Did you go home?"

Front-Page looks at Jim and tries to shrug. "Doanmumber."

"He doesn't remember," Bills translates for the frowning Edgar. He hands his glass of beer to Front-Page and watches him take a long slug.

Jack Fedogan strolls across and places the pitcher of frothy beer on the table, puts a glass in front of each person. "How's he doing?"

"Not good," says Edgar.

"He's worse than not good," says Bills. "He's dead."

Nobody speaks.

Front-Page looks from one wide-eyed face to another while in the background, from Jack Fedogan's bar speakers, Ellis and Branford Marsalis play a haunting version of "Maria".

"I think," says Front-Page, "he's right." The words come out straighter and coherent and he looks as surprised at that as everyone else looks as a result of Bills Williams's revelation. "It happens sometimes," Front-page says. He gives the table a single knock with his knuckles.

"It happens sometimes that people die and walk into a bar to see their old friends?" Edgar says, his voice getting higher with each word.

Front-Page shakes his head. "My voice," he says. "Sometimes it sounds almost normal. The beer helps."

"But, yes, Edgar, it does happen sometimes that people walk around after they've . . . *passed on*," Bills says. "I seen it once before, down in New Orleans." He reaches across to Front-Page's open shirt-neck, pulls a silver chain there until he exposes a circular medallion depicting an old man carrying someone on his shoulders. "Saint Christopher," Bills says.

"Who's he?" asks Jim Leafman.

"Patron Saint of travellers," Front-Page says. "Protects anyone on the road . . . looks after them."

"Why did you not shake McCoy's hand?" Bills asks. "When you came over to the table."

"Bad luck to shake hands across a table," Front-Page answers. "Everyone knows that." He looks around at the blank faces. "Don't they?"

"Why'd you keep rapping the table," Edgar asks, making it sound like he already knows the answer.

"Knocking wood," Front-Page says. "Keeps from tempting fate."

McCoy Brewer says, "Keeps from tempting fate to do what?"

Front-Page shrugs. "From exercising irony. You say something is this way – the way you want it to be – then you knock wood to make sure it keeps on being that way."

"You very superstitious?" Bills asks.

Front-Page seems to be settling into his chair more now, though he keeps flexing his mouth, opening it wide like he's in pain. "No more than the next guy," he says.

"Tell us about Betty," Bills says to him.

Front-Page McGuffin visibly winces. He closes his eyes and shakes his head slowly. "She's not here anymore, Bills . . . and I miss her. I surely do miss her."

"I know you do," Bills says. "Tell us about the time she was in the hospital. Is that when the superstitions started?"

"I guess so."

"What did you do?" Jack Fedogan asks, crouching down by the table. He's checked the counter to make sure nobody's waiting for drinks. In the background, the Marsalis father-and-son team is playing "Sweet Lorraine".

"She had a tumour."

"I know that," Bills says. "Tell us how the superstitions started."

"Number 13," Front-Page says. "They wanted to put her in Room 13. I remember now. That's when it started."

"You weren't superstitious before then?" Jim asks.

"They – the doctors – they told me wasn't anything going to help Betty now. Then this other one, nice guy, he puts his hand on my shoulder and he says to me, 'You can try praying'." Front-Page leans onto the table, knocks it a couple of times, and continues.

"So I tell him I'm not a religious man. Wouldn't know how to even begin talking to God . . . even if I thought he *did* exist. And this guy, he looks at me with this sad smile, and he says to me, 'That's all you have now, Mr McGuffin. That's all your *wife* has.' He says to me, 'Whyn't you give it a try?'

"So, that night – the first night she was in hospital – I got down on my knees in the bedroom, right alongside her side of the bed, and I prayed. I cried like a baby – and that's something else I don't do – and I prayed." He raps the table and shifts his weight in the chair, looking like he's uncomfortable.

"Next day, I go into the hospital and they tell me Betty's had a good night. But they tell me they're moving her into another room." He looks across at Bills and gives a single nod. "Room 13.

"'I take it you're not superstitious, Mr McGuffin?' this nurse says to me, all sweetness and light. Anyway, I think to myself for a minute; and I think about how Betty has had a better night and how – maybe coincidentally, but hell, who knows? – how I did all that praying. And I wonder if maybe it *did* have an effect. And if it did, how maybe

I should try to avoid anything that could work against her. So I say to the nurse that I don't want Betty in Room 13."

"What did they say?"

Front-Page looks aside at Edgar and says, "They did it. They found her another room. They weren't *happy* about it, but they found her another room."

Edgar snorts a *Way to go!* snort, chuckles and pats Front-Page on the hand, which feels very cold just lying there on the table.

"Then," Front-Page says, sounding kind of tired, "everything started to get really intense.

"I went home and started to think about all the little superstitions and sayings folks use to get them through one day into the next. Totems and talismans they employed to keep them well and happy."

Suddenly remembering the pitcher, Jack gets to his feet and pours beer into the glasses.

Watching the beer froth up, Front-Page says, "I knew a few but I wondered how many there really were . . . wondered if I really went to town on these things that maybe Betty would be . . ." He lets his voice trail off and takes a long slug of beer.

"So," he says, setting the glass back on the table, "I went down to the library and I read up on them. You wouldn't believe how many books there are on superstition." He takes hold of the medallion about his neck and rubs it gently between his thumb and forefinger. "Got this from a book titled *Dictionary of Saints* by D. Attwater, 1965. Got another one from M. Trevelyan's *Folk-lore of Wales*, 1909."

"What was that one?" McCoy asks.

"That told how a posthumous child could charm away a tumour by putting his or her hands over the appropriate spot."

"What the hell's a—"

"It's a child born after its mother has died," Bills Williams says to Jack Fedogan.

"You found one of these . . . posthumous children?" Edgar says.

Front-Page nods. "Guy in the newsroom knew somebody." He waves his hand. "You don't want to know the details. It's a depressing story. Anyway, he arranges for this guy's daughter to visit Betty with me." There's a strange sound from Front-Page's throat that could be a chuckle, although there's no sign of amusement on his face. "Betty didn't know what the hell was going on – she was in a lot of pain, mind you. So I kept her talking while this girl – she was a woman actually . . . the tragic events surrounding her birth having taken place some time ago – she rubs Betty's stomach.

"And, you know . . . I think it helped her. Course, it could just've been the rubbing that helped but I didn't think so. Anyway, I wasn't taking any chances. So the girl came with me to the hospital another couple of times and then she didn't want to come any more. I can't say as how I blamed her. Hospitals can be downbeat places at the best of times and I was bad company to go with."

McCoy takes a slug of beer and rests his glass on the table. "So what did you do then?"

"By this time I had gotten so many of these folk-stories, sayings, homilies, and who knows what else that I was taking a whole bunch of stuff in there every day . . . and I was visiting with Betty morning, afternoon and evening, each time with something else to slip under her pillow or in her bedside cabinet."

"Things like what?" Jim asks.

"Oh, good luck coins – pennies with her year of birth printed on them – taped-up saltpot, a model of a black cat, piece of wood from an altar, rabbit's foot . . . there were so many I kind of lost track what I was doing there for a while." Front-Page shakes his head and altar the table. "And I had started doing things by myself, too."

Jack is back down on the floor and he shifts his weight from one knee to the other. "Like what?" he asks.

"Knocking wood all the time," he says, rapping the table to demonstrate, even though no demonstration was necessary, "spitting when I saw the back of a mail-van, spinning around when I inadvertently walked across cracks in paving stones, moving one hand in an arc to join the other hand when I saw a nun or a priest – you'd be surprised how many nuns and priests you see when you're doing this kind of stuff."

"It's a wonder they didn't lock you up," Jim observes and then winces when Edgar kicks him in the shin.

"That's okay," Front-Page says, and he raps the table just to make sure.

"But Betty . . . Betty didn't make it," he says quietly.

There's a world of regret in that simple statement and, even though Front-Page's voice is low, the two guys at the bar look around, just for a second, not knowing why they're looking around but simply responding to the sudden sense of loss that permeates the bar and mingles with the sound of Art Pepper's alto on "Why Are We Afraid?".

Edgar and McCoy and Bills and Jack and Jim just sit there, taking it in turns to nod, Edgar and Bills squeezing Front-Page's shoulders.

Front-Page shakes his head. "By then, I was too heavily into this stuff to back off. Even tried to change her burial day."

"Why?" asks Jack

"I read that, in County Cork in Ireland, it's bad luck to be buried on a Monday and that's when . . . when Betty was scheduled. They wouldn't change it. Said that it wasn't as simple as just changing days. I was devastated. There was a whole lot of spitting and knocking and turning the night after I found out, I can tell you that for nothing! But then I read someplace else that it was okay to be buried on a Monday so long as at least one sod was turned on the grave-site a day or two beforehand. So I went down to Lawnswood and dug over a small section. Then I was . . . heh, I was going to say *happy* – I was *placated*."

"How come you never told us any of this?" Edgar asks. "We saw you the night after Betty died and you seemed . . . well, you seemed normal. I mean, you were upset – hell, that was obvious – but I didn't know about any of this other stuff." He turns to the others. "Anyone know about this?"

There were several shakes of heads and a few grunted "*No*'s".

"Well, I'm pleased to hear that," Front-Page says. "I tried to keep it to myself . . . though I'm pleased that nobody happened to see me when I could see a nun!"

Sometimes it happens that a conversation just naturally takes a pause and this one does right here. A time to take a drink and to watch the guy at the bar throw a couple of bills on the counter before making his way to the stairs and up to the waiting streets of New York; a time to nod to the music, like you were listening to it all along; a time to take a drink.

"So," Jack Fedogan says, his voice kind of lilting, phrasing the question like he's asking what Front-Page thinks to the new album by Jimmy Smith, "what took you down to Battery Park?"

"Just walking," comes the reply. "I spent the past three years just walking . . . walking and thinking . . . and rapping, and spitting, and turning, and who knows what else. And I just fell right over, felt like a truck ran over my chest. Then I got up. Went somewhere . . . like I say, I don't remember. Wasn't until a couple of days later, after I'd stopped eating and sleeping and drinking, I felt for my pulse and there wasn't one. Put my hand on my chest—" He puts his hand on his chest to demonstrate. "—No heartbeat."

Front-Page opens his mouth wide. The inside is grey and dry and, just for a second, before he turns his head away, Jim Leafman thinks he sees something wriggle across the back of Front-Page's mouth, down near the top of the throat. "No saliva," Front-Page explains. "Gets so I can hardly open my mouth sometimes. The drink helps though . . . I think," he says as he takes a slug of beer and swishes it around his mouth, then swallows.

"So why'd you come here?" Jack asks. "I mean, why'd you wait until tonight?"

"Well, for a time there, I didn't want to see anybody who would remind me of what I had and don't have any more. Kept myself to myself. Lived out on the streets . . . down in the subway tunnels sometime. Met some strange people. Met some nice people, too. It's like I say, there's good and bad everywhere.

"Then, when I'd . . . you know; when I'd died . . . I met this guy in an alley and I told him pretty much everything I just told you guys. And he says – after we'd established the fact that I *was* dead . . . and he was mighty surprised at *that*, I can tell you – he says maybe I need to do it again."

"Huh?" says Jim, a thin trickle of beer dribbling down his chin. "Do it again? Do *what* again?"

"Die."

The five men stare at Front-Page McGuffin wondering if they heard him right.

"He says to me – this guy I met – he says that maybe, every once in a while, it doesn't take the first time and I need to do it again. So—"

Edgar Nornhoevan shakes his head and pushes his chair back. "Hey, do I want to hear this?"

"No," says Front-Page. "It's okay. Really.

"So, we think of ways I can do it. He says, why don't I throw myself under a car or onto the subway under a train. Now I don't want to do that because it'll maybe mess up the driver of that car or train. But I say, yes, I'll try the subway track because it's electrified, but only when the train has been through.

"So we go down onto 42nd Street, buy the token, the whole business, and we wait until a train comes through. Then when it leaves, I climb down onto the track and lie against the third rail. Nothing happens. I mean, I took hold of that thing and there was nothing. By the time I'm climbing out, commuters are coming onto the platform for the next train. They look at me and the other guy like we're scum of the earth and we high-tail it out of there as quickly as we can, with folks shouting after us, calling us names.

"So then he suggests I go up somewhere high and jump down. This sounds like a good idea to him – I mean, what could be more final, right? – but I always had this fear of heights and, well, I just couldn't do it. And another thing was that if it didn't work, and I was still conscious but with every bone in my body mushed to pulp, I wouldn't even be able to get around.

"So I say how's about I drown myself. He thinks this is a good idea.

"We go up to Central Park – out to the lake? – and I wade on out into the water, which I have no sensation of, incidentally, and I keep walking until it covers my head. And I keep on walking. Then I just stand there, looking up through the water at the stars twinkling up there in the sky. I can hear this other guy shouting to me – a kind of half-shout, half-whisper . . . because it's late at night, you know, and the muggers are out – he's shouting asking me if I'm okay. And I'm trying to answer him. There I am, in ten feet of water, trying to talk. I stayed there for about fifteen minutes and then came out."

Front-Page shakes his head and takes a slug of beer.

Edgar suddenly notices that beer is dripping onto the floor from Front-Page's chair but he doesn't say anything.

Shrugging, Front-Page says, "And I tried other things. Hanging myself. No good. I think it broke my neck, which is maybe why I have trouble swallowing, but it didn't do anything else. I only thank God that I did it with this other guy near at hand. I mean, I just kicked away a wastebasket – we were in the Park again, under cover of darkness – and swung there from the branch of this tree. I felt fine . . . well, I felt no different. If he hadn't have been there, I'd have been found in the morning, still swinging there, still trying to talk and ask someone to please get me down.

"Then I tried poison. You see, I was trying things that, if they didn't work, wouldn't make me look any different than the way I always look. I mean, if I'd tried fire, then I may have burned all my body into a blackened mass which I would still maybe have to walk around with."

Front-Page shakes his head again and knocks wood.

"Then this guy, he says maybe he's not the one to give me any advice. He means by this, maybe nobody *alive* can give me advice on this one. So I ask him what he means by this. And he says I should think about trying to speak to somebody who's already dead."

At this point, Front-Page McGuffin turns to Bills Williams and says, "I want you to help me talk to Dawdle O'Rourke."

Without saying a word, Jack Fedogan gets to his feet and walks over to the counter. A couple of minutes later he comes back to the lilting piano of Herbie Hancock playing "My Funny Valentine", carrying another pitcher of beer. Nobody has said anything while he's been away, like it was some kind of performance which couldn't continue while one of the actors was taking a leak.

Jack pulls over a chair and sits down at the table, setting the pitcher next to the empty one. "This should be bourbon," he says. To which Edgar gives a short snigger and then does the honours of freshening everyone's glass.

"Can you do it, Bills?" McCoy asks.

Bills nods and looks down at the playing cards in his hands. "I can try," he says. "But are you sure Dawdle is the one? You don't want me to call on Betty instead?"

"Uh uh," says Front-Page. "She'd worry. I mean, I should be up there – or 'out' there . . . or wherever the hell '*there*' is – and the fact that I'm not with her will mean I must still be alive. If she knew all this was happening, she'd worry. It has to be Dawdle. Dawdle and me go way back. If he can't help me, then nobody can. I know I can trust him not to say anything to anyone else . . . mainly to Betty. He's the only one. I love the others but they'd think they were doing me a favour by speaking to Betty. I can't take that chance."

Only Herbie Hancock has anything to say after that, and he's doing his talking with his piano.

After a while, Front-Page says to Bills, "Will you do it?"

Bills nods. "I'll do it."

As they're preparing one of the tables over near the wall, Jack Fedogan is going around telling the other folks that he's closing up for the night, closing up early. It's a credit to him and the Working Day itself that the other patrons accept this as just the way things are. They leave with smiles and nods, pulling on scarves and overcoats as they prepare to venture up the wooden stairs and out into the January streets of Manhattan.

Pretty soon there's just the six of them.

Eleven if you count Coleman Hawkins, Eddie "Lockjaw" Davis, Tommy Flanagan, Ron Carter and Gus Johnson, whose mellow "There Is No Greater Love" is wafting around the bar, filling the corners and all the nooks and crannies of The Land at the End of the Working Day, preserving the mystery of those hidden places while removing their threat.

Front-Page himself is not taking part in the preparations. He's sitting at the old table, the one near the bar, sitting by himself and occasionally looking up, looking around, and then looking back at his drink, sometimes taking a slug, the pool of beer around his chair widening all the while.

"All his insides are shot," Edgar explains to Jim Leafman as they throw a green cloth over the designated table. "Liver, kidneys, heart, lungs, bowel, colon . . . all rotted to mush."

"Yeah?" says Jim, sneaking a glance across.

"It's what happens," Edgar says matter-of-factly. "Happens to us all." He pulls a face. "You catch the smell?"

Jim frowns and shakes his head.

"You should've been sitting next to him. Poor guy. Smells like an open sewer."

Bills Williams comes out of the bathroom with McCoy Brewer. "What he's done," he's saying to McCoy, "is mess up his natural forces with protective talismans and totems. Maybe it's the sheer number and frequency, maybe it's just the interaction of one or two . . . I don't know."

They stop at the table and look across at Front-Page.

"And in doing so, he's made it so that *he* . . . his soul, his id, his karma . . . whatever you want to call it – he's made it so that his very essence has been imprisoned. Maybe he was protecting himself – for a while anyways – from *external* influences, but he died from what sounds like a heart attack. It was an *internal* force that killed him. I don't think you can protect yourself from what's happening in your own body. Don't think you should even try." Bills gave a small smile, without humour. "We are born, we live and we die. That's the way it is . . . and that's the way it has to be. When Front-Page's time came and his body could no longer continue, his essence should have been free to go. We're going to do this thing – contact Dawdle O'Rourke – but I don't know as how it'll do any good."

"Okay, everybody ready?" says Jack Fedogan.

"As we'll ever be," says Bills. "Front-Page?"

The time of inaction seems to have taken its toll and Front-Page is once again moving with extreme difficulty. So much so that Jack and McCoy have to go over and help him to the new table.

When they are all seated evenly around the table, Bills starts to speak.

"Okay, here's the way it's going to work. We all link hands palm-down on the table. Nobody breaks the link, whatever happens. If this thing is going to work, it'll work right away. If it doesn't, then it isn't going to work. Okay?"

Everyone nods and grunts assent.

"No talking or sounds of any kind, okay?"

Without waiting for a response, Bills Williams takes a hold of McCoy's and Jack's hands and allows his head to fall forward onto his chest.

"Dawdle O'Rourke?" Bills says, his voice sounding deep and strange, sitting on the sound of Tommy Flanagan's piano like a cork on an ocean. "Dawdle O'Rourke, I need to speak with you. A friend of yours needs your help. His name is Front-Page McGuffin. Please respond."

They wait in silence.

After a couple of minutes, Bills repeats the message word for word. Still no response.

"Dawdle O'Rourke, you are urgently needed. This is Bills Williams in The Land at the End of the Working Day. *Please* respond."

Front-Page tries to smile and pulls his hands away from Edgar and Jack. "It's no good," he says as he tries to pull his eyelid up. "It's just not going to work."

They all break their hand-holds.

Jack Fedogan leans forward on the table. "Hey," says Jack, "you ever hear about those cases where folks lift automobiles off of kids who are trapped beneath . . . just regular scrawny people who suddenly have this amazing strength?"

"Yes?"

"Yep."

"Uh huh?"

"Well," says Jack, "why is that?"

"You think this is the time for—"

"No, Edgar, this could be important," says Jack. "It's the power of the mind, isn't it? That's what does it."

"Yeah, that's what they say on Cable TV, Jack," says Edgar, "so what's your point?"

"My point is . . ." He turns to look at Front-Page and sees his old friend's wrecked face, sees the black rings around the eyes, pieces of lip that seem to be coming away – he never noticed those before – and tufts of hair that stand proud of the scalp which itself is going kind of blue and mottled, like hands that have been in water too long. And, taking hold of Front-Page's hand again, he asks, "Do you trust me?"

The voice that comes back is deep and resonant, the voice on an old vinyl record that's playing when the power cuts out on the player. "I trust you, Jack," Front-Page says, and he blinks his eyes closed.

"Front-Page?" Edgar says.

"He's gone," says Bills.

"Where's he gone?" says Jim. "He's right there. Where could he—"

"Give me a hand with him," Jack Fedogan says. He stands up and pulls Front-Page up to his feet by his arm. "Jeez, his arm!"

"What's wrong with his arm?" asks McCoy.

Bills rushes around the table and takes hold of Front-Page McGuffin's other arm, hoisting it around his own shoulder. "The muscles have atrophied," he says. "Gone to mulch."

Jim Leafman scowls. "Yeuch."

Edgar kicks nudges him and says, "Shh!"

With Front-Page on his feet, but his eyes still closed, and his arms around Jack's and Bills's shoulders, Bills says, "What now?"

"Help me get him to the stairs."

"Where you going?" asks Bills.

"Out."

"*Where* out? It's below zero out there," says McCoy getting to his feet.

"I'm going to teach him the power of the mind," says Jack.

"Wear your coat at least," Jim shouts as Jack starts up the stairs, his arm around Front-Page's waist.

"You want me to come with you?" says Bills.

"Uh uh." Jack grunts. "He's still carrying a weight."

Bills Williams thinks Front-Page is carrying lots of things around with him, but he doesn't say anything.

"I'll be back," Jack shouts, in his best Arnie impression. "Serve yourselves."

Out on the street it's cold.

It's dark and there's a wind blowing and snow's in the air, though right now it's trying to rain . . . but most of all it's cold.

But somehow . . . it's okay.

Sometimes the City carries its magic on the surface for all to see. Right now, at a little before 9:00 pm, on a Tuesday evening after the longest Happy Hour in the brief history of Jack Fedogan's Land at the End of the Working Day, the streets are empty of people. Jack looks along 23rd and then down Fifth and there's not a single person to be seen. Not even any traffic.

Then, its tyres swishing along the rain-washed streets, a single Yellow cab turns the corner into Fifth just a block down and heads their way, its light glowing like a beacon in the darkness.

Jack hefts Front-Page up against him and waves his free arm. "Hey!" he yells into the gloom.

The cab pulls up alongside them, the cabby calls, "Get in."

"Thanks." Jack pulls open the door and manoeuvres Front-Page into the back seat. It smells of cheap perfume and cigarette smoke, for which Jack is grateful. His companion would not win any prizes in a sweet-smells competition.

"Where to?" the driver asks as Jack pulls the door closed.

"Central Park."

"Where in Central Park, friend? It's a big park."

"Anywhere, but quickly." He pushes a rolled-up twenty through the grill.

"You got it," comes the reply.

As they drive, Jack starts patting Front-Page's face. "Front-Page," he says, "can you hear me?"

"Hear you," says Front-Page.

"Hang on in there, buddy," says Jack. "Hang on in there."

Front-Page lets rip with a fart. It sounds like material tearing.

"He okay?" the driver calls over his shoulder. "He gonna throw up, you tell me, okay?"

"It's just wind," Jack shouts. Then, to Front-Page, "Hang on, buddy."

The driver lets them out on the corner of Central Park South and Fifth, seemingly relieved to have made the trip without his passengers redecorating the back seat.

Jack holds onto Front-Page, his shoulders hunched over at the biting cold wind, and watches the cab drive on up Fifth Avenue.

"Okay," says Jack, "I want you to walk with me."

"Where . . . going?" says Front-Page.

"We're gonna sit ourselves down on a bench along here a ways and we're gonna look up at the city."

As they start to walk, Front-Page McGuffin says, "Nice."

Maybe it's something in the air, maybe it's the promise of rain coming down as a fine spray, but Front-Page starts to improve as they move along and it doesn't take as long as Jack thought it would to reach his destination.

Then they're there.

A bench on one of the pathways that cross and re-cross Central Park. Over across from them as Jack lowers Front-Page onto the seat, they can see the buildings up Central Park West, their lights twinkling like fairy lights in the gloom.

"This is where Phyllis and me used to come," says Jack Fedogan. He leans forward on his knees and looks up through the branches at the glittering lights. "We used to come here and make plans," he says, either telling Front-Page McGuffin or simply reminding himself. If you were to ask him which one it was, he wouldn't be able to tell you. Not for sure.

"You. Miss. Her?" Front-Page's voice is stilted and echoing, hollow, more like the memory of voice than the voice itself.

"I miss her very much, my friend," says Jack. "And I look forward to seeing her again. But only when the time is right."

By his side, Front-Page nods. "Time. Is. Right," he says.

For a few seconds they sit in silence and then Jack says, "What I was saying back in the Working Day? About the power of the mind?"

Front-Page's head lolls on his neck.

Jack shakes his friend's arm and says it again.

"Yes?"

"You have that power."

Jack takes the single grunt to be an ironic laugh. "I have no power."

"Yes you *do*," Jack says. "Okay, you can't lift an auto right now . . . and maybe you couldn't even if Betty were here and lying right underneath. But you'd have a college try, am I right?"

Front-Page nods.

"So try."

"Wha— What? No. Auto. Here."

"Try to get to her, for Chrissakes. Just . . . just leave it all. Let it *go!*"

"How?"

"Your body is finished. It's *you* who've trapped yourself here . . . nobody else. You and all those dumb superstitions . . . all that spitting and rapping and twirling. You've got— Listen." Jack turns around and takes hold of Front-Page's jacket lapels. "If I could change places with you right now, I'd do it. You hear what I'm saying to you, Front-Page? If I could be as close to seeing Phyllis again as you are to seeing Betty, I'd change places right now. All you have to do is try."

"Try," says Front-Page. "Yes" Then, "How?"

"Just . . . just close your eyes and let it go. Don't fight it. Use that power of the mind that folks use to lift automobiles."

Front-Page McGuffin blinks at Jack Fedogan and then looks down at his friend's hands. "You. Can . . ."

Jack takes his hands away. "Sorry. Getting carried away there."

"S'okay," says Front-Page and he moves his head to face the twinkling lights on the buildings through the trees. "Quite. A. City," he says, his voice now sounding like a door rubbing on a piece of coal trapped beneath it. "New. York," he says.

Even the words themselves have a magical sound, Jack thinks. He rubs his shoulders and shivers. "You trying?"

"Trying," says Front-Page.

They sit like that for a few minutes, silent.

"Jack?"

"Yeah?"

"Something . . . You. Good. Man. Jack."

"So they tell me."

"Something. Happening."

Jack Fedogan turns around and looks at his friend's face. Is it his imagination or is it the light filtering through the trees . . . or does Front-Page look more peaceful now?

"Hold. Hand," says Front-Page McGuffin. "Going."

Jack takes hold of Front-Page's hand and grips it tight, trying hard to let him feel the warmth. "Front-Page?" he whispers.

"Yessss . . .?" Sleepy-sounding now.

"Tell Phyllis I said, 'Hi'."

Front-Page's head lolls forward. And now there is just one person sitting on the bench in Central Park, breathing in the fine mist and watching the lights twinkling through the trees. Jack sits there for a while like that, his arm around Front-Page McGuffin's shoulder and Front-Page's head leaning against his own like a sleeping lover, just watching the city and listening to its sounds.

It takes Jack Fedogan almost two hours to walk back to The Land at the End of the Working Day. Two hours in which he has re-lived weeks and months and years of memories. When he arrives at the familiar entrance at the corner of 23rd and Fifth, it's raining hard and Jack is already sniffling.

"Where you been?" Edgar says as Jack clumps down the stairs. "It's almost midnight!"

"Where's Front-Page?" asks McCoy Brewer.

"Right now?" says Jack. "Right now I'd say he's catching up with someone he's been missing for a long time."

"Where'd you leave him?" asks Bills Williams.

Jack walks across to the counter and lifts the hatch. "In the park."

Bills smiles. "And I bet I know where," he says.

"Coffee anyone?" asks Jack. "It's been a long—"

Suddenly the lights flicker.

A wind blows down the stairs and swirls around them, a wind so strong that the five of them shield their eyes.

Then, as quickly as it appeared, the wind drops.

The lights return to their full intensity.

And a solitary shimmering figure stands at the foot of the stairs.

"Someone call me?" asks Dawdle O'Rourke.

SIMON STRANTZAS

It Runs Beneath the Surface

SIMON STRANTZAS WAS BORN in the harsh darkness of the Canadian winter over thirty years ago. He is the author of two short story collections – *Beneath the Surface* (Humdrumming, 2008) and *Cold to the Touch* (Tartarus, 2009) – and his work has not only appeared in such award-winning magazines as *Cemetery Dance* and *Post-Scripts*, but also in the previous volume of *The Mammoth Book of Best New Horror*.

He is currently working on a third collection of weird fiction; after which he plans to catch up on a voluminous amount of reading, and then perhaps begin work on a short novel.

"There is something about city life that fascinates me," explains Strantzas. "I find myself musing to no end about the effect it has on its inhabitants. I know I'm not alone in that regard – some of the greatest examples of the urban supernatural are in the work of Fritz Leiber, especially in stories such as "Smoke Ghost" and "The Black Gondolier". Both these tales no doubt infected my mind when I was dreaming up "It Runs Beneath the Surface", but it was an inchoate mess until I chanced to hear a stray line from an unassuming pop song. Suddenly all my disparate thoughts coalesced and I knew exactly what the tale was about, what should happen in it and, most importantly, how it should end.

"On reflection, I'm particularly proud of the dot the final line puts on things."

THE SUBWAY CAR PIERCED the darkness, rattling along its thin track and filled with faces carrying a burdensome weight. Pale, sallow, as if the city had drained them, the passengers shook quietly, packed together in the tiny metal box.

Philip Kirk had managed to find a seat for the ride in but he regretted taking it once bodies filled the space around him and stole oxygen from his lungs. He adjusted his rumpled jacket, trying to alleviate its restrictiveness and find a few extra inches in which to move. The yellow lights of the car buzzed and flickered intermittently with every power surge, and they drew the shadows that confined him closer.

The jittering train came to a stop at Carlton Street Station. Philip peered through his window at the sullen people moving like automatons across the opposite platform. They seemed to have already conceded failure; it was in their stances, in the way they walked.

An eruption of movement caught his eye. A vagrant covered in grime ran erratically across the platform, clutching at himself, ripping his tangled beard and unkempt hair. He screamed, his mouth a dark and bottomless pit, but the noise was ineffectual; no one but Philip appeared to notice, and even then it was inaudible over the roar of the train unsteadily moving forward. The filthy man reached the end of the platform just as the train passed before him, and Philip only caught a glimpse of arms from the shadows stretching to catch the man.

When Philip finally arrived at the Eastside Mission he found he had the place to himself. He sat at his desk and ran wrinkled hands over case reports and worn files, re-reading the data that he had already memorized. The grey words of each report read the same: there was nothing more that could be done for any of them, no magic wand to be waved that assimilated his clients back into the world they left so long ago. No one wanted to bear the trouble. No one wanted to do anything but forget.

"Sorry," Philip heard, and looked up to see Allan picking his blue topcoat free of lint before hanging it on the shared rack. "I had to make a stop." Across the back of his pressed trouser leg was a large smear of mud. Philip noted it with suspicion but said nothing.

Clients arrived in a steady flow, their amorphous shadows darkening the translucent window to the waiting room. The two men took turns using the counselling room that sat through a door on the right wall, though Allan's sessions often ran overlong. He was still enthralled by all the pains and troubles that flowed through his clients like darkened blood, but for Philip they were merely further evidence of a rotted world that tainted its cowed populace. At the end of every session he felt soaked through with despair and secretly he envied Allan and the hopes the young man still held in his clear blue eyes.

Those eyes clouded, however, upon the conclusion of his afternoon session. Philip had observed Allan's new client but briefly, and – though he was perhaps less kempt than the rest – there was nothing beside his height that marked him as different. Even that wasn't very peculiar, yet Allan appeared disturbed.

"I've never spoken to someone that far gone before."

Philip's eyes did not move from his work. "How so?"

"What he said didn't make any *sense*. He just kept warning me about something. I'm not sure he ever told me about what."

"You'll get used to that," Philip said. "They all imagine some disaster is happening."

"I suppose." Allan trailed off, looking out the window for a long time. Philip noticed and turned, but saw only amassing rain clouds through the glass. Allan eventually excused himself, rubbing his eyes. By the time Philip finished with his last client Allan and his topcoat had already disappeared for the day. Philip left a short time later.

His ride home was not as cramped as the morning's commute, but even so an empty seat eluded him. He stood near the doors, looking for some respite from the crowd, and too late he realized the pole he grasped for support was soiled by a murky slick film. He was revolted by the filth that seeped from those around him and fouled everything they touched.

He scrubbed his hands raw once safe within his dingy apartment, watching the bowl of the sink tint pale brown as the world washed away from him, but nothing he did could remove the feel of grease that had crept between his fingers.

The lumps of his bed resisted his weight as he lay down, but he was far too tired to fight them. His head throbbed from exhaustion, and he closed his eyes to avoid seeing the walls he could not escape.

He dreamt of himself fixed to a seat at the end of an empty subway car, watching passing stations flicker in the windows like a silent film. Their light illuminated the entire car, exposing the mosaic of muddy footprints, thick and dark, that were scattered along its length. Murky shadows gathered at the opposite end of the car and Philip noticed wisps of movement within the darkness, like a black pool beginning to swirl. Two pseudopods gradually formed from the shadows, then grew larger and stretched across the floor towards him. He struggled, but his feet were caked in black muck and fused to the floor. The shapes formed a pair of figures that closed in as the subway sped faster. They raised their hands, their fingers becoming long tendrils that crawled towards his face, and just as they made contact Philip found himself awake and panting in his own bed, his skin burning and covered with sweat.

Philip's first session ran long, and thus he was unaware of when precisely Allan arrived at work. The young man was simply there, sitting at his desk uncharacteristically withdrawn and contemplative, seemingly unaware of Philip until he spoke.

"You still have your coat on."

Allan jumped in his seat, and then, after Philip repeated himself, looked at his blue topcoat.

"Yeah, I guess I do," he said. "Listen, can I ask you something?"

Philip shrugged.

"How do you do it? Deal with all of this day after day after day?"

"You'll get used to it. You're young."

"I don't know. I keep thinking about everything the clients say. Sometimes I find myself lying awake at night thinking about it."

Philip's nightmare subway sped through his thoughts. "You have to learn to forget it. Forget it all."

Allan sat silent, weighing the words, his furrowed brow working them like a bone. Philip sighed and regretting what he was about to ask.

"Do you . . ." he said. "Do you really want to know how it works?"

Allan turned his desperate blue eyes to Philip, and the older man almost reconsidered.

"Everybody," Philip said as he turned away, "starts this job thinking they'll make a difference. Yet no one does. All you'll be doing is passing time. At best, you'll help a few people to suppress their fears and pains and desires for a little while, but soon it will all come bubbling back up stronger than before. Your only job is to get them in and out with as much paperwork as possible."

Allan sat stunned, as though Philip had reached in and twisted his soul.

"It's true. You'll see for yourself once you've been around a little longer."

Allan sank, inspecting his hands and muttering in disbelief. Philip returned to his paperwork and pretended not to notice the young man's pain. Allan would have to make a choice: either accept it or burn out trying to change it. There wasn't a third option.

The ring of Allan's telephone interrupted the silence. He answered it and put the receiver to his ear. Then, after only a minute and without saying a word, he hung it up again. In his hand he held his blazer, and it trailed behind him as he darted out of the office, the door closing firmly in his wake. His dark shape faded in the translucent window, and then rematerialized a moment later with another. The two shadows moved to the right and disappeared into the counselling room. Their mumbling soon penetrated the walls.

It was unlike Allan to act so secretively about a client, and Philip feared he had pushed him too far.

He approached the counselling room with care. He wanted to hear the session without betraying his presence. Allan's voice, dry and shaky, spoke only briefly, interrupting the fragments of babble delivered by his client.

". . . can't keep . . . contained . . . oozing . . . "

". . . liquid . . . fills my . . ."

". . . hot . . . tar . . . do you understand?"

Philip took flight when he heard the sound of scraping chairs. He reached his desk just as Allan emerged from the counselling room, and realized immediately that he had forgotten to close the door between them. Philip could feel the error had been noticed, but he refused to acknowledge it.

Allan and his towering client stood in the waiting room and spoke quietly. Philip now recognized the man from the previous day, yet in that time he seemed to have acquired a year's worth of filth. His pants were torn completely away below his right knee, exposing a leg smeared with dark grime. His coat, too, held together only by dried stains, hung from his shoulders as though soaked through. From where Philip sat an odour, like ammonia, burnt his nostrils.

Finally, the tall man left. Allan still seemed agitated, wiping his hands repeatedly with a handkerchief. He took his seat, exhausted, eyes red and puffy as though he had just been crying. Philip felt awkward and discreetly left to fill his mug with water from the waiting room cooler. Once there, he saw the series of dirty footprints that made a trail across the carpet and into the hallway.

Familiar faces crowded the subway home, each passenger staring ahead with dull dark eyes as he or she passed the time without a word. Upon their collective sagging shoulders was borne the weight of all their troubles, and Philip felt the same heaviness as it coursed through his withering veins and wrapped around his soul.

Hidden among the sex-shops, his building stood squat and lifeless, its bricks stained by the filthy air. Soot clung to his hands as he pushed through the entrance and he wiped them clean against the side of his trouser leg.

He discovered the broken light bulbs as he emerged from the stairwell. They left the entire corridor in darkness, yet what seemed to be his shadow remained cast on the wall at the opposite end, traced impossibly by the remaining lights behind him. He watched the uneven mass roll towards him as he approached his apartment. It seemed wrong somehow, as though it were actually growing as it advanced toward him. He stopped at his door, but for a moment thought the shadow continued, its movements slightly out of time with his own through some illusion of the lowered light. He felt a chill but he shook it off, and inserted his key into the lock.

He woke the next day with his head throbbing and his stomach burning its way into his throat. He struggled to the washroom and took a long drink from the rusted faucet, replacing one sour taste with another. His yellow, sagging face stared at him from the mirror, and with clarity knew that he had been forsaken. His hopes and dreams had been surreptitiously drained, leaving nothing but sorrow to fill the void. He stuck out his tongue and was horrified by the grey filmy protrusion.

Just above the reddish stubble that outlined his cheekbone he found the mark. Black, about an inch in length, it stretched further when Philip put his thumb to it, leaving a greasy smudge across his cheek that soap and water could not completely eliminate.

Philip stepped aboard the subway train amazed – it was barely half-full. The passengers there were pressed into the far end of the car. Between him and them lay the bulk of the seats, empty and coated in a brown viscous substance that infected the entire car with a foul stale odour he could not stand to breathe.

When the next stop arrived, he hurried off and stood gasping for air on the edge of the platform as he watched the subway train leave the station, the hazy shadows of its passengers fading into the darkness.

The platform was nearly as empty as the train. Only a few commuters were left along the narrow stretch of concrete, their faces weighted down, eyes cast blankly upward. Along the periphery, Philip saw shadows disappear quickly behind the commuters, those new arrivals looking for a place to stand. He could feel eyes from the small crowd upon him, but when he turned he saw nothing but blankness.

The next train could not arrive soon enough. When it did, he was relieved it was uncontaminated by the odour, though he found its passengers gave him a wide berth. He sniffed his sleeve and coughed. His jacket smelled foul.

He aired it out as best he could at the office, but the odour proved too resilient. Just a whiff of it sent his stomach churning.

Allan's desk was vacant, his coat-hook bare. Philip frowned. The man was becoming increasingly tardy and unreliable.

Fortunately, Philip had no trouble handling things alone; his morning was devoid of clients. They simply failed to show up. Instead, he caught up on paperwork still pending. A fine drab mist covered the streets outside, making uneasy shadows of the obscured pedestrians.

Philip began to get fidgety by noon, his anger over Allan breaking his concentration. Unable to sit still any longer, he paced the room, growing more enraged by Allan's unexplained absence. He swung open the office door, half-expecting to see the young man there with an arm wrapped around the water cooler and acting as if he'd been at the office all along, but instead Philip found the waiting room empty. The door to the counselling room, however, was closed, and its tiny window was lit.

Within the room, pressed into the far corner, sat Allan's bearded client, dirty and bloodied knees pressed tightly to his chin. He shook as if with fever, head pressed sideways into the tatters of his blackened clothes, the grime of his face streaked with tears. He blubbered uncontrollably.

"Are you hurt?" Philip took a hesitant step forward.

The man's head turned, his one exposed eye bloodshot and filled with terror. The room became startlingly quiet. The entire left side of the man's face was covered in a thick oily mud that clogged his orifices and disguised what lay underneath. It caked his greying beard and stained his clothes and skin. Philip retreated to the door as the man scrambled to his feet, leaving marks across the wall while sounds gurgled from his fouled lips. He pushed past Philip, leaving a long smudge across the counsellor's chest, and Philip could do nothing but watch him escape. After he'd gone, Philip retreated to the office shaken, and sat quietly at his desk.

He'd never seen anything so bizarre and upsetting before. His hands shook and he placed them upon the desk hoping to steady them. Underneath his fingers, Allan's files stared up and the sight of them began to transform Philip's fear into anger. Where *was* Allan? Of all the days to skip work, he chose *this* day? Philip dialled Allan's home number and at the sound of the answering machine hung up. Loathing filled him.

He was relieved at the end of the day to find the train home nearly deserted as he wanted only solitude. He sat facing the front window, and watched the dark tunnel advancing upon him. Lights ran across the few passengers who sat like gargoyles, heads hung low, waiting for life to pour from their drooping mouths. Each door opening brought a glare that blinded them, and they squinted until their stop arrived. They then trudged with difficulty onto the cold platform, leaving Philip further alone.

He looked back through the rear window along the line of cars behind him. They all seemed empty, passengers having departed them one by one until only Philip remained. As his train took the turn at Union Station and Philip realized he was wrong: near the other end of the train, he saw the briefest shape of someone sitting. Immediately the figure was gone, hidden behind so many empty cars.

The distance between the penultimate stop and his own stretched for an eternity. When Philip stood to collect his things he noticed, upon his seat, a black gelatinous streak. He craned his head, looking for a stain upon his clothes and found it spread across his leg. Brushing only made it worse. He stepped from the car annoyed.

The train hurried off, leaving him in his filthy clothes alone on the platform. The exit was bathed in its orange light, and as he walked towards it a strange sound followed. Like the suction of a foot leaving mud, it repeated, echoing off the walls. He looked around but the platform was empty. The noise continued and he wondered if he was really alone, or if someone else had left the subway train while he was too preoccupied to notice. He looked back again, and then moved faster towards the orange stairwell.

Light spilled from it and flooded the blotched tiles. Philip saw illuminated a dark stream of footprints that curled around the concrete walls and into the stairwell. From the first stair he could just barely see the surface level above and the dark night that already clogged the sky. He climbed the stairs, anxious to escape the shrinking walls and the awful sound behind him, and tried to ignore the feel of the railing, still slick with the sweat of an entire city's hands.

A pair of figures crested the top stair. They stood side-by-side, silhouetted by the pale light behind them. They filled the width of the stairwell and began to descend towards him. He stood to the side, unsettled by their approach, to let them pass.

But when they were almost upon him, Philip recoiled in horror.

They were six or seven foot tall, coated in some foul black crude like thickened oil; it slowly rippled over their bodies, obscuring their faces and mouths. It seemed to eat the light, and – like two black holes – reflected nothing under the orange glow.

Philip found the first stair behind him, and then the next, and soon scrambled back down them to the platform. He needed to escape from those barren faces and find his way free.

He turned the corner and there were more faceless shadows awaiting him. They grabbed his shoulders, black stuff swimming frantically over their hands, and touched his face. He felt numb instantly and his legs crumbled, dropping him to his knees. Philip's stomach constricted, muscles convulsing, lungs filling, and he coughed up a thick, viscous fluid. With a shudder, his gut exploded, and a torrent of black grease poured from him like blood, covering the ground. Dark figures stood around him, their faces a swirling mass, black sputum pooling at their feet, as one by one Philip's muscles failed. His whole body revolted, liquid spilling out, and he collapsed onto the drowned square tiles.

Slowly, the world stopped moving, and for a brief moment threatened to never resume.

Then, drop after drop, the congealed oil crept back towards Philip's lifeless body. It crawled onto his chest, into his hair, through his clothes. More followed, faster, coating his body in a layer of sludge, of bile, of everything that had filled him for so long. It covered him, flowing thick like a river across the surface of his cooling skin. Eddies swirled in his eyes, finding banks in the angles of his bones. It was a torrent flooding over him, a tumultuous sea, as silent as the shadows that looked on.

Eventually the waves subsided, and the liquid began to calmly move beneath the dull orange lights of the deserted subway platform, swirling in odd patterns.

Then, something stood, and one more shadow joined the night.

LYNDA E. RUCKER

These Things We Have Always Known

LYNDA RUCKER CURRENTLY lives in Athens, Georgia in a rambling old house with her partner and lots of books, an overgrown yard, and one fussy cat imported from Ireland.

This is her third appearance in *The Mammoth Book of Best New Horror*. Her fiction has also appeared in *Black Static* and *Supernatural Tales*, among other magazines, and she has a story in the forthcoming anthology *Apparitions*, due out from Screaming Dreams Press in 2010.

"On an afternoon break from one in a series of deadly dull office jobs I once held," Rucker recalls, "this narrator's voice stole into my head and started telling me about the very strange sort of work that *he* did and the even weirder place where he lived.

"I wrote it all down on a yellow legal pad (possibly pilfered from an office supply cabinet) and, consumed as I was at that time with that 'anywhere-but-here' feeling, I really did think that Cold Rest, creepy and apocalyptic as it was, seemed preferable to the place I found myself in that day."

C OLD REST IS THE NAME of this hard town scratched out on the side of a Georgia mountain ridge, so far to the north it's bleeding over into North Carolina, really, although it doesn't seem much to belong to either place. The people here have a certain way of talking, like you'll find in isolated regions, the kinds of places no one ever really leaves and that outsiders never move to, or even visit.

I have always known that there was something wrong in Cold Rest. People round here laugh when they say, something in the water, but it's true that the community my wife was raised in is not like other places. And there is a hardness about every single resident of Cold Rest – Sarah included – that is, in the end, like living alongside something rigid and alien. It hasn't been a perfect relationship; in twenty years we've had plenty of opportunity to hurt one another. I think Sarah still gets the occasional note or e-mail from the man she thought about leaving me for (though she never would have) five years ago. You learn to overlook these things. Here in Cold Rest, things are different, as I have said.

That something was always waiting in Cold Rest we all knew. You often had the feeling that you were in a room with someone, even when alone, who was getting ready to speak, making barely audible noises prior to forming actual words. You felt it sometimes like a seismic rumble deep in the earth. When you dreamed it you never could remember the following day, just a kind of uneasiness like something had crawled into your brain in the night and left the faintest of markings behind, a gloss of breath where your own thoughts used to lie.

"That one's lovely, Neil." Until Sarah spoke I didn't know she'd been watching me. She came forward and touched the robin I'd been carving as gently as if it had been alive. Dusk had descended while I was out there in my little workshop at the back of the house. I had lost track of time.

Sarah frowned when she saw what else I was working on, an abstract sculpture about half her height, rusted wire twisted into irregular angles broken by slivers of mirror. Everywhere that the robin whittled out of oak was warm and comforting, this seemed designed to inflict a kind of wound upon the observer. I worked on the robin when I got blocked on the other piece.

"I wish you'd just stick to carving birds and dogs like you used to," she said. "You never made anything like this before."

I just shrugged.

"Dinner's ready. And Gary's here."

That surprised me. I hadn't heard my brother's truck – though it's true that I sometimes get so engrossed in my work that I am not really aware of anything outside it – and Gary hadn't dropped in to see us in a long time. He lived a couple of hours away, so it wasn't as though he'd just stop in casually.

I looked over the robin I'd been carving, ran one finger along its breast, felt something stirring. It seemed finished.

"What does he want?"

Sarah said, "I think he wants a job."

My brother's a writer – no, you probably haven't heard of him; when he tells people the names he writes under you can see them being sorry they've asked, anxious in case it turns out the names *ought* to ring a bell.

Gary prefers to think of himself as a regular guy. I know because he's told me so many times. He writes horror, thrillers, crime, whatever he can get paid for – Sarah says a romance novel here and there, though he's never admitted it to *me* – and that seems all right to him because it's regular-guy fiction.

We were sitting down to dinner, the four of us – our teenaged daughter Emma crept out of her room and joined us – and I said it outright. "I don't know, Gary. I mean, I'm sure I could get you on at the yard, but why in hell you want to go and do something like get a job? And why here?"

Gary looked at his food and mumbled. "Headaches. I've been getting these damn fierce headaches. I don't have any health plan and I'm scared to see a doctor. Something's really wrong, I could be paying them off for the rest of my life."

There was a silence round the table, except for the sound of Emma's chewing with her mouth open.

Gary tried to laugh. "Thought I'd try to get me some of that sick leave you working folks are always talking about. Imagine getting paid to lie in bed all day and puke!"

I said, "It doesn't really work that way," but Sarah cut me off with a look.

"Besides," Gary went on, "the things that go on here sometimes with those carvings you do, I figure maybe I could use a jolt of that for my books."

Sarah said, "It doesn't happen the way you tell it to, Gary. Neil's carvings come to life under his hands sometimes, but it's not anything he can control. You can't use it for your own purposes."

When Sarah says *come to life* you understand that she is not speaking figuratively. I have told that you Cold Rest is not like other places.

"Well," Gary said, "I'd sure like a chance to try."

Sarah changed the subject. "How's Barbara?" she asked, referring to Gary's long-time, on-again off-again girlfriend.

"She got married last month."

Emma scraped her chair back and announced that she was going out. Her hair was black as pitch that night and falling across her face. The week before it was emergency-red. It was as though someone different sat down to dinner with us every few nights, although even without the outlandish hair I felt like I didn't know her any longer. She's grown so tall in the last couple of years, and her hands are long and delicate, pianist's hands, except she hasn't touched Sarah's grandmother's baby grand in the living room since she reached her teens. She has dark eyes and her mouth is sulky, at least around Sarah and me. Sarah said she was sure Emma and her boyfriend were having sex, but that she didn't know what to do about it. I said, I'm sure you'll handle it, because I didn't even want to think of it, and I didn't know why we had to *do* anything. That boyfriend of hers, Sam or Simon . . . What kind of a name is Simon anyway? I tried not to look at him when he came to visit. He had soft, puffy hands. I imagined saying something to him like, "You'd better not touch my daughter with those hands!" fully realizing how ridiculous that made me. I said to Sarah, "For God's sake, she's only sixteen years old," and she said, "But don't you remember sixteen? She seems like a baby to us but at sixteen you think you're all finished growing up."

But. Sixteen! She still looked like a child.

"I'll see what I can do for you," I said to Gary. "You can stay here if you need to. There's not much in town in the way of rentals."

"Why don't you take Gary out to your shop and show him what you've been working on?" Sarah suggested. "Maybe he'll like them better than I do."

Gary always feigned, or perhaps genuinely felt, a polite interest in even my most banal creations. We walked out there while Sarah was brewing coffee. Evenings in Cold Rest are beautiful. There's a special way the sun slips down the mountain and leaves everything glowing. Tonight we were just in time to see the sky deepen and blaze in all its twilight glory. I dragged a couple of the things I'd been working on out of my shop, because I'd noticed that when the light was right – at about that time of day – the metal I was using glowed like it was plugged into an electrical outlet.

Gary didn't touch any of it like he usually does. He stood back a bit and pointed at one of them. "What's going on there?" he asked.

I had stretched and hammered torn strips of canvas across an irregularly shaped cage I'd built, and along the sides threaded teeth from the skulls of dead animals I'd come across in the woods.

"I don't know," I said. "I just felt like it had to look that way."

Gary didn't say anything for a long time. Finally, "I don't like it."

That shocked me, and it hurt a little. Gary always liked what I did. He was younger than me, but I treated him more like an older brother, anxious for his approval. I'd never been real proud of my woodworking before, mediocre stuff I could've sold at inflated prices in some of the tourist towns to folks who didn't know any better. For the first time, making these sculptures that came to me in dreams, I felt like I was doing something that mattered.

"I think you ought to get rid of them and go back to making birds and baby rabbits, even if some of them do get away from you," he said, and then he was heading for his truck just like he hadn't said he was going to sit a while and have coffee with Sarah and me, and she came out the back door when she heard his engine and looked at me with a question in her eyes. Had we argued? I shook my head, to show her I didn't know.

The following evening, when I got out to the shop after work, I found the robin with its neck broken. I'd forgotten to set it outside before I closed up for the night, and it had flown repeatedly against the windows.

I cradled it in my palms and carried it in to show to Sarah and Emma. I felt so bad, like I'd taken it up in my own two hands and dashed it against the wall. Like I'd created something just so it could suffer and die. We buried it in the backyard because it didn't seem right to just throw it out, and Emma set a little ring of stones round its grave.

Sarah teaches English at the local junior high school in town. At night sometimes, to help me unwind, she reads me poems. I like the ones that rhyme. I know that's not very sophisticated of me, but there it is. My favourite poet is Robert Frost. Emma said, "Sean (or Stan, or Steve, or whatever his name is) is a poet and he said Robert Frost was supposed to have been a real dick." Sarah said, "Emma!" and Emma said, "What? I'm just saying," and I didn't say anything at all. Instead I repeated lines of poetry to myself. I like the one about miles to go before I sleep.

Sarah had Emma's boyfriend in her class a few years ago. She said he "had quite a way with words for such a young person". This made me feel like she was taking sides with Emma and that boy, against me. Sarah writes poetry, just for herself. Once in a while she'll read one to me. They don't rhyme, and I don't understand them, although I pretend like I do. I think this is one of the things she liked about the man she had the affair with. He was a poet of moderate renown – if you move in those circles, which I don't; I took Sarah's word for it – and she met him when she taught in a special program down south for gifted children a few summers ago. I remember how she was for a while afterwards. Not better, not worse, just a different Sarah; their intimacy drew out dormant parts I'd not known in her. She used words and turns of phrases she hadn't before. Her mind strayed to subjects I was unaccustomed to. They weren't his words, his subjects. They belonged to Sarah, but it was all hidden geography in the context of *our* relationship.

Maybe that was why she and Gary didn't like what I was working on. Maybe it was as simple as that, the unaccustomedness, the fact that they were used to seeing me work with wood and blade to make cosy scenes like fox families or spring fawns. I told myself that while she read to me that night by the fire, got lost in the words she was speaking till I fell asleep dreaming of the bird pitching itself against the glass, trying to get free, until it shattered the bones in its neck, and she had to wake me to send me to bed.

I knew that Emma was gone almost before she actually left. I thought afterwards about that word – *almost* – such a little word, six letters and the difference between what was and what might have been. I woke covered in a bad dream, and I felt something wrong in the night. Something gone out of the house. Later, when I talked to Sarah about it, she said I must have woken up earlier, unknowing, when Emma closed the front door, or heard the engine of whatever car swept her into the night and away from us. I told her she must be right. But I knew what woke me was the simple fact of her absence, unnatural and complete. The house fairly vibrated with the lack of her. Had I known, in my dreams, that she was going? Had I let her go, to find out how far away she could get?

I was right all along not to trust that boy.

The week after Gary came to dinner – before Emma had left us – he accompanied me to the yard for the first time. I showed him round a little bit, and he went to talk to Human Resources, a phrase which has always had a little too literal a turn to it for my liking.

Gary talked a good game about honest manual labour but he's never been the type to break a sweat, and I knew he'd wind up taking a position in the office. I can't blame him for that. It gets unbearably hot in the yard in summer, and in the winter the ground freezes hard. I've seen folks felled by heat stroke and frostbite and worse things, because of what it is we're digging out of the ground there. And we sink mine shafts deep into the earth, even though it's getting harder to find people willing to go under the ground like that. Mostly just the old-timers'll take that kind of work.

Gary moved into our spare room, and he got up and went to work every day, and locked himself away when he came home, only venturing out for dinner. I figured he must be getting a lot of writing done. It got so we were seeing more of Emma than him, and that's saying something. I didn't pay him much attention, to be honest, because I'd been dreaming again about what I wanted to work on next, and the dreams were strange and left me with a taste in my mouth like cold metal. I didn't have clear pictures in my head of the devices I needed to build next, but the designs seemed etched into the movement of my hands.

And then Emma was gone, and the work was all that could soothe me, take my head somewhere it wasn't worried sick about what was happening to her. The police said they'd do all they could, and none of her friends knew a thing. Sean's – or Seth's – or Sam's mother visited Sarah one day; I couldn't bear to be around her, a wan, ineffectual woman. I headed out to the shop.

After a while Gary joined me. I was painting sheets of tin in coat after coat of black paint. I wanted to get a deeper black than I'd ever seen in nature. I asked Gary if he thought it was working. He didn't answer me.

"How are things going?" I said. "You seem pretty busy."

He shrugged and wouldn't look at me. "I've been writing," he said, "but when I get back and look at the pages, I don't remember putting down what I see there, and what I see scares me."

"What do they have you doing in the office there?" I was curious; there was no mixing between the blue- and white-collar folks at the yard.

"I print reports and collate them, and compare long lists of figures with other long lists, but listen to this, after I get far enough down the lists they stop being numbers and they start being other kinds of marks, things I've never seen before. Also, I write letters for some of the executives. I wrote down the names of some of the places they were being sent to, places I never heard of, but when I looked them up later I could never find any of them." His face looked clammy and pale when he was telling me this.

"You made an appointment to see a doctor about those headaches yet? I know one in town'd see you."

He shook his head. "I don't think this has anything to do with those headaches."

"Still." I had a feeling Gary'd come to us because he was at the end of his rope, that it had been more than headaches and fear of skyrocketing medical bills that had driven him. I didn't know how to ask him if he had any money at all, but I didn't need to; knowing Gary, he'd have offered to pay us for room and board if he'd been able.

"Listen, Neil, I got to ask you something that sounds crazy. Do you ever think maybe you wind up in a place and everything in your life has been about moving you to that moment, preparing you for something momentous even? Like your life's work?"

"I hope you're not talking about Cold Rest. Anything moving you toward something here can't be good."

"Why'd you stay?"

"Why do people stay anywhere? My family's here."

"Why do *they* stay?"

They don't, I wanted to say, but I couldn't think that way. Emma would come back to us. It was simply not possible to acknowledge any other outcome. "It's different for folks born here."

Gary put his hand out to touch the piece I was working on. "Careful," I said, "wet paint," but wet paint or no, I didn't want anyone touching those structures but me.

"What are they?"

"Instruments," I said. "Instruments for the summoning of dead races."

"The hell's that supposed to mean? That sounds fucked up."

"It came to me. In a dream. I thought about trying to put on some kind of show, you know, like a real artist, and I pictured that title printed up on little cards and hanging above them."

"I don't think that's such a good idea."

"In a way, I don't either. Anyway, I'd have to hold it out here in the shop. Cold Rest isn't much for art exhibitions."

Gary reached in his shirt pocket and took out a pack of cigarettes. "I thought you quit."

"I did." He lit one, took a long drag, staring off into the woods, and said, "I think we ought to go look for Emma."

"Where would we start?"

"You don't want her to come back here, do you?"

I said, "I miss her so much sometimes I can't breathe."

Gary watched me for a while. "Over at the yard, Neil, who runs that place?"

"Nowadays," I said, "Bree Cold and her brother Ambrose. He's kind of a half-wit, though. The Colds always ran it. Town wouldn't be here without the company. They came here from – well, hell, nobody knows where, but they started it up during the Depression, and people came from all over that couldn't get work anywhere else."

"What goes on there? What are y'all digging out of the ground all day?"

"What are you pushing papers round the office for?"

Gary finished his cigarette and lit another one off that. "I don't know," he said. "I got some ideas. I think it's time I cut my losses and hit the road, but there's something I haven't told you and Sarah."

"You don't owe us any explanations."

"That last book, though, it sort of tanked. They've been doing that for a while, actually."

"Well." I put down my paintbrush. I wondered if he was going to try to borrow some money; we didn't have anything to give him. "It's not all bad here. Sarah says at least in Cold Rest we can get at the edges of something miraculous." *The price of living is dying,* Sarah had told me, *and even when Cold Rest has swallowed up the last of you whole you know you've been in the presence of something divine.*

"Something miraculous," Gary said. "Is that how she sees it?"

Emma called us last night.

Her voice sounded so far away on the telephone. Sarah started crying. She asked Emma if she needed anything, if we could send her money, if there was anything at all she'd let us do. Emma said no. She just wanted to let us know she was all right.

"Baby, sooner or later you'll have to come home," Sarah said, but Emma had already hung up.

I couldn't sleep after that; I'd be dropping off and I'd think I heard her voice. Then a storm moved over us, thunder and lightning and wind to wake the dead. I got up and prowled around for a while, looking out the windows like I was waiting for something, and finally I braved the torrent of rain to make a sprint out to my workshop. I tried to work on a new piece. Sarah had stopped going out there at all. She said it upset her stomach to see the things I was making nowadays. She said she couldn't even look at them, that she had to look *around* them, because they just seemed like objects gone wrong somehow.

It occurred to me while I was out there hammering bits of bone I'd salvaged from carcasses of deer and dead birds – filthy work – that I could do the kind of thing a decent man would never do. I could leave. I could just disappear and put Cold Rest behind me. I could make the last twenty years of my life vanish just like that. Start anew. I was still young enough to have another family even.

At the same time I had a funny feeling I'd missed the chance to do anything like that, that whatever was set in motion couldn't be stopped any longer.

We have always known in Cold Rest that we were waiting on something. We didn't know what, or if we'd see it in our lifetimes, but without ever talking about it among ourselves we all knew we were preparing for something bigger than any of us could conceive.

There is not much of a social life in Cold Rest except among the teenagers. Sarah and I had never had any real friends. I wondered what kind of devices other people were constructing behind the walls of their homes. I wondered what kind of poems Sarah was writing that she wasn't showing to me.

Gary found me in my workshop just as dawn was breaking. The storm had blown over but the sky had a tattered look about.

"I got the truck all loaded," he said. "I'm taking off. Sure you don't want to join me?"

I said, "I don't think it would do me any good." And, "What about your headaches?"

His eyes, I realized with a shock, were bright with tears. "I tell you," he said. "I've been scared shitless all along it's a brain tumour. I think something's bad wrong. I just want to get somewhere bright and warm. Thinking of heading down to Tybee Island. Remember, when we were kids?"

Laughing like fools splashing into waves big as houses. Crab legs at the restaurant with the red and white checkered oilcloth where you threw the shells into a hole in the middle of the table. The 178 steps to the top of the old lighthouse and the rumours of pirate gold.

I had a couple of twenties on me, but he wouldn't take them. "I just want to sit on the beach and take it all in," he said. "I don't think I'll need that."

"For gas money, then," I said. It seemed important that I try to do something for him. I watched him leave, his taillights disappearing down the driveway, and then I turned back to my sculptures. In the gathering morning light they glowed and seemed to sing to me.

Sarah was fixing breakfast when I went in, pancakes and sausage. "Gary left," she said, not a question. I nodded anyway and helped myself to some coffee. The clock above the sink that played Westminster chimes on the hour struck, and went on striking, and both of us counting and trying to look like we weren't. Fifteen, sixteen, seventeen.

"Goodness, that was strange," Sarah said when it finished, with a nervous laugh.

I have never tasted a meal less than I did that breakfast.

I looked out the window toward my workshop, and I kept seeing things. Holes in my vision like Sarah describes when she gets one of her migraines, only my head felt fine. I think I said I better head on to work. Sarah looked anxious and said, did I have to go?

Once I turned onto the main road through town I saw I might not get far. The storm had been worse up that way; tree limbs torn and blown into the road, pieces of asphalt chunked into rubble like there'd been an earthquake. It was still passable, barely, but I couldn't see any reason to pass. I turned around and headed back home.

Only now I'm here and Sarah's gone. I've called her name, and I've gone looking for her, and her cup of coffee is half-drunk and still on the table where she was sitting when I left. I tell myself she went on to work, too, but there's only one road into town and I didn't pass her on my way back. I don't dare look in the garage because I don't want to see her car there. I don't dare leave the house now, in fact, or even look out the windows.

It has gone blacker than night outside, although I believe it is about eleven in the morning; I cannot be sure because my watch has begun running in reverse and the clock is chiming weird hours at uncertain intervals. A little while ago there was a splitting sound, and I heard things scuttling and then swarming the sides of the house; it is only a matter of time now before what is out there gets in. We have always known there was something hidden in Cold Rest, something murmuring in a pitch not known to us, something waiting just outside our field of vision. We have obliged it with our reticent ways; we have nurtured it in our guarded, secret souls; we have made it potent with our lies; and now it is upon us all, all of us dreamers, whispering of promises we didn't mean to make, and cold as the stars.

NEIL GAIMAN

Feminine Endings

OVER THE PAST COUPLE of years, Neil Gaiman has co-scripted (with Roger Avary) Robert Zemeckis' motion-capture fantasy film *Beowulf*, while both Matthew Vaughn's *Stardust* and Henry Selick's *Coraline* were based on his novels.

Next up, his Newbery Medal-winning children's novel *The Graveyard Book* is being adapted for the movies, with Gaiman on board as one of the producers.

The ever-busy author also has out a book of poems, *Blueberry Girl*, illustrated by Charles Vess; *Crazy Hair*, a new picture book with regular collaborator Dave McKean, and the graphic novel compilation *Batman: Whatever Happened to the Caped Crusader?* (with art by Andy Kubert). *The Tales of Odd* is a follow-up to the 2008 children's book *Odd and the Frost Giants*, while *The Absolute Death* and *The Complete Death* from DC/Vertigo feature the character from the author's *Sandman* comic.

The author is also working on a non-fiction volume about China, following his visit to that country in 2007.

"'Feminine Endings' was written for a book of love letters," explains Gaiman.

"In my head it is set in Krakow, in Poland, where the human statues stand, but it could be anywhere that tourists go and people stand still.

"Readers have assumed that the person writing the letter is male, and they have assumed the person writing the letter is female. I have been unable to shed any light on the matter.

"There is an odd magic to writing love-letters, I suspect, even if they are scary-strange fictional love letters. Shortly after I wrote this story I met and, eventually, fell in love with a former human statue, and have been trying to tease out the cause and effect ever since – and, of course, whether or not I should be worried . . ."

MY DARLING,

    Let us begin this letter, this prelude to an encounter, formally, as a declaration, in the old-fashioned way: I love you. You do not know me (although you have seen me, smiled at me, placed coins in the palm of my hand). I know you (although not so well as I would like. I want to be there when your eyes flutter open in the morning, and you see me, and you smile. Surely this would be paradise enough?). So I do declare myself to you now, with pen set to paper. I declare it again: I love you.

I write this in English, your language, a language I also speak. My English is good. I was some years ago in England and in Scotland. I spent a whole summer standing in Covent Garden, except for the month of Edinburgh Festival, when I am in Edinburgh. People who put money in my box in Edinburgh included Mr Kevin Spacey the actor, and Mr Jerry Springer the American television star who was in Edinburgh for an Opera about his life.

I have put off writing this for so long, although I have wanted to, although I have composed it many times in my head. Shall I write about you? About me?

First you.

I love your hair, long and red. The first time I saw you I believed you to be a dancer, and I still believe that you have a dancer's body. The legs, and the posture, head up and back. It was your smile that told me you were a foreigner, before ever I heard you speak. In my country we smile in bursts, like the sun coming out and illuminating the fields and then retreating again behind a cloud too soon. Smiles are valuable here, and rare. But you smiled all the time, as if everything you saw delighted you. You smiled the first time you saw me, even wider than before. You smiled and I was lost, like a small child in a great forest never to find its way home again.

I learned when young that the eyes give too much away. Some in my profession adopt dark spectacles, or even (and these I scorn with bitter laughter as amateurs) masks that cover the whole face. What good is a mask? My solution is that of full-sclera theatrical contact lenses, purchased from an American website for a little under 500 euros, which cover the whole eye. They are dark grey, of course, and look like stone. They have made me more than 500 euros, paid for themselves over and over. You may think, given my profession, that I must be poor, but you would be wrong. Indeed, I fancy that you must be surprised by how much I have collected. My needs have been small and my earnings always very good.

Except when it rains.

Sometimes even when it rains. The others as perhaps you have observed, my love, retreat when it rains, put up the umbrellas, run away. I remain where I am. Always. I simply wait, unmoving. It all adds to the conviction of the performance.

And it is a performance, as much as when I was a theatrical actor, a magician's assistant, even when I myself was a dancer. (That is how I am so familiar with the bodies of dancers.) Always, I was aware of the audience as individuals. I have found this with all actors and all dancers, except the short-sighted ones for whom the audience is a blur. My eyesight is good, even through the contact lenses.

"Did you see the man with the moustache in the third row?" we would say. "He is staring at Minou with lustful glances."

And Minou would reply, "Ah yes. But the woman on the aisle, who looks like the German Chancellor, she is now fighting to stay awake." If one person falls asleep, you can lose the whole audience, so we would play the rest of the evening to a middle-aged woman who wished only to succumb to drowsiness.

The second time you stood near me you were so close I could smell your shampoo. It smelt like flowers and fruit. I imagine America as being a whole continent full of women who smell of flowers and fruit. You were talking to a young man from the university. You were complaining about the difficulties of our language for an American. "I understand what gives a man or a woman gender," you were saying. "But what makes a chair masculine or a pigeon feminine? Why should a statue have a feminine ending?"

The young man, he laughed and pointed straight at me, then. But truly, if you are walking through the square, you can tell nothing about me. The robes look like old marble, water-stained and time-worn and lichened. The skin could be granite. Until I move I am stone and old bronze, and I do not move if I do not want to. I simply stand.

Some people wait in the square for much too long, even in the rain, to see what I will do. They are uncomfortable not knowing, only happy once they have assured themselves that I am a natural, not an artificial. It is the uncertainty that traps people, like a mouse in a glue-trap.

I am writing about myself perhaps too much. I know that this is a letter of introduction as much as it is a love letter. I should write about you. Your smile. Your eyes so green. (You do not know the true colour of my eyes. I will tell you. They are brown.) You like classical music, but you have also ABBA and Kid Loco on your iPod Nano. You wear no perfume. Your underwear is, for the most part, faded and comfortable, although you have a single set of red-lace brassière and panties which you wear for special occasions.

People watch me in the square, but the eye is only attracted by motion. I have perfected the tiny movement, so tiny that the passer can scarcely tell if it is something he saw or not. Yes? Too often people will not see what does not move. The eyes see it but do not see it, they discount it. I am human-shaped, but I am not human. So in order to make them see me, to make them look at me, to stop their eyes from sliding off me and paying me no attention, I am forced to make the tiniest motions, to draw their eyes to me. Then, and only then, do they see me. But they do not always know what they have seen.

I think of you as a code to be broken, or as a puzzle to be cracked. Or a jigsaw puzzle, to be put together. I walk through your life, and I stand motionless at the edge of my own. My gestures – statuesque, precise – are too often misinterpreted. I want you. I do not doubt this.

You have a younger sister. She has a MySpace account, and a Facebook account. We talk sometimes on Messenger. All too often people assume that a medieval statue exists only in the fifteenth century. This is not so true: I have a room, I have a laptop. My computer is passworded. I practise safe computing. Your password is your first name. That is not safe. Anyone could read your email, look at your photographs, reconstruct your interests from your web history. Someone who was interested and who cared could spend endless hours building up a complex schematic of your life, matching the people in the photographs to the names in the emails, for example. It would not be hard reconstructing a life from a computer, or from cell phone messages. It would be like filling a crossword puzzle.

I remember when I actually admitted to myself that you had taken to watching me, and only me, on your way across the square. You paused. You admired me. You saw me move once, for a child, and you told a woman with you, loud enough to be heard, that I might be a real statue. I take it as the highest compliment. I have many different styles of movement, of course – I can move like clockwork, in a set of tiny jerks and stutters, I can move like a robot or an automaton. I can move like a statue coming to life after hundreds of years of being stone.

Within my hearing you have spoken many times of the beauty of this small city. How, for you, to be standing inside the stained-glass confection of the old church was like being imprisoned inside a kaleidoscope of jewels. It was like being in the heart of the sun. Also, you are concerned about your mother's illness.

When you were an undergraduate you worked as a cook, and your fingertips are covered with the scar marks of a thousand tiny knife-cuts.

I love you, and it is my love for you that drives me to know all about you. The more I know, the closer I am to you. You were to come to my country with a young man, but he broke your heart, and still you came here to spite him, and still you smiled. I close my eyes and I can see you smiling. I close my eyes and I see you striding across the town-square in a clatter of pigeons. The women of this country do not stride. They move diffidently, unless they are dancers. And when you sleep your eyelashes flutter. The way your cheek touches the pillow. The way you dream.

I dream of dragons. When I was a small child, at the home, they told me that there was a dragon beneath the old city. I pictured the dragon wreathing like black smoke beneath the buildings, inhabiting the cracks between the cellars, insubstantial and yet always present. That is how I think of the dragon, and how I think of the past, now. A black dragon made of smoke. When I perform I have been eaten by the dragon and have become part of the past. I am, truly, 700 years old. Kings come and kings go. Armies arrive and are absorbed or return home again, leaving only damaged buildings, widows and bastard children behind them, but the statues remain, and the dragon of smoke, and the past.

I say this, although the statue that I emulate is not from this town at all. It stands in front of a church in southern Italy, where it is believed either to represent the sister of John the Baptist, or a local lord who endowed the church to celebrate that he had not died of the plague, or the angel of death.

I had imagined you perfectly pure, my love, pure as I am, yet one time I found that the red lace panties were pushed to the bottom of your laundry hamper, and upon close examination I was able to assure myself that you had, unquestionably, been unchaste the previous evening. Only you know who with, for you did not talk of the incident in your letters home, or allude to it in your online journal.

A small girl looked up at me once, and turned to her mother, and said, "Why is she so unhappy?" (I translate into English for you, obviously. The girl was referring to me as a statue and thus she used the feminine ending.)

"Why do you believe her to be unhappy?"

"Why else would people make themselves into statues?"

Her mother smiled. "Perhaps she is unhappy in love," she said.

I was not unhappy in love. I was prepared to wait until everything was right, something very different.

There is time. There is always time. It is the gift I took from being a statue – one of the gifts, I should say.

You have walked past me and looked at me and smiled, and you have walked past me and other times you barely noticed me as anything other than an object. Truly, it is remarkable how little regard you, or any human, give to something that remains completely motionless. You have woken in the night, got up, walked to the little toilet, micturated, walked back to your bed, slept once more, peacefully. You would not notice something perfectly still, would you? Something in the shadows?

If I could, I would have made the paper for this letter for you out of my body. I thought about mixing in with the ink my blood or spittle, but no. There is such a thing as overstatement, yet great loves demand grand gestures, yes? I am unused to grand gestures. I am more practised in the tiny gestures. I made a small boy scream once, simply by smiling at him when he had convinced himself that I was made of marble. It is the smallest of gestures that will never be forgotten.

I love you, I want you, I need you. I am yours just as you are mine. There. I have declared my love for you.

Soon, I hope, you will know this for yourself. And then we will never part. It will be time, in a moment, to turn around, put down the letter. I am with you, even now, in these old apartments with the Iranian carpets on the walls.

You have walked past me too many times.

No more.

I am here with you. I am here now.

When you put down this letter. When you turn and look across this old room, your eyes sweeping it with relief or with joy or even with terror . . .

Then I will move. Move, just a fraction. And, finally, you will see me.

GARY McMAHON

Through the Cracks

GARY McMAHON'S FICTION has appeared in various magazines and anthologies in the UK and USA, and has been reprinted in both *The Mammoth Book of Best New Horror* and *The Year's Best Fantasy and Horror*.

He is the British Fantasy Award-nominated author of the collections *Rough Cut*, *All Your Gods Are Dead*, *Dirty Prayers*, *How to Make Monsters* and *Different Skins*, plus the novel *Rain Dogs*. McMahon has also edited an anthology of original novelettes titled *We Fade to Grey*. Forthcoming is another collection, *To Usher, the Dead*, and his first mass-market novel, *Hungry Hearts*, is published by Abaddon Books in 2009.

"I saw a picture online that was meant to be a Mid-Eastern Djinn crawling through a narrow crevice in a subterranean cave," explains the author. "The picture was a fake of course, but the ideas behind it were not.

"'Through the Cracks' examines the fascination we all have with what might lurk between the cracks in reality; and what monsters we might have summoned with our unquenchable desire to see beyond the mundane.

"As you can see, the basic idea for this one came relatively easily, but it was very difficult to write – the tone of the piece evaded me for a long time, until the last paragraph (which is a kind of homage to the work of the great Joel Lane) popped into my mind fully formed.

"After that, I was flying – and I began to see the cracks everywhere."

T HERE WAS A CRACK in the train window. Emma stared at the fine imperfection, imagining that in a sudden wind the crack would open and everyone inside the speeding vehicle would be sucked out and killed on the tracks.

Or perhaps when the train thundered through an underground tunnel, something older than the railways would crawl inside through the crack – summoned by the flickering electric lights, the smell of human sweat and the low sound of murmured conversations, it would feast upon the commuters.

When her mobile phone began to vibrate, signalling an incoming call, Emma suddenly forgot where and when she was. Her mind had drifted to a time many years ago, when such cracks had threatened to appear in the substance of reality all because of the insanity of one man – a man whose name and face she could never forget.

She had not spoken to Prentiss in three years, so when his name appeared on the screen on the front of the phone, accompanied by a shrill version of some forgettable chart hit, Emma's initial instinct was to hang up without speaking. But she didn't. Instead she calmly watched the blocky text flashing on the small rectangular screen, wondering what he could want, and why she'd left his details in the gadget's memory anyway.

"Hello," she finally answered, holding the handset tight against her ear to minimize the noise of the train as it hurtled over uneven tracks towards Newcastle. "Hello. Prent, is that you?"

Nothing. Not even the familiar whispery hiss of static. Just a long, almost baleful silence on the other end of the line. Then she heard a sound like glass or crockery breaking – a loud crunching crackle that made her pull her hand away from the side of her head and screw up her face in an expression of distaste. Was he toying with her, testing what reaction he might receive after all this time?

"*Hello*," she said, loudly, one more time, finger hovering over the green hang-up button.

"*Em?* Emma, it's me. It's Prentiss." His voice was faint, as if coming to her across a vast distance. Then there was a surge in volume and she could hear him more clearly. "How are you?"

"Hi, Prent. I'm good. Long time no hear." It was typical of him to call her up out of the blue, as if nothing had happened between them. That complete disregard for the social rituals had been part of why they'd split up in the first place. That and about a million other things: half-hidden cracks in his personality that had become all-too apparent during their time together.

"I've been thinking about you." The statement sent a faint chill of anticipation along her nerve endings, culminating between her legs. No matter how weird Prentiss had become, how strange his behaviour had been, Emma had long ago resigned herself to the fact that she would always be attracted to him.

"Oh." The train went under a tunnel; the connection broke for a few seconds so she could not be completely sure of what he said next.

"—so I've been a bit low lately. Things have been strange." What had she missed? It seemed important, but she didn't want to ask him to repeat whatever he'd said; her feelings were always so damn messy when it came to dealing with Prentiss that she was unable to act in anything approaching a normal, rational manner.

"Can I see you?"

"I live in London now, Prent. I left the north-east eighteen months ago."

"Really? Well that one took me by surprise."

"I'm visiting my sister this weekend." She regretted telling him this as soon as the words passed her lips. "I guess I could meet you somewhere."

"It's like fate, isn't it?"

Emma did not reply.

"I'm having . . . *difficulty* leaving the house. Could you come round? I'm still living in the same place."

"Yes. Okay. Tomorrow evening." She hung up before she could even question her response. The train carried her towards home, and towards yet another ill-thought out meeting with her ex. As bright winter sunlight battered her with harsh lightning strokes through the long carriage windows, Emma wondered why, wherever Prentiss was concerned, she could never bring herself to say no.

She arrived in Central Station just after mid-day, and dodged the bustling December crowds to catch a Metro to her sister's place out near the airport. Yet another capsule rocketing through underground caverns. Somehow this seemed like a metaphor for a part of her life she'd tried so very hard to leave behind. The stations flew by in a blur: MONUMENT. HAYMARKET. JESMOND (rendered dark with memories of Prentiss). ILFORD ROAD. Place names now meaningless because of her relocation to the Smoke. A group of youths in regulation white tracksuits got on at South Gosforth, the only feature distinguishing one from the next being the colour and brand of their baseball caps. The boys – aged between fourteen and sixteen – lounged with their feet up on the seats and drank cheap cider from dented cans. Emma felt relieved to be getting off the train at the next stop.

Nicci's house was a five minute walk from the station, past tired-looking shop fronts with dusty window displays consisting of canned and boxed goods Emma hadn't seen advertised in over ten years. Steel bars and vandal-proof glass marked the way; the sacred landscape of her youth was deteriorating a little more each day she stayed away. Certain parts of the footpaths seemed cracked beyond repair, big gaping fissures opening up in the grubby concrete paving slabs to reveal the dark grasping earth beneath.

Emma hurried towards Nicci's house, and when she approached the door it was opened without her having to announce her arrival.

"Em! Welcome home!" Her sister's chunky arms went around her, and she was bustled inside and into the warm environment. Food smells accosted her nostrils, the sound of a radio greeted her from another room. This was better. This was more like home.

They chatted over coffee and biscuits, Emma trying not to comment on Nicci's recent weight gain. It seemed that her sister's husband had started a new job, long-distance lorry driving between the UK and Germany. Ed was away for long stints, but according to Nicci this made the time he spent at home with her and the kids all the more worthwhile.

Emma's nephews, Olly and Jared, were over at a friend's house for some pre-teenage birthday party, and would return much later, stuffed to idleness with the unhealthy delights of chocolate and cake. Emma was glad of the time alone with her sister. Quiet moments like these happened all too rarely these days, and their intimacy helped remind her that she hadn't just the left bad things behind.

"Mum and dad send their love," Nicci said, smiling broadly. "I got an e-mail last night."

"I've been a bit lazy in contacting them. My computer crashed a few weeks ago, and I seem to have forgotten how to use the phone . . ."

Nicci grinned, appreciating that Emma had never been a strong communicator, and that she'd never approved of their parents' emigration, designed so that they could spend their retirement in the sun. "It's expensive to call Australia," she said, reaching out across the table to brush Emma's hand in a rare show of solidarity. "I'm sure they understand."

The rest of the afternoon passed quickly, and all too soon the kids arrived back from the party. Olly was unable to hide his affection for his aunt, and smothered her with rich candy-flavoured kisses; Jared was more insular, and merely pecked at her offered cheek before slouching off to the bathroom to get ready for bed.

The travelling had tired Emma more than she cared to admit, and when she started to doze in front of the television Nicci ordered her up to bed. "You're in the spare room, the one next to the boys' room. I've put fresh sheets on the bed, and there's a stereo set up in there in case you want to listen to some music before turning in."

Emma hugged her sister hard, afraid that if she let go this moment might shatter like glass. When Nicci broke free, a look of amused concern on her face, Emma shook her head and trotted silently upstairs.

Sleep teased her mercilessly, staying just out of reach, jerking away from her mind whenever she got close enough to grab its tenuous, mist-like essence. She thought of Prentiss, and of his obsessions. The way he'd become convinced that reality was shredding like old wallpaper in a derelict house and something nasty was peering through from the other side.

It was these frightening notions that had finally led to the break-down of affection between them. Emma had loved him right up until the end, but had eventually been forced to admit that sometimes love isn't enough. He refused to seek professional help, remaining con-vinced that he was sane and stable, despite the protestations of the few friends he had left. When Emma had walked away for the last time, Prentiss was too afraid of his own phantoms to even follow her out the door.

And now, three years later, did the same madness still drive him? Was he still seeing demons, or had he rid himself of the fantasy life that had driven a wedge between them?

Finally, she slept, but dark smudges stained her dreams, shapeless fractures that gaped in the corners of her imagination, put there by Prentiss too long ago to trouble her waking mind.

"For God's sake, Em, don't tell me you're going to see him?" Nicci's face was contorted into a snarl – she couldn't mention Prentiss' name without it scarring her features. "The bloke's a psycho. Didn't he run off chasing monsters, or something?"

"No," Emma replied, placing her teacup on a floral-patterned coaster. "He locked himself away so that they couldn't get him."

"Oh, well excuse my mistake. That makes a *big* difference." Nicci stood and walked to the window, looking out at her boys playing football in the huge back garden. A smile played across her face at the sight, but then she remembered that she was supposed to be angry. Emma loved her unquestionably in that moment, gaining a glimpse into the heart of motherhood, a peek at a state of mind that she someday dearly wished to experience for herself.

"He sounded rational, Nic. Like he's got himself together."

Her sister turned away from the window, an apple tree framing her, giving the illusion of devil horns sticking out of the sides of her head. "You always went back to him," she said, the anger having fled in the face of genuine concern. "And he always exploited that."

"Things are different now. I have my own life, a new start. I'm strong now; I don't need him to lean on."

"No," said her sister. "You have that all wrong. It was always him who leaned on you."

The taxi arrived at 6:30 pm, and Nicci walked her to the door. "Be careful," she said, tenderly. "Don't let him use you again."

Emma kissed Nicci's cheek and climbed into the cab, watching the suburban view unfurl as they neared the outskirts of the city. Prentiss lived in a shared house in Jesmond, a huge Victorian terraced property with rooms so big each one could have contained her entire flat in Bermondsey with enough space left over to squeeze in a single bed.

All too soon the ride was over, and Emma paid the driver and watched him pull away from the kerb. Trees lined the verges, their branches bare. Some of them bore splits in their wide flaking trunks, possibly the result of some kind of elm disease. The footpaths here were in better condition than the ones in Nicci's neighbourhood, but still the area seemed to be falling slowly into ruin. Gardens were overgrown; the brickwork of some of the houses was badly in need of repair. Even the sky looked broken, shattered into giant slivers, like a damaged picture window.

She could remember the place as if she'd visited it only yesterday. Surely Prentiss' housemates would have changed a few times by now, but she knew his room would look exactly the same. The last time she'd been inside, there had been newspaper clippings stuck to the walls, stories about environmental disasters, nuclear meltdowns, landmark buildings crumbling into dereliction.

Prentiss' obsession with social decay had been only the start of it. From there, his preoccupations had taken a darker turn. When the books about atrocities had turned up on his shelves, Emma had finally spoken out and begged him to talk to a doctor. It wasn't natural, she claimed, to read constantly about the Holocaust, Bosnian war crimes, the muddied hell of First World War trenches.

Prentiss had explained it all away by saying that modern society needed to embrace the darkness at its core, if only to prevent that darkness from taking hold of us all over again. To stop it reaching through the gaps to pull us down.

Thinking about all of this, Emma almost walked away. Her hand hovered over the doorbell, and she conducted an interior argument with herself as to whether or not she should return to Nicci's and order a Chinese takeaway.

The door opened. A figure stood well back from the threshold, visible only as shadow, and beckoned her inside. "Hurry," said the shadow. "Come on in."

It was Prentiss. He'd been waiting for her.

"I thought you might not come," he said as she followed him along a damp, badly decorated hallway. The stairs creaked ominously as they climbed to his room, but Emma was beyond being nervous under such conditions. Prentiss was a shred of the man he'd used to be. His clothes hung on him like rags, his hair was thinning at the scalp, and his skin had taken on a sickly yellow sheen. He looked ill, and Emma knew that if things got out of hand she could easily send him to the floor with a well-placed right-hook.

"I thought you might be . . . better," she said, following him into his room, the interior of which proved her prognosis to be utterly without foundation.

Prentiss sat on the bed, clearing a space with his hand. Papers scattered to the floor, but he made no move to pick them up. Emma could see they were covered in scrawled notes, unintelligible handwritten theories that still had a grip on his mind.

"Thank you for coming," he said, smiling nervously. As he was now, Emma had great difficulty understanding exactly what it was about him that had attracted her in the first place. He was a shell, a self-abused puppet flopping on severed strings.

Suddenly she became aware of the smell – a damp, flat odour that was difficult to place. Then, when she saw the state of what parts of the walls and ceiling remained visible, she realized what it was. Wet plaster. Opened plastic pots of Polyfilla repair paste and crack sealant sat on the windowsill, battered cutlery sticking up out of the white doughy mass within.

Prentiss had been filling cracks. The stuff hung in abstract stalactites from the ceiling, in frozen drips down the walls. Any crack –

however superficial – had been stuffed and inexpertly covered with the malleable material and left to set.

If it were not for his debauched and denuded appearance, Emma would have fled. But even now, in this vastly reduced state, he still retained a magnetic pull on her emotions. She gravitated towards him, even though the stench of urine and halitosis that rose from him in a cloud made her want to back away. He cut a pathetic figure in his stained T-shirt and ripped black jeans. His torso flashed white and spare under the baggy clothing. Emma had never seen him so thin. He looked positively malnourished.

"Why did you ask me here?" She thought a direct approach might at least yield one or two vaguely coherent answers.

Prentiss stood up from the mattress, a hand going up under his shirt to scratch a dry sore on his concave belly. Emma drew in a breath; as he turned, she could clearly define his ribs and the vicious ripple of spine through the scant covering of skin and atrophied muscle. Prentiss, she realized, was visibly wasting away.

"One of my housemates knows your sister – he drinks in the pub where she sometimes does shifts behind the bar. I knew you were coming, Emma . . . I'm sorry. I needed to talk to someone, and you were the only one who ever believed me. The only one who *listened*."

"I never believed you." The truth was her only recourse now; Prentiss had been fooling himself for too long and she no longer wanted to be complicit in the deception. "All I ever did was humour you. And when you didn't get the message, I left."

His smile was grim, like a widening crack that slowly crawled over the lower part of his waxy face. Emma had the insane urge to plug it with sealant from the tubs lined up on the floor by the end of the bed.

"I see," he said, sitting back down and rubbing the side of his head with an open palm, wincing as something – some undefined pain – bothered him. "I understand."

"You need help, Prent. You've needed it for a long time."

"Nobody can help me." His face softened, becoming both more and less than the sharp angles of his bone structure. It was as if a form more solid than his features could hint at was trying to push through from inside his skull. "I've spent all these years looking for them, examining the gaps, and now that they're finally here no one believes me.

"They're coming, Emma. Coming through the cracks."

Emma suddenly felt very afraid, not only for her own physical well-being, but also for her old boyfriend's sanity. This was real madness, close to the bone and way out over the edge. Prentiss had completely lost his mind.

"I'm going now," she mumbled, slipping her hands into her pockets and trying to act like this situation was the most normal thing in the world. "I have to get back – Nicci will be wondering where I am."

Prentiss said nothing; just stared at a spot on the floor, eyes wide and seeing beyond the worn weave of the carpet.

Emma opened the door and glanced back over her shoulder. Prentiss was now on his feet, moving slowly towards her, a large scrapbook held out like an offering. "Take it," he said. "Please. Just take it and read what's inside."

She turned to face him and took the book, smiling coldly as she stepped backwards through the door and out onto the landing. The door closed in her face; Prentiss did not pursue her out of the strange world that was his grubby double room. She took the stairs two at a time, forgetting about the book in her hand. Once out on the street, she ran towards the nearest Metro station, jumping the cracks in the pavement and praying that she would not have to wait long for a train.

At some point during the journey, she remembered that she was holding the scrapbook. Carefully, as if she were handling some extremely fragile artefact, she opened the book. The pages were stained and dog-eared from overuse, and the narrow spine was torn. Inside were pasted articles from obscure periodicals, smudged prints of digital images downloaded from amateur Fortean websites, and yet more hand-written notes.

Emma scanned a few of the articles, her blood seeming to thicken in her arteries.

A report of a Djinn terrorizing a cave network somewhere in the desert outside Dubai in the United Arab Emirates. The caves were fed by underground streams that were part of some immense subterranean network of gulfs and chasms – cracks in the belly of the earth.

An earthquake in Argentina, and the subsequent sightings of a strange spider-limbed demon prowling in the foothills of some local mountains.

Cave divers reported missing in the Yorkshire Dales.

Babies stolen from a hospital in Mexico, whose basement was recently damaged in a terrorist bomb blast, the foundations splitting open to reveal a deep underground crevasse.

They were coming. *Coming through the cracks.*

Emma shook her head, trying to dislodge Prentiss' crazy statement. This was not evidence; it was merely random information used to support his own delusion, a framework upon which he could hang his fantasies. You could prove anything to yourself if you were desperate enough, even this utter nonsense.

When she eventually made it back to Nicci's place, Emma remained withdrawn and pensive until it was time for her nephews to go to bed. Then she read them a bedtime story before soaking in a hot bath. She lay in the steaming tub with her eyes open, staring at the ceiling. There was a crack above the toilet she'd not noticed the day before.

Her aimless dozing was interrupted by a knock on the door; Nicci's voice drifted in to break her reverie: "Em, you okay? Can I come in?"

"No, I'm fine. Really. Just a bit down after seeing Prentiss. But you can rest easy. It's over. I won't be seeing him again."

"Okay, hon. I'm here to talk if you need me."

Emma glanced over at the scrapbook she'd balanced on the rim of the sink. She almost called Nicci back, asked her to look at what was inside the tatty covers. But no, to do so would have felt too much like willingly entering Prentiss' nightmares. The only cracks she knew of were the ones in his sanity.

Bath time over, she dried herself off and went to bed, looking forward to the end of her stay. She was due to return to London the next day and any enjoyment she'd taken from the trip had been tarnished by her communication with Prentiss. Even now, he was able to ruin small parts of her life, and she resented the power he had over her.

"I'll miss you," said Nicci, holding her tight on the doorstep. "Come back soon, big sis."

Emma returned the hug, and wished that she felt more like staying; it would cost her nothing to extend her trip, to spend more quality time with her family, but right now the thought of leaving Prentiss' ever-widening circle of influence seemed like a very good idea. "I'll be back at Christmas," she said. "In three weeks time. I promise."

Olly and Jared followed her outside, trailing her along the street as she headed for the Metro. They were good boys, full of life and energy, and she brushed away a tear as they ran off towards the park, waving and calling her name. Even Jared had seemed sad to see her go.

The next train was delayed by ten minutes, and Emma felt herself drawn to her mobile phone. She took it out of her pocket, dialled Prentiss' number, but didn't press the button to connect the call. She repeated this procedure three more times before finally giving in to temptation.

The phone rang out at the other end. No one was home.

Feeling deeply uneasy, Emma checked her watch. The London train wasn't scheduled to leave Newcastle until 3:00 pm. It was just after one. If she was quick, she could call in on him, just to check that he hadn't done anything foolish.

The train arrived. She got on, knowing exactly at which station she'd disembark. She made it to the house in plenty of time, telling herself that all she was planning to do was check on Prentiss' well-being. If he'd had an accident, or even tried to kill himself, she would never be able to look at herself in the mirror again. Despising her own weakness, and his passive strength, she rang the doorbell.

The door opened and a stranger stepped outside. "Oh, hi," he said, pulling a woollen hat down over his shaven head. "You here to visit someone?"

"Yes, Prentiss O'Neil." She realized this must be one of the people he shared the house with.

"Ah. I think the queer bugger's still in his room. I haven't seen him for days. If he is in, tell him he owes me fifty quid for the gas bill, would you." Then he was gone, jogging along the street towards the bus stop outside a tiny video rental shop that, judging by the window display, seemed only to stock titles she'd never heard of.

Emma pushed open the door and went inside, wiping her feet on the threadbare doormat. The house was silent; a stale heaviness hung in the air. She climbed the stairs to Prentiss' first floor room and knocked on his door, her touch lighter than intended. When no answer came, she knocked again, louder this time. The door swung open under the increased pressure from her knuckles.

Emma took a step inside, smelling that same dry yet moist odour and sensing that something was very wrong. Something crunched under her feet. The room was dark, with the blinds pulled over the single window, and it looked in even worse disarray than during her last visit.

"Prent. You here?" She expected no reply, and none came.

There was a naked figure kneeling on the bed, its body turned to face the wall. It was male – she could at least make out that pertinent detail in the gloom – and his hands were flattened against the peeling wallpaper. Drawing closer, she noticed that the floor was covered in a layer of crumbled plaster; the cracks Prentiss had crudely attempted to repair had opened up, shedding their DIY skin.

"Prent?" She could tell it was him from the familiar curvature of his spine, and the small tattoo of a rose on his left shoulder.

"What the hell—?"

She stopped in the centre of the room, poised to take another step but not quite managing it.

From this angle it looked as if he had tried to force his head into the long diagonal crack in the wall that ran in a jagged line from the corner of the window frame. She could see the soles of his feet on the bed, his legs, taut and skinny, his pallid back, his neck . . . but nothing above that.

Then, with growing horror, she realized her mistake.

Prentiss had not stuck his head into the crack; the crack had spread across the wall, passing through flesh and bone to shear off most of his head above the jaw-line. Prentiss' skull had become part of the fracture, a jagged black rent through which only darkness could be viewed.

As Emma watched, the wall around the crack seemed to shiver and the area of damage widened. Its messy Rorscharch edges sent out spidery limbs to breach plasterboard and brickwork and splinter the dead matter of Prentiss' rigid torso.

The crack was growing; something was trying to climb out.

Emma ran from the room, slamming the door to shut the monstrosity inside. She stumbled to the station and jumped on the first train to arrive, heading into the heart of the city. Perhaps safety lay in numbers, surrounded by crowds. But there were cracks everywhere – cracks in buildings, in road surfaces, even in people.

When she reached the station she sat in a glassed-walled waiting room under a row of stark fluorescent bulbs. At least where there was too much light she would see them coming, be alerted to their presence before they reached her. She pulled up her feet onto the bench, listening to the groan of plastic, hoping that it would not break. Or crack.

TIM LEBBON

Falling Off the World

TIM LEBBON IS A *New York Times* best-selling writer from South Wales. He has had almost twenty novels published to date, including *The Island, The Map of Moments* (with Christopher Golden), *Bar None, Fallen, Hellboy: The Fire Wolves, Dusk* and *Berserk*, as well as scores of novellas and short stories.

Lebbon has won three British Fantasy Awards, a Bram Stoker Award and a Scribe Award, and has also been a finalist for the International Horror Guild Award and the World Fantasy Award. In 2004, *Fangoria* magazine named him "One of the 13 Rising Talents Who Promise to Keep Us Terrified for the Next 25 years". So, no pressure then.

Several of his novels and novellas are currently in development as movies in the US and UK, and he is working on some new novels, screenplays and a TV series.

"I've always wondered how many helium-filled balloons you'd have to give someone before they lifted off," he explains. "There's that wonderful apocryphal story about a man tying hundreds to a deck-chair and drifting up into the airlines' flight paths with nothing more than a four-pack and a pin to ensure his descent.

"But I got to thinking what else could be up there, just floating around, and how perhaps the sky isn't as empty as it first appears."

A T FIRST THEY ALL CAME running after her, panic sewn onto their faces and a stitch in their sides. She could have been a stone plucked from a pond in defiance of gravity and they were the ripples in reverse, flowing in from all direction to the point of her egress. All

colours, all shades, sunburnt or pale, bald or long-haired, they ran
with their hands held out to catch the trailing rope.

She had not been lifted that high yet, and the end of the rope still
kissed the ground below her, drawing a snaking trail in the dusty
ground surrounding the lush field. One man leapt and missed it by a
finger; he stumbled and fell, and Holly smiled. Dust rose around him
in a cartoon halo. A woman managed to grab the rope but then let
go, screeching as it ripped through her hand and burned the skin. She
blew on her palm, and Holly laughed out loud, waiting for the smoke
and fire. Other people jumped for the rope and missed, and somewhere a woman screamed.

But by then the breeze had Holly held in its breath, and one great
gust clasped the balloon and made her truly airborne. Holly looked
up at the balloon but that made her dizzy, so she looked down at the
ground again, at the people slowing from a run to a walk behind her,
and then from a walk to a standstill, hands on hips, faces pointed
skyward but darkening quickly as their owners looked down to their
own level again. Some of them turned and walked away, shaking
their heads as if forgetting what they had been doing. Others started
chatting now that circumstance had brought them unexpectedly
together. One face remained aimed up at Holly. The shape waved
its arms over its head, and she heard a distant voice. She did not
understand the words. They were of the ground and she was of the
air, and the language was wholly alien.

She drifted westward towards where the sun would set in a couple
of hours, and thought that maybe she would beat it there. It hung
high in the sky before her, a smudged yellow behind the hazy cloud
cover. It was so *slow*. She concentrated on the sky next to it, trying to
detect the sun's movement out of the corner of her eye, but it must
have known she was looking because it did not move. There was *no
way* it would beat her. She was travelling *so fast*. The wind had her
firmly in its grasp now, tugging hard at the flabby pink balloon
above her, dragging it across the sky and leaving only a trail of her
sighs behind.

The rope was long and old, frayed here and there where it had
been tied an unknown number of times, worn by constant striving
for aerial freedom. It was stained too, darkened by the sweat of a
thousand people who had tried to hold the balloon down. But old
and frayed, rough and dark though it was, still the rope sat snugly
and comfortably beneath Holly's armpits, encircling her twice
around the chest and shoulder blades, tied in some random fashion
that seemed to mimic the very best knot she had ever been taught in

Brownies. Those knots had been designed to restrain and hold back; ironic that now, here, they gave her such freedom.

Holly twisted and looked back over her shoulder. She could just make out the field in the distance, a splash of deep green in a patchwork of otherwise pale, wan fields and meadows. A firework rose above the field and splashed a red smear across the sky, much lower than she but obviously so high up for those observing from the ground. Another followed it up, and then another, silent explosions flowering in the air like reflections from oily water.

The rope tugged at her once, hard, and she turned her attention forward again.

The show was going on without her, it seemed. She could hardly blame them. It was not as if they had meant this to happen, and guilt, as her mother often muttered between remorseful silences, was such a waste of time.

Holly was growing cold. She had come to the show dressed in summer finery; a flowery dress, sandals, a sun hat that had been flipped from her head the second the balloon had broken from its mooring, wrapped itself around her chest and tugged her hard at the sky, even though there was no discernible breeze that day. No wind, no gale, no breath in the air, except when the balloon needed it. She looked up, but the pink balloon did not stare back down. She shivered, then smiled as they entered a stream of warmer air. It rushed by her face faster than before, lifting her hair from her forehead, and it was warm and comforting. She even began to feel tired.

Holly looked down, and between her dangling feet she saw a splash of water. It could have been a paddling pool in someone's back garden, filled to the brim at the break of day and slowly draining as the sun made its traverse of the sky, the black flecks drowned insects, the pool ignored already for some more urgent plaything. Or perhaps it was a lake, a mile across at its widest, speckled with insect-like boats tearing at its surface tension in their eagerness to sport or fish. She kicked off one of her sandals to see how long it took to fall, but the balloon moved her faster across the sky and she lost sight of it before the splash came.

She imagined some lonely fisherman mourning a dearth of catches that day, amazed at the footwear in his net. She giggled. Then she wondered what the little boy in his pond would think at the floating footwear, and she laughed so hard she wanted to pee.

She could, she supposed. There was no one here to see. But she held back, because modesty was really all about herself.

Holly's arms were aching slightly, and the rope had begun to chafe her armpits through the thin summer dress. But the sensations were not unpleasant. Sometimes after a day riding her bike or running through the woods with her friends she would ache, muscles burning, face scorched by the sun, but it was always a good feeling. It was the evidence of a day well spent. Here and now, that feeling was more profound than ever.

The ground grew dark before the sky. The fields and roads faded into uniformity, and here and there the speckled lights of civilization marked unconscious territory against the wild, the dark, the unknown that lived everywhere. It was as though the ground were fading away into nothing, and only these isolated pockets of humanity held out for a few hours more, their artificial light cementing them to reality.

Holly had always been aware of the unknown, so near that it touched her every day, so familiar and so much a part of life that it was almost impossible to make out from everything else. She talked about it to her mother, but her mother sighed and shook her head and lit another cigarette, not knowing that the smoke made languages in the air. Holly would run through the garden, brushing by plants and flowers and letting them coat her in pollen. Her mother's shout from the kitchen doorway would dislodge the pollen from the fine hairs on Holly's arms, perhaps drifting to find other plants, aiding the spread of flowers. The land had language, and Holly was keen to translate.

As the sun dipped down into the west, winning the race, she looked up and saw several bright specks hanging in the air around her. They could have been stars but they seemed much closer, close enough to reach out and touch. She started to stretch her hand but the rope bit in. By the time the pain faded away the sky had grown dark, and whatever the setting sun had been hitting high up in the atmosphere had cloaked itself in night.

For Holly, night was a time of revelation. Lying in bed at home, clouds covering the sky, streetlights turning off at midnight, she had always imagined darkness to be a blanked canvas of history upon which the new day could be drawn. There were always noises linking the day passed by to the new one to come, but whatever made them were more secretive and self-conscious, more aware than when the life-giving light illuminated them. The sun had shunned them after all, spinning its way beyond their land to bless faraway places. They should be shamed at its leaving them. They should be humbled at its return.

And then the new day would dawn, and all night fears would burn away in the sun.

Here, now, above the clouds, Holly knew that true darkness must exist only in death. Because above the sleeping land, starlight made her shine. The light of the sun was minutes old, her mother had once told her, reading in stilted sentences from a book. That had made Holly feel grimy and grubby with age, but then her mother read that the light from stars was years old, centuries, millennia, five billion years, and that most of what you saw in the night sky was no longer there. The feeling of grime had been swept away by time, turning Holly into little more than a fossil. She was an artefact waiting to be found, a blip in time, and that idea of immateriality pleased her immensely. As her mother closed the book and left the room, Holly had stared from her window, straight out and up at one particular star. She wondered whether she could be staring directly into the eyes of a little alien girl a trillion miles away . . . and she knew that if that were the case, that alien girl was a long time dead and gone. All Holly could see of the universe were echoes. Nothing was quite as it seemed.

Stars floated here. They were the specks of light the sun had glanced from as it dipped down to bed, reflective shapes in the sky, and now they caught moon and starlight, shedding the primeval radiance without a care. Holly tried to steer their way. The breeze had her up here, and she was submitted to its will, but she still thought that if she leaned to one side, left, left, she could edge herself that way. She looked up but the balloon was merely a shadow blocking out a circle of the night sky. The shapes came nearer. Holly was cold and hungry and she closed her eyes as her bladder let go. Her pee warmed her legs for a time, but then she thought it had turned to ice.

One of the shapes seemed to manifest from the silvery night, drifting closer to her as if steered by someone else, and it was as dawn exploded leisurely in the east that she saw it was another balloon.

There was a boy hanging beneath this one. He seemed excessively tall, as if stretched by however long he had been hanging up here, and though at first Holly thought he was waving, perhaps it was simply his limp, dead arm swinging in the wind. His balloon was a bright silver, as if it had swallowed and retained the starlight. It veered away, taking the boy so that Holly could not make him out in any great detail, for which she was glad. He had looked very thin.

As the sun rose once again, warming her back, she looked around her at the reflections or dark specks that marked other shapes. She was amazed at how many people seemed to have been taken by balloons and blown up here. Perhaps somewhere, there was someone she knew.

When she was eight one of her school friends, Samuel, had gone missing. His parents had come to the school with red-rimmed eyes and thin, sunken faces, their hands so tightly twisted into each other that they looked like an old knotted tree. They had sat on the stage with the headmaster during morning assembly and then, when called upon, Samuel's mother had made a tearful plea to the children to tell them where Samuel may be. Holly had been shocked. She had no idea why Samuel's parents would assume that she knew where their son was. She had looked around at her friends, and they all appeared to be thinking the same.

Samuel had never been found, and Holly had soon cast him from her mind. But now maybe she would see him again. Perhaps he was up here, with all the other people caught beneath balloons, and perhaps even now her own mother was standing red-eyed on a stage, pleading with a hall full of children for Holly's safe return.

She looked down at the new ground created by this sunrise, and far, far below she could see a road. It had no dimension from this altitude, it was merely a grey line stretching across the land. It twisted here and there, avoiding hills she could not see. Branches sprung from it and snaked away to places where few people went, withering eventually to nothing. Holly thought that was strange. All the roads she remembered went somewhere, not nowhere. Maybe there were so many more roads left untravelled, there simply to exist. There were no signs of cars travelling these routes, but then maybe she was too high up to see. They would certainly not see her, she was sure of that. She kicked off her other sandal, giggled as it span away below her, and she watched until distance had swallowed it up. Its eventual fate would remain a mystery.

She warmed up nicely in the morning sun, though her arms and legs had grown stiff during the night. The rope was still making her armpits sore, but the worst pain now came from her shoulders and chest, stretched and strained as they were by the unaccustomed weight they were supporting. The rope was holding her in position, true, but it was her shoulders taking most of the strain. She tried to shrug herself into a more comfortable position. The rope shifted. She smiled, satisfied, and then screamed out loud when she realized that the rope was still shifting. It was slowly pulling her arms up, as if forcing her to flap the slow wings of a wounded butterfly, and if that happened the loop would slip over her arms and past her head, and the balloon would no longer have her.

Holly forced her arms down, crying, screaming out at the unknown people in the unseen cars far below to help her. The sandal must have landed by now, surely? They couldn't just ignore it, could they? Swerve around the footwear that had bounced across the concrete road, clip it with their wheels, send it skimming into the ditch to rot there and become home to ants and woodlice and other things?

It took all her strength to stop screaming and squeeze the rope to herself. It tightened. The wind caught the balloon and snapped it this way and that, and the rope tugged, and it tightened some more. Whatever unseen knot held her here must have been twisted and knotted again, because suddenly she felt safe once again.

She looked down at the strange ground far below, glad she had not gone. Things were much nicer up here.

Minutes later, and the brief scare seemed a lifetime ago. The speckled sky of night felt like two lifetimes, and the memory of those people chasing the rope as the balloon whisked her away was someone else's entirely. She may have been up here forever. She wondered what she ate and drank, but she felt neither thirst nor hunger.

The sun was chasing her. The breeze carried her westward, ever westward, but after yesterday she had serious doubts over whether she could ever beat the sun. It was gaining on her even now, furtively following its path of old and aiming to bypass her to the south, arc over her head and win the race again. She could see it if she glanced over her shoulder, feel its heat on her left cheek, arm, leg. She willed her balloon on, but will was not enough. There was wind, and the balloon's own improbable desire, and that was the only power her flight was allowed.

As the sun reached its zenith Holly saw another balloon drifting in from the north. Its path seemed to match hers for a while, several miles away but clearly defined by the reflected glare from its filled expanse. Holly crossed her arms and watched its progress. There was a shape hanging below this one too, a long thin shape dangling apparently lifeless, though it was still too far away for Holly to make any rash judgments as to its true status. She would have to wait, see if it came any closer, and make up her mind then.

It did come closer. Slowly, almost indefinably, its approach only apparent in the fresh detail Holly could make out. Like the hour hand of a clock she could not perceive its movement, yet still that movement was obvious. Her own internal clock was not attuned to such subtle changes. She wondered at all the intricacies of the world she missed because of this; the growth of plants, the blossoming of flowers, the lengthening of her own hair, the ageing of her skin, the erosion of a rock, the melting of glass. If she could speed up time she would see all these things, like a time-delayed camera showing her the birth, life and death of a mayfly. But time would not be changed by the likes of her. She would have to change herself.

Holly closed her eyes and tried to blank her mind, think of nothing, focussing on one single point of light in her mind's eye. When she opened her eyes again the balloon was noticeably closer, and the shape below had resolved into a hanging body. She closed her eyes again, that spot of light, nothing else, the light, the light.

Eyes open, reality crashed back in a welter of sensations, and the balloon was closer. The body had turned its head. It had a skeletal face, skin dried and pressed to the bones by the breeze. Long hair flared around its skull. Some of its clothes had been ripped off, and those that were left were bleached by the sun. Holly could not tell whether it was a boy or girl. Not even when it spoke.

"Hello," it said.

"Hello," Holly replied. She had observed this balloon's journey and perceived its dangling cargo's progress across the skies. So much else must have changed that she had not noticed, and she looked around to see what. Down below, the road had vanished and the ground was smothered in a silvery sheen of distance. She wondered how high up she was, and how much higher she could go.

"Don't you think it's amazing," the hanging body said, "how many people are taken by balloons and carried up here?"

Holly nodded, went to speak and realized that there was no need. The person looked away, seeming to agree. There was not that much to say.

They drifted together for some time, until the sun had overtaken them once again and was on its homeward descent. Holly used her newfound talent to close off time, concentrate on the light, the light, and when she opened her eyes again she had seen the sun move. She wondered if the Earth was aware of those things on its surface or floating way above, or whether it was so old and slow that these fleeting things were all but invisible to its grand perception. She and the body glanced at each other often, and she even smiled. The other person's balloon looked larger than Holly's, but perhaps that was a trick of the light, or distance deceiving her again.

She thought of the many things she could ask: *How do we get down? What is down? Has there ever been a down, or did we dream it?* But she did not wish to spoil the moment with awkward questions. So she averted her eyes for a time and watched the Earth moving beneath them.

At some point the other balloon must have been tugged away by an errant breeze, because when Holly looked again it was gone.

She thought about falling. It was not the falling that killed, she remembered her mother once telling her, it was the impact. Looking down between her feet now, the ground hidden by a layer of cloud, she thought that maybe she could fall forever.

That did not frighten her. What frightened her was immobility, apathy and an absence of wonder. She knew that she had a choice. The rope slipped again as if to remind her of this; if she raised her elbows and pointed up at the balloon, the loop would slip over her shoulders and head and she would begin her new journey.

She raised one hand, felt the rope slide up her arm and lock at her elbow. It would be as simple as that.

She hung and watched the sunset, specks of light emerging across the heavens as star- and moonlight picked out other balloons. And she closed her eyes and concentrated on the light, to see whether she would feel herself making that choice.

PAUL FINCH

The Old Traditions Are Best

PAUL FINCH IS A FORMER police officer and journalist, now turned full-time writer. He first cut his literary teeth penning episodes of the British TV crime drama *The Bill*, but has also written extensively in the field of animation, contributing numerous scripts to various children's television shows.

However, he is probably best known for his work in the horror genre. To date, he has had eight books and nearly 300 short stories and novellas published on both sides of the Atlantic. His first collection, *Aftershocks*, won the British Fantasy Award in 2002, and he received the award again in 2007 for his novella "Kid". That same year he won the International Horror Guild Award for his story, "The Old North Road".

Finch co-scripted the UK horror movie *Spirit Trap* (2004) starring Billie Piper, while more recently he adapted *Leviathan*, one of his father's *Doctor Who* scripts from the mid-1980s, for a brand-new audio release starring Colin Baker.

He is currently working on three movie adaptations of his own stories, *Cape Wrath*, *Charnel House* and *Hunting Ground*, and on *Dark Hollow*, a film adaptation of Brian Keene's horror novel of the same title.

The author lives in Lancashire, northern England, with his wife Cathy and his children, Eleanor and Harry.

"I've long been fascinated by the old traditions of Britain," Finch reveals, "of which there are too many to count – but how many of these are really old or were simply Victorian inventions designed to attract tourists to village festivals?

"The origins of the custom I focus on in this particular story are shrouded in mystery. It certainly predates Victorian

times. In fact, there are references to it from the sixteenth
century.

"The medieval explanation, which I extrapolate in the story,
sounds fanciful and almost certainly owes to folklore rather than
any similar event in history. But it adds colour to the occasion, which
I'm glad to say is celebrated as much now as it ever was. Anyone who
travels down to Cornwall to experience it is guaranteed a good time.
I've visited Padstow twice on these occasions, and found a near-
Bacchanalian atmosphere – a real throwback to the sort of feast that
you could genuinely believe would have a pre-Christian basis.

"As for the dark undertones, I think that's purely a personal thing.
As my wife is fond of saying – usually quite wearily – anything can
have a dark undertone where I'm concerned."

S COTT WALKED INTO THE PUB, checked the two fivers in the pants
  pocket of his new shell-suit, then marched up to the bar and
ordered a pint of lager.

The landlord was someone he thought of as a typical Cornishman:
huge and well-built; red-haired and apple-cheeked; grinning from ear
to ear. His rolled-back shirt sleeves revealed immense, beefy forearms
complete with naval tattoos. His smart tie bore a crest and a coat of
arms. He gazed jovially down at the newcomer.

"And how old are you, son?" he asked.

Scott, who was sixteen, but small and skinny for his age, immediately realized the game was up, even on a day of celebration like
this. He dropped his false smile, became surly. Rotten teeth showed
between his curled lips. "It's probably piss-water anyway."

The landlord chuckled. "*You* won't be finding out, that's for
sure."

There were amused sniggers from his bar-stooled regulars.

"I'll send some firm round here!" Scott warned him.

Still grinning, the landlord pointed at the hostelry door. "So long
as they're over eighteen, that's fine with me. Now go out and watch
Obby Oss."

Furious, but sensing a different breed from the weary, apathetic
Mancunians he was more used to dealing with, Scott backtracked
towards the door. He'd only been in Cornwall two days and already
he hated it.

"We call them hobby-horses where I come from," he retorted.
"And you know what, they're like . . . fucking kids' stuff!"

"Out you go, son."

"Wanker!" Scott spat, to gales of scornful laughter from the men in the pub.

Outside, he was irritated to be confronted by the Kidwells. How the hell had they found him so quickly in this whirling mass of revelry?

"Where've you been, Scott?" Russ Kidwell demanded, taking his pipe out, but looking more concerned than angry. Mary, Russ' wife, seemed equally anxious. Scott wanted to hoot with laughter. He'd been missing, what – five minutes, and they were already worried about him. About *him*. Not about what he might get up to while he was out of their supervision. Typical air-head probation officers.

"I was looking for you," he said, pulling his usual stunt, which was to pass the onus of blame back onto the person who was accusing him.

"Oh." Russ puffed on his pipe again, and gazed at his charge thoughtfully.

Russ was a tall, lean man – in good condition for someone of his age, which was probably fifty or so – but he had a genial disposition and seemed incapable of thinking the worst of anyone. His shock of white hair, and taste for canvas pants, deck shoes and roll-neck jumpers, gave him a sort of "eccentric uncle" look. His wife, Mary, who was twenty years younger at least, but more rounded, in fact dumpy, which contrasted oddly with her bobbed fair hair and very pretty face, was even more of a pushover.

"We thought you'd done a bunk," she said, in a tone that was more apologetic than reproachful.

Scott merely shrugged. "Where to in this shit-hole?"

He turned and began walking, elbowing his way through the cheering, dancing crowd. Russ glanced at his wife, rolled his eyes, and set off after him.

There was no way Padstow could truthfully be described as a "shit-hole".

Granted, it was more a town than a village these days, but it still had to be regarded as one of the quintessential Cornish holiday resorts.

First built as a fishing hamlet on the western corner of scenic Padstow Bay – a vast and winding estuary of the beautiful River Camel – it had steadily expanded throughout the twentieth century, but had never quite lost its nautical character. Its quaint cottages, which seemed to tumble over each other down the narrow, zigzagging streets to the waterside, were exclusively built from local granite, but were also whitewashed and permanently bedecked with flowers, even in winter-time, because the climate was so benign. Many gardens were filled with sub-tropical vegetation, while rumour held that some of the ancient oaks in the nearby deer-park were evergreens.

The harbours themselves, of which there were several, each contained their individual quota of fishing-boats (the local oyster-beds, in particular, were still very busy, as were the pilchard grounds), but greater by far were the numbers of yachts, dinghies, and other leisure craft. The quaysides were gaggles of shops, restaurants and atmospheric pubs but, though endlessly thronging with visitors and tourists, the mood down there was unfailingly friendly.

It was no real surprise, perhaps, that such a charming and picturesque little backwater should still play host to the weird and wonderful tradition of "Obby Oss", as the locals referred to it.

When the Kidwells and their reluctant responsibility arrived at the next set of crossroads, the creature in question was again close at hand, now spinning madly around its "teaser", a guy dressed as Punch, armed with a balloon on a stick. The procession of May Day celebrants still dashed and jumped on all sides of it, hurling blossoms and confetti, singing and shouting at the tops of their voices.

The Oss itself bore no actual resemblance to a horse, being essentially a long and heavy-looking oval of black-painted wood, with a hole cut in the centre so that it could be worn on the shoulders. Whoever had the job of wearing it was clearly robust, judging by the speed with which he was cavorting.

He'd stuck his head up through the hole, though his own features were hidden from view by the preponderance of red and black streamers flowing down from his conical hat (to render him even more indistinct, his face had also been painted, one half black, the other red).

His body was concealed too, in this case by heavy skirts attached around the rim of the oval and hanging to the floor. The tail was a chunky length of rope, but the creature's most alarming feature was its head, which was fixed at the front but jutted up and outwards at a predatory angle. It was handsomely carved and polished, but was again painted red and black, and had a fearsome countenance. It was almost demonic, more dragon-like than equine. Its lower jaw, inlaid with a full set of gleaming white teeth, was articulated and would *clack* up and down loudly, no doubt operated by some internal device.

Every part of the bizarre effigy was adorned with bells and ribbons, the purpose presumably being that no one, however uninterested in the ancient customs, could ignore the thing when it came prancing along their street, looking for donations.

Despite Scott's natural antipathy to anything he didn't understand, he was momentarily fascinated enough by the weird sight to wonder what it was actually supposed to represent. "What the hell's all this about, anyway?"

"I suspect an old fertility rite," Russ replied, still puffing on his pipe. "You know . . . a hangover from the Celtic days."

And indeed, Scott did now notice that it was mainly girls – all dressed to the nines in colourful rural regalia – who, while seeming reluctant to make physical contact with the Oss, would dart forwards to pluck at its ribbons, then scurry away again, squealing and giggling as it chased them.

"'Scuse me sir," someone said, "but that's not strictly right."

It was one of the musicians who'd been accompanying the Oss. He was a Morris-dancer type, with bells adorning his knees and elbows, and bunches of leaves fastened to his bowler hat. Again, he struck Scott as a typical Cornishman, being large and red-haired, with a bushy red beard. He had a heavy accordion slung down over his corpulent stomach; he'd broken off playing in order to sink a pint of chilled cider. A second passed as he finished the drink, wiped his mouth, then handed the glass back to a girl, who'd just come out of a pub with a tray.

He looked at Scott and Russ again. "There *is* a fertility reference in the old story, that's true. But the Padstow Oss has a much more aggressive role than that. That's why Peace Oss was brought in to moderate it."

"Peace Oss?" Russ said.

The accordion man continued. "Obby Oss has a combined role these days. As well as being a fertility symbol, he's used by Padstow folk to repel thieves and raiders. Story is he was granted diabolic powers for this very purpose. So what do you think of that, young fella?" And he prodded Scott's shoulder.

Scott was bewildered by the gesture, but also frightened, and because he was frightened, angry. "I dunno, why you asking *me*?"

"Because," said the man, who prodded Scott again, "you look like someone who needs to know."

Scott usually tried to avoid violence. His long list of criminal offences mainly comprised house burglaries, carried out during the day when the householders were absent. This wasn't because he didn't like confrontation, but because if he indulged in it, he was usually the one who came off worse. But, like any trapped rat, he *could* fight if he had to.

As now.

He'd already spat on the accordion man's sissy costume and was about to kick the bastard in the shins, when Russ and Mary dragged him away.

"You pair of tossers . . . you said no one would know," he snarled as they hustled him through the crowds.

"No one *does* know," Russ tried to reassure him.

"You said you wouldn't tell anyone!"

"It'd be more than our job's worth to tell someone."

"You said . . ."

"For God's sake, Scott, give it a rest!" Mary hissed. "You're drawing even more attention to yourself."

And it was true. Even in the midst of such noise and gaiety, Scott saw that several people were directing curious stares at him. More than a couple of their smiles had faded.

Half an hour later, the three of them were seated around a table on an outdoor terrace, waiting for their lunch to be served.

Mary pushed an open packet of crisps across the tabletop to Scott. He took a few out but didn't bother to thank her. The terrace was attached to a pub-restaurant called The Old God's Rest, and gave startling views over the estuary. It was early May, but the sun was now high and very warm. Seagulls dipped and looped over the rippling blue inlet. The windowboxes to either side of the pub's rear door were a riot of colourful late-spring blooms. A decorative cartwheel, painted a vivid green, was fixed on the pub wall, just under the triangular apex of the roof.

"According to this," Russ said, reading from a guidebook, "'the Obby Oss celebration, while not unique to Padstow, has some unique Padstow modifications.'" He glanced over at Scott. "It's true what that bloke said, it *does* have something to do with raids on the town."

Scott said nothing. He was barely listening.

"Check this out." Russ read a selected passage. "'In 1346, during the Hundred Years War, England's king, Edward III, commenced a lengthy siege of the port of Calais. The French fleet was unable to break it, and thus launched a series of tit-for-tat raids on English coastal towns. One such was Padstow in north Cornwall, which was assaulted in the April of 1347. The town, denuded of defenders as the bulk of its male population was involved at Calais, could only offer resistance by carrying the town's traditional spring-time symbol, the Hobby-Horse – or Obby Oss – down to the harbour, and threatening to invoke demonic forces with it.

"'The French scoffed at this, but legend holds that, when they landed, the Obby Oss did indeed come to life and attack them. Several Frenchmen were borne away into the sea by it, before their comrades fled.'"

Scott still wasn't listening. He was too preoccupied with the incident earlier, and what, if anything, it might signify.

As far as he understood, the "Safari Programme", as the popular press scornfully termed it, was designed to provide short holidays for young offenders as an aid to their rehabilitation. It was supposed to be good for everyone: ease up pressure on the prison system, and show the offender that a different and more rewarding lifestyle was possible.

But surely the people who actually lived in the place the offender was being taken to weren't supposed to know about it? Surely the whole thing would be carried out as secretly as possible? This had worried Scott from the outset. Thoughts of mob vengeance were never far from a young criminal's mind. Back in Manchester, he knew of one lad who'd been tied to a lamp-post and had paint poured over him. Another had been locked in a shed with a savage dog, and had almost died from his injuries.

Russ read on. "'Owing to the infernal forces that allegedly worked through it on that long-ago spring day, the Padstow Oss has developed a reputation for defending the town aggressively, even cruelly. This is not entirely out of keeping with other hobby-horse legends. Scholars have suggested that the name itself, 'hobby-horse', derives from the old English word 'Hobb', which means 'Devil', though in the case of Padstow events have clearly gone a little farther than most. Even now, in modern times, the Padstow Oss has a disquieting appearance, and in a grim reversal of the role commonly played by fertility gods, is said to draw its power from violence rather than love.'"

"Didn't know this place was so interesting," Mary said, taking a sip of lemonade.

Russ looked again at Scott, who hadn't touched his own drink. "Just shows though, doesn't it, Scott. You thought that bloke was having a go at you, but all he was doing was telling you about the history of the place."

Scott grunted. He wasn't convinced. Or satisfied. Even if it was true that the strange conversation had been a coincidence, he wasn't having some carrot-crunching yokel pushing him round, making fun of him. He came from the inner city, from a concrete jungle where he'd had to fight and scratch for everything he got, while these fat, lazy slobs down here sat in the sun all day and danced around painted animals. He'd show them. He'd break their cosy little world in half.

Russ quoted the guidebook again. "'In fact, Obby Oss' reputation grew so fearsome over the years that Peace Oss was introduced to counteract it.'"

"That Morris-man mentioned something about a 'Peace Oss', didn't he?" Mary put in, concerned by Scott's sullen indifference and trying to generate some interest in him. "What's that then, Russ? Tell us about it."

Russ shrugged, flipped a couple of pages. "We haven't seen it yet because apparently it dances its way in from the other side of the town." He read more. "'Peace Oss, which was introduced after the bloodshed of the First World War, is the spiritual opposite of Obby Oss. It is blue and white instead of red and black, and is noticeably of a less mischievous and frolicsome disposition. It was brought into the festivities not to arrest Obby Oss' behaviour as such, but to moderate it, to reduce it to an acceptable level.

"'However, as the two sides of Nature, the negative and the positive, are deemed indivisible from one another, Padstow's two horses must inevitably meet. The May Day celebrations in the town thus culminate when the two creatures, having paraded through different neighbourhoods, drawing ever larger crowds behind them, finally unite and perform a ritual dance, their numerous supporters capering around them. This in itself is a raucous occasion and may touch off a rowdy, drunken party that could well go on all night.'"

Russ laid the book down and grinned. "All's well that ends well, then."

Scott stood up.

The Kidwells watched him.

"Need a leak," he said. "Fancy coming giving me a hand, Mary?"

"Don't be long," she replied in a patient tone. "Your pie and chips is coming."

He sidled away into the pub, and as soon as he was out of sight nipped through the front door and out into the street. It was still a chaotic scene in the town, every road and avenue thronging with merry-makers. He wondered what they'd all do if it suddenly started pouring with rain, but, though it would give him a certain malicious pleasure to see their celebrations dampened, he decided he preferred it this way, warm and sunny, with everyone out of doors – and their houses undefended.

First off, of course, he'd have to put as much distance as he could between himself and The Old God's Rest.

On realizing that he'd eluded them again, the Kidwells would initially search by themselves. Because of the embarrassment it would cause, they wouldn't want to alert the coppers until they were absolutely sure he was up to no good. But by then he'd have had plenty time to wreak havoc.

As he slipped down a side street, and found the crowds dwindling, Scott felt a tremor of excitement. He was on the job again, and there was no better feeling. He'd had it with playing stupid games: watching fancy-dress parades; sitting in beer-gardens, drinking lemonade for Christ's sake! What next, sandcastles on the beach? Fuck all that.

He walked for several minutes, doing his best to look nonchalant but already casing properties for possible weak points. He didn't have any tools with him, of course, but then he'd never got into the habit of using tools, owing to the way the police up in Manchester were quick to nab you for "going equipped". Nevertheless, things looked good. He was now descending towards the waterfront, but was still in a residential district, and the potential for break-ins seemed promising.

The houses round here, though small and often terraced, were quality. They were uniformly whitewashed – probably a local by-law or something – and were all in good nick. Again, profusions of flowers poured from their windowboxes, front doorsteps were scrubbed, woodwork was brightly painted. At the rear, they nearly all had gardens, tiny but well kept.

If there was any drawback, it was that the neighbourhood was a little cluttered. The streets were narrow, labyrinthine, and had the tendency to turn suddenly into flights of steps between different levels; you were never quite sure if someone was overlooking you or not.

A couple of times, Scott almost ran into trouble because of this. On the first occasion, he found a car parked up with its front-passenger window wound down, and a handbag in full view on a seat. He loitered for a second, glancing around, but only at the last minute did he look up and, directly overhead, see an elderly lady leaning from a window, watching him.

A few moments later he was wandering along another alley when he spotted a rear-gate standing ajar, and on the other side of that a window that had been propped open. Beside it, on the step, a row of uncollected milk bottles suggested the occupants were away. Again Scott dallied, considering – but then spotted a child in the next-door garden. Only its head was visible – it was probably on top of a climbing-frame or something – but it was gazing at him curiously. Scott gave the child the finger, and stalked on.

Neither of these incidents worried him unduly. At least, not as much as the sudden wooden *clack* he heard a few minutes later.

He came to an abrupt halt. Paused. Listened.

He stared to the front and back, but saw nothing and no one. The alley was still deserted. All he could hear now was a distant cheering from the town centre. But that *clack* – it had been sharp, abrupt. Like a gunshot echoing in the narrow streets. Anything could have made it, but Scott had the odd feeling that it had been for his benefit.

That was ridiculous, of course. But even so, when he moved on he moved cautiously, ears attuned. He ventured thirty yards to the next junction, looking warily both ways before crossing it. Leftwards, the passage ran up to a parked car and a closed garage door. Right-wards, it bent out of sight under a whitewashed brick arch. As Scott peered down that way, he heard another, very distinctive *clack*.

He tensed, wondering.

Had the noise come from down there, beyond the arch?

But even if it had done, what the hell? There was probably a perfectly logical explanation for it.

Not that he could think of one.

Scott decided he wasn't going to hang around to find out. He pressed on quickly, feeling as though someone was watching him. He was quite close to the seafront, he told himself. Once down there, he'd be among other people again. He could take a rain-check on the whole situation.

But suddenly, the seafront wasn't easily to be found.

Gulls called overhead, he could smell salt in the gentle breeze, but every passage he now took seemed to switch back on itself and send him uphill again.

He glanced though the gaps between houses, but instead of masts and blue sky, and the low, distant woods of the estuary's eastern shore, he saw only more houses. What was worse, now it seemed there was nobody around to ask. Ten minutes ago, the knowledge that every front door and window was firmly closed because there was nobody at home would have encouraged him. Now, it disconcerted him. Surely the festival wouldn't empty the residential neighbourhoods this completely? Surely people had other things to do?

He started violently – having just heard hooves.

At least, they'd sounded like hooves.

On concrete.

His ears strained.

Had it been hooves, that eerie but fleeting *clip-clop-clip* from somewhere close behind? He glanced backwards, but again saw no one. However, as before, the alley curved quickly out of sight, so someone could be close by and remain concealed.

But why should they be? And anyway, it couldn't have been hooves. They wouldn't have stopped after two or three beats. He'd have heard them fading off into the distance.

CLACK!

Much louder, much nearer.

Unable to stop himself, Scott began to run. He hared down the nearest passageway, taking pot luck rather than trusting to his sense of direction, and this time, ironically, shooting straight out onto the harbour-side esplanade, almost knocking over a couple of teenage girls as they walked cheerfully past, chomping on pasties.

He slid to a halt, aware that he was red-faced and dishevelled, acutely conscious that he'd drawn several querying glances from the numerous people dotted here and there.

One old boy seemed particularly interested; he was seated on a mooring-pillar, smoking a clay pipe. He had a grizzled, leathery face and white mutton-chop whiskers, and over the top of both he wore a faded seaman's cap. He was typical of the sort Scott would expect to find on a Cornish dockside: a living, breathing cliché, probably sat here every day bemoaning the fact that he no longer had regular access to his shipmates' arseholes. Still, the old git had clearly spotted Scott and was no doubt wondering who he was and what he was up to. The young hoodlum realized he'd already muddied these waters too much to continue trawling them.

He strolled across the esplanade to the edge of the dock, and gazed down at the green wavelets lapping the pilings. Striations of oil were visible on their surface, but ducks were bobbing about on them, and healthy fronds waved back and forth just underneath.

It was a pleasant enough scene, but Scott wasn't taking it in; he was thinking. He glanced right. Beyond the old guy on the mooring-pillar – who was still watching him – he saw jetties, a forest of masts and, on the far side of those, shops and arcades. In the other direction, however, the buildings ran out fairly quickly. A stone quay jutted into the estuary, with a miniature lighthouse on the end of it, and beyond that there was nothing but sand-flats running steadily northwards.

Not sure why, but thinking this was worth investigating, Scott strode off in that vague direction. When he reached the quay he walked a few yards along it, and glanced northwards again. What he'd thought were sand-flats he now saw were an extension of beach; the tide was so low that much more of it was exposed than usual. With the sun at its zenith, it would normally be heaving with visitors, but, thanks to the festivities in the town, there was currently no one out there at all.

And then he saw something else.

Which pleased him no end.

Perhaps half-a-mile away, at the far end of the beach, there was a headland, and on that headland a cluster of four or five white bungalows.

Holiday-homes, almost certainly. They had to be, out in a favourable position like that. Which likely meant that many of their occupants, if not all, would be up in the town, enjoying the fun. Add to that the headland's isolated position – it was probably only linked to the town by a narrow country lane, which would slow down the police response – and you had a handful of burglaries just waiting to happen.

Scott trotted down a flight of steps onto the sand and, with his hands thrust into his pockets, commenced an idle and apparently leisurely stroll north.

It wasn't the first time he'd visited the seaside and found his visual perceptions distorted.

After twenty minutes at least, the headland still seemed a good half-mile away, though Scott had now left the environs of the town well behind.

To his left, there were high, rolling dunes crowned with tussocky marram grass, and beyond those were wooded hills. To his right lay the estuary, the glittering waterline of which suddenly seemed substantially closer. The sand, though flat and rippled, as it tended to be on quiet beaches, had dried out in the sun and was becoming crumbly, difficult to walk on.

He'd already taken his trainers off to avoid leaving identifiable sole-prints, but he soon had to put them on again; fragments of shells, crab-casing and small twists of black, hardened seaweed were littered everywhere, and cut like glass. On top of this, to increase his discomfort, the sea breeze was stiffening and freshening, and Scott was wearing nothing beneath his flimsy shell-suit jacket.

He shrugged, strode on determinedly. Hell, it wasn't as if he wasn't used to the cold. He'd absconded from custody numerous times, spending whole winter nights dossing in subways or under motorway flyovers.

By the same token, though, he wasn't as fit as someone of his age should be. For one thing, he was undernourished: by choice, he spent most of his money on booze, cigs and drugs rather than food, while these, in their turn, had further damaged his health.

Even after twenty minutes he was tired and footsore, having trouble getting his breath. Still, who gave a shit? If he finished today with a pocket full of someone else's jewellery, he'd be perfectly happy for a week or so.

He carried on walking, only for it to then strike him that, out here alone on this huge expanse of sand, he made a conspicuous figure. Anyone currently in residence on the headland would spot him easily.

It might have made more sense to approach along the road, where he could have kept a lower profile. But it was too late to do anything about that now. And, in any case, Scott didn't really expect to get away with what he was doing here. Okay, they'd send him back to the clink, but they were going to do that come what may.

The main purpose of today, rather than make a major score that he could retire on, was to grab a bit of extra cash; that, and to get his own back on these fucking hicks who thought they were so cool taking the piss out of him.

But still the headland was no nearer. And now Scott had noticed something else. It wasn't a clear stroll to it. A line of rocks had appeared in front of him, extending all the way down to the sea. He'd have to scramble over those before he got anywhere near the headland, and they weren't small; they were more like outcrops than loose boulders. He'd probably be able to thread his way through them, but it wouldn't be easy. It might also mean there'd be people around; youngsters and their grandparents investigating rock-pools and such.

"Shit," he muttered.

This wasn't running exactly to plan, but he'd keep going. If nothing else, he would give the Kidwells a good run-around for half a day. That should teach the do-gooding bastards a lesson.

So he plodded on defiantly, progressively narrowing the distance between himself and the rocks, which grew taller and taller, until soon they were towering over his head.

By this time his view of the headland had been blotted out. It was as though the last trace of fellow human life had been extinguished. That was an outlandish but nonetheless discomforting thought, rather like his experience down in the harbour-side neighbourhood, when he'd suddenly found himself eerily alone.

Scott stopped for a moment, breathing hard, his abused lungs working overtime. He glanced towards the water; the estuary had noticeably widened and its far shore was barely visible. Ahead, the rocks weren't just tall, they'd adopted curious shapes; all jagged peaks and crooked spires, no doubt carved by the weather and the sea, but reminiscent of an alien planet rather than the Cornish coast.

And then – his thief's sixth sense began to tingle.

He tensed, unsure what it meant. Was someone close by? If so, where? A moment passed, during which he scanned his immediate vicinity, seeing and hearing nothing. And then, slowly, he turned and stared behind him.

He couldn't believe his eyes; but that didn't make any difference to what he was seeing.

A large object – a large, red and black object – was in pursuit of him. It seemed to have come from the town, and it was approaching fast along the beach, unnaturally fast.

It was still well over a hundred yards away but he could clearly see the jutting, dragon-like head, the great oval body, the fluttering ribbons and streamers. And now he could hear it jingling, the bells on it, the harness.

At first Scott was bemused rather than frightened. How the hell could one man carry such a bulky costume, at such speed, over such a distance? And where were all the others who were with him? Where were the revellers, where was the "teaser" dressed as Punch?

Scott tried to scoff, tried to laugh at the ridiculous, garish object, though it didn't look quite so ridiculous any more.

It was still awkward, clumsy, but it was also large and powerful, and even over this distance he could hear the ferocious, repeated *clacking* as its jaws snapped open and shut. And the question begged again, how could one man move like that under such an encumbrance?

If it *was* one man.

But then it *had* to be? Whoever he was, the guy's head was in place in the middle of the hobby-horse's broad back. The conical hat gave it away, but with all the paint and ribbons adorning it, it melded so comfortably into the rest of the creature's livery that, in truth, it wasn't really distinguishable.

And still the thing was coming.

Scott now fancied he could hear the thunder of galloping feet.

No – not *galloping*. That was ludicrous. Humans didn't *gallop*.

All right, the thunder of *pounding* feet. But more than one pair.

And still it was coming. Now it was less than a hundred yards away, much less. Unquestionably, there was no human who could move that fast, or show such endurance.

By sheer instinct, Scott started to retreat.

He reached the rocks in record time, and hurriedly began to clamber among them.

As he'd hoped, there were many clefts and crannies that he could follow, some of which were narrow, their side-surfaces slick with weed or serrated with barnacles; not ideal avenues for something as large as Obby Oss.

Yet somehow Scott didn't think this would pose a problem for it. And indeed, less than a minute later, he heard the jingle of its bells and harness again, the thumping and clopping – yes, the *clopping* – of its feet, as it came racing into the rocky enclave.

"This is not . . . happening," he wheezed. "Not . . . happening . . ."

He found himself at the head of a narrow defile shaped like an inverted triangle. It was cluttered with boulders and pebbles, and slippery with weed.

He tottered down it, falling at least twice, gashing his arms, ripping holes in his shell-suit. But none of that mattered because he had to get away, and he *would* get away. He was Scott Sinclair, and he'd done jobs all over Manchester. He'd evaded some of the toughest cops in the whole of Great Britain. Of course, his options now weren't quite as wide as when running for broke through the benighted sprawl of the city.

At the end of the defile, for example, he had to scale a sheer rock-face, skinning his fingertips, spraining his wrists. On the other side of that, he dropped downwards again. He didn't mean to drop so quickly, but gravity took over and he found himself sliding on his arse over another near-vertical face, slashing yet more holes in his clothing and flesh.

The next thing he knew he was on sand again but, though it was easier to land on than rugged rock, it was problematic for different reasons. He'd alighted in a natural cove, with no obvious way out – other than the sea.

The walls hemming him in on all sides were probably not un-climbable, but they were hugely steep, and Scott was now exhausted. He hobbled forward, tripping and falling onto his knees.

Immediately, there was a scraping and clattering of what sounded like wood and – yes, hooves – behind him. He turned. Like some immense, armoured insect, Obby Oss had appeared over the parapet behind, and was now perched on the incline just below it, at an angle that was surely impossible.

Briefly it was still, the sun embossing its brilliant but demonic colours, glinting greasily from its thick whorls of oil paint, from its flashing crimson eyes and clamped white teeth.

Scott crab-crawled backwards, rose, turned, tried to run, and tripped and fell again.

He heard it start to descend. He glanced back; unbelievably, it was climbing down the rock-face head first, bulky and clumsy, swaying from side to side, but negotiating the perilous footing with astound-ing ease.

With no other options, he jumped to his feet and ran towards the water – but he'd never been a confident swimmer. Beyond the line of surf, it deepened quickly, and the first wave to hit his legs bowled him over. He plunged beneath the surface, and for seconds was in a frantic, twilit world of swirling, salty bubbles and lashing strips of kelp. Even then, he might have tried to make progress, might have risked everything to swim out farther – had he not suddenly spotted certain *things* beneath him.

When he re-emerged he was coughing and gasping. He threw himself back onto the shore, drenched but shivering more with horror than with cold. When he managed to regain his feet, he stumbled backwards, retreating from the waterline but staring down at it all the same.

He'd have liked to think that the ivory ribs, broken teeth and multiple fragments of skull scattered across the shifting sands down there were all that remained of the French pirates who'd come here in 1347. But deep inside, he knew the real truth: they represented raiders of a more recent vintage.

Instinctively, he glanced up at the rocky ridges encircling him. He wondered if he'd see Peace Oss at this point: smaller, slighter, and with gentler curves than its mean-spirited cousin; decked in blue and white, its polished wooden head a reminder of graceful carousel rides rather than brutish, pagan feasts.

But there was no sign of it. And why should there be? Peace Oss had not been introduced to halt Obby Oss' activities, merely to temper them, to moderate them, to restrain them – perhaps, just for the sake of argument, to once a year?

Scott nodded, smiled bitterly. And a jingle of harness alerted him to the presence now standing directly behind him.

It was a couple of hours later when Mary Kidwell finally looked at her husband, and said: "Okay?"

Russ Kidwell nodded amiably. "Absolutely fine."

"I suppose I ought to inform the police that he's gone?"

Russ, who was puffing on his pipe at the far side of the table, shook his head. "Give it another half-hour or so. Let's enjoy ourselves a little longer."

The pub garden and all the adjacent streets were teeming with revellers. The noise, laughter and song was astonishing, the music of drums and flutes almost deafening. Mary took another sip of wine. "It's a fun night on the town, that's for sure."

Russ nodded again. "It is *now*."

"The old traditions are always the best," she sighed.

Her husband smiled. "That's why I like coming home now and then."

RAMSEY CAMPBELL

The Long Way

AFTER TWENTY YEARS (five of them as co-editor), Ramsey Campbell
should need no introduction to the readers of this anthology series.

In fact, he has recently contributed a marvellous Introduction to,
and has a story in, the omnibus compilation *The Very Best of Best
New Horror*, forthcoming as a limited edition from US imprint
Earthling Publications.

Campbell's other recent projects include a new novel, *Creatures of
the Pool*, and another collection, *Just Behind You*, both out from PS
Publishing, who also produced a special edition in a shared slipcase,
with an extra story in the collection. He is also working on another
novel, *The Seven Days of Cain*.

"On Sunday morning at the World Fantasy Convention in Sar-
atoga Springs, Tom Doherty took a bunch of us to breakfast," recalls
Campbell. "The conversation turned to people's ghostly experiences,
and Kim Greyson mentioned that when he was a boy he'd been told
that a house he had to pass on the way to a friend's was haunted.
Because of this he used to take the long way round.

"That was the whole of his anecdote as I recall, but it immediately
started me thinking what might happen if the house wasn't so readily
avoided. The thought became this tale. Thanks, Kim!"

I T MUST HAVE BEEN late autumn. Because everything was bare I saw
inside the house.

Dead leaves had been scuttling around me all the way from home.
A chill wind kept trying to shrink my face. The sky looked thin with

ice, almost as white as the matching houses that made up the estate. Some of the old people who'd been rehoused wouldn't have known where they were on it except for the little wood, where my uncle Philip used to say the council left some trees so they could call it the Greenwood Estate. Nobody was supposed to be living in the three streets around the wood when I used to walk across the estate to help him shop.

So many people in Copse View and Arbour Street and Shady Lane had complained about children climbing from trees and swinging from ropes and playing hide and seek that the council put a fence up, but then teenagers used the wood for sex and drink and drugs. Some dealers moved into Shady Lane, and my uncle said it got shadier, and the next road turned into Cops View. He said the other one should be called A Whore Street, though my parents told him not to let me hear. Then the council moved all the tenants out of the triangle, even the old people who'd complained about the children, and boarded up the houses. By the time I was helping my uncle, people had broken in.

They'd left Copse View alone except for one house in the middle of the terrace. Perhaps they'd gone for that one because the boards they'd strewn around the weedy garden looked rotten. They'd uncovered the front door and the downstairs window, but I could never see in for the reflection of sunlight on leaves. Now there weren't many leaves and the sun had a cataract, and the view into the front room was clear. The only furniture was an easy chair with a fractured arm. The chair had a pattern like shadows of ferns and wore a yellowish circular antimacassar. The pinstriped wallpaper was black and white too. A set of shelves was coming loose from the back wall but still displaying a plate printed with a portrait of the queen. Beside the shelves a door was just about open, framing part of a dimmer room.

I wondered why the door was there. In our house you entered the rooms from the hall. My uncle had an extra door made so he could use his wheelchair, and I supposed whoever had lived in this house might have been disabled too. There was a faint hint of a shape beyond the doorway, and I peered over the low garden wall until my eyes ached. Was it a full-length portrait or a life-size dummy? It looked as if it had been on the kind of diet they warned the girls about at school. As I made out its arms I began to think they could reach not just through the doorway but across far too much of the room, and then I saw that they were sticks on which it was leaning slightly forward – sticks not much thinner than its arms. I couldn't distinguish its gender or how it was dressed or even its face. Perhaps it was keeping so still in the hope of going unnoticed, unless it was challenging me to object to its presence. I was happy to leave it alone and head for my uncle's.

He lived on Pasture Boulevard, where he said the only signs of pasture were the lorries that drove past your bedroom all night. The trees along the central reservation were leafy just with litter. My uncle was sitting in the hall of the house where he lived on the ground floor, and wheeled himself out as soon as he saw me. "Sorry I made you wait, Uncle Philip," I said.

"I'll wait for anything that's worth the wait." Having raised a thumb to show this meant me, he said "And what's my name again, Craig?"

"Phil," I had to say, though my parents said I was too young to.

"That's the man. Don't be shy of speaking up. Ready for the go?"

He might have been starting a race at the school where he'd taught physical education – teaching pee, he called it – until he had his first stroke. When I made to push the chair he brought his eyebrows down and thrust his thick lips forward, which might have frightened his pupils but now made his big square face seem to be trying to shrink as the rest of him had. "Never make it easy, Craig," he said. "You don't want my arms going on strike."

I trotted beside him to the Frugo supermarket that had done for most of the shops that were supposed to make the estate feel like a village. Whenever a Frugo lorry thundered past us he would mutter "There's some petrol for your lungs" or "Hold your breath." In the supermarket he flung a week's supply of healthy food from the Frugorganic section into the trolley and bought me a Frugoat bar, joking as usual about how they'd turned the oats into an animal. I pushed the trolley to his flat and helped him unload it and took it back to Frugo. When I passed his window again he opened it, flapping the sports day posters he'd tacked to the wall of the room, to shout "See you in a week if you haven't got yourself a girlfriend."

I had the books I borrowed from the public library instead, but I didn't need him to announce my deficiency. I knew he disapproved of girls for boys my age – they sapped your energy, he said. "I'll always come," I promised and made for Copse View, where the trees looked eager to wave me on. The wind gave up pushing me as I reached them, and I stopped at the house where the boards had been pulled down. As I peered across the front room, resting my fists on the crumbling wall, my eyes began to ache again. However much I stared, the dim figure with the sticks didn't seem to have moved – not in an hour and a half. It had to be a picture; why shouldn't whoever used to live there have put a poster up? I felt worse than stupid for taking so long to realise. My parents and the English teacher at my school said I had imagination, but I could do without that much.

Ten minutes brought me home to Woody Rise. "Well, would he?" my uncle used to say even after my parents gave up laughing or groaning. The houses on this edge of the estate were as big as his but meant for one family each – they looked as if they were trying to pass for part of the suburb that once had the estate for a park. My father was carrying fistfuls of cutlery along the hall. "Here's the boy who cares," he called, and asked me "How's the wheelie kid?"

"Tom," my mother rebuked him from the kitchen.

I thought he deserved more reproof when I wasn't even supposed to shorten my uncle's name, but all I said was "Good."

As my father repeated this several times my mother said "Let's eat in here. Quick as you like, Craig. We've people coming round for a homewatch meeting."

"I thought you were going out."

"Just put your coat on your chair for now. We've rescheduled our pupils for tomorrow. Didn't we say?"

She always seemed resentful if I forgot whichever extra job they were doing when. "I suppose you must have," I tried pretending.

"Had you found some mischief to get up to, Craig?" my father said. "Has she got a name?"

"I hope not," my mother said. "You can welcome the guests if you like, Craig."

"He's already looked after my brother, Rosie."

"And some of us have done more." In the main this was aimed at my father, and she said more gently "All right, Craig. I expect you want to be on your own for a change."

I would rather have been with them by ourselves – not so much at dinner, where I always felt they were waiting for me to drop cutlery or spill food. I managed to conquer the spaghetti bolognese by cutting up the pasta with my fork, though my mother didn't approve much of that either. Once I'd washed up for everyone I was able to take refuge in my bedroom before all the neighbours came to discuss watching out for burglars and car thieves and door-to-door con people and other types to be afraid of. I needed to be alone to write.

Nobody knew I did. My stories tried to be like the kind of film my parents wouldn't let me watch. That night I wrote about a girl whose car broke down miles from anywhere, and the only place she could ask for help was a house full of people who wouldn't come to her. The house was haunted by a maniac who cut off people's feet with a chainsaw so they couldn't escape. I frightened myself with this more than I enjoyed, and when I went to sleep despite the murmur of neighbours downstairs I dreamed that if I opened my eyes I would see a figure standing absolutely still at the end of the bed. I looked once and saw no silhouette against the glow from the next street, but it took me a while to go back to sleep.

For most of Sunday my parents were out of the house. As if they hadn't had enough of teaching at school all week, my mother did her best to coax adults to read and write while my father educated people about computers. They couldn't help reminding me of my school, where I wasn't too unhappy so long as I wasn't noticed. It was in the suburb next to the estate, and some of the boys liked to punch me for stealing their park even though none of us was alive when the estate was built, while a few of the girls seemed to want me to act as uncouth as they thought people from it should be. I tried to keep out of all their ways and not to attract any questions in class. My work proved I wasn't stupid, which was all that mattered to me. I liked English best, except when the teacher made me read out my work. I would mumble and stammer and squirm and blush until the ordeal was done. I hated her and everyone else who could hear my helplessly unmodulated voice, most of all myself.

I wouldn't have dared admit to anyone at school that I quite liked most homework. I could take my own time with it, and there was nobody to distract me, since my parents were at night school several evenings, either teaching or improving their degrees. It must have been hard to pay the mortgage even with two teachers' salaries, but I also thought they were competing with each other for how much they could achieve, and perhaps with my uncle as well. All this left me feeling I should do more for him, but there was no more he would let me do.

Soon it was Saturday again. I was eager to look at the house on Copse View, but once it was in sight I felt oddly nervous. I wasn't going to avoid it by walking around the triangle. That would make me late for my uncle, and I could imagine what he would think of my behaviour if he knew. The sky had turned to chalk, and the sun was a round lump of it caught in the stripped treetops; in the flat pale light the houses looked brittle as shell. The light lay inert in the front room of the abandoned house. The figure with the sticks was there, in exactly the same stance. It wasn't in the same place, though. It had come into the room.

At least, it was leaning through the doorway. It looked poised to jerk the sticks up at me, unless it was about to use them to spring like a huge insect across the room. While the sunlight didn't spare the meagre furniture – the ferny chair and its discoloured antimacassar, the plate with the queen's face on the askew shelf still clinging to the pinstriped wall – it fell short of illuminating the occupier. I could just distinguish that the emaciated shape was dressed in some tattered material – covered with it, at any rate. While the overall impression was greyish, patches were as yellowed as the antimacassar, though I couldn't tell whether these were part of the clothes or showing through. This was also the case with the head. It appeared to be hairless, but I couldn't make out any of the face. When my eyes began to sting with trying I took a thoughtless step towards the garden wall, and then I took several back, enough to trip over the kerb. The instant I regained my balance I dashed out of Copse View.

Perhaps there was a flaw in the window, or the glass was so grimy that it blurred the person in the room, though not the other contents. Perhaps the occupant was wearing some kind of veil. Once I managed to have these thoughts they slowed me down, but not much, and I was breathing hard when I reached my uncle's. He was sitting in the hall again. "All right, Craig, I wasn't going anywhere," he said. "Training for a race?"

Before I could answer he said "Forget I asked. I know the schools won't let you compete any more."

I felt as if he didn't just mean at sports. "I can," I blurted and went red.

"I expect if you think you can that counts."

As we made for Frugo I set out to convince him in a way I thought he would approve of, but he fell behind alongside a lorry not much shorter than a dozen houses. "Don't let me hold you up," he gasped, "if you've got somewhere you'd rather be."

"I thought you liked to go fast. I thought it was how you kept fit."

"That's a lot of past tense. See, you're not the only one that knows his grammar."

I was reminded of a Christmas when my mother told him after some bottles of wine that he was more concerned with muscles than minds. He was still teaching then, and I'd have hoped he would have forgotten by now. He hardly spoke in the supermarket, not even bothering to make his weekly joke as he bought my Frugoat bar. I wondered if I'd exhausted him by forcing him to race, especially when he didn't head for home as fast as I could push the laden trolley. I was dismayed to think he could end up no more mobile than the figure with the sticks.

I helped him unload the shopping and sped the trolley back to

Frugo. Did he have a struggle to raise the window as he saw me outside his flat? "Thanks for escorting an old tetch," he called. "Go and make us all proud for a week."

He'd left me feeling ashamed to be timid, which meant not avoiding Copse View. As I marched along the deserted street I thought there was no need to look into the house. I was almost past it when the sense of something eager to be seen dragged my head around. One glimpse was enough to send me fleeing home. The figure was still blurred, though the queen's face on the plate beside the doorway was absolutely clear, but there was no question that the occupant had moved. It was leaning forward on its sticks at least a foot inside the room.

I didn't stop walking very fast until I'd slammed the front door behind me. I wouldn't have been so forceful if I'd realised my parents were home. "That was an entrance," said my father. "Anything amiss we should know about?"

"We certainly should," said my mother.

"I was just seeing if I could run all the way home."

"Don't take your uncle too much to heart," my mother said. "There are better ways for you to impress."

On impulse I showed them my homework books. My father pointed out where the punctuation in my mathematics work was wrong, and my mother wished I'd written about real life and ordinary people instead of ghosts in my essay on the last book I'd read. "Good try," she told me, and my father added "Better next time, eh?"

I was tempted to show them my stories, but I was sure they wouldn't approve. I stayed away from writing any that weekend, because the only ideas I had were about figures that stayed too still or not still enough. I tried not to think about them after dark, and told myself that by the time I went to my uncle's again, whatever was happening on Copse View might have given up for lack of an audience or been sorted out by someone else. But I was there much sooner than next week.

It was Sunday afternoon. While my mother peeled potatoes I was popping peas out of their pods and relishing their clatter in a saucepan. A piece of beef was defrosting in a pool of blood. My father gazed at it for a while and said "That'd do for four of us. We haven't had Phil over for a while."

"We haven't," said my mother.

Although I wouldn't have taken this for enthusiasm, my father said "I'll give him a tinkle."

Surely my uncle could take a taxi – surely nobody would expect me to collect him and help him back to his flat after dark. I squeezed a pod in my fist while I listened to my father on the phone, but there was silence except for the scraping of my mother's knife. My hand was clammy with vegetable juice by the time my father said "He's not answering. That isn't like him."

"Sometimes he isn't much like him these days," said my mother.

"Can you go over and see what's up, Craig?"

As I rubbed my hands together I wondered whether any more of me had turned as green. "Don't you want me to finish these?" I pleaded.

"I'll take over kitchen duty."

My last hope was that my mother would object, but she said "Wash your hands for heaven's sake, Craig. Just don't be long."

While night wouldn't officially fall for an hour, the overcast sky gave me a preview. I was in sight of the woods when I noticed a gap in the railings on Shady Lane. Hadn't I seen another on Arbour Street? Certainly a path had been made through the shrubs from the opening off Shady Lane. It wound between the trees not too far from Copse View.

As I dodged along it bushes and trees kept blocking my view of the boarded-up houses. I couldn't help glancing at the vandalised house; perhaps I thought the distance made me safe. The scrawny figure hadn't changed its posture or its patchwork appearance. It looked as if it was craning forward to watch me or threatening worse. Overnight it had moved as much closer to the street as it had during the whole of the previous week.

I nearly forced my own way through the undergrowth to leave the sight behind. I was afraid I'd encouraged the figure to advance by trying to see it, perhaps even by thinking about it. Had the vandals fled once they'd seen inside the house? No wonder they'd left the rest of the street alone. I fancied the occupant might especially dislike people of my age, even though I hadn't been among those who'd rampaged in the woods. I was almost blind with panic and the early twilight by the time I fought off the last twigs and found the unofficial exit onto Arbour Street.

I was trying to be calmer when I arrived at my uncle's. He seemed to be watching television, which lent its flicker to the front room. I thought he couldn't hear me tapping on the pane for the cheers of the crowd. When I knocked harder he didn't respond, and I was nervous of calling to him. I was remembering a horror film I'd watched on television once until my mother had come home to find me watching.

I'd seen enough to know you should be apprehensive if anyone was sitting with his back to you in that kind of film. "Uncle Philip," I said with very little voice.

The wheelchair twisted around, bumping into a sofa scattered with magazines. At first he seemed not to see me, then not to recognise me, and finally not to be pleased that he did. "What are you playing at?" he demanded. "What are you trying to do?"

He waved away my answer as if it were an insect and propelled the chair across the room less expertly than usual. He struggled to shove the lower half of the window up, and his grimace didn't relent once he had. "Speak up for yourself. Weren't you here before?"

"That was yesterday," I mumbled. "Dad sent me. He—"

"Sending an inspector now, is he? You can tell him my mind's as good as ever. I know they don't think that's much."

"He tried to phone you. You didn't answer, so—"

"When did he? Nobody's rung here." My uncle fumbled in his lap and on the chair. "Where is the wretched thing?"

Once he'd finished staring at me as if I'd failed to answer in a class he steered the chair around the room and blundered out of it, muttering more than one word I would never have expected him to use. "Here it is," he said accusingly and reappeared brandishing the cordless phone. "No wonder I couldn't hear it. Can't a man have a nap?"

"I didn't want to wake you. I only did because I was sent."

"Don't put yourself out on my behalf." Before I could deny that he was any trouble he said "So why's Tom checking up on me?"

"They wanted you to come for dinner."

"More like one did if any. I see you're not including yourself."

I don't know why this rather than anything else was too much, but I blurted "Look, I came all this way to find out. Of—"

One reason I was anxious to invite him was the thought of passing the house on Copse View by myself, but he didn't let me finish. "Don't again," he said.

"You'll come, won't you?"

"Tell them no. I'm still up to cooking my own grub."

"Can't you tell them?"

I was hoping that my father would persuade him to change his mind, but he said "I won't be phoning. I'll phone if I want you round."

"I'm sorry," I pleaded. "I didn't mean—"

"I know what you meant," he said and gazed sadly at me. "Never say sorry for telling the truth."

"I wasn't."

I might have tried harder to convince him if I hadn't realised that he'd given me an excuse to stay away from Copse View. "Don't bother," he said and stared at the television. "See, now I've missed a goal."

He dragged the sash down without bothering to glance at me. Even if that hadn't been enough of a dismissal, the night was creeping up on me. I didn't realise how close it was until he switched on the light in the room. That made me feel worse than excluded, and I wasn't slow in heading for home.

Before I reached the woods the streetlamps came on. I began to walk faster until I remembered that most of the lamps around the woods had been smashed. From the corner of the triangle I saw just one was intact – the one outside the house on Copse View. I couldn't help thinking the vandals were scared to go near; they hadn't even broken the window. I couldn't see into the room from the end of the street, but the house looked awakened by the stark light, lent power by the white glare. I wasn't anxious to learn what effect this might have inside the house.

The path would take me too close. I would have detoured through the streets behind Copse View if I hadn't heard the snarl of motor-cycles racing up and down them. I didn't want to encounter the riders, who were likely to be my age or younger and protective of their territory. Instead I walked around the woods.

I had my back to the streetlamp all the way down Arbour Street. A few thin shafts of light extended through the trees, but they didn't seem to relieve the growing darkness so much as reach for me on behalf of the house. Now and then I heard wings or litter flapping. When I turned along Shady Lane the light started to jab at my vision, blurring the glimpses the woods let me have of the house. I'd been afraid to see it, but now I was more afraid not to see. I kept having to blink scraps of dazzle out of my eyes, and I waited for my vision to clear when a gap between the trees framed the house.

Was the figure closer to the window? I'd been walking in the road, but I ventured to the pavement alongside the woods. Something besides the stillness of the figure reminded me of the trees on either side of the house. Their cracked bark was grey where it wasn't blackened, and fragments were peeling off, making way for whitish fungus. Far too much of this seemed true of the face beyond the window.

I backed away before I could see anything else and stayed on the far pavement, though the dead houses beside it were no more reassuring than the outstretched shadows of the trees or the secret darkness of the woods, which kept being invaded by glimpses of the house behind the streetlamp. When I reached the corner of the triangle I saw that someone with a spray can had added a letter to the street sign. The first word was no longer just Copse.

Perhaps it was a vandal's idea of a joke, but I ran the rest of the way home, where I had to take time to calm my breath down. As I opened the front door I was nowhere near deciding what to tell my parents. I was sneaking it shut when my mother hurried out of the computer room, waving a pamphlet called *Safe Home.* "Are you back at last? We were going to phone Philip. Are you by yourself? Where have you been?"

"I had to go a long way. There were boys on bikes."

"Did they do something to you? What did they do?"

"They would have. That's why I went round." I wouldn't have minded some praise for prudence, but apparently I needed to add "They were riding motorbikes. They'd have gone after me."

"We haven't got you thinking there are criminals round every corner, have we?" My father had finished listening none too patiently to the interrogation. "We don't want him afraid to go out, do we, Rosie? It isn't nearly that bad, Craig. What's the problem with my brother?"

"He's already made his dinner."

"He isn't coming." Perhaps my father simply wanted confirmation, but his gaze made me feel responsible. "So why did you have to go over?" he said.

"Because you told me to."

"Sometimes I think you aren't quite with us, Craig," he said, though my mother seemed to feel this was mostly directed at her. "I was asking why he didn't take my call."

"He'd been watching football and—"

I was trying to make sure I didn't give away too much that had happened, but my mother said "He'd rather have his games than us, then."

"He was asleep," I said louder than I was supposed to speak.

"Control yourself, Craig. I won't have a hooligan in my house." Having added a pause, my mother turned her look on my father. "And please don't make it sound as if I've given him a phobia."

"I don't believe anyone said that. Phil's got no reason to call you a sissy, has he, Craig?" When I shook or at least shivered my head my father said "Did he say anything else?"

"Not really."

"Not really or not at all?"

"Not."

"Now who's going on at him?" my mother said in some triumph. "Come and have the dinner there's been so much fuss about."

Throughout the meal I felt as if I were being watched or would be if I even slightly faltered in cutting up my meat and vegetables and inserting forkfuls in my mouth and chewing and chewing and, with an effort that turned my hands clammy, swallowing. I managed to control my intake until dinner was finally done and I'd washed up, and then I was just able not to dash upstairs before flushing the toilet to muffle my sounds. Once I'd disposed of the evidence I lay on my bed for a while and eventually ventured down to watch the end of a programme about gang violence in primary schools. "Why don't you bring whatever you're reading downstairs?" my mother said.

"Maybe it's the kind of thing boys like to read by themselves," said my father.

I went red, not because it was true but on the suspicion that he wanted it to be, and shook my head to placate my mother. She switched off the television in case whatever else it had to offer wasn't suitable for me, and then my parents set about sectioning the Sunday papers, handing me the travel supplements in case those helped with my geography. I would much rather have been helped not to think about the house on Copse View.

Whenever the sight of the ragged discoloured face and the shape crouching over its sticks tried to invade my mind I made myself remember that my uncle didn't want me. I had to remember at night in bed, and in the classroom, and while I struggled not to let my parents see my fear, not to mention any number of situations in between these. I was only wishing to be let off my duty until the occupant of the derelict house somehow went away. My uncle didn't phone during the week, and I was afraid my father might call him and find out the truth, but perhaps he was stubborn as well.

I spent Saturday morning in dread of the phone. It was silent until lunchtime, and while I kept a few mouthfuls of bread and cheese down too. I lingered at the kitchen sink as long as I could, and then my mother said "Better be trotting. You don't want it to be dark."

"I haven't got to go."

"Why not?" my father said before she could.

"Uncle Phil, Uncle Philip said he'd phone when he wanted me."

"Since when has he ever done that?"

"Last week." I was trying to say as little as they would allow. "He really said."

"I think there's more to this than you're telling us," my mother warned me, if she wasn't prompting.

"It doesn't sound like Phil," my father said. "I'm calling him."

My mother watched my father dial and then went upstairs. "Don't say you've nodded off again," my father told the phone, but it didn't bring him an answer. At last he put the phone down. "You'd better go and see what's up this time," he told me.

"I think we should deal with this first," said my mother.

She was at the top of the stairs, an exercise book in her hand. I hoped it was some of my homework until I saw it had a red cover, not the brown one that went with the school uniform. "I knew it couldn't be our work with the community that's been preying on his nerves," she said.

"Feeling he hasn't got any privacy might do that, Rosie. Was there really any need to—"

"I thought he might have unsuitable reading up there, but this shows he's been involved in worse. Heaven knows what he's been watching or where."

"I haven't watched anything like that," I protested. "It's all out of my head."

"If that's true it's worse still," she said and tramped downstairs to thrust the book at my father. "We've done our best to keep you free of such things."

He was leafing through it, stopping every so often to frown, when the phone rang. I tried to take the book, but my mother recaptured it. I watched nervously in case she harmed it while my father said "It is. He is. When? Where? We will. Where? Thanks." He gazed at me before saying "Your uncle's had a stroke on the way home from shopping. He's back in hospital."

I could think of nothing I dared say except "Are we going to see him?"

"We are now."

"Can I have my book?"

My mother raised her eyebrows and grasped it with both hands, but my father took it from her. "I'll handle it, Rosie. You can have it back when we decide you're old enough, Craig."

I wasn't entirely unhappy with this. Once he'd taken it to their room I felt as if some of the ideas the house in Copse View had put in my head were safely stored away. Now I could worry about how I'd harmed my uncle or let him come to harm. As my father drove us to the hospital he and my mother were so silent that I was sure they thought I had.

My uncle was in bed halfway down a rank of patients with barely a movement between them. He looked shrunken, perhaps by his loose robe that tied at the back, and on the way to adopting its pallor. My parents took a hand each, leaving me to shuffle on the spot in front of his blanketed feet. "They'll be reserving you a bed if you carry on like this, Phil," my father joked or tried to joke.

My uncle blinked at me as if he were trying out his eyes and then worked his loose mouth. "Nod, you fool," he more or less said.

I was obeying and doing my best to laugh in case this was expected of me before I grasped what he'd been labouring to pronounce. I hoped my parents also knew he'd said it wasn't my fault, even if I still believed it was. "God, my shopping," he more or less informed them. "Boy writing on the pavement. Went dafter then." I gathered that someone riding on the pavement had got the bags my uncle had been carrying and that he'd gone after them, but what was he saying I should see as he pointed at his limp left arm with the hand my mother had been holding? He'd mentioned her as well. He was resting from his verbal exertions by the time I caught up with them. "Gave me this," he'd meant to say. "Another attack."

My parents seemed to find interpreting his speech almost as much of an effort as it cost him. I didn't mind it or visiting him, even by myself, since the route took me nowhere near Copse View. Over the weeks he regained his ability to speak. I was pleased for him, and I tried to be equally enthusiastic that he was recovering his strength. The trouble was that it would let him go home.

I couldn't wish he would lose it again. The most I could hope, which left me feeling painfully ashamed, was that he might refuse my help with shopping. I was keeping that thought to myself the last time I saw him in hospital. "I wouldn't mind a hand on Saturday," he said, "if you haven't had enough of this old wreck."

I assured him I hadn't, and my expression didn't let me down while he could see it. I managed to finish my dinner that night and even to some extent to sleep. Next day at school I had to blame my inattention and mistakes on worrying about my uncle, who was ill. Before the week was over I was using that excuse at home as well. I was afraid my parents would notice I was apprehensive about something else, and the fears aggravated each other.

While I didn't want my parents to learn how much of a coward I was, on another level I was willing them to rescue me by noticing. They must have been too concerned about the estate – about making it safe for my uncle and people like him. By the time I was due to go to him my parents were at a police forum, where they would be leading a campaign for police to intervene in schools however young the criminals. I loitered in the house, hoping for a call to say my uncle didn't need my help, until I realised that if I didn't go out soon it would be dark.

December was a week old. The sky was a field of snow. My white breaths led me through the streets past abandoned Frugo trolleys and Frugoburger cartons. I was walking too fast to shiver much, even with the chill that had chalked all the veins of the dead leaves near Copse View. The trees were showing every bone, but what else had changed? I couldn't comprehend the sight ahead, unless I was wary of believing in it, until I reached the end of the street that led to the woods. There wasn't a derelict house to be seen. Shady Lane and Arbour Street and, far better, Copse View had been levelled, surrounding the woods with a triangle of waste land.

I remembered hearing sounds like thunder while my uncle was in hospital. The streets the demolition had exposed looked somehow insecure, unconvinced of their own reality, incomplete with just half an alley alongside the back yards. As I hurried along Copse View, where the pavement and the roadway seemed to be waiting for the terrace to reappear, I stared hard at the waste ground where the house with the occupant had been. I could see no trace of the building apart from the occasional chunk of brick, and none at all of the figure with the sticks.

I found my uncle in his chair outside the front door. I wondered if he'd locked himself out until he said "Thought you weren't coming. I'm not as speedy as I was, you know."

As we made for Frugo I saw he could trundle only as fast as his weaker arm was able to propel him. Whenever he lost patience and tried to go faster the chair went into a spin. "Waltzing and can't even see my partner," he complained but refused to let me push. On the way home he was slower still, and I had to unload most of his groceries, though not my Frugoat bar, which he'd forgotten to buy. When I came back from returning the trolley he was at his window, which was open, perhaps because he hadn't wanted me to watch his struggles to raise the sash. "Thanks for the company," he said.

I thought I'd been more than that. At least there was no need for me to wish for any on the walk home. I believed this until the woods came in sight, as much as they could for the dark. Night had arrived with a vengeance, and the houses beyond the triangle of wasteland cut off nearly all the light from the estate. Just a patch at the edge of the woods was lit by the solitary intact streetlamp.

Its glare seemed starkest on the area of rubbly ground where the house with the watchful occupant had been. The illuminated empty stretch reminded me of a stage awaiting a performer. Suppose the last tenant of the house had refused to move? Where would they have gone now that it was demolished? How resentful, even vengeful, might they be? I was heading for the nearest street when I heard the feral snarl of bicycles beyond the houses. Without further thought I made for the woods.

Arbour Street and Shady Lane were far too dark. If the path took me past the site of the house, at least it kept me closer to the streetlamp. I sidled through the gap in the railings and followed the track as fast as the low-lying darkness let me. More than once shadows that turned out to be tendrils of undergrowth almost tripped me up. Trees and bushes kept shutting off the light before letting it display me again, though could anyone be watching? As it blazed in my eyes it turned my breaths the colour of fear, but I didn't need to think that. I was shivering only because much of the chill of the night seemed to have found a home in the woods. The waste ground of Copse View was as deserted as ever. If I glanced at it every time the woods showed it I might collide with something in the dark.

I was concentrating mostly on the path when it brought me alongside the streetlamp. Opposite the ground where the demolished house had been, the glare was so unnaturally pale that it reduced the trees and shrubs and other vegetation to black and white. A stretch of ferns and their shadows beside the path looked more monochrome than alive or real. My shadow ventured past the lamp before I did, and jerked nervously over a discoloured mosaic of dead leaves as I turned my back on the site of the house. Now that the light wasn't in my eyes I could walk faster, even if details of the woods tried to snag my attention: a circular patch of yellowish lichen on a log, lichen so intricate that it resembled embroidery; the vertical pattern on a tree trunk, lines thin and straight as pinstripes; a tangle of branches that put me in mind of collapsed shelves; a fractured branch protruding like a chair arm from a seat in a hollow tree with blanched ferns growing inside the hollow. None of this managed to halt me. It was a glimpse of a face in the darkness that did.

As a shiver held me where I was I saw that the face was peering out of the depths of a bush. It was on the side of the path that was further from Copse View, and some yards away from my route. I was trying to nerve myself to sprint past it when I realised why the face wasn't moving; it was on a piece of litter caught in the bush. I took a step that tried to be casual, and then I faltered again. It wasn't on a piece of paper as I'd thought. It was the queen's portrait on a plate.

At once I felt surrounded by the deserted house or its remains. I swung around to make sure the waste ground was still deserted – that the woods were. Then I stumbled backwards away from the street-lamp and almost sprawled into the undergrowth. No more than half a dozen paces away – perhaps fewer – a figure was leaning on its sticks in the middle of the path.

It was outlined more than illuminated by the light, but I could see how ragged and piebald the scrawny body was. It was crouching forward, as immobile as ever, but I thought it was waiting for me to make the first move, to give it the excuse to hitch itself after me on its sticks. I imagined it coming for me as fast as a spider. I sucked in a breath I might have used to cry for help if any had been remotely likely. Instead I made myself twist around for the fastest sprint of my life, but my legs shuddered to a halt. The figure was ahead of me now, at barely half the distance.

The worst of it was the face, for want of a better word. The eyes and mouth were little more than tattered holes, though just too much more, in a surface that I did my utmost not to see in any detail. Nevertheless they widened, and there was no mistaking their triumph. If I turned away I would find the shape closer to me, but moving forward would bring it closer too. I could only shut my eyes and try to stay absolutely still.

It was too dark inside my eyelids and yet not sufficiently dark. I was terrified to see a silhouette looming on them if I shifted so much as an inch. I didn't dare even open my mouth, but I imagined speaking – imagined it with all the force I could find inside myself. "Go away. Leave me alone. I didn't do anything. Get someone else."

For just an instant I thought of my uncle, to establish that I didn't mean him, and then I concentrated on whoever had robbed him. An icy wind passed through the woods, and a tree creaked like an old door. The wind made me feel alone, and I tried to believe I entirely was. At last I risked looking. There was no sign of the figure ahead or, when I forced myself to turn, behind me or anywhere else.

I no longer felt safe in the woods. I took a few steps along the path before I fought my way through the bushes to the railings. I'd seen a gap left by a single railing, but was it wide enough for me to squeeze through? Once I'd succeeded, scraping my chest and collecting flakes of rust on my prickly skin, I fled home. I slowed and tried to do the same to my breath at the end of my street, and then I made another dash. My mother's car was pulling away from the house.

She halted it beside me, and my father lowered his window. "Where do you think you've been, Craig?"

His grimness and my mother's made me feel more threatened than I understood. "Helping," I said.

"Don't lie to us," said my mother. "Don't start doing that as well."

"I'm not. Why are you saying I am? I was helping Uncle Phil. He's gone slow."

They gazed at me, and my father jerked a hand at the back seat. "Get in."

"Tom, are you sure you want him – "

"Your uncle's been run over."

"He can't have been. I left him in his flat." When this earned no response I demanded "How do you know?"

"They found us in his pocket." Yet more starkly my father added "Next of kin."

I didn't want to enquire any further. When the isolated streetlamp on Copse View came in sight I couldn't tell whether I was more afraid of what else I might see or that my parents should see it as well. I saw nothing to dismay me in the woods or the demolished street, however – nothing all the way to Pasture Boulevard. My mother had to park several hundred yards short of my uncle's flat. The police had put up barriers, beyond which a giant Frugo lorry was skewed across the central strip, uprooting half a dozen trees. In front of and under the cab of the lorry were misshapen pieces of a wheelchair. I tried not to look at the stains on some of them and on the road, but I couldn't avoid noticing the cereal bars strewn across the pavement. "He forgot to buy me one of those and I didn't like to ask," I said. "He must have gone back."

My parents seemed to think I was complaining rather than trying to understand. When I attempted to establish that it hadn't been my fault they acted as if I was making too much of a fuss. Before the funeral the police told them more than one version of the accident. Some witnesses said my uncle had been wheeling his chair so fast that he'd lost control and spun into the road. Some said he'd appeared to be in some kind of panic, others that a gang of cyclists on the pavement had, and he'd swerved out of their way. The cyclists were never identified. As if my parents had achieved one of their aims at last, the streets were free of rogue cyclists for weeks.

I never knew how much my parents blamed me for my uncle's death. When I left school I went into caring for people like him. In due course these included my parents. They're gone now, and while sorting out the contents of our house I found the book with my early teenage stories in it – childish second-hand stuff. I never asked to have it back, and I never wrote stories again. I couldn't shake off the idea that my imagination had somehow caused my uncle's death.

I could easily feel that my imagination has been revived by the exercise book – by the cover embroidered with a cobweb, the paper pinstriped with faded lines, a fern pressed between the yellowed pages and blackened by age. I'm alone with my imagination up here at the top of the stairs leading to the unlit hall. If there's a face at the edge of my vision, it must belong to a picture on the wall, even if I don't remember any there. Night fell while I was leafing through the book, and I have to go over there to switch the light on. Of course I will, although the mere thought of moving seems to make the floorboards creak like sticks. I can certainly move, and there's no reason not to. In a moment – just a moment while I take another breath – I will.

MICHAEL BISHOP

The Pile

MICHAEL BISHOP'S ACCLAIMED novels include *And Strange at Ecbatan the Trees*, *Stolen Faces*, *A Little Knowledge*, *Transfigurations*, *Under Heaven's Bridge* (with Ian Watson), *No Enemy But Time* (Nebula Award winner), *Who Made Stevie Crye?* from Arkham House, *Ancient of Days*, *Unicorn Mountain* (Mythopoeic Award for Best Fantasy Novel), *The Secret Ascension (or, Philip K. Dick Is Dead, Alas)*, *Count Geiger's Blues* and *Brittle Innings* (*Locus* Award for Best Fantasy Novel).

His short story collections include two other Arkham volumes, *Blooded on Arachne* and *One Winter in Eden*, plus *Close Encounters with the Deity*, *Emphatically Not SF Almost*, *At the City Limits of Fate*, *Blue Kansas Sky (Four Novellas)*, *Brighten to Incandescence*, and a volume of mainstream pieces, *Other Arms Reach Out to Me: Chinaberry Stories*, which is still seeking a publisher.

The author's novelette "The Quickening" won the Nebula Award in 1980. His short story "Dogs' Lives" appeared in the 1984 edition of *Best American Short Stories* edited by Gail Godwin, and his novelettes "The Door Gunner" and "Bears Discover Smut" each won Southeastern Science Fiction Awards for Best Short Fiction.

Bishop has also edited the anthologies *Changes* (with Ian Watson), *Light Years and Dark* (winner of the *Locus* Award for Best Anthology), three volumes of *Nebula Award Stories* (#23, #24 and #25), *A Cross of Centuries: Twenty-Five Imaginative Tales About the Christ*, and *Passing for Human* (with Steven Utley), which features a wraparound dust-jacket by his son, Jamie, a teacher and a graphic artist who died in the shootings at Virginia Tech on April 16, 2007, along with thirty-one other innocent people.

"I wrote this tale based on the first of ten notes for stories that Jamie left on one of his computers after his murder," reveals the author. "I have turned these notes into three stories, including 'Purr', which recently appeared in *Weird Tales*, and 'The Library of Babble', which is scheduled to appear in *Subterranean Online*. I will eventually try to get to some of the others, but these three narratives struck me as the most engaging of his suggestions.

"'The Pile' is named for a conglomeration of trash that residents of Jamie's townhouse complex in Carrboro, North Carolina, left beside the dumpsters there. Stuff that some residents reclaimed and used again, stuff that got hauled away almost immediately, and stuff that had possibilities for reclamation, if anyone cared enough to effect the necessary changes in it.

"Jamie observed that some items in The Pile cycled through a number of residents, adding that he thought this phenomenon could make a good horror story if 'some other element' were developed to give the tale extra depth and dimension.

"I tried to find a suitably spooky additional element to provide the complementary *oomph* that he wanted, and so it pleases me to note here that 'The Pile' is one of six finalists for the 2008 Shirley Jackson Award in the short story category. This honour would have tickled Jamie silly. No kidding."

T HE DAY AFTER Roger and Renata Maharis – brother and sister, *not* a married couple – moved into a Fidelity Plaza townhouse that their father in Savannah had bought as a residence for them while she attended university and he raised money to return to classes, Roger carried some boxes out to the Dumpsters at the far end of the swimming pool and ran smack-dab into The Pile.

The Pile: that's how he had to think of it because that's what it was. It consisted of the discards of the Fidelity Plaza community: the cast-offs and leavings of its residents, stuff too good to feed to the Dumpsters' maws, jettisoned junk with potential adaptability to other people's uses: *The Pile*.

Roger marvelled at the items there: dilapidated home-made bookshelves, crippled rocking chairs, coffee tables made of converted telephone-line spools, chipped planters, moribund banana trees, elaborate metal floor lamps that (obviously) no longer worked, hideous plastic bric-a-brac, cheaply framed paintings of cats, clipper ships, or long-dead celebrities (not a few on black velvet), fast-food action figures from ancient film flops, scrap lumber, and a lonely plaid lounge chair that had declined from recliner to outright reject. Wow, thought Roger: A treasure-trove for the budget-conscious – a category into which most Fidelity Plaza residents naturally fell.

After all, Renata was a doctoral candidate in marsh ecology, Roger worked part-time at the college in IT, and their immediate neighbours, Nigel and Lydia Vaughan, who had helped Daddy Maharis find this place, were bluegrass musicians who sold lapidary jewellery – or jewellery makers who often mangled bluegrass – to make ends meet. Other residents were retirees on Social Security, language tutors, rookie cops, or administrative assistants with live-ins who tended bar, stocked shelves, or schlepped out to the corner every morning to wait with the Hispanics, druggies, and dropouts for pickup day jobs. Despite the rundown elegance of its townhouses, then, Fidelity Plaza hardly qualified as upscale, and a murder at the swimming pool three years ago had earned it the mocking sobriquet *Fatality Plaza*. Ha-ha.

Roger half-coveted the plaid lounger, even though he and Renata had no place to put it. But if he could think of a place (maybe tossing out an old chair to make room), he should grab it *now* – before a downpour turned its cushions into waterlogged gunnysacks.

Whereupon a thirty-something woman and a really young teen-ager showed up at the Dumpsters to interrupt his musings.

"You interested in that thing?" the woman asked.

"Excuse me," said Roger, startled.

"I mean, if you are, well, you can tote it off, because you got here first, but if you aren't, I'd like to haul it to our place for Brad." She jerked her thumb toward the boy and introduced herself as Edie Hartsock.

Brad looked through Roger as if Roger's black-and-white Springsteen T-shirt bestowed on him total invisibility.

Roger smiled in spite of a sudden uneasiness. "It's yours. Haul away."

"Could you give us a hand? I'm a woman and he's just a kid, you know?"

So, after handing the boy the fattest cushion and warning Mrs Hartsock to watch her feet, Roger wrestled the Laz-E-Boy all the way from the Dumpsters to the Hartsocks' townhouse, dragging and rocking it like a lone stevedore struggling with a crated nuclear warhead. He even manhandled it up the steps and into their front hall, finishing there in a streaming sweat.

"Great!" Mrs Hartsock said. "You'll have to come sit in it some time. When you do, I'll give you an Orange Crush."

The Pile provided the ever-coming-and-going folks of Fidelity Plaza with a *resource* – Roger's apt term – for losing what they no longer wanted or needed, and for acquiring what they hoped they could put to life-brightening use. It changed more often than the residents. Items appeared and disappeared every day, some rapidly and some with such vegetable slowness that it seemed they would take root beside the Dumpsters and grow up next to them like scrub trees or Velcro-suckered vines.

Roger and Renata settled in. They added to The Pile a burned-out portable TV set, a used wicker picnic hamper, and the plastic dishes, now scratched, that had come with it. Each of these items, Roger noted with satisfaction, vanished overnight. Somebody had found them worth taking, and that was good. Roger visited The Pile every other day or so, more out of curiosity than need, but usually hung back several yards to avoid seeming overeager to loot its ever-mutating mother lode.

After he returned one evening with a working steam iron – an iron that looked almost new – Renata started visiting The Pile herself. Occasionally she went with Roger to help him appraise its inventory, and together they salvaged a rustic coffee table that Renata assigned to the back porch as a "garden table". Later, friends for whom Roger grilled burgers and vegetable kebabs on this makeshift patio told them that the table had first belonged to Graig and Irene Lyons, and then to Kathi Stole in Building F, and then to a sickly man in the nether corners of the complex, and finally to Roger and Renata. Renata, bless her, had refinished the table herself.

"The old guy's son put it on The Pile the day after he passed," Nigel said. "Don't worry, though. I don't think he croaked from anything catching."

Lydia sipped her virgin Bloody Mary. "But we're not saying it isn't *haunted*."

She could have, though: that table was about as haunted as a kumquat.

The iron proved more problematic. Using it, Renata burned iron-shaped prints in a new blouse, an old tablecloth, and a pair of Roger's favourite chinos. Once, for no reason either of them could discern, it leapt off the shelf on which Renata had left it and gouged a hole in a linoleum countertop.

"Haunted," Roger told her, joking.

"Defective," she countered. "That's why it wound up on The Pile."

"I'll put it back out there."

"You will not. A decent soul would dump it where nobody else could get it."

"Okay: I'll dump it where nobody else can get it."

"Yes you most certainly will," Renata said. "Today."

And because Big Brother did as Little Sis said, that was the end of that.

The Pile remained an attraction, though, and neither Roger nor Renata could resist going out there periodically to see what had manifested on, or departed from, it.

Roger, although good at his job, found his IT work only intermittently satisfying ("We're all trapped in the tar pit of technology," he once told his unamused boss); and so The Pile became for him not only a resource for items with which to furnish or decorate their place, but also a source of stuff that he could repair, remake, or put to good aesthetic use in imaginative artefacts of his own creation.

He converted a broken floor lamp into a bona fide light-giver that also served as a hat-tree. He painstakingly perforated a cymbal – *one* cymbal – to turn it into a colander-cum-projector with which a person could drain canned vegetables, *or* give an impromptu planetarium show (by shining a flashlight through its underside). He made a colourful banner for the front porch out of scraps of old material and pieces of balsa wood daubed with model-airplane paint. He used a discarded drum for the base of a revolving chess platform, whose board he assembled from coping-sawed squares of white pine and red cedar. When he couldn't find what he needed on The Pile, he extracted from it items to barter with local merchants for stuff he *could* use.

Renata, working toward her doctorate, encouraged Roger in these activities; she even ceded to him the decoration of the living room and the upstairs bedrooms, areas that many women fight to control, and they prospered by this arrangement. If anybody razzed them or expressed surprise, they offered a united front.

Renata: "A major victory in the war for female emancipation."

Roger: "An expansion of the territories suitable for male exploration."

Of course, few of their friends expressed surprise. Any surprise, given the well-established theoretical bases of gender equality, centred on the fact that they actually put into practice what Renata preached – even if, after the iron episode, she might have said that she too often *wielded* that instrument while Roger *hung out* at The Pile talking with his scavenger pals and assessing its contents.

Roger added to his acquaintances by hanging out there, though. He saw an oddly slow-moving Brad Hartsock put some nested TV trays on The Pile. He met a college cop, Douglas-Kenneth Smith, who anted up the well-oiled derailleur of a road bike. (Roger grabbed this, wiped it dry, and hung it in a closet as a bartering chip.) He talked baseball with a grandmother, Loretta Crider, whose nephew unloaded a sewing machine, and he foraged out a set of yellowing place mats (with inset pen-and-ink sketches of Big Ben, Westminster Abbey, the Tower of London, etc.) that a high-school teacher, Ronald Curtis, had left on the Incredible Heap in a pretty aqua carton.

"You know why we call this place Fidelity Plaza?" Mr Curtis asked Roger.

"Because the couples here only screw around with their own spice?"

Mr Curtis scowled in consternation. "Their own what?"

"Their own *spice* – plural of *spouse*."

"Ah, that's very funny." But Mr Curtis declined to smile.

"Then why *is* this place called Fidelity Plaza?" Roger lifted a hand. "Does it have anything to do with insurance?" He lowered his hand. "Forget that. I don't have a clue."

"It's because everyone who lives here – or nearly everyone – is as faithful as Fido to caring for and worshipping The Pile."

"Well, I guess it beats watching *Wheel of Fortune*."

"I don't know." Mr Curtis at long last smiled. "I've always liked the pretty Letter Turner."

"I prefer her sister Lana. Or did until Daddy said she made her last film the year I was born. And now poor Lana's kaput."

"I hope you and your sister enjoy the place mats." And whistling the theme to *The Andy Griffith Show*, Mr Curtis slipped his hands into his pockets and walked poker-faced back to Building G.

One evening, after Roger had had another annoying tiff with his boss, he went out to The Pile to cool off. Renata was at the library, and he was grateful for the relative quiet near the pool and the Dumpsters.

Then Brad Hartsock sauntered over from Building M and stopped maybe twenty yards away. He held a furry doll wearing a red scarf around its neck and, under its hairy chin, an ebony breastplate like those worn by Roman legionaries in epic Biblical flicks – except, of course, for its size and colour. Also, the kid holding this figure – a gorilla doll? – looked different this afternoon. On his and Roger's first meeting at the plaid Laz-E-Boy, Brad had appeared no more than fourteen, with a morose face and eyes of such opaque iciness that Roger had been mildly freaked and entirely convinced that the teen had an IQ lower than the average Atlanta temperature in February. Today, though, he looked older and smarter – his eyes boasted a fiery spark – but, in his hipshot stance out by the Dumpsters, no less spooky.

"Hey, Brad, what you got?"

Brad studied the object in his hands as if his wit had fled. Then he swallowed and his smarts flooded back.

"A singing and dancing ape that doesn't do either anymore," he said. "Why? You want this piece of crap?"

"No thanks. I'm holding out for a piccolo-playing orang-utan."

"Smartass," Brad snarled, like an adult gang-banger. His torso had some bulk, as if he'd been working out, and his jaw showed reddish-brown stubble. In starched denims and a striped pullover, though, he was dressed like a grade-school preppy.

An evil imp made Roger say, "You seem a tad mature to be toting around an ape doll, Bradley me lad."

"And you seem pretty friggin' *infantile* for a grownup."

My God, thought Roger, the boy has panache. He raised his hands in appreciative surrender. "Touché, kid: touché."

"Besides, this thing's Mama's. My bastard daddy gave it to her. Now it's broken. All I want to do is chunk it on The Pile and go home. Okay?"

"Sure. It's a free townhouse complex – even *freer* if you can get somebody else to put up your rent." He backed away from The Pile.

Brad shook his head as if Roger undermined his dream of a crap-free world, but shuffled up in his expensive gym shoes and set the ape doll on an unpainted particleboard nightstand that would certainly blow apart in a light wind. Then he turned and sashayed straight toward Building M.

Again, Roger couldn't help it: he approached The Pile, scrutinized the twenty-inch gorilla from a squat, and at length snatched it off the nightstand. It was his, or his and Renata's, for Renata would love it. She loved animals and funny effigies of animals, and the red scarf around this ape's throat – along with the needle-like scarlet tongue in its rubbery mouth – would win her over faster than a loaf of fresh-baked Syrian bread.

And Renata did love it. She rocked it in her arms like an infant. She cuddled it to her neck on the sofa. She laid it beside her in her bed and took pains not to roll over on it during the night. "What a cutie," she said a dozen times a day.

Because of its skin colour and quirky smile, she named it *Andruw*, after a favourite ballplayer, totally heedless of the fact that many people would think naming a gorilla doll after a black man racist. But she loved the ballplayer and thought his given name and its unusual spelling quite as endearing as his Mona Lisa smile.

Roger told her why she just couldn't call the toy Andruw, and Renata said she would shorten the name to Andy. Roger said this dodge wouldn't work because there'd once been a TV show, *Amos and Andy*, which many people now regarded as illustrative of racial attitudes best forgotten. Renata rolled her eyes, but, being an intelligent young woman, understood the strictures with which a monstrous past not of one's own making could tint the present, and so gave in.

"I'll call it Q.T.," she said. "Who can argue with that?" She added that it would be fabulous, though, if Roger could restore its ability to sing and dance. As cute as she found it, "bringing it to life again" would greatly heighten its adorability.

"If it gets any more adorable," Roger said, "I'll jump under a train."

Renata gave him an adorable up-yours grimace, and Roger got busy on the doll's adorable innards, to see what miracles he could perform.

A day later, still working on the issue, he went out to the pool for some air and glimpsed Brad Hartsock perched on a patio chair with a poncho over his shoulders. (It had begun to get cool.) Brad gazed into the bland aqua ripples with such alarming world-weariness that he looked, well, about thirty, with a grown man's five-o'clock shadow and violet circles under his eyes.

Briefly, Roger thought the person must be Brad's older brother, on a visit from out of town. However, Mrs Hartsock was nowhere near old enough to have given birth to this fellow, and maybe a trick of the autumn light had deceived Roger. Or maybe the guy was Mrs Hartsock's younger brother or . . .

"Brad?" he said. "Brad, is that you?"

The figure in the chair turned a cold hard gaze on him. "Yeah, it's me. Who'd you think it was, President Bush?"

"Nearly," Roger said. "Sorry. I just thought you looked a little puny."

"Seasonal allergies." Brad flung back his poncho, disclosing a big aluminium can of malt liquor. "Plus this, I guess."

"Your mama lets you drink?"

"Why you think I'm out here?" The voice belonged to Brad, as did the features – but the galoot at the pool was a worn near-future avatar of the young teen Roger had met on his first visit to The Pile.

"Do *you* think that's a good—?"

"Hey, I'm self-medicating, all right?"

"Whatever." Roger didn't want to leave. True adults didn't let teens drink, even if they looked like flea-bitten thirty-year-olds. "By the way, I took your mama's gorilla off The Pile – it just sort of spoke to me."

Brad toasted him with the malt-liquor can. "May it bring you true happiness." He chug-a-lugged for a good fifteen seconds, wiped his mouth with the back of his hand, and gazed back down into the water – dismissively, Roger thought.

The gorilla, as Roger soon learned without even Googling "*Gorilla Dolls*" on his P.C., sang a novelty number called "The Macarena" to the tinny-sounding band in its back. It moved its rubbery lips, showed its pointed red tongue, and swayed its apish hips like a mutant hula-dancer.

When Renata returned from the library that evening, Roger took the toy to her, set it on their kitchen table, and flipped its switch. Q.T. did his thing, loudly and repeatedly. Renata laughed aloud. She knew the gestures that went with the dance (even though Q.T. clearly didn't) and performed them for Roger several times in a row.

"My God, what a cheesy routine," Roger said, switching Q.T. off.

"Thank yew, thank yew." Renata curtsied to him and to make-believe spectators elsewhere in the room. "What a terrific gift." She tickled Roger's chin and mockingly rubbed his upper arms.

"Thank Edie Hartsock, the gas-company secretary over in 13-M. The ape was hers before I rescued him from The Pile."

"I certainly will." Renata stopped rubbing her brother's arms. "But what if she gets jealous? What if she wants it back, now that it works again?"

"Losers, weepers," Roger said. "Finders, keepers."

But then a series of events turned Renata's appreciation of Q.T. into something like distaste. Roger hit the doll's switch so often that soon even he had learned the hip movements and hand gestures that enlivened Q.T.'s ditty. A better than average dancer, he *kept* hitting the switch, triggering the tinny music, Q.T.'s pelvic swivels, and his own pseudo-Latin moves, which he busted in the kitchen, the dining room, and Renata's room as she struggled to study.

"Stop it!" she shouted, covering her ears. "Have you gone bazooka?" This was a facetious Maharis family term for *berserk*.

"You bet – totally bazooka. Forgive me. It's just so damned addictive."

"For a while it was funny. Now it's annoying. So, for God's sake, stop."

"I will. I promise. I'll stop."

But he couldn't. He'd stop briefly, to watch a TV programme or fix a meal, but then the contagiousness of Q.T.'s act would call to him, and he'd turn the toy on again and jig about the townhouse, upstairs and down, extending his arms, crossing them, clutching his head, and doing every other move dictated by the song's choreographic protocols. Even when the music ran down and the ape ceased gyrating, Roger kept singing, kept doing his manic St Vitus dance. He had become the Irksome Dervish of Building D.

"Stop it!" Renata cried. "Stop it! *Stop it! STOP IT!*"

"Yes. You're right. I'll stop."

He did stop, for a while, but then he started again. Renata screamed "*Arrrrrrgh!*" (as he'd never heard her scream before), trotted downstairs with an old walking stick, and poked its tip into his bellybutton.

"Put Q.T. back on The Pile, Roger! Put him back out on The Pile!"

"A decent soul would dump him where nobody else could get him."

Renata twisted the stick. "Give it to me," she said. "*Now.*" Roger passed her the ape. "Good. Now we're going to give it back to Mrs Hartsock. She might never have had Brad toss it on The Pile if it hadn't stopped working."

"Maybe he started doing what I've been doing."

"Only a baboon" – Renata started over – "Only a buffoon would do what you've been doing. Come on. We *will* take it back." They each grabbed sweaters and met at the door. "I'll carry it, bro' – I, myself, not you."

"Come in," Edie Hartsock called out in a gravelly voice.

They entered the townhouse's smoky lower floor. Renata waved off offers of an orange soda and a mint-flavoured cigarette and thrust the doll into Mrs Hartsock's arms while explaining that Roger had repaired it and that it only seemed right to give it back to her now that it worked again.

"I don't want it," Mrs Hartsock said.

"But—" Renata began.

"From almost the get-go it gave me the willies. I was glad when it wore out."

"But—"

"And I hate its stupid song. My ex gave it to me as a gag, if not as a torment."

Roger noticed that the plaid Laz-E-Boy had emerged into visibility (of a limited kind, anyway) from the drifting cigarette smoke. Brad lay in this chair, whose footrest he had extended and whose arms he clutched like an astronaut enduring a rocky launch. But what most disturbed Roger was the fact that several large manikins, marionettes, or dolls either stood about the room or hung from pieces of wire from the ceiling. He made out an evil-looking Howdy Doody, a lifelike Creature from the Black Lagoon, and a less adept facsimile of Godzilla. Other simulacra haunted the corners and the stairwell so that 13-M now seemed a bizarre conflation of a menagerie and Madame Tussaud's.

As for Brad, he dully ogled his visitors through eyeballs that appeared pollen-dusted. His bottom lip hung down, and strands of hair on his balding pate rose and fell in the updraft of a heating vent on the floor. Tonight, as opposed to Roger's last encounter with him at The Pile, he looked not only ill but also middle-aged – forty-five, at the very least. He'd lost weight and taken on wrinkles, and his skin had the sallow cast of a man long pent in a damp basement.

"Brad?" Roger said. "Brad, is that you?"

"Yeah," Brad drawled mockingly. "Who'd you think I was, Beyoncé?"

"Those are powerful *allergies* you're fighting," Roger said. He wanted to point out that Mrs Hartsock shouldn't smoke around him, but how could he in her own outré place? Besides, she ought to know that.

"Allergies?" Mrs Hartsock said. "Is that what he told you?"

"Yes ma'am, he did."

"Oh, Bradley." Then: "Oh, no. You see, he's got this condition."

"What condition?" Renata gazed about the townhouse in evident discomfort and perplexity. Roger could see that she thought Halloween much too far away to justify such freaky décor now.

Edie Hartsock said in an annoyed-sounding stage whisper, "I really don't like to talk about it in front of him."

"Why?" Brad whined. "Because I'm fourteen and look forty? Or do I look even older tonight?"

"*Fourteen?*" Renata said. "How can this person be *fourteen?*"

"It's really fast, his condition," Mrs Hartsock said.

"What condition?" Renata asked again, almost demanding.

"Progeria," Brad said from the Laz-E-Boy. "I got progeria."

Roger pondered this. The only case of progeria he'd ever heard about – in a book about bad shit happening to good people which his father had made him tackle when their mother died of breast cancer – occurred in a kid who'd begun looking like a little old man at three and who died at – well, at *fourteen*.

Brad's progeria, if that's what this was, had *started* at fourteen and was moving a lot faster than the disease of the kid in the book, as if to make up for lost time. It seemed impossible, but Roger had learned from his mama's death that "impossible" crap could drop on you like a grand piano at any time and then resound smashingly in your head and your kicked-asunder life forever.

"This is a pretty weird sort of progeria, isn't it?" Roger asked Mrs. Hartsock. "I mean, if weirdness has degrees." (The Hartsocks' townhouse suggested that it had *many* degrees.)

"Yeah," Brad said weakly. "My doctor calls it an allelomorphic progeria, a sort of one-gene-off kind."

Renata stared at Brad Hartsock. "He's a very smart fourteen."

"But I look forty," Brad said. "Or is it fifty? Mama, is it fifty? Or is it like" – his adult voice poignantly broke – "maybe even *six*-tee?"

"You look twenty-five, Brad: a handsome twenty-five."

"Right," Brad said, but he visibly relaxed.

"What can we do?" Renata asked. "To help, I mean."

"Maybe a little entertainment," Roger said. He took the ape doll from Renata and switched it on: "The Macarena" blared into the room, and both he and the doll began hip-swivelling. Brad screamed. Mrs Hartsock grabbed the doll away from Roger and fumbled to switch it off.

"Brad can't abide it anymore," she said, not unkindly. "I can't either."

"Nor can I," Renata said, giving Roger a look. "I'm sorry – so sorry."

"Well, you could put the obnoxious thing back on The Pile for me."

"Yes, Mrs Hartsock. We'll do it tonight."

"Edie," Brad's mother said. "Call me Edie." They had bonded over their disgust with Roger's asininity and their concern for Mrs Hartsock's dying son.

Mrs Hartsock stepped onto the porch with them and unburdened herself as if they were paid confessors. "I divorced Bradley's father seven years ago. He was never home much, and when he was, well, he was an abuser."

"What sort?" Renata asked. "Physical?"

"That depended. He never hurt the boy, though. All that stuff in there – he makes models for movies, theatres, and Halloween festivals. When I told him by telephone that Bradley was – uh, terminally sick, he sent that hideous junk and had these guys who work for him come install it, just to cheer the boy up, and—" She began to cry.

Renata embraced her. "Does Bradley like it, all that stuff? *Does* it cheer him up?"

"I don't know. He says so. But it may scare him. He'd rather his daddy came to see him, I think, but he won't say that for fear of hurting my feelings. It wouldn't – hurt my feelings, I mean – it would just scare me too."

"Has he threatened you?" Renata asked. "I mean, since your divorce."

"Not so I could ever convince anybody of it. But he's always liked to hurt me, and I can't help thinking that all this" – she waved one hand vaguely – "is all part of his plan to do that and to spread the hurt as far as possible."

Renata carried Q.T. to The Pile and set the ape gently on the shelf of a flimsy, lopsided bookcase.

"Don't fetch him back," she told Roger. "Or I'll kick you out and get daddy to back me a hundred per cent." This was at once a joke and not a joke. It gave Roger all the incentive he needed to obey, for his otherwise sweet sister ruthlessly carried out even her most extravagant threats.

"All that work," Roger said looking at the gorilla doll.

"You replaced a battery," Renata said, "maybe two. Don't pretend it was this big deal. Now maybe somebody sane can enjoy it."

"Until they're driven bazooka," Roger said.

"Just don't bring it back."

He didn't. And Q.T. – under a wholly different name, if under any name at all – vanished from The Pile into the townhouse of another resident.

In fact, Nigel Rabe appropriated it and set it up on a chest-of-drawers against the inner wall of Renata's office. Whenever he or Lydia played it, Renata ground her teeth in chagrin and frustration.

At length, she knocked on Nigel and Lydia's door and offered fifteen dollars for the doll. Its "Macarena" binges irritated her even more than did their weekend bluegrass jams, because the doll sounded off on nights when she studied. Faced with her complaint, Nigel declined Renata's money but returned the doll to The Pile himself. A friend indeed was Nigel. And, by returning it to The Pile, he side-stepped the punishments, deliberate or accidental, that possessing the thing often inflicted.

Thereafter the doll began making the rounds of those Fidelity Plaza residents who visited The Pile. Kathi Stole took the singing and swaying ape after Nigel and Lydia, but put it back on The Pile when her two kids began fighting over it like piranhas flensing a baby pig. The next time it appeared, however, several people expressed interest in it, and Mr Curtis, who didn't care at all about the ape, became the comptroller of this item, the guy who decided who could have it. He inaugurated the ritual of handing a small piece of red string to whomever he deemed its next legitimate inheritor.

After Kathi Stole unloaded the gorilla, Mr Curtis wandered into the crowd hanging out around The Pile like flea-market vultures and gave this red string to Creed Harvin, a political-science grad student. Creed took the toy home and promptly broke two knuckles thrusting them into a doorjamb while doing the hand motions that accompany "The Macarena". (It was dark, and Harvin was drunk.)

After Harvin, Bill Wilkes in Building J received the red string and of course the doll. The next morning, after he and his wife had hosted an intimate soirée at which the little ape did his repetitive stuff, a city trash truck rear-ended their Audi in the parking lot, and Bill Wilkes immediately returned the ape to The Pile.

Then D-K. Smith, the campus cop, slipped Mr Curtis (whom no one suspected of bribe-ability) a ten for the red string and put the doll in a window of his townhouse as a symbol of defiance against the rumour that the toy precipitated misfortune on its owners. But working security the next day, he got into an argument with a middle-aged man, who insisted on entering an athletic dormitory without proper ID, and wound up handcuffing the troublemaker. Later that afternoon, at the insistence of the offended man (an alumnus and a high-level donor), Smith was summarily fired, with no chance of appeal. With his rent paid through the month, Smith carried Bonzo – formerly Q.T. – out to The Pile and slung the ape into a discarded baby carriage.

Mr Curtis was visiting relatives in Macon and so could neither pass the red string along to the doll's next hapless soul nor accept another bribe. And although Roger could not imagine too many residents vying for the doll now, he saw two other persons waiting for the ape when Smith jettisoned it, both bachelors, a bartender and a dry-waller, and they reached for it simultaneously, knocking the pram over and rolling in the ambient litter to establish ownership. In fact, they grunted and grappled barbarously. Finally, one wrestler yanked the doll away from his rival, rolled through the detritus on the edge of The Pile, gained his feet, and took off along one fenced side of the swimming pool. The other man, slimmer and swifter, pursued with blood in his eyes.

Roger trotted down his own porch steps to keep both in view and marvelled as first the larger man leapt the chain-link fence and then the slimmer gracefully took the same hurdle. It was late afternoon, and cool, but a small group of residents had gathered at the farther end of the pool beside the bathhouse; and, near the diving board in front of these people, the slimmer man caught the tail of his rival's shirt and spun him about so that he bounced off the board's butt end, flailed for balance without releasing his prize, and fell with a huge splash into the leaf-mottled water. The pursuer then jumped on the board and began pushing down on the bigger man's head with one wet shoe, apparently doing all in his power to drown the guy.

"*Hey!*" Roger opened the gate to the pool and burst through to the diving board. Two people seated before the bathhouse – a burly man and a woman in a floral dress and a loose beige sweater – hurried to help Roger drag the assailant from the board. A siren on a light pole, a siren used for fire drills and tornado warnings, started to keen, and the man in the water sank beneath churning ripples as the doll went down with him.

Fully clothed, Roger plunged in after both. He had no coherent plan for saving either and so much fierce headache-inducing noise in his head that he despaired of ever hearing anything else again.

Renata knelt beside the supine, spread-eagled bartender with a nursing student from their building, a matter-of-fact young woman who said, "This poor dude is gone." D-K. Smith, the sacked campus cop, held the elbow of the unresisting dry-waller who had just shoe-dunked the drowned man to a depth impossible to rise from. Although the Fidelity Plaza siren had stopped wailing a short while ago, the sirens on, first, an ambulance and, then, two city squad cars had superseded it.

The ambulance left with the bartender; one of the squad cars, with the dry-waller. Two policemen stayed to take statements from the on-site witnesses.

They began with Roger, who'd seen far more than he cared to admit, and moved on to D-K. Smith, the student nurse, Renata, and the group at poolside. The woman who had helped Roger halt the dry-waller's assault on the bartender (too late to prevent his death) turned out to be Edie Hartsock.

When this fact penetrated Roger's brain – as he stood on the slick concrete dripping like a spaniel in a cloudburst – he realized that the frail, wheelchair-bound figure at a round metal table in front of the bathhouse was Brad, drastically transfigured. Or was it? Could it possibly be?

Roger squelched over to this mysterious personage.

The man in the wheelchair squinted up at him out of a piggy grey eye in a deep-dug socket. He had a few thin wisps of hair across his skull and skin like wax-laminated tissue paper. He smelled of greasy menthol and stale pee.

"Are you Brad Hartsock?"

The codger blinked once and then blinked again. "Who'd you think I was?" he cackled faintly. "Methuselah?"

Roger found he was clutching the sodden simian doll over which the barkeep and the dry-waller had fought. Despite Brad's screaming fit earlier in the week, he felt that he should give it to the "kid" as a wonky pool-party favour, a charm against early oblivion. Apparently, Renata telepathically parsed his intentions.

"Roger!" she shouted. "Roger, don't you do it!"

But Q.T., or Bonzo, or Little King Kong, fell from Roger's hands into Bradley's plaid-blanketed lap. Brad gawped at the doll.

Then he opened his mouth, which continued slack. No scream issued from it – no scream, no word, no whimper, no breath.

It was rumoured that Edie Hartsock had a small closed-coffin family funeral for her son in her home town. No one from Fidelity Plaza received an invitation to this event, and when Mrs Hartsock returned a week or ten days later, she cloistered herself in her townhouse like a nun in a convent. Some residents speculated that she had had the gorilla doll buried with Brad, whereas others argued that she had weighted it with used flashlight batteries or old tractor lug nuts and spitefully committed it to an alligator hole in the swamp near her birthplace. These speculations were so outlandish, though, that Roger could not easily imagine what had prompted them.

A few evenings after Mrs Hartsock's return, Renata saw a crowd gathered at The Pile in the twilight. She called Roger to her side on the porch. "There's something new out there. Do you want to see what it is?"

"I don't know." Despite their satisfaction with a couple of salvaged items (their garden table and an elegant little medicine cabinet), Roger had grown wary of The Pile.

"Come on," Renata said. "It might be worth it to look."

So they went to look. People parted for them – people gawking but not speaking, people stunned into a near-trancelike state.

The Maharis siblings moved gingerly through them to a point where each felt like a supplicant in the presence of some august, or richly uncanny, superluminary – for they beheld in the lee of one cardboard-filled Dumpster a plaid Laz-E-Boy in which sat a pale white figure reminiscent of Bradley Hartsock before the advent of his virulent variety of progeria. This effigy wore a powder-blue T-shirt, multi-pocketed grey shorts, and some of the prettiest Italian sandals Roger had ever seen. Had the figure had any nerve endings, it would have been cold – but, given Brad's death after fast-forward progeria, it existed only as a detailed manikin, not a living being, and Roger and his sister gaped at the real-looking humanoid artefact in bewilderment and awe.

D-K. Smith handed Roger a lace-bearing sign.

The sign's legend read TAKE ME HOME. Its obverse read CHAIR AND ITS OCCUPANTS NOT TO BE SEPARATED.

"The Brad-thing was wearing this sign," D-K. told the Maharises.

"'Occupants'?" Renata said. "Why is that word plural?"

Loretta Crider stepped up and showed them the worrisome little "Macarena" ape. "This was in the Bradley-thing's lap," she said. "It freaked D-K. out, so I just picked it up and held it."

"Right," D-K. said. "Thanks. I'm leaving this spooky bullshit with you all. Take care, okay? I mean it: *take care.*"

And he left them all standing there at The Pile.

Well, why not? There were laws against child abandonment, but none that Roger knew of against *effigy abandonment*.

After a while, Loretta Crider said, "Mrs Hartsock's disappeared. Her townhouse is empty, flat-out empty. Who knows where she or all her stuff's gone? It's a mystery, is what it is."

She set the ape doll back in the lap of the Bradley-thing, and the remainder of the uneasy onlookers dispersed to their own places.

After a longer while, Roger said, "Renata, I could make something with this Laz-E-Boy and this creepy Bradley-thing."

"What, for God's sake?"

"I don't know – a sort of found-art installation, maybe."

Renata crossed her arms. Her face had grown lavender in the darkness.

No moon shone. The pool lights cut off. A wind rose.

Roger could feel the night, the month, and in fact the year itself all going deeply and dreadfully *bazooka*.

For my son Jamie, on whose notes this story is based.

TANITH LEE

Under Fog

IN 2009 TANITH LEE was the recipient of the Grand Master Award from the World Horror Convention and, coincidentally, announced as one of the Guests of Honour at the 2010 event, to be held in Brighton, England.

In a writing career that has spanned nearly four decades, she has worked in many genres for both adults and children. She has won the British Fantasy Award and two World Fantasy Awards, as well as being a Nebula Award nominee.

In the US, Wildside Press has issued two volumes of *The Selected Stories of Tanith Lee: Tempting the Gods and Hunting the Shadows*, while Norilana Books is reprinting her entire "Tales from the Flat Earth" series plus two new volumes. She recently completed a contemporary novel, *Ivorian*, and is currently working on a new fantasy novel, *The Court of the Crow*, along with several short stories for various markets.

About the following story, the author explains: "This really just sprang from the name of the original anthology in which the story appeared: *Subterfuge*.

"In Latin, *subter* means beneath (under), of course. And my dyslectic reader's eye can happily render *fuge* as fog. A sort of pun, then.

"The narrator and all other characters, including the noble Iron, arrived immediately, since the nature of the story grew at once from the image of deeds enacted under fog cover."

Oh burning God,
Each of our crimes is numbered upon
The nacre of your eternal carapace,
Like scars upon the endless sky.

> —"Prayer of the Damned"
> (found scratched behind the altar
> in the ruined church at Hampp)

W E LURED THEM IN. It was how we lived, at Hampp. After all, the means had been put into our grip, and we had never been given much else.

It is a rocky ugly place, the village, though worse now. Just above the sea behind the cliff-line, and the cliffs are dark as sharks, but eaten away beneath to a whitish-green that sometimes, in the sunlight, luridly shines. The drop is what? Three hundred feet or more. There was the old church standing there once, but as the cliff crumbled through the years, bits and then all the church fell down on the stones below, mingling with them. You can still, I should think, now and then find part of the pitted face of a rough-carved gargoyle or angel staring up at you from deep in the shale, or a bit of its broken wing. The graveyard had gone, of course, too. The graves came open as the cliff gave way, and there had been bodies strewn along the shore, or what was left of them, all bones, until the sea swam in and out and washed them away. Always a place, this, for the fallen then, and the discarded dead.

By the days of my boyhood, the new church was right back behind the village, uphill for safety. The new church had been there for 200 years. But we, the folk of Hampp, we had been there since before the Domesday Book. And sometimes I used to wonder if they did it then too, our forebears, seeing how the tide ran and the rocks and the cliff-line. Maybe they did. It seemed to be in our blood. Until now. Until that night of the fog.

My first time, I was about nine years. It had gone on before, that goes without saying, and I had known it did, but not properly what it was or meant. My nine-year-old self had memories of sitting by our winter fire, and the storm raging outside, and then a shout from the watch, or some other man banging on our door: "Stir up, Jom. One's there." And father would rise with a grunt, somewhere between annoyance and strange eagerness. And when he was gone out into the wind and rain, I must have asked why and Ma would say, "Don't you fret, Haro. It's just the Night Work they're to."

But later, maybe even next day, useful things would have come into our house, and to all the impoverished houses up and down the cranky village street. Casks of wine or even rum, a bolt of cloth, perhaps, or a box of good china; once a sewing machine, and more than once a whole side of beef. And other stuff came that we threw on the fire, papers and books, and a broken doll one time, and another a ripped little dress that might have been for a doll, but was not.

On the evening I was nine and a storm was brewing, I knew I might be in on the Work, but after I thought not and slept. The Work was what we all called it, you see. The Work, or the Night Work, although every so often it had happened by day, when the weather was very bad. Still, Night Work, even so.

My father said, "Get up Haro." It was the middle of the night and I in bed. And behind the curtain in my parents' bed, my mother was already moving and awake. My father was dressed. "What is it, Da?" I whispered. "Only the usual," said my father, "but you're of an age now. It's time you saw and played your part."

So I scrambled out and pulled on my outdoor clothes over the underthings I slept in. I was, like my father, between two emotions, but mine were different. With me that first time, they were excitement, and fear. Truly fear, like as when we boys played see-a-ghost in the churchyard at dusk. But in this case still not even really knowing why, or of what.

Out on the cliff the gale was blowing fit to crack the world. There were lanterns, but muffled blind, as they had to be, which I had heard of but not yet properly seen.

Leant against the wind, we stared out into the lash of the rain. "Do you spot it, Jom?"

"Oh ah. I sees it."

But I craned and could *not* see, only the ocean itself roughing and spurging, gushing up in great belches and tirades, like boiling milk that was mostly black. But there was something there, was there? Oh yes, could I just make it out? Something like three thin trees massed with cloud and all torn and rolling yet caught together.

"You stay put, Haro," said my father. "Here's a light. You shine that. You remember when and what to do? As I told you?"

"Yes, Da." I said, afraid with a new affright I should do it wrong and fail him. But he patted my shoulder as if I were full-grown, and went away down the cliff path with the others. Soon enough I heard them, those 300 feet below me, voices thin with distance and the unravelling of the wind, there under the curve of the crumbled white-green cheese of the cliff-face. Though I was quite near the edge, I knew not to go too far along to see, but there was a place there, a sort of notch in the crag, whereby I could see the glimmer of the lamps as they uncovered them. And I knew to do the same then, and I uncovered my lantern too.

So we brought it in. The thing with the clouded trees that was adrift on the earthquake of great waters. The thing that was a ship.

She smashed to pieces on the rocks below, where the tallest stones were, just under the surface at high tide, against rock and shale, and the faces of angels and devils, and against their broken wings.

This was our Night Work then. In tempest or fog we shone our lights to mislead, and so to guide them home, the ships, and wreck them on the fangs of our cliffs. And when they broke and sank, we took what they had had that washed in to shore. Not human cargo, naturally. That counted for nothing. It must be left, and pushed back, and in worse case pushed under. But the stores, the barrels and casks, the ironware and food and, if uncommon lucky, the gold, those were rescued. While they, the human flotsam, might fare as wind and darkness, and their gods – and we – willed for them, which was never well.

I saw a woman that night, just as the great torn creature of the vessel heaved in and struck her breast, with a scream like mortal death, to flinders on our coast. The woman wore a big fur cloak, and also clutched a child, and in the last minute, in intervals of the storm-roil, I saw her ashen face and agate eyes, and he the same, her son, younger than I, and neither moved nor called, as if they were statues. And then the ship split and the water drank them down. But there was a little dog, too. It swam. It fought the waves, and they let it go by. And when it came to land – by then I craned at the cliff's notch, over the dangerous edge – my father, Jom Abinthorpe, he scooped up the little dog. And my reward for that first night of my Night Work was this little innocent pup, not yet full-grown as neither I was. Because, you will see, a dog can tell no tales, and so may be let live.

But the ship and her crew, and all her people, they went down to the cellars of the sea.

I was always out to the Work with the men after that. By the time I was eleven, I would be down along the shore, wading even in the high savage surf among the rocks, with breakers crashing sometimes high over my head, as I helped haul in the casks, and even the broken bits of spars that we might use, when dried and chopped, for our fires.

Hampp is a lorn and lonely place; even now that is so. And when I was a boy, let alone in my father's boyhood, remote as some legendry isle in the waste of the sea. But unlike the isles of Legend, not beautiful, but bony bare. There were but a dozen trees that grew within a ten-mile walk of the village, and these bent and crippled by the winter winds. In summer too there were gales and storms, and drought also. What fields were kept behind their low stone walls gave a poor return for great labour. And there was not much bounty given by the ocean, for the fish were often shy. The sea, they said, would as soon eat your boat as give you up a single herring. No, the only true bounty the sea would offer came on those nights of fog or tempest, when it drew a ship toward our coast and seemed to tell us: *Take it then, if you can.* For to do the Work, of course, was not without its perils. And to guide them in too required some skill, hiding the light, then letting out the light, and that just at the proper angle and spot. But finally the sea was our accomplice, was it not, for once drawn into that channel where the teeth of the rocks waited in the tide, and the green skull faces of the outer cliffs trod on into the water and turned their unforgiving cheeks to receive another blow, the ocean itself forced and flung each vessel through. It was the water and the rocks smashed them. We did not do it. We had not such power, nor any power ever. And sometimes one of our own was harmed, or perished. Two men died in those years of my boyhood, swept off by the surge. And one young boy also, younger than I was by then, he broken in a second when half a ship's mast came down on him with all its weight of riven sail.

But ten ships gave up their goods in those years between my ninth and fourteenth birthdays, and I was myself by then a man. And the dog had grown too, my rescued puppy. I called him Iron, for his strength. He had blossomed from a little, black soft glove of a thing to a tall and long-legged setter, dark as a shadow. He was well-liked in our house, being quiet and mannerly. Also I trained him to catch rabbits, which he killed cleanly and brought me for my mother's cooking. But he hated the sea. Would not go even along the cliff path, let alone to the edge with the notch, or down where the beaches ran when the tide was out. Whenever he saw me set off that way to fish, he would shift once, and stare at me with his great dark eyes that were less full of fear than of disbelief. Next he would turn his back. And here was the thing too; on those nights when the weather was bad, and the watch we posted by roster spied a ship lost and struggling, Iron would vanish entirely, as if he had gone into the very air to hide himself.

I thought after all he did not know what we were at. Certainly, he would eat a bowl of the offal of any beef or bacon or whatever that came to my family's portion out of a wreck. By then, I suppose, it had no savour of the sea.

He had not known either that we let his ship, his own first master likely on that ship, be drowned. Iron only knew, I thought, that my father, and next I, had plucked him from the water after all else was gone.

For a while I had recalled the cloaked woman and her son. I said nothing of it, and put it from me. And soon I had seen other sights like that, and many since that time. The worst was when they tried to save each other, or worse yet, comfort each other. Those poor souls. Yet, like my dog, I would stare then turn my eyes away. I could not help them. Nor would I have, if I could. We lived by what we took from them, lived by their dying. All men want and will to live. Even a dog does, swimming for the shore.

Iron is here now. He leans on my leg and the leg of the chair. Strange, for there is iron metal there also, but he does not know this. They are kind, compassionate to have let him in. Well then. Let me tell the rest.

I had seen fogs often, and of all sorts. Sea-frets come up like a grey curtain but they melt away at Hampp and are soon gone. The other sort of fog comes in a bank, so thick you think you might carve it off in chunks with your rope-knife. And it will stay days at a time, and the nights with them.

In such a fog sometimes a ship goes by, too far out and never seen, yet such is the weird property of the fog that you will *hear* the ship, hear it creak and the waves slopping on the hull of it, and the stifled breathing of the sails if they are not taken in and furled. It was often worthwhile to go down with extra lanterns then, and range many lamps too along the cliff by the notch, for the ship's people would be looking for landfall and might see the lights, even in the depths of the cloud. But generally they did not. They passed away like ghosts. After they were gone men cursed and shrugged, wasting the lamp-oil as they had and nothing caught. But now and then a ship comes in too far, mislead already by the fog and by the deep water that lies in so near around our fanged rocks. For surely some demon made the coast in this place to send seafarers ill, and Hampp its only luck. These ships we would see, or rather the shine of their own lanterns, and they were heard more clearly, and soon they noticed our lamps too, and sometimes we called to them, through the carrying silence, called lovingly in anxious welcome, as if wanting them safe. And so they turned and came to us and ran against the stones.

That night of the last fog I was seventeen years, and Iron my dog about eight, with a flute of grey on his muzzle.

I had been courting a girl of the village, I will not name her. But really I only wanted to lie with her and sometimes she let me, therefore I knew we would needs be wed. So I was preoccupied, sitting by the fire, and then came the knock on the door. "Stir up, Jom Abinthorpe. Haro – waked already? That's good. There is a grey drisk on the sea like blindness, come on in the hour. And one's out there in it, seen her lamps. Well lit she is, some occasion she must have for it. But sailing near, the watch say."

So out we went, and all the village street was full of the men, shouldering their hooks and pikes and hammers, and the lanterns in their muffle giving off only a pale slatey blue. By now I did not even look for my dog Iron, though a few of the men had their dogs with them, the low-slung local breed of Hampp, with snub noses and big shoulders, that might help too pulling the flotsam to shore.

We went along the cliff, near the edge now all of us, but for the youngest boys, three of them, that we posted up by the notch. Then the rest of us went down to the beach.

It was a curious thing. The fog that night was positioned like a fret, one that stayed only on the sea, and just the faintest tendrils and wisps of it drifted along the beach, like thin ribbons of smoke from off a fire.

The water was well in, creaming clear on the shale, the tide high enough, and not the tips of the fangs below showing, even if the vessel could have made them out. But the ship was anyway held out there, inside the box of the fog, under the fog's lid, like a fly in thick grey amber.

It was a large one, too, and as our neighbour had said, very well lit. In fact crazily much-lit, as if for some festival being held on the decks. We all spoke of it, talking low in case our words might carry, as eerily they did through these fogs. The watchman came and said he reckoned at first the ship had caught fire, to be so lighted up. For she did seem to burn, a ripe, rich, flickering gold. How many lamps? A hundred? More? Or torches maybe, flaming on the rails—

A dog began barking then behind us, a loud strong bell of a bark. Some of the men swore, but my father said, "It's good. Let them know out there land is here. Let them hear and come on. Let's show the lanterns, boys. I'll bet this slut is loaded down with cash and kickshaws – we'll live by it a year and more."

And just then the vessel slewed, and the line of it, all shown in light, altered shape. We knew it had entered the channel and was ready to run to us.

Something came rushing from the other way though, and slammed hard against my legs, so I staggered and almost fell. And turning, I saw my dog there. He was standing four-square on the shale, panting and staring full at me with eyes like green coals. Brighter than our uncovered lamps they seemed.

I said Iron would never come to the sea, nor anywhere near it.

"Wonders don't cease," said my father. "The dog wants to help us with it too. Good lad. Stay close now—"

But Iron turned his eyes of green fire on my father, and barked and belled, iron notes indeed that split the skin off the darkness. And then he howled as if in agony.

"*Quiet!* Quiet, you devil, for the sake of Christ! Do he want to sour our luck?" And next my father shouted at me. I had never seen him afraid, but then I did. And I did not know why. Yet my whole body had fathomed it out, and my heart.

And I grabbed Iron and tried to push him back. "Not now, boy. Go back if you don't care for it. Go home and wait. Ask Ma for a bit of crackling. She knows when you ask. She'll give it you. Go on home, Iron."

And Iron fell silent, but now he sank his teeth in my trouser and began to tug and pull at me. He was a muscular dog, though no longer young, and tall, as I said.

The other men were surly and restless. They did not like this uncanny scene, the flaming ship that drove now full toward us and cast its flame-light on the shore, so the cliffs were shining up like gilt, and the opened lanterns paled to nothing – and the dog, possessed by some horrible fiend, gnawing and pulling, his spit pouring on the wet ground in a silver rain, as if he had the madness.

And then there came the strangest interval. I cannot properly describe how it was. It was as if time stuck fast for a moment, and the moment grew another way, swelling on and on. Even Iron, not letting go of me, stopped his tugging and slavering. And in the hell of his eyes I saw the wild reflection of the gold fire of the ship growing and moving as nothing else, for that moment, might.

"By the Lord," said my father softly, "it's a big one, this crate." It was such a foolish, stupid thing to say. And the last words I ever did hear from my father.

They call them she; that is, the seafarers call each ship *she*. As if she were a woman. But we did not. We could not, maybe, seeing as how we killed them in the Night Work. Just as we ignored the women who died with the ships, and the children who died.

But now I must call it she. The ship, the golden ship.

Believe this or not, as you will.

I do not believe it, and I saw it happen. I never will believe it, not till my last breath is wrung from me. And then, I think, I shall have to.

The moment which had stuck came free and fled. We felt time move, felt it one and all. It was as if the two hands of a clock had stuck, and then unstuck, and the ticking of it and the moving of it began again.

But as time moved, and we with it, it was the *ship* instead that froze. Out there at the edge of the grey slab of the fog, under it, yet visible now as if only through the flimsiest veil. She was well in on the last stretch. She could not stay her course. No vessel, mighty or slight, could have stayed itself now. So far she had driven in, she must hurl on towards her finish against the rocks, and on the faces of the cliffs around, those that crowded out into the sea to meet her. Yet – she did not move. Our clock ran, hers had halted. But oh, something about her there was that moved.

I behold her still in my mind's eye. So tall, six or seven decks she seemed, and so many masts, and all full-laden with her sheets. There was not a man on her that I could see. None. Nor any lamps or torches to light her up so bright that now, almost free of the fog, half she blinded me. No, she blazed from something else, as if she had been coated, every inch of her, in foil of gold, her timbers, her ropes, her sails – coated in gold and then lit up from within by some vast and different fire that never could burn upon this world, but maybe under it – or high above. Like the sun. A sun on fire at her core, and flaming outward. Lampless. *She* was the lantern. How she burned.

Not a sound. No voice, no motion. Even the ocean, quiet as if it too had congealed – but it moved, and the waves came in and lapped our boots, and they made, the waves, no sound at all.

And then the dog, my Iron, he began to worry at me, hard, hard, and I felt his teeth go through the trouser and he fastened them in my very leg. I shouted out in pain and turned, not knowing what I did, as if to cuff him or thrust him away. And by that the spell on me was rent.

I found I was running. I ran and sobbed and called out to God, and Iron ran by me and then just ahead of me. It seemed to me he had me fast by an invisible cord. I had no choice but to fly after him. And yet, oddly, a part of me did not want to. I wanted only to go back and stand at the sea's brink and look at the ship – but Iron dragged me and I could not release myself from the phantom chain.

I was up on the cliff path when I heard them screaming behind me and some 150 feet below. This checked me. I fell and my ankle turned and a bone snapped, but I never heard the noise it made, for there was no sound in that place but for the shrieking of the men, and one of them my father.

Of course, I could no longer stir either forward or back. I lay and twisted, feeling no pain in my foot or leg, and stared behind me.

And this is what I saw. Every man upon that shore, every lad, even the youngest of them, ten years old, and the dogs, those too, and those screaming too as if caught in a trap, all these living creatures – they were racing forward, not as I had inland, but out toward the sea, toward the fog, toward the golden glare of the ship – but they howled in terror as they did so, men and beasts, nor did they run on the earth. They ran on *water*. They ran through the *air*. The three children from the cliff-top – they too – off into the air they had been slung, wailing and weeping, and whirling outward like the rest. And up and up they all pelted, as if racing up a cliff, but no land was there under their feet. Only the ship was there ahead of them, and she waited. The thin veil of the outer fog hid nothing. The light of her was too fierce for anything to be hidden. The men and the boys and the dogs ran straight up and forward, unable to stay their course until, one by one, they smashed and splintered on the cliff-face of the golden ship, on the golden fangs and cheek and rock of the ship. I saw so clear their bones break on her, and the scarlet gunshot of their blood that burst and scattered away, not staining her. As they did not either, but fell down like empty sacks into the jet black water. Till all was done.

After which, she turned aside, gently drifting, herself as if weightless and empty, and having moved all round she returned into the fog, under fog, and under night and under silence. She slid away into the darkness. Her glow went soft and melted out. The fog closed over. The night closed fast its door, and only then I heard the waves that sucked the shale, and the pain rose in my leg like molten fire.

They will be hanging me tomorrow. That is fair; it is what I came to the mainland for, and made my confession. At first I never said why I had had to. How I had crawled up the path, with my dog helping me.

And in the village of Hampp, all the faces, and seeing that each one knew yet would not speak of it. My mother, she like the others. How I stayed two months there, alone, until I could walk with a stick, and by then almost everyone had left the place, the empty houses like damp caves. And then I left there also. But I came here, and my dog quite willing to cross water, and I found a judge, and was judged.

Men have gone to search the waters off the coast, below Hampp. They find nothing of the dead ships. We took all there was to take. As for corpses, bones, theirs and ours are all mingled, like the gargoyles and angels in the stones of the beach.

When I did tell the priest of the ship, he refused to believe me. So I have told you now and let it be written down, since I was never learned to make my letters.

You see there is an iron manacle on my ankle, but it is quite a comfort. It supports the aching bone that snapped. The rope perhaps will support my neck and then that will be crushed, or it will also break, and then I will leave this world to go into the other place, from which golden things issue out.

It is kind they let me say farewell to Iron, my dog. Yes, even though he is no longer mine. They have told me a widow woman, quite wealthy, is eager to have him, since her young son is so taken with Iron, and Iron with him likewise. I have witnessed it myself, only this morning from this window, how the dog walked with the child along the street, Iron wagging his strong old tail that is only a touch grey to one side. The child is a fair boy too, with dark sad eyes that clear when he looks at Iron. And certainly his mother is wealthy, for her cloak is of heavy fur.

That is all then. That is all I need to say.

No. I am not sorry for my village. No. I am not afraid to go to the scaffold. Or to die. No, I am not afraid of these things. It is the other place I fear. The place that comes after. The place they are in, the men of Hampp, and my father too. The place where she came from. The Ship. I cannot even tell you how afraid I am, of that.

CHRISTOPHER FOWLER

Arkangel

CHRISTOPHER FOWLER'S FIRST BOOK, *How To Impersonate Famous People*, was published in 1984. However, it is as an author of horror and mystery fiction that he is best known.

His first thriller was the 1988 bestseller *Roofworld*. Subsequent novels include *Rune*, *Spanky*, *Psychoville*, *Disturbia* and the "Bryant & May" series of classic mysteries featuring two elderly, argumentative detectives.

His short fiction has been collected in two volumes of *City Jitters*, *Bureau of Lost Souls*, *Sharper Knives*, *Flesh Wounds*, *Personal Demons*, *Uncut*, *The Devil in Me* and *Demonized*.

Fowler has worked in the movie industry for more than thirty years. He has written comedy and drama for BBC Radio, has a weekly column in the *Independent on Sunday* newspaper, and has written articles and columns for *The Times*, *Time Out*, *Black Static*, *Smoke*, *Pure*, *Dazed and Confused*, the *Big Issue* and many others, including penning BBC Radio 1's first-ever broadcast drama in 2005.

His 1997 graphic novel for DC Comics was the critically acclaimed *Menz Insana*. His short story "The Master Builder" became a CBS movie entitled *Through the Eyes of a Killer* starring Tippi Hedren and Marg Helgenberger, while his filmed short stories include "Left Hand Drive", "On Edge", "Perfect Casting", "The Most Boring Woman in the World" and "Rainy Day Boys".

In fact, the author has achieved several ridiculous schoolboy fantasies, including releasing a Christmas pop single, writing a stage show, being used as the model for a Batman villain, appearing in *The Pan Book of Horror Stories* and standing in for James Bond. He lives in a glass penthouse overlooking London's King's Cross area. His autobiography, *Paperboy*, was published in 2009.

His fiction has been regularly nominated for awards, including the Bram Stoker Award and the Dilys Award. His collection *Old Devil Moon* received both the 2008 Edge Hill Award and the British Fantasy Award, while *The Victoria Vanishes* won the 2009 Last Laugh Award for a humorous crime novel at Bristol CrimeFest.

"I was at a very Gothic wedding in Poland," recalls Fowler, "in a walled town filled with amazing churches – the kind of place that has changed so little in sixty years that I half-expected to see troops stepping around corners.

"The wedding was the kind complete with family dramas, a hair-raising last-minute dash to the church, a wedding feast that lasted a day and a night, and a trip on an ancient deserted train through the countryside with Izabella, the beautiful bride, her new husband Roger, and a bunch of party animals.

"I love train travel, and we started making up stories, hanging out in the corridor with bottles of beer. We reached Gdansk, but by this time I could no longer remember where I was staying, so we checked into an entirely different town where – for some bizarre reason – the Chinese Terracotta Warriors were being displayed in an old cinema. The odd mix of crazy people and Gothic images created this."

*T*HE RIVETS WERE WHITE GOLD, *fading to crimson and blood brown before they had been fully hammered into place. Iron plate and tempered steel, rods and bolts glimpsed through fire and steam in the cuprous stench of annealing metal. The world of the engines was ever like this.*

The result was a magnificent piece of craftsmanship, but perhaps they were punished for showing too much pride. One of the workers brought in from Wolsztyn Depot had the four fingers of his right hand sheared off in the engine's coupling joint just hours before the dedication ceremony, and the cheap Russian grease they used on the plates infected the wound so badly that by the time the ambulance reached the hospital, his arm was a livid poison sac. Amputation should have caught the contagion, but no; they buried him beside the track less than twenty-four hours after the Arkangel rolled out of its shed. No one pretended the work was easy, but jobs were hard to come by back then and the line brought hope, even if the means of achieving such prosperity also carried lasting shame.

He caught every third word, then realized he was falling asleep. Josh

Beckmann wasn't much of a reader. He threw the guidebook aside and wiped the condensation from the car window, complaining about how long it was taking to reach the town. It was getting too dark to read anyway, and the journey was taking longer than he'd expected. Fields, grey woodlands and factories at low light levels, every Eastern European nation was like this. There was nothing out there to give a clue of what the country was really like.

Nick looked over at his old friend and wondered again what they were doing here. There was no real reason why he and Josh should still be friends; they had nothing much in common. At art college they had been as close as knives in a drawer. As an adult Josh was a collection of passions and skills to which he could barely relate. A degree in graphic design. A career in real estate. Hobbies that included calligraphy and rebuilding an old Camaro. Josh never kept his girlfriends longer than nine months. He was a reliable man to call in an emergency. He never forgot birthdays. He always spent Passover with his family. He had a temper. He had fallen in love with a girl he'd only met twice. That didn't explain why Nick should agree to accompany him on a pair of cheap, appalling Ryanair flights to a country he knew nothing about. Perhaps he was just curious.

And who am I? he thought idly. *I have a job I hate. I have a scrubby beard I stubbornly refuse to shave off. I have few opinions of my own, no faith and no loyalties to speak of. I am unformed and unfinished. And I have no idea – literally or figuratively – where I might be heading.*

The backfiring Mercedes powered past a sulphurous smelting plant, a low modern brick factory that glowed in the country night like the site of a nuclear accident, its rotten-egg reek forcing the driver to close the last inch of his window. A housing estate had been constructed next to the sinister block, its dark gardens bristling with frozen washing and plastic children's toys.

"Does it often smell as bad as that?" Nick asked the driver.

"All the time."

"How can people live so close?"

"The houses were cheap," the driver answered with a shrug. "They can keep their doors shut."

The dank green forest of spruce closed in about them. By the side of the road, an incredibly drunk old man was being helped home by his friend. The going must have been slow, because neither of them had much use left in their rubbery legs. The Mercedes had passed quite a few drunks on the way. One had toppled from his bicycle right in front of them. The driver had swerved around him, acting as if it was the most normal thing in the world to do. October in rural North-Eastern Poland; Nick figured there wasn't a whole lot else for them to do except get smashed during the lengthening autumn nights.

They reached Chelmsk at 9:00 pm, and saw even fewer people on the streets than they'd passed in the countryside. Beyond the smeared taxi windscreen were the high, featureless outer walls of the town, punctuated by nine immense dark churches. There had been fifteen before the war, according to the driver.

The town was stripped of features, silent, dead. No advertising hoardings, no pedestrians, no lit windows. Bare wide streets without cars of any description, a few shuttered shops, a windswept concrete town square with a green metal barn used for a vegetable market and yet another church at its centre, this one even more vast and forbidding. A plasticky orange pizza parlour was tucked into the ground floor of what looked like the only building to be built in the last sixty years. It was shut.

"Where is everyone?" asked Josh, pulling his holdall together as the driver pulled over. "Jesus, it's Saturday night. Danuta is going to owe me for getting her out of here."

The hotel was a surprise, a gabled coaching inn with a cobbled courtyard like the ones in Hammer horror films, empty white stables and a well that was too perfect to be real. The whole place was so freshly painted, planted and preserved that it might have been built a week ago. Johann, the boy running the inn, was younger than either of them. He could not take credit cards, so Nick and Josh gave him cash for two nights. Johann took them up to their rooms, leading the way to a corridor that cut through the middle of the first floor. He eagerly insisted on carrying the bags by himself, smiling with a hopeful innocence that would not survive his youth.

Danuta was waiting for them in the bar, unaccountably nervous and fidgety.

Nick had forgotten how stunning she was, large black eyes set in a heart-shaped face, framed with glossy bobbed hair as black as obsidian. She wore plenty of make-up – her arms were paler than her cheeks – but the look suited her perfectly. A tiny waist and long legs accentuated by her black dress, silver buckled shoes, and the clincher – black-framed glasses that had the odd effect of making her appear demure and dangerous. There was a sense of purpose about her. She constructed her English sentences with a determination that conveyed meaning by emphasis. It gave her an attractive way of stressing certain words. Unlike most of the girls Josh picked up in clubs, she listened and responded in a way that showed she thought carefully about everything he said. She knocked the rest of them out of the field, and Nick couldn't for the life of him see what she admired in his friend, unless she really was planning to use Josh as a means of escape. Nobody could have called him attractive. He was stout and dark, with thinning corkscrew hair, but could be smart and quick-witted, even charming when he made the effort, and she responded enthusiastically to that.

He had met her in one of those Soho clubs that were doomed to disappear after three months, and was a lucky dog for having done so. She had been standing at the bar in the same black dress and silver heels she was wearing tonight. He had singled her out among the bony suburban stalkers, recognizing a timeless appeal in her that eluded the other girls in the room, who were dressed like Victoria Beckham and were out of date in the latest outfits. Danuta was visiting London with her sister, and had managed to slip away for a few precious, thrilling hours. She had come to enjoy the atmosphere of a London bar, and wasn't interested in meeting anyone. Her lack of desperation separated her from the crowd. The three of them had danced together, and ended up back at Josh's flat.

Danuta stayed around the next day, although there were urgent whispered arguments with her sister on the phone. Tousled and hungover, she peered out from Josh's white towelling robe with the sleeves rolled up, the dark flame of a votive candle. There was an indefinable sadness beneath her surface that flickered in moments of lost concentration.

Nick cooked them all breakfast. Danuta read the papers, commenting on stories. Josh sat at the kitchen table, smoking and looking anxious. The situation felt unusual.

Josh's suggestion – to come to Poland and bring her back to London – caught them all by surprise. Two months had passed since they met, and in that time he had not mentioned her once.

Danuta accepted a bottle of oak-flavoured vodka from the barman, and set it down before them. As they drank, she picked at the silver label with an ebony nail and confided in Josh, outlining her reservations about the elopement. The couple had an intensity that left Nick feeling aware of his status as the single friend dragged along for support.

Looking around the bar, he studied the carved wooden rabbits and chickens on the counters and side tables. They covered virtually every surface, inane but curiously touching. Yellow gingham curtains, pickled fruits in great glass jars, bouquets of dried flowers, plaited loaves of bread suspended on the walls; it was like being in some kind of fairytale woodcutter's cottage. The place was cosy and comfortable, and the vodka dropped a warming root through his chest. There were only four other people in the place, all old men. It felt like four in the morning.

He heard Josh ask Danuta where everyone was, and she told them that people stayed home most of the time.

"It's not a typical Polish town," she explained. "They don't like strangers here and barely even talk to each other, except in church or the shops."

"Why is that?" Nick asked.

Danuta shook the fingers of her right hand, a universal gesture of dismissal. "Oh, you know, bad things. Old history. They don't like to forget, even though they should let go of the past."

"That's why you have to leave this place," said Josh. "Did you tell your parents about your plans?"

"I wanted to, but I could find no way of explaining." Josh had suggested that she should post them a letter before she left, then come to London and get waitress work until something better came along.

"So you didn't tell anyone at all?" Josh asked.

"Well." She thought for a moment, framing her words. "I told some of my closest friends – but not my family. It is difficult for them to know how I feel. My father is old. He would not understand."

And there the matter was left.

Grandpapa should have been proud to be selected for such an important position, but a sense of foreboding crept through his bones every time he hauled himself up onto the footplate of the Arkangel. Men had died building the train, and what was this grand machine to be used for? Ferrying the directors and a lucky handful of the town's best families on pleasure trips to the seaside!

Food had been scarce in the town of late. Even the price of turnips had soared so much that people no longer fed shavings to the pigs. But no expense was to be spared on the train. The priests said it would bring new prosperity to the town, but lately they had been proven wrong every time they opened their mouths.

Sighing, grandpapa adjusted his cap and signalled to the driver. With an angry blast of steam, the shining behemoth rolled forward out of the station.

Nick had the impression that Danuta thought Josh would get serious with her when they returned to London, and then she could tell her sister and her father. But to anyone who knew him, settling down was clearly the last thing on Josh's mind.

The distance between their future dreams made Nick uncomfortable, because he saw the situation from both sides. He wanted to encourage Josh to be honest, but did not know how best to broach the subject.

While they ate platefuls of *perogi* and drank more vodka, Nick figured out what to do. Knowing that Danuta would have to go home to her parents' house tonight, he decided to take Josh to a bar in town, where he could sit him down in a quiet corner.

Except that nothing went according to plan. When he suggested going for a late drink Danuta announced that she was coming with them, and they could hardly turn her down. The trio left the inn and headed toward the only open bar in Chelmsk.

The great dark churches dominated the town, forbidding and somehow unwholesome, their decaying walls patched and repaired where wartime bullets had taken their toll. It was so quiet that the click of their shoes echoed against the peeling buildings. A series of tin lamps, suspended across the empty cobbled street, formed sharp cones of yellow light. They passed a peculiar poster for gypsum cement that featured three bald plasterers, a gate topped with a statue of a bear in striped trousers, and a shop with a giant carrot in the window. On every street there was at least one building with a disproportionately tall Gothic tower. There was no graffiti anywhere.

"I've never been anywhere as weird as this," Josh said. "It's like everyone's gone away."

"They just remain asleep," Danuta replied, somewhat mysteriously. "The people here are very private. Too many years of trouble. Twice before in the last century nearly everyone in this town suffered badly. First during the war, then under the communists. Many were taken away. Many died. The ones who survived do not like to forget."

"Are you sure this bar will be open?" Josh was shivering. He hadn't brought a sweater with him, and a chill wind was pushing down the temperature.

"It is owned by an old friend of mine," she assured them. "He knows I am going away. He will be open for us tonight."

A small blue neon sign, ARTYK BAR, hung behind railings in the basement of a tall grey building with scabby cement walls, as if ashamed to announce that it was open at all. Danuta held the gate back for them. Inside was another cosy, wintry room filled with the smell of spiced roast pig, but the spit had been cleaned and there was no indication that the place had ever experienced custom. The CD player was spinning something Nick took to be Polish pop, or possibly an album of Eurovision Song Contest winners.

The man behind the counter was wearing a richly patterned sweater of the kind you could only find in rural Europe. There were red and yellow elks dancing around his neck. He shook their hands with an old-world solemnity that belied his youth, introducing himself as Idzi, short for something unpronounceable. He was pleased to see Danuta, less thrilled to meet her new male friends. After a few vodkas he warmed and became talkative, but it was obvious that he used to go out with her and wished they had not broken up. He asked about London, the music, the clubs, the cost of clothes. He had come here from Gdansk when he was fourteen. Gdansk was cool, there was a lot to do at night, this town was too quiet for him. They answered his questions and drank. You could smoke in the bar – Idzi was surprised when they asked permission.

A couple of young guys in grey hoods and leather jackets came in, regular customers. They looked bored and vaguely angry. As they ordered beers at the bar they kept looking across at Danuta, and were clearly talking about her.

"Do you have a history with these guys?" asked Josh.

"No," said Danuta vehemently. "They go to the same church as my parents."

The boys kept looking. When Idzi was called over to share their drinks, a rift formed in the company. Small towns were the same the world over; everyone knew each other, outsiders were to be pitied or envied in equal measure.

Idzi asked Danuta to come over and join his pals. He was polite enough, seeking his guests' permission to take her away, but as she rose Nick felt something bad. "She's Catholic," he reminded Josh. "She's clearly torn up about the idea of leaving her home and family behind. Would you do that for her? Just don't screw around with her when we get back to London."

"What do you mean?"

Josh was excited about having such a breathtaking girl hanging around with him, but he wasn't going to stay faithful for long. He liked Nick, he was someone whose advice you'd listen to. He was earnest and corruptible.

"She wants to get out of here, Nick."

"She seems conflicted."

"I'm not dragging her away. She's old enough to look after herself."

"You're not just going to dump her on the street if you break up with her."

"Let's drop it."

They drank too much. Another bottle of vodka was opened, and that was soon reduced to empty glasses and a few sticky rings on the table. Idzi and Danuta came back to join them with a fresh bottle, a local brand without a label, possibly homemade. That was when the trouble kicked off.

Idzi and Danuta had been arguing in their own language, and it was obvious that the barman thought his former girlfriend was making a big mistake.

"Hey, she can make up her own mind," Josh interrupted.

"I know what I am doing," Danuta agreed. "I am not a child."

"You went to London and he seduced you," accused Idzi. "You broke your vows."

"Oh Idzi, don't be such a child—" They lost the rest of her reply as she switched into Polish.

Idzi started to shout. The change in him was sudden and frightening. Danuta was too good for them, they were fucking English pigs who should stay away from good Catholic girls, they should forget they ever met her and go back to their own country, where everyone knew the girls were all whores.

Josh pushed back from the table as Nick and Danuta attempted to keep him down. Idzi's pals looked as if they'd been waiting for this moment, and came over to join in. When Josh threw his shot-glass on the floor and tried to land a punch on Idzi he found himself pinned down by the others, who slammed him back against the food counter. He kicked out at them, but one of Idzi's friends picked up the grill's steel carving fork and swung it over Josh's face like a pendulum.

The Europop disc jammed on a particularly inane phrase. It took Nick a moment to work out what was happening. He suddenly imagined Josh stuck like a moth on a pin, pierced through the cheek as one of the fork's tines held him in place on the counter's oak carving board. The boys were feinting at each other, jabbing and dancing back to a safe distance, but somehow the fork connected and raised a single crimson tear just below Josh's eye.

As Josh threw himself at the others, Nick pushed Idzi out of the way and snatched the fork back before any more damage could be done. Danuta screamed "*Stój!*", and Nick was finally able to pull Josh aside.

The trio followed them, tumbling out of the club, with Nick and Danuta pulling at Josh. The wound on his face was mean but not serious. Idzi was throwing out a good line in nationalistic slurs, but the worst seemed to be over. At least the police hadn't been called.

Idzi must have landed one insult too many, because suddenly Josh slipped from their hands and ran back, kneeing the barman in the groin, kicking at his head as he went down. Nick forced Danuta to stay where she was, but by the time he got there things were serious. Josh kicked hard at Idzi's face, the alcohol instantly drawing blood to his flesh. Nick tried to haul him back, but could not stop the blows from hammering down. He heard the sound of Idzi's head repeatedly cracking against the foot of the railings, and it made him feel sick because he knew that the boy was being killed.

When Josh stopped, it was as if he suddenly realized what he was doing. Swaying from side to side, he seemed barely able to stand. He stared down blankly at the writhing body on the pavement. Nick examined Idzi's face. Under the blue neon his blood was black as spilled oil. He was still conscious, moaning softly. Nick realized there was a good chance that his skull had been damaged.

Danuta pulled at the pair of them, repeating "You have to go," over and over again. Idzi's pals had run off, but she felt sure they would soon return with others.

The hotel was silent and asleep. They had not unpacked their bags, so it was easy to leave. Idzi knew where the visitors were staying – there wasn't anywhere else in town. His friends would quickly figure it out. As soon as Danuta said she would settle up with the manager, Nick knew that she wasn't planning to come back with them.

"It's the only way," she said. "They'll see that I'm still here and will realize they beat you. That's all they want."

Danuta kissed Nick and gave Josh the briefest of hugs; she could not bring herself to do more. She watched them go, but Josh did not look back. There was no chance of finding a taxi – they had picked up the incoming one at the airport – but the train station was less than a mile away, so they set off on foot.

Heading along streets that sloped away to open parkland, they passed the biggest cemetery they had ever seen, hundreds of identical bone-white headstones stretching away to the tree-line. They tried to keep moving along the shifting edge of the shadows, but the moon was bright enough to reveal them. Nick was convinced that they were going to be jumped and dragged back into the dark reaches of the undergrowth.

They were making a run for it across the clear green space of the park when the others came back, six or seven of them pounding at the ground with planks and iron rods, yelling and wheeling from beneath the trees. Nick could see that the only chance they had of outrunning the gang was to ditch their cumbersome travel bags. It meant losing his new iPod, but that was a small price to pay for not being kicked to death. He shouted at Josh and they threw their cases onto the grass, hoping their pursuers would stop to gather the spoils. Pelting towards the shuttered cafeteria that stood on the far side of the park, they ran into the alley behind and found that it connected through the backs of houses on the main street. By keeping to the pathway they were able to stay shielded in darkness. Nick could hear Josh gasping raggedly beside him. His chest burned with the effort of drawing breath, but he kept up the pace until he could be sure that they had not been followed.

The squat, featureless whitewashed station stood at the end of a straight lane of pollarded trees, and was entirely in darkness. It was around 3:00 am, and according to the notice board the first train out was not due for six hours. They could only hope Idzi's pals would not bother heading for the station once they realized that Danuta had elected to stay behind.

Nick and Josh walked the length of the platform and saw that the waiting room was open. It was dry and clean, and smelled of coal dust. There were wooden benches to sleep on. The authorities were clearly more trusting in Poland – in London, Josh said, the room would have been filled with rough-sleepers and junkies.

They were stone-sharp and sober now. "Keep near the door," Nick told him. "We have to be able to get out fast if they turn up."

Josh's face was still weeping blood. His right eye was sore and darkly crusted. Nick had a fierce headache, but he had left the aspirins behind in his overnight bag. He knew they could probably pay to jump an earlier flight, but they still had to reach the airport in one piece. After a few minutes their breathing returned to normal and they settled down on the benches, sinking low beneath the waiting room window, out of sight.

Nick pulled his coat tight. The sky was as glossy as black leather, studded with stars to the tops of the trees. There were no friendly lights to be found in the landscape. Nothing but the barren ice-chill of a country night.

A few minutes later he was disturbed by a faint noise. Twisting his neck, he looked up at the window. The planets above had all but vanished. Clouds were blotting them out.

He heard the noise again, an uneven *tinging* sound like ice splitting under a frozen lake. As he listened it evolved and grew, a steady clink like keys swinging from a chain, a rattle backed by the hiss of compressed air. His muscles had frozen on the hard bench, but he swung down his legs and forced himself outside.

The wind was rising, blasting bitter gusts along the platform. He saw two things: at one end of the canopy, the zigzag of electric torches backed by dark human shapes, moving quickly toward them. At the other end, the distant black bulk of an engine riding the silvered track. Jets of vapour appeared above it.

"Get up," he hissed at Josh, "I think there's a train."

"It's not due for hours."

"You'd better hope there is one, 'cause I think they've found us."

Josh stumbled out onto the platform and looked along the line. "It has to be a goods train, it won't stop, otherwise it would have been on the timetable."

Nick could clearly discern the outlines of several men now. They were silently running across the coal-black shale between the tracks, heading for the station stairs. He looked back at the train, a wavering shape that announced its arrival through the singing steel below the platform. Squares of yellow light bounced over the scrubland beside the line. "It's a passenger train," he confirmed.

The maiden voyage of the Arkangel *set the pattern for trips to come. The directors occupied the front carriage. Their respected guests spread through the second and third. As the train chuntered amiably through Wolsztyn, the parents pointed it out to their children; this was where the carriages had been so expertly crafted. Sandwiches were consumed as the train plunged on through dense forest. Conversation became more sporadic. The fathers fell quiet while their wives tended to the children. It was only when the conductor passed through the car with two officers at his back that the mood changed to uncertainty.*

The rhythm of the wheels beat further apart. The train was slowing. As the engine passed trailing clouds of steam, Nick registered the elaborate brass plate fixed below the driver's door: ARKANGEL. He looked over his shoulder and saw that the men were already on the platform. He could hear them shouting. They would attack long before the train could be boarded.

As the two events converged, one overtook the other. The men were less than thirty metres away. The train was not slowing fast enough. Its brakes squealed, but the windows continued to flash past. Nick watched in helpless panic.

Suddenly the group stopped running. They came no closer.

The end-of-carriage door appeared beside Josh. It had an old-fashioned brass handle, not the electric kind controlled by the driver, and they were able to haul themselves inside. Idzi's gang stood motionless, staring at them in bewilderment.

The *Arkangel* had barely come to a halt before it began to draw out of the station once more. Beyond the far end of the platform was a level crossing. Perhaps it had merely slowed down as a safety precaution.

They made their way along the corridor. The windows threw harsh light on the startled faces of their enemies. They showed neither anger nor disappointment at the escape. As the train cleared the platform, Nick lowered the nearest window and watched the station recede into blackness. The men had clicked off their torches and were already starting to disperse. It made no sense. Nothing about the night was making any sense.

Nick took in their surroundings. The locomotive was an old steam engine, attached to a tender. It rode the rails sounding as if it had a beating metal heart. He had seen such machines in movies, but had never been aboard one. The carriages were old and shabbily luxurious, compartmented salons finished in green and cream paint work, with inlaid wood panels and opaque glass light mantels.

Letting themselves into one of the single compartments, they settled on green baize seats. The heating was off, but at least they were getting away. Nick smelled mothballs and damp wood, coal, tobacco and cracked old leather.

The train had picked up speed and was now racing through dark woodlands.

"I had a map," he announced. "It was in my travel bag. I think there's only one railway line running out of Chelmsk. We have to reach the coast eventually."

Josh wiped a bloody smear across his cheek and closed his eyes. There was nothing to do but settle back and wait for the ticket inspector to reach them. They still had their wallets, passports and credit cards.

"Have you looked at this train?" Nick asked him. "The sconces have brass birds on them."

"*Sconces?*" repeated Josh, opening one eye, incredulous. "What the hell are you on about?"

"The fittings, the light fittings. They're carved like birds of prey. The same design is etched on the mirrors."

Josh squinted up. "Are they wearing crowns?"

"Yeah."

"They're eagles," he said, yawning. "Polish eagles. It's an old train, what do you expect."

The weather was turning. The clouds that had buried the stars were now lowering over the treetops. Rain began to patter against the windows. The train laboured up an incline. Blasts of steam were rhythmically expelled from the engine's lungs. The carriage rocked back and forth like a crib, but Nick was too wired to sleep. The rain beat audibly on the roof.

He felt the carriage pass over a set of points. Rising, he swayed out into the corridor, pushed down the window once more and looked over. The train had passed onto a branch line that consisted of single track. The forest was so close now that the branches of trees were brushing the sides of the carriage.

"I'm going to see if there's anyone else on board," he called back to Josh. "I think we just left the main line."

"Do what you want." Josh rolled his head against the seat's antimacassar, summoning sleep.

Nick tacked along the rocking corridor. The crowned brass eagles were on the walls here, too, their wings outstretched. Josh was right; it was the Polish eagle. But these were different. Their talons were knotted together by a coiled, scaly snake. Brass door handles were anchored with spiked, feathery wings. There were more snakes, cut into the moiré patterns of the woodwork, stitched into the green linen blinds, etched in the glass panels of the compartment windows.

There were only three carriages. In the third he found an elderly conductor, avuncular and dusty, with a luxuriant grey moustache. Seated on a tiny fold-down banjo stool, he had managed to fall asleep, which was a skill in itself. His uniform was not standard Polrail issue. A badge sewn onto his cap depicted the eagle tethered by the serpent. Nick shook him gently. The conductor seemed surprised to see him, and asked him something in Polish.

"I'm sorry, I don't understand."

"I am asking where did you get on?"

"At Chelmsk."

"We do not often stop there anymore." He sounded as if he might fall back to sleep at any moment.

"Well, you slowed down long enough to climb aboard." Nick tugged his wallet free of his jeans pocket. "Can I buy two tickets?"

"You do not need tickets."

"Surely I have to – ah—"

"You have made a mistake by boarding this train."

"You don't go to the coast?"

"No, we don't."

"Well, is there a station where we can get a connection?"

"There is, and we must stop there, but it is not for you." He checked his watch and rose on old bones, grimacing. "If you knew about us you would not be here at all."

"It slowed down, so we got on."

"Well, you would not have done so." The conductor was turning to go, moving with difficulty, as if he was walking on artificial legs. Nick noticed that the knees of his trousers had been ripped and badly restitched by hand.

"Hey, it was an innocent mistake." Nick had no idea why he was apologising.

"No one is innocent on board the *Arkangel*." He passed through the connecting passage into darkness.

Nick made his way back along the carriages, passing the length of the train, but there was no one else in any of the compartments. He returned to the sleeping Josh and sat opposite with his forehead against the cold glass, watching the streaking rain. A sudden compression of air in the carriage told him they were rushing through a station. A sign flashed before his eyes, defying him to comprehend it: WOLSZTYN. Then it was gone and they were back out in open countryside.

The wheels beat against the rail joints with a comforting *dickety-dack*. You never heard that sound on British trains anymore. The carriage rocked back and forth. The window shades rattled. A white flash illuminated the horizon, throwing the forest into relief. Seven, eight seconds, then thunder. The next gap was smaller. They were rolling into the storm.

Josh twisted in his sleep. In the mists of his mind he could discern the faint outlines of menacing grey faces with dark eyes and open mouths. He was backing away from them along an endless raised platform, but was moving too slowly to stay beyond their reach. The poor yearning creatures were ragged and thin, barely corporeal, more like charcoal drawings than flesh and blood. They extended their arms desperately in his direction, moving nearer, yet even as he felt the brush of their cold fingers he thought they would not harm him. They merely sought human warmth. Their unwashed stench rose in his throat as they swarmed on every side, pressing their filthy hands into his mouth, pushing down against his ears and eyes, pulling him away from the world of the living . . .

He awoke with a jolt and fled into the corridor, just as the storm broke overhead. Shaking, he made his way to the end of the carriage.

It was impossible to tell how long Nick had been asleep when the change of rhythm began to dispel his dreams. The train was slowing, emerging from a forest of silver birches. He opened his eyes and found the seat opposite empty. Stretching, he wiped a fan of condensation from the window and peered out.

A station, even colder and darker than the one they had left.

Hearing a carriage door bang open, he jumped up and left the compartment. Josh was ahead of him, already on the station platform. The train was bright and silent, the only source of light.

"Josh, what are you doing? Wait for me." Nick ran after him, grabbing his arm. "What's the matter?"

Josh looked back wildly. A moment later, his eyes dulled. "I had a dream." He looked around. "Where the hell are we?"

There was a green metal sign on a pole. It read: ORDZANDZIN DEPOT. There was no one on the platform. The station looked as if it hadn't been used in years. The waiting train was silent, its bright empty compartments far more appealing than the derelict station. They saw the silhouette of the conductor pausing to look at them as he passed along the carriage.

Josh walked along the platform to the stationmaster's office. He tried the door but it was locked. On the elaborate wooden arch above the lintel, picked out in red and gold, was the same carved symbol of the Polish eagle, its feet tethered by a coiling, fanged serpent.

"What do you think that means?"

"I don't know," Josh shrugged. "Eastern European shit. Look around. This place is shut. Why would they even stop here?" Beyond the station canopy rain continued to fall in a thick grey mist, removing all visual cues, deadening all sound.

Against the wall stood a row of rusting trolleys. Each one contained an empty leather sack with an unknotted drawstring at its mouth.

A square of yellowed paper blew along the platform, sticking itself against Nick's shoe. He reached down and picked it up. A flyer of some kind, dense Polish handwriting, a crude drawing of the train with the smoke from its stack transformed into a pointing hand. Exclamation marks, incomprehensible bullet-pointed commands of some kind. He screwed it up and let it fall.

The papers handed out to the passengers had a strange request printed upon them. For the sake of safety, it was desired that all valuables were to be handed to the officers for safekeeping before the train's arrival at Ordzandzin Depot. This included all wrist and pocket watches, wallets, fountain pens, rings, brooches, necklaces, tie-clips, bracelets, earrings, cufflinks, money clips and loose change. Furthermore, any important documents, including all identity papers, deeds of covenant and documents pertaining to property or wills should be handed in at the same time. In certain cases, the gentlemen would be required to write a short note of explanation to their nearest relatives in Chelmsk.

The uncertainty turned to fear now, especially when one of the children saw his family's belongings being unceremoniously tipped into a leather station bag and carted away on a trolley.

"What do you think we should do?"

"Man, anywhere has got to be better than here."

Nick cocked his head. "What is that noise?"

"I don't hear anything."

"You can't hear that?" He loped along the platform of the derelict depot, listening to the sounds beneath the falling rain. Distant voices, a great many of them, but low and keening, now rising together in sorrow, crossing from harmonious melancholy to grotesque discord with such ease that he might have been listening to the wind in the trees. He tried to see beyond the canopy, but a sheet of rainwater was falling from the broken gutter on the roof, obscuring his view. There were darker patches just past the platform edge that looked like forlorn human figures standing in the rain, defined by raindrops.

There were hundreds of them, watching expectantly.

"We have to get out of here," he called back, but received no answer. Turning, he found Josh holding a brown sack against him. The sack had a head of glossy black hair.

"Danuta?"

She was shaking with cold. "I couldn't stay," she explained, letting the burlap fall to the floor.

"How did you get here?"

"I borrowed Johann's car. I went to the station but saw the others arrive on the platform. I couldn't go in. Then I saw the train come through."

"How did you manage to beat it here?"

"The road is new, it is much faster."

"You knew the train would stop at this station?"

"It has to. The Ordzandzin Depot is a supply stop."

Josh looked back at the idling train. "But it isn't picking anything up."

"No, the station is here to receive supplies, not provide them. You cannot get out here. There is nowhere to go."

"What do you mean? Where does the train stop next?"

"There is one further destination beyond this. The Lubicza Terminus. That is the only reason why the *Arkangel* exists. Then the train heads back along the same line, but on the way back it does not call at Ordzandzin Depot. For now we are safer on board the train. But we will have to find a way to escape."

"You're not making any sense," said Josh, exasperated. The rain-battered shapes beyond the platform were shifting back and forth, becoming more agitated by the second. Their voices were rising above the wind and rain.

Behind them, the train's whistle blew. Moments later, the carriages started to move along the platform.

Danuta pulled at their sleeves. "We must go." They paced alongside the departing train and hauled themselves back on board just as it began to pick up speed. Nick watched the retreating figures of the naked dead standing beside the station in the downpour, his face pressed against the cold glass.

"What is going on here?" he asked Danuta. "Why would a train like this run when it has no passengers?"

"It does have passengers." She stared at him anxiously, willing him to understand. "It has us."

"Come in here." Nick pushed her into the compartment. "Why won't you tell us the truth? You saw those people back at the depot, didn't you?"

"They would not have let you leave. I told you, no one like you can survive for long at the Ordzandzin Depot."

"Then how did they let you get through onto the platform?"

"I am from Chelmsk. I am one of them."

"You're not making any sense, Danuta!" he shouted at her.

"It is our fault that the train is here." She took his hand. "We don't have long before we reach the terminus. Listen to me carefully."

The mood on board was very different now. Even the children had begun to sense that something was wrong. A couple of them cried that they wanted to go home, but were sternly admonished by their parents. No one could truly believe their worst fears. It was a modern world. An explanation would be proffered, belongings would be returned with profuse apologies, the day would end well enough.

Calculations were made about how long it would take to reach the coast. The fathers attempted to jolly their wives and children into happier moods.

Then, as the Arkangel *slowed across the windswept plain toward its final stop, they saw the great dark bulk of the Lubicz Terminus approaching and began to fear for their children's lives.*

Danuta looked anxiously at the darkening fields. "My town – you ask why there are so many churches – three hundred years ago there were many more. All the priests in this part of our homeland came from our small town. It was one of the most pious and holy places in the country. But priests are supposed to be celibate, and even if our men of God were not, the children they sired were drowned in secret. In time our population declined. The farms began to die. The shops closed. The town elders met to decide what must be done. To increase the population they needed people who were not Catholic. They brought in Jews."

She glanced nervously from the window. The train was racing at great speed through forests of rain-lashed larches.

"The town grew again. By 1935 it was more prosperous than it had ever been – too prosperous. We were far from the German border, but not so far that we could ever forget what might happen, either. We were one of the first towns to suffer, but few knew of our plight. The piety of Chelmsk went against us; over the centuries, its ancient fortifications had been repaired and strengthened. Walls that had once been designed to keep invaders out now kept the residents in. Still, my grandparents thought they were safe. No one saw that the churches which sheltered us would eventually be used to imprison our own families until the train could arrive. Who knew such things then?"

Nick could feel the train starting to slow down. Danuta rose in alarm, but he pushed her back into her seat. "Keep talking," he warned.

"We did not know that members of the *Sicherheitsdienst* were living among us. One day the newly appointed security officers announced that the town was to be closed for reasons of racial impurity. For too long there had been much mixing of blood. It was our great strength, and it was to become our curse. A work camp had been opened at Lubicza, and although we did not know then, our people were to fill it.

"My town had many blacksmiths and factory workers, men used to tempering metal. In 1940 we were instructed to build a train, a special express under the sole command of the *Sicherheitsdienst* commandants. It was to be a great honour for our town. They asked our families to choose the most well-loved man on the council to become the conductor in charge of the train. He would be privileged to oversee every level of its daily operation. That man was my grandfather."

"The *Arkangel* was used to deliver your townsfolk to the work camp," said Nick. Suddenly he understood the meaning of the symbol; the crowned Polish eagle restrained by a mighty serpent, the symbol of a new German empire being tested out here for the first time, a dry run for the entire world.

"Each time the train left Chelmsk, a few of the town's finest families were taken along with the commandants. There was no panic, only deception. They were told there was a spa resort – that they would return in a few days. When the train reached Ordzandzin, they were ordered to surrender all their valuables, their personal property. Money, watches, even the deeds to their houses, everything they had been advised to bring on the journey. It was collected and thrown out into the leather bags at the Depot. Sometimes people made a run for it when the train stopped. They would push their children out on the platform, only to see them shot dead before their eyes."

"How long was it before the townspeople realized what was happening?"

"The commandants insisted that those families who left had elected to stay on the coast in places of greater safety. Sometimes they returned keepsakes that had been collected at the Ordzandzin Depot as proof of their well-being. When people ask how could the Nazis do this under the very noses of the people, this is how; by keeping any whisper of truth carefully hidden. People can be very naive when they want to believe. My grandfather knew, because he stayed on the train until it had been emptied at Lubicza. But he could not live with the terrible burden of his work. One night, he called a secret meeting at the town council, and told them about the true purpose of the *Arkangel*. But among the people he told was a junior member of the *Sicherheitsdienst*. They took him to the siding where the train waited, and slowly drove it over his legs. They wanted the names of those he told. He took three days to die."

She looked to the window, but might have been seeing the world from a million miles away. "Before the war there were nearly three-and-a-half million Jews living in Poland. By the time it ended, less than 300,000 were still alive."

"What are you saying, that this is a ghost train?"

"No, I said you would never understand. There is no secret to this story. I told you, people remember the past. They know what happened. It's said that after the war, the train was left in the sheds at Chelmsk. The engine was broken up for spare parts, and finally the carriages were sold to Polrail for use on the passenger line. But there were stories, things seen and heard that could not be possible. So the *Arkangel* really did become a ghost train – in the sense that it was shunned by the living."

The train was leaving the larch forest, heading out into the open plain that stood before the terminus. "Believe what you like. The train is real. It runs when it has to. It cannot take me back to Chelmsk. I must alight at the Terminus."

"You must tell me everything, Danuta. What will happen to us?"

She was trying not to cry. "After the war the town was almost deserted. Those with any so-called impurity had been removed. Every remaining resident became precious to us. The town could not lose any more of its inhabitants. This is why the train exists. To keep the families of those who survived from leaving, and to remove those who are tainted, or who would lead them away. This is all my fault. I never saw the *Arkangel* before it appeared tonight." She pressed the back of the hand against the cold metal door. It felt as solid and real as any national Polrail train she had ever caught. "I am so sorry."

The *Arkangel*'s brakes screeched and they were thrown forward. Out in the corridor, they could see the dark mass of the Lubicza Terminus thrown into relief against the night sky.

The convex roof of the train shed was backed by a large brick building topped with a square tower at either end. In a stroke of architectural arrogance, the crematorium chimneys had been built into the very fabric of the terminus. The building's crenellated gables reminded Nick of those on London's own railway cathedral, St Pancras Station. Between the chimneys, beneath the mocking spiked spires that rose along the edge of the steep roof, the eagle symbol was repeated in iron – but here it had changed form. The eagle had been crushed entirely by the triumphant snake that entwined its body.

There was only one railway track into the terminus. The platform extended on either side of the train. Here, grey linen sacks stood in metal frames, ready to receive the clothes of the passengers. They would panic now, of course, sensing their fate just as cattle led to the slaughterhouse would fear the smell of death. But everything about the station was designed to do one thing, and one thing only – to herd the passengers forward toward the building's interior, through its great iron gates.

When the officers demanded that they strip their children and then themselves, a raw terror set in. From the windows they could see the passengers in the carriage ahead of them stumbling onto the platform. Their bare white nudity was profoundly shocking. The children were screaming and sobbing now, their naked mothers pawed and prodded by the guards, the men sometimes punched in the low spine with the butts of rifles if they questioned what was happening. Some of the older ones fell, and were trampled underfoot. An old woman with bloody dentures hanging from her mouth lay screaming and clutching at the passing legs until one of the officers of the Sicherheitsdienst stuck a bayonet into her soft lower belly and dragged it upward, eviscerating her. After that, it was decided that no one should ever be killed on the concourse; the terrified crowd became too difficult to control. Lessons were quickly learned in the management of the damned.

"Where is Josh?" Danuta asked, looking around. "He must not get off the train." She looked into Nick's uncomprehending eyes. "He's a Jew who seduced a daughter of the town."

"He didn't seduce you, Danuta, you know what happened, it was a crazy night, we were all drunk and fooling around, we got carried away—"

"I'm pregnant, Nick. And I don't know whose child I'm carrying, whether it's Josh's or yours. What does that make me in the eyes of the dead? At best I am a whore. At worst, I'm carrying the child of a Jew who is also a murderer. Idzi is dead. He died on the street while you were reaching the station. Josh will be taken and so will I. None of us is innocent. We're not like those who died before."

"Last stop," called the conductor from somewhere further along the carriage. "All those for Lubicza Terminus alight here."

"Have you told Josh about the baby?"

"No, I thought if I hid the truth from him he would be able to leave, and perhaps there was even a chance for me. I should have known there was no way out."

"Your grandfather, can't he do something?"

"He is as much a prisoner here as everyone else."

"There." Nick pointed along the corridor at the figure framed in the doorway. "Josh, stay on the train!"

Josh was stepping out onto the platform. Behind him, the conductor, Danuta's grandfather, stood impassive and unable to prevent any change in the fate of his passengers.

"God, look at this," Josh called, looking up at the span of the roof as he walked further onto the concourse. Behind him a wall of sound was rising, a cry of terror so dense and discordant that it seemed like one great voice. It broke over them in waves, splintering into individual human voices, pleading, panicked, fearful, the voices of those who would do anything at all in order to draw one more breath.

Nick had no choice but to go after him. Josh was walking away. There was no time to explain. He grabbed Josh's wrist and tried to pull him back. "We have to stay on board," he warned, tugging hard.

"What, and go all the way back again, are you crazy? Listen to that, what the hell is that?" The wave was growing, towering above them, ready to crash.

"Josh, stay with me." The distance between them and the *Arkangel* was lengthening. Nick knew that the further he moved from the train, the less chance he would ever have of getting back.

Danuta stepped down and joined them on the platform, but just as she did so they were hit by the breaking force of passing bodies. It was like being caught in a sudden rush-hour; as though everyone who had ever passed through the terminus had reappeared at the exact same instant, a living wall of flesh and bone that broke them apart with great force and swept them aside.

Josh's fingers rose and pawed the air to grasp at Danuta's hand. For a moment the connection was made and held, but then Danuta was torn from him, dragged down by those even more desperate. Nick launched himself forward and scrambled toward the pair of them, climbing on the backs and shoulders of the dispersing dead.

He could see the others clearly, but they were moving out of reach in the great churning sea of flesh. He was surrounded by the fearful faces of those about to die, each held in impression rather than detail. Their tormentors – men merely recruited to perform a duty, after all, replaceable faceless servants – were corporeally unrepresented in this seething nightmare. Goaded and panicked, the naked howling mass rushed forward toward the gates. High above them, crimson sparks danced in the ash-laden smoke that belched from the glowing chimney furnaces. The entrance to the crematorium was packed with rushing bodies; everyone who had passed this way, all at once. No fires of Hell had ever born witness to such eager damnation.

Nick fought to stay afloat in the eddying mass, shouting after Josh as he was borne away toward the gates. Danuta resurfaced near him, and his fist connected with her raised wrist. He pulled hard. He would return her to the carriage and force her to ride the train back to Chelmsk. He would persuade her to surrender her unborn child, a trade that meant saving her own life. She had known the consequences of boarding the *Arkangel*. He owed her a debt of honour. More, he knew he loved her. He yelled at her to hold on, but the sound of his voice was lost beneath a million others.

He felt himself being carried backwards toward the open door of the train carriage, turning and tipping until he had lost all sense of balance or direction. When he managed to upright himself he saw the *Arkangel*'s pistons starting to pump, saw the conductor haul himself up into the train on shattered legs. Before the carriage door was slammed shut he glimpsed Danuta one last time.

She had found Josh close beside her, and although they could not touch she seemed to draw comfort in his proximity. She looked around for Nick, saw him climbing to his feet in the doorway of the train, and placidly studied his face. Her eyes told him something else, that the child in her belly was his. As if she was freed by imparting this knowledge, she no longer resisted the movement of the crowd but complied with her fate, twisting toward the gates and brick chambers beyond like an exhausted swimmer drifting through an ocean of souls.

When Nick looked back at the scene through a caul of tears, he found that she and Josh were already lost from view.

The whistle shrieked and the train began to shunt once more. Through blasts of steam and acrid coal-smoke Nick saw the station roll back and fade like a scene fragmented by migraine.

When he was finally able to raise his head once more and look from the window, all that remained was the empty plain, the ancient meadowlands, and the approaching forest of silver birches.

IAN R. MacLEOD

The Camping Wainwrights

IAN R. MacLEOD HAS BEEN making occasional forays into horror fiction for most of his professional career (including four previous appearances in *Best New Horror*). In fact, pretty much his first professional sale was to *Weird Tales* twenty-odd years ago, and involved strange things happening in an ordinary suburban environment – which has turned into a fairly regular theme.

His most recent novel, *Song of Time*, won the 2009 Arthur C. Clarke Award, and he is just putting what writers like to tell their agents, editors and families are "the finishing touches" to a new novel set in an alternative version of Golden Age Hollywood.

"I came up with the idea for 'The Camping Wainwrights' after reading about a bipolar dad in one of the Sunday newspapers," recalls the author, "whose family always knew things would soon be turning wild when he started singing to himself and wearing shorts."

I T'S A STRANGE SMELL. Part-familiar, yet feral and strange. Deep odours of trodden grass and wormcasty earth mingle with canvas and fresh air. Even folded fully dry and rolled up and brushed clean of that year's harvest of grass and beetles, then put away to slumber its winters in our attic, our family tent had a presence. I could imagine it, smell it, resting above me the dark joists beyond my ceiling as I lay in bed – its lumpen shape reminiscent of some alien mummy surrounded by cobwebbed summer offerings of frying pan, peg, groundsheet, folding chair. On those other occasions when I went up into the attic, those seasonal visits to collect the Christmas decorations or put away my year's worth of school exercise books, its aura was far stronger than anything else. Stronger than that of my old toys, or my rusty pram. Stronger than Christmas itself, even in the times when I still believed in the promises made by tinkling strings of half-dead fairy lights.

We Wainwrights – Dad, Mum, my elder sister Helen and I – were a camping family. We camped. Even back then in the early 80s, the word *camp* had other meanings, but Dad could get away with such statements standing talking to the neighbours, or to the blokes he encountered down at the pub. He probably announced it to the kids he taught at his school as well, and most likely didn't get a single snigger. Camp. Camping. To camp. That was us: the tent, the sizzle of bacon, the great outdoors and the midnight walk to the shower block carrying a damply unravelling roll of toilet paper. We were all defined by the two weeks each summer, and the several weekends, which we routinely spent under canvas.

Camping, for Dad, was an endless adventure. There were the plans, the trickily unfolded maps, the plastic patchings of the groundsheet and the trips to renew the gas canister which powered the cooker. There were his camping clothes – his shorts, of course, canvas as well – which he kept folded away in a special drawer. There were the winter's nights of slide shows. I can still hear him humming in the way he only did when he was involved in anything to do with that tent. The compressed atonal sound comes back to me now, along with the endless *tink tink tink* as, crouched out on the patio in freezing mid-November, he gleefully hammered pegs straight in preparation for next summer's trip.

We were all involved. There was no alternative. There were the family sessions, which he scheduled, proclaimed, for whole weeks in advance, during which he would spread out his latest collection of leaflets, brochures and Ordnance Surveys across the kitchen table before Mum, Helen and I, and explain at unstoppably great length exactly what we would be doing in the summer ahead. I remember how the tart and musty smell of the tent seemed to seep down from the attic on those evenings to pervade the house. Later in the night, when I wrestled with sleep, Dad's voice still droned through the bedroom wall as, punctuated by Mum's monosyllabic replies, he talked about the drives we would take, the many historic sites and morally improving locations we would visit.

I wouldn't say that my sister Helen and I were particularly close – we had our separate interests, and were three years apart in age – but we'd occasionally discuss our schoolfriends' holidays, which involved package flights to some sunny part of southern Europe.

The idea of those bright, white concrete apartments with their proper beds and sea views, a private toilet – shower, even – and chairs that didn't fold up when you tried to sit on them, seemed an impossible dream. We wondered over the idea of beaches so hot that the sand was impossible to walk barefoot, of lands where you didn't have to shelter in the damp-smelling "family room" of some out-of-the-way pub from the endless rain or, worse still, sit huddled playing endless rounds of Travel Scrabble in the dripping communal space of our tent. Once, I ducked into a travel agents on the way back from school and grabbed up some package tour brochures on the mumbled pretext of a geography project. I smuggled them home with all the guilty excitement other lads might have experienced with a copy of *Penthouse*. It was all there in those glossy pages, even the sex: those beaches sprawled with bikinied bodies instead of a deserted expanses dotted with a few hardy families huddled behind wind-breaks and some locals exercising their dogs. I could almost feel the sun, and taste the absence of canvas. Then, one evening, I lifted the brochures out from their hidden space under my bedroom carpet and found their pages savagely creased and muddied. As if a dog, although we Wainwrights didn't own a dog, had dragged them across several wet gardens. But what could I have said? Even if I'd confronted Dad, he would have denied all knowledge, or come up with a semi-plausible explanation.

After all the months of preparation and talk, the day would loom when we were finally to set out again for our summer camping holiday. Mum, who was quiet at the best of times, became quieter, whilst Dad grew louder. His hummings broke into song, or simple ringing shouts of excited affirmation. The process of bringing the tent and all the other camping accoutrements down from the loft was protracted. Everything had to be cleaned, re-assessed, mulled over. There would be lightning trips to obscure shops to buy new alumi-nium pans or a peg hammer. And it all required an audience, and small delegations. Little tasks which Mum and Helen and I were all expected to perform, and which generally went wrong in strangely unpredictable ways.

Our tent was a reasonably modern affair; mid-green, with separate inner compartments, and a metal-poled frame which was high enough for even a man as tall as Dad to be able to move around freely within it. The mummy-like sack which it filled was too big to sit in the back of the Volvo, and was laid out in one of those awninged trailers for it which you still often see on summer roads. When the early morning start of our holiday eventually arrived, with the trailer and the car and all our bags and supplies packed and every possible detail itemized, re-checked and accounted for, we would crawl yawning into the car and set off through a world made strange by dawn mists and buzzing milk floats. The route was scheduled long in advance, as were the stops we were supposed to take on it. Dad disliked motorways, so Mum was constantly occupied in deciphering his complex hand-written directions as we veered along A and B roads. The accompaniment to these journeys was Dad's humming and occasional shouts, along with the cassette tapes which he banged into the slot mouth in the Volvo's dashboard with all his typical holiday relish. Being the age he was, a child of the '50s, Dad had an especial liking for the works of Mantovani, Syd Lawrence and Perry Como.

"Listen to *that*!" he'd shout over the saccharine racket whilst Mum struggled with all the spewing bits of paper. "So much better than today's rubbish!"

Inevitably, we ended up getting lost, although nothing could dent Dad's holiday mood as we repeatedly circled a roundabout or sat at a junction as holiday traffic growled up behind us. For him, one of the highlights of these long hours of travel was to slow down on the street of an obscure village, wind down the Volvo's window and beckon some wandering indigene towards him. *Absolutely lost*, he'd declare. *No use asking my navigator. Absolute waste of time. But perhaps you . . .?* Whether or not the randomly-chosen local had the faintest idea where we should be going, the one-sided conversation would continue. *We're campers, you see, us Wainwrights. Always have been. Can't beat the great outdoors, the British Scenery . . .* One of Dad's favourite occupations was talking pointlessly with strangers.

After several such stops, and occasional pauses for Helen, who grew carsick, to hunch retching over a verge whilst Dad kept the motor revving and sang along to "What Did Della Wear Boy", and after he'd taken the navigation over from Mum and cheerily pointed out to us all exactly where she'd gone wrong, we'd finally arrive at the site, and the proper process of camping began.

Everything had to be choreographed. We all had responsibilities. *Found the drinking water tap yet, our Terry?* he'd say to me, *think it must be over there*, after previously sending me off in the opposite direction. All the pegging and the hammering and my getting the guyropes *twang-tight,* as Dad liked to call it, and searching for this and that small but essential item, which one or other of us were supposed to have packed – and it was never Dad – and which had either gone missing or turned up strangely damaged. That pale, disappointed look on his face again, beneath the smile, now with the two bright red spots on his cheeks which the outdoors always brought out in him.

Cloudy skies, damp grass. Uneven fields scarred by the yellowed outlines of previous camping families. The smell of slurry from a nearby farmyard, the twittering of skylarks. Further off, the drone of some arterial road. Dad, already in his shorts, and humming, whistling, occasionally letting off those weird shouts, would soon be off to *test the lie of the land* or *reconnoitre the toilet block* or *check out what the site shop has to offer* whilst us other three Wainwrights were still struggling to perform our allotted tasks. Hands deep in his voluminous pockets, clayey white legs protruding, he'd strike up conversations with the families of nearby tents, and even some of the caravans, although he disapproved of the latter as *too easy* and *not quite the real camping experience*. Then he'd join in with the football match that many of the younger kids spent most of their holidays playing, calling vigorously for the ball.

"Ah, this is the life . . ." he'd pronounce as he eased himself back down into one of our folding chairs. "Isn't the tea up yet, darling? What on earth have you lot all been doing over here . . .?"

After the traditional camping meal of burnt yet undercooked sausages which Mum had struggled to prepare with some vital utensil missing, the evening, and the even longer night, drifted in. Summer nights are surprisingly dark in Britain, especially in the sort of low, deep, river-strewn valleys which are generally set aside for camping. Surprisingly cold, as well. By ten or ten thirty, as I braced myself for what I hoped would be, but probably wouldn't, my last trip to the reeking, slippery cavern of the shower block, I would already be shivering.

"Not going to bed already, our Terry?" said Dad, jiggling his knees in his shorts. "Warm, beautiful night like this! Call yourself a camper, eh?"

But I knew that the dew would have already have dampened my sleeping bag. And that, just I was unentangling my underpants from my feet before pulling on my pyjamas, my inner tent would unzip, and Dad's head would appear. *Everything alright in there our Terry?* he'd enquire cheerily with those two red spots flaring on his cheeks as I hopped about, freezingly naked. Eventually, I worked out that Dad could see what I was doing from the shadows my torch threw against the tent's lining, and I got changed in darkness instead.

A chorus of goodnights. Hawks of sputum. Dad's humming.

Canvas zipping and unzipping. That tent-smell, compounded now by the rank rubber of the lilo. Twisting about as you try to find comfort without losing your precious core of bodily heat. The debate, which can fill whole excruciating hours, as to exactly when the moment will come when you'll have to get up and head for the toilets. Despite the tent's separate inner compartments, any sense of isolation was illusory. Along with the sounds of the night, you could hear every sigh, move, scratch, swallow, fart or breath anyone else made. Dad snored – snored with the same loud relish with which he did everything else when he was on holiday – but in the proximity of the tent, I was also party to the sounds of his and Mum's love-making. It would start with a lower-sounding version of Dad's usual humming. Then, after enough shuffling of sleeping bags and squealing of lilos to set the entire tent swaying, came a stutter of surprised sobs from Mum: the sort of noises you'd expect someone to make in the throes of grief rather than any sort of ecstasy. Followed by owl calls and the tick of the rain as the tent subsided and Dad's breathing slowed into the rhythm of his snoring, all of it overlaid with the aching sense of my bladder's imminent over-brimming.

For all that, there's something strangely *right* about camping. It's where we humans come from – the more northerly sort, anyway, who were never free to sleep under the stars. When I say *right*, I don't mean that camping ever felt good, and it certainly wasn't homely. There was just this mustily atavistic sense of doing something which already lies deep under your skin. I felt it when we visited a Neolithic tomb on one of our camping holidays. Stooping under the ancient lintel into the earthy space beneath, I realized instantly from the smell, and the whole dark, damp sense of confinement, what my ancestors had had in mind when they had raised this mound. They had wanted to create a long-lasting replica of the sort of space their dead chieftain would have spent his entire life living in: it was a stone tent.

Such visits were a common part of Dad's schedules for our holidays, and we'd be quizzed about them afterwards on the drive back to the site. *Now, tell me, Helen, according to the latest geological research, were those lintels brought here from Brittany, or from Cornwall?* We were never right, and Dad – who'd been studying the leaflets and guidebooks all winter – was never wrong, but those upturned bowls of earth, upright slabs and vaguely defined ditches spoke to me with a kind of sympathy. I almost felt awe, standing on low hills in the freezing rain, watching the wind-driven mist shimmer around teeth-like circles of stones. Gods were worshipped up here, I realized, and they were the gods of this muddy earth, of this rain, of lives lived barely sheltered in fluttering constructions of leaking animal hide. Something cold arose as I gazed down at the puddled grass and thought of the blood that had once been let here, the sacrifices which had long been made. Lying in our own tent that night after a meal of greasy chicken in another pub's family room, and listening to continuing rain, the presence of these demanding and capricious beings remained. They drew me closer than I had ever been to making some kind of sense of what it meant to be a camping Wainwright.

Ever since I could remember, there had always been a feeling of things being marginally askew, of a universe perpetually misbehaving. Early incidents are hard to separate from childhood's general mess and chaos. Like my favourite Corgi car vanishing, only to resurface months later rusting in the flowerbeds, or the Action Man doll which was left to writhe and melt on the cooker after I'd placed it somewhere else. Such things happen to all kids, and perhaps sometimes I was responsible for them, but I'm as sure now as I was then that, mostly, I wasn't. Mum, when I came up to her hot-faced and uncomprehending after some new incident, would patiently tidy things up with promises about putting them back together, or dispose of whatever it was straight away if it was clearly ruined. Helen was little better. They had something similar at the back of their eyes – a smudge of resignation which asked *What else did you expect, our Terry*? This, I soon understood as balls of wool unravelled in Mum's occasional stabs at knitting and Helen's dolls lost their eyes, was part of their lives as well. Dad, though, was always solicitous, caring, fascinated as he turned over the evidence of the latest disaster over in his long-fingered hands. *Perhaps you dropped it, eh, our Terry? We don't always remember exactly what we did with things . . . Maybe a cat took it – they do come into the house sometimes. Perhaps it was blown off the table by the wind. Or perhaps you forgot, eh lad? Perhaps it's that, our Terry. Perhaps you just simply forgot about what you really did with it . . .* As I grew older and the incidents and Dad's explanations grew more baroque, I learned to hide whatever was especially precious to me, although, as with those package holiday brochures, that tactic sometimes failed. It was just another part of our lives, of being a Wainwright – the existence of this capricious poltergeist, which could remain dormant for months, then visit you with some trivial destruction and kneel down afterward to inspect the damage with a broad smile and two pale pinks spots on the cheeks of its equine face. It wasn't something we other Wainwrights discussed. After all, these things – the dead mouse which turned up in Helen's old doll's house, or the lines of Mum's washing which were repeatedly torn and muddied as they fell across the lawn – are part of the life of every family. As I grew older and Mum's mutterings became more clipped and monosyllabic, and Dad remained happy as ever to explain things in his own inimitable way, it seemed that there was little else we other Wainwrights could do, other than get on with the life that we were living.

Camping was always at the core of these odd happenings. Holidays of any kind are prime times to loose, damage or forget things, even if they don't involve laying out all your belongings in some windy field. So it was always especially hard when we were camping to tell exactly how much of what went wrong involved any external assistance. You didn't need Dad to discover a frog in your sleeping bag, or dead beetles in the bottom of your plastic beaker of Fanta. Or perhaps you did. Where did it start? Where, beyond all the humming and Mum's sad groans and getting ridiculously lost on the way to the site and then finding that the holiday pack of cards had got themselves smeared with dogshit, did being a camping Wainwright end and ordinary life begin? In our tent the cold, mustily playful fingers of those vicious outdoor gods were always threatening, demanding some small new sacrifice or abasement. There was no escape.

The journey to Wales for the last holiday all four of us camping Wainwrights ever took together was just like every other journey. We got lost to Mum's directions along B roads as Dad hummed and banged the dashboard and sang along to Perry Como. *Hope you've got your passports*, he shouted as we crossed the border. *Can't you even* try *to repeat that Welsh phrase I told you, our Terry?* He was as happy as I'd ever seen him, and revved the Volvo's engine into cheery clouds of fumes as Helen crouched coughing and retching at the roadside. His only disappointment came when the old woman he pulled up beside didn't understand his version of Welsh. And it started raining. Of course it started raining; on Wainwright camping holidays, it always rained. When we finally reached our site, which was too wreathed in wet cloud for us to have any idea of its surroundings, Dad climbed out and stopped humming for long enough to sniff the air loudly and proclaim, *Good, fresh, Welsh precipitation!* just as he had praised the rain of the Lake District, Cornwall, the Scottish Highlands and other portions of Wales on previous holidays. We, the tent and all our belongings were soaked by the time everything had been transferred and erected.

Opening out my bag that evening in the wan light of the dripping tent, I discovered that several of the cassettes of current hits which I had carefully taped off the radio on my portable player had unravelled themselves into balls of shining brown ribbon. I didn't feel particularly shocked as my fingers slid through them. In fact, this was far too petty, too trivial . . .

"Problem there, our Terry?"

I looked up. Stupidly I'd left my inner tent hanging open and Dad's long face, smiling as ever, was looking in on me.

"Just this . . ." I remembered the hours I'd spent with my finger hovering over press the record and stop buttons. But I wasn't going to let him see me cry.

"Those tapes, eh? Well, never mind. Must have got jolted loose in the car. I've told you before that every cassette really needs to be kept neatly in its case."

"That's impossible," I said. "You did it."

Dad's smile scarcely changed. "Like I say, Terry. These things happen—"

"No they don't!"

"But there's the evidence right in front of you." He gazed down at the balled-up mess of ruined cassettes.

I drew back. I could tell that he longed to touch and inspect them.

"I suppose it's no great loss," he mock-sighed. "After all, there's nothing to beat the old crooners, the classics."

"Just leave me alone! It's like all the other stuff – everything in our lives that's ever been wrecked or ruined or broken!"

"Now, Terry . . ." For a moment, there was a change at the corners of Dad's smile, and those bright points of pink which always flushed his cheeks on holiday darkened. ". . . you really think *I* did all of those things?" There was something else in his gaze. Something which I had never seen. It could have been denial, or wonder, or a sort of anger, or a kind of sorrow, even. Then he retreated, leaving me shivering.

Despite the drum of rain, such conversations in a tent are never private, and its chilly echo lingered as we ate dinner off plastic plates. The food was semi-cold: Dad had delegated to Mum the task of replacing the gas canister this year, and the thing now turned out to be empty. *Maybe you just picked up the old one by accident . . . You are sure you actually went . . .? Of course, it could have leaked. This modern so-called workmanship . . .* We'd heard the same or similar explanations a million times and Mum, in particular, seemed frail and hollow-eyed at the start of this holiday – far older and wearier than her forty-something years. Iller, too, although almost everyone looks unwell in the greenish light of canvas. Apart from Dad, that is. I kept glancing at him as he ate, hating the pink spots which had returned to his cheeks, the open-mouthed way in which he chewed and how he rested his plate on his bald, bared knees and drummed his fingers on the arms of his folding chair to the beat of the rain. That night, I lay in bed listening to the continuing rain, re-acquainted with that feeling both of stifling confinement and empty exposure which you only ever experience in a tent. Dad's face loomed. I cowered, drowning in canvas. The drenching clouds swept by, and I dreamed of sacrifices to the gods of a windswept earth until I was awoken in the still dark by the absence of the rain and the soft, nearby sound of something mewling. A mouse, I thought at first, being slowly dismembered by a fox or a cat in a nearby hedgerow; the sound was that high, that hopeless. Then it was punctuated by a characteristic series of soft "ohs" and I realized that it was Mum. And I knew that this had nothing to do with anything resembling love. She was simply crying.

Something extraordinary happened next morning; we awakened to find the Welsh hills bathed in sunlight, and what looked like the whole blue Atlantic glinting beckoningly beyond a low fence. The breeze was warm and mild – barely enough to flutter the sides of the tent as Dad, hands stuffed deep into the pockets of his shorts, strode around it, muttering about the forecast being wildly wrong; how he'd been expecting, had *planned for* far harsher weather. The day, which had started deliciously warm, soon grew warmer. By noon, even the deep pools of mud outside the shower block had started to shrink.

For the first part of our holiday, everything basked in incredible heat, and everyone on the site bore a dazedly cheerful expression. This, after all, wasn't how camping holidays anywhere in Britain were supposed to be – especially in Wales. There was a small village nearby with a whitewashed pub, giddy cliff walks, and steps which led down to a vast, rock-strewn, beach. I remember the clean smell of the salt as I splashed in and out of the tepid shallows in the swimming costume I normally only wore on the afternoons when we escaped into some municipal swimming pool from the rain. Mum and Helen lounged on towels on and read doorstop novels. We all got mildly sunburnt. This was nothing like a usual Wainwright holiday. This, in fact, was almost like those brochures that I'd once smuggled home from the travel agents. Dad, for whom camping was all about battling storm and tempest, did his best to hide his disappointment. He wandered resentfully in his holiday sandals, boring the neighbours with his endless stories, scowling at the blazing sky and joining in the kids' football match which had decamped itself to the beach near to a place where Mum and Helen sunbathing. Unsurprisingly, and although I don't think it was Dad who actually kicked it, the ball once hit Mum in the face.

At night, lying in the clean dryness of my inner tent and feeling the pinprick itch of my sunburn, I wondered at all these new sensations. Was this how other families lived their lives, had their holidays? Was this what it meant to be actually *happy*? But I knew it couldn't last. When I climbed out of our tent on Saturday morning the sun was still blazing, but already there was a different tang to the air. Dad was walking briskly up the grassy slope from his trip to the camp shop with a bag full of sausages and bacon and his copy of the *Daily Telegraph* rolled like a baton. His shorts flapped in the breeze. I'd never seen him grinning so broadly.

"Haven't you heard, our Terry? I'd make the best of today if I were you – your pretend-swims. And better tell that lazy sister and mother of yours to wake up and start getting things shipshape." Cheeks redly gleaming, he scanned the Welsh horizons, then let out a shout – a yelp – of sheer joy loud enough to set the seagulls screaming. "There's a big storm coming. Good job I managed to find a gas canister to replace the one your Mum forget to get fixed. We'll need something warm inside us this evening . . ."

Already, people were packing up. Tent poles tinked and car engines revved as cheery voices called farewell to holiday acquaintances they knew they would never see again. *Not going yet, then?* someone called. We shook our heads. After all, we were the camping Wainwrights, and Dad loved a big storm. Just like that Carpenters song which, despite its relative modernity, he was humming and singing in odd barks as he organized things, he was on top of the world.

By noon, the sky had clouded over and the site was already near-deserted. Those few other hardy beings who were planning on staying were tautening canvas, knocking blocks under the wheels of their caravans, hammering in more tent pegs. Grass shivered, briars creaked, clumps of hawthorn waved their limbs, and there was a sense of siege as I hung my sodden trunks to flap from the guyropes after what I knew would be my last *pretend-swim*. All those recent happy days of warmth and sunlight already seemed like a dream. Even now, the tent was starting to give off its characteristic odour of soured canvas. The old, capricious gods of wet earth, of drumming rain, and of endless small destructions and sacrifices, were returning . . .

Then a loud gasp came from within the tent. I ducked inside, and saw Mum crouched beside Helen in her inner tent. They were both looking down into my sister's clothes bag, and what seemed for a moment like blood was smeared over their hands.

"This is everything I've got left to wear," Helen muttered, gazing at the inky mess where the two or three of her girlishly multi-coloured biros had seemingly leaked simultaneously across most of her clothes. "God knows how we're going to get them clean."

"Isn't there a washing machine in the block by the office?" I asked hopefully.

"For what good that will do." In this bilious light, Mum's eyes were black. Her face, as if lit like a Hallowe'en lantern, had a waxy, greenish glare. She pulled out a tissue from her pocket and began to wipe her fingers. "I suppose I'd better get started before the storm kicks in. I mean . . ." She balled the tissue hard inside her fist so hard I heard it squeak. "I mean, it could be worse . . ." She trailed off. The sides of the tent bellied as the wind moaned. "I mean, it could be . . ." She trailed off again. I heard something in her throat click. "It's like that bloody gas canister. It's like – we can't go on like this, can we? We've got to—"

She stopped as the sound of Dad's humming and the tramp of his sandaled feet grew close across the grass outside. We heard the jingle his keys as he shoved his hands into his shorts. He was standing right beside us now, a dark shape looming just beyond the canvas. He let out an abrupt shout.

"Talk of a bit of rain, and look what happens," he called. "Half the campsite disappears. But we'll show them, eh? Us Wainwrights'll have the time of our lives, eh? Eh?"

In the late afternoon, the site owners drove their beaten-up Land-rover around the field, offering the shelter of a mouldy caravan which lay at the edge of the site. Dad, legs apart, stripped down to nothing but his shorts, fists planted on his bony hips as he stood in front of our tent, the absolute epitome of Wainwright resilience, smilingly shook his head. By now, huge, boiling banks of cloud, the far-flung arm of some tropic tempest which had reached all the way to us from across the Atlantic, were massing. There was a second leave-taking as most of the remaining campers decided against braving the elements on this exposed Welsh field. The sun gave a final bloody glare as it poked through the mountainous horizon, and

I rechecked the guyropes and the pegs and the rubber hoops and the tent-ties and the metal poppers which held the frame together. I was looking for the flaw, the fault, the strain or rip or tear or twist or breakage, which I was sure lay hidden somewhere amid all Dad's cheery preparations. But I couldn't find anything – and that absence, as the tent's canvas began to throb whilst Mum set about boiling up a meal of Vesta curry beneath the dripping remains of Helen's stained clothing, was the wrongest thing of all.

Mum, Helen and I ate stoically. Dad, though, was taut as a guyrope, and humming, smiling, jiggling. In its way, it *was* exciting to be here inside our tent as it began to bow and creak when the first heavy drops of rain started to thud against it. Then the heavens opened, and we just sat there wishing the hours away, for this was far too much, despite our many wet nights us camping Wainwrights had experienced. Normally, we'd have played cards, but the hissing, flapping roar of the storm as it beat against the tent was all-absorbing. Shining runnels of water pooled. The frame leaned and creaked in each roaring hammer-blow, dimming our dangling gas lantern. Even in raincoat and plastic trousers, I was instantly drenched on my last trip to the toilet. There was a moment of blind panic on the way back when I slipped in the mud and found my torch illuminating nothing but streaming rain. I was sure I'd lost our tent. But there it was: inner-lit, standing out against the pouring dark, it really did look almost safe; nearly welcoming.

"Bit of a breeze out there?" Dad shouted in his typically yo-ho-me-hearties way as I wrestled to zip the flap back up. "You lot can all just go to bed. I'll keep watch for all us Wainwrights, make sure every-thing stays absolutely shipshape . . ." Pulling off my wellingtons and plastic overthings, too tired to bother with anything else, I crawled into my sodden sleeping bag and curled up there. Sleep, I told myself in the moment before I tumbled headlong into it, was impossible.

And I dreamed. Although the sun was so bright I could barely see, I knew that we all us Wainwrights were here, and I stumbled in search of Mum's and Dad's and Helen's holiday-happy voices. Slowly, I realized that the gleamingly painful light came from the gloss of the pages of the brochures into which I had fallen, with their bright poolside bars and plasticky palm trees. And, being mere pictures, the whole thing was flat; a disappointing wasteland. *Come on, our Terry!* Dad's voice remained typically hearty. *Could do with some help here* . . . But I was still faltering, trying to work out exactly where on earth *here* was. My feet skidded and my hands slid. My fingers tore at the paper in my anger and frustration, which clumped and grew damp. Everything was sodden and filthy now, wet and reeking of soil and canvas as it closed over me, weighing down my flailing arms, wrapping my face and blocking my mouth in a filthy, turfy, earthy, musty reek. I fought against it. I couldn't move, scream, breathe—

Could do with some help here, Terry, Dad was still saying as I rose out from my dream to find that I was still choking, wrestling with flapping sheets. His torch danced amid the storm, showing streaming turf, blurring rain, a glimpse of his bare white knees. Dad, who was still wearing only his canvas shorts, was battling to secure my corner of the tent before the wind lifted the whole thing away.

"Well done, our Terry! Are you awake in there, Mum? Helen – you as well! Could really do with a little more help out here . . ."

His voice came and went over the thwack of the tent and the wild roar of the wind. Half-buried in mud and canvas, batting away flailing bits of rope, I struggled against the wet grip of my sleeping bag until I finally managed to scramble my way out. The noise was tremendous. Your feet slid. Your legs buckled. The air was sucked from your lungs. Dad's torch played across his face. He was smeared in grass and mud, and the rain streamed off him, but still he was grinning – and that he was humming, singing, letting out those bizarre shouts.

"This is it, eh? Some wind! But could do with a bit of extra help here . . ." He grappled with a stretch of canvas. "Keep a hold of this for us, our Terry."

I did as he said, even though the whole nightmare force of the storm seemed to buck against me. Mum and Helen crawled out from their corners of the tent just as the frame started twisting. Lightning flickered. They looked like muddy zombies. I suppose I did as well.

"Ah! There you are! See that guyrope, Helen? Try to keep a hold and stop it from lifting— And you, darling . . ."

But it was too late. With a splintering screech, the frame broke, tearing as it did so a widening rent in the canvas. There was an odd glimpse of the fragile indoor normality of our camping life: the towels and the tins and the games and the cooking things and all the flip flops and the wellingtons and the hanging stuff we'd vainly hoped would dry, and then the night ripped through it, pulling everything apart. Pack of playing cards and Scrabble letters spewed. An empty water bottle took flight. Someone's lilo slalomed downhill. There was a wild anger about this storm, a sheer physical presence which, as the edge of the tent which I'd been struggling to keep hold of ripped finally itself from my fingers and slapped viciously against my face, I knew it was impossible to fight.

Dad, though, was having none of it. He was still laughing and barking out orders. For him, no matter how bad things got, this was just another story he could tell the neighbours and the kids at his school and those unwary strangers he stopped at the roadside, another camping adventure, a fresh wave of destruction which he'd brought to our lives and would grinningly inspect and discuss with us across the kitchen table through all the endless evenings afterwards. I realized, even as my feet buckled and I slipped back into the mud, there would be other nights, other tents, other holidays – that the lives of us camping Wainwrights would continue to go stupidly and unbelievably wrong.

Lightning flashed as I scrambled back to my feet, and I saw that Mum was gripping the famous blue gas canister, about which there had been such dispute this holiday, in her hands. The thing was heavy now that Dad had had it refilled, but she held it as if weighed nothing. Dad, who was crouching as he attempted to stop the tent frame's last straight leg from twisting, looked up as she stood over him. The rain had washed Mum's nightdress pale. Her hair streamed black around her white face. Lightning flared again, and Dad's grin broadened. Even though Mum looked strange and eerie and angry, he probably imagined she was going to use the canister to weigh down our rapidly collapsing tent.

"That's great, darling, if you could—"

With a strength I didn't imagine she possessed, Mum swung the canister down and around. Dad looked surprised when, with a wet, splitting sound, it struck the side of his head. " . . . careful . . . could really have hurt—" His grin loosened as Mum swung and struck him again. The side of his skull had become oddly shaped, and his voice was slurred. "Could *still* do with a bit of help here . . ." His mouth began to bubble with dark fluid. "If you could just—" The gas canister flashed for a third time, and all expression dropped from Dad's face. He wavered for a moment, then toppled forward, landing in a splash of limbs amid what was left of our tent. Mum just stood watching, the dripping canister still in her hands, as his body gave a series of spasming jerks. So did Helen. Dad had dropped his torch as he fell. I stooped to pick it up from where it had slid across the mud.

"Turn it off!" Mum shouted.

The torch was darkly slippery. Its beam seem to brighten and fan out as my fingers struggled with the switch, lancing across the field.

"Here – give it . . ." Helen, nearly falling across Dad and the mess of the tent, wrenched it from me. But still the light wouldn't go out. Mum joined in, and our struggles with that stupid and unobeying object filled our attention for what could have been seconds, minutes. Then the wind gave a surging moan, a wall of wet darkness slammed into us, and we realized as the torch finally blinked out that something strange was happening to Dad and the tent. It was mainly a sound at first, a huge ripping and tearing. Then, as the clouds flared again, we saw that the whole thing was rearing itself up in the wind. Dad had become part of it. We saw the flail of his limbs tangled in ropes and canvas as poles twisted and parted, then the bony white mask of his face. He even seemed to be struggling grinningly against the stripes of rope and bloody canvas that had wrapped themselves around his body, although more likely it was merely the storm which was animating him. The tent streamed up and out. Then, as some last restraint gave in a groaning tear, it took off and began a tumbling movement down across the campsite, lit by the lightning's stuttering flares, and bearing Dad with it. It was one of those things that you see and yet don't see; that your mind struggles to grasp even as you witness it. Amazed, we followed. The storm tore with wild hands, straining to lift us as well as we stumbled across the sodden field and the thing danced ahead like some weird black jellyfish. Shedding aluminium pans, wire hangers and plastic plates – the whole detritus of our lives as camping Wainwrights – in its wake, it finally snagged against the fence which separated the land from the sea. There was a loud bang as one of the posts snapped. Then another was ripped from the earth and barbed wire unravelled in a series of bright screams until the whole edge of the land gave way and Dad and our tent tumbled off into the night.

The rescue services were incredibly busy that night, but there was still a rigorous search. As Mum, Helen and I sat huddled in blankets and waiting for news in the bland florescent glow of the campsite owner's kitchen, I still half-imagined that Dad would be found alive. After all, it was just like one of this stories, the whole way he explained the world. *Well, the tent caught certainly me up, but it acted as a sort of parachute, and then it floated . . . Sounds strange, near-impossible, I know . . .*

CAMPING MIRACLE – MAN BORNE ALOFT IN GALE
SAVED BY TENT

I could see the headlines, and the twin red spots on his cheeks above his smile. But Dad was dead. They found his body not long after dawn at the far edge of the same beach on which Mum and Helen had sunbathed, and I'd paddled. He'd died, we were told, from the injuries sustained from his fall off the cliff. Most probably, we were reassured by several doctors and policewomen, he hadn't suffered.

We returned home to find the house wrapped in its usual holiday post-drowse, and a note on the doormat from the local camping shop apologising for having accidentally given Mum an empty gas canister the week before. The place seemed quiet, empty, ridiculously dry and clean and spacious, but then, at the end of holidays, it always did. There was a spate of the things which happen after someone dies – visits from relatives, an inquest, many forms to fill in, more relatives, solicitors, a funeral – and then life returned to what us three remaining Wainwrights would eventually come to think of as normality, even if the evenings did seem longer and quieter as autumn set in. The pension and insurance policies which Dad had paid for through his school and his teaching union were quick to pay up, and Mum soon bought a new car – a much smaller, sportier, redder, prettier thing than Dad's old Volvo. It took the three of us out on expensive meals quite different to those you eat in the family rooms of pubs, or to the cinema to see the kind of stupidly comedic films of which we knew Dad would never have approved. We sat there in the dark gazing up at the screen, listening to the sound of other people laughing. And then we went home again.

Christmas, as anyone will tell you who's lost someone, is a hard season. The idea of going up into our loft and rummaging around for the lights and the tinsel close to the space where all our camping stuff had laid – *have you sorted out those new bulbs like I asked you to, our Terry. Pity about what happened to that plaster Santa Claus* – was never something about which any of us felt happy. Instead, Mum came home one evening with bright handfuls of brochures for holidays in parts of the world which are still warm at that time of year, and it was almost like the old times as we spread them out over the kitchen table and looked at the vistas of palm trees and swimming pools, and talked of times and dates and facilities. The odd thing was how often things continued to go wrong for us. The downstairs sink cracked, my schoolbooks got unstapled and Helen's favourite perfume evaporated – all seemingly spontaneously. The only thing that was missing was Dad's humming, those bright spots on his cheeks, his occasional cheery shouts, and his bizarrely pointless explanations as he stroked the ruined objects with his fingers.

Then school term ended, and Christmas came, and all three of us were kept quietly busy wondering what to bring with us to this strange, hot land where people swam and sunbathed and ate fresh salads in December. The pots, the pans, the folding chairs, the games of cards and Travel Scrabble, were all gone anyway, although it was odd to be getting ready to go somewhere without them, and without the pervasive smell of our lost tent. But the flight itself was early in the morning, and the business of going to bed early knowing you wouldn't sleep was familiar. But I slept anyway, and dreamed that Dad was crouching in front of me in his canvas holiday shorts, and that he was turning over and over in his long fingers something which looked like his own ruined head. *You really imagine I do all those things, our Terry?* he was asking with a strange, sad and wounded look on his face. Then the alarm went off, and I dragged myself up from darkness to get dressed.

I paused outside my sister Helen's door as I hauled my suitcase towards the stairs. We didn't normally enter each other's rooms, but something about the way she was standing by her windowledge made me go in. She had one of her favourite new multi-coloured biros in her hand, and it was covered with streaks of blue and black and red.

"I left it last night on the radiator," she explained. "And see what's happened – it's leaked. Just from the heat. It was probably the same with those ones I had in my bag last summer. I mean, you remember how hot it got inside our tent."

I looked down at her hands, which were stained and twisting. "I suppose some things do just happen by pure accident," I acknowledged. "But not all of them. I mean, my cassettes—"

Helen barked a laugh. "Those ridiculous tinny recordings you make! Your taste is even worse than Dad's – you really thought any of us could bear listening to those terrible, stupid songs of yours all the time cooped up in our tent?" Taking her ruined biro more firmly in her right hand, she mimed holding something with her left, and then stabbing it, twisting it through the heart and turning and turning with the biro's tip. I realized that she was miming unravelling one of my cassettes.

"You never said."

She shrugged, and was about to say more when her expression

changed as she glanced behind me. I turned, and saw that Mum was standing in the doorway. For all that she had her hair done more prettily now, the look in the dark of her eyes was impenetrable and her face was pale. "Better get your stuff downstairs," she muttered, and we three remaining Wainwrights carried our bags down to the car and headed off on our first non-camping holiday through a world made strange by dawn mists, buzzing milk floats and the absent sounds of Mantovani, Syd Lawrence and Perry Como.

REGGIE OLIVER

A Donkey at the Mysteries

REGGIE OLIVER HAS BEEN a professional playwright, actor, and theatre director since 1975. Besides being a writer of original plays, he has translated the dramatic works of Feydeau, Hennequin, Maupassant and others. *Out of the Woodshed*, his biography of the author of *Cold Comfort Farm*, Stella Gibbons, was published by Bloomsbury in 1998.

Besides plays, his publications include four volumes of supernatural horror stories: *The Dreams of Cardinal Vittorini* (Haunted River, 2003), *The Complete Symphonies of Adolf Hitler* (Haunted River, 2005), *Masques of Satan* (Ash Tree Press, 2007) and *Madder Mysteries* (Ex Occidente Press, 2009), which includes "A Donkey at the Mysteries".

"In 1971, before going up to Oxford, I travelled around Greece for several months by myself," Oliver reveals, "and this story is based on those experiences.

"In my wanderings I came to an island on which was the site of an ancient mystery cult. Next to the ruins there was a hotel whose only guests, beside myself, were an archaeological draughtsman and the widow of the man who had excavated the site.

"The Ancient Greeks have a reputation for reason and ideal beauty, but they, like all of us, had a dark irrational side which was all the darker for the contrast with their better-known aspects. This darker side is to be found in their so-called 'mystery' religions."

DOLPHINS HAD FOLLOWED the little ferry boat that afternoon all the way from Alexandroupolis to Thrakonisos, their polished pewter backs arcing in and out of the sapphire and diamond waves. They seemed to me like an escort, a guard of honour, seeing me safe to the little island, celebrating my voyage. I was eighteen at the time, an age when, if you are reasonably lucky, the whole world can seem to be in your favour.

At first Thrakonisos was no more than an indigo smudge on a stretch of brighter blue. Then the golden rocks that crowned its heights, intersected by deep green gorges, began to define themselves; and finally the white lines of houses that composed the island's principal town and harbour of Chora, glittering in the unclouded sunlight. I knew little about the island except that there were some archaeological remains there connected with an ancient mystery cult. This was the reason for my visit.

As I stepped off the ferry onto the jetty at Chora I was surrounded by schoolchildren who had come with me from the mainland in their bright sky-blue uniforms. The teacher in charge was talking to the captain of the boat, and the children, taking advantage of their release from control, surrounded me, chattering and asking me questions.

My Greek was only sufficient to understand simple, slow inter-rogations and to give equivalent replies, so I smiled and waded through them towards an inviting looking bar on the sea front. One of the children pointed to the paperback I was carrying and which I had occasionally tried to read on the choppy voyage out to the island. He was indicating the strangely distorted human figures outlined in turquoise green on its cover, and seemed to be asking me what the book was. It would have been impossible for me to explain that it was a copy of E. R. Dodds' *The Greeks and the Irrational,* a book my future tutor in Greek Literature had recommended I read before coming up to Oxford. Up till now the book had interested without engrossing me.

I sat down at one of the tables on the pavement outside the bar and ordered a beer. In those days I travelled hopefully. I knew I wanted to visit the site of the Sanctuary of the Great Gods, and that near it was a Xenia Guest House, but I had no idea how to reach it or whether there would be accommodation for me.

When the barman came out with an icy, perspiring bottle of FIX beer I asked if there was a bus going to the Sanctuary. He shook his head several times. What about a taxi? He looked doubtful and gave an ambiguous reply. He suggested I do the six kilometres to the Xenia guest house *meta podia*, on foot. It was a razor-bright, cloudless Greek afternoon, and the prospect of doing six kilometres with a heavy rucksack was not inviting. I would decide what to do when I had finished my drink.

The local habitués of the bar sat inside playing draughts or clacking their worry beads. The tables on the pavement were occupied only by myself and a man and a woman drinking ouzo.

They seemed an odd couple. The man, balding, fifty-ish, sandy-haired, wore a shapeless linen jacket and baggy trousers. He looked like an English schoolmaster on holiday. The woman, slender and in her thirties, wore an immaculate black trouser suit which could have come straight from a Paris couturier. A little diamond brooch glittered on her lapel. Her hair was covered in a vivid scarlet and black silk headscarf and she wore dark glasses. From what little I could see of her face she must have been something of a beauty with high cheekbones and a perfectly formed mouth. Her skin was a smooth creamy white. She might have been taken for a film star trying to travel incognito.

I thought of approaching them, but in those days I was very shy. It was one of the reasons I had decided to spend some of the eight months or so between school and Oxford travelling around Greece and Italy on my own. Though I missed the pleasure of companion-ship, I was entirely free. I could stay or go where I liked. If I missed a bus, or failed to book ahead and had to sleep on a beach, I needn't feel guilty about having inconvenienced anyone but myself. I took a sip of beer and read from Chapter Five of the book I had been carrying:

> *There is no domain where clear thinking encounters stronger unconscious resistance than when we try to think about death . . .*

A shadow fell across my page. It was the barman and beside him was a nut brown, wizened man with teeth the colour of his amber worry beads. The barman explained that this was Stavros who would drive me the six kilometres to the Xenia Guest House. He named a price that was high even by London cab standards. I wondered if I was meant to haggle but I was too tired and full of beer to bother. Out of the corner of my eye I saw the sandy-haired man rise, as if he were about to come over to me; but the lady gripped his arm and he subsided into his seat. I noticed her fingernails for the first time: painted scarlet and honed to a point, like little blood-stained arrowheads.

The road out to the Xenia ran along the coast. It was little better than a dirt track and Stavros drove fast. Whenever we bumped particularly violently over a stone or into a pothole he would turn to me and grin. It was not reassuring: I would rather he had kept his eyes on the road, especially as his breath smelled strongly of garlic. Several times he asked me questions which I could not hear above the racket of the car, so I simply nodded and smiled.

We roared up the drive of a long low modern building, which was the Xenia Hotel. I paid Stavros the sum we had agreed upon, at which he seemed slightly embarrassed. He asked me a question which this time I understood. Was I here to see "*ta archeea*", the ancient things? I nodded and said I was. Stavros took something out of his pocket and pressed it into my hands. It was a small set of yellow plastic worry beads with a little metal cross attached to them by a chain. I protested only slightly as I could see he would be offended if I refused the gift.

Something about Stavros's suddenly earnest manner brought to mind a snippet about Thrakonisos that I had picked up from one of Montague Summers' books, *The Vampire in Europe:*

> Greece too has its Vampire tradition. Commonly known as katakhanadhes or vrykolakes they inhabit mostly the mountain villages and the islands. One island in particular, Thrakonisos, is famous for its vampires, so much so that "vrykolakes to Thrakonisos" is their colloquial equivalent of our "coals to Newcastle".

It was 1971 when all this happened, a time when the Colonels were ruling Greece. In those days the state-owned Xenia Hotels were clean, cheap places, often run with an almost military efficiency. The staff at this particular establishment was exclusively female: pasty-faced, unattractive middle-aged creatures, all dressed in identical blue overalls. The woman on the reception desk told me that I could only stay one night. This surprised me as the place seemed deserted, but I was offered no explanation. I was shown to a room of simple comfort that faced the sea.

I did not spend much time in my room as I was determined to get out and explore the place before supper. The Xenia was perched on a small hill facing the sea. To one side of it there was a broad, shallow valley where lay the remains of the Ancient Greek sanctuary. The sun was getting low in the horizon, and making the crystalline marble slabs and columns that lay about shine like gold. Further up the valley the authorities had reconstructed four Ionic columns of an ancient temple, thus providing the focus for a scene that otherwise would have looked entirely chaotic and desolate. Across the valley on another bluff overlooking the sea was a little white chapel. Apart from this, the hotel, and a distant farmhouse on the hillside beyond the Sanctuary no other habitable buildings could be seen. I decided to save my exploration of the Sanctuary for the following morning and walk to the chapel instead.

I wandered along the steeply raked shingle beach. There was not a boat, let alone a bather, in sight. I could see far into the sea's clear blue depths. Then I climbed a sheep track that snaked around the bluff and up to the chapel.

Like many Greek Island chapels this one seemed improbably small, incapable of holding any sort of congregation. It was entirely white on the outside, but within it was painted an intense cobalt blue. Western light shone in through tiny deep-set lancet windows. Apart from a brass sanctuary lamp suspended from the ceiling and two blackened icons, there was no decoration. There was a plain stone altar, and on it was a coffin.

I was so shocked by this unexpected encounter with death, that it was some time before I noticed that there was something odd about the coffin itself. No flowers rested on it. Instead it seemed to have some thing or things wound around it, rather like the straps round an old-fashioned trunk. I approached the altar just near enough to determine what they were. They were long strands of brambles or thorns, tightly plaited together. It looked as if someone had taken a great deal of trouble to bind the lid to the box, as if to prevent anyone or anything from getting into it, or out.

I can't say that I was deeply affected by the sight. I simply made a note of it, as a picturesque local detail that I must remember to put into the travel journal I was keeping.

By the time I had got back to the hotel it was supper time, and before going into the dining room I loitered for a while in the entrance hall, curious to see if there were any other guests. There were not. I studied the rack of picture postcards at the reception desk, most of them dull, deckled-edged black and white images of the excavations. There was also a slim paperbacked book on sale in two piles, one labelled GERMAN, the other ENGLISH. The cover was grey with the image of an ancient Thakonisian coin printed on it in black, but there was no writing on it to tell me what the book was about. I took one from the ENGLISH pile and opened it at the title page:

A Guide to the Excavations of the Sanctuary of the Great Gods, Thrakonisos by Dr Dietrich Leichenfeld, Honorary Doctor of Ancient Languages at the University of Tübingen

It was not perhaps the most thrilling of titles, but I bought a copy because I would feel safer with it when I entered the dining room. I had found on my solitary voyage round Greece that reading at meals in restaurants not only protected one from unwanted attention, but was a pleasure in itself.

The dining room contained some twenty tables gleaming with stainless steel, glass and pristine white napery. I was firmly directed by one of the blue-overalled women to a particular table in a far corner, in spite of the fact that all but one of the other tables were unoccupied. In the opposite corner of the room to mine sat the man and woman whom I had seen outside the bar in Chora. They were looking at me intently. I smiled and nodded at them; I may even have waved. They immediately pretended not to have noticed me, suddenly taking a great interest in each other's conversation, pouring out orange-coloured retsina into glasses, crumbling bread rolls. I felt no inclination to challenge their unsociability, so ordered my food and a carafe of the orange-coloured wine (surprisingly drinkable) and settled down to the book I had bought.

The frontispiece was a photograph of its author, Dr Dietrich Leichenfeld. This assertion by the writer of his own personality in an archaeological monograph impressed me. Leichenfeld was shown standing in the ruins of the Sanctuary, one foot on the earth, the other on a slab of masonry, as if it were the neck of a lion and he an Edwardian game hunter. He had one of those big, squat Germanic heads with small regular features, glittering currant eyes, and a long thin mouth turned down at the corners, of the kind frequently called "cruel" by lovers of the cliché. His toad-like face reminded me a little of photographs I had seen of Göering at the zenith of his grotesque power; but Leichenfeld's look was more intellectual, more formidable even.

Most of the book was taken up with a rather dry description of the various structures found on the site and the artefacts discovered in them. It was illustrated with foggy black and white photographs, one or two plans and several speculative elevations of the buildings. I skipped through much of this, but there was a short final section that looked more promising. It was headed:

THE MYSTERIES OF THE GREAT GODS

The word mystery derives from the Greek word *muein*, to be silent or blind. If it was true of the Mysteries of Eleusis that this silence was preserved by its devotees, it was even more closely guarded by the Initiates of Thrakonisos. The penalties in both this life and the next for divulging the mysteries were said by Diogenes Laertius to have been of the utmost savagery, though he did not specify what they were. For this, and no doubt for other reasons, the secrets of the Great Gods were faithfully maintained throughout antiquity.

What little is known of the cult can be summarized as follows.

Traces of a religious site have been found dating from as far back as the middle of the Bronze Age, around 1500 BC.

It was a chthonic cult, probably of Phrygian, certainly of Middle Eastern origin. The earliest cult objects found are small votive images of the god who appears to be hermaphrodite. By the end of the Bronze and beginning of the Iron Age (around 950 BC) the deity (or deities) has become a strange creature with a somewhat amorphous but bestial body and two heads, one bearded and masculine, the other female. Until well into the fifth century this image remained on Thrakonisian coinage.

We know for certain that from around 600 BC these deities became associated with the Hellenic Gods of the underworld, Hades (or Pluto) and his consort Persephone, the daughter of Demeter, goddess of fertility and the seasons. A recently discovered papyrus fragment from Oxyrinchus associates these deities directly with Thrakonisos. The fragment, written in hexameters, appears to be part of an Orphic hymn. Language and style dates it to the late epic period of literature, around the time of the composition of the earliest Homeric Hymns. Some have even boldly ascribed these lines to Hesiod:

. . . the trim-ankled daughter of yellow haired Demeter
Gathering flowers in a soft meadow of sea-girt Thrakonisos.
With her, her companions, the lovely white-skinned daughters of
    Okeanos
Picked violets and roses, and the sweet-scented hyacinth,
Beautiful to behold . . .
There the Son of Kronos, he who has many names, saw her,

And longed to embrace the white-armed daughter of Demeter.
He caught her up, reluctant, into his dark-hued chariot.
Bitter pain and fear seized her heart as she cried out
To her lady mother who was distant and did not hear,
But the dusky horses of the dread son of Kronos
Bore her down into the empty halls beneath the earth,
And he seized her with violence, and held her down on the black
*   earth*
With his death-dealing arms. Three times her terrible cries
Echoed across the wide plains of sea-girt Thrakonisos,
And the pale-skinned daughters of Okeanos heard the pitiful
*   lament,*
As they gathered flowers, but heeded it not . . .

Neither Pluto nor Persephone is mentioned by name in these
fragmentary verses in accordance with the ancient superstitious
dread of naming the deities of the underworld. From these
verses we may assume that the tradition, mentioned in Pausa-
nias, that one of the entrances to the Underworld was in
Thrakonisos had become well-established by the sixth century
BC. The rest of the poem appears to follow the well-known
version of the legend. Demeter complains to Pluto's brother
Zeus and obtains a reprieve for Persephone whereby she can
spend four months of the year above ground with her mother.
The only departure from the common version is that the
Daughters of Okeanos in the Oxyrinchus fragment are punished for their failure to heed Persephone's cries by being made
to become her perpetual handmaidens both below and upon
the earth.

The priesthood at the Shrine of the Great Gods in Thrakonisos was all female. Like the legendary Daughters of Okeanos,
these priestesses were known as the *leukoparthenoi* or "white
maidens" because of the exceptional whiteness of their skin.
This pallor, says Herodotus, may be attributed to the fact that
"in ecstatic states the Priestesses frequently cut themselves with
knives and bleed upon the altars of the Great Gods".

At breakfast in the dining room the next morning the only other
person present was the woman with the headscarf, Chanel suit, and
dark glasses. She ate nothing but drank large quantities of black
coffee.

It was another cloudless, crystalline Greek day, as I set out,

Leichenfeld's guidebook in hand, to explore at leisure the Sanctuary of the Great Gods. I found a rather listless Greek official lounging by the little museum and bought a ticket to the site: ten drachmas, and Eleusis had only been five.

Wandering over the site, I could occasionally see where there had been excavations, but for the most part the place was green and overgrown. It was May and the vegetation had not yet turned yellow in the withering heat of a Greek summer. The place was larger and more complex than I had expected. I saw the foundations of innumerable buildings: colonnades, temples, treasuries most of them built in honour of the Great Gods by some Hellenistic despot or other. The Sanctuary had had powerful friends.

One of the last buildings I came to was a large round structure which, according to my guidebook, was the Tholos of Olympias. Though the walls had not remained standing to a great height it was somehow impressive, unusually large for a circular classical building. Beside it a series of steps led down into a space surrounded on all sides by finely-cut dressed stone: "possibly a ritual bathing area", said the guide. On these steps sat the man I had seen at the bar in Chora and in the dining room of the hotel. He had a large drawing board on his knees and a neat array of sharpened pencils, rubbers, pens and ink bottles by his side on the step. He was drawing a long rectangular slab of masonry on which a number of human figures had been carved in low relief. They were women in flowing robes, either processing or dancing in one direction. The leading figure carried what looked like a small curved knife.

The draughtsman looked up at me, shading his eyes against the sun. His normally pink complexion flushed even pinker.

"Don't worry," I said. "I'm not going to disturb you."

"No, no no! Not at all!" The voice was high, cultivated and a little pedantic with its clipped enunciations. "I thought you were English when I saw you arriving at Chora. The way you negotiated your way through those dreadful Greek schoolchildren – 'blood will tell,' I thought!" He gave a short nervous laugh.

There was a pause and I wondered if he was going to apologise for not having offered me a lift up to the hotel the previous day. He must have heard me asking how to get there.

"Are you and your wife involved with the excavations then?" I asked.

"What? My wife? Oh, I see! Oh, dear me, no! Oh, good lord no! Oh, no! Oh, no!" Again, the nervous laugh; but this time it was longer, and even more nervous. "No, I am a confirmed bachelor. For

my sins! Ha ha! No, the lady you saw was . . . is . . . Madame
Leichenfeld. The widow of . . . er . . ."

"Dr Dietrich Leichenfeld who wrote this?" I said, holding up the
guidebook.

"Exactly so! Yes. You'll see some of my drawings in there. Let me
show you." I handed him the book, he searched through it, then gave
it back to me open at a half-page illustration. He nodded several
times, obviously proud of his achievement. It was a reconstruction of
the large sacred enclosure known as the Temenos of Seleucus,
complete with sculptures and a solitary woman in classical dress
walking in the shadow of its long colonnade. She too carried a knife.
The drawing was meticulous, elegant, a little soulless. In the bottom
left hand corner he had left his signature in tiny capital letters: S.P.
WHITTLE.

"Mr Whittle?" I said.

"Yes! That's me. I also teach Classics at Sedbergh. This is more . . .
what you might call . . . a holiday task. Interesting enough. Rewarding in its way, but it has its frustrations. It's extremely irritating
having noisy Greeks and their even noisier children scrambling all
over the place and peering at my drawings. Then one of their brats
goes missing and they come back and start jabbering at me as if I'm
to blame. You'd think it's a quiet life being an archaeological
draughtsman, wouldn't you? Believe me, it's not. Take up a nice
peaceful profession, like road mending with a pneumatic drill. At
least nobody will want to ask you dam' fool questions in a foreign
tongue."

Having unburdened himself of this, he sighed and asked me a few
questions about who I was and what I was doing here. There was
another pause after he had taken in all he wanted to hear. I asked him
whether "Madame" Leichenfeld was in charge of the excavations.

"'Oh, goodness yes! You see Leichenfeld – he died just over a year
ago – was a rich industrialist. I expect you've heard of Leichenfeld
Pharmaceuticals? He always had this passion for archaeology. About
ten years ago he left his sons by his first marriage to look after the
business and came out to finance the diggings here. He became very
involved. He met his second wife in Thessaloniki actually, but
Madame – her birth name is Aspassia Aidonides – actually comes
from Thrakonisos."

"Did Leichenfeld die out here?"

Whittle looked away. "I believe so. I wasn't around at the time.
Oh, no! I was at Sedburgh. For my sins! Yes. He was a good
archaeologist, I think. Full of enthusiasm . . . full of ideas . . ." A

pause followed during which Whittle seemed to be debating with himself whether to confide in me. He looked at me once more and spoke, this time in a subdued tone, as if afraid of being overheard.

"He became obsessed with the existence of what he called the *koile aguia*."

Whittle was searching my face for signs of curiosity and I obliged him.

"A couple of years ago, six months before he died, we uncovered a midden which contained a large number of potsherds – black figure calyxes and amphorae mostly – dating from around 500 BC The midden was situated not far from the great Temenos of Seleucus and was obviously a dump where they had thrown all the vessels containing offerings that were no longer required or had got broken. There were one or two interesting inscriptions incised on them. The most complete of these ran something like this: 'Hipponikos made this offering, having returned from the *koile aguia*.' And again, on another: 'the Great God (or Goddess)' – then something, indecipherable – 'may he (or she) bring me back safely from the *koile aguia*.' And there were other more fragmentary inscriptions on several of which parts of the words *koile* and *aguia* could be made out."

I had been searching the very inadequate Ancient Greek Dictionary in my head, and had come up with a rough translation. "*Koile Aguia* . . . Empty . . . Street?"

Whittle made a pedantic face: I knew I had not got it right. "Hmm, yes. That is a perfectly adequate *literal* translation, of course, but it can also mean . . . well, we puzzled over it for some time until Dr Leichenfeld – I think it was – suddenly remembered Pindar . . . Ah, yes! You haven't gone up to Oxford yet, have you? You won't have read any of the Odes of Pindar. Tricky stuff. Look at Olympian Nine, lines 33 and following; translates roughly as: 'Death keeps not the rod unshaken wherewith he brings down men to the hollow city of the dead.' *Koile aguia* in Pindar's highly poeticized language translates as 'hollow city', you see.

"Of course, this was tremendously exciting, because Dr Leichenfeld believed – and I think I follow him here – that those potsherd inscriptions were actually referring to the secret mystery rites of the shrine, mysteries that had remained unrevealed for nearly 2,500 years! Well, Leichenfeld became a man possessed. He conceived all sorts of theories about this hollow city, but the one he became fixated with was this. I won't give you all his reasons but here it is. He was convinced that there was an actual hollow city underground, in subterranean caves, carved out of the rock beneath our feet, and that its entrance was somewhere to be found on this very site. This would account for the legend about the entrance to the Underworld . . . Persephone and so on . . .

"He believed that the would-be initiates were taken down into the Hollow City by the Leucoparthenoi – the white maidens – and there underwent an initiation ceremony which in some way replicated their final journey through the underworld in death. Now we know that something like this happened at Eleusis, the other great site of Ancient Greek mystery religion, but this one, he thought, was on a much vaster scale. Of course, you might say, that was just the good Doctor's megalomania talking, but there were some possible indications. Have a look at this."

Whittle leapt up, looking about sharply as he did so. After mounting the steps, he clambered over the remains of the tholos wall and furtively beckoned to me to follow him into the centre of the rotunda. There he indicated what looked like a large smooth paving stone in one corner.

"Get out your handkerchief or something and brush away the sand and what not from that stone."

I did so.

"That's right. Now what do you see?'

I could see some very faint marks incised on the smooth stone surface. They looked geometrical in that they consisted of straight lines, right angles, and a few regular curves, but they did not look exactly like decoration.

"What do you make of it?" asked Whittle.

"I don't know. Some sort of hieroglyphic writing? A code?"

"No. Not exactly. What does it remind you of?"

"Well, it looks a bit like . . . a ground plan?"

"Aha! Yes. Precisely. That is what Dr Leichenfeld believed. And there are several of these, very similar, dotted around, inscribed on paving slabs. There are resemblances between these maps – as I might call them – and the general plan of the buildings you see around you here in the shrine, but there are crucial differences too. These plan things, for instance, are much more complicated. Labyrinthine, you might say. Unless you knew the way, you might get lost in them. Especially in the dark. Mmm?"

The look he gave me had no warmth. I had the feeling that the information he was imparting had a purpose, but that it was for his own benefit rather than mine. I asked if Dr Leichenfeld had actually found the entrance to the Hollow City.

"We don't know,' he said abruptly. I saw his eyes stray away from me to a point beyond my left shoulder.

"Well, well," he said brushing the knees of his trousers quite unnecessarily. "Mustn't stand around here gossiping. Must get on! No peace for the wicked . . . time and tide . . . etcetera." Again his eyes strayed from me. I looked round and saw a figure standing between two Ionic columns about fifty yards away. The sun was in my eyes, but I identified her from the tall, slender figure, the head-scarf and the film star dark glasses.

On returning to the Xenia from the site I was informed by one of the Blue Overalls that I could, after all spend another night there, but that I would have to occupy another room. I agreed and was shown the new room to which my belongings had already been moved. This one was almost identical to the last, except that it did not face the sea but looked out across the valley where lay the remains of the Sanctuary of the Great Gods.

One of the odd pastimes I had invented for myself during my travels was the "nocturnal visit to the ruins". I would take a torch and, in the dark, visit archaeological remains by its light. The strange shadows cast by the torch and its selective illuminations often created the illusion that I was walking by night in a living city, or that I was paying homage at a shrine whose god still breathed and demanded blood. Aided by imagination and silence, it would turn dusk into an ancient evening. That night I decided to go to the Sanctuary of the Great Gods.

I supped late and alone in the dining room: Whittle and Madame Leichenfeld had perhaps had their meal earlier. When I had finished I took care to leave the hotel unnoticed. I am not quite sure why, but perhaps the carafe of retsina had heightened my sense of the dra-matic. There was a near full moon, and so I hardly needed my torch. My whole body embraced the silence and the stillness. For a while, as I wandered among the moonlit ruins, occasionally stumbling over a stone or two, but not letting it bother me, I barely thought at all; I simply was. I don't share Longfellow's opinion that "the thoughts of youth are long, long thoughts". He may have imagined that *his* were, but mine in those days were brief or blissfully non-existent.

I had walked some distance, had rounded the Tholos and was just approaching the little Ionic temple erected in honour of the Great Gods by Arsinoe, wife and sister to Ptolemy of Egypt, when I heard a noise. It was not a particularly alarming noise, but it was strange to hear it at night, and it brought me to my senses. It was the sound of heavy stones being moved. I switched off my torch and stood still, just listening, to make sure I was not deceived. No. Someone in the dead of night was shifting rocks or blocks of masonry and dropping them onto others.

It was hard to tell the direction from which the sound came, but it seemed to be emanating from beyond and to the left of the Ionic temple. I placed myself carefully so that I could escape easily if I were challenged and then switched on my torch again. The beam swept across the Ionic columns and into the space beyond where it encountered nothing, literally nothing, neither earth nor scrub, nor stone. I switched off the torch and looked once more without its aid. The noise of moving stones had stopped.

Beyond the temple was a black space which reflected nothing. It was an absence, an emptiness without form or content. For several moments I stared at the void. It seemed to drain me of thought and will. Then the noise of rock moving began again; this time, nearer. It came horribly close, like someone suddenly breathing into your ear. I turned and did not stop running until I had reached the drive of the hotel. There I paused to catch my breath.

I did my best to look normal when I walked into the Hotel, but the Blue Overall behind the reception desk gave me a very searching look.

I am not sure what I was planning to do the next morning, but I had it determined for me before I had entered the dining room for breakfast. The Blue Overall at reception handed me a large brown manila envelope. There was no writing on it.

I entered the dining room and said good morning to Madame Leichenfeld, at her usual table. She was wearing a charcoal dress with belted waist and gently gathered skirt, and was drinking black coffee. She made no acknowledgment, but I was sure she was watching me covertly, so I waited till I had got back to my room to open the envelope. As I had somehow expected, it was from Whittle.

It contained two full plate photographs, both of Whittle's drawings. I recognized them from the style and the initials S. P. W. in the corner. The first was sketchier and more expressive than any of his designs I had hitherto seen. It depicted what looked like some sort of cellar or undercroft, vast in size. The low and rather irregular roof was held up by a line of stout Doric columns that extended infinitely into an obscure distance. In recesses between the columns were a number of grotesque classical sculptures. I spotted Cerberus, the Chimera, Pan and the she-goat, and others, but between two of the columns was a black doorway towards which a draped figure of indeterminate sex was crawling on its hands and knees. The second photo seemed to be the ground plan of some kind of building complex, similar to but more detailed and elaborate than the scratches I had seen on the paving stone in the Tholos. One notable feature was an arcade of columns which stretched the whole length of the diagram. About halfway down the colonnade an entrance was marked which gave access to a labyrinth of passages. In the centre of the labyrinth was a circular space which Whittle had marked by hand with a blob of red ink. On the back of the diagram some words had been scrawled hastily in pencil: "If you do not see me today, go again tonight."

I folded up both pictures, put them in my inside pocket and went out to explore the site again. I went first to the Tholos but saw no one. On the steps where I had first seen Whittle I found a tiny bottle of red India ink, that was all. Naturally I explored the area beyond the Ionic temple, but could see nothing. It was just scrub, punctuated by a few fallen slabs of masonry. Here and there I noticed that attempts had been made at excavation, but there was nothing of interest. Beyond that point there was an olive grove where a donkey cropped its stubborn grasses, after which the ground rose slowly towards Mount Aidoneos, the highest peak of Thrakonisos's central massif. Distant sheep bells clanked peacefully from its slopes; the donkey brayed like a sick man in distress.

The rest of the day I spent alone on the beach, swimming and reading. Towards evening I paid a second visit to the little chapel on the hill above the sea. The coffin had gone, and I almost persuaded myself that it had never been there. At supper Madame Leichenfeld and I were the sole occupants of the dining room. She wore black, relieved only by a small rope of pearls. I drank mineral water.

The moon shone full, but clouds had blown in from the East and sometimes they muffled the light. I believe no one had seen me leave the hotel. Was I afraid? I don't remember. All I know is that I could not possibly have turned back; something pushed me onwards. When I was standing by the Tholos I shone my torch. I swung it onto the Ionic temple and then to the left where the beam met void and was gobbled up by it. I turned the torch onto the ground just ahead of me and began to walk forward.

By the time I had gone twenty yards or so, the temple was on my right and I realized that the ground was sloping downwards, quite gradually at first. I kept my torch on the way ahead of me. Presently I came across some wide shallow marble steps and I continued on my way down. Silly things kept slipping into my mind, like the tag of Virgil: "*facilis descensus Averno*" – the way down to Hades is easy. The steps became steeper and began to twist and turn. I descended into the earth.

For a while darkness completely enveloped me. If I pointed my beam anywhere but at my feet, it met nothing; it did not even cast a faint shaft of light through the surrounding blackness. It was a long descent, in my mind that is, because I had no idea what the clocks would have to say about it: I had left my watch at the hotel.

Finally I stood on the black earth and felt rather than saw a faint grey light surrounding me. I switched off the torch so as to see my general surroundings better. What I saw gave me the impression that I was on the lonely street of a great city at night. To my right a long colonnade of marble Doric columns stretched into the distance. It resembled the drawing that Whittle had sent me, but the effect was far vaster.

I switched on the torch and saw the sculptures peering out from between the columns: Cerberus, the three-headed dog; the Chimera, Pan and the she-goat. In one of the recesses was the marble statue of a Harpy which looked like a bird of prey except for the head which was that of a beautiful blank-faced woman. I followed the colonnade along until I came to the dark entrance marked in the drawing and went in.

I was now in a labyrinth of stone clad passages, just wide enough and high enough to allow me to walk upright. I took out Whittle's plan and shone the torch on it. Why was I doing this? Was I imagining it all? What did I hope to find? I still don't know. This is only what I remember.

As I came nearer to the core of the maze I began to hear noises. Someone was groaning faintly and breathing hard. I turned a corner and almost fell over a man in shirtsleeves and pale, baggy trousers crawling away from me. He looked up. It was Whittle. He was pale and there were red scratches or gashes on his throat. I stooped to pick him up but he shook his head at me and pointed in the direction that he had been crawling. The more I hesitated the more urgently he pointed forwards. Now I could hear both his gasps for breath and someone else panting ahead of me. So I left him behind and, with the help of his map, came to the circular space, about fifteen feet in diameter, at the heart of the maze.

My torch flashed about the round chamber whose roof went up to a single central keystone at the apex. It was like being inside a smaller version of the beehive tombs at Mycenae. My torch beam continued to travel until it halted on the thing which I had heard panting in the dark. It squatted on the floor in the very middle of the chamber. What I saw first were two human heads facing me, one above the other. I then made out their white bodies, the larger clasped to the other's back, like a pair of mating toads. The body on top was that of a man, his face bloated and heavy with small glittering eyes and a long, lipless crack of a mouth that gaped uselessly. My heart began banging against my ribcage because I had recognized the face from the frontispiece of the guide. It was Dr Leichenfeld, and the face beneath his was that of his wife Aspassia. I saw for the first time her savage eyes stripped of their shades, and her hair uncovered. It was long, silky and white.

They remained there in the centre of the hive, heaving slightly, locked in their sweating, animal embrace, and though they made no move to attack me, the loathing and rage in their eyes was palpable. My right hand held the torch, my left felt in my trouser pocket and gripped Stavros's worry beads with the little metal cross.

I did not turn. I backed out of the beehive tomb and slowly retraced my steps. When I came on Whittle again I lifted him up and together we staggered out of the Hollow City, up infinite numbers of steps and into the overworld where a reluctant sun was beginning to creep up from behind Mount Aidoneos.

The hotel seemed to be empty when we staggered in. I took Whittle to his room and locked myself in mine. Later that morning I told the Blue Overalls to prepare my bill because I was going. They seemed rather indignant about this: I could not leave, they said; no bus was going from the hotel that day into Chora. I asked them to order a taxi. No, there were no taxis on Thrakonisos. Very well, I said, I would walk to Chora, "*meta podia*". They had no answer to this, so I went into the dining room, feeling that I had scored a victory.

There I received a final shock. Whittle and Madame Leichenfeld were sitting at their usual table taking breakfast. At least, he was devouring bread and jam while she was drinking her black coffee. She did not look at me at all, but Whittle stared at me for a while, blankly, without a trace of recognition on his face, while he crammed great gobbets of bread into his mouth. His skin seemed unnaturally waxy and smooth; his formerly pink complexion was as white as Madame Leichenfeld's.

Immediately after breakfast I packed my rucksack and walked the six kilometres into Chora. There I spent the morning at the bar, drinking beer and reading Dodds until the afternoon ferry took me across the sea to the mainland.

I find it rather surprising now that these events did not have more effect on me at the time. Perhaps it was because the mind goes numb when it encounters what it cannot understand; and I had been, as the Ancient Greeks used to say, "a donkey at the Mysteries". So I simply continued my tour of Greece and saw many lovely things. If there was a change in me, it was that I was less earnestly interested in the classical antiquity of the places I visited, and more generally concerned with their beauty and their people.

In this way I came to the Meteora in central Northern Greece to the East of the Pindus mountains. The place is famous for the strange rock towers, great bony fists of stone, that thrust their way upwards from the Thessalian plain. The wind whistles round them with a sound like the sea, and on them are perched the monasteries of the Meteora. Some are inhabited by large colonies of monks, and these are the most accessible and frequently visited ones, but I was determined to visit them all if I could.

The Monastery of St Simeon can only be reached by coming up from the valley floor and climbing the several hundred steps that are carved into the living rock of the pinnacle. I met no one during my ascent. At the top of the steps I rang a bell at the monastery gate. A dark-robed monk with a long black beard, sunglasses and a limp answered my summons and in perfect silence escorted me round his domain, of which he was the sole human inhabitant. At the top of some clumsy wooden steps a cat arched its back and stared at us with indifference. The monk showed me the winch and pulley system by which he hauled up provisions from the ground below, then he took me to a chapel stained with mildew but painted all over with scenes from the life of Christ.

He moved about the chapel silently pointing out to me the various images painted on the walls. Several times I noticed him staring at me; then, with a sudden, impulsive movement, he led me over to a tiny side altar, no more than an apsidal niche.

In the apse was the fresco of a scene which I later identified as the Anastasis: the Harrowing of Hell. Jesus, in a dynamic pose, unusual for the conventionally iconic style of painting, is dragging the dead from their tombs, his whole body redolent of the energy of the Risen Christ. I have come across this image many times since in Greek Orthodox iconography, but one detail, as far as I know, was unique to this particular image. The figure on the right whom Christ is dragging by the arm from his sarcophagus, was here being held back by a curious, pale, toad-like creature whose two long forelimbs were clasped round the man's legs. The spectator is witnessing a moment of perfect equilibrium and suspense, the outcome of which remains forever uncertain. Will the dead man be dragged free into Paradise, or is he to be hauled down again into the tomb?

The monk said nothing to me but his finger pointed towards the scene for a long time, indicating first the toad, then Christ, then the toad again, then Christ. Finally he made the sign of the cross over me and led me into a small painted cell where he indicated that I should sign a visitor's book. When I lifted my eyes from this task I found him standing by me with a small tray on which was a glass of ouzo and a piece of Turkish delight. While I consumed these he watched me in the same grave silence.

I had climbed down the pinnacle St Simeon, and was walking along the road back to Kalambaka when I ran into an old school friend, Mark Hutton. Like me he was going up to Oxford in the autumn to read Mods and Greats, and before leaving England we had made vague arrangements to meet up on our travels. I was surprised by how relieved I felt to see his hearty, cherubic face.

As we walked back to the village I told him about the classical sites I had visited. Without consciously avoiding the subject, I made no mention of Thrakonisos. At the end of my recital Mark stopped and studied me. A tiny frown wrinkled the freckled space between his eyebrows, a characteristic expression. My memory of it was dug up only last week while I was attending his memorial service.

"Yes," he said "I can see you haven't been lounging about on beaches, soaking up the sun and ogling maidens in bikinis. Are you sure you're not taking all this classical archaeology a bit too seriously? No, really. There's hardly any colour in your cheeks. You look like death warmed up. Come with me. A few glasses of FIX should fix it. They shall be to you as the waters of Lethe were to the departed spirits in the Underworld."

STEVE DUFFY

The Oram County Whoosit

STEVE DUFFY LIVES in North Wales. His short stories have appeared in numerous magazines and anthologies in Europe and North America. His forthcoming collection, *The Moment of Panic*, will be his third, and includes the International Horror Guild Award-winning tale, "The Rag-and-Bone Men".

Of "The Oram County Whoosit", Duffy says: "The story comes from my long-standing appreciation of the works of two true American one-offs: Charles Hoy Fort and Howard Phillips Lovecraft.

"Running their idiosyncratic world-views together in a two-fisted tale of the Yukon seemed like a fun thing to try, and I can honestly say it never once felt like hard work."

MAYBE FOR THE REST of the welcoming committee it was the proudest afternoon of their lives; I remember it mostly as one of the wettest of mine. We were standing on a platform in Oram, West Virginia, waiting for a train to pull in, and it hadn't stopped raining all day. It wasn't really a problem for anybody else at the station: the mayor had a big umbrella, and his cronies had the shelter of the awning, over by the ticket office. I had my damn hat, was all.

They belonged to the town, you see, and I didn't. I'd been sent down from Washington the day before, like the guest of honour on whom we were all waiting. Our newspaper had sprung for him to travel first-class, having sent me up ahead in a rattling old caboose – to pave the way for his greatness, I guess. Because he was some kind of a great man even then, in newspaper circles at least. Nowadays, you'll find his stories in all the best anthologies, but back then the majority of folks knew Horton Keith mostly from the stuff they read over the breakfast table; which was pretty damn good, don't get me wrong. But then so were my photographs, or so I thought, so why was I the one left outside in the cold and wet like a red-headed stepchild? It's a hell of a life, and no mistake; that's what I was thinking. I was younger then, in case you hadn't guessed: twenty-four, as old as the century. That didn't feel so old then – but it does now, here on the wrong side of 1980. Then again, the century hasn't weathered too well either, has it?

Away down the track a whistle blew, and the welcoming committee spat out their tobacco and gussied themselves up for business. Through the sheets of rain you could barely see the hills above the rooftops, but you felt them pressing in on you: that you did. Row upon row of them, their sides sheer and thickly forested, the tops lost in the dense grey clouds that had lain on the summits ever since I arrived. By now, I was starting to wonder whether there *was* any sort of blue sky up there, or whether mist and rain were the invariable order of the day. Since then I've looked into it scientifically, and what happens is this: the weather fronts blow in off the Atlantic coast, and they scoot across Virginia like a skating rink till they hit the Alleghenies. Then, those fronts get forced up over the mountains by the prevailing winds, and by the time they're coming down the other side, boy, they're dropping like a shot goose. And *then*, the whole bunch of soggy-bottom clouds falls splat on to Oram County, and it rains every goddamn day of the year. Scientifically speaking.

A puff of smoke from round the track, and then the train came into view. The welcoming committee shuffled themselves according to rank and feet above sea-level; one of them dodged off round the side of the station, and hang me for a liar if he didn't come back with a marching band, or the makings of one at least – a tuba, trombones, a half-a-dozen trumpets and a big bass drum. The musicians had been waiting someplace under shelter, or so I hoped: if not, then I wasn't going to be standing too close to that tuba when it blew. It might give me a musical shower-bath on top of my regular soaking.

The first man off the train when it pulled in was a Pullman conductor, an imperturbable Negro who looked as if he'd seen this kind of deal at every half-assed station down the line. Next was a nondescript fat man packed tight into a thin man's suit, weighed down by a large cardboard valise. If he looked uncomfortable before, you can bet he looked twice as squirrelly when the band struck up a limping rendition of "Shenandoah" and the mayor bore down on

him like a long-lost brother. One look at that, and the poor guy
jumped so high I practically lost him in the cloud – his upper slopes,
at least. In many ways he was wasted on the travelling-salesman
game; he ought to have been trying out for the Olympics over in
Paris, France. Instead, he was stuck selling dungarees to miners. Like
I said before, it's a hell of a life.

While that little misunderstanding was being cleared up, a few
carriages down my man was disembarking, quietly and without
any fuss. You may have seen photographs of Horton Keith – you
may even have seen *my* photograph of him, which just happens to
be the one on the facing-title page of his *Collected Short Stories* –
but it seems to me he always looked more like his caricature. Not
a bad-looking man: hell no! That sweep of white hair and the jet-
black cookie-duster underneath meant he'd always get recognized,
by everyone but the good folk of Oram, West Virginia at any
rate. And there was nothing wrong with his features, if you liked
'em lean and hungry-looking. But the hunger was the key, and it
came out in the drawings more vividly than in any photo I ever
took of him. I never saw a keener man, nor one more likely to
stick at it till the job got done. As a hunting acquaintance of mine
once put it: "He's a pretty good writer, but he'd have made one
hell of a bird-dog."

"Sir?" I presented myself as he stepped down from the train. He
looked me up and down and said, "Mister Fenwick?" Subterranean
rumble of a voice. I nodded, and tipped the sopping straw brim of my
hat. "Good to meet you, sir."

"Nice hat," he said, still taking my measure as he shook my
outstretched hand. "Snappy." No hint of a joke in those flinty eyes. It
was 1924, for God's sake. *Everyone* wore a straw hat back then.

"I guess it's had most of the snap soaked out of it by now," I said,
taking it off and examining it. "We could dry it out, maybe, or else
there's a horse back there on the hitching rail without a tooth in his
head. He could probably use it for his supper, poor bastard."

Keith smiled at that. Didn't go overboard or anything; but I think I
passed the test. Then, the welcoming committee were upon us.

The guest of honour was polite and everything; that is to say, he
wasn't outright rude, not to their faces. He shook all their hands, and
listened to a few bars more of "Shenandoah" from underneath the
mayor's big umbrella. I was fine, I had my snappy straw hat, which
had more or less disintegrated by now. But then the mayor, a big
moose called Kronke, wanted to cart him off in the civic automobile

for some sort of a formal reception with drinks, and Keith drew the line at that.

"Gentlemen, it's been a long day, and I need to consult with my colleague here. We'll meet up first thing in the morning, if it's all the same to you." *My colleague.* That was about the nicest thing I'd heard since I'd arrived in Oram County. It did my self-esteem a power of good; better than that, it got me a lift in the mayoral flivver as far as the McEndoe Hotel, which was where Keith and I had rooms.

The McEndoe was a rambling old clapboard palace, one of the few buildings in town that went much above two storeys. It had a view over downtown Oram that mostly comprised wet roofs and running gutters, and inevitably you found your eyes were drawn to the wooded hills beyond, brooding and enigmatic beneath their caps of cloud. Here and there you saw scars running down the hillside, old landslides and abandoned workings. Oram was a mining town, and you weren't likely to forget it; at six in the evening the big siren blew, and soon after a stream of men came trudging down main street on their way home from the pits. Watching them from the smoking lounge window as I sipped bootleg brandy from my hip flask – their pinched sooty faces, the absolute deadbeat exhaustion in their tread – I told myself there were worse things in life than getting my hat a little wet. I might have to work for a living, like these poor lugs.

"It's funny," Keith said, close up behind me. I hadn't heard him come in.

"Sorry?" I guessed he meant peculiar; God knows there was little enough that was comical about the view.

He was staring at the miners as they shuffled along in their filthy denim overalls. "I was up in the Klondike round the time of the gold rush, back in '98," he said. "Dug up about enough gold to fill my own teeth, was all. It was like that with most of the men: I never knew but half-a-dozen fellows who ever struck it rich; I mean really rich. But my God, we were keen sons-o-bitches! We'd jump out of our bunks in the morning and run over to those workings, go at it like crazy men all the length of a Yukon summer's day till it got dark, and like as not we'd be singing a song all the way home. And were we singing because we were rich? Had we raised so much as a single grain of gold? No, sir. Probably not." He took a panatella from his pocket and examined it critically. I waited for him to carry on his story, if that's what it was.

"Now these fellers," he said, indicating with his cigar: "each and every one of them will have pulled maybe a dozen tons of coal out of that hill today. No question. They found what they were looking for, all right. Found a damn sight more of it than we ever did. But you don't see them singing any songs, do you?" He looked at me, and I realized it wasn't a rhetorical question: he was waiting for an answer. I was sipping my drink at the time, and had to clear my throat more quickly that I'd have liked.

"They're working for the company," I said, as soon as I could manage it through my coughing. "You fellers were working for yourselves. Man doesn't sing songs when he knows someone else is getting eighty, ninety cents out of every dollar he earns."

"No," agreed Keith. "No, he doesn't. But that's just economics, after all. You know what the main difference is?" I had a pretty good idea, but shrugged, so that he'd go on. "We were digging for gold," he said simply, "and these poor bastards ain't. Call a man an adventurer, send him to the top of the world so he's half-dead from the frostbite and the typhus and the avalanches, and he's happy, 'cause he knows he might – just might! – strike it rich. Set him to dig coal back home day in, day out for a wage, and he's nothing but a slave. It's the difference between what you dream about, and what you wake up to."

It sounds commonplace when I write it down. That's because you don't hear the way his voice sounded, nor see the animation in his face. I don't know if I can put that into words. It wasn't avaricious, not in the slightest. I never met a man less driven by meanness or greed. It was more as if that gold up in the Klondike represented all the magic and excitement he'd ever found in the world; as if the idea had caught hold of him when he was young and come to stand for everything that was fine and desirable, yet would always remain slightly out of reach, the highest, sweetest apple on the tree. That he kept reaching was what I most admired about him, in the end: that he knew he wasn't ever going to win the prize, and yet still reckoned it was worth fighting for. The Lord loves a trier, they say, but sometimes I think he's got a soft spot for the dreamer, too.

"Well, these fellows here might have been digging for coal," I said, offering him a light, "but seems as if a couple of 'em may have lit on something else, doesn't it?"

"Indeed," said Keith, glancing at me from beneath those jet-black bushy eyebrows before bending to the flame of the match. "Now you mention it, I guess it is kind of time we talked about things." He fished out another stogie and offered it to me.

I sat up straight and gave it my best stab at looking keen and judicious. Keith probably thought I'd gotten smoke in my eyes.

"What do you think we actually have here, Fenwick?" He honestly sounded as if he wanted to know what I thought. Back in my twenties, that was still pretty much of a novelty.

"Toad in a hole," I said promptly. "There's a hundred of 'em in the newspaper morgue – seems like they pop up every summer, around the time the real news dries up."

"Toad in a hole," said Keith thoughtfully. He gestured with his cigar for me to continue. Emboldened, I did so.

"The same story used to run every year in the papers out West," I said, to show I'd done my homework and wasn't just any old newspaper shutterbug. "Goes like this: some feller brings in a lump of rock split in half, it's got a tiny little hole in the middle. See there, he says? That's where the frog was. Jumped clean out when I split the rock in two, he did. Here he is, look – and he lays down some sorry-looking sun-baked pollywog on the desk. Swears with his hand on his heart: 'it happened just the way I'm telling you, sir, so help me God'. And the editor's so desperate, he usually runs with it." I spread my hands. "That's about the way I see it, Mr Keith."

Keith nodded. "So you don't believe such a thing could happen?"

"Huh-uh." With all the certainty of twenty-four summers. "Toads just can't live inside rocks. Nothing could. No air. No sustenance." Speaking of sustenance, I offered him a pull on my hip flask. Keith accepted, then said:

"But these miners here – they don't claim to have found a toad exactly, now, do they?" He was watching my face narrowly all the while through a pall of cigar smoke, gauging my reactions.

"No sir. They say they've found a whoosit."

"A whoosit."

"Exactly that. A whoosit, just like P. T. Barnum shows on Broadway. A jackalope. A did-you-ever. An allamagoosalum."

"Jersey devil," said Keith, entering into the spirit of the thing.

"Feegee mermaid," I amplified. "Sewn-up mess of spare parts from the taxidermy shop. Catfish with a monkey's head. That's the ticket." I felt pleased we'd nailed the whole business on the head. Maybe we could be back in Washington by this time tomorrow evening.

Keith was nodding still. He showed every sign of agreeing with me, right up until he said – musing aloud it seemed – "So, how does a thing like that get inside a slab of coal, do you suppose, Mr Fenwick?"

"Well, that's just it. It doesn't, sir." Had I not made myself clear?

"But this one did." His deep-set eyes bored into me, but I held my ground.

"So they say. I guess we'll see for ourselves in the morning, sir."

Unexpectedly, Keith dropped me a wink. "The hell with that. I was thinking we might take a stroll down to the courthouse after dinner and save ourselves a night of playing guessing games. Skip all the foofaraw the mayor's got planned. That is, unless you have plans for the rest of the evening?" A wave of his cigar over sleepy downtown Oram.

I spread my hands, palms up. "What do you know? Clara Bow just phoned to say she couldn't make it."

And so, in the absence of Miss Bow's company, I found myself walking out down the main street of Oram with Horton Keith, headed for the courthouse. We'd passed it in the mayor's car earlier that afternoon; Kronke had told us that was where the whoosit was being kept, under lock and key and guarded by his best men. If the man who was on duty out front when we arrived was one of Kronke's best, then I'd have loved to have seen the ones he was keeping in reserve. He was a dried-up, knock-kneed old codger with hardly a tooth left in his head, and when Keith told him we were the men from Washington come to see the whoosit, he waved us right through. "In there," he said, without bothering to get up off his rocking chair. "What there is of it, anyways."

"What there is of it?" Keith's heavy brows came down.

"Feller who found it, Lamar Tibbs? Had him a dispute with the mine bosses when he brung it up last week. They said, any coal comes out of this shaft belongs to the company, and that's that. So Lamar, he says well, thisyer freak of nature ain't made of coal though, is it? Blind man can see that. And they say, naw, it ain't. And Lamar, he says, it's more in the nature of an animal, ain't it? And they say, reckon so. And Lamar says, well, I take about a thousand cooties home out of this damn pit of yours ever' day, so I reckon this big cootie here can come along for the ride as well. And he up an took it home with 'im." The caretaker cackled with senile glee at Lamar's inexorable logic. I guess it was a rare thing for anybody to get the better of the company, let alone some poor working stiff. But more to the point:

"You're saying the whoosit isn't actually in there?"

"No sir. It's over to Peck's Ridge, up at the Tibbs place. Mayor's plannin' to take you there in the automobile tomorrow, I believe – first thing after the grand civic breakfast."

This was starting to look like a snipe hunt we'd been sent on. Keith jabbed his cigar butt at the courthouse. "So what *have* you got in here?"

"Lump o' coal it came out of," said the caretaker proudly. "Got an exact imprint of the whoosit in it, see? Turn it to the light, you can see everything. Large as life, twice as ugly."

"Is that right?" Keith said. "Company hung on to the lump of coal, I guess?"

"That they did," agreed the last surviving veteran of the Confederate army. "All the coal comes out of that mine's company coal – them's the rules. Mayor's just holdin' it for safekeeping, is all."

"Exactly so," said Keith. "Well, thank you, sir." He slipped a dollar into the caretaker's eager hand – assuming it was eagerness that made it tremble so. "Now if you could see your way to showing us where they're keeping it, we'll quit bothering you."

"They got it in the basement," said the caretaker, leaning back in his rocker and expelling a gob of tobacco juice. "Keep goin' down till you can't go down no more, mister, an' that'll do it."

The basement of that courthouse was like a mine itself; you might almost have believed they'd dug the whoosit out right there, in situ. Keith and I came to the bottom of a winding flight of stairs and found ourselves in a musty sort of crawlspace, its farther corners filled with shadows the single electric bulb on the ceiling couldn't hope to reach. The ceiling was low enough that we both had to stoop a little, and most of the floor was taken up with trunks and boxes and filing cabinets full of junk. Thank God we weren't looking for anything smaller than a pork barrel. We'd have been down there all night. As it was, we began on opposite sides of the basement and aimed to get the job done in something under an hour.

"This is annoying," Keith called over his shoulder. "These damn rubes don't realize what they've got a hold of here."

"Toad in a hole," I called back. Keith ignored me.

"This miner fellow—"

"Lamar Tibbs," I sang out in a poor approximation of the caretaker's Virginian twang.

"—he probably thinks he's sitting on a crock of gold, just like the mayor here and the mining company with their slab of coal. But the two things *apart* don't amount to a hill of beans, and they don't have the sense to see it."

"How so?" I didn't think the whole thing amounted to much, myself.

"Because the one authenticates the other, don't you see? Look here, I'm the authorities, okay? This here's some sort of a strange beast you claim to have found in the middle of a piece of coal. Who's to say it's not a, a, what-d'ye-call-'em . . .?"

"Feegee mermaid."

"Feegee mermaid, exactly." A grunt, as he moved some heavy piece of trash out of the way. "Nothing to make a man suppose it ever saw the inside of a slab of coal – *without the coal to prove it*. The imprint of the beast in the coal goes to corroborate the story, see?"

"Yes, but—" I was going to point out that you didn't find beasts, living or dead, inside slabs of coal anyway, so there was no story there to corroborate, only a tall tale out of backwoods West Virginia. But Keith didn't seem to be interested in that self-evident proposition.

"And it's the same thing with the coal. Suppose there is an imprint of something in there? What good is it without the very thing that *made* that imprint? It's just the work of a few weekends for an amateur sculptor, is all." He bent to his task again, shoving more packing-cases out of the way. "They don't understand," he muttered, almost to himself. "You need the two together."

"Even if you did have the two things, though . . ." I wasn't letting this one go unchallenged ". . . it still wouldn't prove anything, in and of itself. It might go some way towards the *appearance* of proof – hell, it might even make a good enough story for page eight of the newspaper, I guess. That's your business. I just take the pictures, that's all. But at the end of the day . . ."

At the end of the day, Keith wasn't listening. I happened to glance in his direction at that moment, and saw as much immediately. He was standing in the far corner of the basement, hands on hips, staring at something on the floor – from where I was, I couldn't make it out. I called his name. I had to call again, and then a third time, before he even noticed. When he did, he looked up with an odd expression on his face.

"Come over here a second, Fenwick," he called, and his voice sounded slightly strained. "Think I've found something."

I crossed to where he was standing. In that corner the light was so dim I could hardly see Keith, let alone whatever it was he'd found, so the first thing we did was lay ahold of it and drag it to the centre of the basement, right beneath the electric bulb. It was heavy as hell, and we pushed it more than carried it across the packed-mud basement floor.

It was lying inside an open packing-case, all wrapped up in a bit of old tarpaulin. You could see the black gleam of coal where Keith had unwrapped it at one end. "You raise it up," muttered Keith, and again I heard that unusual strain in his voice; "I'll get the tarpaulin off of it."

I laid hold of it and heaved it upright, and Keith managed to get the tarp clear. It was just one half of the slab, as it turned out; its facing piece lay underneath wrapped in more tarpaulin. Stood on its end, the half-slab was roughly the size of a high-back dining chair: it would have weighed a lot more, more than we could have dreamed of shifting, probably, except that it was all hollowed out, as if someone had sawn a barrel in half right down its centre.

The hollow space was nothing more than an inky pool of shadow at first, till I tilted the slab toward the light. Then, its shiny black surfaces gave up their secrets, and the electric light reflected off a wealth of curious detail. I gave a low whistle. Whoever's work this was, he was wasted on Oram. He ought to have been knocking out statues for the Pope in Rome. For it was the finest, most intricately detailed job of carving you ever saw – *intaglio*, I believe they call it, where the sculptor carves in hollows instead of relief. There was even a kind of *trompe l'oeil* effect: if you looked at the cavity while turning the whole thing round slightly, the contours seemed to stand out in projection, that strange hollow form suddenly becoming filled-out and real. I'd have to say it was actually a little bit unsettling, for a cheap optical illusion. It was as if you were looking at the sky at night, the black gulf of space, and the stars all of a sudden took on a shape, the shape of something vast and unimaginable . . .

"My God." A fellow would have been hard put to recognize Keith's voice. It made me turn from the slab of coal to look at him. He was staring open-mouthed at the hollow space at the heart of the slab, with an expression I took at first to be awe. Only later did I come to recognize it as something more like horror.

"It's pretty good at that," I allowed. "The detail . . ."

"It's exact in every detail," said Keith, in wonderment. "You could use it for a mould, and you'd cast yourself a perfect copy." He shook his head, never taking his eyes off of the coal slab.

"Copy of what, though?" I squinted at the concavity, turned it this way and that to get a sense of it in three dimensions. "It's like nothing I've ever seen – it's a regular whoosit, all right. Are those things supposed to be tentacles, there? Only they've got claws on the end, or nippers or something. And where's its head supposed to be?"

"The head retracts," said Keith, almost as if he was reading it from a book. "Like a slug drawing in on itself."

I stared at him. "Beg your pardon, sir?"

"You said it's like nothing you've ever seen," said Keith. "Well, I've seen it. Or something exactly like it"

"You *have*?" It was all I could think of to say.

Keith nodded. "Let's get out of this damn mausoleum," he said abruptly, turning away from the packing-case and its contents. "I'll tell you up in the real world, where a man can breathe clean air, not this infernal stink." And with that he turned his back and was off, stumping up the wooden steps and out of the basement, leaving me to rewrap and repack the slab of coal as best I could before hastening after him.

I was full of questions, all of them to do with the strange artefact we'd been looking at. I have to confess, the level of realism the unknown sculptor had managed to suggest had impressed me – not to say unnerved me. I mentioned before the optical illusion of solidity conjured out of the void, that sensation of seeing the actual thing, not just the impression it had made. That actually began to get to you after a while. Three-dimensional, I said? Well, maybe so. But the longer you looked at it, the dimensions started to looked wrong somehow; impossible, you might say.

On top of that was Keith's admission that he'd seen the like before. What did he mean by that? And over and above everything . . . well, Keith was right. We needed to be in the fresh air. Fact was, it stank in that damn basement: I've never known a smell like it. It was as if a bushel of something had gone bad, and been left to fester for an awful long time.

An awful long time, at that.

Back at the hotel Keith went straightaway up to his room for about an hour, leaving me to pick at my evening meal in the all-but-empty dining room. The smell down in that basement had killed my appetite, pretty much; in the end I pushed my plate aside and went to the smoking lounge. That was where Keith found me.

He looked better than he had back outside the courthouse, at least. I'd found him leaning against the side of the building, looking as if he was going to be sick: he had that grey clammy cast to his face. I asked him was he all right, and he waved me away. Now, there was a little more colour in him, and his eyes were focussing properly again, not staring off into the middle distance the way they do when a fellow is on the verge of losing his lunch.

"You got any of that brandy left?" he said, taking the chair opposite mine. "Medicinal purposes, you understand."

"You're in luck, as it happens," I said, offering him the flask. "I've just taken an inventory of our medical supplies."

"Good," said Keith, and took a long swallow. His eyes teared up a little, but that was only natural. It had kind of a kick to it, that bathtub Napoleon. You could have used it to open a safe, if you'd run out of blasting gelignite.

"Well, then." Keith handed me back the flask. "I believe I owe you a story, Mr Fenwick. Recompense for leaving you with the baby, down there in the basement."

I waved a hand, which could equally be taken to mean, *no problem, don't trouble yourself about it*, or – as I hoped Keith would read it – *go on, go on, you interest me strangely*. The reason I waved a hand instead of actually saying either of those things was because I'd just taken a pull on that flask myself, and was temporarily speechless.

Keith settled back in his armchair and crossed his long thin legs. "It might help explain why I took this assignment," he said, throwing me a cigar and lighting one himself, "why I asked for it." He puffed on his stogie till it was properly lit, sending up a wreath of smoke above his head. Then from the heart of that smokescreen he told me the following tale, in about the time it took us to reduce those big Havanas down to ash.

"I was thirty at the time: a dangerous age, Mr Fenwick. You'll learn that, soon enough. I was working on the *Examiner* in San Francisco when gold fever hit up in the Yukon, back in '98. The news came at exactly the right time, so far as I was concerned – a lot of other folks too, among that first wave of prospectors and adventurers. I was missing something, we all were: the frontier had been closed, and the wild days of excitement out West were history, or so it seemed. For better or worse, the job of shaping the nation was finished, over and done with, and us latecomers had missed the chance to leave our stamp on it. We felt as if we'd all been running West in search of something – something magical and unique, that would make real men out of us – only once we'd gotten there, it had already set sail out of the Golden Gate, and there was no way we could follow. The Gay Nineties, you say? I tell you, there were folks dying in the street in San Francisco. Hunger, want . . . maybe nothing more than heartbreak.

"So you can bet we jumped at the chance to go prospecting, away up in the frozen wastes. That was a new frontier, sure enough: maybe the last frontier, and we weren't about to miss it. And we piled on to those coffin-ships out of Frisco and Seattle, hundreds of us at a time;

'stampeders', we called ourselves. There was about as much thinking went into it as goes into a stampede.

"The Canucks wouldn't let you into the country totally unprepared, though. You had to have a ton of goods, supplies and suchlike, else they'd stop you at the docks. And that took some getting together; 1,100 pounds of food, plus clothing and equipment, horses to carry it with, that sort of thing. I was travelling light – reckoned to hire sled-dogs up in Canada – but even so, my goods took some lugging at the wharf.

"So we sailed North. A thousand miles out of Seattle we made the Lynn Canal, which was where every one of us bold prospectors had to make his first big decision. Where was he going to disembark? 'Cause there were two trails, see, up to Dawson and the gold-fields, 600 miles due north. You could take the easy route, avoiding all the big mountains – that was Skagway and the White Pass. The other route started in Dyea, and it took in the Chilkoot Pass, leading on to the lakes. Even us greenhorns knew about the Chilkoot by that time.

"A lot of folk chose Skagway, but I never heard anything good about that town. In Indian it's 'the place where a fair wind never blows', which pretty much sums it up, I guess. Leave it to the Indians to know which way the wind blows. Soapy Smith's gang ran the town – he was an old-time con-artist out of Georgia, and he knew a hundred ways to pick the pockets of every rube that staggered down the gangplank. Twenty-five cents a day wharf rates on each separate piece of goods. Lodging-houses where they fleeced you on the way in and the way out. Saloons and whorehouses; casinos with rigged wheels and marked cards. Portage fees. Tolls all the way along the trail – and bandits too, armed gangs and desperadoes, hand in glove with the 'official escorts', like as not. No sir: I chose Dyea, which was not a hell of a lot more salubrious, but at least you didn't have Soapy's hand in your britches all the while.

"There was ice all over the boat as it hove into Dyea. It looked like a ghost ship, and I guess we were a sorry-enough looking bunch of ghosts as we stumbled off. The mountains came right down to the outskirts of town; took us two weeks of hard going to climb as far as Sheep Camp, at the base of the Chilkoot. I tell you: there were lots of men took one look at that mountainside and gave it up on the spot, stayed on in camp and made a living for themselves as best they could. You couldn't call them the stupid ones, not really. A thousand feet from base to summit, sheer up and down, straight as a beggar can spit? Any sane man would have turned round and said 'scuse me, my mistake, beg your pardon.

"We were obliged to stay in Sheep Camp for the best part of March, till the pass came navigable. Bad weather, and the worst kind of terrain; even the Indian guides wouldn't touch it in those conditions. It was just before spring thaw, and the weather was ornery in the extreme. Minus sixty-five one night, by the thermometer in Lobelski's General Store. It stayed light from nine-thirty in the morning to just before four in the afternoon. The rest of it was pitch dark and endless cold.

"They were building some sort of a hoisting-gear up the Chilkoot, the tramway they called it, but I never saw it finished. I hauled my goods up there, the old fashioned way. I could have paid the Indians to do it for me, a dollar a pound, but I didn't have 2,000 dollars to spare. That was why I was bound for the Yukon in the first place. So I hauled every last case up that mountainside, forty trips in all. I was raw from the chafing of the ropes on my shoulders, and I was nigh on crippled by the exhaustion and the cold – but I managed it. Somehow. Don't ask me how. It'd kill me now if I tried it.

"Truth is, I don't know how it didn't kill me back then. Fifteen hundred toeholds in the ice, up a trail no more than two feet wide. Take a step to left and right, and you were in the powder stuff, loose and treacherous. If a man slipped, it was all up with him; you never saw him again. That pass was filled with the bodies of good men.

"Anyway! Come April I was over the Chilkoot and heading toward Dawson, a mere 550 miles off. The trail led along Lake Lindeman and Lake Bennett: if you waited for the thaw, the sheer volume of melt coming down off the mountains turned the rivers into rapids. If you went early, like I did, it was just a question of praying the ice wouldn't break. You put it out of your mind, till it came time to camp at night and you'd hear the ice creaking and groaning below you. We rigged up the sleds with sails, and the wind used to push us along at a fine clip. All we had to do was trust in the Lord and watch out for the cracks.

"The lakes weren't properly clear of ice till the end of May, and by that time we bold sled-skaters were already in Dawson, just six months after we'd first set out to strike it rich. Dawson was a stumpy, scroungy kind of town at the bend of the river, set on mudflats and made of nothing much but mud, or so it seemed. Five hundred people lived there as a rule: gold fever pushed that up to 12,000 by the start of the year, 30,000 by that summer's end. It was a breeding ground for typhoid – I stayed clear of the place, except when I made my victualling run once a week.

"I was working my claim south-east of Dawson city, out among the dried-up river beds. That was where I got my crash-course in mining – a year earlier, I'd have thought you just scuffed around in the dirt with the toe of your boot till you turned up some nuggets. Not in Yukon territory. You had to dig your way down to the pastry, we called it, the layers where the gold lay, through forty, fifty feet of rock and frost-hard river muck; tough going? Yes, sir. You broke your back on nothing more than a hunch and a hope. Besides that, all you had was the comradeship of your fellows and the one chance in a hundred thousand your claim would pay out big. I almost came to value the one more than the other, because when the chips were down you could rely on the comradeship at least. Money ain't everything, not in those latitudes. Maybe not in these.

"All through that summer I dug away in the dried-up beds, till it came autumn, and time to make another big decision. The last boat out of Dawson sailed on September the sixteenth, and a lot of fellows I knew were on it, the ones who'd struck it rich and the ones who'd simply had enough. I didn't fall into either camp: I waved that boat away from the landing, and made my plans to stay on through the winter. Plenty did: the proud and foolish ones like me, who couldn't quite bring themselves to admit defeat and go home with only a few grains of gold in their pokes; the optimists, who couldn't believe that the best was over, that the juicy lodes were already worked out and the rest only dry holes; and worst of all the hard core, the ones who'd caught it worst of all, who had no place left for them back in the real world. Quite a bunch.

"I remember one evening in that October of '98, standing up on the banks outside my camp and looking out over the dry gulches. Some of the fellows were burning fires at their workings, trying to melt the frost so the digging would go easier. It lit up all that strange and beautiful landscape like the surface of some alien planet, the fires like lanterns shining out in the gloom, and the way the wood-smoke smell drifted up across the bluffs . . . I could have stayed there for the rest of my life, or so I told myself. I sat and watched those fires till it got full dark, anyway, and later on that night I saw the aurora for the first time, the Northern lights, how they flickered green and magical in the moonless sky.

"The week after, it began to snow for real, and I had to strike camp and head back for Dawson. Some didn't; some stayed out on the flats, and that's where the story really begins.

"I must've been back in Dawson a couple of months, because it was nigh on Christmas when we got word from out on the workings that they'd found something strange – not gold, which would have been strange enough by that time, but something weird, something the likes of which nobody had ever seen. At least, that's what Sam Tibbets told us, when he come in to Dawson for supplies. It was the three Tibbets brothers worked the claim, along with a half-dozen other fellows all hailed from Maine: they were a syndicate, all for one and one for all. They hadn't found a lot of gold – hardly enough for one man to retire on, let alone nine – but Sam reckoned if the worst came to the worst, they could always go into the exhibition business with this thing they'd dug up out of the frost.

"'It's a new wonder of the world, or maybe the oldest one of all', I can hear him saying it, hunkered down by the stove in the saloon with the frost melting in his moustache and the steam rising off his coat; 'I reckon it must 'a turned up late for last boarding on the ark, or else Noah throwed it overboard on account of its looks.'

"'What d'you mean?' I asked him.

"'Aw, Horton, you never saw such a cretur as this,' he said earnestly – he was straight-ahead and simple, was Sam Tibbets. He was one of the original ice-skaters from back on the lakes in the spring: I liked him a lot. 'It's like a plug-ugly dried-up old thing the size of one of them barrels there . . .' he pointed at a hogshead in the corner '. . . and about that same shape, 'cept maybe it comes to sort of a narrow place up top. It's got long thin arms, only dozens of 'em, all around, and there's nippers on the end, same as a lobster? I swear there ain't never been such a confusion. Wait till we haul it back out of here, come the thaw. They'll pay a dime a head back in Frisco just to clap eyes on it, I tell you!'

"It was a plan at that, and if nothing else it made me mighty curious to take a look at this thing, whatever it was. The way Sam told it, they'd been digging through the frozen subsoil when they turned it up: he thought it must have gotten caught in the river away back, stuck in the mud and froze up when the winter came. How deep was it, I asked him, thinking the deeper it lay, the older it must be; 'bout twenty feet, he reckoned.

"'So it's dead, then, this thing?' That was Cy Perrette, who was not the smartest man in the Yukon territory, not by a long chalk. He was staring at Sam Tibbets like a dog listening to a sermon.

"'It better be,' said Sam. 'It's been buried in the earth since Abraham got promoted to his first pair of long pants, ain't it?' Men started laughing all through the saloon, and pretty soon Sam had a line of drinks set down before him. Dawson folks appreciated a good tale, see: something to take their minds off the cold and dark outside, and the endless howling winds. I remember the aurora was particularly strong that night; when I staggered out of the saloon and the cold knocked me sober, there it was, fold upon fold, glowing and rippling from horizon to horizon. I remember thinking, that's what folk mean when they say 'unearthly'. Something definitively not of this planet, something more to do with the heavens than the earth.

"Come morning there was quite a little gang of us, all bent on following Sam Tibbets back to his camp for a look-see at the eighth wonder. Sam was agreeable, said he'd waive our admission fees just this once, on account of the circumstances, and we set off towards the workings. It was a cheerful excursion; the sleds were always lighter when you had company along the trail.

"Sam broke into a run when we reached the banks of the river bed; wanted to welcome us to the site of their discovery, I suppose, like any showman would. He clambered up a snowdrift; then, when he reached the top, he stopped, and even from down below I thought he looked confused. He let go his sled; it slithered down the bank and I had to look sharp, else it'd have taken me off at the shins. 'Sam!' I called him, but he didn't look round. I scrambled up after him, cussing him for a clumsy oaf and the rest of it; then I saw what he'd seen, and the words got choked off in my throat.

"Straight away you could see something was wrong. Sam and his partners had built themselves a cabin by the workings, nothing fancy, but solid enough to take whatever the Yukon winter could throw at it, they'd thought. Now, one end of that cabin was shivered all to pieces. The logs were snapped and splintered into matchwood, just exactly as if someone had fired a cannonball at it. Only the cannon would have had to be on the inside of the cabin, not the outside: there was wreckage laying on the ground for a considerable distance, all radiating out and away from the stoved-in part.

"That wasn't the worst part, though. In amongst the wreckage you could see the snow stained red, and there was at least one body mixed in with the blown-out timber. I saw it straight away; I know Sam had too, because he turned around and looked at me as I grabbed his arm, and I could hear this high sort of keening noise he was making, like some kind of machine that's slipped its gears, about to break itself to pieces. It was the purest, most fundamental sound of grief I'd ever heard coming out of a human being. I've never forgotten it to this day.

"My first thought as we began running down the banks was: dynamite. Plenty of the miners used it to start off an excavation, or to clear whatever obstructions they couldn't dig around. It wasn't unusual for a camp such as this to have a few sticks laying around in case of emergencies. Now, if you got careless . . .? You understand what I'm saying. That was my first assumption, anyway. It lasted until I got in amongst the wreckage.

"Dynamite couldn't account for it, was all. It couldn't have left cups and bottles standing on the table, and still blown a hole in the cabin wall big enough to drive a piled-up dogsled through. It wouldn't have left a man's body intact inside its clothes, and taken his head clean off at the neck. And it couldn't have done to that head . . . the things I saw done to the head of poor Bob Gendreau. Put it this way: my second assumption was bears; them, or some other wild animal. Bears roused too soon from their hibernation, hungry and enraged, coming on the camp and smashing it all to pieces. But again, when you looked at all the evidence, that didn't sit right either.

"There was a side of bacon hanging on the wall still; bears would have taken that. And they wouldn't have stopped at knocking off the head of Bob Gendreau; that's not where the sustenance lies, and all a bear ever looks for is sustenance. Whatever took Bob's head off, then mauled it so his own mother wouldn't have known it; that thing wasn't doing what it did out of blind animal instinct, nor yet the need for nourishment. That thing was doing what it did because it wanted to – because it liked it, maybe. Some say man is the lord of all creation because he's the only creature blessed with reason; others, that he's set apart from the rest of the beasts because he takes pleasure in killing, and there's no other animal does that. But up in that cabin I learned different. Now, I believe there's at least one other creature on this planet that draws satisfaction from its kills, and not just a square meal. I got my first inkling of that when I saw what was left of Harvey Tibbets.

"He was jammed into an unravaged corner of the cabin. It looked as if he'd been trying to dig clean through the packed-mud floor; there was a hole in the ground at his feet, and his fingers were all bloodied and torn. You could see that, because of the way he was laying; hunkered down on his haunches, facing out towards the room, for all the world like a Moslem when he prays to Mecca. His forehead was touching the earth, and his arms were stretched out before him. His hands were clenched in the dirt, still clutching two last handfuls of it even in death. There was no mistaking his attitude: he'd been grovelling before whatever had passed through that cabin. Begging it for mercy.

"And whatever it was had looked down upon him as he crouched there; listened to his screams, I guess. And had it granted him mercy? I don't know. I can't speak as to its motivations. What it *had* done, was sever both his hands, cut 'em clear off at the wrists. Remember before, when I said he appeared to have been digging in the dirt, trying to escape? Both his hands were still there, torn-up and bloody like I said. And he was kneeling down with his arms outstretched; you remember that. But in between the stumps at the end of his forearms and the tattered beginnings of his wrists, there was nothing but a foot of blood-soaked earth. Whatever had killed him had cut off both his hands, and watched him bleed out on the floor while he begged it for leniency. Now what sort of a creature does that sound like to you?

"Indians, was what some of the men thought; Indians touched with the windigo madness. But how could any man, crazy or sane, have knocked an entire gable end out of the cabin that way? There was an Indian with us, one of the portageurs, a quiet, dark-complected fellow named Jake: he wouldn't come within ten yards of the devastation, but he told me it wasn't any of his kin. 'Not yours either,' he said after a pause, and I asked him what he meant by it.

"He took me aside and pointed in the snow. There was a mess of our prints, converging on the cabin so that the ground outside the blasted-out place was practically trampled bare. All around the snow was practically virgin still, and Jake showed me the only thing that sullied it. A single set of tracks, leading from the cabin and headed away north, down along the gulch. I say leading from the cabin, mostly because there wasn't anything in the cabin could have made those prints, living or dead. If it wasn't for that, then I don't know that I could have told you what direction whatever made the prints was travelling in. They weren't regular footmarks, you see, and they were all wrong in their shape, in their arrangement – in their number, even. And the weirdest thing about them? They stopped dead about fifty yards out. A step, then another, then nothing but the undisturbed snow, as far as the eye could see.

"Later on, once the shock of it had passed, I asked Jake what could have made those prints, and he told me an old legend of his people, about the time before men walked these northern wastes, when it was just gods and trolls and ogres.

"Back then, he said, there were beings come down from the sky, and they laid claim to the Earth for a long season of destruction. They were like pariahs between the stars, these beings: not even the Old Ones, the gods without a worshipper, could bear to have them near. They were cast out in the end, as well as the Old Ones could manage it: but the story goes that some of them escaped exile by burrowing down into the earth and waiting their time, till some cataclysm of the planet might uncover them. They could wait: nothing on Earth could kill them, you see. They couldn't die in this dimension. They would only sleep, through geologic ages of the planet, till something disturbed them and they came to light once more.

"That was the legend: I got it out of Jake later that same day, when the party had split up and we were searching all the low land around the arroyo. The mood of the party was shocked and unforgiving: something had done this to our friends, and we were bound to avenge them the best we could. The trail of footprints had given some of the fellows pause for thought, but I think most of them just took the prints as simple evidence of something they could go after, some critter they could corner and shoot. They didn't reflect too much on what could have made them. If they'd stopped and thought it through, I doubt whether any one of them would have been prepared to do what we ended up doing that night: lying in ambush and waiting for the culprit to come back to the cabin.

"The reasoning – so far as it went – was, if it's an animal, it'll come back where there's food. If it's a man, it'll come back because that's what murderers do: revisit the scene of the crime. Pretty shaky logic, I know, but the blood of the party was up. We were really just looking for trouble, and we damn near found it, too.

"As night fell we set up an ambuscade in the ruins of the cabin. We'd buried the bodies by then, of course, but inside the cabin still felt bad; stank, too, like something had lain dead in there all through the summer, and not just a few hours in the bitter icy cold. We had the stove going: we had to, else we'd have froze to death. We had guards at all the windows, and a barricade at the wrecked end of the cabin. It didn't matter what direction trouble might be coming at us from, we had it covered. Or so we thought.

"God, we were so cold! The wind died down soon after dark, and that probably saved us all from the hypothermia. Still it was like a knife going through you, that chill, and you had to get up and move around every so often, just to prove to yourself you were still alive. We passed around a bottle of whiskey we found among the untouched provisions, and waited.

"All across the wide northern sky there was a glow, cold and mysterious, as far removed as you could imagine from the world of men and their paltry little hopes and fears. The aurora was so vivid that night, you might have read a newspaper by it. All the better to see whatever's coming, we thought; at least it can't creep up on us and take us unawares, not in this light.

"Somewhere in the very pit of the night, just when the body's at its weariest and wants only to drop down and sleep, an uncanny sort of stillness fell across the snowed-up river bed. What was left of the wind dropped entirely, and the only sound beneath the frozen far-off stars seemed to come from the creaking of the stove round which we sat, the cracking and spitting of the logs that burned inside it. A few of us looked round at each other; all of us felt it now, the heightened expectation, the heightened fear. Without words, as quietly as we could, we moved away from the stove and took up our places at the barricade.

"I remember – so clearly! – how it felt, crouching behind that mess of planks and packing-cases, waiting to see what might show its head above the snow-banks. A couple of times I thought I saw something, away out beyond the bounds of night vision. Even under the greenish radiance of the aurora I couldn't be sure: *was* that something moving? *Could* it be? One time Joe McRudd discharged his rifle, and scared us all to hell. 'Sorry,' he mouthed, when we'd all regained our senses. He cleared his throat. 'Thought I saw sump'n creepin' round out there.'

"'Save your ammo,' grunted Sam Tibbets, not even bothering to look at poor Joe. 'Keep your nerve.' That was all. Directly after that it was upon us.

"It came from the only direction we hadn't reckoned on: overhead. There was a thump on the roof of the cabin, and then a splintering as the boards were wrenched off directly above our heads. It caused a general confusion: everyone jumped and panicked, and no one really knew what was happening. Joe McRudd's rifle went off again; some of the other fellows shot as well, I don't know what at. Before I could react, Sam Tibbets was snatched up from alongside me – something had him fast around the head and was dragging him off of his feet, up towards the hole in the roof.

"I grabbed him around the waist, but it was no use: I felt my own feet lifting clear of the floor as Sam was hoisted ever upward. He was trying to call out, but whatever had snatched him was laying tight hold around the whole of his head and neck, and all I could hear was a muffled roar of anger and pain – fear, too, I guess. It was as if he was being lynched, hung off a high bough and left to swing there while he throttled. I called to the rest of them to help, to hang on to us: a couple of them laid ahold of my legs and heaved, and for a moment we thought we had him. Then there came an awful sound, like something out of a butcher's shop, and suddenly we were all sprawled on the floor of the cabin, with Sam Tibbets' headless body lying dead weight on top of us.

"I don't remember exactly how the next few seconds panned out. All I remember was being soaked with Sam's blood: the heat of it, the force with which it gushed from his truncated neck, the bitter metallic stink. The fellows told me afterwards that I was screaming like a banshee on my hands and knees, but I know I wasn't the only one. Jake the Indian brought me out of it: he dragged me away from the shambles in the middle of the room and slapped me a couple times till I quit bawling. As if coming round from a dream I goggled at him slack-mouthed; then I came to myself in a dreadful sort of recollection. Before he could stop me, I'd grabbed the big hunting-knife from its sheath at his waist and pushed him out of the way.

"By climbing up on top of the hot stove, I just about managed to reach the hole in the roof. I had Jake's knife between my teeth like the last of the Mohicans; I was covered all over in Sam Tibbets' blood, and I was filled with the urge to vengeance, nothing else. I hoisted myself up so my head and shoulders were through the hole. With my elbows planted on the snow-covered shingles, I looked around.

"It was crouched by the farther end of the roof like a big old sack of guts, mumbling on something. Sam's head. I made some sort of a noise, and it looked up: I mean, the thick squabby part on top of it suddenly grew long like an elephant's trunk, and one furious red eye glared out at me from its tip. The noise it made: good God, I never heard the like. It damn near deafened me, even out in the open; it went ringing through my head like the last trump.

"Some part of its belly opened itself up, and Sam Tibbets' head was gone with a terrible sucking crunch. Then all those tentacles that fringed the trunk suddenly came to life, writhing and flailing like a stinging jellyfish. One of them caught in my clothing – I slashed out at it with Jake's knife, but I might as well have tried to cut a steel hawser. It had me fast; it was like being caught in a death-hold. The thing let rip a revolting sort of belch, and started to haul me in, and I had just enough time to feel the entire sum of my courage vanish in a wink as fear, total and absolute, rushed in to fill up every inch of my being. It's a hell of a thing, to lose all self-respect that way: to know that the last thing you'll feel before death is nothing but abject, craven panic. God, let me die like a man, I prayed, as the thing dragged me up out of the hole towards its gulping maw – that glaring gorgon's eye—

"It was Jake down below contrived to save my life. He grabbed me by the ankles and swung on them like a church bell, and there came a sharp rip as my coat came to pieces at the seams. It didn't have proper hold of me, only by the fabric, you see: that was what saved me, that and the Chinee tailor back in San Francisco who'd scrimped on the thread when he put that old pea-coat together. I went sliding back through the hole on the roof, while the thing struggled to regain its balance on the icy shingles. It let out another of those blood-freezing hollers, and then I was lying on top of Jake, in amidst all of the blood and the panic down below.

"All of the breath had gotten knocked out of me by the fall, and the same for Jake, who was underneath me, remember. The two of us were pretty much *hors de combat* for a while; plus, I dare say I wouldn't have been much use even with breath in my lungs, not after the jolt I'd took up on the roof. I was aware that the rest of the fellows were running round like crazy, firing into the rafters and yelling fit to raise Cain. For myself, right then, I figured old Harvey Tibbets'd had the best idea, digging himself a hole – or trying to. I knew if it wanted to come down and try conclusions, we none of us stood a chance in hell, guns or no guns. I thought it was all up with us still, and to this day I don't know why it wasn't.

"Because after a while, in amongst all the raving and the letting-off of guns and the war-whoops and hollers and what have you, it gradually dawned on the fellows that there was no movement from up on the roof. Nothing coming through the hole at us, no fresh attack; no sound of creaking timbers, even – though I doubt we'd have heard it, we were making so much noise ourselves. In the end a couple of men ran outside to look up on the roof: nothing there, they yelled, and I thought to myself, no, of course not. It won't show itself so easy. I figured it had only gone to earth for a while, that it would pick us off one by one when we weren't expecting it.

"Then one of them happened to look upwards – I mean straight up, towards the sky. What he saw up there made him let out such a shout, it brought us all out of that broke-up shambles of a cabin. We joined him out in the snow: I remember us all standing there, staring up into the heavens as if God in all his glory was coming down and the final judgement was upon us.

"Silhouetted against the wraithlike flux of the aurora, the thing was ascending into the night sky. It had wings, but they didn't seem to be lifting it, or even bearing its weight; it was as if it simply rose through the air the way a jellyfish rises through the water. That sound – that terrible piercing howl – echoed all across the wide expanse of the landscape, from mountain to lakeshore, through all the sleeping trees, and I swear every beast that heard it must have trembled in its lair; must have whined and cowered and crept to the back of its cave and prayed to whatever rough gods had made it, *Lord, let this danger pass.*

"Up it rose, till we could hardly make it out against the green-wreathed stars. Then, there came one last throb of phosphorescence, bright as day – and it was as if a circuit burned out, somewhere in the sky. The aurora vanished, simple as that; and in the brief interval while our eyes adjusted to the paler starlight, I believe we all screamed, like children pitched headlong into the dark.

"As soon as we could see what we were doing again, we lost no time in getting out of that hateful place. Without waiting to bury our dead – poor Sam Tibbets – we beat a retreat back to Dawson, and there was never a band of pilgrims more relieved to see the sun come up. It shone off the frozen river in bright clean rainbows of ice; it showed us the dirty old log cabins we called home, and we wept with joy at the sight. Exhausted as I was, and scared too, and bewildered at all I'd seen, I believed we might be safe at last. Until the night came; that first night, and all the other nights that followed through that long Canadian winter.

"The nights were bad, you see. I took to sleeping in the daytime, when I could, and once it got dark I'd sit with Jake and the rest of the men in a private room at the back of one of the saloons, playing cards and drinking through to sun-up, very deliberately not talking about what we'd been through that evening. I was never really any good after that; not till I made it out of Dawson with the first thaw. Another season of that, and I'd have ended up a rummy in the streets of Skagway, telling tall tales for the price of a pint of hooch. Some of the men had heard of a fresh strike in Alaska, up on the shale banks at Nome – me, I'd lost heart, and could only think of getting home to San Francisco, where such things as we'd seen up on the roof of the cabin couldn't be. Or that's what I thought back then. What do *you* think, Mr Fenwick?"

For a second I thought he just wanted me to pass judgment on his tale – to say *yes, I believe you*, or *hold on a minute, are you sure about that*? Then I realized the import of his words. "You mean that thing down in the basement, don't you?" I said, slowly, almost reluctantly, and he nodded. I opened my mouth, but nothing came out, and after a moment or two I shut it again.

"It looks every inch a match," Keith said, through his hands. He sighed, and leaned back in his chair, staring up at the nicotine-yellow ceiling. "It was like some sort of damnable optical illusion – didn't you get that? – the longer you looked at that black void, the more it seemed as if the creature was projected into the empty space." With hands that trembled hardly at all, he lit up another cigar.

"A thing can't come to life after so long," I asserted, without a fraction of the confidence that had illuminated Keith's entire narrative. "Nothing of this earth—" and there I stopped, remembering what the Indian Jake had had to say on that subject.

"—Could last so long trapped inside a layer of coal," finished Keith, helpfully. "It's bituminous coal hereabouts; laid down during the Carboniferous age. That's, what? Three hundred million years ago, give or take a few million. Imagine the world back then, Fenwick: the way it looked, the way things were all across the land. Dense humid forests; sodden bogs and peat swamps. The stink of rot, of decomposition; of new life forming, down amongst the muck and the decay. The first creatures had just crawled up out of the warm slimy seas, lizards and snails and molluscs, is all. Trilobites and dragonflies. Nothing much bigger than a crawdad. And then *they* arrived.

"God, they would have been lords of the earth, Fenwick! They could still be now, if—" He broke off, and his hands went once more to his thin eager face. "If enough of them got turned up." His voice was muffled somewhat, but in another way it was remarkably clear – clear-headed, at least.

"Three hundred million years." I was having trouble with the concept – you could say that. Yes, you could certainly say that the concept was troubling me. "You're saying that a thing . . . a thing—"

"Not of this earth," put in Keith helpfully.

"Whatever . . . could keep alive for so long, under such incredible pressure; no air, no sustenance . . . why, it's fantastic."

"It's fantastic, all right," said Keith, and for the first time there was a hint of impatience in his deep even voice. "I thought I made it clear this wasn't a tale you'd hear every day. But look at the facts. These miners here – they didn't find a fossil, a chunk of rock! No more than the Tibbets found a fossil up there in the Klondike. Set aside your preconceptions, Fenwick. I had to. Look at the facts."

"That's just what I aim to do," I said. "Tomorrow, when we get a look at this damn stupid whoosit of theirs."

And on that note, though with a deal more talk thereafter, we agreed to leave it; and I went up to bed with a head full of questions and misgivings. The brandy helped me get off to sleep, in the end. If I dreamed, I'm glad to say I don't remember it. And in any case—

There are many less-than-pleasant ways to be woken from even the most fitful of slumbers, I guess: but let the voice of experience assure you that there's no more absolute way of rousing a fellow than the sound of a monstrous siren going off in what sounds like the next room down the corridor. I was practically thrown out of bed and into the corridor, where I bumped into Keith. He was already dressed; or more probably hadn't been to bed yet.

"Accident at the mine," I croaked. By this time I'd managed to remember where the hell I was, or just about.

"Maybe," was all Keith would say. "Get your pants on, news-paperman."

By the time we made it out into the street people were milling around in their night-shirts, asking each other was there trouble up to the mine. For a while no one seemed to know, and everyone expected the worst; then, we saw the Mayor's Ford barrelling down main street, and Keith practically flung himself in the way of it. Before Kronke or any of his stooges could complain, we were scrambling into the rumble seat and pumping them for information.

"Had us a report of some trouble, up on Peck's Ridge," was all Kronke would say. He looked grey with panic; the flesh practically hung off his face.

"Peck's Ridge?" We'd heard that place name before, of course. "Isn't that where Lamar Tibbs lives?" The mayor didn't answer at first; Keith leaned forwards and gripped his shoulder. "Tibbs? The man who found the creature?"

"Up near there," Kronke said, shaking loose his arm. H tried to regain some of his mayoral authority: "'Tain't rightly speaking none of your business anyways, mister—"

"Drop that," Keith said impatiently. "Drop that straightaway, or else I'll make sure you come across as the biggest hick in all creation when the story makes it into the papers. How's that gonna play with the voters come election time, Mr Kronke?"

The two men stared angrily at each other, but there was only ever going to be one winner of that contest. After a second Kronke told his chauffeur "Drive on," and we were off, away down main street heading out of town, up into the hill country.

That was some drive, all right. The middle of the night, and not a light showing in all that desolate stretch; only the headlamps of the car on the ribbon of road ahead. Trees crowding close to the track, and between their ghostly lit-up trunks only the blackness of the forest. Overhead, a canopy of branches, and no starlight, no sliver of the moon; it felt as if we were going down into the ground as much as climbing, as if we'd entered some miner's tunnel lined with wooden props, heading clear down to the Carboniferous.

Alongside me on the rumble, Keith sat, hands clenched on the back of the seat in front. He was willing the automobile on, it seemed to me, the way a jockey pushes his horse along in the home straight. His old man's mop of hair showed up very white in the near darkness, but that didn't fool me any: underneath it all was still the dreamer he'd always been and would remain, the thirty-year-old who'd walked out on his safe job with Mr Hearst and headed up North to the Klondike on nothing more than a notion and a chance. Hero worship? I should say so.

Maybe seven or eight miles out of town, we saw light up ahead: fire. The Ford swung round and down a trail so narrow, the branches plucked at our sleeves and we had to cover our faces from their lash, and then we came out into a natural dip between two high sides of hills, with a farmhouse and outbuildings down the bottom of the hollow. All hell was breaking loose down there.

People were running back and forth between the main house and the outhouses, the farthest of which was well ablaze. You could hear the screams of animals trapped in the sheds; I couldn't be sure there weren't the cries of people in there too.

Before we even came to a halt, an old man in biballs came running up, crying out unintelligibly. "Was it you phoned?" Kronke bellowed at him above the tumult. Whether he expected any answer, I don't know. It was clear the fellow was raving mad, for the time being at least. Keith passed him over to Kronke's buddies, who were very pointedly not setting foot outside the automobile, and beckoned me follow him down towards the house.

Kronke hung back, unwilling to leave the safety of the car; why he'd even bothered coming out there in the first place was hard to say. Perhaps he thought it was his chance to get the whoosit back, on behalf of the mining company. Perhaps – I think this is not unlikely, myself – perhaps there was always some sort of a trip planned for that night, Kronke and a few men armed with pistols, up to Peck's Ridge on company business. Well, they might have had a chance at that, I guess, had things only panned out just a little differently.

Down by the sheds Keith managed to get a hold of one of the people fighting the fire; a teenager, no more, in a plaid shirt and patched drawers. "What's going on here?" he yelled.

"They're trapped!" the kid hollered back, his eyes round with panic. "Uncle Jesse and Uncle Vern! In there! They were a-watchin' over it!"

"Watching over what?" The kid tried to shake free, but Keith had him tight. "Were they keeping guard? What over?"

"Over Pap's thing!" The kid made to break loose again, without success. "That what Pap found, down to the mine! Lemme go, mister . . ."

"Your pap Lamar Tibbs?" Keith was implacable. I felt for the youngster, I did. But I wanted to know as well.

The kid nodded, and Keith had one more question. "Where is he?"

"*I don't know!*" screamed the boy. "*I DON'T KNOW!*" Keith was so shocked at the ferocity of it, the sheer volume, that he let him go. The kid stood there for a second, surprised himself I guess, then shook himself all over like a dog coming out of the creek and ran off towards the burning barn. We followed on behind.

Some of the men had formed a chain, and were passing buckets of water up from the pump. The fellows nearest the door were emptying the buckets into the smoke and flames; Keith brushed straight past them and was inside before anyone could stop him. I went to follow him, but one of the men in the doorway grabbed me. "It's gonna come down!" he yelled in my ear.

I was just about to holler after Keith when he appeared through the smoke, coughing and staggering. "It's not in there," he wheezed, soon as he could talk. Then there came a mighty creaking and splintering, and we all sprang back as the roof collapsed in a roaring billow of sparks.

"It's gone," Keith insisted, as we stood and watched the barn burn out from a safe distance. "But it was there, though." I was about to ask him what he meant, how he could have known that, when a stocky little man came running up from the house shouting, and interrupted me.

"You see anything of Vern and Jesse in there, mister?" His face was blackened, eyes white and staring; I learned later they'd dragged him out of the barn once already, half-dead from the smoke. "It's my brothers – I'm Lamar Tibbs."

Keith nodded. The man was about to ask the next, the obvious, question, but I guess Keith's expression told him what he wanted to know. Tibbs' own features crumpled up, and he bowed his head.

After a little while he said: "It all up with them?" Keith nodded again. "Fire?"

"Before the fire," Keith said. The miner looked up, and he went on: "They were over in the far corner. They weren't burned any." I think he meant it kindly; that was the way Tibbs took it, not knowing any better then. But Keith's eyes were flinty hard, and I for one had my misgivings.

"Was it that thing caused it?" Tibbs' voice was all but inaudible. "That thing I brung up from the mine?"

"I believe so." Keith's voice sounded calm enough, the more so if you couldn't take a cue from his face. "It's not there any more: it looks to have busted out the back before the roof went."

That got Tibbs' attention. "You sure?"

"Can't be certain that's the way it got out," said Keith, picking his words with care. "It wasn't in there when the roof fell in, though – that, I'm sure of."

Tibbs looked hard at Keith, who stared levelly back at him. What he saw seemed to make his mind up. "Wait there, mister," he said shortly, and started back towards the house. Over his shoulder, he shouted: "You in the mood for a dawg hunt?"

I began to say something, but Keith stopped me with a upraised hand. "What about you, Mr Fenwick? You in the mood for a dawg hunt, sir?"

What could I say? Understanding that no matter what, Keith would go through with it, I nodded miserably. Then there was no more time to think: Tibbs was running back from the house with three of the mangiest, meanest-looking yaller hounds you ever saw in your life. The chase was on.

The dogs picked up a trail directly we got round the back of the barn. They shivered uncontrollably – as if they were passing peach pits, as Keith memorably put it later that same night – and set off at a good fast clip into the trees. Tibbs had them on the end of a short leash, and it was all he could do to keep up the pace. Keith loped along after him, and I brought up the rear. A few of Tibbs' relatives from back in the yard joined in – thankfully, they'd thought to bring along lanterns. There were a half-dozen of us in all.

"I thought it was a goner," panted Tibbs from up in front. He'd pegged Keith for a straight shooter more or less from the beginning, that was clear: I suppose it was watching Keith dive straight into that burning barn had done it. I doubt it came easy for him to trust anyone much, outside of his extended family circle, but he damn near deferred to Horton Keith. "We'd been blastin' on the big new seam, see: I swung my hammer at a big ol' chunk of coal fell out the roof, 'bout the size of a barrel – the fall must 'a cracked it some, 'cause one lick from me was all it took. That chunk split wide open like a hick'ry nut, clean in two – an' there it was, the whoosit, older than Methuselah. Fitted in there like a hand inside a glove, it did."

"I know," Keith wheezed. For a man well into his fifties, he was keeping up pretty good, but Tibbs was setting a punishing pace. "Seen it – back at the courthouse."

"You seen that? You seen the coal? Then you got a pretty good idea what we brung back here." *He's got a better idea than that, maybe*, I thought to myself, but I didn't say anything. For one thing, I doubt my aching lungs would have let me – nor yet my growing panic, which I was only just managing to keep in check.

"Anyhow, it was deader'n Abel slain by Cain – I'll swear to that, an' these men here'll back me up. You never seen a thing so dried out an' wrinkled – nor so ugly, neither. Jesus Christ, it made me sick to look at it! – but it was my prize, an' I swore it was goin' to make me a rich man. Me an' all my kin . . ." He choked up at that, and we none of us pressed him; we ran on, was all, with the rustling thud of our footfalls through the brush warning the whole forest of our approach, probably.

The dogs were still straining hard after the scent, when all of a sudden they stopped and gathered round something underfoot, down by a little stand of dwarf sumac. I thought it was a rock at first – I couldn't see through the bodies of the hounds. It was Tibbs' cry that made me realize what it *might* be – that, and the story Keith had told me not half-a-dozen hours previously, rattling round my mind the way it had been ever since.

Tibbs couldn't pick it up, that roundish muddy thing the dogs had found. That was left to Horton Keith. He lifted it just a little, enough for one of the other men in the party to gasp and mutter "Jesse". Tibbs repeated the name a few times to himself, while Keith replaced the thing the way he found it and straightened up off his haunches. Then Tibbs gave it out in a howl that made the dogs back off, cower on their bellies in the leaf-rot as if they'd been whipped. I swear that sound went all the way through me. I hear it still, when I think about that night. It's bad, and I try not to do it too much, mostly because the next thing I think of is what I heard next – what we all heard, the sound that made us snap up our heads and turn in the direction of our otherworldly quarry.

You'll probably remember that Keith had already taken a stab at describing that sound. If you go back and look at what he said, you'll see he compared it to the last trump, and all I can say is, standing out there in the middle of the forest, looking at each other in the lantern light, we all of us knew exactly what he meant. It turned my guts to water: I damn near screamed myself.

It was so close; that was the thing. Just by the clarity, the lack of muffling, you could tell it wasn't far off – five, maybe ten score of paces on through the trees, somewhere just over the next ridge. Tibbs got his senses back soonest of us all, or maybe he was so far gone then that sense had nothing to do with it: he was off and running, aiming to close down those hundred yards or so and get to grips with whatever cut down his brothers and took a trophy to boot. The dogs almost tripped him up; they were cowering in the dirt still, and there was no budging them. He flung down the leash and left them there.

It was Keith started after him, of course. And once Keith had gone, I couldn't not go myself. Then the rest of then followed on; all of which meant we were pretty strung out along the track. It may have saved Keith's life, that arrangement.

I heard Tibbs up ahead, cursing and panting; then, I heard a strange sort of a whizzing noise. I once stood at a wharf watching a cargo ship being unloaded, and one of the hawsers broke on the winching gear. The noise it made as it lashed through the air; that was what I heard. Whip-crack, quick and abrupt; and then I didn't hear Tibbs any more.

What I thought I heard was the sound of rain, pattering on the leaves and branches. I even felt a few drops of it on my face. Then one of the men in the rear caught up and shone his lantern up ahead. It lit first of all on Keith as he staggered back, hand to his mouth. Then, it lit on Tibbs.

At first it seemed like some sort of conjuror's trick. He was staggering too, like a stage drunk, only there was something about his head . . . At first your brain refused to believe it. Your eyes saw it, but your brain reported back, no, it's a man; men aren't made that way. It's a trick they do with mirrors; a slather of stage blood to dress it up, that's all. Then, inevitably, Tibbs lost his balance and fell backwards. Once he was down it became easier to deal with, in one way – easier to look at and trust your own eyes, at any rate. At last, you could look at it and see what there was to be seen. Which was this: Tibbs' head was gone, clean off at the neck.

I said you could look at it; not for long, though. Instead I turned to Keith, who was pressed back up against a tree trunk, still with his hand to his mouth. He saw me, and he tried to speak, shaking his head all the while, but he couldn't find the words.

Then we both heard it together: a rustling in the branches above our head, the sound of something dropping. We both looked up at about the same time, and that was how I managed to spring back, and so avoid the thing hitting me smack on the crown of my head. It hit the ground good and hard, directly between the two of us: the soft mud underfoot took all the bounce off it, though. It rolled half of the way over, then stopped, so you couldn't really see its features. There was no mistaking it, though, even in the shaky lantern-light; I'd been looking at the back of Tibbs' head only a moment ago, hadn't I?

A dreadful realization dawned in Keith's eyes, and he looked back up. Instinctively I followed suit. I guess we saw about the same thing, though Keith had the experience to help him evaluate it. It was like this:

The branches were close-meshed overhead, with hardly any night sky visible in between. What you could see was tinted a sickly sort of greenish hue: the way those modern city streetlights will turn the night a fuzzy, smoky orange, and block out all the stars. Through the treetops, something was ascending. I'd be a liar if I said I could recognize it; there was just no way to tell, not with all those shaking, rustling branches in the way. All I got was a general impression of size and shape; enough for me to stand in front of that slab of coal in the courthouse basement the next day and say, yeah, it could have been; I guess. Keith was with me, and so far as he was concerned it was a deal more straightforward; but as I say, he had the benefit of prior acquaintance.

Up it went, up and up, till it broke clear of the canopy, and we had no way of knowing where to look. The sky gave one last unnatural throb of ghoulish green, as if it was turning itself inside out; and it was over. All that was left was the bloody carnage down below: Lamar Tibbs' body, that we dragged between us back to the farmhouse, and the bodies of his brothers covered up with a tarpaulin. One entire generation of a family, wiped out in the course of a single night.

What with the weeping and the wailing of the relatives, and the never-ending questions – most of them from that fat fool Kronke, who hadn't even the guts to get out of his damn automobile – that business up on Peck's Ridge took us clear through dawn and into the afternoon of the next day to deal with. It stayed with us a good while longer than that, though; in fact, it's never really gone away. Ask either of my wives, who will surely survive me through having gotten rid of me, as soon as was humanly possible. They'll tell you how I used to come bolt upright in the middle of a nightmare, hands flailing desperately above my head, screaming at the ghosts of trees and branches, babbling about a sky gone wrong. Ask them how often it happened, and what good company I was in the days and weeks that followed. Yes, you could say it's stayed with me, my three days' visit down in Oram County.

* * *

I had the pleasure of Keith's acquaintance for a dozen more years in all, right up until the time he set off for the headwaters of the Amazon with the Collins Clarke archaeological party and never came back. Missing, presumed dead, all fifteen men and their native bearers; nothing was ever found of them, no overflights could even spot their last camp. Keith was well into his sixties by then, but there was never any question that he'd be joining the expedition, once he'd heard the rumours – the ruins up above Iquitos on the Ucayali, the strange carvings of beasts no one had ever seen before. He'd done his preparation in the library at Miskatonic with Clarke himself, cross-referencing the Indian tales with certain books and illustrations – and with that slab of coal from the Oram County courthouse, one-half of which had made its way into the cabinets of the University's Restricted Collection. There was no stopping him: he was convinced he was on the right track at last. "But why put yourself in their way again?" I asked him. "With all you know; after all you've seen?" He never answered me straight out; there's only his last telegram, sent from Manaus, which I like to think holds, if not an answer, then a pointer at least, to the man and to the nature of his quest.

DEAR FENWICK (it said): FINALLY FOUND SOMEPLACE WORSE THAN SKAGWAY. AND THEY SAY THERE'S NO SUCH THING AS PROGRESS. WE SET OFF TOMORROW ON OUR SNIPE HUNT, NOT A MOMENT TOO SOON FOR ALL CONCERNED. WISH YOU WERE HERE . . . ON THE STRICT UNDERSTANDING THAT WE'RE SOON TO BE SOMEWHERE ELSE. WITH ALL BEST WISHES FROM THE NEW FRONTIER, YOUR FRIEND, HORTON KEITH.

My friend, Horton Keith.

STEPHEN KING

The *New York Times* at Special Bargain Rates

AFTER TWENTY YEARS I am delighted to finally welcome the world's most successful, popular and influential horror writer to these pages.

Born in Portland, Maine, in 1947, Stephen King's first novel, *Carrie*, appeared in 1974. Since then he has published a phenomenal string of bestsellers, including *Salem's Lot*, *The Shining*, *The Stand*, *Dead Zone*, *Firestarter*, *Cujo*, *Pet Sematary*, *Christine*, *It*, *Misery*, *The Dark Half*, *Needful Things*, *Rose Madder*, *The Green Mile*, *Bag of Bones*, *The Colorado Kid*, *Cell*, *Lisey's Story* and *Duma Key*, to name only a few.

His short fiction and novellas have been collected in *Night Shift*, *Different Seasons*, *Skeleton Crew*, *Four Past Midnight*, *Nightmares and Dreamscapes*, *Hearts in Atlantis*, *Everything's Eventual*, *The Secretary of Dreams* (illustrated by Glenn Chadbourne), *Just After Sunset: Stories* and *Stephen King Goes to the Movies*.

He has written the non-fiction volumes *Danse Macabre*, *Nightmares in the Sky: Gargoyles and Grotesques* (with photographs by f-stop Fitzgerald) and *On Writing: A Memoir of the Craft*. He also contributes the occasional "The Pop of King" column for *Entertainment Weekly*, and in 2007 he guest-edited a volume of *The Best American Short Stories*.

Many of King's books and stories have been adapted for movies and television, most recently with *1408*, *The Mist*, *Dolan's Cadillac*, *Everything's Eventual* and a TV remake of *Children of the Corn*.

The winner of numerous awards – including both the Horror Writers Association and World Fantasy Convention Lifetime

Achievement Awards, and a Medal for Distinguished Contribution to American Letters from the National Book Foundation – King lives with his wife, novelist Tabitha King, in a reputedly haunted house in Bangor, Maine.

The following ghost story is both poignant and disturbing, and would not have been out of place in the old *Twilight Zone* TV series . . .

S HE'S FRESH OUT OF THE shower when the phone begins to ring, but although the house is still full of relatives – she can hear them downstairs, it seems they will never go away, it seems she never had so many – no one picks up. Nor does the answering machine, as James programmed it to do after the fifth ring.

Anne goes to the extension on the bed-table, wrapping a towel around herself, her wet hair thwacking unpleasantly on the back of her neck and bare shoulders. She picks it up, she says hello, and then he says her name. It's James. They had thirty years together, and one word is all she needs. He says *Annie* like no one else, always did.

For a moment she can't speak or even breathe. He has caught her on the exhale and her lungs feel as flat as sheets of paper. Then, as he says her name again (sounding uncharacteristically hesitant and unsure of himself), the strength slips from her legs. They turn to sand and she sits on the bed, the towel falling off her, her wet bottom dampening the sheet beneath her. If the bed hadn't been there, she would have gone to the floor.

Her teeth click together and that starts her breathing again.

"James? Where *are* you? *What happened*?" In her normal voice, this might have come out sounding shrewish – a mother scolding her wayward eleven-year-old who's come late to the supper-table yet again – but now it emerges in a kind of horrified growl. The murmuring relatives below her are, after all, planning his funeral.

James chuckles. It is a bewildered sound. "Well, I tell you what," he says. "I don't exactly know where I am."

Her first confused thought is that he must have missed the plane in London, even though he called her from Heathrow not long before it took off. Then a clearer idea comes: although both the *Times* and the TV news say there were no survivors, there was at least one. Her husband crawled from the wreckage of the burning plane (and the burning apartment building the plane hit, don't forget that, twenty-four more dead on the ground and the number apt to rise before the world moved on to the next tragedy) and has been wandering around Brooklyn ever since, in a state of shock.

"Jimmy, are you all right? Are you . . . are you burned?" The truth of what that would mean occurs after the question, thumping down with the heavy weight of a dropped book on a bare foot, and she begins to cry. "Are you in the hospital?"

"Hush," he says, and at his old kindness – and at that old word, just one small piece of their marriage's furniture – she begins to cry harder. "Honey, hush."

"But I don't *understand*!"

"I'm all right," he says. "Most of us are."

"Most—? There are *others*?"

"Not the pilot," he says. "He's not so good. Or maybe it's the co-pilot. He keeps screaming, 'We're going down, there's no power, oh my God.' Also 'This isn't my fault, don't let them blame it on me.' He says that, too."

She's cold all over. "Who is this really? Why are you being so horrible? I just lost my husband, you asshole!"

"Honey—"

"Don't call me that!" There's a clear strand of mucus hanging from one of her nostrils. She wipes it away with the back of her hand and then flings it into the wherever, a thing she hasn't done since she was a child. "Listen, mister – I'm going to star-sixty-nine this call and the police will come and slam your ass . . . your ignorant, unfeeling *ass* . . ."

But she can go no further. It's his voice. There's no denying it. The way the call rang right through – no pick-up downstairs, no answering machine – suggests this call was just for her. And . . . *honey, hush*. Like in the old Carl Perkins song.

He has remained quiet, as if letting her work these things through for herself. But before she can speak again, there's a beep on the line.

"James? *Jimmy*? Are you still there?"

"Yeah, but I can't talk long. I was trying to call you when we went down, and I guess that's the only reason I was able to get through at all. Lots of others have been trying, we're lousy with cell phones, but no luck." That beep again. "Only now my phone's almost out of juice."

"Jimmy, did you know?" This idea has been the hardest and most terrible part for her – that he might have known, if only for an endless minute or two. Others might picture burned bodies or dismembered heads with grinning teeth; even light-fingered first responders filching wedding rings and diamond ear-clips, but what

has robbed Annie Driscoll's sleep is the image of Jimmy looking out
his window as the streets and cars and the brown apartment buildings of Brooklyn swell closer. The useless masks flopping down like
the corpses of small yellow animals. The overhead bins popping
open, carry-ons starting to fly, someone's Norelco razor rolling up
the tilted aisle.

"Did you know you were going down?"

"Not really," he says. "Everything seemed all right until the very
end – maybe the last thirty seconds. Although it's hard to keep track
of time in situations like that, I always think."

Situations like that. And even more telling: *I always think.* As if
he has been aboard half a dozen crashing 767s instead of just the
one.

"In any case," he goes on, "I was just calling to say we'd be early,
so be sure to get the FedEx man out of bed before I got there."

Her absurd attraction for the FedEx man has been a joke between
them for years. She begins to cry again. His cell utters another of
those beeps, as if scolding her for it.

"I think I died just a second or two before it rang the first time. I
think that's why I was able to get through to you. But this thing's
gonna give up the ghost pretty soon."

He chuckles as if this is funny. She supposes that in a way it is. She
may see the humour in it herself, eventually. *Give me ten years or so,*
she thinks.

Then, in that just-talking-to-myself voice she knows so well: "Why
didn't I put the tiresome motherfucker on charge last night? Just
forgot, that's all. Just forgot."

"James . . . honey . . . the plane crashed two days ago."

A pause. Mercifully with no beep to fill it. Then: "Really? Mrs
Corey *said* time was funny here. Some of us agreed, some of us
disagreed. I was a disagreer, but looks like she was right."

"Hearts?" Annie asks. She feels now as if she is floating outside
and slightly above her plump damp middle-aged body, but she hasn't
forgotten Jimmy's old habits. On a long flight he was always looking
for a game. Cribbage or canasta would do, but hearts was his true
love.

"Hearts," he agrees. The phone beeps, as if seconding that.

"Jimmy . . ." She hesitates long enough to ask herself if this is
information she really wants, then plunges with that question still
unanswered. "Where *are* you, exactly?"

"Looks like Grand Central Station," he says. "Only bigger. And
emptier. As if it wasn't really Grand Central at all but only . . .

mmm . . . a movie set of Grand Central. Do you know what I'm trying to say?"

"I . . . I think so . . ."

"There certainly aren't any trains . . . and we can't hear any in the distance . . . but there are doors going everywhere. Oh, and there's an escalator, but it's broken. All dusty, and some of the treads are gone." He pauses, and when he speaks again he does so in a lower voice, as if afraid of being overheard. "People are leaving. Some climbed the escalator – I saw them – but most are using the doors. I guess I'll have to leave, too. For one thing, there's nothing to eat. There's a candy machine, but that's broken, too."

"Are you . . . honey, are you hungry?"

"A little. Mostly what I'd like is some water. I'd *kill* for a cold bottle of Dasani."

Annie looks guiltily down at her own legs, still beaded with water. She imagines him licking off those beads and is horrified to feel a sexual stirring.

"I'm all right, though," he adds hastily. "For now, anyway. But there's no sense staying here. Only . . ."

"What? What, Jimmy?"

"I don't know which door to use."

Another beep.

"I wish I knew which one Mrs Corey took. She's got my damn cards."

"Are you . . ." She wipes her face with the towel she wore out of the shower; then she was fresh, now she's all tears and snot. "Are you scared?"

"Scared?" he asks thoughtfully. "No. A little worried, that's all. Mostly about which door to use."

Find your way home, she almost says. *Find the right door and find your way home.* But if he did, would she want to see him? A ghost might be all right, but what if she opened the door on a smoking cinder with red eyes and the remains of jeans (he always travelled in jeans) melted into his legs? And what if Mrs Corey was with him, his baked deck of cards in one twisted hand?

Beep.

"I don't need to tell you to be careful about the FedEx man anymore," he says. "If you really want him, he's all yours."

She shocks herself by laughing.

"But I did want to say I love you—"

"Oh honey I love you t—"

"—and not to let the McCormack kid do the gutters this fall, he works hard but he's a risk-taker, last year he almost broke his fucking neck. And don't go to the bakery anymore on Sundays. Something's going to happen there, and I know it's going to be on a Sunday, but I don't know which Sunday. Time really *is* funny here."

The McCormack kid he's talking about must be the son of the guy who used to be their caretaker in Vermont . . . only they sold that place ten years ago, and the kid must be in his mid-twenties by now. And the bakery? She supposes he's talking about Zoltan's, but what on *Earth—*

Beep.

"Some of the people here were on the ground, I guess. That's very tough, because they don't have a clue how they got here. And the pilot keeps screaming. Or maybe it's the co-pilot. I think he's going to be here for quite a while. He just wanders around. He's very confused."

The beeps are coming closer together now.

"I have to go, Annie. I can't stay here, and the phone's going to shit the bed any second now, anyway." Once more in that I'm-scolding-myself voice (impossible to believe she will never hear it again after today; impossible *not* to believe), he mutters, "It would have been so simple just to . . . well, never mind. I love you, sweetheart."

"Wait! Don't go!"

"I c—"

"I love you, too! Don't go!"

But he already has. In her ear there is only black silence.

She sits there with the dead phone to her ear for a minute or more, then breaks the connection. The non-connection. When she opens the line again and gets a perfectly normal dial tone, she touches star-sixty-nine after all. According to the robot who answers her page, the last incoming call was at nine o'clock that morning. She knows who that one was: her sister Nell, calling from New Mexico. Nell called to tell Annie that her plane had been delayed and she wouldn't be in until tonight. Nell told her to be strong.

All the relatives who live at a distance – James', Annie's – flew in. Apparently they feel that James used up all the family's Destruction Points, at least for the time being.

There is no record of an incoming call at – she glances at the bedside clock and sees it's now 3:17 pm – at about ten past three, on the third afternoon of her widowhood.

Someone raps briefly on the door and her brother calls, "Anne? Annie?"

"Dressing!" she calls back. Her voice sounds like she's been crying, but unfortunately, no one in this house would find that strange. "Privacy, please!"

"You okay?" he calls through the door. "We thought we heard you talking. And Ellie thought she heard you call out."

"Fine!" she calls, then wipes her face again with the towel. "Down in a few!"

"Okay. Take your time." Pause. "We're here for you." Then he clumps away.

"Beep," she whispers, then covers her mouth to hold in laughter that is some emotion even more complicated than grief trying to find the only way out it has. "Beep, beep. Beep, beep, beep." She lies back on the bed, laughing, and above her cupped hands her eyes are large and awash with tears that overspill down her cheeks and run all the way to her ears. "Beep-fucking-beepity-beep."

She laughs for quite a while, then dresses and goes downstairs to be with her relatives, who have come to mingle their grief with hers. Only they feel apart from her, because he didn't call any of them. He called her. For better or worse, he called her.

During the autumn of that year, with the blackened remains of the apartment building the jet crashed into still closed off from the rest of the world by yellow police tape (although the taggers have been inside, one leaving a spray-painted message reading CRISPY CRITTERS LAND HERE), Annie receives the sort of e-blast computer-addicts like to send to a wide circle of acquaintances. This one comes from Gert Fisher, the town librarian in Tilton, Vermont. When Annie and James summered there, Annie used to volunteer at the library, and although the two women never got on especially well, Gert has included Annie in her quarterly updates ever since. They are usually not very interesting, but halfway through the weddings, funerals, and 4-H winners in this one, Annie comes across a bit of news that makes her catch her breath. Jason McCormack, the son of old Hughie McCormack, was killed in an accident on Labor Day. He fell from the roof of a summer cottage while cleaning the gutters and broke his neck.

"He was only doing a favour for his dad, who as you may remember had a stroke the year before last," Gert wrote before going on to how it rained on the library's end-of-summer lawn sale, and how disappointed they all were.

Gert doesn't say in her three-page compendium of breaking news, but Annie is quite sure Jason fell from the roof of what used to be their cottage. In fact, she is positive.

*   *   *

Five years after the death of her husband (and the death of Jason McCormack not long after), Annie remarries. And although they relocate to Boca Raton, she gets back to the old neighbourhood often. Craig, the new husband, is only semi-retired, and his business takes him to New York every three or four months. Annie almost always goes with him, because she still has family in Brooklyn and on Long Island. More than she knows what to do with, it sometimes seems. But she loves them with that exasperated affection that seems to belong, she thinks, only to people in their fifties and sixties. She never forgets how they drew together for her after James's plane went down, and made the best cushion for her that they could. So she wouldn't crash, too.

When she and Craig go back to New York, they fly. About this she never has a qualm, but she stops going to Zoltan's Family Bakery on Sundays when she's home, even though their raisin bagels are, she is sure, served in heaven's waiting room. She goes to Froger's instead. She is actually there, buying doughnuts (the doughnuts are at least passable), when she hears the blast. She hears it clearly even though Zoltan's is eleven blocks away. LP gas explosion. Four killed, including the woman who always passed Annie her bagels with the top of the bag rolled down, saying, "Keep it that way until you get home or you lose the freshness."

People stand on the sidewalks, looking east toward the sound of the explosion and the rising smoke, shading their eyes with their hands. Annie hurries past them, not looking. She doesn't want to see a plume of rising smoke after a big bang; she thinks of James enough as it is, especially on the nights when she can't sleep. When she gets home she can hear the phone ringing inside. Either everyone has gone down the block to where the local school is having a sidewalk art sale, or no one can hear that ringing phone. Except for her, that is. And by the time she gets her key turned in the lock, the ringing has stopped.

Sarah, the only one of her sisters who never married, *is* there, it turns out, but there is no need to ask her why she didn't answer the phone; Sarah Bernicke, the one-time disco queen, is in the kitchen with the Village People turned up, dancing around with the O-Cedar in one hand, looking like a chick in a TV ad. She missed the bakery explosion, too, although their building is even closer to Zoltan's than Froger's.

Annie checks the answering machine, but there's a big red zero in the MESSAGES WAITING window. That means nothing in itself, lots of people call without leaving a message, but—

Star-sixty-nine reports the last call at eight-forty last night. Annie dials it anyway, hoping against hope that somewhere outside the big room that looks like a Grand Central Station movie set he found a place to re-charge his phone. To him it might seem he last spoke to her yesterday. Or only minutes ago. *Time is funny here*, he said. She has dreamed of that call so many times it now almost seems like a dream itself, but she has never told anyone about it. Not Craig, not even her own mother, now almost ninety but alert and with a firmly held belief in the afterlife.

In the kitchen, the Village People advise that there is no need to feel down. There isn't, and she doesn't. She nevertheless holds the phone very tightly as the number she has star-sixty-nined rings once, then twice. Annie stands in the living room with the phone to her ear and her free hand touching the brooch above her left breast, as if touching the brooch could still the pounding heart beneath it. Then the ringing stops and a recorded voice offers to sell her The *New York Times* at special bargain rates that will not be repeated.

SARAH PINBOROUGH

Our Man in the Sudan

SARAH PINBOROUGH IS THE British author of six horror novels from Leisure Books, the most recent being *Feeding Ground*. Her short stories have appeared in several anthologies and she has also written a *Torchwood* novel, *Into the Silence*, for BBC Books.

She has recently completed *A Matter of Blood*, the first of a supernatural thriller trilogy for Gollancz, which will be published in 2010.

The author has twice been shortlisted for the British Fantasy Award for Best Novel, and when she's not writing she can normally be found laughing with friends and drinking wine, probably with a cat in her lap.

"When I was a little girl back in the early 1980s," she recalls, "my dad was posted to Khartoum. One night, when I was about ten, I had a sleepover at another girl's house. We decided – completely missing the point of a *sleep*over to try and stay up all night. At around 6:30 am, in a final attempt to stay awake, we went outside and mucked around in the dusty street in front of her house.

"By 6:45 we could see the sandstorm rolling towards us from the desert and were totally transfixed by it. It wasn't my first, but it was the first time I'd seen one approach like some kind of tidal wave. We stayed outside as it rolled over the ramshackle city and didn't go back inside until we couldn't take the sting of the sand on our skin anymore. It was an experience and sight I'll never forget.

"My mother also dragged me out to sit in the baking desert to hear a historian talk about the battle of Omdurman. As much as I hadn't wanted to go, I found his stories of the men with swords who hid in the sand dunes and slashed at the horses quite terrifying and, like the sight of the haboob, they have stayed with me.

"This story gave me an opportunity to blend those two memories into something with a life of its own and, I hope, also create a photograph of a city that I loved very much as a child."

"I WANT TO SEE the body," Fanshawe said.

His eyes burned and his sockets were gritty as he blinked, as if the infernal dust that covered everything in this back end of beyond hell hole had somehow also coated the inside of his eyelids. Sat stiffly as he was in the leather-backed chair in Clift's office, sweat itched under his collar and he fought his fingers' urge to creep up and at least loosen his tie. Instead, he just lifted his chin slightly and made a valiant effort to ignore it.

His shirt clung soaking to his back. It wasn't helping his rising irritation. He was tired, not so much from the flight that had landed at two o'clock that morning, but from the constant heat. It had been a baking black furnace when he'd walked across the runway to fight for his suitcase in the tatty terminal building, and there'd been no respite since. It seemed the air-conditioning on some floors of the Nile Hilton was refusing to work and unfortunately, he'd been placed on one of those floors. He suspected from the weary expressions of all those who made it to the buffet breakfast, that it was all rooms that were affected, but the management refused to confirm or deny.

Blasted heat. He hated it. Crisp, elegant European winters were his choice; civilized and organized. This African climate left him cold, and even his own poor joke couldn't raise his mood.

On the other side of the desk, Clift smiled. But then it was probably easier for him to do so, dressed casually as he was in shorts and a T-shirt and making no apology for it. The First Secretary poured thick sweet black tea from a tall metal pot.

"We'll have to have it local style today, I'm afraid. Had a blasted power cut and the night watchman didn't start the genny." He slid a cup and saucer across the desk. "He was probably asleep. Wouldn't be the first time. Anyway, all the long life's gone off."

Fanshawe stared at the cup but didn't touch it. How anyone could drink anything hot in these temperatures was beyond him.

"The body?" he repeated.

"Ah yes. The body. Well, that is a touch embarrassing as it happens." Clift took a sip of his own tea and sat back in his chair. With his tan and easy grin he didn't look at all perplexed by the heat. It didn't endear him to Fanshawe. Neither did his next sentence.

"I'm afraid we don't have the body. Not anymore."

Fanshawe stared. Outside, in the white brightness below, car horns blared loudly and two torrents of guttural Arabic raged over each other.

"What do you mean, you don't have it?" His own Queen's English was as dry as the occasional patches of Khartoum grass and scrub that he'd passed on his way to the Embassy.

Spreading his fingers, Clift shrugged. "It was the coffin, you see. God only knows where our standard issue has got too. We haven't needed one since that poor sod flipped his Land Rover and broke his neck on the way back from Port Sudan, and that was a couple of years ago now." He shook his head slightly and frowned. "I'm not even sure it was replaced. I'd only been in post a couple of months then, and you know how these things are."

Fanshawe wasn't entirely sure that he did. In the cool sophistication of Europe's Embassies, those on her Majesty's diplomatic service wore suits and ties and typed everything in triplicate. He swatted a fly away and raised an eyebrow. "Go on."

Clift took another sip of his tea and leaned forward, his arms resting on the desk. "We tried to borrow one from the Germans but then one of their buggers bloody went and died too and so they needed it back. Didn't want to ask the Yanks or the Russians. They'd have had a bloody field day with that." He peered at Fanshawe. "We telexed the FCO. They said he had no next of kin so, to be honest, we didn't think anyone would be that concerned. In the end we just buried him."

Fanshawe sighed and looked over to the window. Even through the thick mosquito gauze stretched across it, he thought he'd have to flinch in the white of that sun. Maybe it reflected back up from the dusty, dirty cream of the ground. Perhaps that's why it seemed so endlessly bright under the empty blue skies of North Africa. He chewed the inside of his mouth slightly. He'd wanted to see the body. There were things he needed to verify.

Clift rummaged in the desk drawer and pulled out a folder. "The doctor examined him and was pretty sure he'd had a heart attack." He slid the death certificate over so that it sat next to Fanshawe's untouched tea.

"Local doctor?" Happy to bring his eyes back to the more comfortable view of the 70s furniture that had seen better days, Fanshawe picked up the paper.

"Yes, we're a minimum staff in a post like this. He's a good chap, though. Did his training in London." Clift lit a cigarette, the match barely touching the side of the box before bursting into flames. "I have to say, I don't really understand this interest in Cartwright's death. He seemed like an ordinary Second Secretary. So, what's the story?"

Fanshawe refused the offered cigarette, even though he was a smoker himself. The smoke and the dust combined would probably make him choke. Watching Clift, he wondered how long you had to spend in a place like this before you acclimatized. Too long, was the only conclusion he could reach.

"He was MI6," he said, eventually. "He'd had some trouble behind the Iron Curtain so he was laying low here. Having some R and R while things quietened down."

Clift laughed. "Well, a year out here is certainly long enough to be forgotten. Are you worried the Russians tracked him down? If so, I wouldn't be overly concerned. It's too hot for spying games out here. I doubt they'd have the energy for it." He laughed again.

Fanshawe smiled tightly. "Probably not."

"It seems like you may have had a wasted journey. Sorry about that."

Fanshawe stood up and shrugged. His shirt was still stuck unpleasantly to his skin. "It's a week until the next BA flight back to London, which gives me time to take a look around. Perhaps check his files. Just to be sure."

Clift nodded. "Of course. Anything I can do to help just let me know."

"I'm going to want a full report on his death and this . . . irregular burial procedure." He paused. "Where did you bury him? The cemetery?"

Under Fanshawe's superior tone, Clift lost a little of his laid-back manner. "Um, no. It takes forever to get the paperwork for a foreign national to get a plot there, and in this heat and with the power cuts we've been having . . ." he paused. "Well, you just can't keep a body in it for long."

"So, where did you bury him?"

As he fed a fresh sheet of paper in the typewriter before answering, Fanshawe noted that at least Clift had the decency not to look up as he spoke.

"Out on the edge of the desert near where he lived. Like the locals do. There are bodies in unmarked graves all along the border of Omdurman and the Sahara."

Unmarked. Fanshawe reconsidered the cigarette.

The first time Cartwright had telexed back to London they'd had the whole team working for ten hours trying to unscramble the message. He wasn't supposed to be in any kind of contact while lying low in Khartoum let alone sending encrypted sentences at two o'clock in the morning local time. Fanshawe had smoked a lot that night. Cartwright was one of the best. It wasn't unfeasible, if a little against the unwritten rules of play, for one of his opposite number to have tracked him down.

Eventually, a very tired young woman knocked on his office door, shaking her head. "We've been through all the codes, sir. It doesn't make sense in any of them." She shrugged and Fanshawe waved her away. He looked down at the original sheet of telex paper with the single sentence printed out on it:

IT'S ALL IN THE SAND.

What the hell could Cartwright mean?

As it was, Cartwright was silent for just over a month before the next telex landed on Fanshawe's desk. It had been a long five weeks at the London end, during which Fanshawe maintained the protocol of radio silence to protect his hidden man. If Cartwright had something to tell them, he was going to have to get in touch again. In the meantime, all the encryptions were frantically being re-written. Perhaps they were compromised. Perhaps that's why Cartwright had chosen an ambiguous statement instead of using his allocated code. When the next message came it was as indecipherable as the first:

I CAN HEAR THE THUNDER OF HOOVES;
THE SCREAMING OF THE DYING BEASTS.

After staring at both messages side by side for far too long for sanity, Fanshawe was ready to scream himself. He felt as if he were stuck on the last clue of *The Times* crossword with no hope of getting the answer. The sentences were imprinted on the back of his eyes. He carried them everywhere with him.

He waited for Cartwright to get in contact again. But there was nothing. Instead, two months later came the Telex that said he'd been found dead in his house in Khartoum. And so here Fanshawe was. Hot, bothered and no closer to being able to solve the puzzle.

"I think I might go back to the hotel for a while. Catch up on some sleep."

Clift nodded, and Fanshawe was sure there was just a touch of relief in the way the younger man's shoulders dropped slightly.

"The driver downstairs will take you, sir. Call me if you need anything. Otherwise I'll pick you up tomorrow morning on my way into the office."

By the third day when Clift picked him up from the Hilton, Fanshawe had given up on the shirt and tie completely, settling in favour of an aertex collared T-shirt over cream slacks. His eyes burned from lack of sleep. It seemed that no one in the building had been capable of fixing the air-conditioning beyond the ground floor level. Fanshawe had stopped asking when that might be rectified. This was primarily because he was mildly concerned that he might commit an act of murder if anyone else was foolish enough to give him the answer "*Bukrah, in sh'Allah.*" *Tomorrow, if Allah wills it.* So far, Allah was very much against the idea.

As the Land Rover bounced across the uneven, rocky and pot-holed dusty tracks that served as roads, Fanshawe squinted out through the open window. Beyond the shallow ditches that ran along each side of the street, old women sat on low stools hawking their piles of paper bread and watermelons to any passers-by. Their skin was as cracked as the ground they came from, eyes black suspicious raisins in a desert of wrinkles as they watched the two white men drive by.

Clift paused at a crossroads, waiting for the melee of trucks and buses so over-loaded with people hanging from the sides that they looked like they might tip right over to stop blaring horns and figure out whose right of way it really was. Fanshawe was so busy trying to decide which potential accident was going to happen first that he didn't see the man approaching and jumped when he appeared at the window, waving the necklace at him.

"Jesus Christ." He pulled in a little, away from the leathery hand intruding his space trying to force him to touch the jewellery as if perhaps that would oblige Fanshawe to buy it. The metal and ivory pendant dangling from the shoelace strap looked tarnished and battered.

"*Y'ella,*" he muttered in disgust at the skinny man on the other side of the car door, whose free arm below the hem of the well-worn Adidas T-shirt, was loaded with necklaces and bracelets all with the same charm attached. The man's response was to lean in closer, words rushing in thick guttural Arabic, too fast for Fanshawe to follow.

Clift revved the engine and pulled the Land Rover forward, leaving the man standing in the street behind them, still waving and shouting at the dust trails of their tyres.

"Sorry about that," Clift said. "Seems they've been selling those bloody things everywhere. Must be the latest local fashion."

Winding the window up a little to prevent further intrusion, but to still allow in whatever hot breeze the car's motion could create, Fanshawe shook off the unsettled feeling and stared at the strange dips at the side of the road.

"What are the ditches for?" he asked Clift. Around them the huts and corrugated iron shacks slowly turned into rows of low, one-story buildings that made up the houses and shops as they came nearer into the centre of the capital city. They looked like they'd been forged from the sand around them. Maybe there was brick and plaster somewhere under their creamy surfaces, but it was well-hidden. The dust had claimed them, as it seemed the dust claimed and coated everything.

"There's your answer," Clift nodded over to the right. A thin man who could have been anywhere between twenty-five and forty lifted the folds of his white djellabah and squatted at the edge. Fanshawe frowned.

"Is he . . .?"

"Yes, 'fraid so." The car bounced past the man. "The ditches are the closest you'll come to public lavatories in Khartoum. Damned health hazard, but there's no telling the locals." Clift continued, swerving to get past a battered truck that pulled out without even pausing. "The German that died? That was because of those ditches. We had the first of the big rains. Came out of nowhere and flooded the roads. The German's jeep got stuck in a pothole and he got out to try and clear the wheel. Found himself knee deep in sewage. He must have had a cut that got infected, because it was dysentery and then blood poisoning and then all over. Poor chap."

Fanshawe said nothing for a while. He couldn't imagine water in these streets. The ground must devour it within a day; no amount of rain could be enough to quench the thirst of this parched land. The car made its way through the increasingly busier streets. Wild brown dogs panted under parked cars, ready to dart out to claim dropped food or to snarl at anyone that got too close. Men and women talked and laughed and sat outside shops or on the wrecked pavements in dusty mixes of tatty western clothes, Arab djellabahs and bright tribal dresses; a melange of fabric and dark skin. Flies settled unnoticed on dark flesh.

Somewhere in the distance a Muezzin began a call to prayer. Slowly all activity ceased and prayer mats were unfurled, for a few moments the majority of the city on their knees, facing Mecca. Fanshawe wondered if the man crouching by the ditch had finished in time. Turning into the Embassy car park, they passed three exceptionally tall and ebony black men who stood frozen on the corner, staring impassively in at Clift and Fanshawe. They carried long sticks, which for a moment Fanshawe thought might be spears. Tribal men, not Arab men.

He sighed as the Land Rover came to a halt. "It's not quite Bonne, is it?" he said, eventually.

"No, sir." Clift stepped out into the heat. "It's not quite Bonne."

By midday, Fanshawe had finished his second sweep of Cartwright's office. He'd taken the phone apart, checked the light sockets and even the air-conditioning vent and there was no sign of any bugs. Sweating and fed up, he sat back in the desk chair. Maybe Clift was right. Maybe it was too damned hot out here for spying games. Maybe Cartwright had just got a touch of sunstroke and then died of a heart attack. These things did happen.

He pulled at the top drawer of the desk, tugging it open even though it was stiff. He wasn't convinced by his own argument though. Cartwright had undergone a full medical after the fiasco in Moscow and passed it with flying colours. His heart had been in perfect working order.

He yanked the drawer open and checked its contents again. Pens, paper, a stapler. All basic and ordinary and as expected. He pushed the drawer and it caught again. Something was stopping it running smoothly. He frowned as he slid a hand over the rough surface of the drawer's base. An envelope was cellotaped there. Fanshawe ripped it free and emptied the contents onto the desk.

Photographs. At least twenty. Spreading them carefully out so he could study each one, Fanshawe clenched his teeth slightly. They were pictures of the desert. There wasn't a single soul in any of them, just the endless sand and occasional black rocky outcrop under the bright cloudless sky. He searched their edges to see if maybe they lined up, like some kind of jigsaw puzzle, but it was a fruitless task. To all intents and purposes, they were just random images, holiday snaps. So why had Cartwright felt the need to hide them? Were the Russians or East Germans planning to use part of the desert in some way? It didn't seem likely. So what the hell had the man been playing at?

The office door opened and a trolley appeared, carrying white mugs and a large urn, and pushed by a grinning Sudanese man, the darkness of whose skin was emphasized by the crisp cleanliness of his white djellabah.

"Tea, sir?" There was surprisingly only a hint of the thick Arab accent in his intonation; a far cry from the dusty Sudanese who had thrust his arm so rudely into the Land Rover that morning. The second surprise was that Fanshawe did indeed feel like a cup of tea, despite the acrid heat.

"Yes please. With milk if there is any."

"Certainly, sir." With one hand he poured a splash of milk into a cup and then placed it under the urn. The tea poured, hot steam rising up from it, and then with the same hand the man carefully placed it on the desk. He looked at the pictures and smiled.

"Interesting photographs. Deceptive, aren't they?"

Fanshawe had been about to sip his tea, and he paused. "How do you mean?"

"When you see the desert like that it looks flat. But of course, it is not."

Fanshawe stared at the images spread out in front of him. The ground looked level to him.

"Look there," the tea *wallah* pointed to a slight undulation in the sand. "It looks just like a ripple on the surface, yes?"

Fanshawe nodded in agreement.

"But," the local continued, "it is not. Just beyond that is the drop of a dune, maybe six feet or more. The desert is full of them." He shook his head slightly. "But to those that do not know the Sahara, it appears flat."

Fanshawe stared at the picture more closely and thought he could just see, in the hint of the shadows on the golden ground, what the man meant. "Tell me," he said. "Are there such drops in all of these photos?"

The man's eyes scanned the display and nodded. "Yes, I think so. When the Mahdi fought the British at Omdurman, they used the land's deception as part of a battle strategy. While some stood and lured the British forward on the flat sand, others would wait in the drops between the dunes with their swords ready. As the cavalry charged at the enemy they didn't see the drop until it was too late. The Mahdi's men would hack at the surprised horses' feet with their swords as they galloped and both beast and man would fall screaming into the pit." He smiled at Fanshawe. "Not bad for native thinking, eh, sir?"

Fanshawe nodded. "Not bad, at all."

Looking at the clean cups, the perfect whiteness of the man's outfit and the way he stood tall and with dignity, Fanshawe's curiosity got the better of him. "You seem a little over-educated for your current position. And your English is perfect. Surely you could be better employed elsewhere."

The man shook his head sadly and then revealed the stump at his right wrist. "Like many others, I've moved up from the South. I was a teacher of Politics at the university in Juba." He shrugged. "But then, apparently I stole a small item from the market and despite my protests of innocence . . ." His words drifted off, and Fanshawe stared again at the man's missing right hand.

"A man with a criminal record finds it hard to get good employment, even here in the north. But I can't complain. I have good pay and conditions." The tea man smiled. "God save the Queen."

"Yes, quite," Fanshawe muttered, but any slight empathy he'd felt for the man disappeared as something else he'd said gripped his thoughts. He sipped his tea as Cartwright's second telex typed itself out in his head.

I CAN HEAR THE THUNDER OF HOOVES;
THE SCREAMING OF THE DYING BEASTS.

"Tell me," he was surprised to find the tea was good; strong and hot and not even a hint of sourness in the milk. "Did you know the man in this office? The man that died?"

The tea *wallah's* eyes slipped away and he shrugged. "A little." He paused. "Did he take these pictures?"

"Yes."

"I thought so."

Fanshawe frowned. "How did you know they were his?"

The man sighed. "They say we all walked out of Africa in those first days of mankind and then spread to the four corners of the globe. Perhaps the desert calls some of us back. I think maybe your friend was one of those people." He started to wheel his trolley out. "I think he became fascinated with the desert. The sand was in his eyes from his first *haboob*. He became different."

The Sudan Club was a small oasis of green in the middle of the dry city. Sprinklers turned on the vast lawns and from where he sat in the bar, Fanshawe could see the swimming pool glinting blue under the floodlights that kept the dark away. Perhaps somewhere else, people would notice the tattiness of some of the paintwork and the chips in the floor tiles, but after four days of African dust and heat, even to Fanshawe, the private club whose membership was only open to those with British passports seemed like an idyll; a visit back to the glory days of the British Empire.

And at least the air was cool, fuelled by a generator that ran somewhere out at the back of the building, its throb like gentle background music. It seemed that the city danced to the beat of the generator drum, always one or two roaring somewhere, so that in the end you barely heard them. Maybe the silence of bare feet on sand would be more disturbing.

He leant on the marble bar and sipped his drink. It was the perfect mix of gin and tonic, just a large enough splash of the first, poured over huge rocks of ice, before being topped up with mixer. Enough of these and he wouldn't need his anti-malaria pills. Still, it felt like it had been a long day.

He'd spent the afternoon at Cartwright's house across on the western side of the wide muddy Nile, out past the edge of the town of Omdurman. He'd hoped to find an answer there for why the agent had moved from the centre of Khartoum, to the dustier, disappeared streets that bordered the desert, where only scrubby dry grasses and bare-footed goat herders lined what should be the pavements. At least in the capital Cartwright could have gone to the hubbub of Street 15 and bartered for eggs, sure that at least two or three of them wouldn't have been broken on the uneven journey by the time he got home. Instead he'd moved to the back end of the back end of beyond. It didn't make sense.

Impressive as the Omdurman house appeared – rising up on two levels, with a balcony that ran all round the top floor and three gates to get in – there was a sense that it was unfinished. Where there should have been gardens surrounding the building, there was only dirt, the lawns never having been laid, and although at the front of the property there was a high, metal gate and impressive walk up to the double fronted heavy wooden door, it seemed that Cartwright favoured the low gate at the back that squealed open onto a short path leading up to the servant's quarters on the right, and the door into the kitchen, straight ahead. It was by that gate that his car was parked.

The servant's quarters were empty, although there was evidence that Mahmood, the boy, was still living there even though Clift claimed not to have seen him since Cartwright's death. A small jar of coffee and a pot of rice sat on a low chipped Formica table by the narrow camping bed, above which, on the uneven walls that looked made of mud, hung an amulet of ivory and tarnished metal. Its diamond shape was less regular than the one that had been thrust so rudely through the Land Rover window that morning. This one looked older. The symbols or letters that were battered into its surface made no sense to Fanshawe and he left it where it was and headed to the main house.

In the spotless kitchen, the fridge was empty apart from a bottle of Gordon's gin. A case of Schweppes tonic sat on the clean tiles alongside it and for a moment Fanshawe stared at them. The city of Omdurman, unlike Khartoum and the Nile Hilton, seemed to be fine for electricity. The gin was cold and smooth blocks of ice filled the trays in the small freezer section. Tempted as he was to pour himself a drink, as much to fight his frustration as cool himself down, he resisted, and instead methodically did as he was trained to do, and worked his way through the various electrical appliances, searching for cameras and bugs, sweeping each room. It was painstaking and slow work, but as with Cartwright's office at the Embassy there was nothing.

All he found was precise neatness, a well-made bed, and ironed shirts in the closet. Not even any photographs, although there were slight tacky marks on the walls of the second bedroom as if perhaps pictures of some kind had been stuck up until recently. He'd stared at those marks for a long time but they refused to speak to him.

Eventually he went out on the balcony. The sun-baked tiles burned his feet through his shoes and shading his eyes with his hand, he looked out over the ocean of the desert that filled his view. Was this why Cartwright had moved? Simply to be closer to the desert? He stared at the dunes which looked flat even though he knew better and bit the inside of his cheek. But why? What was so special about the desert? The desert glared back at him.

Clift had picked him up at 5:00 pm, just as the heat of the day was turning its rage inwards, and they'd driven in almost silence to the club. Fanshawe was sure there had been a slight edge of smugness in Clift's expression as he'd peered over and asked, "Everything in order?" Fanshawe could hear the unspoken words echoing underneath the louder ones. *Sometimes heart attacks just happen.* Maybe it was just the heat addling his tired brain, but experience told him that smugness like that normally came from someone who thought they'd got away with something.

He wiggled his glass at the barman who nodded and waited for Clift to finish the last mouthful of his food before he spoke.

"So why did he move from the first house? Omdurman's a good forty-five minutes drive from here. It doesn't seem practical."

"He got an infestation of ants. Red ones. Those bastards really sting when they bite." Clift pushed away the remains of his chicken and chips in a basket so that it sat next to Fanshawe's, ready to be silently cleared away.

Fanshawe stared at it, as he mulled over Clift's words. Meat still hung uneaten from the tiny half-skeleton; just more greasy Western waste in a starving country. No one would boil those bones for chicken stock. Fanshawe idly wondered how the local men that worked at the club continued with their benign smiles and nods of subservience. Perhaps one day someone would drive by the Sudan club to find confused white heads stuck on poles at its gates, mimicking Gordon, brows still furrowed. *What did we do?*

"He moved out while it was being fumigated. And just never moved back."

Fanshawe looked up from the basket, firmly back on his very Western business. "There was no mention of ants in his file. That just shows that he requested a move. To that particular house, in fact."

As if appearing to support Clift's argument, a small black ant industriously carried an impossibly unwieldy crumb over to the far edge of the bar. It seemed to Fanshawe that ants and flies were a way of life in this part of the world. Ants wouldn't bother Cartwright, however painful their bite was. And he would know better than to draw attention to himself, even in a minor way.

"Paperwork isn't one of our strong points." Clift shrugged. "Not on the admin things like housing. The Embassy's too small for a dedicated housing officer."

The barman replaced Fanshawe's empty glass with a fresh, full one. Around them the room was relatively quiet apart from a fat man sitting further down from them who was laughing loudly, either with or at, a much thinner middle-aged man and his rather bored-looking pale wife. Fanshawe thought that perhaps Khartoum was not the best place for the pale-skinned to find themselves. He had a feeling you could burn in the shade here if your skin was so inclined.

"What's a *haboob*?" he asked suddenly, and was sure Clift twitched.

"*Haboob*?" The twitch again; a small tic in the man's cheek. "Where did you hear that word?"

"It was something the tea boy said." *Cartwright changed after the first* haboob. That's what the *chai wallah* had implied.

Clift lit a cigarette. "It's the local name for a desert sandstorm. We've had a few over the past couple of months. The season for them really starts now. You can feel the potential for one in the air most days." He drained his glass; almost half his drink gone in one go. "They're quite a sight."

Fanshawe thought he could make out the first beginnings of a bead of sweat on the younger man's hairline, even within the cool embrace of the chugging air-conditioning. He lit a cigarette of his own.

"The tea boy said Cartwright was quite fascinated with them."

Clift's eyes slid away. "Yes, I suppose . . . although he only saw his first one a couple of months ago. By the end of the season I'm sure he would have got used to them." He sucked almost a centimetre of the Marlboro into blazing red and orange.

Fanshawe watched him. How old was the first secretary? Thirty maybe? He suddenly looked younger. Clift may well go far within the ranks of her Majesty's Diplomatic service, but he would never make MI6. Not with that tic telling in his cheek. He sipped his drink. It really was very good.

"Perhaps," he said softly, "he moved to be nearer to the desert?"

Clift stared at the bar. "Maybe."

Behind them, the thin man and his pale-skinned wife said their goodbyes and headed out into the night. The fat man stayed where he was, a fresh drink placed in front of him. He smiled at the barman.

"*Shookran.*"

"*Afwan.*"

"*Afwan yourself.*"

Over Clift's shoulder, Fanshawe could see the barman laughing along with the man's English/Arabic joke, but there was a sense that he'd heard it far too many times before. He took the tip though, before returning to cleaning and polishing glasses.

The bar paused in silence for a moment and then Clift pushed his stool away and stood up. "I think I'll head home." He busily picked up his wallet and car keys, avoiding eye contact. "Do you want a lift to the Hilton?"

Fanshawe shook his head. "I'll get a taxi later. Think I'll enjoy the air-conditioning for a little while longer."

Clift nodded. "I'll pick you up in the morning then." As Clift moved, Fanshawe caught a glimpse of shoelace around his neck. Thin, black and local.

"I'll be there."

Sliding his glass round in his fingers, enjoying the cool condensation, Fanshawe watched him go. *Heart attack. Haboob. Omdurman. Sahara.* All of those words were wrapped up in the tic in his young colleague's face. But what was he hiding? Cartwright going mad? Maybe he was poisoned with a slow-acting agent. Maybe that's why he changed. *After his first haboob.* And why was Clift wearing a pendant like the one they'd seen this morning?

He turned back to the bar and found that the fat man was watching him, sharp eyes peering out from sockets dragged downwards with the weight of his cheeks. Despite the jowls, he managed a grin.

"Jasper Vincent. Freelance journalist." He raised his glass as a welcome. "How are you finding Khartoum?"

"Is my newness that obvious?"

Vincent laughed, and although it was loud and brash, there was an earthy warmth there. "Your skin doesn't look like leather yet."

"Fair enough comment. Alan Fanshawe. It's a flying visit for me. Just checking up on some things at the Embassy. Routine paperwork stuff. Freelance, you say?"

Vincent nodded. "Even the BBC doesn't keep a man out here full time anymore. Not now things have calmed down. I started out with them, but then went native and couldn't face heading back to London anywhere else for that matter." He paused. "I presume you're here about that British dip that died."

Fanshawe carefully sipped his drink. "You heard about that?"

"It's a small town. Where ex-pats are concerned, word travels." Ice that clung to the last hope of solidity clinked within his glass. "And I was in here when that chap that just left and the doctor came in afterwards. They seemed pretty shaken up. They drank a lot at any rate, and neither of them was laughing."

Signalling the barman to replenish their glasses, Fanshawe was far too well trained to push for more information. It would come soon enough he suspected, from a man like Vincent. And asking was often the very best way of not finding out.

Vincent stood up, sweat holding the creases and crumples in his linen trousers from where he'd been sitting. "Let's take these onto the terrace. It should be pleasant out there now."

They left the cool brightness of the bar and Fanshawe followed the fat man out to a metal table and chairs on the red dusty tiles. Yellow bulbs gave out a warm glow above them, and although the air was hot there was just the lightest touch of breeze. As he took his seat Fanshawe listened for a moment to the loud calling of the crickets and other insects who, in the gloom of the lawns and cacti and bushes, seemed determined to drown out the generator's soft thrum.

Under the glow of one of the lamps, a small sea of black lay in the pool of light. He tossed an abandoned bottle top into it, and the mass rose as one for a moment before fragmenting, the huge flying ants clattering their wings into each other as they hovered before settling back down, drowning the discarded metal disc. Fanshawe shivered a little in disgust. The place was all wrong; dark, alien and wild.

"How on earth could you choose to stay here rather than go back to London?"

Vincent stared out into the darkness, his stomach and arms overflowing from the metal confines of the chair.

"Africa is a strange place," he said, eventually. "And maybe Sudan is one of the strangest within it. Some people view it as a kind of *terra media*, lying between and linking Africa and the Arab world. Others see it as lying on the fault line between two peoples, torn between them and unable to unite. Maybe it's both of those things. They certainly have their share of problems with the South. That's what brought me here in the first place, reporting on the civil war. But Sudan is more than that. In the face of the white man its peoples are all one. The Dinka, the Arabs and the Nuer and the other smaller tribes, they can do what we can't begin to – they all understand the land. They understand the power and truth of living on the edge of poverty and with the vast Sahara challenging them to survive it."

He paused, and Fanshawe smiled. The man had a way with words. He could have made a good career for himself away from this filthy hellhole. "And you fell in love with that challenge?" Fanshawe was cynical. With his wide girth and the ruddy face of someone destined for an early grave due to far too much enjoyment of the finer things in life, Vincent did not look like a man that wanted the challenges of living on the edge of poverty. In fact, he looked like a man a year away from a heart attack. Fanshawe would believe *that* death of this man with as much conviction as he couldn't believe it of Cartwright.

Vincent grinned. "No. I fell in love with a Dinka woman. A tall, ebony beauty full of the strength and quiet promise of the desert. You don't get women like that back in England. Trust me."

Fanshawe watched Vincent's chubby wrist as it reached for his glass and his own smile fell a little. Around it hung ivory and battered metal.

"What *is* that bracelet? They seem to be everywhere. Some damned local tried to sell me one today and even Clift's wearing one."

Vincent's chubby fingers teased the charm for a moment. "Ah, my magic charm. The wife gave it to me. She insists I wear it in *haboob* season, and I'm not going to argue with her."

That word again. *Haboob*. Fanshawe's jaw clenched. "I don't understand the fascination with the bloody desert and the sandstorms," he muttered, the gin not strong enough to relax him.

Vincent's convivial appearance had melted away. He looked thoughtful. Almost pensive. "Your man lived out in Omdurman, didn't he? I heard stories about him, you know. Wandering out in the desert in the full heat of the day, taking photograph after photograph of the dunes."

Fanshawe sighed. In his years in the service he'd learned there was no point in being secretive with information that was already out there. "It would appear that he had become a little obsessive about the desert in the weeks before his death, yes." *It's all in the sand*. He paused. "After his first *haboob*."

Vincent nodded as if all the things that were leaving Fanshawe so confused, were making perfect sense to him. "Yeah, the natives said the spirits in the *haboob* had got him." He sat back in his chair, comfortable in the heat.

"People think that Sudan is a Muslim and Christian country, most of its people one or the other. And in some ways that's true. It seems so the Western world anyway, where we have a habit of only seeing the people we think matter. But the Dinka and the other tribes from the south, they have their own religions. Older ones. And maybe darker and more powerful ones too."

The crickets roared louder and Fanshawe could help but wonder if they were trying to silence the journalist who considered himself native, but was so obviously not of this land.

"*Haboobs* are amazing to see." Vincent looked up into the night sky around them. "You might see one tonight if this wind holds to its promise." Fanshawe lifted his head. The other man was right: the breeze was getting stronger.

"And sandstorms are all *haboobs* had been for maybe centuries, until the Dinka started fleeing from the south, crossing the desert and bringing their old religions with them. It was as if perhaps they woke something with their steady march across the sand. Something that had slept for too long and was happy to be woken." He smiled. "The true religion of the desert dwellers."

Fanshawe wondered for a long moment if the journalist was slightly mad or maybe had a touch of sunstroke or was just plain drunk. Perhaps there was no real information to be had here. The flying ants shifted a little in the pool of light and he fought a ripple of revulsion.

"What did the doctor say was the cause of death?" Vincent asked.

Fanshawe peered over at the fat man. "Heart attack. Why? What else could it have been?"

Vincent laughed a little. "Well, that would depend on whether you believe in the spirits in the desert."

"I don't understand." Fanshawe wondered if perhaps he was just being lured into a game with the jaded ex-pat; some old public school trick of getting one over on the new boy.

"The Dinka believe a great God lives in the hot earth beneath the endless layers of sand. Most of the time he sleeps in the coolness of the ground away from the sun. But for two or three months of the year, he's restless and sometimes wakes and reclaims the land, striding through the desert and leaving a huge rolling storm of dust in the wake."

Vincent looked over at Fanshawe. "The Dinka say that when he walks the desert so do the spirits of those that died in it, all of those that fell or are buried there. They can revisit the living, carried in the cloud. That's why some of the locals bury their loved ones out on the edge of the city – they hope that they'll return."

Fanshawe sniffed. Bloody native hokum-pokum. "That's an appealing legend." Perhaps he should have got a lift back to the hotel from Clift. "But you don't expect me to believe it, do you?"

Vincent grinned, his cheeks squashing his glinting eyes. "No, I don't. But I'll tell you this, just so you know." He leaned forward, resting his forearms on the table. "It wasn't Clift and the Doctor that buried him out in the desert. It was Mahmood, his servant." He paused, Fanshawe was sure for effect, before continuing.

"The story goes that your man wandered out in that last *haboob*, right into the middle of it, to see if the things he thought he'd glimpsed and heard were true. He came back hours later, a walking dead man; his eyes and ears full of sand and muttering incoherently."

Fanshawe stared. If Vincent hadn't used Cartwright's houseboy's name he'd have been laughing and on his way to find a taxi. As it was his mind was racing. Could Vincent be in the pay of the Russians? And why would the Russians create such an elaborate story when he'd already been told by his own people that Cartwright had died of a commonplace heart attack? Around him it seemed that the hot black night crept closer, threatening to smother him.

"How do you know this?"

"I told you, word travels. And I'm married to a Dinka. The white man who thought he saw the dead walking in the *haboob* has been the talk of the Dinka for a few months. They take these things seriously."

Fanshawe appeared smooth and relaxed as he leaned back in his chair, despite the edge in his nerves. "Go on."

"Mahmood wanted to call the *Faquih* to purge the spirits, but the Englishman collapsed on the floor and filled with sand, gripped his arm and wouldn't let him go. He held him like that for a full five minutes until the desert really claimed him and he died. They had a pact you see. Mahmood had promised that if anything happened to him, he'd bury him in the old traditional ways out by the desert. He called the Embassy man out and when he saw the state of the body and went for the doctor and was in a panic about a bloody coffin, Mahmood took the body to the edge of the desert and buried it before disappearing with whatever money your man had given him."

"Isn't Mahmood an Arab name? Why would he believe any of this?"

"Arab father, native mother," Vincent shrugged. "Most Sudanese have a healthy respect for all the religions. When you live in poverty and with disease and death always ready to grab you, it's advisable to keep your options open."

They sat in silence, and behind them a light bulb flickered but kept its hold on the rare stream electricity. The outside of Fanshawe's gin and tonic glass was damp under his fingers as he finished his drink.

"So, you think Cartwright really believed that the dead walked in the *haboobs* and wanted to become like them? And you believe that?"

Vincent shook his head slightly. "I believe that *he* believed it." He held up his fat wrist with the charm on it. "The amulet is supposed to keep the desert spirits from touching your soul. It protects you from the *haboob*." He smiled. "Maybe I've been here long enough to start hedging my bets too."

It was at about five o'clock in the morning that Fanshawe felt the breeze carrying the tiniest particles of dust through the mesh of the mosquito gauze stretched across the open hotel room window. He sat up, his heart thumping hard in his chest for no good reason. Wind tickled his face. More breeze than he'd felt in nearly a full week in the Sudanese capital.

He pushed back the covers, pulled on his trousers and without stopping for a shirt strode to the balcony doors and stepped outside. Despite the hours of darkness that had passed, the tiles under his feet were still pleasantly warm as was the metal rail that he gripped with his fingers. He barely felt them though, as he stared out at the land on the other side of the river, the wind dancing around him, teasing him, laughing at him.

He'd never seen anything like it. In the distance, small white one level houses disappeared into the foaming sand that surged across the land. A tidal wave of brown stretching across the width of his view thundered across the furthest parts of the city. Watching it rise up from the flat cream land, its facing edge billowing like clouds ballooning forward, Fanshawe could only guess at its height. Maybe fifty feet? Sixty? Or was it as much as a hundred feet in the air, endlessly rising towards the African sky.

Fanshawe's mouth dropped open in awe, as it claimed more of the city below, battered trucks and cars lost beneath its rolling movement, the desert like a murky cloud so huge and heavy that it had dropped from the sky, spreading out on the land and swallowing everything it touched in the whistle of its wind.

Against the silent backdrop of the pale pink horizon, the *haboob* raged. Fanshawe squinted. Despite the grit that pelted painfully into his bare skin he leaned forward. It couldn't be. It just couldn't be. For a moment out in the wild madness that had been the desert, he thought that the sandy shape of a huge horse's head, its mouth wide against the bit as it galloped, rose up through the cloudy edges of the sand storm before collapsing back below, as if something had . . . cut it down.

Gripping the edge of the balcony so tightly the bones of his knuckles threatened to tear through his skin, he blinked the screaming horse away. It was replaced by another. And another. And as the sand charged forward, Fanshawe was almost sure he could hear the battle cries, both orderly and foreign carried on the wind that brought the sand from Omdurman to the borders of Khartoum and was sure, just for a second, beneath the wailing and screeching of the wind, that the cry of "*Al nasr lana!*" Victory is ours.

He stared until his eyes were bleeding water from the onslaught of dust, and then just as the foamy surf of the desert tidal wave reached the far shore of the Nile, the wind dropped. Within moments the desert had fallen, becoming simply silent dust and sand covering everything it had touched.

He stood there for a long time, feeling the small particles of crushed ground fall slowly through the still air, pulled back by gravity, their tiny weight still too heavy to sustain their flight without the power of the wind. They tickled at Fanshawe's skin and scalp. It seemed to him that in that dawn moment of complete peace, the city sighed.

The day was quiet in the city. Fanshawe made some pretence of working in Cartwright's office, but in fact spent much of his time staring at the desert photographs, spread out in front of him, a code within a code. Clift seemed relieved that he had no more questions for him and kept himself hidden away, and when the *chai wallah* came round he merely watched Fanshawe cautiously for a moment or two before sinking into his subservient role and pouring out the tea and milk with his one good hand before wheeling his trolley away again. Fanshawe caught a glimpse of metal and ivory around the man's neck just before the door closed behind him.

The burning air was thick as honey and seemed so still that Fanshawe thought that not the breath of any god could lift it, but at four in the afternoon the slightest hint of a breeze teased its way into the hubbub of Khartoum. Away from the desk and looking out of the window, the glass panes blurred with dust in front of the mosquito screens, Fanshawe chewed on his lip and was convinced that he felt the city and its various people tense up.

He slipped out of the Embassy without saying a word to Clift and told the reluctant driver to take him to Omdurman. Staring at the shapeless streets and hawkers that lined them, he watched the wind tug at the djellabahs and yashmaks and Adidas T-shirts, making its presence increasing felt. Somewhere beyond the pretence of civilization the desert was stirring. Breathing. Claiming its life.

At Cartwright's house, he let himself in. His heart thudded to a stop for the briefest moment before he slowly closed the door behind him and crouched to examine the floor more closely. His eyes narrowed.

Where the day before the marble had been spotlessly clean, sandy footprints now wandered aimless through the house, as if they'd come looking for their owner.

Fanshawe's cool MI6 trained eyes scanned the room, and he walked carefully to the sink, picking up the glass that sat on the draining board. Around its edge were crusty brown lip prints that glittered in the fading light.

With the glass in one hand, he stared at both it and the footprints scattered on the ground and thought of the photographs still in his pocket, and the horses heads that had rose through the storm that morning, and that final cry of *Al Nasr Lana*, until eventually the wind outside howled as the sun set and his reverie was broken.

He left the lights off and put the dirty glass down. He took a clean one from the cupboard and made himself a large gin and tonic. The ice cubes tinkled loudly as he padded into the gloom of the large lounge. In the cushioned high back chair, he casually crossed one leg over the other, sipping his drink before letting the glass rest on the scratched wooden arm of the regulation Embassy furniture. He'd mixed it perfectly and as the gin tingled to his head, the tonic buzzed sharply on his tongue.

After half an hour the first tendrils of sand began to whip at the sides of the house. Fanshawe, perfectly still in the chair, smiled. He'd come to Khartoum for answers. In the encroaching embrace of the desert *haboob*, he wondered if perhaps he'd get them from Cartwright himself.

MARK SAMUELS

"Destination Nihil"
by Edmund Bertrand

MARK SAMUELS IS THE AUTHOR of three short story collections: *The White Hands and Other Weird Tales* (Tartarus Press, 2003), *Black Altars* (Rainfall Books, 2003) and *Glyphotech & Other Macabre Processes* (PS Publishing, 2008), as well as the short novel *The Face of Twilight* (PS Publishing, 2006).

His tales have appeared in both *The Mammoth Book of Best New Horror* and *Year's Best Fantasy and Horror*. His fourth collection of stories, *The Man Who Collected Machen & Other Stories* is scheduled to appear from Ex Occidente Press in 2009. He is also literary executor for the late Edmund Bertrand.

"How I came to be Bertrand's literary executor is a convoluted affair and too long to go into here," explains Samuels. "In any case, it's certainly ironic, given that Bertrand (an American citizen, but of French ancestry, as his name suggests) was a staunch Anglophobe.

"Bertrand was born in Memphis, sometime during 1957, and died in a mysterious hotel fire whilst attending a convention in England, two years ago. His stories chart the far reaches of madness, and were never collected together in a single volume. His main influences were European authors such as Stefan Grabinski, Roger Gilbert-Lecomte, Dino Buzzati and Jean Lorrain."

"I SAID, 'CAN I SEE your ticket please, sir'."

The man to whom the instruction was issued gave a start and appeared to wake from a trance-like state. He rummaged in the pockets of his worn corduroy jacket and finally drew out a crumpled and aged card.

The conductor, however, did not touch the ticket but leant forward in order to scrutinize it. At no point did his hands leave his pockets of his staff jacket. His face, shaded by a cap, appeared strangely paralytic and expressionless. It was devoid of healthy pallor, being of a bloodless yellow hue. The eyes were too far back in their sockets, as if sinking in the quicksand of bodily decay. Overall, it was too much like a dead face.

"Have a pleasant trip Mr Grey."

The man who had been addressed as "Mr Grey" examined the ticket, squinting at the print through his horn-rimmed eyeglasses. The name on the ticket read "Robert Grey", but it meant nothing to him. No starting point or destination was indicated although the name of the train company NORACH was emblazoned at the top.

I assume then, the man thought, that I must be Robert Grey. He tried to keep down the wave of panic that threatened to wash over him. Since I cannot recall what I am doing here on this train, he reasoned, the only logical conclusion is that I am either an amnesiac or suffering from some form of dementia affecting my memory, perhaps with hallucinations thrown in for good measure. The cadaverous appearance of the train conductor was surely an example of mental turmoil externalized by a diseased imagination.

Grey examined his hands. A few liver spots dappled the skin and blue veins were prominent. He turned his head to the dusty window and saw his reflection, slightly hazy but still mirror-like in the darkness outside the car. His face was paunchy and lined. Thinning white hair crowned his head. His neck had turkey folds. Grey calculated his age to be somewhere between sixty-five and seventy. Perhaps it's senile dementia, he thought, since he appeared to be at the prime age range for its onset. His breath caught in his throat and he fought back a second wave of panic.

Across from him, on the far side of the dividing table and resting on the seat opposite, was a large black valise. Its leather surface was scuffed, particularly at the edges, and it looked to have seen a great deal of use. Perhaps there might be an answer in there. If it were his property then the familiar possessions within might kick-start his memories, or at least give him a foothold in his own identity.

The valise was atrociously heavy. Grey gasped with the effort as he hauled it onto the table, and then unbuckled the two binding straps that kept the lid down. Once he'd pulled the top open, the smell that wafted out alerted him to its contents before he'd even laid eyes on the interior. The valise was full of densely packed earth. And when Grey put his hand inside, turning over the moist and pungent soil, he discovered that it was infested with innumerable wriggling maggots. He closed the lid with a cry of disgust and brushed his hands clean of the black dirt that clung damply to them.

There was no question now of keeping panic in check. Grey loped off along the aisle of the car in search of the conductor, or of the first person he encountered. A few rows further down he saw a man slouched in his seat, dressed in a rain mac and a wide-brimmed floppy hat that obscured his face. Grey hesitated before addressing the stranger, because he feared the face concealed in shadow. Would it be like that of the conductor? If it were, then he feared he would have reached a tipping point and might scream himself to death.

But the stranger was conscious of Grey at his elbow. He looked up and revealed himself to be an ordinary, living man, possessed of an ordinary face, albeit one marked by concern at Grey's agitation.

"Are you alright?" The stranger said, "You look dreadful. Here, sit down."

Grey hesitated for a moment, staring hard at the stranger's face, searching for any sign of abnormality. He could find none. It was the face of a harmless middle-aged man, slightly wrinkled around his blue eyes, clean-shaven, nondescript, bland in the extreme. It was the face of a million men who are passed on the sidewalk every day without leaving any impression in the memory.

"Something's wrong," Grey burbled out, "I don't know how I got here. I don't know where I am. I don't even know who I am. You must help me. That conductor, for example, there's something . . ."

"Calm down," the stranger interrupted, "you seem to me to be in shock. I know what it's like. Take it easy. Tell me about it."

Grey lowered himself into the seat adjacent to the man, let out a deep breath and tried to control himself. He ran his hand over his forehead, transferring a cold sheen of sweat to his palm.

"My name is Black," the middle-aged man said.

Grey replied, "Where's this train bound for?"

Black grimaced. He'd kept his hands hidden within the outside pockets of his mac and had not removed them since Grey had first spotted him. Now he made circular movements as if twisting them around inside his coat.

"Black, what is this train's destination?" Grey asked again.

"Shush." Black whispered, "If the conductor hears you . . . the destination is not important. The journey is the thing."

"What do you know about this train? Look around you." Grey persisted.

Black's steady eyes looked over the enclosed expanse of the car in which the two men were seated. Sickly green paint flaked from the walls. Half of the lamps were broken. The spring suspension in the seats had given way long ago, and deep hollows indicated the presence of thousands of former passengers. The inside of the windows was coated with a layer of dust. In the overhead racks there were dozens of valises, all apparently without owners.

"What I know," said Black, "is that if you insist on making a fuss like this, you're liable to be thrown off the train."

"Thrown off the train just for asking a straightforward question?" Grey was now regarding Black with incredulity. Grey had anticipated some anchor in reality, a counterpoint to his own confused mental state, rather than an individual who seemed in an even worse condition than himself.

"Of course. But I see you don't yet understand. Have you just woken up? Obviously you've not had the chance to see what's outside yet. Still too dark I suppose." Black said.

Grey momentarily turned to the window. It was impossible to discern what was outside. Even after he had managed to scrub away some of the grime from the pane with the cuff of his jacket, all he could see was his own reflection peering back at him and an impenetrable blackness beyond.

"I suppose, in a manner of speaking, I have just woken up," Grey said, shifting back into the seat opposite Black with a long drawn-out sigh, "but it feels as if I've gone insane."

"It's said that if you die in your dreams you die in the waking world. But what if you went mad in your dreams? What if you couldn't wake up and the dream went on and on and on . . ."

"What about if you tell me what's really going on here?" Grey interjected, thumping his fist on the table between them. This was no dream, he was certain of that much. There was no blurring around the edges, no non-lineal procession of events, none of the recognized attributes that accompany dreaming.

"Perhaps it's not your dream, perhaps it's mine. Perhaps you're just a made-up character and I haven't filled you with memories and a past," Black said.

"I need to find someone talking sense, excuse me," Grey said, getting to his feet and loping off along the aisle again, swaying slightly with the rocking motion of the car.

*　　*　　*

Grey had gone through sixteen deserted cars before he paused for breath. Some were almost in ruins, with seats torn out and there were even signs of fires having been started in half a dozen. He had not encountered another person. He wondered whether all the passengers had deserted the train, alighting at an earlier station after having wreaked havoc in the cars like rampaging Brit soccer hooligans. Only the elusive ticket inspector could provide an answer, but Grey feared that he might already be in a car even further forward in the train, at such a distance that exhaustion would intervene before he could be intercepted.

Grey tried not to think about the prospect any more deeply, and trudged onwards, picking his way through several more cars choked with debris until he came to a luggage coach. He noticed at once the moist and pungent smell of earth and was not surprised to find dozens of large valises piled up in the storage area. A couple of their poorly fastened lids had come loose and the soil within had spilled out on the wooden floor, along with the writhing grubs who'd formerly been its inhabitants. The mass of valises was not properly secured and they teetered with each sideways lurch of the train.

He leaned down to get a closer look at one of the sickly-yellow grubs wriggling around blindly. It was, like its companions, considerably larger than the ones he'd seen back in the valise he'd opened just after awakening. These specimens appeared more developed and Grey noticed that each one was wriggling along the floor, towards the back of the coach, around and beyond the pile of valises.

Grey followed in the wake of the grubs, taking care not to crush any underfoot, since he thought it would be loathsome to see one of them squashed.

Behind the valises he discovered more than a dozen black canvas sacks and secured at the top end by rope. Each contained something that struggled to escape. They were piled up, one on top of another, in a mound. Grey thought that he detected the sound of a low groaning coming from a couple of the formless heaps.

The grubs were not making for the occupied sacks but for the empty ones even further back in the coach.

Terrified, but unable to resist discovering some part of the solution to the riddle in which he was trapped, Grey pulled one of the sacks from the mound and untied the rope securing the opening.

Grey couldn't make out the thing within clearly as it huddled up its stunted body to itself, as if avoiding the light. But he had the impression of a squashed and boneless parody of humankind. He did, however, see the creature's face before it had turned away. Its lidless eyes were wholly white. Drool oozed from its groaning, gummy mouth.

The moaning from the other occupied sacks intensified, as if they were aware of Grey's presence, and were pleading either for his attention or to be left alone. He tied up the end of the sack he'd just opened, returning its occupant to its former state, and hauled the squirming object back onto the mound to rejoin its companions.

He stumbled out of the car, his legs weak beneath him, shocked and terrified by what he'd seen. Were those half-formed beings the train's hidden cargo, on their way to be exterminated – the remains of scientific experiments that had gone horribly wrong?

In the corridor, there was half-light. Dawn had broken, providing feeble illumination across the landscape that could now be seen through the train windows. Grey pulled up the nearest window and leant outside. A chill blast of air buffeted his head, rumpling his white hair and making his eyes water. As far as he could see was a vast and dusty plateau, its monotony broken only by a myriad of tumbleweeds and lunar craters. The sky was a sheet of total blackness. It could not account for the dying dawn creeping across the landscape, trailing gaunt shadows in its wake.

Grey tried to see the end or beginning of the train, but it appeared to be turning a huge curve on the railroad and he was looking at the outside bend. He passed to the opposite side of the corridor and threw open a window there, so he could see the length of the inside bend of the train. Straight ahead, across almost a mile, he spotted a white-haired man staring back at him.

The train charted a circle, a gigantic wheel turning endlessly, a self-enclosed universe of railroad cars, without end or beginning.

ALBERT E. COWDREY

The Overseer

ALBERT E. COWDREY WAS BORN in New Orleans and attended Tulane and Johns Hopkins Universities. Equipped with a doctorate, he spent thirty years working as a historian, mostly in Washington, DC – teaching, writing for trade and university presses, and turning out official histories for the US Army.

At retirement he uttered a silent but heartfelt vow that henceforth he would do what he had to, and what he wanted to, but never again what he ought to. The result has been a second career in science fiction and fantasy.

His new bibliography includes a novel from Tor Books, *Crux* (2004), as well as forty-five novellas and short stories already published or soon to appear in *The Magazine of Fantasy & Science Fiction*. His work has been much anthologized in English and reprinted in languages he can't read, including Russian, Polish, Czech, Romanian, Hebrew and Chinese.

He has received awards both from the American Historical Association (1984) and the World Fantasy Convention (2002). Not many writers can make that statement; perhaps not many would want to.

" 'The Overseer' " is the product of a long wrestling match between the historian and the writer of fantasy," admits Cowdrey. "First it was mostly history and didn't work as a story; then Felix Marron came stalking out of some trapdoor in my subconscious, took the tale over and gave it point and meaning.

"Demons are of course quite real, though fortunately rare, and without a single exception they all are or have been human."

T HOUGH APPROPRIATELY RUNDOWN, Nicholas Lerner's big house on Exposition Boulevard in uptown New Orleans was not haunted. The same could not be said of its owner.

That spring morning in 1903 the old man was getting ready for the day. Or rather, Morse was making him ready.

"So, Mr Nick," murmured the valet, applying shaving soap to his employer's face with an ivory-handled brush, "are you writing a book?"

Damn him, thought Lerner. *He knows I detest conversation with a razor at my throat.*

"My memoirs," he muttered. "A few jottings only. Waiting to die is such a bore, I write to pass the time."

Was that the real reason he'd become a late-blooming scribbler – mere boredom? Most of his life had been devoted to hiding the truth, not revealing it. And yet now . . .

"I think you must be writing secrets," smiled Morse, piloting the blade beneath his left ear. "The way you lock your papers in the safe at night."

"I lock them up," Lerner snapped, getting soap in his mouth, "because they are *private.*"

And had better remain so, he thought wryly. The other memorabilia in his small safe – an ancient, rusted Colt revolver; a bill from a Natchez midwife; a forty-year-old spelling book; a faded telegram saying RELIABLE MAN WILL MEET YOU RR LANDING STOP – would mean nothing to any living person.

Then why should he write the story out, give evidence against himself? It seemed to make no sense. And yet, having started, somehow he couldn't stop.

Humming an old ballad called "Among My Souvenirs", he pondered the problem but reached no conclusion. He closed his eyes and dozed, only to wake suddenly when Morse asked, "Who is Monsieur Felix?"

Lerner heard his own voice quaver as he replied, "Someone I . . . knew, long ago. Where did you hear of him?"

"Last night, after you took your medicine, you spoke his name over and over in your sleep."

"Then I must have seen him in a dream."

Shrewd comment. Morse knew that the opium he obtained for the old man caused intense dreams, and would ask no more questions.

Without further comment he burnished his employer's face with a hot towel, combed his hair, and neatly pinned up his empty left sleeve. He removed the sheet that protected Lerner's costly, old-fashioned Prince Albert suit from spatter, and bore all the shaving gear through the door to the adjoining den and out into the hall. Remotely, Lerner heard Morse's voice – now raised imperiously – issuing orders to the housemaid and the cook.

Good boy! thought Lerner, checking his image in a long, dusky pier glass. *Make 'em jump!*

He was rubbing his smooth upper lip to make sure no bristles had been left, when suddenly he leaned forward, staring. Then, with startling energy, his one big hand whirled his chair around.

Of course nobody was standing behind him. A trick of his old eyes and the brown shadows of his bedchamber with its single door, its barred and ever-darkened window. Or maybe a result of talking about Monsieur Felix, whom he would always associate with mirrors, fog, winter darkness, summertime mirages – with anything, bright or dark, that deceived the eye.

"Ah, you devil," he muttered, "I'll exorcise you with my pen. Then burn both you and the damned manuscript!"

Maybe that was the point of his scribbling – to rid himself of the creature once and for all. Smiling grimly, he trundled into his den.

Like its owner, his safe was an antique, the combination lock encircled with worn red letters instead of numbers. He dialed a five-letter word – *perdu,* meaning lost, a word with many meanings as applied to its contents. He jerked open the heavy door, drew out a pack of cream-laid writing paper and carried it to his old writing desk, a burled walnut monster honeycombed with secret compartments.

On the wall above, his dead wife smiled from a pastel portrait. Elmira as she'd been when young – conventionally pretty, not knowing yet that her short life would be devoted mainly to bearing stillborn children. On her lap she held their first boy, the only one born alive, but who, less than a month after the artist finished the picture, had suffocated in his crib, in the mysterious way of small children.

Bereft, surrounded by servants who did everything for her, idle, dissatisfied, Elmira had died a little too. Her husband had granted her everything she wanted except entry into his head and heart.

"Why don't you trust me?" she'd asked him a thousand times, and he'd always answered, "My dear, I trust you as I do no other human being."

She'd never quite found the handle of that reply. Morse's father and mother would have understood the irony – the fact that he really trusted no one – but of course they were dead too.

They saw into my soul, Lerner thought, *but it didn't save them, either one.*

He shrugged, dismissing Elmira and all the other ghosts. Time to introduce the Overseer into his story. But first he wanted to sharpen his unreliable memory by rereading what he'd written so far. He drew the papers closer to his nose and flicked on a new lamp with a glaring Edison bulb that had recently replaced the old, dim, comfortable gaslight. Squinting balefully at his own spidery, old-fashioned handwriting, he began to read.

CHAPTER THE FIRST

Wherein I Gain, Then Lose, My Personal Eden

As I look back upon the scenes of a stormy life, filled with strange adventures and haunted by a stranger spirit, I am astonished to reflect how humble, peaceable and commonplace were my origins.

My ancestors were poor German peasants, who in 1720 fled the incessant wars of Europe and found refuge on Louisiana's Côte des Allemands, or German coast, near the village of Nouvelle Orléans. Their descendants migrated northward to the Red River country, still farming the land but, like the good Americans they had become, acquiring slaves to assist their labours.

Here in 1843 I was born into the lost world that people of our new-minted Twentieth Century call the Old South. The term annoys me, for to us who lived then 'twas neither old nor new, but simply the world – our world. I first saw light on a plantation called Mon Repos, a few miles from the village of Red River Landing, and there spent my boyhood with Papa and Cousin Rose. Our servants were three adult slaves and a son born to one of them, whom Papa had named Royal, according to the crude humour of those times, which delighted in giving pompous names to Negroes.

Our lives resembled not at all the silly phantasies I read nowadays of opulent masters and smiling servants. Our plantation was but a large ramshackle farm, its only adornment a long alley of noble oaks that Papa had saved when felling the forest. Our lives were simple and hard; many a day at planting or harvest-time Papa worked in the fields beside the hands, his sweat like theirs running down and moistening the earth.

In our house Cousin Rose counted for little, for she was but a poor relation whose parents had died in the same outbreak of Yellow-Jack that claimed my mother. Ever pale and fragile as a porcelain cup, she spent most days in her bedroom, more like a ghost than a girl. The slave boy Royal, on the other hand, counted for much – at least in my life.

How I envied him! He never had to study, and went barefoot nine months of the year. I was beaten often by the schoolmaster, but Royal escaped with a scolding even when he was caught stealing flowers from the garden, or roaming the house above stairs, where only the family and the housemaid were allowed to go. Indeed, Papa so favoured him that I came to understand (though nothing was ever said) that he was my half-brother.

Spirits, too, inhabited our little world. All who dwelt in that benighted region believed in divining rods and seer stones, in ghosts and curses, in prophetick dreams, buried treasure, and magical cures. Royal and I were credulous boys, like those Mark Twain so well describes in Tom Sawyer, *and we met often in the bushes near the servants' graveyard at midnight to whisper home-made incantations, half-fearing and half-hoping to raise a "sperrit" that might shew us the way to an hoard of gold – though none ever appeared.*

In these expeditions Royal was always bolder than I, as he was also in our daylight adventures. He dove from higher branches of the oak overleaning our swimming-hole than I dared to; he was a better shot than I, often bearing the long-rifle when, as older boys, we fire-hunted for deer. Ah, even now I can see and smell those autumn nights! The flickering of the fire-pan; the frosty crimson and gold leaves crackling under our feet; the sudden green shine of a deer's eyes, the loud shot, the sharp sulphurous smell of burnt powder, and the dogs leaping into the darkness to bring down the wounded animal!

Are we not all killers at heart? Scenes of death having about them a kind of ecstasy, however we deny it, greater even than the scenes of love.

Preceded by a clink of china, Morse spun the door handle and backed into the den, hefting a tray with a dish under a silver cover, a folded napkin, and a goblet of red wine.

"When," demanded Lerner testily, "will you learn to knock, my boy?"

"Mr Nick, I ain't got enough hands to carry the tray, open the door and knock, too."

A doubtful excuse, thought Lerner; a table stood in the hallway convenient to the door, where Morse could have rested the tray. Frowning, he turned his pages face down on the desk.

Morse set his lunch on a side table, moved the wheelchair, shook out the stiff linen napkin and tied it around Lerner's neck.

"Should I cut the meat for you, Mr. Nick?"

"Yes, yes. Then leave me alone. And don't come back until I ring."

"You'll be wanting your medicine at the usual time?"

"Yes, yes. But wait for my ring."

In leaving, Morse took a long look at the half-open safe, a fact that did not escape the old man. Lerner ate lunch slowly, pondering. His dependence on Morse reminded him all too clearly of how his father had become the servant of his own servant after Monsieur Felix entered Mon Repos. That had been the beginning of many things, all of them bad.

I will not suffer that to happen again, he thought.

Lerner had an old man's appetite, ravenous at the beginning but quickly appeased. Without finishing his lunch, he hastily swallowed the wine at a gulp, wheeled back to his desk, took up his manuscript and again began to read.

The Eden of my childhood did not last long. In the Fifties the world's demand for cotton soared, and Papa began to dream of growing rich.

He was not alone. The steamboats that huffed and puffed up and down the Mississippi began delivering carven furniture, pier-glasses, and Paris fashions to our community of backwoodsmen. Ladies – it seemed overnight – graduated from sun-bonnets to hoopskirts, and the men were as bad or worse, with their sudden need for blooded horses and silk cravats and silver-mounted pistols and long Cuban segars.

In this flush atmosphere, Papa borrowed from the banks and cotton factors and bought new acres, though land had become very dear. He made trips to New Orleans to barter for workers in the slave markets at Maspero's Exchange and the St Charles Hotel, and he rebuilt our comfortable log house as a mansion with six white columns, which – like our prosperity – were hollow and meant only for shew. But he remained a farmer, not a businessman; he overspent for everything, and could not make the new hands work, for he was too soft to wield the whip as a slave-driver must. Soon he was in debt and facing ruin, and so in 1855, during one of his trips to the city, he hired an Overseer to do the driving for him.

'Tis hard for me to remember Felix Marron as a man of flesh. I see him in my mind's eye as the sort of shadow that looms up in a

morning fog, briefly takes human form, then fades again into a luminous dazzle.

Yet when first we met, he seemed merely freakish. Royal and I were returning from a fishing jaunt when we espied him talking to Papa, and we stared and giggled like the bumpkins we were. I suppose he was then about forty, but seemed ageless, as if he never had been born – a strange creature, very tall and sinewy, his long bony face a kind of living Mardi Gras mask with grotesquely prominent nose and chin. Though 'twas August, he wore an old musty black suit, and I remember that despite the stifling Delta heat, his grey face shewed not a drop of sweat.

When Papa introduced us, he ignored Royal but swept off his stovepipe hat to me, loosing a cloud of scent from his pomade, and in a penetrating stage whisper exclaimed, "Bonjour, bonjour, 'ow be you, young sir?" Shifting an old carpetbag to his left hand, he clasped my right in his cool bony grip, causing a braided whip he carried over that arm to swing and dance. Then Papa led him away to view the quarters, and Royal and I laughed out loud – thereby proving that neither of us was gifted with prophecy.

Papa hired Monsieur Felix (as he preferred to be called) upon the understanding that he would have a free hand to extract profit from our people and our acres. At first the bargain seemed to be a good one, for the Overseer was restless and tireless, keeping on the move (as the slaves said) from can't-see in the morning to can't-see at dusk. He had a strange way of walking, lunging ahead with long silent strides that ate up the ground, and appearing suddenly and without warning where he was not expected. And woe to any slave he found idling! Not one escaped flogging under his regime, not even Royal, whose days of idleness and indulgence came to an abrupt end. Soon he learned to dread the hoarse whisper, "Aha, tu p'tit diable," the Overseer's sole warning before the lash fell.

At first Papa resisted this abuse of his darker son. But the Overseer argued that to favour one slave was to corrupt all by setting them a bad example; further, that Royal (then twelve years of age) was no longer a child, and must be broken in to the duties of his station in life. Finally, that unless he could impose discipline on all our hands, Monsieur Felix would leave Papa's employ, and seek a position on a plantation that was properly run. So Papa yielded, and by so doing began to lose mastery over his own house.

I watched Royal's first beating with fascination and horror. My own floggings at the schoolmaster's hands were but the gentle flutter of a palmetto fan compared to the savage blows administered by

Monsieur Felix. Had I been the victim, I would have raised the whole country with my howls; but Royal remained obstinately silent, which the Overseer rightly saw as a kind of resistance, and added six more to the six blows first proposed, and then six again, leaving Royal scarce able to walk for three or four days.

Thus began several years of tyranny. Even when he grew older and stronger, Royal could not strike back – for a slave to assault a white man, whatever the provocation, meant death – nor could he flee, for the patterollers (as we called the cruel men of the slave patrols) scoured the neighbourhood. And so he bore his whippings as the others did, and let his hatred grow. In my innocence I loathed the Overseer, for I was too young to understand that he flogged our people not out of cruelty, nor indeed of any feeling at all, but as an herdsman prods his ox or a plowman lashes his mule – to wring work from them, and wealth from his acres.

In that he succeeded. With the crops heavy – with the hands hard at work – with prices rising, and dollars rolling in, Papa felt himself no longer the descendant of Westphalian peasants, but rather a great planter and a member of the ruling class. He bought leather-bound books by the linear foot, and installed them in his den, though he did not attempt to read them; he drank from crystal goblets, though his tipple was corn whiskey drawn from his own still. He paid Monsieur Felix well, and built him a substantial house midway between Mon Repos and the slave quarters, which was where the Overseer himself stood, in the southern scheme of things. Papa thought he would be content to live there and receive wages that grew from year to year, and mayhap marry in time some poor-white slattern of the neighbourhood. But in this he misjudged the Overseer's ambition.

Applying still more pomade to his lank black hair, he took to invading our house, supposedly to talk business with Papa, but in reality to ogle my cousin Rose – then fifteen and almost of marriageable age. Though I was but a great clumsy overgrown boy with long skinny shanks and feet like keelboats, I well understood that the Overseer designed to marry into our family as the first step toward gaining control of Mon Repos. In a rage, I summoned up my smattering of French and called him cochon to his face, for his English was so poor I feared he might misunderstand if I called him swine. I ordered him never again to set foot in the house, at which he laughed in his strange soundless way. He would have loved to give me a taste of his whip, but the caste system protected me, for only the schoolmaster was allowed to beat the heir of Mon Repos.

To get rid of me, Monsieur Felix told Papa I deserved to finish my *education in the North, saying how 'twould honour our family if I won a degree from a famous school. With money weighing down his pockets, Papa agreed, and in the summer of 1860 I was compelled to say goodbye to everyone and everything I knew, and set out for the land of the Puritans, as I imagined it. I wished to take Royal to Yale College as my valet, but Monsieur Felix warned Papa that he would run away, once in the free states. So he was doomed to stay behind, whilst I boarded a Cincinnati-bound steamer at Red River Landing for the first leg of my journey.*

I was seventeen years of age, as fresh and proud as a new ear of corn, and as green. Wearing varnished boots and carrying my shiny first top hat, I stood upon the hurricane deck, gazing down at ragged and dusty Royal, who had come with the family to say farewell. We who had been playmates now were clearly master and slave. Yet we shared a secret plan, devised during many a night-time meeting at the graveyard. If, as I anticipated, Monsieur Felix laid hands upon Rose, Royal was to kill him, and give himself up to the sheriff without resistance. I would return post-haste and testify that he had merely obeyed my orders, as a slave should, to protect my cousin's honour. As his reward, when I inherited him I would set him free. Upon this understanding, I left my rifle in a place only Royal knew – wrapped in oily rags, and tied atop a rafter in the cabin of the slave quarters where he slept.

I raised my hand to him as one conspirator to another, and he nodded in reply, his face smooth and immobile as a mask of bronze. Rose wept, Papa honked into his handkerchief, and Monsieur Felix vouchsafed a thin arid smile, like an arroyo dividing his blade of a nose from his large blue chin. Then the whistle blew, the bell chimed, the gangplank lifted, and the muddy bank – like my youth – began drifting away from me.

Siesta time had come. Lerner returned the manuscript to the safe, closed the heavy door and spun the dial. He picked up a little silver bell, rang it briskly, and within ten minutes Morse appeared like a household genie. He removed the lunchtime clutter, spread and adjusted the old man's lap robe, put a pillow behind his head, and vanished again, quietly closing the door.

Since the back injury that had left him unable to walk, Lerner had needed such coddling to shield him against severe pains that otherwise spread up and down his spine. Yet he understood that his immobility was killing him. He could almost feel the systems of his body rusting in place, shutting down slowly. *How tiresome it is,* he thought, *to die by inches,* and with an effort of will concentrated his mind upon his story. He'd come to the end of what he'd already written; tomorrow he must carry the tale forward, weaving fragments of memory into a narrative.

He dozed until five-thirty, waking when Morse turned on the electric chandelier and set down his dinner tray with a folded evening newspaper beside the plate. Lerner ate while perusing the unexciting developments of the day – the end of the Philippine Insurrection, the galumphing of that damned cowboy in the White House. Then the long ritual of putting him to bed began. Morse worked with the deft expertness of a hospital nurse, and by seven-thirty the old man was resting in bed, propped up on a hillock of cushions and covered with spotless linen. He sniffed the penetrating, somehow frigid smell of grain spirits left by the alcohol rub Morse had given him, then folded his hands and smiled, awaiting the high point of his day.

"Come, come, Morse," he whispered.

The indefatigable one returned with a gleaming salver on which rested a sticky pellet of opium wrapped in rice paper, a crystal flask of amber bourbon, a shot glass, and a silver coffee spoon. Deftly he prepared the laudanum, dissolving the opium in the whiskey with ritualized movements, like a priest mixing water and wine.

"I need to go and buy more of your medicine, Mr Nick," he murmured, presenting the drink.

"Why not buy it from a drugstore?" Lerner demanded. "Those neighbourhoods by the docks are dangerous."

"Mr Nick, I can do that, but it'll cost twice as much. The import tax alone is six dollars a pound, and I can buy decent opium from a Chinaman for five."

Grumbling, the old man extracted a few bills from a drawer in his marble-topped night table and handed them over. Then in three long sips he drank the draught that ended pain and summoned sleep.

His throat burned, he felt a sharp pain in his gut, then a banked fire that burned low, warming and soothing him. A delicious languor began to spread through his old body. He felt his weight lessen, then almost evaporate. He felt dry and light, like a balsa-wood doll floating high on still water.

"Ah," he whispered. "So good, so good."

Morse lingered, watching him, rearranging his bedclothes to make him even more comfortable and secure. When he felt sure that Lerner was asleep, he leaned close to his ear and whispered, "Father? I need to know the word that opens the safe. Tell me the word, Father. Father? What word opens the safe?"

Lerner grunted but slept on.

"Shit," grumbled Morse. "Old bastard, he don't relax even when he's snoring. I bet he keeps a bag of gold in that iron box of his."

From the cache of bills in the night table he took a tenner, added it to the five, thrust both into his pocket, and soon afterward left the house. He slipped away into the lengthening blue shadows, his mind perhaps on pleasure, or merely on escaping for a few hours the dull round of servitude to a dying man that defined his daytime life.

Lerner woke early, tasting ashes. Dun shadows filled the bedroom, but a thin white scar of daylight already ran between the red-plush window drapes, casting the shadows of iron security bars. He seized the silver bell and rang it loudly.

"Morse—" he began as the door opened. But instead of Morse, the yellow face of the housemaid – Cleo, was that her name? – intruded, anxious beneath a spotted kerchief.

"Oh, Mr Nick," she burst out, "don't nobody know where Mr Morse is at. I been up to his room to look, and his baid ain't been slep' in."

Lerner stared at her. If she'd told him the sun had failed to rise in the east, he could hardly have been more astonished.

With Cleo's help he wrestled himself painfully into the wheelchair, but there his abilities ended. A one-armed man with a spinal injury was close to helpless. A manservant had to be borrowed from next door to prepare him for the day. Lerner found the process distasteful; he hated to have a stranger see him unclothed or touch him; the fact that the man obviously disliked the work made it no easier to bear. In shaving him, the fellow nicked his face repeatedly, until Lerner sent him away with a miserly tip and a muttered curse. A barber had to be brought from a nearby shop, and he charged a whole dollar for the visit!

By then Cleo had brought him breakfast, and it was all wrong for a variety of reasons. Yet he failed to complain about the chilly toast, hard egg, and unsugared coffee. As he entered the den a good hour late and dragged out his manuscript, he was worrying over something much more serious: the possibility that Morse might *never* return.

As he'd warned last night, rough characters swarmed on the docks; the knife, the revolver, and the slung-shot were common weapons of choice; the Mississippi with its murky water, vast size, and hidden undertows was perfect for disposing of superfluous bodies – as Lerner knew well from certain experiences of his own.

"And without Morse, how would I *live*?" Lerner demanded aloud, and there was nobody to answer him.

From a desk drawer he took out a new gold-banded reservoir pen, uncapped it with fingers and teeth, filled it from his inkwell by pressing down an ivory piston, and tried to fix his mind on his story. From time to time as he wrote, he raised his head and listened. Despite the thick walls of the house, some street sounds intruded – the horn of a motor-car brayed; a seller of vegetables chanted "Ah got ni-ess al-li-gay-tuh pay-uhs" – and the house itself was never totally quiet, doors opening and closing for no good reason, a woman's starched dress (Cleo's?) rustling past in the hall.

And yet, despite his distraction, the new chapter began taking form. His thoughts might be elsewhere, but his hand travelled over the paper in a sort of automatic writing, like a spirit's message upon a sealed slate.

CHAPTER THE SECOND

Wherein I Encounter War, and a Spirit

Need I say that eighteen-sixty was a poor year for a southern lad to get an education? That winter a storm of rebellion swept the cotton states, and in the spring of '61 the country went to war.

For a time I dawdled, hoping that peace might break out. But after the affray at Fort Sumter, with the whole country responding to the call of the trumpet and the drum, I saw that I must go home. I took a train to Cincinnati, where the steam-packets were still running, war or no war; and after a week spent churning down the Ohio to the Mississippi, and down the Mississippi to the Red, stepped ashore at the same spot I had left a year earlier.

Already the Landing seemed to belong to another and darker age. The village was strangely silent; I learned that my schoolfellows had vanished into the Army, and two were already dead of camp diseases in Virginia. Mon Repos had never deserved its name less. Though I arrived at noon, I found Papa already drunk, and noted with disgust how he wobbled when he walked, like a goose hit with a rock. Royal and the Overseer both had disappeared, and when I asked Papa what had happened to them, he only mumbled and shook his head.

'Twas Rose – all atremble – who told me the story. Monsieur Felix had proposed marriage to her, and, when she declined, threatened to

compromise her honour so that she would have to marry him, willing or not. This she took to be a threat of rape, and many a tear-stained letter had she written, praying me to return and save her. But because of the war, I received none of them. Then the war itself intervened. The men of the slave patrols joined the army and went east, and as soon as they were gone, Royal took down my rifle from its hiding place, shot Monsieur Felix neatly through the eye and ran away, leaving the corpse lying spread out like a hog ready for flaying on the gallery of the nice house Papa had built for him.

At first I felt only pleasure in hearing this tale, and laughed gaily at the thought of being (as I imagined) rid of the Overseer forever. But after I spent a day tramping over our acres, I began to suspect that in reality his death had ruined us all. The crops of corn and cotton stood heavy but weed-choked and in need of hoeing; the hands idled about the quarters, and when I ordered them to work they went but slowly, with deep mutterings that boded no good.

Brooding over these developments, I turned my steps home-ward, passing close by the Overseer's house on the way. I found it a scene of ruin, grown up with vines like a castle in a fairy tale, with cicadas droning in the trees and hot sunlight vibrating upon a weedy mound of earth where he lay buried. A pine board carven only with his name and the date of his death served as his headstone.

I was gazing upon this melancholy scene when something moved upon the vine-shrouded gallery of the house. I shaded my eyes against the fierce light, and espied through drifting red spots Mon-sieur Felix standing in the spot where he had died. His pale face seemed to float amid a dark wreath of cat's-claw, his left eye nothing but an oozing pit, his right gleaming like a splinter of glass. His blue jaw moved and his penetrating whisper etched itself upon my ear-drums, saying, Tu, mon p'tit, serais mon vengeur.

I stepped back – stumbled over the grave marker – staggered, blinked away drops of stinging sweat, and an instant later found myself entering our house, with no sense of time elapsed nor memory of anything I might have seen along the way. Rose was fetching something for Papa, and she stopped and gazed at me, astonished. She brushed a strand of hair out of her eyes and said, "Nick, are you well?"

I answered without knowing what I said.

That night I drank with Papa, paying no attention as his slurring voice complained endlessly of his troubles, but instead thinking of the words of the Phantasm. I could make no sense of them: for what could be greater nonsense than that I (of all people) should become the avenger of my hated enemy, Monsieur Felix?

I went to bed more than half drunk, and slept like the water-logged trees that river pilots call dead-men. When I wakened at first light, the house seemed uncommonly silent. For half an hour I lay at ease, waiting for the usual noises to begin, the murmur of voices, the rattle of pots in the kitchen, the creak of the pump handle. A summer wind passed across the world with a great sigh, and a light rain began to fall. Still I heard nothing from down-stairs, as if the house had died overnight. Then my door opened and Rose slipped in, looking especially thin and pale in her cotton nightdress.

"Nick," she whispered, "where are all the servants?"

I jumped out of bed, threw on some clothes and ran outside. The brief shower having passed, I walked through the slave quarters, finding the cabins all empty, with doors hanging open on leathern hinges, and in the little fireplaces ashes that were still warm. The paddocks were empty, the farm animals all gone, driven into the woods and marshes by the departing slaves. I understood then that the slaves felt no loyalty toward Papa, who had never protected them from Monsieur Felix, whilst the Overseer's death had freed them from the fear that alone had made Mon Repos run.

I stood gazing at the overgrown fields, where little pines had already begun to spring up, whilst afar off, a church bell started to toll in dreary monotone – the notice of a funeral, whose I don't know: perhaps the funeral of our world.

So much Lerner had written, and was staring at an unappetizing lunch that Cleo had brought, when the door to his den opened suddenly and Morse stumbled in.

His hands were tremulous, his face yellow, his shoes muddy, his clothes mussed and odorous. In a hoarse voice he began to complain about the darkness of the house. In fact, it was no darker than usual; but as Lerner perceived, the pupils of his eyes had shrunk to pinpoints that shut out the light.

If anybody knew opium's aftermath, that man was Lerner. Speaking firmly, he ordered Morse to go to bed and, when he sobered up, to return and explain his conduct. He slouched away, looking like some wretched Lascar who sleeps off his drug debauch under the wharves, while the old man, muttering a curse, returned grimly to telling his tale.

*   *   *

Well do I remember those late-summer days in '61 when, like a child, I imagined that the worst had already happened.

I knew that we must abandon Mon Repos, hoping to return in better days, should better days ever come. And yet for weeks Papa refused even to consider flight. Finally, in a rage I threatened to take Rose away with me, and leave him to manage alone. At last he yielded and we became refugees, an early rivulet of the great tide that would flow southward in years to come.

At Red River Landing we bought our way aboard a fishing yawl, for Papa had become very close with a dollar, and refused to buy us passage on a steamboat.

Mostly our fellow-passengers were ordinary country folk, but one caught my eye – a very tall, thin man dressed in black, who sat at the prow, stiff and unmoving like the dragon's-head of a Viking ship. 'Twas evening, and he was hard to focus on against the blaze of the setting sun. I looked away, blinked and looked back: a hefty woman was seating herself in a flurry of skirts; perhaps he was behind her, perhaps not. Intending to make sure whether he was what I feared, I rose to my feet. But the boat was now so crowded and the freeboard so small that the captain shouted at me to sit, or I should swamp her.

Night shut down, the sails were raised, and we began a ghostly voyage down a moon-haunted river, in company perhaps with a Phantom. Does this not sound like a poem by Coleridge, or a tale by Poe? Yet I remember chiefly the discomfort of the wretched craft. I dozed and waked a dozen times; a woman nursed a baby that cried often; some fellow who had managed to fall asleep snorted like a donkey-engine. Once a steamboat blazing with lights pounded by in midstream, and the waves so rocked our burdened craft that we shipped water, and had to bail with cupped hands.

Come morning, we landed at New Orleans, all of us stiff and soaked and blear-eyed. The levee swarmed with shouting labourers; barrels and bales and cannons and gun-carriages were heaped up everywhere, guarded by new-minted soldiers in fancy uniforms. I sought the man in black, but he seemed to have vanished in the confusion. We engaged a porter with a barrow, and traipsed behind him through the Old Quarter, which was saturated with the smell of roasting coffee and noisy as a parrot cage.

In time we reached a house on Rue des Bons Enfants, or Good-children Street, belonging to some of our cousins, and they bade us welcome, having plenty of room to spare. Their warmth was not entirely a matter of family feeling. We again had money, for the city banks were still open, and Papa insisted on paying all our expenses –

as foolish in generosity as he had been in miserliness. From the same sense of pride, when I was commissioned a lieutenant in the Confederate Army, he bought me a fine grey uniform that did not survive my first and only battle.

That fall and winter of '61 I divided my time between Goodchildren Street and a training camp amongst the farmlands of Metairie, where I drilled men who knew as much about marching as I did, which was nothing. Passing through town one evening, I fell captive to the charms of a fair privateer, and caught the clap. 'Twas a light case that I got over in a week, but it occasioned much merriment in camp, where my fellow officers pounded me on the back and chortled, "Now Nick, when you have killed your first Yankee, you will be a real man at last!"

Whilst I was yet ill and feverish, I again saw the Phantom. Three or four nights in succession he rose in my dreams, fixing his one eye horridly upon me. One bright winter day I saw him gazing at me from the shade of an oak-grove hung with streamers of grey moss. Though daunted by the sight, I hastened toward him, but found nothing there. The figure had been only a compound of light and shadow – or at any rate, so I explained it to myself. Then I grew well again, and dismissed the Phantom as the trick of a sickly mind.

In plain fact I had no time for ghosts. The war was speeding up; we began to break camp and load our equipment. A thrill of excitement touched with fear ran through every man of us, for we knew that the day was nearing when at last we would see the Elephant, meaning combat. The order came in the first days of April, 1862, when the fields were covered with white and red clover. My company boarded a train to Jackson, and marched into Tennessee, where twenty-four thousand men were soon to be laid low in the great battle at Shiloh Church.

On the first day of the fight, I led a scouting party that blundered into an enemy picket. The Yankee sentry (a boy whose white, scared face will forever remain in my memory) instantly threw down his musket and fled; the weapon was on half-cock and discharged by itself, the ball smashing my elbow. Whilst the battle raged, the surgeons chloroformed me and cut off all but about eight inches of my left arm. I was laid in a wagon amongst other mutilated bodies and hauled away to the rail-head, screaming at every lurch and bounce.

So began and ended my acquaintanceship with war: but not with the Spectre, who soon seized upon my state of weakness to manifest himself again.

By the time I reached New Orleans, the stump of my arm had become infected (or mortified, *as we said then*), smelling foully and oozing unpleasant matter. Nursed by Rose, I lived through feverish days and haunted nights. Again Monsieur Felix ruled the dark hours, smiling horridly from amid great fields of corpses, where not one was whole – some torsos without arms or legs, some bodies without heads, some heads without bodies that glared from white eyes the size of walnuts.

Then my mind cleared, and I became able to understand the scarcely less frightening news that Rose brought me. I heard of the federal fleet appearing off the Passes, and of hard fighting at the downriver forts; of warships riding high on the flood-swollen Mississippi, with guns pointing down at the city's rooftops; of rioting mobs on the levee, burning warehouses and looting banks; of bluebacks filing ashore and deploying a battery of bronze cannon in front of the plush St Charles Hotel, where Papa used to stay when he was bargaining for slaves.

At home on Goodchildren Street our cousins began to cast bitter looks upon us. Papa had run out of cash, and because the war had severed the connection between city and farm, food had become very dear and hard to come by. Our hosts begrudged us every mouthful we ate, as if we were taking it directly off their plates – as in fact we were. Indeed, we were no longer a promising or even a respectable crew. Papa was customarily drunk, and even when sober, more scatter-brained than ever; Rose was obliged to work as a house servant, but a frail one who never did anything right. As for me, the cousins thought that if I recovered, 'twould be only as a poor cripple who would continue to eat but bring in nothing.

So they moved me out of my comfortable bedchamber, and put me upstairs in a store-room that held a clutter of retired furniture, broken crockery, and dusky mirrors. 'Twas stifling hot under the eaves, and no place for an injured man; but they thought it good enough for me, hoping perhaps that I might die and relieve them of a burden.

One summer morning I woke from a restless sleep. The arm I had lost was aching as no arm of flesh and blood could, every hair upon it like a burning wire. And yet, as the bright hot morning light grew, my eyes shewed me nothing, not even a ghost, lying on the ragged counterpane beside me. Rose slept nearby on a battered chaise, with a fine dew of perspiration upon her pale face, and though the pain of my phantom arm was such that I wished to moan or cry out, I remained silent for fear of waking her.

Restlessly my eyes wandered to an old dim mirror with an irregular dark shadow in the middle of the glass. As I gazed, the shadow began to take shape, like the sort of black paper silhouette that in those days decorated every parlour in the land. 'Twas Monsieur Felix – no, I could not have been mistaken! No man save he ever had such a face. As I watched in fascination, he began to turn slowly toward me, his features emerging like the image on a tintype in its acid bath, until his full face hovered in the glass, picked out in shades of glistening black and bone white.

Unable to bear the empty socket and gleaming eye fixed upon me, I stumbled from bed, my limbs rubbery as those of a new-whelped pup, and in one fierce motion turned the mirror and slammed it against the plaster. The glass shattered and Rose started up and cried out, "Oh Nick, you should be resting, not walking!"

"So should he who roused me," I answered, and her eyes widened in fear, for she thought that suffering had caused me to go mad.

The first sign that the household on Exposition Boulevard was wobbling back toward normal came when supper appeared at the proper hour.

Cleo carried the tray instead of Morse, but the meal was tasty and hot, with terrapin stew, warm bread, and a glass of elderly pale sherry. Lerner dumped half the sherry into the stew, swallowed the rest, and made a better meal than he'd expected.

After dinner Morse appeared, clean and silent, and went to work at the most intimate duties of a body-servant: setting Lerner upon the commode-chair, giving him an alcohol rub, putting his night-shirt on him and settling him in bed. Watching Morse prepare the laudanum, the old man found himself admiring the performance. Instead of making weak apologies, Morse was seeking to demonstrate how much Lerner needed him – and in that he succeeded, the clever fellow.

After drinking the potion, Lerner ordered him to sit down on the foot of the bed, and said quietly: "You know, my boy, this drug should be taken only to subdue pain and give rest, not for a doubtful pleasure that ends in a horrid slavery."

"I'm in pain all the time, Mr Nick," he muttered, looking at the floor. "This stuff gives you ease, so I thought it might do the like for me."

"You're in pain? Are you ill, Morse?"

"No. Yes. My anger eats at me."

"Anger at what?" asked Lerner in surprise, for he'd always thought Morse very comfortably off, for a coloured man.

"At *this*," he said, holding up his left hand with the dark back turned toward Lerner, then turning it over to show the white palm. "Wondering why I could not be like *this*. I have long known you are my father. If I were white, you would have loved and acknowledged me, and I would be a man among men."

For a moment Lerner was too astonished to speak. Unsteadily he asked, "Who told you that I am your father?"

"My mother."

It was on the tip of Lerner's tongue to say, *But you never knew your mother*. Instead he bit his tongue and said slowly, weighing the words, "I'm glad you've spoken out, my boy. Trust me, and I shall yet do you justice."

He sent Morse away, all his secrets intact. But when he was alone, lying in the dark on clean linen, Lerner found sleep difficult to come by. Maybe the laudanum was losing its effect. Or maybe he was finding it hard to grasp the fact that a Morse existed of whom he knew nothing.

What did the fellow do when he wasn't being the perfect servant? Did he read books? Practice voodoo? Engage in orgies with Cleo and the cook, improbable as that seemed? And how could he dare to live some other life, when he depended on Lerner for food, shelter, pocket money, everything? Wasn't that a kind of treason?

In time Lerner fell asleep, the puzzles of reality yielding to gorgeous visions of things that never had existed at all. And as he snored, the next day's instalment of his memoir composed itself, someplace deep beneath the level of his dreaming.

CHAPTER THE THIRD

Wherein the Demon Saves and Enslaves Me

On that day, the day I saw him in the mirror, I dressed and went forth with sleeve pinned up, in search of work.

I found none. The city had always lived by grace of the river, but now 'twas blocked by warring armies. Everything had ground to a halt; the once-busy levee lay empty, save for a few Union warships and a graveyard of decaying hulks, and no work was to be had by anyone, much less a cripple.

After a week of useless tramping about, I turned the mirror in my garret around, for desperation had conquered fear, and I was ready to receive counsel from whatever source. Alas, the shattered glass shewed only fragments of my own gaunt and yellowed image, which I thought grimly appropriate. Gazing at that shattered countenance, I brought to mind a verse or incantation that Royal and I used to chant in the graveyard at midnight: Come ye, take me, lead me on/Shew me gold, and then begone! *Very deliberately, I said it seven times, which was the magic number: but answer there was none.*

Yet that very afternoon, I saw – upon Levee Street, about half a square distant, amid waves of heat rising from the cobblestones – a thin, black-dressed figure loping with unmistakable gait through the trembling mirages. And as the strings of a harp will pick up and faintly repeat distant sounds, although no fingers have touched them, my heart-strings thrilled to a sense of hope and fear.

I hastened after him; he turned the corner of Gallatin Street, as did I a moment later: he had vanished, but in his place an amazing sight met my eyes. A file of coloured men wearing blue uniforms were practising the manual of arms. Royal was drilling them, and his strong nature had already asserted itself, for he wore upon each sleeve three broad gold stripes in the shape of spear-heads pointing down.

When the "Stand at ease" was given, I approached and spoke to him. He threw back his head, and laughed so loud that his men stared. We shook hands and spoke briefly of old times; he queried me about my missing arm, and briefly told me how he had enlisted in one of the new coloured regiments. I admitted to needing food, whilst he revealed an ambition to sign the name he had chosen for himself – Royal Sargent – to the muster-roll, in place of an X. We struck a bargain: he promised to get me army rations, if in return I would make him literate.

That same evening he came to the house on Goodchildren Street, but was not invited in. The cousins pointed out that teaching him to read and write was forbidden under the state's Code Noir; *the fact that the black code was already dead they ignored, having no patience with mere reality. So Royal and I sat down on an iron bench in the patio, and for the first of many times bent our heads over a reading-book that some charitable society at the North had sent his regiment. When he went, he left behind army bacon and coffee and hardtack and cornmeal, which the cousins did not disdain to share that night at supper time.*

When not working, he and I chatted about the past. I asked him how he felt after killing Monsieur Felix, and he answered solemnly, "I took my first breath when he took his last."

Hesitantly I asked if he thought the Overseer's spirit might walk, as those who die by violence are said to do. Royal laughed his loud laugh and said, "So many have died in the war, he'd be lost in the crowd!"

He inquired after Rose, and began to bring her small gifts, oranges and fruit pies and ices that he bought from the sutlers out of his pay of ten dollars a month. She received his gifts in the kitchen, the only room the cousins permitted him to enter. They stood by and glowered as she thanked him, saying how she rejoiced to see him a free man – at which they glowered more.

In this manner we all lived for a time, but had barely grown accustomed to regular eating, when without warning Royal's unit was sent down-river to garrison the forts at the Head of Passes. Then in quick succession fell two more blows: Papa died from a lethal mixture of whiskey and despair; and our cousins, in an excess of Confederate feeling, refused to take the oath of allegiance as ordered by the commanding general. Straightway they were branded Enemies of the United States and expelled from the city; soldiers seized their house as rebel property, and sold it at auction with all its contents.

Rose and I swore allegiance to the old flag, but it did us no good; we were driven into the street anyway, and a most difficult time began.

Ah, how fortunate are those who have never learned the awful truth taught by hunger: that a man will do anything, to live one single day more!

I tried hauling rubbish, but 'twas a two-handed job; I did poorly at it, and was laid off. I was for a time doorman of a brothel frequented by Union officers. One of them, a Major Wharton, was sufficiently moved by the plight of a Yale man to recommend me to a sutler, who sold food openly and bad whiskey secretly to the troops. I began keeping his account books, whilst Rose plied a needle twelve hours a day, repairing blue uniforms in a sweat-shop run by the Quartermaster.

Yet for all our efforts, we existed rather than lived in three poor rooms near the levee, beset with bugs of many species, but all equally blood-thirsty. I sought everywhere for my private Spectre, but found him not; at times my bizarre longing to behold again such an one as he made me wonder whether madness might soon compound my

*other troubles. And then, one night in January, 1863 – I remember
the rapid, mushy impacts of sleet against the shutters – I heard a shot
in the street outside, and feet scampering away.*

*I tumbled out of bed, lit a stump of candle and hastened to the
room's one window. A fat civilian in flash attire (probably a
gambler) lay on the paving-stones amongst glistening pebbles of
ice. Superimposed upon this image, I saw my own reflection in the
dirty window-pane, and something else besides – a tall, thin, black-
dressed man standing just behind me.*

*I whirled around, almost dropping the candle, and of course no
one was there. But as I stood trembling, suddenly my confusion
vanished and I knew what I must do. I blew out the candle, ran
outside in my night-shirt, bent over the dying man and began rifling
his pockets. My fingers slipped into something that felt like warm wet
liver – 'twas his wound – then closed upon his fat leather purse. Back
inside, I hid the money (good greenbacks, near an hundred dollars!)
in a knot-hole in the floor, and moved my bedstead to cover the
hiding place.*

*I washed my bloody hand and went back to bed. Sounds came and
went outside – a mounted patrol clip-clopping past halted, there was
talk, and later a wagon clattered up to remove the body. Meantime
I lay in bed, scratching my bug-bites, and resolved that henceforth I
should take what I needed from the world by force. And though I had
been law-abiding all my life, I knew exactly how to go about it.*

*Next day I used twenty dollars of the gambler's money to acquire
an army Colt revolver (the famous model 1860) in the thieves'
market that flourished in the alleyways near the Hospital Street
wharf. I taught myself to load the weapon one-handed, clamping the
grip under my stump, and using my right hand to tamp in powder
and balls and affix copper caps to the nibs. That same night I
ventured into the narrow fog-bound streets to try my luck. Guided
by the glow of wide-spaced lanterns, listening always for the tramp
of the provost marshal's guard and the clatter and jingle of the
mounted patrols, I robbed two drunks. Though neither yielded as
rich a haul as the gambler, I garnered enough to hand Rose money
that would see us through a few more days.*

*"Where did this come from, Nick?" she asked, and I answered, "I
prayed to Saint Dismas," meaning the patron saint of thieves.*

*Night after night I worked to perfect my technique. My method
was to come up behind my victims and strike them down, using the
heavy pistol as a club; then clamp it under my stump and search their
pockets. 'Twas not an easy life, for others of my own kind were in the*

streets; we snarled at each other like dogs eyeing the same scrap, and twice I had to drive off my fellow jackals with bullets.

Yet these scavengers also became my new acquaintances. I met them in the cheap brothels I began to patronize, and the wretched saloons called doggeries, where I warmed my belly against the night air with dime shots of bad whiskey. From the garish crowd of whores, pimps and rogues who shared my perils and my pleasures, I learned that I was a knuck or a sandbagger when I struck my victims down; that when I searched their pockets I was overhauling them; that my pistol was a barking iron; that when I tracked my prey in silence I was padding my hooves. Yale had taught me none of these things.

There was also a Creole argot, of which I understood a few words: the women called me bras-coupé, after a famous one-armed bandit of an hundred years before, or bête-marron, meaning a tame beast gone wild. I was struck by that term, because it reminded me that the Overseer's half-forgotten surname had also been Marron – as if we had been brothers.

And brothers we might have been, brothers in crime. I saw his shadow often in the streets, slipping past a lantern, or sliding along a wall half lit by a red-shaded coal-oil lamp in the window of a bagnio. I recognized him easily by his strange walk; I envied him his silence of movement, and soon learned to take him as my guide. He was clever at finding the staggering sots who remained my favourite prey, and the shadow of his long arm pointed them out to me. He also led me out of danger. One night, when the cavalry were so close behind me that I saw the sparks their horseshoes struck from the cobblestones, I spotted that angular dark form vanishing into an alleyway, followed it and found safety there.

Later – in that deceptive hour just before dawn, when the eyes cannot tell a cloud from a mountain – I saw him again, dimly through a bank of silver mist. With the mad aim of thanking him for my salvation, I shouted, "Monsieur Felix!" and sprang after him. The shadow turned, and like a razor seen edge-on, instantly disappeared. And later that day I started up in bed, awakened by my own screaming.

Those who never have been haunted can scarcely believe the power of a Phantasm. Soon even the full blaze of noon could not drive him off. Upon a crowded street my eye would fall upon my shadow against a wall, yet 'twas not my shadow but his; and if the shadow raised its arm, I would find my own rising too, as if

*he mocked me, saying by a gesture: you see which of us is real,
after all!*

In my dreams he appeared in many forms: as himself, stalking
about in his old black suit, the whip over his arm; as the host of a
costume ball, where at midnight the dancers all dropped their masks,
revealing the faces of wolves, foxes and rats; as an idol carven of
wood, to which dim crowds were bowing, myself among them.
Awaking sweat-soaked from such visions, I began to comprehend
that the Overseer was no mere ghost – no mere echo or reflected
image of one who had lived. By giving himself up wholly to the
insatiable passion of revenge, Monsieur Felix had become something
stranger than that, more powerful and more utterly lost. And it was
to this demonic power that I bowed down, for I needed to draw upon
it to save myself.

One night in such a dream the idol's stiff jaw moved, and the well-
known voice whispered, Tu, mon p'tit, serais le roi du coton! At
which, upon waking, I could not but laugh. For how should a one-
armed knuck become King of Cotton? And yet that very day upon
the street a Yankee officer with eagles on his shoulder-straps and a
great clanking sabre banging at his knees, called out to me, "Old
Eli!"

'Twas my benefactor Wharton, now promoted to colonel. He
asked if, as a onetime planter, I knew quality in cotton, and when I
said yes, he intimated that a friend of his wanted to deal in Confederate cotton smuggled across the lines.

So I acquired a new profession, more rewarding than the old,
though not less dangerous. Using my knowledge and my weapon
and the wood-craft I had learned as a boy, I guided the dealer – a
gross creature named Klegg, with especially foul breath – into the
rebel-held regions beyond Lake Pontchartrain. There he bought
cotton very cheap, intending (as he told me) to transport it to the
city, ship it out and sell it very dear at the North, where the factories
were starving for the stuff.

My spectral ally guided us well. Twice I saw him standing stiff as a
scarecrow in an overgrown field, pointing a long finger in the
direction we must take. Returning from our jaunt, I was poling
our heavily laden bateau along the sedgy margins of Lake Maurepas,
when I saw him again, this time a deeper shadow in the blue dusk,
pointing directly at Klegg, who was seated in the bow with his fat
back turned to me. Taking the hint, I silently laid down the pole,
drew the Colt from the waistband of my trowsers, and shot the dealer
between the shoulder-blades.

This was my first murder, and as the reeking powder-smoke dispersed I was all a-tremble, gazing at the deep round oozing hole in the man's spine, scarce able to believe what I had done. But then I felt a great surge of power, as if now I could do anything. With some effort, I heaved the carcass into a slough, watched a drowsy alligator wake long enough to play sexton, and then, taking up the pole again, went my silent way.

After selling the cotton, I sought out Colonel Wharton, reported the dealer killed by bandits, and bribed him to select me as manager of a west-bank plantation the government had seized from its rebel owner. With free Negroes as workers and government mules to pull the plows, I was soon making cotton for thirty cents a pound and selling it in New York for a dollar-twenty – all without incurring any danger whatsoever!

Thus I attained the dignity of a war-profiteer, and the golden sun of prosperity began to shine upon me and mine. I freed Rose from her wage-slavery; I freed myself forever from the life of a scavenger. I cut Colonel Wharton a share of my profits, and was rewarded when he brought me – now that I had money to invest – into many a profitable venture. I invited him to the plantation, and visited his home; I came to know his dull wren of a wife, with her deplorable hats and her nasal mid-western twang. For the first time I laid eyes upon his daughter Elmira – then little more than an auburn-haired girl, but already giving promise of voluptuous beauty to come.

At first my mutilation frightened her – she thought me some sort of monster, in which she was more than half right – but in time my ready wit, and the small presents I brought her, made me a great favourite, the more so as she came to pity me. I smiled at her and listened to her chatter, and told her closely cropped versions of my sufferings, for which she pitied me the more.

Elmira, of course, was a project for the future; 'twas pleasant to think that again I had a future. By the winter of 1864 I was back in town for good, and living in fair comfort with Rose in a pleasant cottage in the Third District. And the following spring, peace returned at last.

It had been a fine and busy day – wearying, but the kind of weariness that felt good. A whole new chapter completed, the household running like clockwork, everything normal again, just as it ought to be.

When evening shadows gathered, the old man lay at rest, lapped in clean linen, inhaling the smells of rubbing alcohol, bourbon, and the sour saplike odour of raw opium that lingered in the air. Before sleep took him, he again invited Morse to sit on the foot of the bed, and for a few minutes the two men spoke frankly – or at any rate, one of them did.

"I have no one to be my child save only you, Morse," Lerner told him, feeling a curious finicky unwillingness to call himself Morse's father in so many words.

Morse missed the distinction. "Yes. But because of my skin, you use me as a servant, not a son."

"When I die," said Lerner, "you will learn how much I view you as a son."

Morse gazed at him searchingly, as if to read his true thoughts. "Do you encourage me to have hopes, Father?" asked he, almost in a whisper.

"No," said Lerner. "I encourage you to have expectations."

Morse turned away, and a dry sob seemed to rack his chest. "I am sorry, Father, for the trouble I give you," he said humbly, then turned off the lights and left, closing the door to the den noiselessly behind him.

In the dark, Lerner lay back smiling, and played for a time with the thought of actually leaving Morse some substantial sum. How that would outrage the respectable white society of New Orleans! How it would kill them to see a Negro made richer than they could ever hope to be!

But was that really necessary? Lerner's will, after providing somewhat meagerly for his servants – Morse was down for a hundred dollars and his second-best suit – left most of his millions to found a library. A strange bequest for a man who'd seldom read a book since leaving Yale, but the point (as with the vaster gift made for the same purpose by Andrew Carnegie) was the fact that his name would be chiselled over the building's door.

Anyway, merely by giving Morse hope, which cost nothing, he'd safeguarded his own comfort. Truly, he thought, in walking with a demon one learns many things, including the fact that faith, hope, and love – those supposed virtues – may become chains with which to bind a spirit.

Still smiling, he fell asleep, and all the dark hours his next chapter wrote itself, ready to be transcribed in the morning by his hand.

CHAPTER THE FOURTH

Wherein I Triumph During the Reconstruction

One April evening, as I sat in the little courtyard behind our house, sipping a glass of tolerable whiskey and watching sunset streamers unfurl across the sky, the gate hinges creaked and a well-attired coloured man entered and extended his hand. So quietly did Royal re-enter my life.

Smiling at the stranger who once had been my playmate in Eden, I invited him to sit down and called Rose to bring a clean glass. When she saw Royal, she fairly ran from the kitchen, blushing and smiling in her pleasure. Then she recovered her customary demure ways, and asked him how he did. He said well, and she placed her small hand for an instant in his large one, before returning with a light step to making supper. I poured Royal a whiskey, he offered me a segar, and for a time we sipped and smoked, whilst covertly observing each other to see what changes the years had made.

"Nick, I hear you've become a Union man," he said at length, his voice strong and firm with the habit of command.

"Yes," I replied dryly. "'Twas conversion by the sword."

He laughed. "You were smart to make the change. Now me – I've been discharged from the army, and mean to enter politics as soon as my people get the vote. They'll need leadership, and I can supply that."

I said quietly, "Watch your back."

He leaned forward and peered at my face. "Nick, I hope you ain't like the Bourbons, who learned nothing and forgot nothing."

"You've been reading history, I see."

"Yes. And mean to make some."

"Royal," said I, "this city is full of people who have learned nothing and forgotten nothing. And most of them know how to shoot."

Indeed, they were returning every month by the hundreds – beaten soldiers, political exiles – like red-hot pumice stones raining down in the aftermath of an eruption. I saw them every day about the streets, people with pinched faces and missing limbs, the most desperate bending over garbage heaps behind the great hotels.

Royal was unimpressed. "Well, we'll have to work together to rebuild. I want to offer the former rebels the hand of friendship."

I smiled a little, thinking what was likely to happen to a hand so extended. But I said diplomatically, "Away with the past! Let us live for the future!"

Rose called out that supper was ready, we emptied our glasses, and Royal departed. When I went inside, I saw that she had laid three places at the table. She said in a disappointed voice, "He didn't stay to eat?"

"Why should he stay to eat?"

"Well, he was one of our people, after all."

"No longer," I answered, "now he belongs only to himself."

I piled into my food, still smiling at Royal's notion that Yank and Rebel could work together to rebuild our shattered world. Oh yes, my deals with Colonel Wharton shewed that Blue and Grey could be brought together by the colour Green. But well I knew that the spectrum of the time contained also a deep crimson stripe – the colour of rage, of unburied hate, of blood-vengeance.

As if to confirm my belief, a few days later a strange man with a scarred face limped through our gate at sunset, when as usual I was drinking alone. He introduced himself as Brigadier General Eleazar Hobbs, late of the Confederate Army.

I said quickly, "I am a poor man."

"I haven't come to ask for money," he said with a grim smile. "I've heard that you too wore the grey."

This I acknowledged, and he invited me to join a club he was forming to discuss the current state of affairs in the city, the state, and the South.

For the founder of a debating society, he asked some odd questions. Eyeing dubiously my pinned-up left sleeve, he wanted to know if I were able to handle a weapon. I still went armed, the city being so disturbed; I had long since retired the old 1860 model revolver as a memento of difficult but exciting times, and replaced it with a new-model Remington, a sweet weapon that fired up-to-date brass cartridges in place of loose powder and copper caps.

I drew this gun, cocked it, took aim at a broken flower-pot against the garden wall and blew it to pieces. Hobbs nodded thoughtfully, and for a time we chatted, his preferred topic being the intolerable arrogance of the liberated slaves. When I told him frankly that I had taken the Iron-Clad Oath and knew a number of blue-backs, he was not disturbed.

"We need a friend in the camp of the enemy," he said, and I began to understand what he wanted of me. A new and secret war was beginning, and I was being invited to serve in it – as matters turned out, to serve on both sides!

I found it an odd sort of struggle. Brigadier Hobbs and his friends let strictly alone the blue-coated soldiers who once had been their enemies, for killing them would only bring down upon the South all the calamities of years past. Instead, they shot presumptuous blacks and Republicans of all hues. The Red River in particular proved to be well named, from the hundreds of bodies that floated down it.

'Twas my old neighbourhood, its byways well known to me, and I had a ready-made reason to go there, for I was attempting to regain control of Mon Repos, or what was left of it. The house had been burnt by one army or the other, or by bandits – I never learned which – but the land, with its alley of great oaks, remained. That summer, on a trip upriver I tracked and killed a man I did not know, nor why he needed killing: my sole motive being to prove my bona fides to General Hobbs.

Need I say that Monsieur Felix accompanied me? I first saw him on the boat, seated near the stern-wheel with sparkles of light gleaming through his shadowy form as he gazed at the frothing tumult of the water. A day later, when I had slain my man in a little wood near the levee, and was turning away, I saw him again, standing amongst the cottonwood trees with arms folded – looking on with great interest, but making no sign, like a wise teacher who lets an apt pupil learn by doing.

The thought struck me then that I was different, not only from the man I had been, but also from the man I might have become without his guidance. I might have been a good man; I might have been a dead man. Most likely I would have been both – good and dead!

In any case, why dream of what had not happened? With my latest victim lying at my feet, my whole being hummed with tigerish joy, for again I had broken the bonds of conscience and felt free to do anything. So I nodded to Monsieur Felix in a comradely way, and passed on.

All that busy morning, with the words flowing from his mind as smoothly as the ink from his reservoir pen, Lerner had nothing to complain of, except that Morse in performing his duties seemed a touch too familiar.

Give a nigger an inch, he thought, *and he'll take an ell.* At lunchtime he spoke firmly, saying that discretion was the first thing he would look for in any man who aspired to be his principal heir.

"In short," said Morse, his voice as pettish as a spoiled child, "despite what you said last night, in the sight of the world I am to go on being your nigger-man."

Hearing him use the same word, as if they shared a bond of mind as well as blood, gave Lerner an odd feeling. He answered almost defensively:

"I have never treated you so, but as a member of my household and as my right-hand man. Think about it, and see if I do not tell the truth."

Whether convinced or not, Morse apologised again, and after serving the meal and cutting the meat for him, departed as silently as an Arabian Nights servitor. Smiling, Lerner refilled his pen, set to work, and the tale emerged without a single deletion or correction, like the automatic writing of a seer.

Back in town, I began to find my true role in the Reconstruction. Not as a killer, of whom there were more than enough, but as a peace-maker – a reconciler of differences. Who could be a better go-between than I, who had lost a limb for the Cause, yet had sworn loyalty to the Union? I spoke to each side in their own language, and my tongue moved freely, as if hinged in the middle.

Without undue arrogance, I aver that within a few years I became an indispensable man. Most of my time was spent in the lobby of our statehouse – the pompous, gold-domed, elegantly decaying St Louis Hotel – where blood enemies combined forces to build a new ruling class upon the ruins of the old.

Ah, I can see it now! The walls covered with stained and tattered silk; the floor scattered with spittoons, of which there never were enough, for the Turkey carpet was foul with spittle. I see servants hastening about with tall amber bottles and trays of crystal goblets that ping at the touch. I see the all-male crowd, smell the hazy bitter segar-smoke, hear the whispered conferences, feel between my fingers the stiff smooth rag paper as drafts of pending bills whisper and slide from hand to hand. And amongst the portly scoundrels with their embroidered vests and gleaming watch-chains, I perceive a rail-thin figure that flickers and comes and goes like a mirage, his one good eye gleaming like a splinter of glass.

One day when I was busy conniving, someone touched my shoulder. I turned to find Royal smiling at me. He was rising fast in the post-war chaos – a former slave who could read and write and knew how to exercise power. The tattered slave-boy had become a soldier, the soldier a state senator and a man to reckon with, through his influence over the Negro legislators.

"Nick," he said, "I might have known I should find you in a den of thieves."

"Come, Senator," I jested. "Governor Wharton would not like to hear a fellow Republican so describe his friends and supporters!"

He shook his head, smile broadening. "Nick, there is something uncanny about you. That a one-armed Rebel should emerge as the governor's – what's a polite word for it—"

"Legislative agent, shall we say?"

"Just so. The Master of the Lobby. You know, my constituents are all black folk, and from them I hear whispers that at night you transform into a Klansman – although that I refuse to believe!"

"I hope you disbelieve it, mon vieux, for that is a vile slander put about by the envy and malice of my enemies."

"I rejoice to hear it. Nick, I wonder . . . can you tell me whether the Governor has decided to sign my bill?"

"The one to legalize marriage between blacks and whites? I think he will swallow it, but only if sweetened with a spoonful of sugar."

He made a face. "How much?"

We quickly struck a bargain. The governor wished the Legislature to charter a rather improbable railroad, whose stock promised a handsome return from foreign investors ignorant of the fact that it was to run through a fathomless swamp. Royal agreed to swing the necessary votes in the Senate, and I guaranteed him a certain quantity of the stock to pass around.

He said with relief, "Old Wharton is so greedy, I thought he would want a bag full of gold!"

"No, there's more money in railroads. However, his daughter, the lovely Elmira, is soon to enter society, and a thousand dollars toward the cost of her ball and ballgown would help to seal the bargain."

That was how things were done in Louisiana. But why do I say were? And why do I imply that things were done differently in General Grant's Washington, or Boss Tweed's New York? Yet some differences between North and South did exist: as was proved by a Mardi Gras ball I gave early in March, 1870, and the crisis that followed, making and unmaking so many lives.

Although my house now stands deep within the city, in those times it stood upon the Uptown fringes of settlement. I designed it myself, a place of stained glass and gables and towers and spires, all painted garishly as an Amazon frog, in a deliberate affront to the classical taste of the age I grew up in.

Within, gaslight glittered upon glass and silver, upon long tables piled with steaming food, upon champagne that flowed in sparkling rivers. The noisy throng was a patchwork of colours and a Babel of *languages – a muster-roll of all who were corrupt, entertaining, and important in our world. How different from this dismal twentieth century, when white and black are hardly permitted to breathe the same air!*

I took pleasure in inviting men of all races and factions, and women of all professions, including the oldest. I hoped they might amuse me by striking a few sparks from one another – little dreaming upon what tinder those sparks would fall.

At the time I was still a bachelor; Rose was doing the honours as hostess, and Royal asked her to dance. My dismay was great when I saw Brigadier Hobbs staring at them: they were a handsome couple, carven as it were of teakwood and ivory. But in Hobbs's scarred face burned the eyes of a crouching wolf.

I can hear the music now – a waltz called (I think) Southern Roses – and the stiff rustling of the women's gowns like the rush of wind through dry autumnal trees, and the scrape of dancing feet. When the guests were leaving, an hour or two before dawn, Royal pounced upon me. He was in a strange mood, exalted and more than a little drunk.

"Didn't I tell you that reconciliation would come? May our connection grow ever closer!" he exclaimed, almost crushing my one remaining hand.

"May it be so!" I replied, striving to retrieve my fingers intact.

"'Tis very late, Nick – or rather, very early – but I have a proposal to make. Could we speak privately for a moment?"

The word "proposal" passed me by entirely. I bowed him into my den – into this very room, where as a crippled old man I sit in a wheeled chair, writing. And here he rather grandly announced, in terms even then old-fashioned, that he desired to form "an honourable union" with Rose.

'Twas the worst shock I'd had in years. Rapid visions flashed across my brain of how Brigadier Hobbs and his friends would react, should a member of their society allow such a marriage to take place.

"Brother," I said, swallowing my feelings with difficulty, "I'm honoured by your confidence. Of course, I must commune with my cousin. I fear that your proposal might place her in great peril."

"She is resolved to face it with me."

"That sentiment does her honour. But speak to her I must."

"Of course," said he, bowing like a dancing-master. "I shall return in – shall we say a week? – for your answer."

No sooner had he left than I confronted Rose, who met me with a face both scared and determined. I dragged her into the den and shut *the door to exclude the servants, who were busy gathering up the fragments of the feast.*

"How dare you connive at this lunacy?" I demanded, grinding my teeth.

"I dare, because it is time for me to be born!" she declared. "Here I am, twenty-six years old – almost too old to marry. And what have I ever been but an orphan, a poor relation, a seamstress to the Yankee army, and a housekeeper to you? I have never had a life! And I am resolved to have one now, ere it is too late!"

"This affair must have a long background!" I raged. "Yet you never confided in me, though I stole and killed for you."

"You stole and killed because you are a thief and a murderer!" she replied. "Royal is worth twenty of you. Did you know that long ago when we were children, he would risk a whipping to sneak upstairs and bring me flowers? That he would sit on the floor and tell me about his adventures, whilst you never talked to me at all, except to say good morning and good-bye?"

"What!" I thundered, "has it been going on that long?"

"He is a strong, wise man with a brilliant future. Have you forgotten that he killed that beastly Monsieur Felix to save me?"

It quite maddened me to hear that when I killed I was a murderer, but when Royal did the same he was a paladin.

"Royal shot the Overseer for his own revenge – you were incidental. You have always been incidental, Rose, a mere burden for others to carry, dead weight upon the road of life."

"Cochon!" she cried, and slapped me so hard my head rang. Then, weeping, she flung open the door and fled upstairs to her bedroom.

I closed the door again, took a dusty bottle from the tantalus and poured a triple brandy. I had swallowed about half, when a movement in the corner of my eye caused me to turn.

I can see the room as it was then – indeed, as it still is, save for the electric lights: the heavy red draperies; the dark crouching furniture; the small iron safe; the broad burled walnut desk; and the wavering shadows cast over everything by a gasolier's twelve flickering bluish points of flame. Against a wall covered with expensive French paper, something moved – a black shadow cast by nothing tangible.

"Well," I demanded, "what the devil shall I do?"

A very apt way of speaking, all things considered. And in that instant I knew – knew how to handle the situation – as if I had spent years and years planning every detail.

I finished the drink, climbed the stairs and went to Rose's room, where she lay sobbing upon the bed. Sitting down beside her, I spoke in the quiet, calm voice of a man who has regained his sanity after an emotional storm.

I reminded her that we were linked by blood, that we had been children together, that we had shared many perils and helped each other to survive terrible times. I lamented that we had both said things we should not have said. I said that she ought to have prepared me for Royal's proposal, which had come as a great shock.

"I ask only that you take a little time to be sure, my dear. I have but recently cleared the taxes from Papa's old land near Red River, and must take a brief trip there to get a new survey made. If, when I return, you are still resolved to marry Royal, you shall find me a champion of your right to choose him, and his to choose you. And you shall have a dowry proportioned to my wealth and your deserts."

We wept together; I begged forgiveness a thousand times. She called me her dearest friend, her other self, the best and most understanding of men. I have never known why women believe the things men tell them – or vice versa.

In my bedroom I smoked a last segar, smiling without mirth as I saw with clear, unimpeded vision how the demon had saved and shaped my whole life to this very end. "Damn it all to hell," I exclaimed, "je m'en fiche! I don't care!"

But in that I lied. I cared, but knew that I could no longer change my course, which was fixed for all time. And perhaps beyond time as well.

Next morning, without the slightest warning, after days of quiet, all the arrangements meant to secure Lerner's comfort broke down at once.

He woke from opulent dreams, as rich as those recorded in De Quincey's *Confessions of an English Opium-Eater*. Dreams of caravans pacing across deserts where the light was blindingly intense; of chiming camel-bells and wailing flutes; of dark-eyed houris glancing through silken veils that covered swaying howdahs; of Mameluke guards with crooked swords and prancing horses; of lavish pavilions where dancing girls twirled on rose carpets to the twanging of dulcimers.

And, yes, Monsieur Felix had been there, smiling his razor-thin smile and rubbing his hands like a master of ceremonies whose every gesture seems to say, "What wonders our performers will show you tonight!"

Then Lerner woke, tasting ashes as usual, and saw Cleo's scared face and chignon peeping around the bedroom door like a polka-dotted messenger of doom. He didn't even have time to ask what had gone wrong when she blurted out, "Oh, Mr Nick, Morse he been arrested, him!" And burst into tears.

The rest of the morning was spent unravelling what had happened the preceding night. It wasn't easy. Two years back, with great reluctance Lerner had allowed a telephone to be installed in his house. But Morse had done all the calling, and when the old man wheeled himself into the hall to use it, he discovered that the box had been placed too high on the wall for him to reach.

So his questions had to be passed through Cleo – who was hysterical – and after he sent her away, through the cook, a sullen woman with the improbable name of Euphrosyne, an import from South Carolina with a Gullah accent as dark and impenetrable as a flagstone. The information from the other end of the line (first from Lerner's lawyer, later from a police captain named Hennessy) had to come back by the same cross-African pathway.

But the old man was persistent, and knew how to offer Hennessy a bribe without actually using the word. So he learned that what the captain called "your pet nigger" was the talk of Storyville, where – it now appeared – he'd been a familiar figure for years, known for dispensing money (*whose* money?) with a free hand, and for his rough way with the women in the cribs and coloured brothels. A piano player called Professor Jelly Roll had already produced a "jass" composition in his honour, called "Mr Morse's Blues".

Lerner knew nothing of so-called jass music, except that it was said to be noisy. But as the story unfolded, he began to feel that Morse from his very conception had been headed for this reckoning. Apparently he began his evening with a few pipes of opium at some den near the docks that he'd discovered while procuring the drug for Lerner. Heading home, he entered a street-car while still befuddled and, finding it crowded, sat down on a bench meant for whites. The conductor and motorman ordered him to vacate it and stand behind a yellow sign that courteously stated THIS SECTION IS RESERVED FOR OUR COLOURED PATRONS ONLY. Morse refused, and courtesy perished as the two men hustled him off the car and flung him into a mud puddle.

Considerably dishevelled, Morse repaired to a saloon that served Negroes whiskey through a back window. He swallowed a few quick shots of courage and proceeded to a bawdy-house to seek further comfort. His choice of establishment was either deliberate arrogance or a grave mistake. The Madame, a fearsome mulattress who called herself Countess Willie V. Piazza, had built a fine business by providing handsome coloured women to a clientele of white men only. She took one look at Morse – mahogany-hued, smelling of drink and much the worse for wear – and refused him admittance. When he forced his way inside anyway, she summoned the police, and Morse topped off a busy night by assaulting not one but two brawny Irishmen.

With Hennessy's assistance, Lerner's lawyer found Morse in a cell of Parish Prison, where the police had been amusing themselves by playing drum-rolls on his ribs with their billyclubs. Bribes were necessary merely to preserve his life; when he was dragged before a magistrate, the lawyer had to guarantee his bail. Prison remained a distinct possibility, only (the lawyer warned) to be averted by still more bribes. When Morse at length was returned home by cab, Lerner not only had to pay the hackman, he had to hire a doctor to tend Morse at two dollars a visit. By evening of a day of upheaval, Morse was lying in his room upstairs, the doctor had cleaned his wounds and strapped his ribs, and Lerner was in a greater rage than was safe for an elderly man.

Damn him! he thought. *Were he not a kinsman, I would let him sink or swim! Doesn't he know what can happen to a man of colour in the grip of our police?*

Well, of course he knew. It was just that Morse, Lerner's pet from his birth, protected by the walls of this house, hadn't thought it could happen to him.

Next morning – sleepless, ill-shaven, nerves ragged for lack of his drug, back pains lancing him like sparks of pure white fire – the old man returned ashen-tongued and red-eyed to his task, under a compulsion made somehow worse by the events of yesterday.

CHAPTER THE FIFTH

Wherein the Demon Proves the Real Winner

As a burning sun rose over the Father of Waters, I boarded a steam packet on the levee at Felicity Street. I had already visited a telegraph-office, and sent two local wires, one to Royal and one to Brigadier Hobbs.

Whilst the shore fell away, I stood gazing upon the broad churning wake of the stern-wheel, and the wide, ever-busy river beyond. I watched the crowded riverboats; the sleek steamers from overseas trailing plumes of ash from their smoke-stacks; the sailboats with little patched sails, and the scows with men hauling at the sweeps; the green banks and the low, irregular levees; a party of church-goers clad in white gowns, being baptised in the shallows; and the floating and diving gulls that screamed in harsh voices.

Amidst all this busy life, I felt a strange loneliness, as if for all my wealth and influence I was but a gypsy and a wanderer upon the earth. My earlier homicides had been easy enough, for I had slain men who meant nothing to me. Perhaps I was not yet entirely what my master had designed me to be, for the thought that I must now play the role of Cain lay upon my heart like a stone. Somehow, through many years of dark deeds I had preserved the memory of my time of innocence, in which Royal played so large a part. Even if the tale told in the Bible be true, which I doubt, a vengeful God merely cast Adam out of Eden: he did not demand that he go back and befoul the very fountains of his former Paradise with blood.

Hoping to shake off my melancholy, I started to take a brisk turn about the deck, but stopped when I saw a well-known figure sitting at the bow, still as a carven figurehead. So the Overseer was coming along to see his revenge accomplished. I was not surprised – after all, the patient devil had waited nine years for it.

At Red River Landing, a tolerable inn survived, and I engaged a room. The town was muddy and straggling as in times gone by, but it boasted two or three steamboats tied up and unloading, with black labourers not unlike the slaves of yesteryear – indeed, they were the slaves of yesteryear – chanting work songs as they trotted up and down the gangplanks, with heavy loads miraculously balanced on their heads.

In my room, I laid my pistol upon the usual marble-top table, beside the usual chipped washbasin and flowered pitcher. Then I lay down to rest upon an ill-smelling featherbed, drawing a dusty musketo-net about me. My thoughts were sombre, but I did not have long to indulge them. Came a knock on the door, and the innkeeper – a huge man with smaller eyes in a larger face than I ever saw before – handed me two telegrams, and stood waiting whilst I read. I put the telegrams under my stump and began to fish in my waistcoat pocket for a coin.

"I'm not wanting a tip," he said in a low drawling grumble of a voice. "General Hobbs has contacted me. Where'd you lose the wing?"

"Shiloh. Better come into the room." He nodded and followed me.

"I was there too," he said. "I saw General Johnston killed. The minny-ball broke an artery in his leg; he turned white as cotton and

bled to death in half a minute. Is this a matter of honour, or politics?"

"Both. You'll find that I know how to be grateful."

"I'm sure." Despite omitting the "r", he made two syllables out of sure. "You want the nigger to go slow, or fast?"

"Fast."

"Night or day?"

"He's no fool. He won't go out at night. And you don't want him killed here."

"So it's daytime, then, which means masks and an ambush."

In whispers we completed our arrangements. After engaging his horse and buggy for the morrow, I explained that I had grown up nearby.

"I'm from Arkansaw, myself," he said. "You owned the nigger in the old days?"

"Yes."

"Ah," said he, sadly shaking his massive head. "They was happier then." He left the room with a surprisingly silent tread, for so big a man.

Everything was in readiness. I dined without appetite, slept poorly, but was waiting at the dock with the landlord's buggy when Royal strode ashore from the morning packet. As if impersonating himself, he was all strut and boldness, jaunty and dressed in flash attire – a claw-hammer coat and top hat – at which blacks and whites alike turned and stared. I hailed him, and he leaped into the buggy, which swayed under his weight, and gripped my hand.

"Nick," he exclaimed, "Never did I think we would meet here again, and for such a reason!"

I said, "Since you're a bird with two wings, perhaps you'll drive?"

He took the reins and snapped them with the casual ease of a country-bred man. The horse shook its mane and the buggy rolled with a jingle of little bells along the old familiar road that led to the ruins of Mon Repos. The day was fine, the ground dry and the spring weather cool and bright, with fair-weather clouds above, and great shadows flitting soundlessly over woods and meadows.

As we drove, I plunged into recollection, chattering nervously in a manner most unusual for me. Royal (a great talker) responded in kind, and soon we were pointing and exclaiming as if we were boys again. My school had been reduced to a few scattered bricks, and 'midst the ruins of the church I saw – fallen and rusting – the iron bell that once had tolled for the death of a world. We turned into a dim track, where tall grass brushed the underside of the carriage with the sound of rubbed velvet. Near the stark chimney that alone had survived the fall of Mon Repos, Royal tugged at the reins and we halted.

For a minute or so we sat silent. Then he said, "I was amazed at your telegram, Nick."

"I designed it to be amazing."

"Frankly, Rose and I were prepared to defy you, if need be. But how fine it is that you consent to our marriage – and that you intend this land to be Rose's marriage portion!"

"I could imagine nothing that would please either of you more than to own Mon Repos," I replied. "It's the logical dowry."

I watched covertly as Royal's natural wariness dissolved in the grip of irresistible emotion. "To own the land where I was once a slave!" he exclaimed, his voice choking midway in the sentence.

He gazed like one transfixed down the long alley of noble oaks, where grey streamers of moss floated on the breeze with the silent grace of shadows. I began to talk about the taxes, the difficulty of getting tenants to work the fields, and the need for a new survey, since most of the old landmarks had disappeared.

"Those were to have been my problems," I said. "Now I fear they will be yours. And you must be on your guard, my friend. The Klan's active hereabouts – you're safe enough in daytime, but a prominent coloured man with a white wife should beware the night."

He grinned and raised the tail of his fawn-coloured coat to shew a handsome silver-mounted pistol in a holster of tooled leather hanging from a wide cartridge-belt.

"I am prepared for anything," he said.

I shook my head at his fatal arrogance. How can a man be prepared for anything?

"Ah, look," I said, pointing, "do you remember that path? It led to our swimming-hole, did it not?"

He turned and craned, and as he did so a figure in robe and hood stepped from behind the chimney and raised a rifle. A shot exploded, and the round buzzed past me.

Frightened, the horse reared and whinnied. The buggy tilted; I grabbed at the reins and struggled one-handed to get the animal under control. Meantime, like a good soldier Royal leaped to the ground and rolled and fired.

His shot killed the idiot in spook attire, and the Klansman's hand, contracting in death, squeezed off a round that struck the horse in the brain. The animal crashed in the traces, the buggy overturned, and I was flung out and landed with a thump.

Well, the whole thing was a hopeless mess. I scrambled past a wildly spinning wheel, jumped to my feet, and found that I was alone amid the ruins of Mon Repos.

The assassin lay like a heap of soiled bedclothes on the ground. Royal had vanished into a nearby stand of trees, and I heard shouts and shots and the crashing of men plunging through the dense second-growth of pine and sweetgum saplings.

A shotgun boomed. Silence for six or seven heartbeats, then two revolver shots, Blam! Blam!

Desperate to learn what was happening, I drew my pistol and followed the sounds into the trees. The wind seemed to hold its breath; invisible birds were screaming, but the noise of the fire-fight had slain all movement save mine.

I paused and stood listening. The shotgun boomed again close by, followed by a revolver shot and a strangled outcry. I hastened through the blinding tangle, panting, inhaling the reek of sulphur mingled with the wine-cork smell of spring growth.

In a little glen I found a figure weltering in the grass – another hooded man, a big one. I lifted the hood and saw the landlord's broad face and tiny eyes. He had been shot through the throat, and his sharp little eyes turned to dull pebbles as I watched.

A new fury of shots broke out. A deathly pale young man broke from the thicket and ran past me, his breath rattling like a consumptive's. He ran like a hare, this way and that, either to make aiming difficult or simply in the madness of fear. Then he was gone, and I was alone with Royal.

I whispered bitterly, "You might have spared me this."

I had not forgotten all woodcraft, and slipped without a sound past slender pale trunks and rough pine branches, over thorny mats of wild grape and thick dying undergrowth. In the treetops strong sunlight vibrated, but down in the tangle evening colours – blue and bronze – enveloped me. Then I stumbled on a heap of dry wood, something cracked under my feet, and behind me Royal's voice said, "Hello, Nick."

I turned and faced him. He levelled his revolver and said, "Your weapon."

A smile of relief began to cross my lips, and he said more sharply, "Come, come – your weapon! And let me tell you, brother, you have but little to smile about."

In that he was wrong, for I was watching Monsieur Felix emerge from the ruins of his house. Then that unforgettable voice ground out, Aha, tu p'tit diable!

Royal turned his head, and looked into the one glinting eye and the one oozing pit. That was when I shot him down, and shot him again where he lay.

For a long moment the Overseer and I stood gazing at each other over the body. He smiled, that thin smile I remembered so well, like an arroyo between his blade of a nose and blue hillock of a chin. I hated him then, yet not half so much as I hated myself, for having sold my destiny forever to such a one as he.

Then, like a shadow struck by light, he vanished without a sound.

Strange, very strange, he thought, rereading what he'd written. After all, his tale was a confession. But who was he confessing to? God had long ago departed from his universe, and Royal and Rose already knew his guilt, assuming they knew anything at all.

The slow approach of shuffling footsteps in the hall interrupted his brooding. Hastily he locked up his manuscript and assumed the demeanour of a hanging judge. The door opened, and Cleo and Euphrosyne together helped Morse limp in to face the music.

His face was swollen, one eye was a purple plum, and he winced at every movement from the pain of his ribs, though the doctor had told Lerner that the bones were only cracked, not broken.

The old man greeted him with silence, then waved the women away. For several long minutes Morse stood before him, his one good eye fixed in contemplation of his toes. Finally Lerner spoke in what he hoped were the tones of Fate.

"I suppose you know that you might have been beaten to death."

Morse nodded.

"I can't prevent you from embarking on such adventures again. But I can withdraw my protection. Once more, and you're on your own. Then you'll either die at the hands of the police or else go to prison where, I promise you, you'll learn many things, but nothing to make you grateful to your teachers."

Morse nodded again. He already knew that he would be forgiven one more time. How else to explain the fact that he was here, rather than lying on the oozing brick floor of the prison, watching enormous cockroaches feast on spatters of his own blood? He also knew without being told that he'd reached the end of his rope, that he'd have no more chances, and that his hopes of inheriting a portion of the old man's wealth were probably over.

What he couldn't know were the thoughts passing through Lerner's mind. The old man was looking at Morse but, still full of the story he'd been writing, thinking not of him but of himself and Royal.

Well, we all come to it in time – we are broken down to ground-level, and must construct ourselves anew. If we survive, we become stronger: with few exceptions we do not become better. For most of us, when all else has failed, turn to the demon.

He drew a deep breath, said, "Sit down," and watched Morse relapse, wincing, into the same chair – now battered and dusty – where Rose had sat so long ago.

Opening the safe, Lerner took out a fist-sized parcel of rice paper. He unwrapped it, revealing a sticky dark mass of opium. The doctor had obtained it for him at a handsome mark-up; he used the drug in his practice, and made sure that it was legally bought.

From the tantalus, Lerner lifted a crystal flask of bourbon and two shot glasses. By now Morse had raised his one good eye and was watching as if mesmerized. Lerner prepared two shots of laudanum and offered one to Morse.

After they had both swallowed their medicine, and the mixture was spreading a slow fiery comfort through their veins, Lerner delivered his verdict: "Hereafter, Morse, you will use the drug with me in these rooms, and nowhere else."

"Yes," he mumbled. "Yes, Father."

"I take that as your word of honour," said the old man, noting wryly how odd the word *honour* tasted on his tongue. "If you break it, I will have no mercy on you. Now help me to bed. Tomorrow you'll do only what is most necessary, and otherwise rest."

The bedtime ritual that night was even slower than usual, with Morse wincing – sometimes gasping – with pain, and pausing again and again to recover. Lerner had plenty of time to think, and what he thought about was how, in one way or another, he'd lost everyone who had ever been close to him: Elmira, his and Elmira's children, Papa, Rose, and Royal.

All of them gone. Soon he would be gone too. But it was still within his power to save something from the wreckage, through a man of his blood who would live on after him. *He is, after all, the last of our family and, even if adopted, the only son I shall ever have. But if he continues the way he's going, he will die too, and nobody will be left at all.*

Old people have to decide things quickly, having no time for the long thoughts of youth. He resolved to act tomorrow – summon his lawyer and settle everything while Morse lay resting upstairs in bed. Lerner's old habits of deep suspicion didn't quite leave him, for he also thought: *better not tell the boy. I know what I might do, if one old man stood between me and a great inheritance.*

He smiled craftily, thinking what a surprise ending he could now give his confession. Then leave it to be read once he was safely gone. Confession might be good for the soul, but if incautiously made public might be death to the body. After all, he reflected, his veins and Morse's held much the same blood.

No one instructed me as to how I should conceal my crime (he began to write next day, after the lawyer had come and gone). *Nor did anyone need to.*

I grasped Royal's hand, dragged his carcass down into the glen, and pressed my pistol into the hand of the dead innkeeper. Then I set out briskly enough, rehearsing my story as I went, and after disarranging my clothing, staggered into Red River Landing, crying out a shocking tale of ambush and sudden death.

All who saw me that day knew that I truly grieved, though they did not know why. General Hobbs, of course, knew what had happened, but my secret was safe with him. Rose (I think) divined the truth, but could do nothing, having no protector but myself, and needing one more than ever, because she was with child.

'Twas almost miraculous, how all the pieces fell into place. The hue and cry over the murder was great, for Royal had been a rising star of the Republican Party, and his death became a hook upon which President Grant could hang new and stringent measures against the Klan. In the months that followed, I travelled to Washington thrice to testify, and made (I may say without false pride) a good job of it: in lengthy testimony on the Hill, I never made a serious error; never was at a loss for words; most important of all, never told the truth.

Based largely upon my testimony, Congress concluded that two loyal Union men had been attacked by Klansmen, one being killed and other barely escaping with his life. The outrage led directly to passage of the Ku Klux Act, which caused so much trouble to General Hobbs and his friends: 'twas under that law he was later arrested for some trifling murder, tried by military commission, and sent to Fort Leavenworth, where he died.

Thereafter I was a marked man amongst his followers, as I was already a pariah to all who hated the Yankee occupation. Yet isolation was familiar to me, and I was not unhappy to be rid of so impulsive and violent a friend. For great changes were in the air, and a cool head was needed to take advantage of them. In 1873 a depression devastated the Grant administration, which was already falling by the weight of its own corruption. Another three years, and the Democrats seized power in Louisiana; Governor Wharton was impeached, and departed public life with a fortune (said to be in the range of two millions) to comfort his old age.

He paid me a handsome price for my land near Red River, and there built the grand and intricate monstrosity of a house he calls Réunion. He sited his mansion at the end of the great oak alley, clearing away the old chimney in the process, and the ruins of Monsieur Felix's house as well, which spoiled his view. 'Twas in this house, in rooms that were perfect symphonies of bad taste, that I courted his daughter Elmira, and won her consent to be my bride.

The marriage was sumptuous. Like the great slave-owners he had always secretly admired, the Governor displayed an instinct for magnificence. As the wedding day approached, he imported from South America hundreds of spiders known for the beauty of their webs and turned them loose in the oaks. When their shining orbs had taken form, with his own hand he cast handfuls of gold dust upon the threads.

Up this astounding aisle, more splendid than any cathedral, 'midst golden glitter and dancing sunlight he led Elmira, clad in ashes-of-roses chenille and watered silk and Brussels lace, to where I waited for her beside the soaring staircase of Réunion. There we were wed, and the parson prayed that our marriage might symbolize an end to the strife which had so long bloodied the State and the Nation.

After kissing my bride, I embraced my new father-in-law with one arm, whilst he hugged me with two. Tears leaked into his whiskers as he saw his family joined forever to what he liked to call, in hushed tones, "the old aristocracy".

Rose's story was less glorious. Eight months after Royal's death, she gave birth to an infant which she freely acknowledged to be his.

I was by then a busy man, between my Washington trips and my courting of Elmira, and was at some difficulty to cover things up. In the end I arranged for Rose to visit Natchez in the character of a widow, accompanied by a discreet woman of my acquaintance. There a hale and noisy male infant passed through the gates of life, and entered this world of sin. The final act of the tragedy came when Rose died of a haemorrhage resulting from a difficult labour. Well, she had always been sickly and frail – not a good candidate to bear a large and lusty man-child!

I was somewhat at a loss what to do with this new and (at first) unwelcome kinsman of mine. I expected to have children with

Elmira. Along with the Old South had vanished those easygoing days when a large brood of varicoloured youngsters, some slave and some free, some legitimate and some bastards, could all be raised together under one paternal eye. Since then a certain niceness and propriety had come into life, and appearances had to be preserved.

I named the boy Morse, an uncommon name for a black. At the time I knew not why I chose it, though I now believe 'twas a strangled echo of the remorse I felt over his father's death. I hoped that he might be light in hue and featured like an European, which would have made everything easier. But in a few weeks it became plain that – despite a double infusion of white blood, from his mother and his father's father – robust Africa was stamped firmly and forever upon his visage.

I put him out to be suckled by a wet-nurse in the Creole quarter, and this woman solved the problem for me. Recently she had lost an infant and been abandoned by her lover; she longed for a child, and she needed work. I took her into my household as a maid, where she remained until her death, representing herself to Morse as his mother. I believe that this woman, spotting a certain ghostly similarity in our features, decided that Morse must be my bastard, and in time passed on this bit of misinformation to her charge.

Yet he was my kinsman, and discreetly I watched over his raising, as in the past Papa had watched over Royal's. He grew strong and clever, learned to read and write and cipher to the rule of twelve, and in my service was trained to the duties of an upper servant. The walls of my house shielded him from much that was happening to his people in the outside world where, abandoned by the North, they were made into serfs by the South.

All unknowing, I was preparing a caretaker for myself. Ever since I had angered the Klan, a series of events had placed my life in danger: I but narrowly escaped two assassination attempts, and once had my house set on fire (though so incompetently that the blaze was readily extinguished). I hired Pinkertons to protect me, and for a time the attempts ended. But in '93, on busy Canal Street at noonday, an empty four-horse dray came careening around a corner and knocked me to the ground. The vehicle swerved around the next corner, and vanished: 'twas later found abandoned in a weedy lot near the river, the horses unbridled and peacefully cropping grass. The driver was never discovered – or so the police reported.

Thus by a spinal injury I became an invalid at the age of fifty, when otherwise still vigorous and in the prime of life. Believing that my former associates had forgotten nothing and forgiven nothing, I turned increasingly into a recluse, dependent upon Morse, the only caregiver I felt that I could trust. And so—

Unnoticed by Lerner, dusk had come, and with it came Morse, barging through the door with a touch of his old insouciance, despite his stiffness and the plum over his eye, carrying the dinner tray in which the old man felt no interest, and the drug he truly needed.

Lerner hastily put away his manuscript and closed the safe. Towards the food he made only a gesture, swallowing a forkful here and there and thrusting the rest away. After he had been settled for the night, Morse sat down beside the bed on a footstool, his head resting against the moss mattress, and they shared the opium.

As usual these days, one dose of laudanum wasn't enough for Lerner. The second put him into a state like the trance of a medium. He saw the spectres of the past rising up about him, and whispered, "Look, look there."

"Where?"

"There, in the mirror. Can't you see him? It's Monsieur Felix! Look how his one eye gleams!"

"You're crazy, Father," Morse said, not unkindly.

"He wants me to come with him to his house. It lies halfway to the quarters, and once there I can never leave. Ah Morse, how can I tell him *No*, when I have so often told him *Yes*?"

"Rest, old man," Morse said, "for the past is dead and gone."

"No, no, 'tis a phantom limb that aches more than a real one, for there is no way to touch it, to heal it, to give it ease."

"Sleep," Morse said, and mixed him yet another dose. Lerner drank it off at a gulp, choked, gasped for a moment, then relaxed against his pillows.

Little by little the shadows of the room turned bronze, then brown. For a time the old man seemed still to be conversing with Morse; he heard voices, one of which sounded like his own, and unless mistaken he heard spoken the word *perdu*. But the voices became still; he found himself enjoying a brilliant scene of people waltzing at a masked ball. Then nothing.

Next morning he woke with his head, as usual, filled with ashes. For a time he lay in bed, unable even to reach for the bell. When his mind cleared, he rang as usual, but no Morse appeared. Nor anyone else.

After ringing again and again, Lerner, cursing, stretched out a trembling arm, drew the wheelchair beside the bed and despite a shock of pain, wrestled himself into it. Where the devil was everyone? He trundled to the door of his den and flung it open.

The safe door stood ajar. He rolled into the room and put a trembling hand inside. The manuscript was gone. *Well,* thought Lerner, *he was always a clever fellow.*

The house was utterly silent. Morse must have sent Cleo and the cook away. Lerner spun the chair this way and that. What to do, what to do? The telephone was out of reach, and anyway Morse might be waiting in the hallway. The old man peered back into the bedroom, but with only the one barred window it was a trap without an exit. He couldn't lock himself into the den, for the key to the hall door had vanished years ago – possibly removed by Morse, so that he could enter at will.

And he'd put his life into the hands of this man! Soon he'd be coming to accuse Lerner of murdering his real father. Coming with the razor, but not to shave him.

He turned to his desk, pulled out a handful of ancient bills that stuffed a pigeonhole, pushed aside a panel at the back and touched a hidden spring. A second panel opened into a dark recess. He thrust in his hand and pulled out the Remington. He clamped it muzzle-first in his left armpit, broke it open and checked the load of six brass cartridges. He snapped the weapon shut again. The hammer was stiff, but he cocked it easily with his one hand accustomed to doing the work of two.

He hid the gun under his lap robe and wheeled himself back into the bedroom. Closing the door to his den behind him, he waited for Morse – an old and crippled wolf, but not a toothless one.

Yet his first visitor appeared, not at the door, but in the mirror. Monsieur Felix couldn't bear to miss out on what was about to happen, and suddenly there he stood in the clouded pier glass – one eye gleaming, thin smile widening like an arroyo between the blue chin and the great blade of a nose. Perhaps he was too eager, for Lerner read his mind.

Why, he wondered, *did I ever imagine his vengeance would stop with Royal? Did I not call him swine, connive at his death, supply the weapon that killed him? Did I not write my confession at his command? In an opium dream, did he not cause me to speak the word* perdu *that let Morse open the safe? Is it not his pleasure now to destroy me and Royal's son at one stroke? For either I'll kill him and perish of my infirmities, or he'll kill me and go to the hangman for murder.*

At that moment the door slammed open and Morse entered, razor flickering in his hand. His face was swollen, his eyes drugged to pinpoints, his smile an arid duplicate of the one in the mirror. He whispered, "I've come to scrape your throat, Uncle."

Lerner pulled the revolver from under the lap robe. Morse halted like a man suddenly transmuted into stone. In the fearsome quiet that followed, Lerner spoke to him for the last time.

"Whatever else I've done in a long and mostly foul existence, Morse, remember how at the very end I saved you from the hangman's noose and gave you a new life for my brother's sake."

Two crashes of thunder. The shards of the mirror were still tinkling on the floor when Lerner slumped in his chair, the pistol slipping from his hand.

The smoke was dense, and through it Monsieur Felix, emerging from the shattered mirror, passed like a shadow seen in fog. He stared at Lerner, absolutely baffled. The vatic power he depended upon, the power that enabled him to plan his murders a decade or more in advance – why had it been blind to this possibility?

J'ai perdu son âme, he thought, almost in despair. *I've lost his soul.*

Then he turned his gaze on Morse. His trademark smile slowly rekindled, as he recalled the deepest secret of the young man's life: how, as a child, he'd entered the nursery in this house, turned Elmira's son over in his crib, and pressed the baby's face into the mattress until he suffocated – all out of fear that the white child would take his own place in Lerner's favour.

Now the poor devil needed help, which Monsieur Felix was always happy to supply.

Gradually Morse recovered from his shock. First he'd forgotten to breathe; then panted like a winded animal, heart thundering. Now his breath evened, his heart slowed to a regular beat. He folded the razor and put it into his trouser pocket, while cool thoughts seemed to rise from some unshaken region of his mind.

I must touch nothing. I must telephone the police. I must report the suicide. His illness and the drug will explain everything. And aren't the police identifying people by their finger-marks these days? Well, his finger-marks are on the pistol's grip.

But there was something else. *The police – suppose they decide to bury the evidence and hang me as they've hung other blacks, for the mere pleasure of it?*

A thought tickled the back of his mind. *There's something in the desk.*

He turned back into the den. Took the razor out again and threw it into the safe, so it wouldn't be found on him. He slammed the iron door, spun around, knocked the pile of ancient bills off the desk and reached his arm to the elbow inside the open hidey-hole. What was he touching?

He pulled out a leather purse with a string closure, opened it and grinned at the cylinder of gold double-eagles it contained. *Why, the old devil,* he thought. *Here's his secret cache, and all the time I thought it was in the safe!*

A few bribes would enable him to handle the police, and that was all he knew or cared about now. The fact that he would soon be rich – that he would have power beyond the imagining of ordinary people to exercise an appetite for cruelty that had grown up in him during a lifetime of stifled rage – all that remained to be discovered.

The Demon stood behind him, smiling, lending him useful thoughts, mentoring him, delighted as always to be the Overseer of human destiny.

Aha, le p'tit diable! whispered Monsieur Felix. *Him I won't lose.*

PINCKNEY BENEDICT

The Beginnings of Sorrow

PINCKNEY BENEDICT GREW UP on his family's dairy farm in the mountains of southern West Virginia. He has published two collections of short fiction (*Town Smokes* and *The Wrecking Yard*) and a novel (*Dogs of God*).

He currently serves as a professor in the English Department at Southern Illinois University in Carbondale, Illinois.

"'The Beginnings of Sorrow' evolved out of my long-standing fascination with werewolf tales," explains the author, "from the Roman soldier in Petronius' *Cena Trimalchionis*, for example, up to the fairly recent (and terrific) film *Dog Soldiers*.

"I wanted very much to write a werewolf story in reverse, one in which a dog painfully and protractedly becomes a man.

"Setting that story on a failing farm in the Appalachian highlands seemed natural to me, as did the rapid disintegration of the world outside the farm, communicated as it is by television: a fantasia on the hermetic environment in which I was raised."

> "Whoo-oo-oo-oo-hooh-hoo-oo! Oh, look at me, I
> am perishing in this gateway . . . I howl and howl,
> but what's the good of howling?"
> —Mikhail Bulgakov, *Heart of a Dog*

VANDAL BOUCHER TOLD his dog Hark to go snatch the duck out of the rushes where it had fallen, and Hark told him *No*. In days to come, Vandal probably wished he'd just pointed his Ithaca twelve-gauge side-by-side at Hark's fine-boned skull right that moment and pulled the trigger on the second barrel (he had emptied the first to bring down the duck) and blown the dog's brains out, there at the edge of the freezing, sludgy pond. But that unanticipated answer – any answer would have been a surprise, of course, but this was *no*, unmistakably *no*, in a pleasant tenor, without any obvious edge of anger or resentment – that single syllable took him aback and prevented him from taking action.

Vandal's old man, now: back in the day, Vandal's old man Xerxes Boucher would have slain the dog that showed him any sign of strangeness or resistance to his will, let alone one that told him *no*. Dog's sucking the golden yolks out of the eggs? *Blam*. Dog's taking chickens out of the coop? *Blam*. Dog's not sticking tight enough to the sheep, so the coyotes are chivvying them across the high pastures? *This dog's your favourite, your special pet? You wish I would refrain from shooting the dog? Well, sonny, you wish in one hand and shit in the other, see which gets full first. Blam.* Nothing could stop him, no pleading or promises, and threats were out of the question. But that was Xerxes in his prime, and Vandal wasn't a patch on him, everybody said so, Vandal himself had ruefully to agree with the general assessment of his character. So when Hark said *no*, Vandal just blinked. "Come again?" he said.

No.

Well, Vandal thought. He looked out into the reeds, where the body of the mallard he had just shot bobbed in the dark water. That water looked cold. Hark sat on the shore, blinking up at Vandal with mild eyes. It would have struck Xerxes Boucher as outrageous that the dog should balk at wading out there into that cold, muddy mess, the soupy muck at the pond's margin at least shoulder-deep for the dog where the dead mallard floated, maybe deep enough that a dog – even a sizeable dog like Hark – would have to swim.

But damn it if, on that grey November morning, with a hot thermos of his wife's bitter black coffee nearby just waiting on him to drink it, and a solid breakfast when he got home after the hunt, and dry socks – damned if Vandal couldn't see the dog's point.

"Okay," he said. "This once."

He was wearing his thick rubber waders, the ones that went all the way up to the middle of his chest, so he took off his coat – the frigid air bit into him, made his breath go short – laid the coat down on the bank, set the shotgun on top of the coat, and set off after the mallard himself. The waders clutched his calves as the greasy pond water surged around his legs, and his feet sank unpleasantly into the soft bottom. He considered what might be sleeping down there: frogs settled in for the winter, dreaming their slick wet dreams; flabby catfish whiskered like old men; great knobby snapping turtles, their thick round shells overlapping one another like the shields of some ancient army.

They were down there in the dark, the turtles that had survived unchanged from the age of the dinosaurs, with their spines buckled so that they fit, neatly folded, within their shells; and their eyes closed fast, their turtle hearts beating slow, slow, slow, waiting on the passing of another winter. And what if the winter never passed and spring never came, as looked more and more likely? How long would they sleep, how long could such creatures wait in the dark? A long time, Vandal suspected. Time beyond counting. It might suit them well, the endless empty twilight that the world seemed dead-set on becoming.

Vandal didn't care to put his feet on such creatures, and when his toes touched something hard, he tried to tread elsewhere. The pond bottom was full of hard things, and most of them were probably rocks, but better safe than sorry. He had seen the jaws on snapping turtles up close, the beak on the skeletal face like a hawk's or an eagle's, hooked and hard-edged and sharp as a razor. Easy to lose a toe to such a creature.

When he reached the mallard – it was truly a perfect bird, its head and neck a deep oily green, unmarked by the flying shot – he plucked its limp body up out of the water and waved it over his head for the dog to see. "Got it!" he called.

Hark wasn't paying any attention to him at all. He was sitting next to the tall silver thermos and gazing quizzically at the coat and, cradled on the coat, Vandal's shotgun.

"I told him to go get the duck," Vandal said to his wife, who was called Bridie. Then, to Hark, he said, "Tell her what you told me."

No, said Hark.

Bridie looked from her husband to the dog. "Does he mean to tell you no," she asked, working to keep her voice even and calm, her tone reasonable. "Or does he mean he won't tell me?"

No, the dog said again. It wasn't like a bark, which Bridie would have much preferred, one of those clever dogs that has been taught by its owner to "talk" by mimicking human speech without understanding what it was saying. "What's on top of a house?" *Roof!* "How does sandpaper feel?" *Rough!* "Who's the greatest ballplayer of all time?" *Ruth!*

DiMaggio, she thought to herself. *That's the punchline. The dog says* Ruth! *but really it's DiMaggio*. Vandal laughed. He was a big broad-shouldered good-natured man with an infectious laugh, which was one of the reasons Bridie loved him, and she smiled despite her misgivings. The dog seemed delighted with the turn of events too.

"That's the sixty-four dollar question, ain't it?" Vandal said. He clapped Hark on the head in the old familiar way, and the dog shifted out from under the cupped hand, eyes suddenly slitted and opaque. *No*, it said.

Much as she loved Vandal, and much as she had hated his bear of a father, with his great sweaty hands always ready to squeeze her behind or pinch her under her skirt as she was climbing the stairs, always ready to brush against her breasts – glad as she was that the mean old man was in the cold cold ground, she couldn't help but think at that moment that a little of Xerxes' unflinching resolve wouldn't have gone amiss in Vandal's character, in this circumstance. She wished that the dog had said pretty much anything else: *Yes*, or better yet, *yes sir*. Even a word of complaint, *cold, wet, dark. Afraid*. But this flat refusal unnerved her.

"He takes a lot on himself, doesn't he? For a dog," she said.

"Talking dog," said Vandal, his pride written on his knobby face, as though he had taught the dog to speak all by himself, as though it had been his idea.

Hark had begun wandering through the house, inspecting the dark heavy furniture like he had never seen it or the place before. Not exploring timidly, like a guest unsure of his welcome, but more like a new owner. Bridie thought she saw him twitch a lip disdainfully as he sniffed at the fraying upholstery of the davenport. He looked to her for a moment as though maybe he were going to lift his leg. "No!" she snapped. "Bad boy!"

He glanced from her to Vandal and back again, trotted over to Vandal's easy chair with his tail curled high over his back. He gave off the distinct air of having won some sort of victory. "Come here," Bridie called to him. She snapped her fingers, and he swung his narrow, intelligent head, looking past his shoulder at her.

No, he said, and he hopped up into Vandal's chair. Bridie was relieved to see how small he was in the chair, into which Vandal had to work to wedge his bulky frame.

There was room for two of Hark in the seat, three even, so lean was he, slender long-legged retriever mix. Vandal nodded at him with approval. The dog turned around and around and around as though he were treading down brush to make himself a nest, in the ancient way of dogs. In the end, though, he settled himself upright rather than lying down, his spine against the back of the chair, his head high.

"Xerxes wouldn't never allow a dog up in his chair like that," Bridie said. And was immediately sorry she had said it. Vandal had adored and dreaded his brutal, unstoppable old man, and any comparison between them left him feeling failed and wanting. *Xerxes, Xerxes. Will he never leave our house?*

"Xerxes never had him a talking dog," Vandal said. He handed the dead mallard to her. Its glossy head and neck stretched down toward the floor in a comical way, its pearlescent eyes long gone into death. It was a large, muscular bird.

"Not much of a talking dog," Bridie said. She turned, taking the mallard away into the kitchen when she saw the flash of irritation in Vandal's eyes. She didn't look towards Hark, because she didn't want to see the expression of satisfaction that she felt sure animated his doggy features. She wanted to let Vandal have this moment, this chance to own something that his father couldn't have imagined, let alone possessed, but it was – it was wrong. Twisted, bent. It was a thing that couldn't be but was, it was unspeakable, and it was there in her living room, sitting in her husband's chair. "Not much of one, if all it can manage to say is *no*."

Hark reclined in the easy chair in the parlour. The television was tuned to the evening news, and the dog watched and listened with bright gleaming eyes, giving every appearance of understanding what was said: wars and rumours of wars. Earthquakes and famines and troubles. None of it was good at all, it hadn't been good in some little time, but none of it seemed to bother him in the least. He chewed briefly at his own hip, after some itch that was deeply hidden there, and then went back to his television viewing.

Vandal sat on the near end of the davenport, not appearing to hear the news. From time to time he reached out a hand to pet Hark, but Hark shifted his weight and leaned away, just out of reach. It was what Bridie had always striven to do when Xerxes went to put his hands on her but that she had somehow never managed, to create that small distance between them that would prove unbridgeable. Always the hand reached her, to pet and stroke and pinch, always when Vandal's attention was turned elsewhere. And them living in Xerxes' house, and her helpless to turn him away.

About the third time Vandal put his hand out, Hark tore his gaze from the TV screen, snarled, snapped, his jaws closing with a wicked click just shy of Vandal's reaching fingertips. Vandal withdrew his hand, looking sheepish.

"No?" he asked the dog.

No, Hark said, and he settled back into the soft cushions of the chair, his eyes fixed once more on the flickering screen.

Over Bridie's objections, Hark ate dinner at the table with them that night. Vandal insisted. The dog tried to climb into the chair with arms, Vandal's seat at the head of the table. Vandal wasn't going to protest, but Bridie wouldn't allow it. She flapped the kitchen towel – it was covered in delicate blue cornflowers – at him, waved her hands and shouted "Shoo! Shoo!" until he slipped down out of the chair and, throwing resentful glances her way, slunk over to one of the chairs at the side of the table and took his place.

He ate like an animal, she noted with satisfaction, chasing the duck leg she had given him around and around the rim of the broad plate with his sharp snout, working to grasp the bone with his teeth, his tongue hanging drolly from the side of his mouth. Always, the leg escaped him. Each time it did, she put it carefully back in the middle of the plate, and he went after it again. From time to time he would stop his pursuit of the drumstick and watch Bridie and Vandal manipulate their utensils, raise their forks to their mouths, dab at their lips with napkins. His own napkin was tucked bib-like under the broad leather strap of his collar, and it billowed ridiculously out over his narrow, hairy chest. Vandal watched this process through a number of repetitions, his brow furrowed, before he put down his knife and fork.

"You can't let a dog have duck bones like that," he said. "He'll crack the bone and swallow it and the sharp edges will lodge in his throat."

Good, Bridie thought. *Let him.* The dog stared across the table at her, his face twisted into what she took to be an accusatory grimace. Hark had always been Vandal's dog, never hers, and she had never felt much affection for him, but he had always seemed to her to be a perfectly normal dog, not overfriendly but that was normal in an animal that was brought up to work rather than as a pet. Restrained in his affections, but never hostile. Lean and quick and hard-muscled, with the bland face and expressions of his kind. And now he looked at her as though he knew what she was thinking – an image of Hark coughing, wheezing, hacking up blood on the kitchen floor swam back into her consciousness – and hated her for it.

Was there an element of surprise there too? she wondered. He hadn't known about the bones. An unanticipated danger, and now he knew, and she could sense him filing the information away, so that such a thing would never be a threat to him again. What else was he ignorant about?

Bridie had never disliked Hark before, had never disliked any of Vandal's boisterous happy-go-lucky hunting dogs, the bird dogs, the bear dogs, the coon dogs, all of them camped out in the tilting kennel attached to the pole barn. They shared the long fenced run that stretched across the barnyard, and they would woof and whirl and slobber when she went out to feed them. Dogs with names like Sam and Kettle and Bengal and Ranger. And Hark. Hark the waterdog, a little quieter than the others, more subdued, maybe, but nothing obvious about him to separate him from the rest of them. They were Vandal's friends and companions, they admired him even when Xerxes fed him scorn, and they were kind to him when even she herself wasn't. She didn't fool with them much.

Something had come alive in Hark, something that allowed him, compelled him, to say *no*, and now he was at her table when the rest were outside in the cold and the dark, now he was looking her in the eye. That was another new thing, this direct confrontation; he had always cast his gaze down, properly canine, when his eyes had locked with hers in the past. He'd regained his earlier cocksureness, and the impression of self-satisfaction that she had from him made him unbearable to her.

Vandal was leaning over, working his knife, paring the crispy skin and the leg meat away from the bone. "Here you go," he told the dog, his tone fond. Hark sniffed.

"If he plans to eat his food at the table like people," Bridie said, "then he better learn to pick it up like people."

Vandal stopped cutting. Bridie half-expected Hark to say No in the light voice that sounded so strange coming out of that long maw, with its mottled tongue and (as they seemed to her) cruel-looking teeth. Instead, he nudged Vandal out of his way and planted one forepaw squarely on the duck leg. *He understands*, Bridie thought to herself.

The plate tipped and skittered away from him, the duck leg tumbling off it, the china ringing against the hard oak of the tabletop. The dog looked perplexed, but Vandal slid the plate back into place, picked up the drumstick and laid it gently down.

Just as gently, Hark put his paw on the leg bone, pinning it. He lowered his head, closed his teeth securely on the leg – the chafing squeak of tooth against bone made Bridie squint her eyes in disgust –

and pulled away a triumphant mouthful of duck. He tossed it back, swallowed without chewing, and went after the leg again.

"Good dog," Vandal said. The dog's ears flickered at the familiar phrase, but he didn't raise his head from the plate. Bridie bit into her own portion. Duck was normally one of her favourites, but this meal filled her mouth like ashes. Vandal stopped chewing, leaned down close to his plate, his lips pursed as though he were about to kiss his food, his eyes screwed nearly shut. He made a little spitting noise, and a pellet of lead shot, no bigger than a flea, pinged onto his plate, bounced, and lay still.

After supper, as Bridie retted up the kitchen, Vandal sat cross-legged on the floor in the parlour, the shotgun broken down and spread out on several thicknesses of newspaper on the floor before him. A small smoky fire – the wood was too green to burn well, hadn't aged sufficiently – flared and popped in the hearth.

Hark sat in the comfortable chair, and his posture had become – she felt sure of this – more human than it had been previously. He was sitting like a man now, a misshapen man, yes, with a curved spine and his head low between his shoulders, but he was working to sit upright. He looked ridiculous, as she glanced in at him from where she was working, but she felt no impulse to laugh. Was he larger than he had been? Did he fill the chair more fully? While she watched, he lost his precarious balance, slipped to the side, thrashed for a moment before righting himself again.

The television was on, the usual chatter from the local news, a terrible wreck out on the state highway, a plant shutting down in the county seat, a marvel on a nearby farm, a Holstein calf born with two heads, both of them alive and bawling, both of them sucking milk. *Who could even take note of something like that in these times*, Bridie wondered to herself as she worked to scrub the grease from the plates. The next day it would be something else, and something else after that, until the wonders and the sports and the abominations (*how to tell the difference among them?*) piled up so high that there wouldn't be any room left for them, for her and for Vandal, the regular ones, the ones that remained.

A talking dog? Was that stranger than a two-headed calf? Stranger than poor old Woodrow Scurry's horses eating each other in his stables a fortnight earlier? Every day the world around her seemed more peculiar than it had the day before, and every day she felt herself getting a little more used to the new strangenesses, numb to them, and wondering idly what ones the next day would bring.

How you use? They were Hark's words, clumsy and laughable, coming to her over the din of the voices on the television. There was another sort of show on, this one a game of some type, where people shouted at one another, encouragement and curses. *That thing*, Hark said.

"So," Vandal said, "you can say more than *No*."

How you use that thing, Hark said again. A demand this time, not a question.

The shotgun, Bridie thought, and she dropped the plate she was washing back into the sink full of lukewarm water and dying suds and hurried into the den, drying her hands on a dishtowel as she went.

"Don't tell him that," she said.

Vandal looked up at her, startled. Just above him on the wall hung a picture that his mother had hung there as a young woman. She had died young. In the decades since it had been hung, the picture, it occurred to Bridie, had taken in every event that had occurred in that low-ceilinged, claustrophobic room. It depicted Jesus, a thick-muscled Jesus, naked but for a drape of white cloth, getting his baptism in the river Jordan. The Baptist raised a crooked hand over his head, water spilling from the upraised palm.

Vandal was fitting the barrels of the shotgun – which had been his old man's but which was now his, like the house, like the farm – back into the stock. The metal mated to the wood with a definitive click. "Why in the world wouldn't I tell him?"

Bridie was at a loss for a cogent answer. It seemed obvious to her that Vandal ought not to impart such information to the dog just for the asking, but he didn't share her worry at all, it was clear. How to explain? The dog looked at her with, she thought, an expression of feigned innocence. "A dog ought not to know how to use a gun," she said.

Vandal chuckled. "He doesn't even have hands. He has no fingers."

"So why tell him how a gun works?"

"Because he wants to know."

"And should he know everything he wants to, just because he wants to know it?"

Vandal shrugged. Bridie felt heat flooding her face. How could he not understand? He thought it was terrific, the way the dog had decided to talk, the way he could sit there with it and watch television, the way it asked him questions, the way it wanted to know the things that he knew. He was happy to share with it: his table, his food, his house, his knowledge. He was treating the dog like a friend, like a member of the family. Like a child, his child.

"What he wants is to have hands. What he wants is to be a man. To do what you do. To have what you have."

She caught Hark gazing at her intently, his eyes gleaming, hungry, his nose wet, his broad flat tongue caught between the rows of his teeth.

"What's wrong with that?" Vandal wanted to know.

He is not your boy, she wanted to tell him. He is not your son. He is a dog, and it's wrong that he can talk. You want to share what you have with him, but he doesn't want to share it with you. He wants to have it instead of you.

The dog wrinkled his nose, sniffing, and she knew suddenly that he was taking her in, the scent of her. A dog's nose was, she knew, a million times more sensitive than a man's. He could know her by her scent. He could tell that she was afraid of him. He could follow her anywhere, because of that phenomenal sense of smell. In prehistoric times, before men became human and made servants out of them, Hark and his kind would have hunted her down in a pack and eaten her alive. Her scent would have led them to her. Hark's eyes narrowed, and her words clung to her jaws. She couldn't bear to speak them in front of the dog. She blinked, dropped her gaze and, under the animal's intense scrutiny, fled the room.

Behind her, Vandal spoke. "This here's the breech," he said. The gun snicked open. "This here is where the shells go." The gun thumped closed.

Vandal always wanted her after a meal of game meat: duck, venison, bear, it didn't matter what. It was something about the wild flavour, she thought, and the fact that he had killed the food himself. It made him happy, and when he was happy he always came to her in bed, his hands quick and his breath hot. He was at her now, pushing up her nightgown, slipping the straps off her shoulders, throwing one of his heavy, hairy legs across hers. She shoved at him.

"Don't," she said. "He'll hear."

After supper, after television and the lesson about the gun – he could name all the parts of it now, Hark could, and his speech was becoming rapidly clearer, the words coming to him swiftly and easily; and maybe that was true of his thoughts as well, slipping like eels through that clever brain in its dark prison in the dog's skull – Hark had refused to go outside to sleep in the kennel. He had simply braced his legs at the house's threshold and bared his teeth and muttered at them, *No*.

"For God's sake," Bridie had said to Vandal.

"What's the harm?" Vandal had asked. Plenty of people, he had told her in a patient voice, owned dogs that lived indoors.

"Not you," she said to him. "Never you."

No, he agreed, he'd never owned an indoor dog before. Xerxes wouldn't allow such a thing.

Xerxes. He couldn't understand what was happening to him, to them, because of Xerxes and the shadow he cast, even from the grave. Vandal had always wanted an indoor dog, a pet, and Xerxes wouldn't hear of it.

So Hark became an indoor dog, sleeping in the parlour. Bridie had tried to lay down a couple of old rag rugs on the floor for him, but he had just stared blankly at her from the chair, and she had left him there rather than risking having to hear that flat refusal another time.

"He won't hear anything," Vandal said. Bridie knew how sharp a dog's hearing was. Vandal knew it even better than she did, but he was saying what he imagined she needed to hear, because he wanted to get hold of her. A dog's hearing was like its sense of smell, a million times or more what humans are capable of. "He's downstairs. He's probably asleep," Vandal said. He nuzzled her, took the lobe of her ear between his teeth and nipped. He slid her nightgown down to her waist, his hands on her breasts, his palms and the pads of his fingers tough with callus. Her breathing quickened as he pushed her hard against the mattress and pressed her legs apart. "Who cares if he hears us?"

"I care," she said. She knew that Hark would not be asleep, not on his first night in their house. In his first moments alone and unguarded in a human place. He might not even be in the parlour anymore. She pictured him creeping down the hallways, clambering up the stairs, sloping through their rooms, looking at everything, that keen nose taking in the odours of the house and its denizens, possessing them, filing them away. He might be climbing up on Xerxes' bed – the guest bed, she corrected herself, Xerxes was gone – right now.

"We'll be quiet then," Vandal assured her, and she meant to protest, but he put his hands under her hips and lifted her, and she groaned and opened to him. He gave a sharp cry of delight. She shushed him, but he continued to exclaim as he moved against her, his voice growing louder with every fierce thrust of his hips, until he was calling out wordlessly at the top of his voice. By then she was far gone too, her voice mingling with his, and under it all the sharp metallic crying of the bedsprings.

In the night, while Vandal slept, Bridie considered Xerxes. X, as he had told her to call him, all his friends called him X. He had many friends on the neighbouring places and in town, the men he hunted with, roistered with, brawny old men like himself who had fought in one war or a couple, men who took no shit from anyone. Terrible X, Mountain-Man X, X the Unknown and Unknowable, his eyes on her always, his hands on her too whenever Vandal was out of the house, when he was out hunting or tending to his dogs in the kennel. Sometimes when Vandal was in the house, too, sometimes when he was in the same room. X wasn't afraid, he wasn't afraid a bit.

Be quiet, he would say to her.

She never told Vandal because she was afraid of what he would do. What was she afraid of, exactly? That he would confront Xerxes, Daddy Xerxes, Daddy X as Vandal called him. Was she afraid that Vandal would challenge Xerxes, fight him, shoot him, kill him? Or was she afraid that he wouldn't? She could imagine no happy outcome to her revelation, and so she chose not to make it.

"No," she would tell Xerxes as he pawed her, plundered her. He didn't even hear her, she didn't believe. She might as well have been speaking another language, or not speaking at all. "No."

When a brain stroke had taken him one wonderful day – he had cornered her in the parlour, was squeezing her breasts, crushing her to him, one great hand pressed hard in the middle of her back so that she couldn't escape him – she had simply stood away from his stumbling, twitching, stiffening body, had watched him topple over like a hewn tree, had watched him spasm and shudder on the floor, his mouth gaping, hands clawing at his own face, one of his eyes bulging grotesquely, rolling upward independent of its twin to take her in where she stood.

She stared back into the rogue eye, in which the pupil was contracting, swift as a star collapsing, until she realised that X's gaze was no longer fixed on her, but on something behind her, above her. She was seized with an awful terror, and the effort of turning left her shaken, exhausted. Nothing. Nothing but the picture on the wall, which was as it had always been since the hand of Xerxes' wife had placed it there: Jesus and, standing over him, John, the Baptist, clothed all in ragged unfinished animal hides. She turned back to the dying man before her.

The eye reeled farther, impossibly far – it was funny to see, really, or would have been in any other circumstance – to fix on the ceiling, until finally the iris and the pupil disappeared altogether and the eye turned over white.

She leaned down to him, breathing hard from the fright he had given her over the picture, and put her mouth right up against his thick cauliflower ear, its whorls filled with stiff grey hair like the bristles of a boar-hog. This time, she wanted to make sure that he heard. "No," she told him.

Some folks, the voice said, *have too much life in them to die all the way*.

Bridie snapped awake, sure that the words had come to her in X's voice. That gruff commanding voice, weirdly distorted with wolf-tones and as full of echoes as though it were being broadcast from the moon. *How else should the voice of a dead man sound?* she asked herself. *He's come a long way back to say what he has to say to me.*

The gruff voice, and an answering sound, staccato: Hark's mirthless laughter. The sound of it chilled her. She had never cared much for loud laughter. The bared teeth, the closed eyes, the contorted features of the face, the shuddering, it all looked too much like pain to her, like convulsions or madness. She herself always laughed behind her hand, her eyes down. The voice went droning on below. It sounded like it was giving advice, and Hark's laughter had stopped. She could picture him soaking in whatever notions Xerxes was giving him.

"He's watching TV." Vandal's voice at her shoulder startled her. His eyes glinted in the weak light that filtered in through the window, the moon's final quarter. His good straight teeth glittered. He slid his hands to her breasts, kneaded her flesh. He wanted to go again. "He ain't paying any attention to us, is he?"

"How did he turn it on, Vandal?" she asked him. Another voice was speaking now, this one lighter, quicker, with a peculiar accent. She couldn't make out the words. Was it Hark's voice? Was he having conversation? Vandal urged her over prone, prodded her up onto her elbows and knees. His hands were shaking. He was as eager as a teenager, and rough, too rough. She liked him when he was sweet, and mostly he was, he was sweet, but there was no sweetness in him now. Nothing was strange, nothing was outside the realm of possibility. The television was talking to the dog, and the dog was talking to the television. She pressed her face into the smothering whiteness of the pillow, which smelled to her of her own soap and night sweat. Nothing was too strange to happen anymore.

*   *   *

The next day, as he went out the door, Vandal told Bridie that he'd gone colour blind. Hark was sitting in his place at the table, waiting on his breakfast to be brought to him. He looked from one of them to the other with eager eyes.

"You mean you can't tell red from green?" She'd had an uncle with the same problem. Except for dealing with stoplights and some problems matching clothes, it hadn't seemed to bother him much. As far she knew, though, it was a problem he'd had his whole life, not something he'd acquired.

Vandal waved a hand in front of his face, as though he were demonstrating actual blindness. "The whole ball of wax," he told her. "It's all shades of grey out there."

"You've got to see a doctor," she said to him. "This ain't natural."

"Natural," he said. "Ha. I wouldn't know natural these days if it came up and bit me in the ass."

"Seeing colours. That's natural."

"It's winter coming down," he said. "Just winter, and the colour goes out of everything. It just looks like it's all an old movie."

She shook her head, and he drew her to him with a hand on her waist, another in the middle of her back. He pressed against her, and she felt the warmth that spread out from him, felt his hardness. His need for her was palpable, and it made her sad and excited all at once. She peeled his hands from her body because the dog was watching, too avidly. There was something in Vandal's touch that wasn't just for her, and wasn't just for him either, it wasn't just selfishness. There was something in it that was for the dog too, and she couldn't stand that.

Vandal withdrew. "Who has the money for a doctor?" he said. "Who has the leisure?" His brow was furrowed. Already his thoughts had turned from her to his work. Seldomridge, their neighbour to the east, had called to say that a half dozen of his cattle were dead in the night, no telling what had killed them but the condition of their bodies was very strange, and could Vandal bring over the skid-steer and help him plant them? It was a full morning's labour lost from their own place, but there was no way a man could refuse to help in such a situation. No time to worry about little things like the colour of the world going away.

His expression cleared briefly. "It's the winter time. That's what's got everything all turned around. Come spring and the colour will come back. You watch."

*   *   *

After Vandal left the house, Bridie shooed Hark down off the chair and away from the kitchen table, hustled him out the door with gestures and cries. She made as if she might kick him, and he went, but she could tell by the set of his shoulders that he knew no blows were coming, and he went at his own pace. She kept waiting for him to tell her *no* as she drove him across the yard towards the dog run.

She had decided upon rising that morning what she would do if he refused her, if he refused to do anything she told him. She was expecting it, she was waiting for it, she was even hoping for it: reason to take down the choke collar that Vandal kept for training and slip it over Hark's head and cinch it tight as a noose around his neck. Watch the chain links cut into his thick pelt and the delicate flesh of his throat. Force him to do what she wanted. Hiss her orders into his sensitive ears. Show him what a dog was, and what a human was, and what the proper relationship between them should be.

And if Hark grew angry, lashed out, bit her? Then she should show Vandal the marks on her skin, and he would understand at last how utterly wrong the situation was, how obscene, and he would do what was necessary. She allowed the ball of her foot to come in contact with Hark's rump – was she tempting him? – but he just hurried on ahead, as though he were suddenly eager to enter the dog run. His tail was up and switching when the steel latch of the kennel door clanged down behind him.

That's that, she thought as she went back into the house. The day stretched out in front of her. Plenty to do, as always, and no Vandal, no Hark, no Xerxes to keep her from it. *That's it for him, returned to the place of his beginnings.*

All day, the voice issued from the kennel. Answered at first by the growling and defiant barking from the other dogs, and then their cowed whimpering, and then silence. They were good dogs, obedient dogs, conditioned to a man's voice. It pained Bridie to think of him out there among them, but what else to do? She had hopes that their good simple natures would remind Hark of what he had used to be, what he ought still to be.

Better out there than in here anyway, she thought. *A kennel's the place for dogs, and what happens out there is no worry of mine.*

It was dusk getting on toward night when Vandal arrived home again, the skid-steer up on the flatbed, his shoulders slumped with weariness. "It's bad over at Seldomridge's," he told her. "Worse than he said." He washed his hands vigorously under the hot water tap, skinning them hard with the scrub brush and the Lava soap, lathering himself all the way up to the elbows. His face was pinched and drawn-looking.

"It's bad over here too," she said. He didn't seem to hear her.

"I'll be back over there tomorrow," he said. "After that, it's no more cattle at Seldomridge's." He looked around the kitchen, ducked into the parlour to check in there. "Where's he at?" he wanted to know.

She gestured out the window toward the silent kennel, and his face hardened. "I had work to do too, you know," she said.

"I didn't say nothing." He was already in motion toward the door.

"I didn't have the time to babysit your new pet," she called after him. His pet. His changeling child. She watched his large awkward figure cross the yard and enter the chain-link run, kneel down just inside the gate. Her heart quailed. All afternoon the silence had worn at her. It worried her as much as the voice had done. More. A kennel was never a silent place, always some kind of choir going out there, a tussle, an alarm over a rabbit or over nothing. The jolly voices of dogs. Vandal was bent over something, shaking his head, mumbling, his shoulders bowed.

She strained in the failing light to make out what he was doing. She had a moment in which she imagined that the normal dogs had torn the strange one to pieces, and her heart leaped. *It will be my fault, just like the death of Xerxes*, she thought, *and he will never forgive me, and I will bear the blame gladly*.

And then he was coming back to the house, Hark slinking along at his side. When they entered the kitchen together, Vandal's face was wreathed in a great smile. The smell of dog, hairy and primeval and eye-wateringly strong, struck Bridie like a blow. Hark trotted into the parlour and climbed wearily onto the davenport, where he lay draped like a rug, his sides heaving.

"Tell her what you told me," Vandal called in to him. No answer. "Tell her what you been doing all day, while we was working."

Humping, came the voice from the living room, muffled against the davenport's cushions.

"Did you hear that?" Vandal asked her.

"I heard," Bridie said.

"Made them line up for him, and then he humped every one of those bitches out there, one right after the other. He's the king of the dogs now, I guess."

"I guess," Bridie said.

"We got to make sure he eats good tonight," Vandal said. "He tells me he wants to do it all over again tomorrow."

When Hark started in to walking on his hind legs, Bridie told Vandal that he couldn't spend his days in the kennel anymore. "I thought you wanted him penned," he said, "to keep him out of your hair."

"It's not right," she said, "a thing that goes on two legs and a thing that goes on four." She couldn't bring herself to call Hark a man. He wasn't a man exactly, not yet anyway. He was like a tadpole, Bridie thought when she looked at him, something in between two other things and not really anything in itself. He was neither man nor dog, and he was both, and he was awful. Nothing could exist for long in that middle condition, she didn't believe. It was unbearable.

"We've got to put him in some clothes too," she said, "to get him covered up." He went around in an excited state half the time, and the sight of him, slick and red, sickened and haunted her.

"Can he wear some of mine?" Vandal asked.

Probably, Bridie thought. He was getting more man-sized and more man-shaped with every day that passed. *And it's probably exactly what he wants to do too.* But she said, "I think we should get him some of his own." *Some coveralls*, she thought, *and a tractor cap to cover that low sloping forehead and the bony ridges above the eyes.*

The more like a man he became, the more he horrified her. She wondered if there was a point at which she would simply be unable to stand his transformation any longer, and what would happen when she reached it? Would she start screaming and be unable to stop? Would he simply turn into another man who lived in their house, like a vagrant brother or an unsavoury cousin? Like Xerxes. Would such a creature be possessed of a human soul? Would it be murder to kill him?

After a couple of wobbly practice laps around the pasture field in the truck with Hark behind the wheel, Vandal yelled at him to stop the vehicle. "There's no way you can drive on the road," Vandal told him. Hark's head barely poked up above the steering wheels, and his thin legs wavered uncertainly over the pedals. He glared at Vandal. Bridie, who was watching, silently applauded. She was glad to see Vandal denying him something, anything. "You'd kill somebody, or die yourself."

You take me, Hark said. There was very little he couldn't say these days. Occasionally he struggled for a word, a phrase, but mostly his speech was fluid. At times his voice could be silky and persuasive.

He had taken to answering the phone when it rang, which was not often, and even to initiating phone calls in which he carried on long, secretive conversations with they knew not whom. There was no one outside the house, outside the farm, that they could imagine him knowing. When they asked, he simply told them that he was *finding out.* "Finding out what?" they inquired. *Finding what's out there,* he said. "What's out there?" Vandal had asked him. *You wouldn't believe me if I told you,* Hark said, staring straight at Bridie. *But you'll know before too long, anyhow. It'll soon be more of me and mine out there than you and yours.*

In the truck, he repeated his demand. *You take me, if I can't drive.*

"Take you where?" Vandal wanted to know.

Into town, Hark said. When Vandal just kept looking at him, he continued. *To get . . . fuck.*

Vandal laughed. "You want to get laid?"

Hark shrugged his narrow shoulders. He wore a youth-size denim work shirt and a pair of Levi's, procured at the Rural King store out on the county line, and they fit him reasonably well, adding considerably to the illusion that he was just a slightly misshapen boy or small man. Sunglasses and a one-size-fits-all John Deere cap helped to obscure his hairy forehead and his unnatural eyes. *Everything wants to fuck,* he said.

Vandal shut off the truck's ignition, pulled the key, and climbed out of the truck's cab.

You won't let me go in amongst the bitches no more, Hark said. His voice was less peremptory now, pleading. *It ain't right, keep me from what I want. What I need.*

"You think you'll find women in town to sleep with you?" Bridie called. "A thing like you are?"

Hark laughed, a short bark that went strangely with his hominid appearance. *There's them in town as would be glad to be with me any way I am. Any way I want.*

"That's why we stay far from town," Vandal said. He stalked away from the truck, his face dark and angry, and marched into the house. Hark stayed where he was, behind the steering wheel, glaring balefully through the dirty windshield. The glass was spider-webbed with fine cracks.

"Get out of there," Bridie said to him. "You're not driving nowhere."

I belong in town more than you do, Hark said without looking at her. *You know it's so. More and more every day. You got no right to keep me out here with you, amongst the cows and the crows.*

She pictured him among people, in some smoky place where she herself would never go, a cigarette tucked in the corner of his mouth, his hat tilted back on his head because he was unafraid of his own peculiar nature, his long teeth gleaming in dim light, his eyes slitted, one of his paws (*his hands*, she corrected herself, *they are much more like hands now*) on the thigh of a giggling, sighing girl beside him. But was she a girl, exactly, this creature in the vision? Wasn't she just a bit too large to be a normal sort of girl, too sleek and well-fleshed, her hair thick and coarse down her neck, her nostrils too wide, her eyes broadly spaced, on the sides of her head, almost? *A pony*, she thought. And the heavily-bristled, barrel-bodied man across the table from them, snorting with laughter, little eyes glittering with nasty delight, his snout buried in his plate . . .

"Probably you're right," she said, and she followed Vandal into the house, leaving Hark where he was.

He found his way into the liquor not long after that. The bottles had belonged to Xerxes. Vandal was strictly a beer man, and Bridie didn't drink at all. It was a holdover from her upbringing, which was hardshell Baptist. Much of that way of thinking and living had left her in the years she had been gone from her parents' house, which had been at once a stern and a gentle place, but her dislike of hard spirits had stayed with her. She found him in the living room, as usual, fixated on the television screen, which was announcing yet another series of nightmares. His eyes were glazed, a half-empty bottle of Knob Hill on the TV tray at his elbow, and he blinked slowly when she entered the room, so that she knew he was aware of her presence. His breathing was loud and stertorous.

This ain't happening just here, you know, he told her. He nodded at the TV, where hail was pelting down from a clear sky, smashing windows, denting the hoods and roofs of cars, sending people scrambling for solid cover, flattening crops. Birds of every description were dropping dead into the streets. *It's happening everywhere.* He burped lightly and covered his mouth with his hairy palm. His tone had sounded mournful before, but now he giggled.

Bridie understood that he didn't mean their own situation, not exactly, not a dog turning into a man, not just (her thoughts turned away, but she forced them back: she had to look at everything that was happening, and not just a part of it) a man turning into a dog, or at any rate something less than a man; but other, equally terrible things, inexplicable things, things that had never happened before. And she knew that he also meant, *There is no stopping them.*

She sat down across from him, close enough that she could touch him. He took his gaze from the television and looked her full in the face, and his eyes were soft and brown, much more like the dog she remembered, and not antagonistic. There was pain written in them – did it hurt, to become a man? – and fear. For the first time, the sight of him didn't fill her with disgust. He sniffed.

It's the foller-man as gets bit. It's the foller-dog as gets hit. His voice was a kind of singsong. Playful. He took another swig from the bottle, waiting on her response. If he had not been what he was, she might have thought he was being flirtatious.

"What's that mean?" she asked him.

You tell me.

She thought a moment. She believed that she had heard a rhyme like it somewhere before. Her girlhood, maybe. A cadence for jumping rope. Was it some kind of a riddle? *The foller-man.* She thought of the head of a snake, then, the dead eyes and the mouth wide, the fangs milky with poison; and she had it.

"It's always the second man on the trail that gets bitten by the snake," she said. Hark nodded, and his head moved so slowly that the gesture seemed wise. "The first man wakes the snake up, and it strikes the second man in the line."

And the lead dog, he said, *judges the distance to get across the road before the car comes. But the dog that comes along just a second later, trailing the first one like he always does, he . . .*

"Gets hit," she said.

Is it a joke? he asked. *That the first one plays on the second one?*

"Not so much a joke," she told him, "as just not giving it any thought. Always looking forward and there's no looking behind."

I never want to be no foller-dog anymore, he said to her. *Nor no foller-man neither. I'm going to be the firstest one along every trail, and the firstest one across every road.* He took another drink, and the level in the bottle dropped appreciably. He coughed and sputtered. *From now on in*, he said.

In other places, some not so very far away, the television informed them, the dead were said to be rising up from their graves. The recent dead, and the long dead: it didn't seem to make any difference. The ones who came back to life most often found their ways back to their homes, their families, back to those who loved them, and when they found somebody who recognized them – assuming anybody was left who did – they cried aloud at the wonders they had seen in the great lightless cities that they inhabited after death.

Would resurrected people have the vote, the television wondered?

Hark closed his eyes and sighed. *Some folks just have too much life in them to die all the way, I guess*, he said. He looked so sad when he said it that she felt a sudden stab of unexpected sympathy for him, and sorrow.

They took to having conversations, short ones, usually, that ended in unsatisfying confusion, because she didn't know the right questions to ask, or he didn't know the right words to tell her what she wanted to know. Sometimes, she swore, he held back his answers, wanting always to get more than he gave. When he asked her about the wider world, outside the borders of the farm, outside the boundaries of the county, she found that she didn't know very much – only what she saw on TV, really, and he saw as much of that as she did; more, in fact – and he quickly became contemptuous of her. Always, though, their exchanges came back to a single question:

"Why wouldn't you go into the water that day?"

There was something waiting for me in that pond.

"What was waiting?"

A spirit. There was a spirit on that water, and it wanted me to come in there with it. The spirit wanted me, the spirit and the water both.

"You were afraid the water would change you?"

I was afraid it wouldn't. I felt the change coming on me that day, and I had the fear that the water might take it off and leave me what I had always been. I wanted to be something else.

"The change didn't feel bad to you? It didn't hurt?"

It felt – exhilarating. He sounded pleased with himself that he had come up with that word, but his face was impossible to read.

Hark was still drinking and watching TV, and the liquor was holding out longer than Bridie had thought (had hoped) it might. Vandal had taken to spending long stretches away from the house, out walking the fields or shuffling about in the granary, sitting alone in the loft of the silent barn, watching over the place as it fell fallow without his labour.

Sometimes he went into the kennel, and she didn't care to ask him what he did there. He didn't touch her in their bed at night anymore, wouldn't undress where she could see him. Under his clothes, he seemed to have shrunk, and his gaze, whenever it fell on her, was cool and distant. At that moment, he was upstairs, asleep in their bed. He slept ten hours a night, sometimes more, and still he seemed always to be exhausted.

Hark dropped an empty bottle and it rolled across the parlour floor and disappeared under the davenport. *It could be*, she thought, *that Xerxes had him a stash that I never knew about. But how did he find it?*

"Hark?" she said.

Ain't my name.

"What?" she asked.

Nefas. That's what you call me now. That's my name now. Not that word you give me, that nothing. That Hark.

"I'm not going to call you—"

Nefas! he shouted. His teeth, still pointed, flashed at her. *Baphomet! Marduk, Shahar, Enkidu! Call me by my God-damned name!*

Her hand flashed out, and her open palm cracked against the sharp bones of his face. The sting of the blow travelled up her arm, to the centre of her chest, and her eyes filled with tears, but she swung again, savagely backhanded him so that spittle flew from his gaping mouth. His right eye closed and his head twisted to the side. She thought that she wouldn't be able to stand the throbbing of her hand. Her fingers; had she broken them?

He flew at her with a snarl, and the momentum of his small, furious body took them both to the floor. He put his teeth on the swelling of her throat just below her jaw, and his breath was hot against the skin of her neck. *He will kill me now*, she thought, and the flaming agony of her arm, and Hark's noisome weight – or Marduk's, or whatever he cared to call himself, Nefas – on her, and the events of these last days, made that idea not at all an unwelcome one.

Instead, he began to squeeze her breasts with both his hands, and his breathing quickened as he fumbled to open her blouse. He pushed a knee between her legs and worked to part them. *This is how he did it*, he said.

"No," she said.

He gave a throaty little chuckle. There was real amusement in the sound. *It's all fine and dandy to tell someone No*, he said. *But the question has to be: can you make it stick?* The stench of whiskey filled her nostrils. His teeth and his lips moved from beneath her chin to the hollow of her throat, and from there to her breastbone. He pressed himself avidly against her.

She willed her wrecked right hand into motion, her fingers and thumb searching for his eyes, her palm forcing his blunt head up and back. The stubble on his cheeks rasped against her like sandpaper, and she cried out with the pain and horror of it. She didn't want to hurt him. She had never wanted to hurt anyone in her life.

She caught sight of the picture of the baptism on the wall, hanging high above her – *I am where Xerxes lay*, she thought, *and this is the angle he saw it from at the last* – while her left hand went seeking, almost on its own, along the wall. In the picture, a great crowd of grey figures, cloaked like ghosts, filled the background, lining the far bank of the river. Seen from a distance, it was possible to take them for clouds, or a line of distant cliffs. *How is it I never noticed them before?* she thought, as Hark (*Nefas!*) fastened his eager mouth on her nipple, as her left hand found the set of fireplace tools that stood on the hearth and brought them all clattering down. As her left hand got purchase on the pair of iron log tongs and whipped them around in a hard arc.

The tongs took him up high, on the temple, and his suckling mouth fell away from her, his limbs spasming. She struck him again, on the shoulder this time, and he screeched and tumbled off of her, scrambling to escape, his limbs scrabbling against the floor. He was like an injured insect. She stood and went after him, straddling his body, thumping him on the back of the head, the spine. He squealed, and she wondered if Vandal might hear the sound and come to investigate. "Your name is Hark!" she shouted at him. Her blows rained down on him.

Nefas, he managed to gasp out.

"You will come when we call!"

Enkidu.

"You will do what we say."

Hark scuttled into a corner of the room, behind the easy chair, where Bridie had a hard time getting at him. She stood with the tongs upraised, waiting on a good moment to strike him again. When she saw his eyes on her, she tugged her blouse closed with her injured hand. A couple of the buttons were missing. Crouched in the corner, his spindly arms crossed over his head for protection, Hark indicated the picture with a lift of his snout.

Okay, he said. His ribs were heaving, and blood stained his shirt and his pants. *You got the upper hand of me. You going to make me get down on my knees and worship him the way that you do?* he said. *Bow down to your water man, your dead man? Your foller-man?*

Vandal lay next to her in the dark, moaning softly, his legs kicking from time to time beneath the bedcovers. He faced the wall, and when she touched him, she could feel the puckered ridge of his backbone. He had always been a thickset man, but now it was as if the flesh was melting off him, leaving his body a skeletal landscape of edges and hollows. She envied him his sleep. She had taken some aspirin, the last in the house, but her right arm continued to pain her terribly.

"What if we're imagining all this?" she asked Vandal's back. She kept her voice low, because she didn't really want to wake him. She hoped, somehow, that he might awake on his own, and be as he had been before. He shivered and whimpered at the sound of her voice. "What if he never talked or changed at all? What if we're dreaming it?" she asked.

Dreaming the same dream, he said. She closed her eyes at the sound of his voice, which was no longer his, little more than a buzzing or gurgling deep in his throat. Eyes open, eyes closed, she found that it was the same darkness all around her.

"Maybe I'm just dreaming it," she said. "Alone."

Vandal made a small snorting noise that she took to mean assent, and went on, like a being in a fairy story, with his impenetrable slumber.

Deep in the night, when she could not tell how long she had been asleep, the voice came to her from outside her bedroom door, whispering in like wind through the crack at the threshold: *The strong will do what the strong will do. And the weak will bear what they must.*

When he surprised her in the kitchen, she understood that this time there would be no lucky hand on the tongs, no surprise blow to the head. He wasn't drunk. He was ready. Nefas (she had come to think of him that way – he wasn't Hark anymore, and it seemed foolish to keep calling him by the vanished dog's name) had grown at least as large as she was, and nimbler, and far faster and stronger, with a beast's terrible speed and strength, and a man's cruelty. If she tried to hurt him, he would hurt her far worse in return, she knew. In some deep part of him, she thought, he hoped that she would fight him, because he very much wanted to hurt her.

Her right arm was immobilized in a sling that she had rigged up for it out of a couple of dish cloths, her fingers bruised, the joints blackened. She had a fever. Vandal was still upstairs, in the bed that was now far too large for him. He slept around the clock, wasting away. She would not have been surprised, upon going into the bedroom, to find him gone altogether.

If I had a pot of water boiling, she thought. *If I had a skillet full of sizzling grease, I would fling it in his grinning face*. There was nothing hot. He had placed himself between her and the great wooden knife block. He wasn't stupid. He had the shotgun in his hand, pointing clumsily downward, at his feet.

She found herself hoping that Vandal wouldn't awake, ever, that he would simply sleep through what was coming, for her, for him, for all of them. She hoped that he could go on forever dreaming for himself a world where the sunshine was bright and golden as in the old days, and untamed birds crisscrossed the sky in their lopsided Vs, and cattle drifted in friendly bunches across the pastures, and game, unending phalanxes of game, deer and clever squirrels and bear and swift wily turkeys that could be hunted and brought down but which did not die, which lent themselves again and again to the eternal chase – she hoped that, in his dreams, all of these filled the emerald mansions of the limitless forest.

God be with you, she thought, and then Vandal, like Hark, was gone from her thoughts.

Nefas set the shotgun carefully on the floor behind him and put his hands on her shoulders. His touch was heavy but not painful. His hands were broad and short-fingered. "Please," she said.

Call me by my name, he said.

"Nefas," she said, choking on the word. "Please."

He leaned into her, cradled the back of her head with his hard palm, sniffed deeply at her hair. *Call me by my name*, he said.

She struggled to remember what he had said she should call him. Why did he need so many names? She couldn't recall them all, and she was terrified of what he would do to her if she couldn't name him properly. Her memory leaped. "Baphomet," she said. "Marduk, please."

He bit the lobe of her ear, hard enough to draw blood, and she cried out. She struggled to free her arm from the sling but it was caught fast. *Call me by my name*, he said, his mouth against her ear. His breath was moist, his tone simultaneously intimate and insistent. He cupped her right breast as though he were weighing it, as though it were a piece of fruit that he was considering buying. His weight against her drew agony from her wounded hand, trapped between her body and his.

"Enkidu," she said. She knew that she could not, must not, resist him, and she steeled herself to surrender. Why, she wondered, was it not possible simply to die? To her astonishment, her uninjured hand, her left, hefted a cumbersome iron trivet from the stovetop. It had belonged to Vandal's mother, and Bridie had never cared much for it, but she had kept it for the sentiment she imagined it provoked in Vandal.

She raised the trivet over Nefas' shaggy head. The fingers of her left hand were bloodless, she was holding it so tightly. He followed its ascent with his eyes, but he did not take his mouth away from her ear. He made a sound that she thought might be laughter. His hand went to the skirt that she was wearing, and he tugged the hem up to her waist.

Shall we fuck each other, or shall we kill each other? he asked. It didn't sound like he much cared which. Both were fine with him. With one of his feet he hooked the shotgun and slid it forward, where he could get a hand on it quickly.

"This doesn't have to happen," she said.

No? he asked. His hands were busy, unbuttoning, unclasping. She was nearly nude, and still her hand stayed poised over his skull. The trivet had a number of pointed projections. It had always seemed a peaceable thing, domestic, sitting patiently atop the stove, but in her hand it had taken on the look of some exotic piece of medieval weaponry. He shucked his baggy Levi's, and the buckle of his belt clattered against the linoleum. *Seems to me it's happening already.*

Spare me, spare me, she thought, but she didn't say it because a creature like him wouldn't spare her anything. He was toying with her. He had come an unspeakable distance and waited an unthinkably long time for the pleasures he was planning to indulge. "You were a good dog," she said. "Can't you be a good man?"

He considered a moment, drew fractionally away from her. Her skin where it had touched his was hot, and the small space between them felt deliciously fresh. The trivet was growing heavy, her hand was trembling with the effort of holding it over him. Nefas jerked a thumb upward, and his hand brushed the metal. He could have taken it from her if he had wanted, but he let it stay. *Is he a good man?* he asked her.

She had to struggle to work out who he might mean. Vandal, asleep in the master bedroom overhead. "He was," she said. "I don't know what precisely he is now."

You think it's only me that gets to choose, he said. *He chooses too. Every minute he chooses.*

Vandal, upstairs, choosing oblivion.

You choose too, just as much as him. Just as much as me. He tapped the trivet with a dense fingernail, and it rang like a bell. *You're choosing right now. What is it you're choosing?* "Not this," she said, indicating his nakedness, and hers. His eyes roamed over her body, and she had the impulse to cover herself, but she resisted it. It took her a great deal of will to open her fingers; wearily, she dropped the iron trivet onto the counter, where it thumped and rolled and left a small scar. "Not this either," she said. Unable to suppress a whimper of pain as she did it, she shucked the sling and flexed the stiffened fingers of her hand.

Nefas returned his gaze to her face. *He ain't fucked you in a while now,* he said. *And you don't want to fuck me. You just planning on doing without it for the rest of your life?*

"That might not be such a very long time," she said. "With the world the way it is."

And yet it might, he said to her. *That's one choice as is not left up to us.*

Stifling her disgust, she reached out and took him by the hand, his broad palm in her swollen fingers. She drew him gently to her, not in the way of a lover, but as a mother might. An expression of shock, unmistakable even on his inscrutable face, crossed his crude features. Slowly he came to her, almost against his will. She gritted her teeth and shut the feel of his hairy hide away from her. He laid his bony head on her bosom, and she embraced him.

With surprise, she felt how meagre he was, how slight his frame. *He's made out of a dog's bones, and he's got a man's mind,* she thought. There was no joy in him anywhere, she could feel that plainly, none of the kind of blind infectious joy that even the least of dogs possesses in abundance. "Why do you think he gave his place up to you?" she asked, meaning Vandal. She could see now that that was precisely what he had done. Slipped away from her, away from the world, and left this twisted creature in his stead. "Being a man isn't what you think it is."

Hark began to cry. His hot tears slipped over her breasts. "I've got my teeth in it now," he said. "I can't ever go back. I don't much want to go forward, but I know for sure I can't go back." He put his arms around her and she stiffened in his embrace, but the lust had passed through him for the moment and left him innocent. It would come back, and the old struggle would rise up between them again; and how it would end she didn't care to contemplate. For the present, they could manage to stand together this way, skin to skin and inextricably linked.

Nefas cocked his head. "I can hear him, you know," he said.

"Always hear him. His voice was quiet. Listen to him as he comes this way. He's pretty near."

"Who?"

Him. Him as sent me on ahead.

She recognized the quality of his fear. It wasn't fear for himself, she realized, and the knowledge clutched at her. "Who can you hear?" she demanded. She struggled to keep her own voice even.

I figured you knew, Nefas said. *I figured you knew all along.* He looked up at her with wide eyes. *He's coming along on my heels, but he ain't your foller-man. It's nothing like that. I don't believe he's any sort of man at all.*

Terror bloomed in her, and her vision dimmed. "X?"

He wanted me to tell as soon as I could talk proper, but I found out I wanted you, so I didn't say it.

"Didn't say what?" she asked. "What were you supposed to say?"

He wanted me to tell you that he don't care about what you said. He supposes he should hold it against you, but he don't plan to pay it any mind at all.

The house felt very small and fragile in that moment, and she felt small and fragile inside it, holding onto this creature, this hairy thing that wasn't her husband, that wasn't her dog either. The world was drawing in around her, the broad fields folding up to the size of handkerchiefs, the once-straight fences crowding and jostling themselves crooked, the barn and the granary and the machine shop butting up hard against the house and the dog run and the kennel, the woods and tangled marshes infiltrating the cleared spaces, humans and beasts colliding, the dead and the living spilling over each other; order failing, pandemonium as all the things that had been separate for so very long came rushing together, splintering one another like ships driven before a storm, until there was no way to know what was one and what was another.

Probably, Bridie thought, this has happened at other times, perhaps countless times before, perhaps every age came to its close in just this way, with no one left alive to tell the tale. Her mind went to the pond, and to the turtles huddled under the shivering surface of the water. *Them*, she thought. *They are the great survivors.*

The house was drawing everything into it and down, like a great whirlpool – all the abhorrent things, all the terrible marvels. Bridie stood at the heart of the catastrophe, and so alone was able to see it for what it was: the end of one thing, and the beginning of another that was infinitely worse.

Perhaps, she thought, Nefas could serve her as a guide, she

thought, a scout among the ruins, blend of senses and mind that he was, a genius of sorts, and utterly unique. It might be possible for her to lose herself in the shrieking bedlam, to hide herself away in the ruins, but for how long? The world's collapse might never end, and X would never stop his returning. "Can you smell him?" she asked. From outside, a whispering as from the tongues of a thousand snakes.

He shook his head. *Not yet. But soon.*

"Will you take my part?" she asked.

His eyes were wide, and he was shivering against her. *You don't have the least idea what you're asking, or who you're asking it from,* he told her. He shrugged and pulled her closer, and she felt him decide in her favour. He leaned down and scooped up the shotgun, and his grip on it looked so clumsy and unpractised that she almost laughed. She had the impulse to take it away from him, but she chose instead not to insult his pride. The understanding between them was brittle enough. "I'll do what I can," he said.

They clung to each other in the midst of the hissing, swaying chaos, murmuring useless reassurances as twilight consumed the kitchen. And Vandal, curled deeply into himself, slumbered away in the upper bedroom, twitching from time to time as dreams of the world, full of infinite life as it had never been, and as it would never be, flitted beautifully across the thin translucent scrim of his mind.

BRIAN LUMLEY

The Place of Waiting

LIKE RAMSEY CAMPBELL earlier, Brian Lumley really should not need any introduction to readers of this anthology series.

His psychological horror story "No Sharks in the Med" graced our very first volume (and appears in *The Very Best of Best New Horror*), and it is always a pleasure to welcome him back to these pages.

Although Lumley has been claiming in recent years that he is cutting down on his fiction output, he still has an impressive number of books being published. Subterranean Press has recently issued *Haggopian*, a fat book of the author's Mythos short stories and a companion volume to the earlier Mythos-related collection *The Taint & Other Novellas*.

Another recent Subterranean volume, *Screaming Science Fiction*, does what it says in the title, while *The Nonesuch* from the same imprint is a trilogy of tales (including an original) about one man's "accidental" confrontations with weirdness.

Lumley's phenomenally successful *Necroscope* series continues with Tor Books publishing *Necroscope: Harry & the Pirates* in the US. In Germany, Heyne has recently commenced republishing the *Necroscope* volumes, while Festa Verlag has now returned to the series, reprinting the books in hardcover.

Necroscope has also been re-optioned as a Hollywood movie for the fourth concurrent year, and a script has finally been approved.

"The thought occurred: I wonder if, when people die, *they* wonder, 'what just happened?'" explains the author. "And if so, do they sit (or float) around waiting to wake up, before realizing that they aren't going to, that they're dead.

"It's the sort of thought, however grim, that if Ronald Chetwynd-

Hayes was alive he and I would have a chuckle over. But he isn't, and forgive me Ron for dealing with you so lightly, but I hope to God you're not in some kind of place of waiting of your own but have moved on to a place of tranquillity and rest.

"I live down in Torquay on England's south-west coast. The locale of 'The Place of Waiting' – Dartmoor, and its scenery – these things are of course, very real, even if the big rock in the story (Tumble Tor itself) isn't. But there are in fact several allegedly haunted Tors, and I would be failing in my craft if I had ignored them any longer. Hence the story . . ."

I SIT HERE by our swimming pool with one eye on my son in the water and the other on the seagulls lazily drifting, circling on high. Actually they're not just drifting; they're climbing on thermals off the nearby fields, spiralling up to a certain height from which they know they can set off south across the bay on their long evening glide to Brixham, to meet the fishing boats coming in to harbour. And never once having beaten a wing across all those miles, just gliding, they'll be there in plenty of time to beg for sprats as the fish are unloaded.

It's instinct with those birds; they've been doing it for so long that now they don't even think about it, they just do it. It's like at ant-flying time, or flying-ant time, if you prefer: those two or three of the hottest days of summer when all of a sudden the ant queens make up their minds to fly and establish new hives or whatever ant nesting sites are called. Yes, for the gulls know all about that, too.

The crying of gulls: plaintive, sometimes painful, often annoying, especially when they're flight-training their young. But this time of year, well you can always tell when it's antflying time. Because that's just about the *only* time when the seagulls are silent. And you won't see a one in the sky until the queen ants stream up in their thousands from all the Devon gardens, all at the same time – like spawning corals under the full moon – as if some telepathic message had gone out into an ant ether, telling them, "It's time! It's time!"

Time for the seagulls, too. For suddenly, out of nowhere, the sky is full of them. And their silence is because they're eating. Eating ants, yes. And I amuse myself by imagining that the gulls have learned how to interpret ant telepathy, when in all probability it's only a matter of timing and temperature: Ma Nature as opposed to insect (or avian) ESP.

And yet . . . there are stranger things in heaven and earth – and between the two – and I no longer rule out anything . . .

My son cries out, gasps, gurgles, and shrieks . . . but only with joy, thank God, as I spring from my deck chair. Only with joy – the sheer enjoyment of the shallow end of the pool. Not that it's shallow enough (it's well out of his depth in fact, for he's only two-and-a-half), but he's wearing his water-wings and his splashing and chortling alone should have told me that all was well.

Except I wasn't doing my duty as I should have been; I was paying too much attention to the seagulls. And well—

—Well, call it paranoia if you like. But I watch little Jimmy like a hawk when he is in the water, and I've considered having the pool filled in. But his mother says no, that's just silly, and whatever it was that I *think* happened to me out on the moors that time, I shouldn't let it interfere with living our lives to the full. And anyway she loves our pool, and so does little Jimmy, and so would I, except . . .

Only three weeks ago a small child drowned in just such a pool right here in Torquay, less than a mile away. And to me – especially to me – that was a lot more than a tragic if simple accident. It was a beginning, not an end. The beginning of something that can *never* end, not until there are no more swimming pools. And even then it won't be the end for some poor, unfortunate little mite.

But you don't understand, right? And you never will until you know the full story. So first let me get little Jimmy out of the pool, dried and into the house, into his mother's care, and then I'll tell you all about it . . .

Have you ever wondered about haunted houses? Usually very old houses, perhaps Victorian or older still? Well, probably not, because in this modern technological society of ours we're not much given to considering such unscientific things. And first, of course, you would have to believe in ghosts: the departed, or not quite departed, revenants of folks dead and long since buried. But if so, if you have wondered, then you might also have begun to wonder why it's these *old* houses which are most haunted, and only very rarely new ones.

And, on the same subject, how many so-called "old wives' tales" have you heard, ghost stories, literally, about misted country crossroads where spectral figures are suddenly caught in a vehicle's headlights, lurching from the hedgerows at midnight, screaming their silent screams with their ragged hands held out before them? Well, let me tell you: such stories are legion! And now I know why.

But me, I didn't believe in ghosts. Not then, anyway . . .

My mother died in hospital here in Torbay some four-and-a-half years ago. And incidentally, I'm glad about that; not about her dying, no of course not, but that she did it in hospital. These days lots of people die in hospital, which is natural enough.

Anyway, it hit me really badly, more so because I had only recently lost someone else: my wife, when we'd divorced simply because we no longer belonged together. It had taken us eleven years to find that out: the fact that right from the start, we hadn't really belonged together. But while our parting was mutually acceptable and even expedient, still it was painful. And I would like to think it hurt both of us, for I certainly felt it: a wrenching inside, like some small but improbably necessary organ was no longer in there, that it was missing, torn or fallen out. And at the time I'd thought that was the end of it; what was missing was gone forever; I wouldn't find anyone else and there would be no family, no son to look up to me as I had looked up to my father. A feeling of . . . I don't know, discontinuity?

But I had still had my mother – for a little while, anyway. My poor dear Ma.

Now, with all this talk of ghosts and death and what-not, don't anyone take it that I was some kind of odd, sickly mother's-boy sort of fellow like Norman Bates, the motel keeper in that Hitchcock film. No, for that couldn't be further from the truth. But after my father had died (also in hospital, for they had both been heavy smokers) it had been my Ma who had sort of clung to me . . . quite the other way round, you see? Living not too far away, she had quickly come to rely on me. And no, that didn't play a part in our divorce. In fact, by then it had made no difference at all; our minds were already made up, Patsy's and mine.

Anyway, Patsy got our house – we'd agreed on that, too – for it had made perfectly good sense that I should go and live with Ma. Then, when it was her time (oh my Good Lord, as if we had been anticipating it!) her house would come to me. And so Patsy's and my needs both would be catered for, at least insofar as we wouldn't suffer for a roof over our heads . . .

Ma painted, and I like to think I inherited something of her not inconsiderable talent. In fact, that was how I made a living: my work was on show in a studio in Exeter where I was one of a small but mainly respected coterie of local artists, with a somewhat smaller, widespread band of dedicated, affluent collectors. I thank my lucky stars for affluent collectors! And so, with the addition of the interest on monies willed to me by my father, I had always managed to eke out a living of sorts.

Ma painted, yes, and always she looked for the inspiration of drama. The more dramatic her subject, the finer the finished canvas. Seascapes on the Devon coast, landscapes on the rolling South Hams, the frowning ocean-hewn cliffs of Cornwall; and of course those great solemn tors on the moor . . . which is to say Dartmoor: the location for Sherlock Holmes' – or rather Arthur Conan Doyle's – famous (or infamous) *Hound of the Baskervilles*.

Ah, that faded old film! My mother used to say, "It's not like that, you know. Well, it *is* in some places, and misty too. But not *all* the time! Not like in that film. And I've certainly never seen the like of that fearsome old tramp that Basil Rathbone made of himself! Not on Dartmoor, God forbid! Yes, I know it was only Sherlock Holmes in one of his disguises, but still, I mean . . . Why, if the moors were really like *that* I swear I'd never want to paint there again!"

I remember that quite clearly, the way she said: "It's not *like* that, you know," before correcting herself. For in fact it is like that – and too much like that – in certain places . . .

After she'd gone I found myself revisiting the locations where we had painted together: the coastlines of Cornwall and our own Devon, the rolling, open countryside, and eventually Dartmoor's great tors, which my dictionary somewhat inadequately describes as hills or rocky heights. But it was the Celts who called them tors or torrs, from which we've derived tower, and some of them do indeed "tower" on high. Or it's possible the name comes from the Latin: the Roman *turris*. Whichever, I'll get to the tors in a moment. But first something of Dartmoor itself.

All right, so it's not like that faded old Basil Rathbone *Hound of the Baskervilles* film. Not entirely like that, anyway; not *all* the time. In fact in the summer it's glorious, and that was mainly when I would go there; for I was still attempting to paint there despite that it had become a far more lonely business . . . often utterly lonely, on my own out there on the moors.

But glorious? Beautiful? Yes it certainly was, and for all that I don't go there any more, I'm sure it still is. Beautiful in a fashion all its own. Or perhaps the word I'm searching for is unique. Uniquely dramatic . . . gloriously wild . . . positively neolithic, in its outcrops and standing stones, and prehistoric in the isolation and sometimes desolation of its secret, if not sacred, places.

As for outcrops, standing stones and such: well, now we're back to the tors.

On Eastern Dartmoor my mother and I had painted that amazing jumble of rocks, one of the largest outcrops in the National Park, known as Hound Tor (no connection to Doyle's hound, at least not to my knowledge.) But along with a host of other gigantic stacks, such as the awesome Haytor Rock or Vixen Tor, the Hound hadn't been one of Ma's favourites. Many a lesser pile or tranquil river location had been easier to translate to canvas, board, or art paper. It wasn't that we were idle, or lacking in skill or patience – certainly not my mother, whose true-to-life pictures were full of the most intricate detail – but that the necessities of life and the endless hours required to trap such monsters simply didn't match up to our limited time. One single significant feature of any given rock could take Ma a whole day to satisfactorily transcribe in oils! And because I only rarely got things right at the first pass, they sometimes took me even longer. Which is why we were satisfied to paint less awesome or awkward subjects, and closer to home whenever possible.

Ah, but when I say "closer to home" . . . surely Dartmoor is *only* a moor? What's a few miles between friends? Let me correct you.

Dartmoor is over 350 square miles of mists, mires, woodlands, rushing rivers, tors carved in an age of ice, small villages, lonely farmsteads and mazy paths; all of which forms the largest tract of unenclosed land in southern England. The landscape may range in just a few miles from barren, naked summits – several over 500 yards in height – through heather-clad moorland, to marsh and sucking bog. There, in four national nature reserves and numerous protected sites, Dartmoor preserves an astonishing variety of plants and wildlife; all of this a mere twenty miles from Plymouth to the south, and a like distance from Exeter to the east.

Parts of the moor's exposed heath contain the remains of Bronze and Iron Age settlements, now home to the hardy Dartmoor ponies; but the river Dart's lush valley – cut through tens of thousands of years of planetary evolution – displays the softer side of rural Devon, where thatched cottages, tiny villages and ancient inns seem almost hidden away in the shady lee of knolls or protective hollows.

Dartmoor is, in short, a fascinating fantasy region, where several of the tors have their own ghosts – which is only to be expected in such a place – but I fancy their ectoplasm is only a matter of mist, myth, and legend. Most of them. Some of them, certainly . . .

I won't say where I went that first time – which is to say the first time anything peculiar happened – for reasons which will become amply apparent, but it was close to one of our favourite places. Close to, but not the precise spot, for that would have meant feeling my mother's presence. Her memory, or my memory *of* her, in that place, might have interfered with my concentration. And I'm not talking about ghosts here, just memories, nostalgia if you like: a sentimental longing for times spent with someone who had loved me all of her life, now gone forever. And if that makes me seem weak, then explain to me how even strong men find themselves still crying over a pet dog dead for months and even years, let alone a beloved parent.

And there is no paradox here, in my remembering yet needing to hold the memories to some degree at bay. I missed my Ma, yes, but I knew that I couldn't go on mourning her for the rest of my life.

Anyway, it was in the late summer – in fact August, this time of year – when less than an hour's drive had taken me onto the moor and along a certain second-class road, to a spot where I parked my car in a lay-by near a crossroads track leading off across the heather. Maybe a quarter-mile away there was a small domed hill, which faced across a shaded, shallow depression one of Dartmoor's more accessible tors: an oddly unbalanced outcrop that looked for all the world as if it had been built of enormous, worn and rounded dominoes by some erratic Titan infant and was now trying hard not to topple over. An illusion, naturally, because it was entirely possible that this was just one massive rock, grooved by time and the elements into a semblance of many separate horizontal layers.

And here I think I had better give the stack a name – even one of my own coining – rather than simply call it a tor. Let's call it Tumble Tor, if only because it looked as if at any moment it just might!

My mother and I had tried to paint Tumble Tor on a number of occasions, never with any great success. So maybe I could do it now and at least finish a job that we had frequently started and just as often left unresolved. That was the idea, my reason for being there, but as stated I would not be painting from any previously occupied vantage point. Indeed, since the moors seem to change from day to day and (obviously) more radically season to season, it would be almost impossible to say precisely where those vantage points had been. My best bet was to simply plunk myself down in a spot which felt totally strange, and that way be sure that I'd never been there before.

As for painting: I wouldn't actually be doing any, not on this my first unaccompanied visit to Tumble Tor. Instead I intended to prepare a detailed pencil sketch, and in that way get as well acquainted as possible with the monolith before attempting the greater familiarity of oils and colour. In my opinion, one has to respect one's subjects.

It had been a long hot summer and the ground was very hard underfoot, the soil crumbling as I climbed perhaps one third of the way up the knoll to a stone-strewn landing where the ground levelled off in a wide ledge. The sun was still rising in a mid-morning sky, but there in the shade of the summit rising behind me I seated myself on a flat stone and faced Tumble Tor with my board and paper resting comfortably on my knees. And using various grades of graphite I began to transpose my oddly staggered subject onto paper.

Time passed quickly . . .

Mid-afternoon, I broke for a ham sandwich with mayonnaise, washed down with a half thermos of bitter coffee. I had brought my binoculars with me; now and then I trained them on my car to ensure that it remained safe and hadn't attracted the attention of any overly curious strangers. The glasses were also handy as a means of bringing Tumble Tor into greater resolution, making it easy to study its myriad bulges and folds before committing them to paper.

As I looked again at that much wrinkled rock, a lone puff of cloud eased itself in front of the sun. Tumble Tor fell into shade, however temporarily, and suddenly I saw a figure high in one of the outcrop's precipitous shoulders: the figure of a man leaning against the rock there, peering in a furtive fashion – or so it seemed to me – around the shoulder and across the moor in the general direction of the road. Towards my car? Perhaps.

The puff of cloud persisted, slowly moving, barely drifting, across what was recently an empty, achingly blue sky, and I was aware of the first few wisps of a ground mist in the depression between my knoll and Tumble Tor. I glanced again at the sky and saw that the cloud was the first of a string of cotton-wool puffs reaching out toward Exeter in a ruler-straight line. Following this procession to its source, I was able to pick out the shining silver speck that had fashioned the aerial trail: a jet aircraft, descending toward Exeter airport. Its long vapour trail – even as it broke up into these small "clouds" – seemed determined to track across the face of the sun.

I looked again at Tumble Tor, and adjusted the focus of my

binoculars to bring the lone climber – the furtive observer of some near-distant event? – into sharper perspective. He hadn't moved except to turn his head in my direction, and I had little doubt but that he was now looking at me. At a distance of something less than 450 yards, I must be visible to him as he was to me. But of course I had the advantage of my glasses . . . or so I thought.

He was thin and angular, a stick of a man, with wild hair blowing in a wind I couldn't feel, some current of air circulating around his precarious position. He wore dark clothing, and as I once again refocussed I saw that indeed he carried binoculars around his neck. Though he wasn't using them, still I felt he gazed upon me. I tried to get a clearer view of his face but the image was blurred, trembling with the movement of my hands. However, when finally I did manage to get a good look . . . it was his narrow eyes that left a lasting impression.

They seemed to glow in the shade of the rock with that so-called "red-eye" complication of amateur photography: an illusion – a trick of the light – obviously. But the way they were fixed upon me, those eyes, was somehow disconcerting. It was as if he was spying on me, and not the other way around.

But spying? Feeling like some kind of voyeur, I lowered my glasses and looked away.

Meanwhile, having swung across the sky, the sun had found me; soon my hollow in the side of the hill, rather than providing shade, was going to become a sun-trap. And so I reckoned it was time to call it a day and head for home. Before I could put my art things aside, however, a tall shadow fell across me and a deep voice said, "Aye, and ye've picked the perfect spot for it. What a grand picture the auld tor makes frae here, eh?"

Momentarily startled, I jerked myself around to look up at the speaker. He was a dark silhouette, blocking out the sun.

"Oh dear!" he said, himself startled. "Did I make ye jump just then? Well, I'm sorry if I've disturbed ye, and more so if I've broken ye're mood. But man, ye must hae been concentratin' verra hard not tae hear me comin' down on ye."

"Concentrating?" I answered. "Actually I was watching that fellow on the tor there. He must be a bit of a climber. Myself, I don't have much of a head for heights."

"On the tor, ye say?" Shading his eyes and standing tall, he peered at Tumble Tor, now bright once more in full sunlight. "Well then, he must hae moved on, gone round the back. I cannae see anyone on the rock right now, no frae here." Then, stepping down level with me, he crouched to examine my drawing close up. And in my turn – now that the sun was out of my eyes – I could look more closely at him.

A big, powerful man, I judged him to be in his mid-fifties. Dressed in well worn tweeds, good walking boots, and carrying a knobbed and ferruled stick, he could well have been a gamekeeper – and perhaps he was.

"I . . . I do hope I'm not trespassing here," I finally mumbled. "I mean, I hope this isn't private ground."

"Eh?" he cocked his head a little, then smiled. "What? Do ye take me for a gillie or somethin'? No, no, I'm no that. And as far as I ken this ground's free for us all. But a trespasser? Well, if ye are then so am I, and hae been for some twenty years!" He nodded at the unfinished drawing in my lap. "That's a bonny piece of work. Will ye no finish it? Ye'll excuse that I'm pokin' my nose in, but I sense ye were about tae leave."

"Was and am," I answered, getting to my feet and dusting myself off. "The sun's to blame . . . the shadows on the tor are falling all wrong now. Also, the back of my neck was getting a bit warm." I stooped, gathered up my art things, and looked at the drawing. "But I thank you for your comment because this is just—"

"—A preliminary sketch?"

"Oh?" I said. "And how did you know that?"

Again he smiled, but most engagingly. "Why, there's paint under ye're fingernails. And ye've cross-hatched all the areas that are the self same colour as seen frae here . . . stone grey, that is. Ye'll be plannin' a painting – am I no right?"

I studied him more closely. He had tousled brown hair – a lot of it for a man his years, – a long weathered face, brown, friendly eyes over a bulbous nose, and a firm mouth over a jut of a chin. His accent revealed his nationality, and he made no attempt to disguise it. The Scots are proud of themselves, and they have every right to be. This one looked as much a part of the moors as . . . well, as Tumble Tor itself.

Impulsively, I stuck my hand out. "You're right, I'm planning a painting. I'm Paul Stanard, from Torquay. I'm pleased to meet you."

"Andrew Quarry," he came back at once, grasping my hand. "Frae a mile or two back there." A jerk of his head indicated the knoll behind us. "My house is just off the Yelverton road, set back a wee in a copse. But – did ye say Stanard?"

"Paul Stanard, yes," I nodded.

"Hmm," he mused. "Well, it's probably a coincidence, but there's a picture in my house painted by one Mary May Stanard: it's a moors scene that I bought in Exeter."

"My mother," I told him, again nodding. "She sold her work through various art shops in Exeter and elsewhere. And so do I. But she she died some nine months ago. Lung cancer."

"Oh? Well, I'm sorry for ye," he answered. "What, a smoker was she? Aye, it's a verra bad business. Myself, I gave my auld pipe up years ago. But her picture – its a bonny thing."

I smiled, however sadly. "Oh, she knew how to paint! But I doubt if it will ever be worth any more than you paid for it."

"Ah, laddie," he said, shaking his head. "But I didnae buy it for what others might reckon its value. I bought it because I thought it might look right hangin' in my livin'-room. And so it does."

Andrew Quarry: he was obviously a gentleman, and so open – so down-to-earth – that I couldn't help but like him. "Are you by chance going my way?" I enquired. "That's my car down on the road there. Maybe we can walk together?"

"Most certainly!" he answered at once. "But only if I can prevail upon ye tae make a little detour and drop me off on the Yelverton road. It'll be a circular route for ye but no too far out of ye're way, I promise ye."

As I hesitated he quickly added, "But if ye're in a hurry, then dinnae fret. The walkin's good for a man. And me: I must hae tramped a thousand miles over these moors, so a half-dozen more will nae harm me."

"Not at all," I answered. "I was just working out a route, that's all. For while I've crossed Dartmoor often enough, still I sometimes find myself confused. Maybe I don't pay enough attention to maps and road signs, and anyway my sense of direction isn't up to much. You might have to show me the way."

"Oh, I can do that easily enough," Quarry answered. "And I know what ye mean. I walk these moors freely in three out of four seasons, but in the fourth I go verra carefully. When the snow is on the ground, oh it's beautiful beyond a doubt – ah, but it hides all the landmarks! A man can get lost in a blink, and then the cold sets in." As we set off down the steep slope he asked: "So then, how did ye come here?"

"I'm sorry?"

"Ye're route, frae the car tae here."

"Oh. I followed the path – barely a track, really – but I walked where many feet have gone before: around that clump of standing stones there, and so on to the foot of this hill where I left the track, climbed through the heather, and finally arrived at this grassy ledge."

"I see." He nodded. "Ye avoided the more direct line frae ye're vehicle tae the base of the tor, and frae the tor tae the knoll. Verra sensible."

"Oh?"

"Aye. Ye see those rushes?" He pointed. "Between the knoll and yon rock? And those patches of red and green, huggin' close tae the ground? Well those colours hint of what lies underfoot, and it's marshy ground just there. Mud like that'll suck ye're shoes off! It would make a more direct route as the crow flies, true enough, but crows dinnae hae tae walk!"

"You can tell all that from the colour of the vegetation? The state of the ground, that is?" He obviously knew his Dartmoor, this man.

He shrugged. "Did I no say how I've lived here for twenty years? A man comes tae understand an awfy lot in twenty years." Then he laughed. "Oh, it's no great trick. Those colours: they indicate mosses, sphagnum mosses. And together with the rushes, that means boggy ground."

We had reached the foot of the knoll and set off following the rough track, making a detour wide of the tor and the allegedly swampy ground; which is to say we reversed and retraced my incoming route. And Quarry continued talking as we walked:

"Those sphagnums . . ." he said, pausing to catch his breath. ". . . That's peat in the makin'. A thousand years from now, it'll be good burnin' stuff, buried under a couple of feet of softish earth. Well, that's if the moor doesnae dry out – as it's done more than its share of this last verra hot summer. Aye, climatic change and all that."

I was impressed. "You seem to be a very knowledgeable man. So then, what are you, Mr Quarry? Something in moors conservation? Do you work for the National Park Authority? A botanist, perhaps?"

"Botany?" He raised a shaggy eyebrow. "My profession? No laddie, hardly that. I *was* a veterinary surgeon up in Scotland a good long spell ago – but I dinnae hae a profession, not any more. Ye see, my hands got a wee bit wobbly. Botany's my hobby now, that's all. All the green things . . . I enjoy tae identify them, and the moor has an awfy lot tae identify."

"A Scotsman in Devon," I said. "I should have thought the highlands would be just as varied, just as suitable to your needs."

"Aye, but my wife was a Devon lass, so we compromised."

"Compromised?"

He grinned. "She said she'd marry me, if I said I'd come live in

Devon. I've no regretted it." And then, more quietly, "She's gone now, though, the auld girl. Gone before her time. Her heart gave out. It was most unexpected."

"I'm sorry to hear it," I said. "And so you live alone?"

"For quite some time, aye. Until my Jennie came home frae America. So now's a nice time for me. Jennie was studyin' architectural design; she got her credentials – top of the class, too – and now works in Exeter."

We were passing the group of tall stones, their smoothed and rounded sides all grooved with the same horizontal striations. I nodded to indicate them. "They look like the same hand was at work carving them."

"And so it was," said Quarry. "The hand of time – of the ice age – of the elements. But all the one hand when ye think it through. This could well be the tip of some buried tor, like an iceberg of stone in a sea of earth."

"There's something of the poet in you," I observed.

He smiled. "Oh, I'm an auld lad of nature, for a fact!"

And, once again on impulse, I said, "Andrew, if I may call you that, I'd very much like you to have that drawing – that's if you'd care to accept it. It's unfinished, I know, but—"

"—But I would be delighted!" he cut in. "Now tell me: how much would ye accept for it?"

"No," I said. "I meant as a gift."

"A gift!" He sounded astonished. "But why on earth would a body be givin' all those hours of work away?"

"I really don't know." I shook my head, and shrugged. "And anyway, I haven't worked on it all that long. Maybe I'd like to think of it on your wall, beside my mother's painting."

"And so it shall be – if ye're sure . . .?"

"I am sure."

"Then I thank ye kindly."

Following which we were quiet, until eventually we arrived at the car. There, as I let Quarry into the passenger's seat, I looked back at the sky and Tumble Tor. The puffs of cloud were still there, but dispersing now, drifting, breaking up. And on that strange high rock, nothing to be seen but the naked stone. Yet for some reason that thin, pale face with its burning eyes continued to linger in my own mind's eye . . .

Dartmoor is criss-crossed by many paths, tracks, roads . . . none of which are "major" in the sense of motorways, though many are modern, metalled, and with sound surfaces. Andrew Quarry directed me expertly by the shortest route possible, through various cross-roads and turns, until we'd driven through Two Bridges and Prince-town. Shortly after that, he bade me stop at a stile in a hazel hedge. Beyond the stile a second hedge, running at right-angles to the road, sheltered a narrow footpath that paralleled a brook's meandering contours. And some twenty-five yards along this footpath, in a fenced copse of oaks and birch trees, there stood Quarry's house.

It was a good sized two-storeyed place, probably Victorian, with oak-timbered walls of typical red Devon stone. In the high gables, under terracotta pantiles, wide windows had been thrown open; while on the ground floor, the varnished or polished oak frames of several more windows were barely visible, shining in the dapple of light falling through the trees. In one of these lower windows, I could only just make out the upper third of a raven-haired female figure busy with some task.

"That's Jennie," said Quarry, getting out of the car. "Ye cannae mistake that shinin' head of hair. She's in the kitchen there, preparin' this or that. I never ate so well since she's been back. Will ye no come in for a cup of tea, Paul, or a mug of coffee, perhaps?"

"Er, no," I said, "I don't think so. I've a few things to do at home, and it's time I was on my way. But thanks for offering. I do appreciate it."

"And I appreciate ye're gift," he said. "Perhaps I'll see ye some other time? Most definitely, if ye're out there paintin' on the knoll. In fact, I shall make it my business to walk that way now and then."

"And I'll be there—" I told him. "—Not every day, but on occasion, at least until my painting is finished. I'll look forward to talking to you again."

"Aye," he nodded, "and so we shall." With which he climbed the stile with my rolled-up drawing under his arm, looked back and waved, then disappeared around a curve in the hedge.

The forecast was rain for the next day or two. I accepted the weatherman's verdict, stayed at home and worked on other paintings while waiting for the skies to clear; which they did eventually. Then I returned to the knoll and Tumble Tor.

I got there early morning when there was some ground mist still lingering over from the night. Mists are a regular feature of Devon in August through December, and especially on the moors. As I left the car I saw four or five Dartmoor ponies at the gallop, their manes flying, kicking up their heels as they crossed the road. They must have known where they were headed, the nature of the uneven ground; either that or they were heedless of the danger, for with tendrils of mist swirling halfway up their gleaming legs they certainly couldn't see where their hooves were falling! They looked like the fabulous hippocampus, I thought – like sea-horses, braving the breakers – as they ran off across the moor and were soon lost in the poor visibility.

Poor visibility, yes . . . and I had come here to work on my painting! (Actually, to begin the second phase: this time using watercolours.) But the sun was well up, its rays already working on the mist to melt it away; Tumble Tor was mainly visible, for all that its foot was lost in the lapping swell; a further half-hour should set things to right, by which time I would be seated on my ledge in the lee of the knoll.

Oh really? But unfortunately there was something I hadn't taken into account: namely that I wasn't nearly as sure-footed or knowledgeable as those Dartmoor ponies! Only leave the road and less than ten paces onto the moor I'd be looking and feeling very foolish, tripping over the roots of gorse and heather as I tried to find and follow my previous route. So then, best to stay put for now and let the sun do its work.

Then, frustrated, leaning against the car and lighting one of my very infrequent cigarettes, I became aware of a male figure approaching up the road. His legs wreathed in mist, he came on, and soon I could see that he was a "gentleman of the road", in short a tramp, but by no means a threat. On the contrary, he seemed rather time- and care-worn: a shabby, elderly, somewhat pitiful member of the brotherhood of wayfarers.

Only a few paces away he stopped to catch his breath, then seated himself upon one of those knee-high white-painted stones that mark the country verges. Oddly, he didn't at first seem to have noticed me; but he'd seen my car and appeared to be frowning at it, or at least eyeing it disdainfully.

As I watched him, wondering if I should speak, he took out a tobacco pouch and a crumpled packet of cigarette papers, only to toss the latter aside when he discovered it empty. Which was when I stepped forward. And: "By all means, have one of these," I said, proffering my pack and shaking it to loosen up a cigarette.

"Eh?" And now he looked at me.

He could have been anything between fifty-five and seventy years of age, that old man. But his face was so lined and wrinkled, so lost in the hair of his head, his beard, and moustache – all matted together under a tattered, floppy hat – it would have been far too difficult if not impossible to attempt a more accurate assessment. I looked at his hunched, narrow shoulders, his spindly arms in a threadbare jacket, his dark gnarled hands with liver spots and purple veins, and simply had to feel sorry for him. Rheumy eyes gazed back at me, through curling wisps of shaggy eyebrow, and lips that had been fretted by harsh weather trembled when he spoke:

"That's kind of you. I rarely begged but they often gave." It was as if with that last rather odd sentence he was talking to himself.

"Take another," I told him, "for later."

"I didn't mean to take advantage of you," he answered, but he took a second cigarette anyway. Then, looking at the pair of small white tubes in his hand, he said. "But I think I'll smoke them later, if you don't mind. I've had this cough, you see?"

"Not at all," I said. "I don't usually smoke myself, until the evening. And then I sometimes fancy one with a glass of . . ." But there I paused. He probably hadn't tasted brandy in a long, long time – if ever.

He apparently hadn't noticed my almost gaffe. "It's one of my few pleasures," he said, placing the cigarettes carefully in his tobacco pouch, drawing its string tight, fumbling it into a leather-patched pocket. Then:

"But we haven't been properly introduced!" he said, making an effort to stand, only to slump back down again. "Or could it be – I mean, is it possible – that I once knew you?" He seemed unable to focus on me; it was as if he looked right through me. "I'm sorry . . . it's these poor old eyes of mine. They can't see you at all clearly."

"We've never met," I told him. "I'm Paul."

"Or, it could be the car," he said, going off at a tangent again and beginning to ramble. "Your car, that is. But the very car . . .? No, I don't think so. Too new."

"Well, I have parked here before," I said, trying my best to straighten out the conversation. "But just the once. Still, if you passed this way a few days ago you might well have seen it here."

"Hmmm!" he mused, blinking as he peered hard, studying my face. Then his oh-so-pale eyes opened wider. "Ah! *Now* I understand! You must have been trying very hard to see someone, and you got me instead. I'm Joe. Old Joe, they called me."

And finally I understood, too. The deprivations of a life on the road – of years of wandering, foraging, sleeping rough, through filthy weather and hungry nights – had got to him. His body wasn't the only victim of his "lifestyle". His mind, too, had suffered. Or perhaps it was the other way around, and that was the cause, not the effect. Perhaps he had always been "not altogether there", as I've heard it said of such unfortunates.

And because I really didn't have very much to say – also because I no longer knew quite *what* to say, exactly – I simply shrugged and informed him, "I . . . I'm just waiting, that's all. And when this mist has cleared a bit, I'll be moving on."

"I'm waiting, too," he answered. "More or less obliged to wait. Here, I mean."

At which I simply had to ask: "Waiting? I didn't know this was a bus route? And if it is they're very infrequent. Or maybe you're waiting for a friend, some fellow, er, traveller? Or are you looking for a lift – in a car, I mean?" (Lord, I hoped not! Not that he smelled bad or anything, not that I'd noticed, anyway, but I should really hate to have to refuse him if he asked me.) And how stupid of me: that I should have mentioned a lift in the first place! For after all I was there to paint, not to go on mercy missions for demented old derelicts!

"Buses?" he said, cocking his head a little and frowning. "No, I can't say I've seen too many of those, not here. But a car, yes. That's a real possibility. Better yet, a motorcycle! Oh, it's a horrid, horrid thought – but it's my best bet by a long shot . . ."

And my best bet, I thought, would be to end a very pointless conversation and leave him sitting there on his own! Yes, and even as I thought it I saw that I could do just that, for the mist was lifting, or rather melting away as the sun sailed higher yet. And so:

"You'll excuse me," I said, with a glance across the moor at Tumble Tor, "but I'm afraid it's time . . ." And there I paused, snapping my head round to stare again at the ancient stack; at its grainy, grooved stone surfaces, all damply agleam, and its base still wreathed in a last few tendrils of mist. ". . . Afraid it's time to go."

And the reason I had frozen like that, albeit momentarily? Because he was there again: the climber on the tor. And despite that from this angle I could see only his head and shoulders, I knew at once that it was the same person I'd seen the last time I was here: the observer with the binoculars – perched so precariously on that same windy ledge – who once again seemed to be observing me! The sunlight reflected blindingly from the lenses of his glasses.

"I paid my way with readings," said the old tramp from his roadside stone, as if from a thousand miles away. "Give me your hand and I'll do one for you."

Distracted, I looked at him. "What? You'll do one?"

"A reading." He nodded. "I'll read your palm."

"I really don't—" I began, glancing again at Tumble Tor.

"—Oh, go on!" He cut me off. "Or you'll leave me feeling I'm in your debt."

But the man on the rock had disappeared, slipped away out of sight, so I turned again to Old Joe. He held out a trembling hand, and however reluctantly I gave him mine. Then:

"There," he said. "And look here, you have clearly defined lines! Why, it's just like reading a book!" He traced the lines in my palm with a slightly grimy forefinger, but so gently that I barely felt his touch. And in a moment:

"Ah!" He gasped. "An only son – that's you, I mean – and you were so very close to her. Now you're alone but she's still on your mind; every now and then you forget she's gone, and you look up expecting to see her. Yes, and those are the times when you're most likely to see what you ought *not* to be seeing!" Now he looked up at me, his old eyes the faded blue of the sky over a grey sea, and said, "She's moved on, your mother, Paul. She's safe and you can stop searching now."

Spiders with icy feet ran up and down my spine! I snatched my hand away, backed off, said, "W-w-what?"

"I'm sorry, so sorry!" he said, struggling to his feet. "I see too much, but so do you!" And as he went off, hobbling away in the same direction he'd come from, he paused to look back at me and called out, "You shouldn't look so hard, Paul." And once again after a short, sharp glance at Tumble Tor: "You shouldn't look so hard!"

Moments later a swell of mist like some slow-motion ocean rose up, deepening around him and obscuring him. His silhouette was quickly swallowed up in grey opacity, and having lost sight of him I once again turned my gaze on Tumble Tor. The moors can be very weird: mist in the one direction, clarity in the other! The huge outcrop continued to steam a little in the sun, but my route over the uneven ground was clearly visible. And of course the knoll was waiting.

Recovering from the shock Old Joe had supplied, determined to regain my composure, I collected my art things from my car's boot and set off on my semicircular route around Tumble Tor. Up there on the knoll twenty-five minutes later, I used my binoculars to scan the winding road to the north of the tor. Old Joe couldn't have got too far, now could he? But there was no mist, and there was no sign of Joe. Well then, he must have left the road and gone off across the moor along some track or other. Or perhaps someone had given him a lift after all. But neither had I seen any vehicles.

There was no sign of anyone on Tumble Tor either, but that didn't stop me from looking. And despite what Old Joe had said, I found myself looking pretty hard at that . . .

I couldn't concentrate on my work. It was the morning's strangeness, of course. It was Old Joe's rambling on the one hand, and his incredibly accurate reading on the other. I had always been aware that there were such people, certainly; I'd watched their performances on television, read of their extraordinary talents in various books and magazines, knew that they allegedly assisted the police in very serious investigations, and that seances were a regular feature in the lives of plenty of otherwise very sensible people. Personally, however, I'd always been sceptical of so-called psychic or occult phenomena, only rarely allowing that it was anything other than fake stage magic and "supernatural hocus-pocus".

Now? Well, what was I to think now? Or had I, like so many others (in my opinion) simply allowed myself to be sucked in by self-delusion, my own gullibility?

Perhaps the old tramp hadn't been so crazy after all. What if he'd merely used a few clever, well-chosen words and phrases and left me to fill in the blanks: a very subtle sort of hypnotism? And what if I had only imagined that he'd said the things he said? For of course my mother, comparatively recently passed on, was never far from my mind . . . anyone who ever lost someone will surely understand that the word "she" – just that single, simple word – would at once conjure her image, more especially now that there was no other "she" to squeeze her image aside.

Psychology? Was that Old Joe's special ability? Well, what or whichever, he'd certainly found my emotional triggers easily enough! Maybe I had worn a certain distinctive, tell-tale look; perhaps there had been some sort of forlorn air about me, as if I were lost, or as if I was looking for someone. But alone, out on the moors? Who could I possibly have been seeking out there? Someone who couldn't possibly be found, obviously. And Old Joe had simply extrapolated.

Stage magic, definitely . . . or maybe? I still couldn't make up my mind! And so couldn't concentrate. I managed to put a few soft pencilled guidelines onto the paper and a preliminary wash of background colour. But nothing looked right and my frustration was mounting. I couldn't seem to get Old Joe's words out of my head. And what of his warning, if that's what it was, that I shouldn't look so hard? I was looking "too hard", he'd said and I was "seeing too much" – seeing what I ought not to be seeing. Now what on earth had he been trying to convey, if anything, by that? One thing for sure: I'd had a very odd morning!

Too odd – and far too off-putting – so that when a mass of dark cloud began to spread across the horizon, driven my way by a rising wind out of the south-west, I decided to let it go and return to Torquay. Back at the car I saw something at the roadside, lying on the ground at the foot of the verge marker where Old Joe had seated himself. Two somethings in fact: cigarettes, my brand, apparently discarded, just lying there. But hadn't he said something about not wanting to be in my debt?

A peculiar old coot, to say the very least. And so, trying to put it all to the back of my mind, I drove home . . .

Then for the next three days I painted in my attic studio, listening to the sporadic patter of rain on my skylight while I worked on unfinished projects. And gradually I came to the conclusion that my chance encounter with Old Joe – more properly with his rambling, indirect choice of words and vague warnings – had been nothing more than a feeble, dazed old man's mumbo-jumbo, to which on a whim of coincidental, empathic emotions I had mistakenly attached far too much meaning.

And how, you might ask, is that possible? In the same way that if someone suddenly shouts, "Look out!" you jump . . . despite that nothing is coming! That's how. But now I ask myself: what if you *don't* jump? And what if something *is* coming?

Early in September, at the beginning of what promised to be an extended Indian summer, I ventured out onto Dartmoor yet again, this time fully determined to get to grips with Tumble Tor. It was a matter of pride by then: I wasn't about to let myself be defeated by a knob of rock, no matter how big it was!

That was my motive for returning to the moor, or so I tried to tell myself; but in all honesty, it was not the only reason. During the last ten days my sleep had been plagued by recurrent dreams: of a stick-thin, red-eyed man, gradually yet menacingly approaching me through a bank of dense swirling mist. Sometimes Tumble Tor's vague silhouette formed a backdrop to this relentless stalking; at other times there was only the crimson glare of Hallowe'en eyes, full of rabid animosity and a burning evil – such evil as to bring me starting awake in a cold sweat.

Determined to exorcise these nightmares, and since it was quite obvious that Tumble Tor was their source – or that they were the outcrop's evil *geniuses loci*, its spirits of place? – I supposed the best place to root them out must be on Dartmoor itself. So there I was once again, parking my car in the same spot, the place where a dirt track crossed the road, with the open moor and misshapen outcrop close at hand on my left, and in the near distance the steep-sided hill or knoll.

And despite that my imagination conjured up an otherwise intangible aura of – but of what? Of something lurking, waiting there? – still I insisted on carrying out my plans; come what may I was going to commence working! Whatever tricks the moor had up its sleeve, I would simply ignore or defy them.

To be absolutely sure that I would at least get something done, I had taken along my camera. If I experienced difficulty getting started, then I would take some pictures of Tumble Tor from which – in the comfort of my own home, at my leisure – I might work up some sketches, thus reacquainting myself with my subject.

As it turned out, it was as well that I'd planned it that way; for weather forecasts to the contrary, there was little or no sign of an Indian summer on Dartmoor! Not yet, anyway. There was dew on the yellow gorse and coarse grasses, and a carpet of ground mist that the morning sun hadn't quite managed to shift; indeed the entire scene seemed drab and uninspiring, and Tumble Tor looked as gaunt as a lop-sided skull, its dome shiny where wan sunlight reflected from its damp surface.

Staring at it, I found myself wondering why the hell I had wanted to paint it in the first place! But . . .

My usual route across the moorland's low-lying depression to the knoll was well known to me by now; and since the ankle-lapping mist wasn't so dense as to interfere with my vision at close range, I took up my camera and art things, made my way to the knoll, and climbed it to my previous vantage point. Fortunately, aware now of the moor's capriciousness, I had brought an old plastic raincoat with me to spread on the ground. And there I arranged the tools of my business as usual.

But when it came to actually starting to work . . . suddenly there was this weariness in me – not only a physical thing but also a numbing mental malaise – that had the effect of damping my spirits to such a degree that I could only sit there wondering what on earth was wrong with me. An uneasy expectancy? Some sort of foreboding or precognition? Well, perhaps . . . but rather than becoming aware, alert, on guard, I felt entirely fatigued, barely able to keep my eyes open.

A miasma then: some unwholesome exhalation spawned in the

mist? Unlikely, but not impossible. And for a fact the mist was thicker now in the depression between the knoll and Tumble Tor, and around the base of the outcrop itself; while in the sky the sun had paled to a sickly yellow blob behind the grey overcast.

But once again – as twice before – as I looked at Tumble Tor I saw something other than wet stone and mist. Dull my mind and eyes might be, but I wasn't completely insensible or blind. And there he was where I had first seen him: the climber on the tor, the red-eyed observer on the rock.

And I remember thinking: "Well, so much for exorcism!" For this was surely the weird visitant of my dreams. Not that I saw him as a form of evil incarnate in himself, not then (for after all, what was he in fact but a man on an enormous boulder?) but that his activities – and his odd looks, of course – had made such an impression on me as to cause my nightmares in the first place.

These were the thoughts that crept through my numb mind as I strove to fight free of both my mental and physical lethargy. But the swirling of the mist seemed hypnotic, while the unknown force working on my body – even on my head, which was gradually nodding lower and lower – weighed me down like so much lead. Or rather, to more accurately describe my perceptions, I felt that I was being *sucked* down as in a quagmire.

I tried one last time to focus my attention on the figure on Tumble Tor. Indeed, and before succumbing to my inexplicable faint, I even managed to take up my oh-so-heavy camera and snap a few shaky pictures. And between each period of whirring – as the film wound slowly forward and I tried to refocus – I could see that the man was now climbing down from the rock but so very *quickly!* Impossibly quickly! or perhaps it was simply that I was moving so slowly.

And now . . . now he had clambered down into the mist, and I somehow knew that my nightmare was about to become reality. For as in my dreams he was coming – he was now on his way to me – and the mental quagmire continued to suck at me. Which was when everything went dark . . .

"What's this?" (At first, a voice from far, far away which some kind of mental red shift rapidly enhanced, making it louder and bringing it closer.) "Asleep on the job, are ye? Twitchin' like ye're havin' a fit!" And then, much more seriously: "Man, but I hope ye're *not* havin' a fit!

"Eh?" I gave a start. "W-what?" And lifting my head, jerking awake, I straightened up so quickly that I came very close to toppling over sideways.

And there I was, still seated on my plastic mac, blinking up into the half-smiling, half-frowning, wholly uncertain features of Andrew Quarry. "G-*God*, I was dreaming!" I told him. "A nightmare. Just lately I've been plagued by them!"

"Then I'm glad I came along," he answered. "It was my hope tae find ye here, but when I saw ye sittin' there – jerkin' and moanin' and what all – I thought it was best I speak out."

"And just as well that you did," I got my breath, finding it hard to breathe properly, and even harder to get to my feet. Quarry took my elbow, assisted me as, by way of explanation, I continued: "I . . . haven't been sleeping too well."

"No sleepin'?" He looked me straight in the eye. "Aye, I can see that. Man, ye're lookin' exhausted, so ye are! And tae fall asleep here – this early in the mornin' – now, that's no normal."

I could only agree with him, as for the first time I actually felt exhausted. "Maybe it was the mist," I searched for a better explanation. "Something sickening in the mist? Some kind of – I don't know – some kind of miasma maybe?"

He looked surprised, glanced across the moorland this way and that, in all directions. "The mist, ye say?"

I looked, too, across the low-lying ground to where Tumble Tor stood tall for all that it seemed to slump; tall, and oddly foreboding now, *and dry as a bone in the warm morning sunshine!*

At which I could only shake my head and insist: "But when I sat down there was a mist, and a thick mist at that! Wait . . ." And I looked at my watch – which was proof of nothing whatever, for I couldn't judge the time.

"Well?" Quarry studied my face, curiously I thought.

"So maybe I was asleep longer than I thought," I told him, lamely. "I must have been, for the mist to clear up like that."

His frown lifted. "Maybe not." He shrugged. "The moor's as changeable as a young girl's mind. I've known the mist tae come up in minutes and melt away just as fast. Anyway, ye're lookin' a wee bit steadier now. So will ye carry on, or what?"

"Carry on?"

"With ye're paintin' – or drawin' – or whatever."

"No, not now," I answered, shaking my head. "I've had more than enough of this place for now."

As he helped me to gather up my things, he said, "Then may I make a wee suggestion?"

"A suggestion?" We started down the hillside.

"Aye. Paul, ye look like ye could use some exercise. Ye're way too pale, too jumpy, and too high strung. Now then, there's this beautiful wee walk – no so wee, actually – frae my place along the beck and back. Now I'm no just lookin' for a lift, ye ken, but we could drive there in ye're car, walk and talk, take in some verra nice autumn countryside while exercisin' our legs, and maybe finish off with a mug of coffee at my place before ye go on back tae Torquay. What do ye say?"

I almost turned him down, but . . . the fact was I was going short on company. Since the breakdown of my marriage (it seemed an awfully long time ago, but in fact had been less than eighteen months) all my friends had drifted away. Then again, since they had been mainly couples, maybe I should have expected that I would soon be cast out, to become a loner and outsider.

So now I nodded. "We can do that if you like. But—"

"Aye, but?"

"Is your daughter home? Er, Jennie?" Which was a blunt and stupid question whichever way you look at it; but having recognized the apprehension in my voice, he took it as it was meant.

"Oh, so ye're no particularly interested in the company of the fairer sex, is that it?" He glanced sideways at me, but for my part I remained silent. "Oh well then, I'll assume there's a verra good reason," he went on. "And anyway, I wouldnae want to seem to be intrudin'."

"Don't get any wrong ideas about me, Andrew," I said then. "But my wife and I divorced quite recently, since when—"

"Say no more." He nodded. "Ye're no ready tae start thinkin' that way again, I can understand that. But in any case, my Jennie's gone off tae Exeter: a day out with a few friends. So ye'll no be bumpin' intae her accidentally like. And anyway, what do ye take me for: some sort of auld matchmaker? Well, let me assure ye, I'm no. As for my Jennie, ye can take it frae me: she's no the kind of lassie ye'd find amenable to that sort of interference in the first place. So now ye ken."

"I meant no offence," I told him.

"No, of course ye didn't." He chuckled. "Aye, and if ye'd seen my Jennie, ye'd ken she doesnae need a matchmaker! Pretty as a picture, that daughter of mine. Man, ye couldnae paint a prettier one, I guarantee it!"

Along the usual route back to the car, I couldn't resist the occasional troubled glance in the direction of Tumble Tor. Andrew

Quarry must have noticed, for he nodded and said, "That auld tor: it's given ye nothin' but a load of grief, is it no so?"

"Grief?" I cast him a sharp look.

"With ye're art and what all, ye're paintin'. It's proved a poor subject."

A sentiment I agreed with more than Quarry could possibly know. "Yes," I answered him in his own words, "a whole load of grief." And then, perhaps a little angrily, revealing my frustration: "But I'm not done with that rock just yet. No, not by a long shot!"

Leaving the car on the road outside Quarry's place, we walked and talked. Or rather *he* talked, simultaneously and unselfconsciously displaying his expertise with regard to the incredible variety of Dartmoor's botanical species. And despite my current personal concerns – about my well-being, both physical and mental, following the latest unpleasant episode at Tumble Tor – I soon found myself genuinely fascinated by his monologue. But if Quarry had shown something of his specialized knowledge on our first meeting, now he excelled himself. So much so that later that day I could only remember a fraction of it.

Along the bank of the stream, he pointed out stag's horn and hair mosses; and when we passed a stand of birch trees just fifty yards beyond his house, he identified several lichens and a clump of birch-bracket fungi. Within a mile and a half, never straying from the path beside the stream, we passed oak, holly, hazel and sycamore, their leaves displaying the colours of the season and those colours alone enabling Quarry's instant recognition. On one occasion, where the way was fenced, he climbed a stile, crossed a field into a copse of oaks and dense conifers, and in less than five minutes filled a large white handkerchief with spongy, golden mushrooms which he called Goat's Lip. When I asked him about that, he said:

"Aye, that's what the locals call 'em. But listen tae me: 'locals', indeed! Man, I'm a local myself after all this time! Anyway, these beauties are commonly called downy boletus – or if ye're really, *really* interested *Xerocomus subtomentosus*. So I think ye'll agree, Paul, *Goat's* Lip falls a whole lot easier frae a *man's* lip, does it no?" At which I had to smile.

"And you'll eat them?" I may have seemed doubtful.

"Oh, be sure I will!" he answered. "My Jennie'll cook 'em up intae a fine soup, or maybe use 'em as stuffin' in a roasted chicken . . ."

And so it went, all along the way.

But in no time at all, or so it seemed, we'd covered more than two miles of country pathway and it was time to turn back. "Now see," Quarry commented, as we reversed our route, "there's a wee bit more colour in ye're cheeks; it's the fresh air ye've been breathin' deep intae ye're lungs, and the blood ye're legs hae been pumpin' up through ye're body. The walkin' is good for a man. Aye, and likewise the talkin' and the companionship. I'd be verra surprised if ye dinnae sleep well the nicht."

So that was it. Not so much the companionship and talking, but the fact that he'd been concerned for me. So of course when he invited me in I entered the old house with him, and shortly we were seated under a low, oak-beamed ceiling in a farmhouse-styled kitchen, drinking freshly ground coffee.

"The coffee's good," I told him.

"Aye," he answered. "None of ye're instant rubbish for my Jennie. If it's no frae the best beans it's rubbish . . . that's Jennie's opinion, and I go along with it. It's one of the good things she brought back frae America."

We finished our coffee.

"And now a wee dram," he said, as he guided me through the house to his spacious, comfortable living-room. "But just a wee one, for I ken ye'll need to be drivin' home."

Seated, and with a shot glass of good whisky in my hand, I looked across the room to a wall of pictures, paintings, framed photographs, diplomas and such. And the first thing to catch my eye was a painting I at once recognized. A seascape, it was one of my mother's canvases, and one of her best at that; my sketch of Tumble Tor – behind non-reflective glass in a frame that was far too good for it – occupied a space alongside.

I stood up, crossed to the wall to take a closer look, and said, "You were as good as your word. I'm glad my effort wasn't wasted."

"And ye're Ma's picture, too," he nodded, coming to stand beside me. "The pencils and the paint: I think they make a fine contrast."

I found myself frowning – or more properly scowling – at my drawing, and said, "Andrew, just you wait! I'm not done with painting on the moor just yet. I promise you this: I'll soon be giving you a far better picture of that damned rock . . . even if it kills me!"

He seemed startled, taken aback. "Aye, so ye've said," he answered, "—that ye're set on it, I mean. And I sense a struggle brewin' between the pair of ye – ye'rsel and the auld tor. But I would much prefer ye as a livin' breathin' friend than a dead benefactor!"

At which I breathed deeply, relaxed a little, laughed and said, "Just a figure of speech, of course. But I really do have to get to grips with that boulder. In fact I don't believe I'll be able to work on anything else until I'm done with it. But as for right now—" I half-turned from the wall, "I *am* quite done with it. Time we changed the subject, I think, and talked about other things."

My words acted like an invocation, for before turning more fully from the wall my gaze lighted on something else: a framed colour photograph hung in a prominent position, where the stone wall had been buttressed to enclose the grate and blackened flue of an open fireplace. An immaculate studio photograph, it portrayed a young woman's face in profile.

"Your wife?" I approached the picture.

"My Jennie," Quarry replied. "I keep my wife's photographs in my study, where I can speak tae her any time I like. And she sometimes answers me, or so I like tae think. As for my Jennie: well now ye've seen her, ye've seen her Ma. Like peas in a pod. Aye, but it's fairly obvious she doesnae take after me!"

I knew what he meant. Jennie was an extraordinarily beautiful woman. Her lush hair was black as a raven's wing, so black it was almost blue, and her eyes were as big and as blue as the sky. She had a full mouth, high cheeks and forehead, a straight nose and small, delicate ears. Despite that Jennie's photograph was in profile, still she seemed to look at the camera from the corner of her eye, and wore a half-smile for the man taking her picture.

"And she's in Exeter, with her boyfriend?"

Quarry shook his head. "No boyfriend, just friends. She's no been home long enough tae develop any romantic interests. Ye should let me introduce ye some time. She was verra much taken with ye're drawing. Ye hae that in common at least – designs, I mean. For it's all art when ye break it down."

After that, in a little while, I took my leave of him . . .

Driving home, for some reason known only to my troubled subconscious mind, I took the long route across the moor and drove by Tumble Tor; or I would have driven by, except Old Joe was there where I'd last seen him. In fact, I *didn't* see him until almost the last moment, when he suddenly appeared through the break in the hedge, stepping out from the roadside track.

He looked at me – or more properly at my car – as it sped toward him, and for a moment he teetered there on the verge and appeared of two minds about crossing the road directly in front of me! If he'd done so I would have had a very hard time avoiding him. It would have meant applying my brakes full on, swinging my steering-wheel hard over, and in all likelihood skidding sideways across the narrow road. And there on the opposite side was this outcrop, a boulder jutting six feet out of the ground, which would surely have brought me to a violent halt; but such a halt as might easily have killed me!

As it was I had seen the old tramp in sufficient time – but only *just* in time – to apply my brakes safely and come to a halt alongside him.

Out of my window I said, "Old Joe, what on earth were you thinking about just then? I mean, I could so easily—"

"Yes," he cut me off, "and so could I. Oh so very easily!" And he stood there trembling, quivering, with his eyes sunk so deep that I could scarcely see them.

Then I noticed the mist. It was just as Andrew Quarry had stated – a freak of synchronicity, sprung into being almost in a single moment – as if the earth had suddenly breathed it out; this ground mist, swirling and eddying about Old Joe's feet and all across the low-lying ground beyond the narrow grass verge.

Distracted, alienated, and somehow feeling the dampness of that mist deep in my bones, I turned again to the old man, who was still babbling on. "But I couldn't do it," he said, "and I shall *never* do it! I'll simply wait – forever, if needs be!"

As he began to back unsteadily away from the car, I said, "Old Joe, are you ill? What's the trouble? Can I help you? Can I offer you a lift, take you somewhere?"

"A lift?" he answered. "No, no. This is my waiting place. It's where I must wait. And I'm sorry – so very sorry – that I almost forgot myself."

"What?" I said, frowning and perplexed. "What do you mean? How did you forget yourself? What are you talking about?"

"It's here," he replied. "Here's where I must wait for it to happen again! But I can't – I mustn't, and won't ever – try to *make* it happen! No, for I'm not like that one . . ."

Old Joe gave a nod and his gaze shifted; he looked beyond me, beyond the car, out across the moors at Tumble Tor. And of course, as cold as I suddenly felt, I turned my head to follow his lead. All I saw was naked stone, and without quite knowing why I breathed a sigh of relief.

Then, turning back to the old tramp, I said, "But there's no one there, Joe!" And again, in a whisper: "Old Joe . . .?" For he wasn't there either – just a curl of mist in the hedgerow, where he might have passed through.

And a few minutes later, by the time I had driven no more than a mile farther along the road toward Torquay, already the mist had given way to a wan, inadequate sun that was doing its best to shine.

I had been right to worry about my state of mind. Or at least, that was how I felt at the time: that my depression under this atmosphere of impending doom which I felt hovering over me was some kind of mild mental disorder. (For after all, that's what depression is, isn't it?) Even now, as I look back on it in the light of new understanding, perhaps it really was some sort of psychosis – but nothing that I'd brought on myself. I realize that now because at the time I *acknowledged* the problem, while psychiatry insists that the psychotic isn't aware of his condition.

In any case, I *had* been right to worry about it. For despite Andrew Quarry's insistence that I'd sleep well that night, my dreams were as bad and even worse than before. The mist, the semi-opaque silhouette of monolithic Tumble Tor, and those eyes – those crimson-burning eyes – drawing closer, closer, and ever closer. Half-a-dozen times I woke up in a cold sweat . . . little wonder I was feeling so drained . . .

In the morning I drove into town to see my doctor. He gave me a check-up and heard me out; not the entire story, only what I felt obliged to tell him about my "insomnia". He prescribed a course of sleeping pills and I set off home . . . such was my intention.

But almost before I knew it I was out on the country roads again. Taken in thrall by some morbid fascination or obsession, I was once more heading for Tumble Tor!

My tank was almost empty . . . I stopped at a garage, filled her up . . . the forecourt attendant was concerned, asked me if I was feeling okay . . . which really should have told me that something was very wrong, but it didn't stop me.

Oh, I agreed with him that I didn't feel well: I was dizzy confused, distracted, but none of these symptoms served to stop me. And through all of this I could feel the lure, the inexplicable attraction of the moors, to which I must succumb!

And I did succumb, driving all the way to Tumble Tor where I parked in my usual spot and levered myself out of my car. Old Joe was there, waving his arms and silently gibbering . . . warning me about something which I couldn't take in . . . my mind was clogged with cotton-wool mist . . . everything seemed to be happening in slow-motion . . . those eyes, those blazing *evil* eyes!

I felt a *whoosh* of wind, heard a vehicle's tyres screaming on the road's rough surface, saw through the billowing mist the blurred motion of something passing close – much too close – in front of me.

This combination of sensations got through to me – almost. I was aware of a red faced, angry man in a denim jacket leaning out of his truck's window, yelling, "You *bloody* idiot! What the bloody hell . . . are you drunk? Staggering about in the road like that!" Then his tyres screeched again, spinning and smoking, as he rammed his vehicle into gear and pulled away.

But the mist was still swirling, my head still reeling – *and Old Joe was having a silent, gesticulating argument with a stick-thin, red-eyed man!*

Then the silence was broken as the old man looked my way, sobbing. "That wouldn't have been my fault! Not this time, and not ever. It would have been yours . . . or *his*! But it wouldn't have done him any good, and God knows I didn't want it!" As he spoke the word "his", so he'd flung out an arm to point at the thin man who was now floating toward me, his eyes like warning signal lamps as his shape took on form and emerged more surely from the mist.

And that was when I "woke up" to the danger. For yes, it was like coming out of a nightmare – indeed it could only have been a nightmare – but I came out of it so slowly that even as the mist cleared and the old man and the red-eyed phantom thinned to figures as insubstantial as the mist itself, still something of it lingered over: Old Joe's voice.

As I staggered there on the road, blinking and shaking my head to clear it, trying to focus on reality and forcing myself to stop shuddering, so that old man's voice – as thin as a cry from the dark side of the moon – got through to me:

"Get out of here!" he cried. "Go, hurry! He knows you now, and he won't wait. He'll follow you – in your head and in your dreams – until it's done!"

"Until what's done?" I managed to croak my question. But I was talking to nobody, to thin air.

Following which I almost fell into my car, reversed dangerously onto the crossover track and clipped the hedge, and drove away in a sweat as cold and damp as that non-existent mist. And all the way home I could feel those eyes burning on my neck; so much so that on more than one occasion I caught myself glancing in my rearview mirror, making sure there was no one in the back seat.

But for all that I saw no one there, still I wasn't absolutely sure . . .

Taking sleeping pills that night wasn't a good idea. But I felt I had to.

If I suffered another disturbed night, goodness knows what I would feel like – what my overburdened mind would conjure into being – the next day. But of course, the trouble with sleeping pills is they not only send you to sleep, they'll *keep* you that way! And when once again I was visited by evil dreams, struggle against them as I might and as I did, still I couldn't wake up!

It started with Old Joe again, the old tramp, a gentleman of the road. Speaking oh-so-earnestly, he made a sort of sense at first, which as quickly lapsed into the usual nonsense.

"Now listen to me," he said, just a voice in the darkness of my dream, the silence of the night. "I risked everything to leave my waiting place and come here with you. And I may never return, find my way back again, *except* with you. So it's a big chance I'm taking, but I had to. It's my redemption for what I have thought to do – and what I have almost done – more times than I care to admit. And so, because of what *he* is and what I know *he* will do, I've come to warn you this one last time. Now you must guard yourself against him, for you can expect him at any moment."

"Him?" I said, speaking to the unseen owner of the voice, which I knew as well as I knew my own. "The man on the tor?"

While I waited for an answer a mist crept into being and the darkness turned grey. In the mist I saw Old Joe's outline: a crumpled shape under a floppy hat. "It's his waiting place," he at last replied. "Either there or close by. But he's grown tired of waiting and now takes it upon himself. He risks Hell, but since he's already halfway there, it's a risk he'll take. If he wins it's the future – whatever that may be – and if he fails then it's the flames. He knows that, and of course he'll try to win . . . which would mean that you lose!"

"I don't understand," I answered, dimly aware that it was only a dream and I was lying in my bed as still and heavy as a statue. "What does he want with me? How can he harm me?"

And then the rambling:

"But you've *seen* him!" Old Joe barked. "You looked beyond, looked where you shouldn't and too hard. You saw me, so I knew you must see him, too. Indeed he *wanted* you to see him! Oh, you weren't looking for him but someone else – a loved one, who has long moved on – but you did it in *his place of waiting!* And as surely as your searching brought me up, it brought him up, too. Ah, but where I only wait, *he* is active! He'll wait no longer!"

Suddenly I knew that this was the very crux of everything that was happening to me, and so I asked: "But what is it that you're waiting for? And where is this . . . this waiting place?"

"But you've *seen* him!" the old tramp cried again. "How is it you see so much yet understand so little? I may not explain. It's a thing beyond your time and place. But just as there were times before, so there are times after. Men wait to be born and then – without ever seeming to realize it – they wait again, to die. But it's when and it's how! And after that, what then? The waiting, that's what."

"Gibberish!" I answered, shaking my head; and I managed an uncertain laugh, if only at myself.

"No, don't!" The other's alarm was clear in his voice. "If you deny me I can't stay. If you refute me, then I must go. Now listen: you know me – you've seen me – so continue to see me, but *only* me."

"You're a dream, a nightmare," I told him. "You're nothing but a phantom, come to ruin my sleep."

"No, no, *no!*" But his voice was fading, along with Old Joe himself.

But if only he hadn't sounded so desperate, so fearful, as he dwindled away: fearful for me! And if only the echoes of his cries hadn't lasted so long . . .

Old Joe was gone, but the mist stayed. And taking shape in its writhing tendrils I saw a very different presence – one that I knew as surely as I had known the old tramp. It was the watcher on the tor.

Thin as a rake, eyes burning like coals in a fire, he came closer and said, "My friend, you really shouldn't concern yourself with that old fool." His voice was the gurgle and slurp of gas bubbles bursting on a swamp, and a morbid smell – the smell of death – attended him. The way his black jacket hung loose on sloping shoulders, it could well have been that there were only bones beneath the cloth. And yet there was this strength in him, this feverish, hypnotic fascination.

"I . . . I don't want to know you," I told him then. "I want nothing to do with you."

"But you have everything to do with me," he answered, and his eyes glowed redder yet. "The old fool told you to avoid me, didn't he?"

"He said you were waiting for something," I answered. "For me, I suppose. But he didn't say why, or to what end."

"Then let me tell you." He drifted closer, his lank black hair floating on his shoulders, his thin face invisible behind the flaring of his eyes, those burning eyes that were fixed on mine. "I have a mystery to unfold, a story to tell, and I can't rest until I've told it. You are sympathetic, receptive, aware. And you came to my place of waiting. I didn't seek you out, you sought me. Or at least, you *found* me. And I think you will like my story."

"Then tell it and leave me be," I replied.

"You find me offensive," he said, his voice deeper and yet more dark, but at the same time sibilant as a snake's hiss. "So did she. But what she did, that was *truly* offensive! Yessss."

"You're making as much sense as Old Joe!" I told him. "But at least he kept his distance, and didn't smell of . . . of—"

"—Of the damp, the mould, and the rot?"

"Go away!" I shuddered, and felt that I was shrinking down smaller in my bed.

"Not until you've heard my story, and then I'll be glad to leave you . . . in peace?" With which he laughed an ugly laugh at the undefined question in his words.

"So get on with it," I answered. "Tell me your story and be done with it. For if that's all it takes to get rid of you, I'll gladly hear you out."

"Good!" he said, and moved closer yet. "Very good. But not here. I can't reveal it here. I want to show you how it wassss, where it wassss, and what happened there. I want you to see why I am what I am, why I did what I did, and why I'll do what I've yet to do. But not here."

"Where then?" I asked, but I'd already guessed the answer. "At your waiting place? Your place on the moor, the old tor?"

"In my place of waiting, yesss," he answered. "Not the old tor, but close, close." And then, changing the subject (perhaps because he thought he'd said too much?) "What is your name?"

I wanted to refuse, defy him, but his ghastly eyes dragged it out of me. "I'm Paul," I replied. "Paul Stanard." And then – as if this were some casual meeting of strangers in a street! – "And you?"

"Simon Carlisle," he answered at once, and continued: "But it's so very, *very* good to meet you, Mr Stanard." And again, as if savouring my name, drawing it out: "Paul Stanaaard, yessss!"

From somewhere in the back of my sub-subconscious mind, I remembered something. Something Old Joe had said to me: "If you deny me I can't stay. If you refute me, I must go." Would it be the same with Simon Carlisle, I wondered? And so:

"You are only a dream, a nightmare," I said. "You're nothing but a phantom, come to ruin my sleep."

But it didn't work! He moved closer – so close I felt the heat of his blazing eyes – and his jaw fell open in a gurgling, phlegmy laugh. Abruptly then he stopped laughing, and his breath was foul in my face. "You would work your wiles on me? On that old fool, perhapssss. But on me? Old Joe came with goodness in his heart, yessss. Ah, but which is the stronger: compassion, or ambition? The old tramp is content to wait, and so may be put aside – but not me! I shall wait no longer. You came to my place, and now I have come to yours. But I can't tell my story here, for I want you to see, and to know, and . . . and to feel."

"I won't come!" I shrank deeper into my bed and closed my eyes, which were already closed.

"You will!" *His* eyes floated down on me, into me. "Say it. Say that you will come to my place of waiting."

"I . . . I won't."

His eyes burned on mine, then passed through them, to burn inside my head. "Say you'll come."

I could resist him no longer. "I'll come," I mumbled.

"Say you *will* come. Say it again, and again, and again."

"I *will* come," I said. "I will come . . . I'll come . . . I'll come, come, come, come, come!" Until:

"Yessss," he sighed at last. "I know you will."

"I *will* come," I was still mumbling, when my bedside telephone woke me up. "I will most definitely . . . what?"

Then, like a run-down automaton, blinking and fumbling, I reached for the 'phone and held it to my ear. "Yes?"

It was Andrew Quarry. "I just thought I'd give ye a call," he said. "See how ye slept, and ask if ye'd be out at the auld tor again. But did I wake ye or somethin'?"

"Wake me? Yes, you woke me. Tumble Tor? Oh, yes – I *will* come – come, come, come."

And after a pause: "Paul, are ye all right? Ye sound verra odd, as if ye're only half there."

God help me, I *was* only half there! And the half that was there was in pretty bad shape. "Old Joe warned me off," I mumbled then. "But he's just an old tramp, an old fool. And anyway, Simon wants to tell me his story and show me something."

"Simon?" Quarry's voice was full of anxiety now. "And did I hear ye say Old Joe? But . . . Old Joe the tramp?"

"Old Joe," I nodded, at no one in particular. "And anyway, he says that I'm to take him back to his place of waiting. He's really not a bad old chap, so I don't want to let him down. And Andrew, I'm . . . I'm not at all well."

Another pause, longer, and when Quarry finally spoke again there was something more than concern in his voice. "Paul, will ye tell me where and when ye spoke to Old Joe? I mean, he's not there with ye this verra minute, is he?"

"He was last night," I nodded again. "And now I must go."

"Ontae the moor?"

"I *will* come," I said, putting the 'phone down and getting out of bed.

There was a mist in the house, in the car, on the roads, and in my mind. Not a really heavy mist, just some kind of atmospheric – and mental? – fogginess that had me squinting and blinking, but without completely obscuring my vision, during my drive out to Tumble Tor.

I had to go, of course, and all the way I kept telling myself: "I *will* come. I will, I will, I will . . ." While yet I knew that I didn't want to.

Old Joe went with me; he kept silent, but I knew he was in the car, relieved to be returning to his place of waiting. Perhaps he was reluctant to speak in the presence of my other less welcome passenger: the one with his cold fingers in my head. As for that one . . . it wasn't just that I could sense the corruption in him, I could smell it!

And in as little time as it takes to tell, or so it seemed to me, there we were where the dirt track crossed the road; and Tumble Tor standing off with its base wreathed in mist, and the knoll farther yet, a gaunt grey hump in the autumnal haze.

I, or rather we, got out of the car, and as Simon Carlisle led me unerringly out across the moor toward Tumble Tor, I knew that Old Joe fretted for me where we left him by the gap in the hedge. Knowing I was too far gone, beyond any sort of help that he could offer, the old tramp said nothing. For after all, what could he do to break this spell? He'd already done his best, to no avail. Half-turning to look back, I thought I saw him by the white-painted marker stone which he'd used as a seat that time. Like a figure carved from smoke, he stood wringing his hands as he watched me go.

But Simon Carlisle said, "Pay him no heed. This is none of his businessss. His situation – in a waiting place such as his – was always better than mine. He has had a great many chances, yessss. How long he is willing to wait is for him to determine. Myself, I am done with waiting."

"Where are you taking me?" I asked him.

"To the tor," he answered, "where else? I want to see just one more time. I want to fuel my passion, as once before it was fuelled. And I want *you* to see and understand. Do you have your glasssses?"

I did. Like him, I wore my binoculars round my neck. And I knew why. "We're going to climb?"

He nodded and said, "Oh yessss! For as you'll soon see for yourself, this vast misshapen rock makes a superb vantage point. It is the tower from which I spied on *them!*"

My soul trembled, but my feet didn't stop. They were numb; I couldn't feel them; it was as if I floated through the swirling ground mist impelled by some energy other than my own. But all I could think of was this: "I . . . I'm not a good climber."

"Oh?" he said without looking back, his clothing flapping like a scarecrow's in the wind, while his magnetism drew me on. "Well I am. So don't worry, Paul Stanaaard, for I won't let you fall. The old tor is a place, yessss, but it isn't the place of waiting. That comes later . . ."

We drifted across the moorland, and despite the shadows in my mind and the mist on the earth I found myself scanning ahead for rushes and sphagnum mosses, evidence of boggy ground. Why I worried about that when there was so much more to concern me, I didn't rightly know. But in any case I saw nothing, and soon we approached the foot of the tor.

Simon Carlisle knew exactly where he was going and what he was doing, and all I could do was follow in his footsteps . . . if he had had any. But we continued to float, and it was only when we began to climb that gravity returned and our progress slowed a little.

We climbed the knoll side of Tumble Tor, where I had first witnessed Carlisle scanning the land beyond. And as we ascended above the misty moor, so he instructed me to place my feet just so, making opportune use of this or that toe-hold, or to secure myself by gripping this or the other jutting knob of stone, and so on; and even a blind man could have seen that he knew Tumble Tor intimately and had gone this route many times before.

We passed carefully along narrow ledges with rounded rims, through stepped, vertical slots or chimneys where the going was easier, from level to striated level, always ascending from one fearful vertiginous position to the next. But Carlisle's advice – his sibilant instructions – were so clear, timely, and faultlessly delivered that I never once slipped or faltered. And at last we came to that high ledge behind its shoulder of rounded stone, where I'd seen and even tried to photograph Carlisle as he scoured the moorland around through his binoculars.

"Now then," he said, and his voice had changed; no longer sibilant, it grated as if uttered through clenched teeth. "Now we shall see what we shall see. Look over there, a quarter-mile or so, that hollow in the ground where it rises like the first in a series of small waves; that very private place surrounded by gorse and ferns. Do you see?"

At first I saw nothing, despite that the mist appeared to have lifted. But then, as if Carlisle had willed it into being, the tableau took shape, becoming clearer by the moment. In the spot he had described, I saw a couple . . . and indeed they were coupling! Their clothing was their bed where they lay together in each other's arms, naked. Their movements, at first languid, rapidly became more frenzied. I thought I heard their panting, but it wasn't them – it was Carlisle!

And then the climax – their shuddering bodies, the falling apart, gentle caresses, kisses, and whispered conversation – the passion quenched, for the moment at least. *Their* passion, yes . . . but not Carlisle's. His panting was that of a beast!

Finally he grew calm, and his voice was as before. "If we were to stay, to continue watching, you'd see them do it again and again, yessss. But my heart was herssss! And as for him . . . I thought he was my friend! I was betrayed, not once but often, frequently. She gave me back the ring which was my promise and told me her love could not be, not with me. Ah, but it *could* be with him! And as you've seen, it wassss!"

I didn't understand, not entirely. "She was your wife? But you said—"

"—I said she gave me back my ring – the *engagement* ring I bought for her. She broke her promissse!"

"She found someone she loved better or more than you."

"*What?*" He turned to me in a rage. "No, she was a slut and would have had anyone before me! She betrayed me – deserted me – gave him what she could never give me. She sent me my ring in a letter, said that she was *sssorry!* Well, I made them sssorry! Or so I thought. But now, in their place of waiting, still they have each other while I have nothing. And if they must wait for ever what does it matter to them? They don't wait in misery and solitude like meeeee! Even now they make love, and I am the one who sufferssss!"

"*Blind hatred! Insane jealousy!*" Now, I can't be sure that I said those words; it could be that I merely thought them. But in any case he "heard" my accusation. And:

"Be very careful, Mr Stanaaard!" Carlisle snarled. "What, do you think to test me? In a place such as this? In this dangerous place?" His red lamp eyes drew me from the stone shoulder until I leaned out over a gulf of air. For a moment I was sure I would fall, until he said,

"But no. Though I would doubtless take great pleasure in it, that would be a dreadful waste. For this is not my waiting place, and there's that which you still must see. So come." As easily as that, he drew me back . . .

We descended from Tumble Tor, but so terribly *quickly* that it was almost as if we slid or slithered down from the heights. As before I was guided by Carlisle's evil voice, until at last I stood on what should have been solid ground – except it felt as if I was still afloat, towed along in the wake of my dreadful host to the far side of the outcrop. But I made no inquiry with regard to our destination. This time I knew where we were going.

And off across the moor he strode or floated, myself close behind, moving in tandem, as if invisibly attached to him. Part of my mind acknowledged and accepted the ancient, mist-wreathed landscape: a real yet unreal place, as in a dream; that was the part in the grip of Simon Carlisle's influence. But the rest of me knew I should be fighting this thing, struggling against the mental miasma. Also, for the first time, I felt I knew for sure the evil I'd come up against, even though I couldn't yet fathom its interest in me.

"Ghosts," I heard myself say. "You're not real. Or you are – or you were – when you lived!"

Half-turning, he looked back at me. "So finally you know," he said. "And I ask myself: how is it possible that such a mind – as dull and unimaginative as yours – lives on corporeal and quick when one as sharp and as clear as mine is trapped in this place?"

"This place? Your place of waiting?"

"No, Mr Stanaaard." He pointed ahead. "Theirs! Mine lies on the other side of the tor, halfway to the bald knoll where first I saw you and you saw me. You'll know it when you see it: the mossesss, reedsss, and rushesss. But this place here: it's theirsss! It's where I killed them – where I've killed them a hundred times; ah, if only they could *feel* it! But no, they're satisfied with their lot and no longer fear me. We are on different levels, you see. Me riding my loathing, and them lost in their lust."

"Their love." I contradicted him.

He turned on me and a knife was in his hand; its blade was long and glittering sharp. "That word is *poison* to meeee! Maybe I should have let you fall. How I wish I could have!"

Logic, so long absent from my mind, my being, returned however briefly. "You can't hurt me. Not with a ghost knife."

"Fool!" He answered. "The knife is not for you. And as for your invulnerability: we shall see. But look, we are there."

Before us the place I had seen from Tumble Tor, the secret love nest surrounded by gorse and tall ferns; the lovers joined on their bed of layered clothing; Carlisle leaping ahead of me, his coat flapping, knife raised on high. The young man's broad back was his target; the young woman's half-shuttered eyes saw the madman as he fell upon them; the young man turned his head to look at his attacker – and amazingly, *he only smiled!*

The knife struck home, again and again. No blood, nothing. And Carlisle's crazed howling like a distant storm in my ears. Done with his rival, he turned his knife on the girl. Deep into her right eye went the blade, into her left eye, her throat and bare breasts. But she only shook her head and sadly smiled. And her eyes and throat and breasts were mist; likewise her lover's naked unmarked body: a drift of mist on the coarse empty grass.

"Ghosts!" I said again. "And this is their waiting place."

Carlisle's howling faded away, and panting like a mad dog he drifted to his feet and turned to me. "Did you see? And am I to be pitied? They pity me – for what they have and I haven't! And I can't *stand* to be here any longer. And you, Mr Stanaaard – you are my elevation, and perhaps my salvation. For whatever place it is that lies beyond, it *must* be better than this place. Now come, and I shall show you *my* place of waiting."

Danger! That part of me which knew how wrong this was also recognized the danger. Oh, I had known the precariousness of my position all along, but now the terror was tangible: this awful sensation of my soul shrinking inside me. I felt that I was now beyond hope. But before my fear could completely unman me, make me incapable of speech, there was something I must know. And so I asked the ghost, ghoul, creature who was leading me on, "What is . . . what *is* a place of waiting?"

"Ah, but that's a secret!" he answered, as we drew closer to Tumble Tor. "Secret from the living, that is, but something that is known to all the dead. They wouldn't tell you, not one of them, but since you will soon *be* one of them . . ."

"You intend to kill me?"

"Mr Stanaaard, you are as good as dead! And then I shall move on."

It began to make sense. "You . . . you're stuck in your so-called waiting place until someone else dies there."

"Ah, and so you're awake at last! The waiting places are the places where we died. And there we must wait until someone else dies in the same place, *in the same way!* To that treacherous dog and his bitch back there, it makes no difference. They have all they want. But to me . . . I was only able to do what I do, to watch as I did in life, to hate with a hatred that will never die, and to *wait*, of course. Then you came along, trying to look beyond life, searching for someone who had moved on – and finding me."

"I called you up," I said, faintly.

"And I was waiting, and I was ready. Yessss!"

"But how shall you kill me? I won't die of fright, not now that I know."

"Oh, you won't die by my insubstantial hand. But you will die of my doing, most definitely. Do you know that old saying, that you can lead a horse to water—"

"But you can't make him drink?"

"That's the one. Ah, but water is water and mire is mire."

"I don't understand," I said, though I was beginning to.

"You *will* understand," he promised me. "Ah, you will . . ."

Passing Tumble Tor, we started out across the low-lying ground toward the knoll. And in that region of my conscious mind which knew what was happening (while yet lacking even a small measure of control) I remembered something that Carlisle had said about his place of waiting:

"You'll know it when you see it: the mossesss, reedsss and rushesss."

"We're very nearly there, aren't we?" I said, more a statement of fact than a question. "The sphagnums and the rushes—"

"—And the mire, yessss!" he answered.

"The quagmire where you killed yourself, putting an end to your miserable life: that's your place of waiting."

"Killed myself?" He paused for a moment, stared at me with his blazing eyes. "Suicide? No, no – not I! Never! But after I killed *them* I was seen on the moor; a chance encounter, damn it to hell! And so I fled. I admit it: I fled the scene in a blind panic. But a mist came up – the selfsame mist you see now – and as surely as Satan had guided me to my deed, my revenge, so God or Fate led me astray, brought me shivering and stumbling here. Here where I sank in the mire and died, and here where I've had to wait . . . but no longer."

We were halfway to the knoll and the mist was waist deep. But still I knew the place. Andrew Quarry had pointed it out on the occasion of our first meeting: the sphagnums and the reeds, pointers to mud that would suck my shoes off. But it now seemed he'd been wrong about that last. Right to avoid it but wrong in his estimation, for it was much deeper than that and would do a lot more than just suck my shoes off.

And it was there, lured on in the ghostly wake of Carlisle – as I stumbled and flailed my arms in a futile attempt to keep my balance, managing one more floundering step forward and wondering why I was in trouble while he drifted upright and secure – it was there that what little remained of my logical, sensible self took flight, leaving me wholly mazed and mired in the misted, sucking quag.

Carlisle, this powerful ghost of a man, as solid to me now as any man of flesh and blood, stood and watched as it began to happen. His gaunt jaws agape, and his eyes burning red as coals in the heart of a fire, he laughed like a hound of hell. And as I threw myself flat on the mud to slow my sinking: "Murder!" he said, his voice as glutinous as the muck that quaked and sucked beneath me. "But what is that to me? You are my third, yes, but they can only hang a man once – and they can't hang me at all! So down you go, Paul Stanaaard, into the damp and the dark. And with your passing I, too, shall pass into whatever waits beyond . . . while you lie here."

It appeared I had retained at least a semblance of commonsense. Drawing my legs up and together against the downward tug of viscous filth, I threw my arms wide and my head back, making a crucifix of my body and limbs in order to further increase my buoyancy. Even so, the quag was already lapping the lobes of my ears, surging cold and slimy against my Adam's apple, and smelling in my nostrils of drowned creatures and rotting foliage; in which position desperation loaned voice to what little of logic remained:

"But where are you bound?" I asked him, aware of the creeping mud. "Do you know? Do any of you know? What if your waiting places are a test? What if someone – God, if you like – what if *He* is also waiting, to see what you'll do, or won't do? What if this was your last chance to redeem yourself, and you're throwing it away?"

"Do you think I haven't – we haven't – asked ourselves the very same questionsss?" he answered. "I have, a thousand times. But think on thisss: if the next place doesn't suit me, I shall move on again by whatever means available. And again, and again . . . alwaysss."

"Not if the next place is Hell!" I told him. "Which I very much hope it is!"

"Wrong!" he said, and burst out laughing. "For my Hell was here. And now it's yoursss!"

I strained against the suction of the mud. I tried to will myself to stay afloat, but the filthy stuff was lapping my chin and surging in my ears, and I could feel my feet sinking, going down slowly but surely into the mire. Weeds tangled my hair and slime crept at the corners of my mouth; immobilized by mud, all I could do was gaze petrified at Carlisle where he stood like a demon god on the surface of the quag, howling his crazed laughter from jaws that gaped in a red-glowing Hallowe'en skull, his lank limbs wreathed in mist and rotten cloth.

Muddy water was in my nostrils, trickling into my mouth. I felt the hideous suction and was unable to fight it. I was done for and I knew it. But I also knew of another world, more real than Simon Carlisle's place of waiting. The world of the quick, of the living, of hope that springs eternal. And at the last – even as I gagged at the ooze that was slopping into my mouth – I called for help, cried out until all I could do was choke and splutter.

And my cries were answered!

"Paul!" came a shout, a familiar voice, which in my terror I barely recognized. "Paul Stanard, is that ye down there? Man, what in the name of all that's—?"

"Help! Help!" I coughed and gurgled.

And Carlisle cried, "No! No! I won't be cheated! It can't end like this. Drink, drown, die, you bloody obstinate man! You are my one, my last chance. So die, *die*!"

He drifted toward me, got down beside me, tried to push at my face and drive my head down into the mud. But his hands were mist, his furious, burning face, too, and his cries were fading as he himself melted away, his fury turning to terror. "No, no, *noooo*!" And he was gone.

Gone, too, the mist, and where Carlisle's claw-like hands had sloughed into nothingness, stronger hands were reaching to fasten on my jacket, to lift my face from the slop, to draw my head and shoulders to safety out of—

—*Out of just six inches of muddy water!*

And Andrew Quarry was standing ankle deep in it, standing there with his Jennie, her raven hair shining in the corona of the sun that silhouetted her head. And nothing of that phantom mist to be seen, no sign of Carlisle, and no bog but this shallow pond of muddied rain-water lying on mainly solid ground

"Did you did you see him, or it?" I gasped, putting a shaking hand down into the water to push myself up and take the strain off Quarry's arms. But the bottom just there was soft as muck; my hand skidded, and again I floundered.

"Him? It?" Quarry shook his head, his eyes like saucers in his weathered face. "We saw nothin'. But what the hell *happened* to ye, man?" And again he tugged at me, holding me steady.

Still trembling, cold and soaking wet – scarcely daring to believe I had lived through it – I said. "It was him, Carlisle. He tried to kill me." As I spoke, so my fumbling hand found and grasped something solid in the muddy shallows: a rounded stone, it could only be.

But my thumb sank into a hole, and as I got to my knees I brought the "stone" with me. Stone? No, *a grinning skull*, and I knew it was him! All that it lacked was his maniac laughter and a red-burning glare in its empty black socket eyes . . .

At Quarry's place, while Jennie telephoned the police – to tell them of my "discovery" on Dartmoor – her father sat outside the bathroom door while I showered. By then the fog had lifted from my mind and I was as nearly normal as I had felt in what seemed like several ages. Normal in my mind, but tired, indeed exhausted in my body.

Andrew Quarry knew that, also knew why and what my problem had been. But he'd already cautioned me against saying too much in front of Jennie. "She would'nae understand, and I cannae say I'm that sure myself. But when ye told me ye'd been warned off, and by Old Joe . . ."

"Yes, I know." Nodding to myself, I turned off the shower, stepped out and began to towel myself dry. "But he's not real – I mean, no longer real – is he?"

"But he was until four years ago." Quarry's voice was full of awe. "He used tae call in here on his rounds – just the once a year – for a drink and a bite. And he would tell me where he had been, up and down the country. I liked him. But just there, where ye parked ye're car, that was where Old Joe's number came up. He must hae been like a wee rabbit, trapped in the beam of the headlights, in the frozen moments before that other car hit him. A tragic accident, aye." Then his voice darkened. "Ah, but as for that *other* . . ."

"Simon Carlisle?" Warm and almost dry, still I shivered.

"That one, aye," Quarry growled, from behind the bathroom door where it stood ajar. "I recognized his name as soon as ye mentioned it. It was eighteen years ago and all the newspapers were full of it. It was thought Carlisle had fled the country, for he was the chief suspect in a double moors murder. And—"

"I know all about it," I cut him off. "Carlisle, he . . . he told me, even showed me! And if you hadn't come along – if you hadn't been curious about my . . . my condition, my state of mind after what I'd said to you on the 'phone – he would have killed me, too. The only thing I don't, can't understand: how could he have drowned in just six inches of water?"

"Oh, I can tell ye that!" Quarry answered at once. "Eighteen years ago was a verra bad winter, followed by a bad spring. Folks had seen nothin' like it. Dartmoor was a swamp in parts, and *that* part was one of them. The rain, it was like a monsoon, erodin' many of the small hillocks intae landslides. Did ye no notice the steepness of that wee knoll, where all the soil had been washed down intae the depression? Six inches, ye say? Why, that low-lyin' ground was a veritable lake of mud . . . a marsh, a quag!"

Dressed in some of Quarry's old clothes, nodding my understanding, I went out and faced him. "So that's how it was."

"That's right. But what *I* dinnae understand: why would the damned creature – that dreadful man, ghost, thing – why would it want tae kill ye? What, even now? Still murderous, even as a revenant? But how could he hope tae benefit frae such a thing?"

At that, I very nearly told him a secret known only to the dead and now to me. But, since we weren't supposed to know, I simply shook my head and said nothing . . .

As for those pictures I'd snapped, of Simon Carlisle on Tumble Tor: when the film was developed there was only the bare rock, out of focus and all lopsided. None of which came as any great surprise to me.

And as for my lovely Jennie: well, I've never told her the whole thing. Andrew asked me not to, said there was a danger in people knowing such things. He's probably right. We should remember our departed loved ones, of course we should, but however painful the parting we should also let them go. That is, if and when they can go, and if they're in the right place of waiting.

Myself: well, I don't go out on the moor any more, because for one thing I know Old Joe is out there patiently waiting for an accident to set him free. That old tramp, yes, and lord only knows how many others, waiting in the hedgerows at misted crossroads on dark nights, and in remote, derelict houses where they died in their beds before there were telephones, ambulances and hospitals . . .

So then, now I sit in my garden, and as the setting sun begins to turn a few drifting clouds red, I rotate these things in my mind while watching the last handful of seagulls heading south for Brixham harbour. And I think at them: *ah, but you've missed out on a grand fish supper, you somewhat less than early birds. Your friends set out well over an hour ago!*

Then I smile to myself as I think: *well, maybe they heard me. Who knows, maybe that flying-ant telepathy of theirs works just as well with people!*

And I watch a jet airplane making clouds as it loses altitude, heading for Exeter Airport. Those ruler-straight trails, sometimes disappearing and sometimes blossoming, fluffing themselves out or pulling themselves apart, drifting on the aerial tides ... and waiting?

Small fluffs of cloud: revenant vapour trails waiting for the next jet airplane, perhaps, so that they too can evaporate? I no longer rule out anything.

But I'm very glad my mother died in hospital, not at home. And I *will* have the pool filled in. Either that or we're moving to a house without a pool, and one that's located a lot closer to the hospital.

And when I think of disasters like Pompei, or Titanic—

—Ah, but I mustn't, I simply mustn't ...

STEVE RASNIC TEM

2:00 pm: The Real Estate Agent Arrives

STEVE RASNIC TEM'S LATEST book is *The Man on the Ceiling* (Wizards Discoveries, 2008), written in collaboration with wife, Melanie Tem. It is a re-imagining/expansion of their award-winning novella. Centipede Press has recently published *In Concert*, a complete collection of their short collaborations.

Also in 2009, Speaking Volumes brought out *Invisible*, a six-CD audio collection of some of Tem's recent stories. He also has new stories upcoming in *Paradox, Interzone, Asimov*'s and numerous other publications.

IN THE BACKYARD, after the family moved away: blue chipped food bowl, worn-out dog collar, torn little boy shorts, Dinosaur T-shirt, rope, rusty can, child's mask lined with sand. In the corner the faint outline of a grave, dog leash lying like half a set of parentheses. Then you remember. The family had no pets.

STEPHEN JONES
& KIM NEWMAN

Necrology: 2008

ONCE AGAIN, THIS COLUMN marks the passing of writers, artists, performers and technicians who, during their lifetimes, made significant contributions to the horror, science fiction and fantasy genres (or left their mark on popular culture and music in other, often fascinating, ways) . . .

AUTHORS/ARTISTS/COMPOSERS

British historical novelist **George MacDonald Fraser** OBE, best known for his popular series of humorous *Flashman* novels (based on a minor character from *Tom Brown's School Days*), died of cancer on January 2, aged 82. As a screenwriter, Fraser contributed to the scripts for the James Bond film *Octopussy* and *Red Sonja*, loosely inspired by the work of Robert E. Howard.

British SF fan **Derek Pickles**, who edited the UK fanzine *Phantasmagoria* (1950–55), died on January 5, aged 79. *Phantasmagoria* contained John Brunner's first published work and was the first fanzine to be available for "the usual" (trade, a contribution, or a letter of comment), rather than by subscription.

Prolific mystery and SF writer and anthologist **Edward D.** (Dentinger) **Hoch** died of a heart attack on January 17, aged 77. Hoch published more than 900 short stories under a variety of pseudonyms for such magazines as *Famous Detective Stories*, *Fantastic Universe*, *Future Fiction*, *Alfred Hitchcock's Mystery Magazine* and, most notably, *Ellery Queen's Mystery Magazine* (he had a story in every issue since May 1973). He was the author of three 1970s SF detective novels about a pair of "Computer Cops", *The Transvection Machine*, *The Fellowship of the HAND* and *The Frankenstein Factory*, while his occult stories about 2,000-year-old Egyptian Coptic priest "Simon Ark" are collected in *City of Brass*, *The Judges of Hades* and *The Quests of Simon Ark*. In 2001 he was named a Grand Master by the Mystery Writers of America and received a Lifetime Achievement Award at BoucherCon.

Japanese *anime* scriptwriter **Jinzô Toriumi** died of hepatocellular carcinoma the same day, aged 78.

Physician Dr **Christine** [Elizabeth] **Haycock**, a member of First Fandom and the widow of editor and critic Sam Moskowitz (who died in 1997), died on January 23, aged 84.

American fan artist **Frank Hamilton** died of cancer on January 28, aged 89. His artwork first appeared in the early 1970s in Robert Weinberg's *PULP* magazine. Best known for his detailed depictions of such pulp characters as Doc Savage, The Shadow, The Spider, The Avenger, G-8 and many others, his artwork also appeared in the pages of *Mike Shayne's Mystery Magazine* and on the cover of his friend Michael Avallone's paperback novel *High Noon at Midnight*. With Link Hullar, Hamilton co-authored the 1989 study *Amazing Pulp Heroes: A Celebration of the Glorious Pulp Magazines*.

Iconic American movie poster artist **John Alvin** died of a heart attack on February 6, aged 59. Best known for his painting of the glowing finger for *E.T. – The Extraterrestrial* and the *Star Wars* 10th Anniversary designs, his more than 135 posters include *The Phantom of the Paradise*, *Young Frankenstein*, *Blade Runner*, *Cocoon* and *Cocoon The Return*, *Gremlins*, *Ernest Scared Stupid*, *Hook*, *Flatliners*, *Arachnophobia*, *Spaceballs*, *Star Trek IV The Undiscovered Country*, *The Golden Child*, *Legend*, *Darkman*, *Innerspace*, *Batman Returns*, *Innocent Blood*, *Pee Wee's Big Adventure*, *The Lost Boys* and *The Goonies*. Among his final work, Alvin contributed design ideas for the advertising campaign for Disney's *Enchanted*.

Comics writer **Steve** (Stephen Ross) **Gerber**, creator of "Howard the Duck" and "Lilith (Daughter of Dracula)", died of complications from pulmonary fibrosis on February 10, aged 60. He began working for Marvel Comics in 1972, where he wrote and edited such titles as *Sub-Mariner*, *Daredevil*, *Man-Thing* and *The Defenders*. Gerber then created *Howard the Duck* and *Omega the Unknown* before leaving Marvel in 1979 over a landmark ownership dispute. After working for DC Comics and Hanna-Barbera, he teamed up with artist Jack Kirby to create *Destroyer Duck* to raise money for their court cases against Marvel. He scripted episodes of TV's *Beauty and the Beast* and *Star Trek: The Next Generation*, and worked on various cartoon series, including *Thundarr the Barbarian*, *The Scooby and Scrappy-Doo Puppy Hour*, *Dungeons and Dragons*, *Transformers* and *The New Batman/Superman Adventures* (for which he won a Daytime Emmy Award). Gerber was diagnosed with lung disease in 2007 and was working on a revival of DC's *Doctor Fate* at the time of his death.

German SF, fantasy and horror author **Werner Kurt Giesa** was found dead at his home on February 14. He was 53. Giesa wrote for the *Perry Rhodan* and *Ren Dhark* SF series, the *Mythor* fantasy series and, under the pseudonym "Robert Lamont", took over the long-running bi-weekly *Professor Zamorra* horror-serial magazine.

British literary agent **Bob Tanner** died after a short illness the same day, aged 88. While Managing Director at New English Library in the 1970s he helped launch the careers of James Herbert and Stephen King. He subsequently formed the literary agency International Scripts, where his clients included Richard Laymon and Simon Clark.

SF scholar **Muriel R.** (Rogow) **Becker**, who wrote the study *Clifford D. Simak: A Primary and Secondary Bibliography* (1980), died on February 15, aged 83. In 2005, the Science Fiction Research Association (SFRA) presented her with a Clareson Award.

British fan and bookseller 90-year-old **Ken** (Kenneth Frederick) **Slater** died on February 16 after developing peritonitis. A major figure in British fandom since the late 1940s, and a founding member of the Science Fantasy Society (SFS), he founded fan group Operation Fantast which eventually became the mail-order service Fantast (Medway) Ltd. For decades, Slater was the major source for American books in the UK, and for many years he was the British agent for publisher Arkham House. He was given the Big Heart Award in 1995, and was Fan Guest of Honour at the 1959 Eastercon and Conspiracy, the 1987 World SF Convention.

Avant-garde French author and film-maker **Alain Robbe-Grillet** died of complications from heart problems on February 18, aged 85. One of the leading figures in the experimental "nouveau roman" literary movement of the 1950s, his offbeat novels include *Jealousy* and *La Belle Captive*. He scripted Alain Resnais' innovative 1961 movie *Last Year in Marienbad*, and was later inducted into the French Legion of Honour.

Joyce Carol Oates' husband **Raymond J. Smith** died of pneumonia the same day, aged 77. A former teacher, he was also editor of *The Ontario Review* (which he co-founded with his wife in 1974).

Peruvian author, playwright and journalist **José B.** (Bernardo) **Adolph** died of a stroke on February 21, aged 74. His short stories were collected in *El retorno de Aladino, Hasta que la muerte, Invisible para las fieras, Cuentos del relojero abominable, Mañana fuimos felices, La batalla del café, Une dulce horror* and *Diario del sótano*.

American SF writer **Milton S. Lesser**, who legally changed his name to **Stephen Marlowe** in the late 1950s and became a successful mystery and literary writer, died of a bone-marrow disorder on February 22, aged 79. Although best known for his globe-trotting private-eye character "Chester Drum" in a series of novels from Fawcett/Gold Medal (1955–68), his early stories regularly appeared in *Amazing, Fantastic* and *Science Fiction Quarterly* under a variety of pseudonyms. He once wrote all seven tales in a 1950 issue of *Amazing* under different bylines. He is also the author of the YA novels *Earthbound, The Star Seekers, Stadium Beyond the Stars* and *Spaceman, Go Home*. His other SF novels are *Recruit from Andromeda, Secret of the Black Planet* and *The Golden Ape* (with Paul W. Fairman), and he edited *Looking Forward: An Anthology of Science Fiction*. He scripted episodes of *Captain Video and His Video Rangers* and the CBS-TV anthology series *Out There*. As Marlowe, he published *The Lighthouse at the End of the World* (1995), a "fictional biography" of Edgar Allan Poe. While living in France, he reportedly appeared in two episodes of the 1980s TV series *The Tripods* as "M. Vichot".

American TV scriptwriter **Richard Baer** died of complications from a heart attack the same day, aged 79. After appearing (uncredited) in *Citizen Kane*, he went on to write scripts for such shows as *The Munsters, Bewitched* and *Turnabout*, along with the TV movie *Poor Devil* (starring Sammy Davis, Jr and Christopher Lee).

Former Tor Books managing editor **Robert** [Paul] **Legault** died of a massive coronary on February 22, aged 58. He also worked as a proofreader and copy-editor for numerous publishers.

British comics artist **Steve Whitaker**, who coloured the DC Comics version of *V for Vendetta*, died of a possible stroke the same day, aged 52. He co-wrote *The Encyclopedia of Cartooning Techniques: A Comprehensive Visual Guide to Traditional and Contemporary Techniques* (1993) with Steve Edgell.

British mystery and historical writer **Julian Rathbone** died after a long illness on February 28, aged 73. A distant relative of actor Basil Rathbone, he wrote more than forty books, including the dystopian SF novel *Trajectories*, and he had a story ("Fat Mary") in the anthology *Dark Terrors 3: The Gollancz Book of Horror*. Rathbone was twice nominated for the Booker Prize.

American SF writer Janet Kagan (Janet Megson), who won a Hugo Award in 1993 for her humorous novelette "The Nutcracker Coup", died of chronic obstructive pulmonary disease on February 29 after a long illness aged 63. She wrote the popular SF novels *Hellspark* and *Star Trek: Uhura's Song*, and six of her "Mama Jason" stories from *Asimov's* were collected in *Mirabile*.

Jane Blackstock, former rights director and publisher at British publishing imprint Gollancz, died of cancer on March 3, two days after her 61st birthday.

Fantasy author and games designer [Ernest] **Gary Gygax** died of an abdominal aortic aneurysm after a long illness on March 4, aged 69. He had suffered a series of strokes in 2004. In 1974, he co-created the first dice-based role-playing game, *Dungeons and Dragons*, with Dave Arneson, and co-founded publishing imprint TSR (Tactical Studies Rules) with Dan Kaye. Although the creators sold their rights in the game in the 1990s, D&D became the basis of a $1 billion worldwide industry of books, films and video games based on its mix of medieval and mythological concepts. As an author, Gygax wrote the fantasy novels *The Anubis Murders*, *The Samarkand Solution* and *Death in Delhi*, along with various titles in the "Greyhawk" and "Gord the Rogue" series.

Two-time Oscar-winning composer **Leonard Rosenman** died the same day, aged 83. In a career that began in 1955 with *East of Eden*, he wrote the scores to such films as *Fantastic Voyage*, *Countdown*, *Beneath the Planet of the Apes*, *The Todd Killings*, *Battle for the Planet of the Apes*, *The Cat Creature*, *The Phantom of Hollywood*, *Race with the Devil*, *The Possessed*, *The Car*, *The Lord of the Rings* (1978), *Prophecy*, *Star Trek IV: The Voyage Home* and *RoboCop 2*. Rosenman also contributed music to such TV series as *The Twilight Zone*, *The Alfred Hitchcock Hour*, *Holmes and Yo-Yo* and Steven Spielberg's *Amazing Stories*.

TV scriptwriter and producer **Richard DeRoy** died on March 8, aged 77. His many credits include episodes of *Shirley Temple's Storybook*, *The Twilight Zone*, *The Girl from U.N.C.L.E.* and *The Flying Nun*, plus the 1971 TV movie *A Howling in the Woods*.

American graphic artist **Dave Stevens**, who created pulp comic hero "The Rocketeer", died after a long battle with leukaemia on

March 10, aged 52. Stevens began his career inking Russ Manning's daily *Tarzan* newspaper strip in the mid-1970s. He also created covers for *Jonny Quest*, worked on the *Star Wars* newspaper strip and did animation art for Hanna-Barbera studios. Stevens joined illustrators William Stout and Richard Hescox in their Los Angeles art studio, and at one time he also shared offices with Steven Spielberg (who hired him to work on storyboards for *Raiders of the Lost Ark*). *The Rocketeer* was filmed by Walt Disney Pictures in 1991. A friend of former 1950s glamour model Bettie Page, he was married to actress Brinke Stevens from 1980–81.

One of the most influential and respected science fiction and popular science writers, Sir **Arthur C.** (Charles) **Clarke** died in a Sri Lankan (formerly Ceylon) hospital on March 19, aged 90. Best known as the co-creator of *2001: A Space Odyssey* (1968) with the director Stanley Kubrick, he was diagnosed with post-polio syndrome in 1988, which made it difficult for him to travel in later years. A winner of three Hugo Awards and three Nebula Awards, among his most notable books are *The Sands of Mars*, *Islands in the Sky*, *Against the Fall of Night*, *Childhood's End*, *The City and the Stars*, *Rendezvous with Rama*, *The Fountains of Paradise*, *2010: Odyssey Two*, *2061: Odyssey Three*, *The Ghost from Grand Banks*, *The Hammer of God* and *3001: The Final Odyssey*. In the 1980s he hosted the thirteen-part TV series *Arthur C. Clarke's Mysterious World*. Clarke is credited with creating the concept of communications satellites in 1945. He was named a SFWA Grand Master in 1986, nominated for a Nobel Prize in 1994, and knighted in 1999.

Belgian comics publisher **Raymond Leblanc**, who co-founded Editions du Lombard and launched the *Tintin* magazine in 1946, died on March 21, aged 92.

Chilean SF writer **Hugo Correa** died on March 23, aged 81. His novel *The Superior Ones* (*Los altísimos*) is considered a classic of Latin American SF.

Norma Vance (Norma Genvieve Ingold), the wife of SF author Jack Vance, died the same day, aged 80.

Comic book artist **Jim Mooney** (James Noel Mooney, aka "Jay Noel") died on March 30, aged 88. He began his long career as part of the Eisner & Iger art studios, briefly illustrating "The Moth" for Fox Publications' *Mystery Men Comics* in 1940. After working at Fiction House and Timely Comics, he started at DC Comics in 1946, ghost illustrating *Batman* for Bob Kane. He went on to draw such strips as "Tommy Tomorrow", "Superboy" and "Dial H for Hero". His best known work at DC was the "Supergirl" strip in *Action*

Comics, which ran from 1959 until 1968. Mooney then moved to Marvel, where he inked John Romita's *The Amazing Spider-Man* and *The Mighty Thor*, along with working on *Marvel Team-Up*, *Man-Thing* and *Omega the Unknown*. After moving to Florida in the mid-1970s, he illustrated Anne Rice's *The Mummy* for Millennium Publications and an *Elvira* comic for Claypool Comics.

Scriptwriter **Robert Warnes Leach**, who worked as a story editor and writer on the 1959–60 TV series *Men Into Space*, died the same day after a long illness. He was 93.

Irish-born SF author and scriptwriter **Johnny** (John Christopher) **Byrne** died in Norfolk, England, on April 3, aged 73. During the 1960s he published five stories in *Science-Fantasy* magazine before going on to write scripts for such TV series as *Space: 1999*, *Tales of the Unexpected* and *Doctor Who*. He also scripted the Turkish movie *Lionman II: The Witchqueen* and the gay comedy ghost film *To Die For*.

TV comedy scriptwriter **Seaman Jacobs**, who regularly worked with George Burns and Bob Hope, died of cardiac arrest on April 8, aged 96. He wrote for such shows as *My Favorite Martian*, *The Addams Family*, *I Dream of Jeannie*, *Sigmund and the Sea Monsters* and *Inch High Private Eye*, along with the movie *Oh, God! Book II*.

Ollie Johnston (Oliver Martin Johnston, Jr), the last surviving member of the "Nine Old Men" of Walt Disney animation, died on April 14, aged 95. He joined the fledgling Disney studio in 1935 and worked on *Snow White and the Seven Dwarfs*, *Pinocchio*, *Fantasia*, *Bambi*, *Song of the South*, *The Adventures of Ichabod and Mr Toad*, *Cinderella*, *Alice in Wonderland*, *Lady and the Tramp*, *Sleeping Beauty*, *One Hundred and One Dalmations*, *The Sword in the Stone*, *Mary Poppins*, *The Jungle Book*, *Winnie the Pooh and the Blustery Day*, *The AristoCats*, *Robin Hood*, *Winnie the Pooh and Tigger Too*, *The Rescuers* and *The Fox and the Hound*. Although he officially retired from Disney in 1978, Johnston continued to work as a teacher, author and consultant, and he was the first animator to receive the National Medal of Arts at a White House ceremony in 2005. With his colleague, Frank Thomas, he wrote the books *Disney Animation: The Illustration of Life*, *Too Funny for Words*, *Bambi: The Story and the Film* and *The Disney Villain*, and both of them can be heard in *The Iron Giant* and *The Incredibles*.

American photo-artist **James** [Allen] **Bearcloud** (aka "Jim Thomas"), whose work appeared on the cover of *Cinefantastique* and inside such magazines as *Amazing Stories* and *Asimov's*, died after a long illness on April 15, aged 58.

American fan and author **Margaret J. Howes**, a member of the Rivendell Group of the Mythopoeic Society since its inception in the early 1970s, died the same day, aged 80. Her stories appeared in *The Tolkien Scrapbook*, she was one of five writers who contributed to the collaborative novel *Autumn World*, and her SF novel *The Wrong World* was published in 2000.

British author **Michael de Larrabeiti** died of cancer on April 18, aged 73. The author of the acclaimed YA dark fantasy trilogy, *The Borribles* (1976), *The Borribles Go for Broke* and *The Borribles: Across the Dark Metropolis*, his 1989 collection *Provençal Tales* was a retelling of historical French fables and folk stories.

American TV scriptwriter, producer and showrunner **Larry** (Lawrence) **Hertzog** died of cancer on April 19, aged 56. His credits include *SeaQuest DSV*, *Nowhere Man*, and *Painkiller Jane*. He also scripted the TV pilot movie *Tin Men* and came up with the original story for *Darkman II: The Return of Durant*. Hertzog wrote his own (amusing) biography on IMDb.

Pioneering electronic music composer **Bebe Barron** [Charlotte May Wind], who created the electronic tonalities for the 1956 movie *Forbidden Planet* with her first husband Louis, died on April 20, aged 82. Her music was also used (uncredited) in *Doomsday Machine* (aka *Escape from Planet Earth*).

British-born electronic music composer **Tristram Cary**, who worked on a number of *Doctor Who* episodes in the mid-1960s, died in Adelaide, Australia, on April 24, aged 82. Instrumental in the invention of the synthesizer, his other music credits include Hammer's *Quatermass and the Pit* and *Blood from the Mummy's Tomb*, along with the BBC-TV show *Late Night Horror* and Richard Williams' animated TV version of *A Christmas Carol* (1971).

British TV scriptwriter and novelist **Donald James** [Wheal] died on April 28, aged 76. His credits include episodes of *The Avengers*, *The Saint*, *The Champions*, *Joe 90*, *Department S*, *The Secret Service*, *Randall and Hopkirk (Deceased)*, *UFO*, *Jason King* and *Space: 1999*, and he also co-scripted the movie *Doppelgänger* (aka *Journey to the Far Side of the Sun*).

American illustrator **John Berkey** died after a long illness on April 29, aged 75. A prolific freelance artist, he created more than 3,000 commissioned paintings, including work for most the major SF publishers, pre-production artwork for *Star Wars* and publicity material for *The Neptune Factor*, *The Towering Inferno*, *Star Trek*, the 1976 remake of *King Kong* and numerous other movies. Some of his work is collected in *John Berkey: Painted Space* and *The Art of John Berkey*.

Danton Burroughs, the grandson of Edgar Rice Burroughs and son of illustrator John Coleman Burroughs, died of a heart attack in the California suburb of Tarzana on April 30, aged 64. He suffered from Parkinson's disease. Danton Burroughs was chairman of the board of Edgar Rice Burroughs, Inc. and publisher of the weekly online fanzine *ERBzine*. On the morning of his death, a fire destroyed much of his historical archive of papers and photographs.

Emmy Award-winning American composer and photographer **Alexander Courage** [Alexander Mair Courage, Jr] died on May 15, aged 88. He had been in declining health since 2005. Not only did he compose the memorable USS Enterprise theme for the original *Star Trek* TV series (reprised in *Star Trek: The Next Generation* and the movies), but also the score for *Superman IV: The Quest for Peace* and episodes of *Voyage to the Bottom of the Sea*, *Lost in Space* and *Land of the Giants*. As an orchestrator, Courage also worked on many classic 1950s musicals, plus *Doctor Dolittle* (1967), *The Poseidon Adventure* (1972), *The Island of Dr Moreau* (1977), *Baby – Secret of the Lost Legend*, *Legend*, *Gremlins 2 The New Batch*, *Hook*, *Basic Instinct*, *Mom and Dad Save the World*, *Matinee*, *Jurassic Park*, *The Shadow*, *Powder*, *Deep Rising*, *Small Soldiers*, *The Mummy* (1999), *The 13th Warrior*, *The Haunting* (1999) and *Hollow Man*.

Mad magazine artist **Will Elder** died the same day from Parkinson's disease, aged 86.

Rory D. Root, the co-founder and long-time sole proprietor of Comic Relief: The Comic Bookstore in Berkley, California, died of complications from hernia surgery on May 19, aged 50.

Humorous fantasy and SF writer **Robert** [Lynn] **Asprin** died on May 22, aged 61. His early SF novels included *The Cold Cash War*, *Cold Cash Warrior*, *The Bug Wars* and *Tambu*, but it was with *Another Fine Myth . . .* (1978) that his career took off. It led to a series of nearly twenty books, many co-written with Jody Lynn Nye. He also wrote the humorous "Phule" series (mostly in collaboration with Peter J. Heck), starting with *Phule's Company* in 1990, and the "Time Scout" series (with Linda Evans), beginning with *Time Scout* in 1995. Other collaborations include *Catwoman* and *Catwoman: Tiger Hunt* (with Lynn Abbey), *License Invoked* (with Jody Lynn Nye), *For King and Country* (with Linda Evans), *E. Godz* (with Esther M. Friesner) and *Resurrection* and *Oblivion* (with Eric del Carlo). His solo 2008 novel *Dragons Wild* was followed by *Dra-*

gon's Luck. Asprin also created the *Thieves World* shared universe, co-editing a dozen anthologies from 1979–89 with his then-wife Lynn Abbey.

Emmy Award-winning American TV composer and orchestrator **Earle H.** (Harry) **Hagen** died after a long illness on May 26, aged 88. He composed the theme for *I Spy*, as well as music for the *Planet of the Apes* TV series.

Graphic artist **Alton Kelley** died after a long illness on June 1, aged 67. During the 1960s he designed iconic psychedelic rock posters of Jimi Hendrix, the Grateful Dead, Country Joe and the Fish and others.

British film historian and collector **John** [Stuart Lloyd] **Barnes** died the same day, aged 87. He wrote the five-volume study *The Beginnings of the Cinema in England, 1894–1901*.

Pulp magazine fan **Edward S. Kessell** died on June 4. A teacher and theatrical director, he ran the dealers' room at the 1969 World Science Fiction Convention in St Louis and in 1972 co-founded the first Pulpcon in the same city.

Role-playing game designer and co-founder of gaming publisher Palladium Books, **Erick Wujcik** died of pancreatic cancer on June 7, aged 57. Among the RPGs he created was the *Amber Diceless Roleplaying Game* based on Roger Zelazny's universe.

Respected German-born Lithuanian SF author, editor, reviewer and teacher **Algis Budrys** (Algirdas Jonas Budrys, aka "AJ") died in Illinois of metastatic malignant melanoma on June 9, aged 77. Although he only wrote a small number of novels (several Hugo-nominated), including *False Night* (aka *Some Will Not Die*), *Man of Earth*, *Who?* (filmed in 1974), *The Falling Torch*, *Rogue Moon* (aka *The Death Machine*), *The Amsirs and the Iron Thorn* (aka *The Iron Thorne*), *Michaelmas* and *Hard Landing*, his short fiction appeared (often under various pseudonyms) in *Astounding*, *Galaxy*, *The Magazine of Fantasy & Science Fiction*, *Amazing*, *Analog*, *The Saturday Evening Post* and *Playboy*, and was collected in *The Unexpected Dimension, Budrys' Inferno* (aka *The Furious Future*), *Blood and Burning*, and *Entertainment*. Budrys worked in various editorial capacities for Gnome Press, *Science Fiction Adventures*, *Ellery Queen's Mystery Magazine*, *Galaxy*, *The Magazine of Fantasy & Science Fiction* and L. Ron Hubbard's Writers of the Future Awards (1984–92), editing a number of the *Writers of the Future* anthologies. He was Guest of Honor at the 1997 World Science Fiction Convention in Texas.

Bulgaria's most famous SF writer, **Lyuben Dilov**, died on June 10, aged 80. His more than thirty-five books include *The Atomic Man*, *The Many Names of Fear*, *The Way of Icarus*, *Cruel Experiment* and the collections *My Strange Friend the Astronomer* and *To Feed the Eagle*.

Sixty-one-year-old American horror writer **James** [Martin] **Kisner** died on June 26 from carbon monoxide poisoning probably caused by a faulty power generator. His wife Phyllis also died. Between 1981–94, Kisner wrote eleven novels for such imprints as Leisure, Pinnacle and Zebra: *Nero's Vice*, *Slice of Life*, *Strands*, *Night Glow*, *Zombie House*, *Poison Pen*, *Earthblood*, *The Quagmire*, *The Forever Children* and *Night Blood* (both published under the pen-name "Eric Flanders"), and *Tower of Evil*. His short fiction appeared in the anthologies *Masques II* and *III*, *Scare Care*, *Urban Horrors*, *Hotter Blood: More Tales of Erotic Horror*, *Predators*, *Vampire Detectives* and *Vampire Slayers: Stories of Those Who Dare to Take Back the Night*.

American comics artist **Michael Turner**, who co-created *Witchblade* for Top Cow Productions, died of complications from bone cancer on June 27, aged 37. He created the covers for such titles as DC Comic's *Superman/Batman*, *The Flash* and *Justice League*, along with *Civil War* and the special 500th issue of *Uncanny X-Men* for Marvel. He also produced online comics for the NBC-TV series *Heroes* and published his own titles, including the bestselling *Fathom*, under the Aspen MLT imprint.

Fan historian **Jack** [Bristol] **Speer**, a member of First Fandom, died on June 28, aged 87. He published the first history of fandom, *Up to Now*, in 1939, and his original dictionary of fan speech, *Fancyclopedia*, appeared in 1944. A book of essays, *Fancestral Voices*, was published in conjunction with his appearance as Fan Guest of Honor at the 2004 World Science Fiction Convention in Boston. Speer is credited by some with inspiring masquerade fandom at the 1940 Worldcon in Chicago, and he was the last surviving member of the Fantasy Amateur Press Association (FAPA).

Estonian-born German editor and collector **Kalju Kirde** (Kalju Frisch) died of Alzheimer's disease and kidney problems on June 29, aged 79. From 1969–79 he edited the influential "Bibliothek des Hauses Usher" series for publishers Insel, which introduced works by H. P. Lovecraft, Clark Ashton Smith, William Hope Hodgson, Arthur Machen, Algernon Blackwood and H. R. Wakefield to German readers. He also edited the anthologies *Das unsichtbare Auge* and *In Laurins Blick*.

Miniaturist, publisher, poet and author **William Buchan**, the 3rd

Baron Tweedsmuir and second son of *The Thirty-Nine Steps* author John Buchan, died the same day, aged 92. Schooled at Eton, where he shared newspaper-reading breakfasts with provost M. R. James, he later worked as an assistant to Alfred Hitchcock and had an affair with actress Peggy Ashcroft. His short fiction was collected in *The Exclusives* (1943) and from 1951–54 he was the London editor of *Reader's Digest*.

Television composer and arranger **David Kahn**, whose best-known work included the themes for *Leave it to Beaver* and *Alfred Hitchcock Presents*, died on July 3, aged 98. After singing and touring with the big band leaders of the 1930s, Kahn ended up at Filmways Television, where he created incidental music for such shows as *Mr Ed* and *The Beverly Hillbillies*. With composer Vic Mizzy he also sang on the theme song for *The Addams Family*.

Acclaimed and often controversial SF and horror writer, poet, editor, playwright and critic **Thomas M.** (Michael) **Disch** died in his New York apartment from a self-inflicted gunshot wound on July 3 or 4. He was 68. One of the most important American SF writers from the "New Wave", his novels include *The Genocides* (1965), *Mankind Under the Leash* (aka *The Puppies of Terra*), *Echo Round His Bones*, *Camp Concentration*, *334*, *On Wings of Song*, *The Businessman: A Tale of Terror*, *The MD: A Horror Story*, *The Priest: A Gothic Romance*, *The Sub: A Study in Witchcraft* and *The Word of God: or, Holy Writ Rewritten*. He collaborated twice with John Sladek, on the novels *The House That Fear Built* (as "Cassandra Kaye") and *Black Alice* (as "Thom Demijohn"), while the Gothic *Clara Reeve* was published under the pseudonym "Leonie Hargrave". Disch's short fiction is collected in *One Hundred and Two H-Bombs and Other Funny SF Stories*, *Under Compulsion* (aka *Fun with Your New Head*), *Getting Into Death*, *The Fundamental Disch*, *The Man Who Had No Idea* and *The Wall of America*. His satirical SF fable "The Brave Little Toaster" was filmed without irony in 1987 by Walt Disney, and he reportedly worked on an early treatment of *The Lion King* for the studio. He also wrote the tie-in books for TV's *The Prisoner* and the movie *Alfred the Great* (as "Victor Hastings"). Disch won the O. Henry Prize in 1975 and 1977, and was involved in founding the Philip K. Dick Award.

Golden Age comics artist **Creig** [Valentine] **Flessel**, who illustrated the original *Sandman* from 1939 onward, died July 17, aged 96. He had suffered a stroke six days earlier. Flessel also contributed work to *More Fun Comics*, the pre-Batman *Detective Comics*, and *Superboy*, and he created the character "Shining Knight" for *Adventure Comics*.

Harriet Burns, who in 1955 was the first woman hired by Walt Disney in a creative capacity, died on July 25, aged 79. She helped design and build prototypes for the Disneyland attractions The Haunted Mansion, Pirates of the Caribbean, the Enchanted Tiki Room and Sleeping Beauty's Castle. She was named a Disney Legend in 2000.

Young adult fantasy writer **Donald** [Bruce] **Callander** died of complications from diabetes on July 26, aged 78. A former travel writer and photographer, his first novel, *Pyromancer*, was published in 1992. He followed it with *Aquamancer*, *Geomancer*, *Aeromancer* and *Mableheart*. His other books include *Dragon Companion* and its sequels, *Dragon Rescue* and *Dragon Tempest*, *Warlock's Bar and Grill* and the posthumously published *Teddybear Teddybear*.

American scriptwriter **Luther** [Berryhill] **Davis**, who won two Tony Awards for co-writing the book of the 1953 Broadway musical *Kismit*, died on July 29, aged 91. He scripted *Lady in a Cage* (which he also produced) and the TV movies *Arsenic and Old Lace* (1969) and *Daughter of the Mind*.

British children's illustrator **Pauline Baynes**, best known for her illustrations for C. S. Lewis' "Chronicles of Narnia" series, died August 1, aged 85. In 1948, J. R. R. Tolkien asked her to illustrate *Farmer Giles of Ham*, and she went on to illustrate Tolkien's *The Adventures of Tom Bombadil*, *Tree and Leaf*, *Smith and Wootton Major* and *Bilbo's Last Song*. She began illustrating Lewis' "Narnia" chronicles with *The Lion, the Witch and the Wardrobe* in 1950, and other books she illustrated included a 1957 edition of *The Arabian Nights*, *The Puffin Book of Nursery Rhymes*, *Spider and Snail*, *The Enchanted Horse*, *The Story of Daniel*, and *A Book of Narnians*. A winner of the Kate Greenaway Medal in 1968 for her work on Grant Uden's *A Dictionary of Chivalry*, Baynes also wrote and illustrated a number of her own children's books.

American SF writer and teacher **George W.** (Wyatt) **Proctor** died after a sudden illness on August 3 while on vacation in Florida. He was 61. The author of such novels as *The Esper Transfer*, *Shadowmen*, *Fire at the Center*, *Starwings*, *Stellar Fist* and the nine-volume "Swords of Raemllyn" series (with Robert E. Vardeman), Proctor also co-edited the anthologies *Lone Star Universe: The First Anthology of Texas Science Fiction Authors* (with Steven Utley) and *The Science Fiction Hall of Fame Vol III: Nebula Winners 1965–1969* (with Arthur C. Clarke). As an author of Westerns, he wrote under the pen-names "Zach Wyatt", "Clay Tanner" and "John Cleve" (with Andrew J. Offut).

Famed EC Comics artist **Jack Kamen** died of cancer on August 5, aged 88. After World War II interrupted his career as a pulp magazine artist, he joined EC, drawing for the line's horror, crime, suspense, SF, humour and even romance titles, where he was renowned for his depictions of attractive women. He later worked in advertising, and illustrated the EC-inspired poster for the 1982 George A. Romero/Stephen King movie *Creepshow*.

Fifty-nine-year-old **Robert Hazard** (Robert Rimato), who wrote the 1983 Cyndi Lauper hit "Girls Just Wanna Have Fun" and toured in the 1980s with his band Robert Hazard and the Heroes, died the same day, following surgery.

Michael Silberkleit, chairman of Archie Comic Publications, died of cancer on August 5, aged 76.

Former editor-in-chief of publisher Farrar, Straus & Giroux, **Robert Giroux**, died on September 5, aged 94.

Star Trek fan **Joan Winston**, who organized the very first *Star Trek* convention in January 1972, died of complications from Alzheimer's disease on September 11, aged 77. She also edited the *Star Trek* fanzine *Number One*, co-wrote *Star Trek Lives* (with Jacqueline Lichtenberg and Sondra Marshak) and was the author of *The Making of the Trek Conventions*.

Acclaimed American author and journalist **David Foster Wallace**, once described as "the voice of Generation X", hanged himself on September 12. He was 46 and had been suffering from depression for many years. Wallace published two novels, *The Broom of the System* and *Infinite Jest*, the latter set in the near future and revolving around a short film that had the power to debilitate its viewers. The book ran to 1,079 pages and had more than 100 pages of footnotes. His short fiction was collected in *Girl with Curious Hair*, *Brief Interviews with Hideous Men* and *Oblivion: Stories*.

Award-winning Motown songwriter and producer **Norman** [Jesse] **Whitfield** died of complications from diabetes on September 16, aged 67. He composed such songs as "I Heard it Through the Grapevine" for Gladys Knight & The Pips, "Too Busy Thinking About My Baby" for Marvin Gaye and "Papa Was a Rolling Stone" for The Temptations.

Editor and author **Brian M.** (Michael) **Thomsen** died of a heart attack on September 21, aged 49. A founding editor at Warner Books/Questar in the 1980s, he went on to work for role-playing imprint TSR and later became a consulting editor at Tor Books. He had around thirty stories published in various anthologies, and was the author of the "Forgotten Realms" tie-in novels *Once Around the Realms* and *The Mage in the Iron Mask*. As an editor, Thomsen's own anthologies included *Halflings Hobbits Warrows and Weefolk* (with Baird Seales), *Furry Fantastic* (with Jean Rabe), *Masters of Fantasy* (with Bill Fawcett), *Novel Ideas: Fantasy*, *Novel Ideas: Science Fiction* and the World Fantasy Award-nominated *The American Fantasy Tradition*. He also helped veteran editor Julius Schwartz to write his 2000 autobiography *Man of Two Worlds: My Life in Science Fiction and Comics*.

American SF author **James P.** (Peter) **Killus** died of a rare form of cancer on September 23, aged 58. He published two SF novels, *Book of Shadows* and *Sunsmoke*, and his short stories appeared in *Twilight Zone Magazine*, *Realms of Fantasy*, *Asomov's* and other magazines.

TV scriptwriter **Oliver** [Kaufman] **Crawford** died of complications from pneumonia on September 24, aged 91. Blacklisted during the Communist witch-hunts of the 1950s, his career successfully recovered and his credits include episodes of *Terry and the Pirates*, *The Outer Limits*, *Tarzan*, *Voyage to the Bottom of the Sea*, *Star Trek*, *The Wild Wild West*, *Land of the Giants* and *The Bionic Woman*.

British historical novelist **Peter Vansittart** OBE died on October 4, aged 88. His first of more than forty books was the SF novel, *I Am the World* (1942), and he also wrote the children's collections of folk stories, *The Dark Tower* and *The Shadow Land*.

Janet Pollock (Janet Machen), the only daughter of author Arthur Machen and patron of The Friends of Arthur Machen society, died on October 10, aged 91. A former actress in Sir Donald Wolfitt's company, she later became a social worker and spirited promoter of her late father's work.

American big band trumpeter and jazz musician, composer and arranger **Neal** [Paul] **Hefti** died on October 11, aged 85. He won a Grammy Award in 1966 for his campy theme to the *Batman* TV show, and he also composed the music for the movies *How to Murder Your Wife*, *Harlow*, *Lord Love a Duck*, *Oh Dad Poor Dad Mama's Hung You in the Closet and I'm Feeling So Sad*, *Barefoot in the Park*, *The Odd Couple*, the TV film *Conspiracy of Terror* and *Won Ton Ton the Dog Who Saved Hollywood*.

Chicago artist-photographer **Harry E. Fassl** died on October 12 from complications related to a flu-like illness. He was 56. Fassel's disturbing photo-art appeared on the covers of *Deathrealm* and

Grue magazines plus various titles published by Chaosium Press, including the anthology *Song of Cthulhu*.

American TV soap opera writer and consulting producer **James E. Reilly**, who created NBC's supernatural serial *Passions* (1999–2008), died while recovering from cardiac surgery the same day, aged 60.

British SF writer **Barrington J.** (John) **Bayley** died of complications from bowel cancer on October 13, aged 71. He began his writing career in 1954 in *Vargo Statten Science Fiction Magazine*, and was later a regular contributor to his close friend Michael Moorcock's *New Worlds*, *Science Fantasy*, *Science Fiction Adventures* and *Interzone*. Bayley's novels include *The Star Virus* (an Ace Double), *Annihilation Factor*, *Empire of Two Worlds*, *Collision with Chronos* (aka *Collision Course*), *Chronopolis* (aka *The Fall of Chronopolis*), *The Soul of the Robot*, *The Garments of Caean*, *The Grand Wheel*, *Star Winds*, *The Pillars of Eternity*, *The Zen Gun*, *The Forest of Peldain*, *The Rod of Light*, *Eye of Terror*, *The Sinners of Erspia* and *The Great Hydration*. His short fiction is collected in *The Knights of the Limits*, *The Seed of Evil* and *Gnostic Endings*.

Sixty-five-year-old British screenwriter **Christopher Wicking** died of a heart attack in Toulouse, France, the same day. During the late 1960s and early '70s he worked on a number of scripts for AIP and Hammer, including *The Oblong Box*, *Scream and Scream Again*, *Cry of the Banshee*, *Murders in the Rue Morgue*, *Blood from the Mummy's Tomb*, *Demons of the Mind* and *To the Devil a Daughter*. His other credits include *Venom* (aka *The Legend of Spider Forest*), *Medusa*, *Dream Demon* and *Lady Chatterley's Lover* (1981). In 1978, Wicking co-wrote the groundbreaking study *The American Vein – Directors and Directions in Television* with Tise Vahimagi.

German co-authors and married couple **Johanna Braun** and **Günter Braun** died on October 24 and November 10, aged 79 and 80 respectively. Among the leading SF writers in the former German Democratic Republic, their often satirical and humorous books include *The Great Magician's Error* (1972), *Uncanny Phenomena on Omega XI*, *The Spheric Transcendental Project*, *The Inaudible Sounds* and *The Hero X-Time Multiplied*. Their short fiction is collected in *The Mistake Factor* and *A Journal from the Third Millennium Found in the Future*.

Edgar Award-winning American novelist **Tony Hillerman** (Anthony Grove Hillerman) died of pulmonary failure on October 26, aged 83. His series of eighteen books featuring Navajo Tribal Police Lieutenant Joe Leaphorn and Sergeant Jim Chee, which include *The*

Ghostway, *Skinwalkers*, *Coyote Waits* and *The Shape Shifter*, often dealt with reports of witchcraft and other apparently supernatural events.

British scriptwriter and sometimes actor **Chris Bryant** [Christopher Bryan Spencer Dobson], who co-wrote Nicolas Roeg's *Don't Look Now*, died on October 27, aged 72. His other credits include the 1975 version of *The Spiral Staircase* and *The Awakening*, the latter based on *The Jewel of Seven Stars* by Bram Stoker.

German composer and arranger **Erwin Halletz** died in Vienna the same day, aged 85. His credits include *Liane Jungle Godness* and its sequel *Jungle Girl and the Slaver*, *Lana Queen of the Amazons*, the "Perry Rhodan" SF movie *Operation Stardust*, *Teenage Sex Report*, *Shocking Asia* and *Shocking Asia II: The Last Taboos*.

Bestselling author, film director, producer and screenwriter [John] **Michael Crichton** (aka "John Lange" and "Jeffery Hudson") died of cancer on November 4, aged 66. The six-feet, seven-inch doctor-turned-novelist wrote such popular SF titles as *The Andromeda Strain*, *The Terminal Man*, *Eaters of the Dead*, *Congo*, *Sphere*, *Timeline*, *Jurassic Park* and its sequel *The Lost World: Jurassic Park* (all filmed), and had more than 100 million copies of his books in print. His other titles include *Prey*, *Next* and *State of Fear*. He directed the TV movie *Pursuit* (based on one of his early pseudonymous novels), *Westworld*, *Coma*, *Looker* and *Runaway*, and co-scripted Steven Spielberg's movie of *Jurassic Park* and the disaster thriller *Twister*. He also created the popular NBC-TV medical show *ER*, and the shortlived SF series *Beyond Westworld*. Crichton was part of the team that won a 1995 technical achievement Oscar for developing a computerized movie budgeting system. A year earlier, he became the only creative artist in America to have the #1 novel, movie and TV series at the same time.

English-born fantasy writer **Hugh** [Walter Gilbert] **Cook** died in Japan after a long battle with non-Hodgkin's lymphoma on November 8. He was 52. Starting with *The Wizard and the Warriors* (aka *Wizard War*) in 1986, he published ten humorous novels in the "Chronicles of an Age of Darkness" (aka "Wizard War Chronicles") series. Cook's other books include *Plague Summer*, *The Shift*, *Bamboo Horses* and *To Find and Wake the Dreamer*. Some of his more than 100 short stories are collected in *This is a Picture of Your God: A Hugh Cook Reader* and *The Succubus and Other Stories*.

American screenwriter **Arthur A. Ross**, who co-scripted *Creature from the Black Lagoon*, died on November 11. His other credits include *The Creature Walks Amongst Us*, *The 30 Foot Bride of Candy Rock*, *The 3 Worlds of Gulliver*, the TV movie *Satan's School for Girls* (as "A. A. Ross") and eight episodes of NBC-TV's *The Alfred Hitchcock Hour*.

Italian screenwriter, director and producer **Marcello Fondato** died on November 13, aged 84. He came up with the original story for the 1959 comedy *Uncle Was a Vampire* (starring Christopher Lee), and scripted Mario Bava's *Black Sabbath* (starring Boris Karloff) and *Blood and Black Lace*. Fondato also wrote and produced the 1979 SF comedy *The Sheriff and the Satellite Kid* and scripted *Aladdin* (1986), both starring Bud Spencer.

Prolific American composer, arranger and musician **Irving Gertz** died on November 14, aged 93. He created the scores (often uncredited) for such films as *The Devil's Mask*, *It Came from Outer Space*, *Cult of the Cobra*, *Abbott and Costello Meet the Mummy*, *The Creature Walks Among Us*, *The Incredible Shrinking Man*, *The Deadly Mantis*, *The Monolith Monsters*, *The Thing That Couldn't Die*, *Curse of the Undead*, *The Alligator People*, *The Leech Woman* and *The Wizard of Baghdad*, along with episodes of the TV shows *Voyage to the Bottom of the Sea*, *The Invaders* and *Land of the Giants*.

Children's writer **Ivan** [Francis] **Southhall** died of cancer on November 15, aged 87. The author of more than fifty books, he was the only Australian writer to win a Carnegie Medal for children's literature (for *Josh* in 1971) and, starting in 1950 with *Meet Simon Black*, he wrote a series of children's SF novels about the eponymous adventurer and inventor.

Prolific Italian screenwriter **Ennio De Concini** died after a long illness on November 17, aged 84. His numerous credits include *Ulysses* (1954), *Hercules* (1958), *Hercules Unchained*, *The Last Days of Pompeii* (1959), *Giant of Marathon*, *Son of Samson*, *The Giants of Thessaly*, *The Colossus of Rhodes*, *The Witch's Curse*, Mario Bava's classic *Black Sunday* (aka *The Mask of Satan*) and *The Evil Eye*, and Antonio Margherti's *Assignment Outer Space* and *Battle of the Worlds*. De Concini won an Academy Award for his script for *Divorce – Italian Style*.

American comedy scriptwriter and director **Irving Brecher**, who wrote vaudeville jokes for Milton Berle and scripted such classic Marx Brothers movies as *At the Circus* and *Go West*, died following a series of heart attacks the same day, aged 94. He also worked as an uncredited script doctor on *The Wizard of Oz* (1939).

American mystery writer **George C.** (Clark) **Chesbro** died of complications from congestive heart failure on November 18, aged 68. Best known for his series of thirteen cross-genre books featuring dwarf private eye Robert "Mongo the Magnificent" Fredrickson, beginning with *Shadow of a Broken Man* in 1977, his other titles include the psychic "Veil Kendry" series and "Chant" series (as "David Cross"), along with a film tie-in for *The Golden Child*.

Scriptwriter **John Michael Hayes**, who wrote Alfred Hitchcock's *Rear Window* (1954), died on November 19, aged 89. He continued to work with the director on *To Catch a Thief*, *The Trouble with Harry*, and the remake of *The Man Who Knew Too Much*, which resulted in a disagreement that ended the relationship.

American research chemist and SF writer **Richard K.** (Kenneth) **Lyon** died on November 21, aged 74. He made his debut in *Analog* in 1973 and published around twenty short stories, some of which were collected in *Tales from the Lyonheart*. In collaboration with Andrew J. Offut he wrote a further half-a-dozen tales, including a 1982 serial for *Analog* and the "War of the Wizards" trilogy of fantasy novels, *Demon in the Mirror* (1977), *The Eye of Sarsis* (1980) and *Web of the Spider* (1981).

Alan Gordon, who co-wrote the 1967 hit "Happy Together" for The Turtles, died of cancer on November 22, aged 64.

American horror writer **Joseph McGee** died of complications from diabetes on November 27, aged 23. Along with stories in various small press magazines, he published the novels *In the Wake of the Night*, *The Reaper* and *Snow Hill*.

British artist, writer and reviewer **James** [Philip] **Cawthorn** – best known for collaborating with his friend Michael Moorcock – died of pancreatic cancer on December 2, aged 78. Cawthorn provided the illustrations for a number of publications edited by Moorcock, including the fanzine *Burroughsania*, *Tarzan Adventures*, the Sexton Blake Library and *New Worlds*. He also supplied the art for early graphic novels based on Moorcock's characters, including *Stormbringer* (1976), *The Jewel in the Skull* (1978) and *The Crystal and the Amulet* (1986), along with two 1962 portfolio's based on J. R. R. Tolkien's *The Lord of the Rings*. Together, Moorcock and Cawthorn wrote the Sexton Blake novel *Caribbean Crisis*, the SF novel *The Distant Suns* (as "Philip James"), the 1988 study *Fantasy: The 100 Best Books* and the script for the 1975 Amicus movie *The Land That Time Forgot*.

Legendary #1 SF fan, editor, literary agent, pulp author, memorabilia collector, Esperantist and film actor **Forrest J** (it didn't stand for anything, so no period) **Ackerman** (aka "Uncle Forry", "Mr

Science Fiction", "Mr Monster" and "Dr Acula" to his fans), died of heart failure at his Los Angeles home on December 4, aged 92. He had been in declining health for several months. Active in the SF field from the 1920s until his death, Ackerman is credited with launching the teenage Ray Bradbury's career and coining the term "sci-fi". He collaborated with C. L. Moore in *Weird Tales*, won the first Hugo Award in 1953, edited the translation of the *Perry Rhodan* series (1969–77), created the comic book character "Vampirella" and edited numerous anthologies and non-fiction books, including *The Frankenscience Monster*, *Mr Monster's Movie Gold*, *Monsters & Imagi-Movies* and *The Gernsback Awards Vol. 1*. However, his greatest claim to fame is as editor of the influential and pun-filled movie magazine *Famous Monsters of Filmland* (1958–82) – along with its companion titles *Spaceman* and *Monster World* – which inspired the careers of numerous professionals, including Stephen King and Steven Spielberg. His numerous movie appearances (often in bit parts) include *The Time Travelers*, *Queen of Blood*, *Dracula vs. Frankenstein*, *The Howling*, *Michael Jackson's Thriller*, *Amazon Women on the Moon*, *Nudist Colony of the Dead*, *Bikini Drive-In* and *Dinosaur Valley Girls*. Ackerman was presented with Lifetime Achievement Awards by the Horror Writers Association in 1997 and the World Fantasy Convention in 2002.

Mystery and non-fiction writer **Julius Fast**, who edited the 1944 SF anthology *Out of This World*, died on December 16, aged 89. He won the first-ever Edgar Award for his 1945 debut novel, *Watchful at Night*.

Screenwriter, playwright and actor **Greg Suddeth** died on December 19, aged 55. He scripted the 1990s movies *Prehysteria!* and *Pet Shop*, and came up with the original stories for *Oblivion* and *Oblivion 2: Backlash*. Suddeth played a gravedigger in the 2007 "Pie-lette" episode of ABC-TV's *Pushing Daisies*.

UK poet and playwright **Adrian Mitchell** died of complications from pneumonia on December 20, aged 76. He wrote the 1970 dystopian novel *The Bodyguard* and the lyrics for a stage version of George Orwell's *Animal Farm*.

Former 42nd Street projectionist, actor and journalist **Bill Landis**, who wrote and edited the groundbreaking exploitation movie magazine *Sleazoid Express* (1980–85), died of a heart attack in Chicago on December 22, aged 49. He revived the magazine for six issues in 1999 with wife Michelle Clifford, and in 2002 the pair edited a book collection of articles from the magazine, *Sleazoid Express: A Mind-Twisting Tour Through the Grindhouse Cinema of Times Square*.

The French-born Landis was also the author of *Anger: The Un-authorized Biography of Kenneth Anger*.

American book editor **Thomas B.** (Boss) **Congdon, Jr.** who, while at Doubleday, edited Peter Benchley's 1974 best-seller *Jaws*, died from Parkinson's disease and congestive heart failure on December 23, aged 77.

Controversial British playwright, screenwriter, director and actor **Harold Pinter** CBE died of cancer of the oesophagus on December 24, aged 78. He scripted the 1990 film adaptation of Margaret Atwood's dystopian *The Handmaid's Tale*, the 1993 version of Franz Kafka's *The Trial*, and the 2007 remake of Anthony Shaffer's *Sleuth* (in which he also had a cameo). Pinter was awarded the Nobel Prize for Literature in 2005.

Legendary pulp illustrator **Edd** (Edward Daniel) **Cartier** died of complications from Parkinson's disease on Christmas day, aged 94. From 1936 onwards, he produced more than 800 illustrations for Street & Smith's *The Shadow Magazine*, and contributed often whimsical SF and fantasy artwork to *Unknown, Astounding, Doc Savage, Planet Stories, Fantastic Adventures* and *Other Worlds*, amongst other titles. Along with newspaper strips and comics, he also produced artwork for Fantasy Press and Gnome Press during the 1950s. Gerry de la Ree published *Edd Cartier: The Known and the Unknown* in 1977, and the artist won a World Fantasy Life Achievement Award in 1992.

American SF writer and scientist **Leo A. Frankowski** also died on December 25, aged 65. His seven-book "Conrad Stargard" series began in 1986 with *The Cross-Time Engineer* and continued with *The High-Tech Knight, The Radiant Warrior, The Flying Warlord, Lord Conrad's Lady, Conrad's Quest for Rubber* and *Conrad's Time Machine*. A nominee for the John W. Campbell Award for Best New Writer in 1987, his other books include *Copernick's Rebellion, The Fata Morgana* and three collaborations with Dave Grossman, *The War with Earth, The Two-Space War* and *Kren of the Mitchegai*.

Scottish author and scriptwriter **Alan W.** (William) **Lear**, whose story "Let's Do Something Naughty" appeared in *The 25th Pan Book of Horror Stories*, died on December 26, aged 55. He suffered from Chronic Fatigue Syndrome for many years. Lear's fiction also appeared *in The Mammoth Book of Ghost Stories 2* and the Haunted Library collection *Spirits of Another Sort: Ghostly Tales of Tompion College*. During the 1980s he scripted a series of amateur *Doctor Who* audio cassettes for Audio Visuals, including

Enclave Irrelative, *Minuet in Hell*, *Cloud of Fear* and *Time Lords*, along with the video drama *Scarecrow City*, starring Nicholas Briggs. *Minuet in Hell* was rewritten in 2001 for an official *Doctor Who* audiobook with Paul McGann playing the Eighth Doctor.

Mystery writer **Donald E.** (Edwin Edmund) **Westlake** (aka "Richard Stark") died of an apparent heart attack on December 31 while on his way to a New Year's Eve dinner during a vacation in Texas. He was 75. Westlake began his career as a SF writer with "Or Give Me Death" in *Universe* (1954), and some of his SF short stories are collected in *The Curious Facts Preceding My Execution and Other Fictions* and *Tomorrow's Crimes*. His more than 100 other books (many written under various pseudonyms, and all on a manual typewriter) include *Anarchaos* (as "Curt Clark"), *Humans* and *Smoke*. With his wife, Abby Westlake, he collaborated on the spoofs *High Jinx* and *Transylvania Station*. Among his crime novels that were filmed were *The Busy Body* (by William Castle), *The Hunter* (as *Point Blank*), *The Hot Rock* and the Oscar-nominated *The Grifters*. Westlake wrote the screenplay for *The Stepfather*, he co-created the Dan Curtis show *Supertrain*, which only lasted for nine episodes on NBC in 1979, and his story "One on a Desert Island" became an episode of Hammer's 1969 TV series *Journey to the Unknown*. A three-time Edgar Award winner, he was named a Grand Master by the Mystery Writers of America in 1993.

PERFORMERS/PERSONALITIES

Finnish-born glamour ghoul and actress **Maila Nurmi** (Maila Elizäbeth Syrjaniemi), better known under her screen persona "Vampira", died of cardiac arrest on January 10, aged 86. Inspired by Charles Addams' vampiric "Morticia" character, and an obvious influence on such later performers as "Elvira, Mistress of the Dark" (who she sued), Nurmi was one of the first "horror hosts" on TV, appearing on KABC-TV in Los Angeles (1954–55). Best remembered for co-starring in Edward D. Wood, Jr's infamous *Plan 9 From Outer Space* opposite an ailing Bela Lugosi, her other credits include *Sex Kittens Go to College*, *The Magic Sword*, *Flying Saucers Over Hollywood: The "Plan 9" Companion* and *The Haunted World of Edward D. Wood Jr. Vampira: The Movie* was a 2006 documentary about her life and career, and she was portrayed by Lisa Marie in Tim Burton's *Ed Wood*.

Rod Allen, lead singer with the British pop group The Fortunes, which he co-founded, died the same day after a short battle with liver cancer, aged 63. In the 1960s and early '70s the group had hits with such songs as "You've Got Your Troubles", "Here it Comes Again", "Here Comes That Rainy Day Feeling Again" and "Storm in a Teacup".

Troubled young actor **Brad Renfro** died on January 15, aged 25. Renfro had a history of drug abuse and was found dead at his home in Los Angeles. Named *The Hollywood Reporter*'s "Young Star" and one of *People* magazine's "Top 30 Under 30" in the mid-1990s, he appeared in the 1998 film version of Stephen King's *Apt Pupil*, *Ghost World*, *The Mummy an' the Armadillo* and *The Jacket*. He was working on an adaptation of Brett Easton Ellis' *The Informers*, starring Winona Ryder, at the time of his death.

Hollywood actress **Susanne Pleshette** died of respiratory failure on January 17, aged 70. She had been battling lung cancer since 2006. Best known as Bob Newhart's TV wife in several series, she appeared in Alfred Hitchcock's *The Birds*, *The Power*, *Oh God! Book II* and Disney's *Blackbeard's Ghost* and *The Shaggy D.A.*, while she contributed two voices to the English-language version of *Spirited Away*. Pleshette's TV credits include *One Step Beyond*, *Sunday Showcase* ("Murder and the Android"), *Alfred Hitchcock Presents*, *The Wild Wild West* ("Night of the Inferno"), *The Invaders* and *Fantasies* (aka *The Studio Murders*). Her first and third husbands were actors Troy Donahue and Tom Poston.

Comedy actor and voice artist **Allan Melvin** died of cancer the same day, aged 84. Best remembered as Bilko's sidekick "Corporal Steve Henshaw" in *The Phil Silvers Show* and Alice's boyfriend "Sam Franklin" in *The Brady Bunch*, he guest-starred in such TV series as *My Favorite Martian* and *Lost in Space*. As a voice actor he contributed to *The Magilla Gorilla Show* (as the titular character), *The Flintstones*, *The Banana Splits Adventure Hour* (as the voice of "Drooper"), *Pufnstuf*, *Kung Fu*, *The New Animated Adventures of Flash Gordon*, *Spider-Man and His Amazing Friends*, *Popeye and Son*, *Scooby-Doo in Arabian Nights* and numerous other shows.

British stage and screen actress **Carole Lynne** (Helen Violet Carolyn Heyman, aka Lady Delfont) also died on January 17, aged 89. In 1941 Lynne co-starred with Arthur Askey and Richard Murdoch in *The Ghost Train*. She was married to actor Derek Farr from 1939–45, and her second husband was entertainment impresario (Lord) Bernard Delfont.

Stage and screen actress **Lois Nettleton** (Lydia Scott) died of lung cancer on January 18, aged 80. A former Miss Chicago, she appeared in *The Bamboo Saucer*, Wes Craven's *Deadly Blessing* and *Mirror*

Mirror II: Raven Dance, plus episodes of TV's *Captain Video*, *Dow Hour of Great Mysteries* ("The Woman in White"), *Great Ghost Tales*, *Twilight Zone*, *The Alfred Hitchcock Hour*, *Night Gallery*, *The Flash* and *Babylon 5*. The actress also contributed voice performances to the 1990s *Spider-Man* cartoon series and *Mickey's House of Villains* from Disney.

California singer-songwriter **John** [Coburn] **Stewart** died of a brain haemorrhage on January 19, aged 68. He had been suffering from Alzheimer's disease. Stewart started out in the early 1960s as a member of the Cumberland Three and The Kingston Trio. His best-known composition was "Daydream Believer", which The Monkees took to #1 in 1967, and his 1969 debut solo album, *California Bloodlines*, is now considered to be influential in launching the folk era of the early 1970s.

Veteran British TV character actor **Kevin Stoney** died on January 20, aged 86. His many credits include episodes of *Hour of Mystery* ("The Man in Half Moon Street" with Anton Diffring), *The Indian Tales of Rudyard Kipling* ("The Tomb of His Ancestors"), *The Avengers* ("Mission . . . Highly Improbable"), *Out of the Unknown*, *Doctor Who* ("The Invasion" and "Revenge of the Cybermen"), *Doomwatch* ("The Plastic Eaters"), *Ace of Wands*, *The Tomorrow People*, *Orson Welles' Great Mysteries*, *Space: 1999*, *The New Avengers*, *Quatermass*, *Hammer House of Horror* ("The Thirteenth Reunion") and *Blakes 7*. His infrequent film appearances include *Shadow of the Cat* and *The Blood Beast Terror* (aka *The Vampire-Beast Craves Blood* with Peter Cushing). Stoney retired from acting in the 1990s, but he continued to attend *Doctor Who* conventions.

Twenty-eight-year-old Oscar-nominated actor **Heath Ledger** (Heathcliff Andrew Ledger) was found dead in a New York apartment on January 22 of an apparent accidental overdose of six different types of prescription drugs, including painkillers, sleeping pills and anti-anxiety medication. The Australian-born Ledger starred in the shortlived heroic fantasy TV series *Roar* (1997) before appearing in such movies as *A Knight's Tale*, *The Order* (aka *The Sin Eater*), *The Brothers Grimm* and *The Dark Knight* (as the Joker). At the time of his death he was working on Terry Gilliam's fantasy movie *The Imaginarium of Doctor Parnassus*.

Sixty-year-old American character actor **Christopher Allport** (Alexander Wise Allport, Jr.) was killed with two other skiers in a freak Californian avalanche on January 25. His credits include *Man on a Swing*, *Savage Weekend*, *Dead & Buried*, *Invaders from Mars* (1986), *Jack Frost* and *Jack Frost 2: Revenge of the Mutant Killer*

Snowman, along with episodes of the 1980s *Twilight Zone*, *Quantum Leap*, *The X Files*, *Kindred: The Embraced*, *The Sentinel* and *The Invisible Man* (2001).

Marlon Brando's troubled eldest son, **Christian Brando**, died of pneumonia at a Los Angeles hospital on January 26. He was 49, and for many years had problems with alcohol, drugs and domestic violence. Brando had small roles in a few movies and, in the early 1990s, spent five years in prison for the manslaughter of his sister Cheyenne's boyfriend, Dag Drollet. She later committed suicide. Brando was also the lover of Bonnie Lee Bakley, who later married actor Robert Blake and was shot to death in 2001.

Humphrey Bogart's personal wig-maker, **Verita Thompson** (Verita Bouvaire), who claimed to have been the actor's secret mistress for thirteen years in her autobiography *Bogie and Me: A Love Story*, died in New Orleans on February 1, aged 92.

British-born actor **Barry Morse** (Herbert Morse), best known as detective Lt Philip Gerard pursuing murder suspect Dr Richard Kimble (David Janssen) in the TV series *The Fugitive* (1963–67), died in London on February 2, aged 89. After appearing in such films as *Thunder Rock* and *Daughter of Darkness*, Morse emigrated to Canada in 1951. His subsequent film credits include *Asylum*, *Welcome to Blood City*, *The Shape of Things to Come* (1979), *The Martian Chronicles*, *The Changeling*, *Funeral Home*, *Whoops Apocalypse*, *Murder by Phone*, *Covenant*, *The Return of Sherlock Holmes* and *Memory Run*. On television he also appeared in the recurring role of "Prof. Victor Bergman" on the first season of *Space: 1999* (1975–76). His other TV credits include episodes of *The Unforeseen*, *Dow Hour of Great Mysteries* ("The Inn of the Flying Dragon"), *Way Out*, *Twilight Zone* (1960s and 1980s versions), *The Alfred Hitchcock Hour*, *The Outer Limits*, *The Invaders*, *The Starlost*, *The Ray Bradbury Theater*, *Dracula: The Series*, *TekWar* and *Space Island One*.

American character actor **Charles** (Fernley) **Fawcett** died on February 3, aged 92. A former wrestler, artists' model, and adventurer who fought in several conflicts, he appeared in many European movies including *I vampiri* (aka *The Devil's Commandment*), *Face of Fire* (uncredited), *The Witch's Curse*, *Captain Sinbad*, *The Secret of Dr Mabuse* and *Kaliman*.

Indian guru **Maharishi Mahesh Yogi**, whose teachings about Transcendental Meditation were adopted by the Beatles, Beach Boys and others in the 1960s, died in Holland on February 5, aged around 91.

Exotic German-born actress, singer and dancer **Tamara Desni** (Tamara Brodsky) died in France on February 7, aged 95. After making a few films in Germany in the early 1930s, she moved to England where she appeared in a number of movies over the next two decades, including *Forbidden Territory* (1934), based on a Dennis Wheatley novel. Her final credit was Hammer's *Dick Barton at Bay* (1950). The fourth of her five husbands was Canadian-born actor Raymond Lovell.

Swedish actress and novelist **Eva Dahlbeck** died of Alzheimer's disease on February 8, aged 87. Best known for her six collaborations with director Ingmar Bergman, she also appeared in *Kvinna I vitt*, a 1949 version of Wilkie Collins' *The Woman in White*. Her other film credits include *Les Créatures* (1966).

American character actor **Robert DoQui** (aka "Bob Do Qui"), who played Sgt Warren Reed in all three *RoboCop* movies, died on February 9, aged 74. His credits include *Visions . . .*, *Cloak & Dagger*, *My Science Project*, *Miracle Mile*, the short *A Hollow Place*, and episodes of *The Outer Limits*, *I Dream of Jeannie*, *The Man from U.N.C.L.E.*, *Tarzan*, *Get Smart*, *The New Scooby-Doo Movies*, *Kolchak: The Night Stalker*, *Tales of the Unexpected* (1977), *Blue Thunder*, *Starman*, *Batman: The Animated Series* and *Star Trek: Deep Space Nine*.

Dependable American stage and screen actor **Roy** [Richard] **Scheider** died in an Arkansas hospital on February 10, aged 75. For two years the two-time Oscar nominee had been treated for multiple myeloma in the hospital's research centre. Best known for his role as Police Chief Martin Brody in the first two *Jaws* films ("You're going to need a bigger boat"), Scheider made his film debut in the low budget 1964 horror movie *The Curse of the Living Corpse*. His other credits include *All That Jazz*, *Still of the Night*, *Blue Thunder*, *2010*, *Naked Lunch*, *The Doorway*, *Dracula II: Ascension*, *The Punisher* (2004) and *Dracula III: Legacy*. For two seasons he starred as Captain Nathan Bridger on the TV series *SeaQuest DSV* (1993–95).

American TV actor **David** [Lawrence] **Groh** died of kidney cancer on February 12, aged 68. Best remembered as Valerie Harper's husband Joe on the 1970s sitcom *Rhoda*, he began his career playing a ghost in ABC's *Dark Shadows* (1968) and his many other credits include episodes of *Buck Rogers in the 25th Century* ("Planet of the Slave Girls"), *Fantasy Island*, *Tales from the Darkside*, *M.A.N.T.I.S.*, *The X Files*, *Black Scorpion* (as regular "Lt Walker") and the TV movie *Last Exit to Earth*.

American character actor **Lionel Mark Smith**, who often worked with playwright and director David Mamet, died of cancer on February 13, aged 62. His eclectic credits include *Galaxina*, *King of the Ants* and an episode of *Batman: The Animated Series*.

French singer and entertainer **Henri** [Gabriel] **Salvador**, credited with introducing his home country to rock 'n' roll under the name "Henry Cording", died of an aneurysm the same day, aged 90. Best known for his novelty songs during the 1960s and '70s, he was appointed a Chevalier de la Légion d'Honneur in 1988.

American character actor **Perry López** died of lung cancer on February 14, aged 78. Often cast in Hispanic or other ethnic roles, he appeared in *Creature from the Black Lagoon* (uncredited), along with episodes of *Alfred Hitchcock Presents*, *The Time Tunnel*, *Star Trek*, *The Man from U.N.C.L.E.*, *Tarzan*, *Voyage to the Bottom of the Sea* and *The Wild Wild West*.

American character actress **Agnes Anderson** (aka "Lynn Anders"), who appeared in *Dracula's Daughter* (uncredited) and *The Shadow Strikes*, died on February 16, aged 94.

Six-foot, five-inch former dancer **Ben Chapman** (Benjamin F. Chapman, Jr.), who famously donned the Gill Man costume for the land scenes in *Creature from the Black Lagoon* (1954), died of congestive heart failure in Honolulu on February 21, aged 79. (Ricou Browning played the Creature underwater.) The cousin of actor Jon Hall, he recreated the role on TV's *The Colgate Comedy Hour* with Abbott and Costello, and his only other genre credit is the Johnny Weissmuller adventure *Jungle Moon Men*. In recent years, Chapman was a regular at movie memorabilia fairs.

Drummer **Buddy Miles**, who played in Jimi Hendrix's Band of Gypsys in the late 1960s, died of complications from heart disease on February 26, aged 60. During the 1980s he sang lead on the animated California Raisins ads on TV.

Right-wing American commentator and spy novelist **William F. Buckley, Jr** died of complications from emphysema and diabetes on February 27, aged 82. During the late 1960s, Buckley appeared in a series of televised debates with author Gore Vidal, and the two famously clashed over the 1968 Democratic Party convention in Chicago. He also participated in a heated live television debate with Carl Sagan following a screening of the 1983 TV movie *The Day After*.

Sixty-four-year-old **Mike Smith**, lead singer and keyboard player with British pop group Dave Clark Five, died of pneumonia in a London hospital on February 28, less than two weeks before the band was to be inducted into the Rock and Roll Hall of Fame in New York City. Smith had suffered a spinal cord injury when he fell from a fence at his home in Spain in September 2003, and was left paralysed below the ribcage with limited use of his upper body. The Dave Clark Five had a string of hits in the 1960s, including "Glad All Over" and "I Like it Like That", and the band starred in John Boorman's debut movie *Catch Us If You Can* (aka *Having a Wild Weekend*), which featured a party guest dressed as the Frankenstein Monster.

Canadian jazz and blues guitarist and singer **Jeff Healey** (Norman Jeffrey Healey), who lost his sight to cancer when he was one-year-old, died of the disease on March 2, aged 41. His biggest hit was "Angel Eyes" in 1988.

Seventy-six-year-old American actor, director and producer **Ivan** [Nathaniel] **Dixon** [III], who portrayed radio technician Sgt James "Kinch" Kinchloe in *Hogan's Heroes*, died of complications from kidney failure and haemorrhage in North Carolina on March 16. He was in the TV mini-series *Amerika* and episodes of *The Twilight Zone*, *The Man from U.N.C.L.E.* and *The Outer Limits*. As a director, his credits include *The Hardy Boys/Nancy Drew Mysteries*, *The Bionic Woman*, *Wonder Woman*, *The Greatest American Hero*, *Tales of the Gold Monkey* and *Quantum Leap*.

British character actor **John Hewer**, who portrayed Captain Birds Eye in the UK TV commercials from 1967–98, died the same day, aged 86. In 1983 he was named the world's most recognized skipper after Captain Cook. He appeared in an episode of the 1950s Boris Karloff TV series *Colonel March of Scotland Yard* (recycled for the "fix-up" movie *Colonel March Investigates*) and starred in the 1961 film *Strip Tease Murder*.

Swedish session musician **Ola Brunkert** also died on March 16 after falling through a glass door in his home in Majorca, Spain, and bleeding to death in his garden from a neck injury. The 62-year-old retired drummer was only one of two session musicians to work on all of Abba's albums in the 1970s and '80s.

Acclaimed British stage and screen actor **Paul Scofield** CBE died on March 19, aged 86. The Oscar, Emmy and Tony Award-winning performer appeared in the movies *Mr Corbett's Ghost*, Franco Zeffirelli's *Hamlet* (as "The Ghost") and *The Crucible*. He also narrated the TV movie *The Curse of King Tut's Tomb* (1980) and voiced "Boxer" in the 1999 version of *Animal Farm*. After breaking his leg, Scofield was replaced by Richard Burton as "O'Brien" in *Nineteen Eighty-Four* (1984). The actor was made a Companion of Honour in 2001 after he reportedly turned down attempts to give him a knighthood.

British TV character actor **Brian Wilde** died on March 20, aged 86. A regular on such BBC comedy series as *Porridge* and *Last of the Summer Wine*, Wilde also appeared in episodes of *The Avengers* ("The Fear Merchants"), *Doomwatch*, *Catweazle*, *Out of the Unknown*, *Ace of Wands*, *Orson Welles' Great Mysteries*, *The Ghosts of Motley Hall* and *Shadows*. His film credits include *Night of the Demon* (aka *Curse of the Demon*), *Corridors of Blood* (uncredited, with Boris Karloff and Christopher Lee), the James Bond adventure *You Only Live Twice* (uncredited), *Goodbye Gemini*, and Hammer's *Rasputin the Mad Monk* (uncredited) and *To the Devil a Daughter* (both also with Lee).

Hollywood tough-guy actor **Richard Widmark** died on March 24 of complications following a fall. He was 93. Best known for his Oscar-nominated debut as giggling psychopath Tommy Udo in *Kiss of Death* (1947), his other films include *Run for the Sun* (based on the short story by Richard Connell), *The Bedford Incident* (which he also produced, uncredited), *Twilight's Last Gleaming*, *Coma* (based on the novel by Robin Cook) and *The Swarm*. In 1976 he was miscast as occult novelist John Verney, battling Christopher Lee's Satanist priest in Hammer's *To the Devil a Daughter*, based on the novel by Dennis Wheatley.

Oscar-winning Hollywood star and former president of the National Rifle Association of America, **Charlton Heston** (John Charles Carter) died of Alzheimer's disease on April 5, aged 84. Best known for the many Biblical and historical figures he portrayed in the movies, from Moses to Michelangelo, in a career that spanned more than sixty years his many films include *The Ten Commandments*, *Touch of Evil*, *The War Lord*, *Planet of the Apes* (both 1968 and 2001 versions), *Beneath the Planet of the Apes*, *The Omega Man* (based on the novel by Richard Matheson), *Soylent Green* (based on the novel by Harry Harrison), *Earthquake*, *The Awakening* (based on the novel by Bram Stoker), the Showscan short *Call from Space*, *Solar Crisis*, *The Crucifer of Blood* (as an unlikely Sherlock Holmes), John Carpenter's *In the Mouth of Madness*, *The Dark Mist*, *Hamlet* (1996), Disney's *Hercules*, *Armageddon* and *Cats & Dogs*. On TV he portrayed Heathcliffe in a 1950 version of "Wuthering Heights" on *Studio One* and The Beast in a 1958 version of "Beauty and the Beast" on *Shirley Temple's Storybook*. Heston also appeared in episodes of *SeaQuest DSV* and *The Outer Limits* (2000).

Busy TV character actor **Stanley Kamel**, who played psychiatrist

Dr Charles Kroger on the USA TV series *Monk*, was found dead of a heart attack in his Hollywood home on April 8. He was 65. Kamel also appeared in *Captain America II: Death Too Soon* (with Christopher Lee), *Automatic* and *Ravager*, along with episodes of *The Sixth Sense*, *Switch*, *The Incredible Hulk*, *The Phoenix*, *Mork & Mindy*, *Knight Rider*, *Star Trek: The Next Generation*, *Probe*, *The Highwayman*, *Beauty and the Beast*, *Dark Skies* and *Dark Angel*.

Australian-born **Lloyd Lamble**, the last surviving actor to have played The Shadow during the golden age of radio, died on April 9, aged 94. He moved to Britain in the early 1950s, where he often portrayed police inspectors and doctors in such films as Hammer's *Quatermass 2* (aka *Enemy from Space*), *Night of the Demon* (aka *Curse of the Demon*), *Behemoth the Sea Monster* (aka *The Giant Behemoth*) and *—And Now the Screaming Starts!*, based on the story by David Case. Lamble also appeared in episodes of TV's *Colonel March of Scotland Yard* (starring Boris Karloff), *The New Adventures of Charlie Chan*, *Invisible Man* (1959), *The Avengers*, *The Prisoner*, *Journey to the Unknown* and *The Rivals of Sherlock Holmes*.

German-born character actor [Heinz] **Dieter Eppler**, a regular in Rialto's Edgar Wallace *krimis* films of the 1960s, died in Stuttgart on April 12, aged 81. He appeared in many European movies, including *The Head*, *The Fellowship of the Frog*, *The Terrible People*, *Slaughter of the Vampires* (aka *Curse of the Blood Ghouls*, as the "Vampire"), *The White Spider*, *The Strangler of Blackmoor Castle*, *The Secret of Dr Mabuse*, *Lana: Queen of the Amazons*, *The Sinister Monk*, Jess Franco's *Lucky the Inscrutable* and *The Blood Demon* (aka *The Torture Chamber of Dr Sadism*, with Christopher Lee).

Hollywood contract player **June Travis** (June Dorothea Grabiner), who only spent three years in films before retiring to concentrate on her marriage, died of complications from a stroke on April 14, aged 93. Between 1934–37 she made thirty movies, including the old dark house mystery *The Case of the Black Cat* (playing secretary Della Street opposite Ricardo Cortez's Perry Mason). In later years she concentrated on stage work and appeared in two more films, her final credit being Bill Rebane's *Monster A Go-Go* (1965).

British-born leading lady **Hazel Court** died of a heart attack in Lake Tahoe, California, on April 15, aged 82. A product of the J. Arthur Rank "charm school", she appeared in *Ghost Ship* (1952), *Devil Girl from Mars*, Hammer's *The Curse of Frankenstein* (with Peter Cushing and Christopher Lee) and *The Man Who Could Cheat Death* (with Lee again), and *Doctor Blood's Coffin*. In the 1960s, she made three films for Roger Corman: *The Premature Burial* (with Ray Milland), *The Raven* (as the "Lost Lenore", opposite Vincent Price, Peter Lorre and Boris Karloff) and *The Masque of the Red Death* (again with Price). Her final film role was an uncredited appearance in the third *Omen* film, *The Final Conflict* (1981). She was also featured in episodes of TV's *The Invisible Man* (1959), *Alfred Hitchcock Presents*, *Thriller* ("The Terror in Teakwood"), *The Twilight Zone* (1964) and *The Wild Wild West* ("The Night of the Returning Dead"). Court married British actor Dermot Walsh in 1949. They divorced fourteen years later, and she was subsequently married to American actor and director Don Taylor from 1964 until his death in 1998. In the 1970s she began a second career as a sculptor, and her autobiography, *Hazel Court: Horror Queen*, was published in 2008.

Danny Federici, long-time keyboard player with Bruce Springsteen's E Street Band, died of melanoma on April 17, aged 58. Federici's playing helped create the band's distinctive sound from "Hungry Heart" to "The Rising".

American actress and scriptwriter **Kay Linaker** (Mary Katherine Linaker), who as "Kate Phillips" co-wrote *The Blob* (1958) for just $125.00, died of heart failure on April 18, aged 94. During the 1930s and '40s she appeared in *Charlie Chan at Monte Carlo*, *The Last Warning*, *Charlie Chan in Reno*, *Charlie Chan at Treasure Island* (uncredited), *Charlie Chan's Murder Cruise*, *The Invisible Woman* (uncredited), *Charlie Chan in Rio* and *Laura* (uncredited), before she retired from acting in 1945.

Norwegian-born actress and Scandinavian sex symbol **Julie Ege** (Julie Dzuli) died of breast and lung cancer on April 29, aged 64. A former Miss Norway and *Penthouse* model, the 36-24-36 actress was promoted by Hammer Films as "The New Sex Symbol of the 1970s" for the prehistoric drama *Creatures the World Forgot*. Her other films include the James Bond adventure *On Her Majesty's Secret Service*, *Every Home Should Have One* (aka *Think Dirty*), *Go for a Take* (aka *Double Take*), *The Final Programme* (aka *The Last Days of Man on Earth*, based on the novel by Michael Moorcock), *Craze* (aka *The Infernal Idol*), *Percy's Progress* (aka *It's Not the Size That Counts*, with Vincent Price), *The Mutations* (aka *The Freakmaker*), Hammer's *The Legend of the 7 Golden Vampires* (aka *The Seven Brothers Meet Dracula*) and the Dutch comedy *De Dwaze Lotgevallen van Sherlock Jones*. She gave up acting in the mid-1970s, and later became a registered nurse in an Oslo hospital.

British actor **Robert Russell**, who portrayed Vincent Price's thuggish sidekick John Stearne in *Witchfinder General*, died of a heart attack on May 12, aged 71. His other credits include *Bedazzled*, *The Sign of Four* (1983) and *Strange Horizons*, plus episodes of TV's *Out of the Unknown*, *The Avengers*, *Randall and Hopkirk (Deceased)*, *The Guardians*, *Doctor Who*, *Space: 1999*, *Blakes 7* and *Hammer House of Mystery and Suspense* ("Czech Mate").

Handsome American leading man **John Philip Law**, best known for playing the blind angel Pygar in *Barbarella*, died on May 13, aged 70. His other films (many shot in Europe) include Mario Bava's *Danger: Diabolik*, *Skidoo*, *The Golden Voyage of Sinbad* (as "Sinbad"), *The Spiral Staircase* (1975), *Un sussuro nel buio*, *Eyes Behind the Wall*, *Tod im November*, *Un ombra nell'ombra*, *Tarzan the Ape Man* (1981), *Night Train to Terror* (aka *Shiver*), *Moon in Scorpio*, *Delirio di sangue*, *Space Mutiny*, *Alienator*, *Scream Your Head Off*, *My Ghost Dog*, *Curse of the Forty-Niner* (which he also associate produced) and *I tre volti del terrore*.

British actor **John Forbes-Robertson**, who replaced Christopher Lee as Hammer's Count Dracula in *The Legend of the 7 Golden Vampires* (aka *The Seven Brothers Meet Dracula*, 1974), died on May 14, aged 80. The son of legendary theatre actor-manager Sir Johnston Forbes-Robertson, he also appeared in *The Vampire Lovers* for the same studio, and his other films include *Bunny Lake is Missing*, *Casino Royale* (1967), *The Vault of Horror*, *Venom*, *Lifeforce* (uncredited) and *Room 36*, along with episodes of TV's *Thriller* (1975), *The New Avengers* and *Crime Traveller*. His last appearance was in the 2008 documentary *The Legend of Hammer – Vampires*.

Czech-born actress, director and author **Hana Pravda** (Hana Beck, aka Hana-Marie Pravda) died in London on May 22, aged 90. An Auschwitz survivor, she appeared in the films *And Soon the Darkness* and *Dracula* (1973, starring Jack Palance), along with episodes of *Department S*, *Catweazle*, *Survivors* (in the recurring role of "Emma Cohen"), *Tales of the Unexpected* and *Hammer House of Mystery & Suspense* ("Czech Mate"). The first of her two husbands was actor George Pravda, from 1946 until his death in 1985.

Eighteen-year-old British actor **Robert** [Arthur] **Knox** was stabbed to death while trying to protect his younger brother during a fight outside a bar in Sidcup, south-east London, in the early hours of May 24. Four days earlier he had completed his role as Marcus Belby in *Harry Potter and the Half-Blood Prince*. A 21-year-old jobless man, who went to the same school as the actor, was charged with Knox's murder.

Eighty-six-year-old **Dick Martin** (Thomas Richard Martin), best-known as one half of the comedy team Rowan and Martin, who hosted the NBC-TV sketch show *Rowan and Martin's Laugh-In* (1968–73), died of respiratory complications the same day. Dan Rowan died in 1987. The pair also appeared together in the 1969 spoof horror movie *The Maltese Bippy*. Martin's acting credits include *The Glass Bottom Boat* and episodes of *Fantasy Island* and *3rd Rock from the Sun*. In the 1970s he became a successful TV director.

Emmy Award-winning American comedian **Harvey** [Herschel] **Korman** died on May 29 of complications from the rupture of an abdominal aortic aneurysm suffered four months earlier. He was 81. Although best known for his TV work (he appeared in *The Wild Wild West*, the infamous *Star Wars Holiday Special*, three episodes of *The Munsters*, and voiced the alien The Great Gazoo in *The Flintstones*), he also appeared in such movies as Disney's *Son of Flubber* (uncredited) and *Herbie Goes Bananas*, *Lord Love a Duck*, *Blazing Saddles*, *High Anxiety*, *The Invisible Woman* (1983), *Alice in Wonderland* (1985), *Munchies*, *Radioland Murders*, *Dracula: Dead and Loving It* and *The Flinstones in Viva Rock Vegas*.

Hollywood actor, director and producer **Mel Ferrer** (Melchor Gaston Ferrer) died of heart failure on June 2, aged 90. He appeared in *The World, the Flesh and the Devil* (based on the novel by M. P. Shiel), *The Hands of Orlac* (aka *Hands of a Strangler*, 1960), *Paris – When It Sizzles* (as "Mr Hyde"), *The Antichrist* (aka *The Tempter*), *Eaten Alive* (aka *Death Trap*), *The Return of Captain Nemo*, *The Norsemen*, *Screamers*, *The Visitor*, *Guyana: Cult of the Damned*, *The Great Alligator*, *Eaten Alive!* and *Nightmare City* (aka *City of the Walking Dead*). His TV credits include episodes of *Search*, *The Fantastic Journey*, *Wonder Woman*, *Logan's Run* and *Fantasy Island* (as "Moriarty", opposite Peter Lawford's Sherlock Holmes). Ferrer also produced the thrillers *Wait Until Dark* (a star vehicle for the fourth of his five wives, Audrey Hepburn), *The Night Visitor* and *W* (starring Twiggy).

Pioneering blues guitarist **Bo Diddley** (Elias Otha Bates) died of heart failure the same day, aged 79. His first single was released in 1955, and among his best-known songs are "Who Do You Love?" and "You Can't Judge a Book by Its Cover". He appeared in *Rockula*, *Blues Brothers 2000* and an episode of the Disney TV show *So Weird*. Winner of Lifetime Achievement at the 1999

Grammy Awards, he was also inducted into the Rock and Roll Hall of Fame.

New Zealand-born TV character actor [William Reginald] **Bruce Purchase**, who played the cyborg villain The Captain in Douglas Adams' 1978 *Doctor Who* episode "The Pirate Planet", died in London on June 5, aged 69. His other credits include episodes of *Doomwatch*, *The New Avengers*, *Supernatural*, *Blakes 7* and *The Tripods*, along with *Alice Through the Looking Glass* (as the Walrus), *The Hunchback of Notre Dame* (1977) and *The Quatermass Conclusion*.

Robert J. (James) **Anderson** (aka "Bobby/Bobbie Anderson"), who played Little George Bailey in Frank Capra's classic Christmas film *It's a Wonderful Life*, died of melanoma on June 6, aged 75. His other movies as a child actor include *Mystery of the 13th Guest* (directed by his uncle, William "One-Shot" Beaudine) and *The Bishop's Wife* (1947). He later became a production manager on *The Time Tunnel* (1966–67), *Goliath Awaits* (featuring Christopher Lee and John Carradine) and *Solar Crisis*, associate produced the 1973 TV movie *The Cat Creature* (scripted by Robert Bloch), and was the executive in charge of production on *Demolition Man*.

Actor turned theatrical producer **Gene Persson** (Eugene Clair Persson) died of a heart attack the same day, aged 74. A juvenile actor in three of the *Ma and Pa Kettle* film series of the 1950s, he was also in *Earth vs. the Spider* and *Bloodlust!* Persson produced Peter Barnes' play *The Ruling Class* in London and the 1967 Off-Broadway *Peanuts* musical, *You're a Good Man, Charlie Brown*. His second wife was actress Shirley Knight.

American actress **Mona Knox** died of heart failure on June 11, aged 79. A former child model, she made her movie debut in the early 1950s. Knox's film appearances include *Tarzan and the Slave Girl* (as an uncredited slave girl), *Aladdin and His Lamp* (as an uncredited dancing girl) and *Rosemary's Baby* (uncredited last film), along with an episode of TV's *Space Patrol*.

South African-born British actor **Bruce Lester** (Bruce Somerset Lister) died in Los Angeles on June 13, aged 96. After appearing in a number of British films from 1934 onwards, he moved to Hollywood in 1938, where he changed his name from Bruce Lister to Bruce Lester. He appeared (often uncredited) in *The Invisible Man Returns* (with Vincent Price), *British Intelligence* (with Boris Karloff), *Man Hunt*, *The Mysterious Doctor*, *Flesh and Fantasy*, *Tarzan's Peril*, *The Son of Dr Jekyll* and *Tarzan and the Trappers*. Lester was also in a 1951 episode of *Fireside Theater* ("Drums in the Night") with George Zucco.

Hollywood dancer and actress **Cyd Charisse** (Tula Ellice Finklea) died of cardiac arrest on June 17, aged 86. With her legs famously insured for $5 million, she danced with Gene Kelly in *Singin' in the Rain*, *It's Always Fair Weather* and the 1954 fantasy *Brigadoon*, and appeared with Fred Astaire in *Ziegfeld Follies*, *The Band Wagon* and *Silk Stockings*. She also appeared in *The Silencers*, *Warlords of Atlantis*, and episodes of TV's *Hawaii Five-O* ("Death Mask") and *Fantasy Island*.

Off-Broadway actress **Jacqueline Bertrand** died the same day from complications following knee replacement surgery. She was 83. In the 1960s she played a ghost on TV's *Dark Shadows*.

Incredibly prolific Canadian-born character actor **Henry Beckman** died of heart failure in Spain on June 17, aged 86. His numerous film and TV credits (usually as a cop or military type) include *Dead Ringer*, *The Satan Bug*, *The Stalking Moon*, David Cronenberg's *The Brood*, *Lion of Oz* and *Epicenter*, plus episodes of 1950s *Flash Gordon* (as "Commander Paul Richards"), *The Twilight Zone*, *My Favorite Martian*, *My Living Doll*, *The Man from U.N.C.L.E.*, *The Munsters*, *The Wild Wild West*, *Tarzan*, *The Flying Nun*, *Bewitched*, *The Monkees*, *I Dream of Jeannie*, *The Immortal*, *Night Gallery*, *The Sixth Sense*, *The Starlost*, *Kolchak: The Night Stalker*, *The Six Million Dollar Man*, *The Lost Saucer*, *Fantasy Island*, *Werewolf*, *The Ray Bradbury Theater*, the 1990s *Outer Limits*, *The X Files* ("Tooms" and "Squeeze") and *Honey I Shrunk the Kids: The TV Show*.

Influential American stand-up comedian and author **George** [Dennis Patrick] **Carlin** died of heart failure on June 22, aged 71. As an actor he appeared as "Rufus" in *Bill & Ted's Excellent Adventure* and *Bill & Ted's Bogus Journey*, and voiced the character in the 1990 cartoon show, *Bill & Ted's Excellent Adventure*. He was also in *Scary Movie 3*, and voiced characters in Disney's *Tarzan II* and *Cars*, *Happily N'Ever After* and TV's *The Simpsons*.

American actor **John T.** (Thomas) **Furlong**, who was the uncredited narrator on Russ Meyer's *Faster Pussycat! Kill! Kill!* (1965), died on June 23, aged 75. Furlong also dubbed all Meyer's screen appearances, and his other credits include *Helter Skelter* (1976), *The Swarm*, *More Wild Wild West*, *Suburban Commando*, John Carpenter's *Vampires* and *Maniacts*, along with episodes of TV's *The Invisible Man* (1975), *Buck Rogers in the 25th Century*, *Fantasy Island* and *Highway to Heaven*.

French-born character actress and drama teacher **Lilyan Chauvin**, who appeared in Ralph Brooke's *Bloodlust!* (1961), died of complications from breast cancer and heart disease on June 26, aged 82. Her many credits include *The Mephisto Waltz, Silent Night Deadly Night, Predator 2, Universal Soldier, Pumpkinhead II: Blood Wings*, Joe Dante's pilot *The Warlord: Battle for the Galaxy* and *The Passing*, plus episodes of TV's *Adventures of Superman, Alfred Hitchcock Presents, One Step Beyond, Thriller, The Man from U.N.C.L.E., Man from Atlantis, Fantasy Island, Darkroom, Earth 2, The X Files, Star Trek: Deep Space Nine* and *Alias*. Her acting students included Raquel Welch and Suzanne Sommers.

Sixty-five-year-old American TV actor **Don S.** (Sinclair) **Davis**, best known for his recurring roles as "Major Garland Briggs" in *Twin Peaks*, and "Major General George S. Hammond" in both *Stargate SG-1* and *Stargate: Atlantis*, died of a heart attack in Canada on June 29. A former US Army captain, his many other credits include the movies *Watchers, Omen IV: The Awakening, Hook, Needful Things, Hideaway, The 6th Day, Savage Island, Seed, Beneath* and *Vipers*, the TV movies *I-Man, Beyond Loch Ness* and *The Unquiet*, and episodes of *MacGyver, Nightmare Café, Highlander, M.A.N.T.I.S., X Files* (as Dana Scully's military father), *The Outer Limits* (1995), *Poltergeist: The Legacy, Viper, The Sentinel, Honey I Shrunk the Kids: The TV Show, The Twilight Zone* (2003), *Andromeda, The Dead Zone, Supernatural* and the Sci-Fi Channel's *Flash Gordon*.

Versatile British character actress **Elizabeth Spriggs** (Elizabeth Jean Williams) died on July 2, aged 78. She appeared in the TV movies *The Cold Room, Alice in Wonderland* (1999), *A Christmas Carol* (1999), and episodes of *Tales of the Unexpected, The Haunting of Cassie Palmer, Simon and the Witch, Doctor Who, The Young Indiana Jones Chronicles, The Casebook of Sherlock Holmes* ("The Last Vampyre"), *The Tomorrow People* ("The Rameses Connection" with Christopher Lee), *Tales from the Crypt* and the revival of *Randall & Hopkirk (Deceased)*. Spriggs also portrayed the Fat Lady in the first *Harry Potter* film, but was replaced by Dawn French in *Harry Potter and the Prisoner of Azkaban*.

Larry Harmon (Lawrence Weiss), who portrayed and licensed popular children's TV character Bozo the Clown in the 1950s, died of congestive heart failure on July 3, aged 83. He was the announcer on the English-language versions of several *Tintin* series and, after acquiring the rights to the comedy duo's names and likenesses, voiced Stan Laurel for the 1966 series *A Laurel and Hardy Cartoon*.

Harmon also produced the controversial 1999 movie *The All New Adventures of Laurel & Hardy in "For Love or Mummy"*, and he used the model of robot Gort from *The Day the Earth Stood Still* for an unsold TV pilot called *General Universe* and the 1950s series *Commander Comet*.

Hollywood actress **Evelyn** [Louise] **Keyes**, best known for playing Scarlet O'Hara's younger sister Suellen in *Gone With the Wind* (1939), died of uterine cancer on July 4, aged 91. She made her movie debut in 1938, and her many credits include *Before I Hang* (with Boris Karloff), *The Face Behind the Mask* (with Peter Lorre), *Here Comes Mr Jordan*, *Ladies in Retirement*, *Strange Affair*, *A Thousand and One Nights* (as the Genie), *Around the World in Eighty Days* (1956), *A Return to Salem's Lot*, *Wicked Stepmother* (with Bette Davis) and an episode of NBC-TV's *Amazing Stories* ("Boo!"). The first of her four husbands shot himself, and she went on to marry film directors Charles Vidor and John Huston, and band leader Artie Shaw. In the 1950s she also had a three-year relationship with film producer Michael Todd, who left her to marry Elizabeth Taylor. She published two tell-all autobiographies, *Scarlett O'Hara's Younger Sister: My Lively Life in and Out of Hollywood* (1977) and *I'll Think About That Tomorrow* (1991).

Former actor turned San Francisco TV talk-show host **Les Crane** (Leslie Stein), known as "The Bad Boy of Late-Night Television", died on July 13, aged 74. In 1971, his Grammy Award-winning spoken-word recording of Max Ehrmann's poem *Desiderata* became a one-hit wonder, reaching #8 in the US music charts and #7 in the UK the following year. Crane also appeared in episodes of *Burke's Law*, *The Virginian*, *It Takes a Thief* and *Ironside* (as himself), and starred in the 1966/73 TV movie *I Love a Mystery* (as detective "Jack Packard"). From 1966–70 he was married to actress Tina Louise.

British comedy actor **Hugh Lloyd** MBE died on July 14, aged 85. He began his career in *Hancock's Half Hour*, before co-starring with Terry Scott in the BBC's *Hugh and I* (1962-67) and *The Gnomes of Dulwich* (1969). Lloyd's other credits include the films *It's Trad Dad!*, *She'll Have to Go* (aka *Maid for Murder*), *The Mouse on the Moon*, *Quadrophenia*, *Venom*, the 1999 TV version of *Alice in Wonderland*, along with episodes of *Doctor Who* ("Delta and the Bannermen"), *Woof!* and the 2000 remake of *Randall & Hopkirk (Deceased)*. He was so popular with the British public that, in a poll conducted by the *Observer* newspaper in the 1960s, he was named by readers as second only to Peter Ustinov as the person they would like to see as President if the Queen was ever replaced. Lloyd's 2002 autobiography was titled *Thank God for a Funny Face*.

Emmy Award-winning American actress **Estelle Getty** (Estelle Scher) died July 22, aged 84. She had been suffering from advanced Lewy Body Disease. Best known as the octogenarian Sophia Petrillo in the NBC-TV sitcom *The Golden Girls* (1985-92), she reprised the character in episodes of *Empty Nest*, *Blossom*, *Nurses* and the short-lived sequel series *The Golden Palace* (1992–93). Getty also appeared in the films *Mannequin* and *Stuart Little*, along with an episode of *Touched by an Angel*.

German actress and voice artist **Eva Pflug**, best known in her native country for portraying Officer Tamara Jagellovsk on the short-lived cult TV series *Space Patrol: The Fantastic Adventure of the Spaceship Orion* (1966), died on August 5, aged 79. She also appeared in Harald Reinl's influential 1959 Edgar Wallace *krimis*, *Face of the Frog*.

British stage and TV actress **Jennifer** [Mary] **Hilary** died of cancer on August 6, aged 65. She portrayed both Laura Fairlie and the title character in the 1966 BBC serial of *The Woman in White*, and her other credits include the 1989 SF movie *Slipstream* and episodes of Hammer's *Journey to the Unknown*, *Out of the Unknown* and *Tales of the Unexpected*.

Blonde American porn actress **Missy** (Maria Christina) was found dead in her Valencia, California, apartment on August 18 from an accidental overdose of prescription medication. She was 41. While working as an administration clerk at a local hospital, she met her future husband, Mickey G., and they became the first married couple to appear in adult movies. After being featured in more than 350 films since 1994, she retired in 2001, having found religion following a mental breakdown.

Fifty-year-old American comedian and actor **Bernie Mac** (Bernard Jeffery McCullough) died of complications from pneumonia on August 9. He had suffered from the tissue inflammation disease sarcoidosis since 1983, but announced it had gone into remission in 2005. Mac's film credits include the remake of *Oceans Eleven* and its two sequels, plus Michael Bay's *Transformers*.

Sixty-five-year-old musician **Isaac** [Lee] **Hayes** died shortly after being found unconscious next to his running machine on August 10. Best-known for his Oscar-winning #1 theme song to the original *Shaft* movie and as the voice of Chef on TV's *South Park*, Hayes also appeared in *Escape from New York*, *Oblivion*, *Oblivion 2: Backlash*, *Uncle Sam*, *Blues Brothers 2000*, *Book of Days*, *Anonymous*

Rex, Return to Sleepaway Camp and episodes of *Tales from the Crypt, Sliders* and *Stargate SG-1*. He was inducted into the Rock and Roll Hall of Fame in 2002.

British character actor **Terence Rigby** died of lung cancer the same day, aged 71. He portrayed Doctor Watson in the 1982 TV movie *The Hound of the Baskervilles*, opposite Tom Baker's Sherlock Holmes, and the following year turned up as Inspector Layton in the *The Sign of Four*, starring Ian Richardson as Holmes. His other credits include *Watership Down, Friends in Space*, the Bond film *Tomorrow Never Dies, Simon Magus* and the Welsh horror movie *Flick*, along with episodes of *Tales of Unease, The Rivals of Sherlock Holmes* and *Spooky*.

American character actor and playwright **George Furth** (George Schweinfurth) died of a lung infection on August 11, aged 75. He appeared in the films *Games, The Boston Strangler, Myra Breck-inridge, Sleeper, Blazing Saddles, Airport '77, Oh God!, Megaforce* and *The Man with Two Brains*, along with episodes of *The Alfred Hitchcock Hour, Honey West, Batman, The Girl from U.N.C.L.E.* ("The Carpathian Killer Affair"), *The Monkees* ("A Coffin Too Frequent"), *I Dream of Jeannie, Night Gallery* (Cyril M. Kornbluth's "The Little Black Bag"), *Salvage 1* and *You Wish*. Furth won a Tony Award for writing the book for the 1970s Stephen Sondheim musical *Company*. The pair collaborated again on the 1981 show *Merrily We Roll Along*, based on a play by Moss Hart and George S. Kaufman, and the 1996 comedy thriller *Getting Away with Murder*.

American character actor **Julius Carry** (Julius J. Carry, III), who co-starred as Lord Bowler in the Fox Network's *The Adventures of Brisco County, Jr*, died of pancreatic cancer on August 19, aged 56. He made his debut in the movie *Disco Godfather*, and his other credits include *World Gone Wild* and episodes of *Misfits of Science, Dinosaurs, Tales from the Crypt* and *Earth 2*.

Legendary Nashville drummer **Buddy Harman** (Murrey Mizell Harman, Jr.) died of congestive heart failure on August 21, aged 79. He reportedly played drums on more than 18,000 recordings, including Roy Orbison's "Pretty Woman", Johnny Cash's "Ring of Fire", Roger Miller's "King of the Road", Tammy Wynette's "Stand by Your Man", the Everly Brothers' "Bye Bye Love" and Elvis Presley's "Little Sister".

Fred Crane, best remembered for his role as Scarlett O'Hara's young beau Brent Tarleton in *Gone with the Wind*, died of a blood clot in the lung the same day, aged 90. He had been suffering from complications related to diabetes. Crane, who was the best man at his friend George (*Superman*) Reeves' first wedding in 1940, later became a classical music radio announcer in Los Angeles. He appeared as an uncredited technician in the pilot for *Lost in Space*, and supplied the voices for Victor Buono's deadly cyborgs in an episode of *Voyage to the Bottom of the Sea*.

Sixty-six-year-old British comedy actor and experimental theatre director **Ken Campbell** (Kenneth Campbell) died on August 31, just days after appearing on stage at the Edinburgh festival. He founded the Science Fiction Theatre of Liverpool in 1976, through which he put on such shows as *The Hitchhiker's Guide to the Galaxy*, the eight-hour *Illuminatus!* (which starred Jim Broadbent), and the twenty-two hour *The Warp*. As a character actor, Campbell also appeared in the films *The Tempest*, *The Bride*, *Dreamchild*, *Alice in Wonderland* (1999) and *Creep*, along with episodes of TV's *Mystery and Imagination* ("Uncle Silas") and *The Adventures of Sherlock Holmes*.

Australian-born character actor **Michael Pate**, who was best known for his villainous roles, died in New South Wales of complications from pneumonia and a chest infection on September 1, aged 88. After relocating to Hollywood in the early 1950s, he appeared in *The Strange Door* (with Charles Laughton and Boris Karloff), *The Black Castle* (with Karloff and Lon Chaney, Jr), *The Maze*, *The Silver Chalice*, *Curse of the Undead* (as vampire gunslinger Drake Robey), *Beauty and the Beast* (1962), *Tower of London* (1962, with Vincent Price) and *Brainstorm* (1965). In the late 1960s he returned to Australia, where he became a producer and director, and played the President in both *The Return of Captain Invincible* (with Christopher Lee) and *The Marsupials: The Howling III*. He also co-wrote the original story ("The Steel Monster") for the 1961 SF movie *Most Dangerous Man Alive*. On TV the prolific Pate played Clarence Leiter in the 1954 *Climax!* adaptation of "Casino Royale" opposite Barry Nelson's James Bond, and he was also in episodes of *Sugarfoot* ("The Ghost", scripted by C. L. Moore), *Men Into Space*, *Thriller* ("Trio for Terror"), *The Alfred Hitchcock Hour*, *Get Smart*, *The Man from U.N.C.L.E.*, *Honey West*, *Batman*, *The Wild Wild West* ("Night of the Infernal Machine"), *The Time Tunnel*, *Tarzan* and *Voyage to the Bottom of the Sea*, amongst many other shows.

Don LaFontaine, who distinctively voiced over 5,000 American movie trailers and 300,000 radio and TV commercials during a career that spanned more than forty years, died of complications from a collapsed lung the same day, aged 68. He appeared as a reporter in the SF mummy movie *Time Walker*, and he narrated the opening credits of TV's *Team Night Rider* (1997–98). LaFontaine's favourite film trailer voice-over was reportedly for the original *Friday the 13th* (1980).

MGM silent actress **Anita Page** (Anita Pomares), who began her film career in 1925 and co-starred with Lon Chaney, Sr in *While the City Sleeps* (1928), died in her sleep on September 6, aged 98. She also had an uncredited bit part in Chaney's *West of Zanzibar* the same year, before retiring from the screen in 1936, after successfully making the transition to sound films. She returned in character roles in the 1990s with appearances in *Witchcraft XI: Sisters of Blood*, *The Crawling Brain*, *Bob's Night Out* and *Frankenstein Rising* (in a cameo, playing Elizabeth Frankenstein).

British actress **Celia** [Christine] **Gregory**, who played the recurring role of Ruth Anderson in BBC-TV's *Survivors* (1976), died on September 8, aged 58. She also appeared in episodes of *Hammer House of Horror* ("Children of the Full Moon"), *Tales of the Unexpected* and *The Casebook of Sherlock Holmes* before giving up work in 1993 to devote more time to her family.

Rick Wright (Richard William Wright), who played keyboards with Pink Floyd, died of cancer on September 15, aged 65. A founding member of the influential British rock band, Wright also co-wrote songs ("Us and Them") and sang on several tracks on such early albums as *The Piper at the Gates of Dawn*, *The Dark Side of the Moon* and *Wish You Were Here*. Roger Walters fired Wright during the recording of *The Wall*, but he returned as a full member to the band a decade later.

American session drummer **Earl** [Cyril] **Palmer**, who worked with the like of the Beach Boys, The Monkees, Frank Sinatra, Barbra Streisand, Sarah Vaughan, Neil Young, Tom Waits, Doris Day and Randy Newman, died on September 19, aged 83. Reputedly the most recorded drummer in history, he played on such hits as Little Richard's "Tutti Frutti", "Long Tall Sally" and "Lucille", Ritchie Valens' "La Bamba", the Righteous Brothers' "You've Lost That Lovin' Feelin'" and Ike and Tina Turner's "River Deep, Mountain High" for producer Phil Spector, and Elvis Costello's "King of America". Palmer also worked on movie soundtracks, including *In the Heat of the Night*, *The Odd Couple* and *Bullitt*, and he was inducted into the Rock and Roll Hall of Fame in 2000.

Philippines-born British character actor and playwright **William** [Hubert] **Fox** died on September 20, aged 97. His credits include an early TV version of *The Two Mrs Carrolls* (1947), episodes of *The*

Avengers ("The Winged Avenger") and *Doomwatch*, and the third *Omen* movie, *The Final Conflict*.

Former child star **Buddy McDonald** (Thomas McDonald) died of congestive heart failure on September 22, aged 85. He appeared in a number of *Our Gang* shorts in the early 1930s and was one of the last surviving members of the *Little Rascals*. After drink problems led to a term in prison for robbery, he recovered in the 1950s and spent the rest of his life helping others with alcohol addiction.

Oscar-winning Hollywood star, director and producer **Paul** [Leonard] **Newman** died on September 26, aged 83. He had been suffering from lung cancer for several months. He made his film debut in *The Silver Chalice* (1954), and his other film credits include *The Towering Inferno*, *Quintet* and *When Time Ran Out* . . . He also voiced the character of Doc Hudson in Disney/Pixar's *Cars* and the spin-off short *Mater and the Ghostlight*. Early in his career, Newman appeared in episodes of TV's *Tales of Tomorrow* and *Suspense*. The founder of the "Newman's Own" range of food products, which has generated more than $125 million to charitable organizations, he was married to actress Joanne Woodward for fifty years.

Singer **George "Wydell" Jones**, a member of the 1950s doo-wop band The Edsels, died of cancer on September 27, aged 71. Jones wrote "Rama Lama Ding Dong", which finally became a hit for the group in the early 1960s.

American character actor and prolific Western player [Robert] **House Peters, Jr**, died of pneumonia on October 1, aged 92. Best known as the original bald-headed "Mr Clean" in a series of TV commercials for a household cleaner in the 1950s and '60s, he made his film debut in 1935 and appeared in *Flash Gordon* (1936), *Batman and Robin* (1949), *King of the Rocket Men*, *The Day the Earth Stood Still* (uncredited), *Red Planet Mars* (uncredited), *Port Sinister* (aka *Beast of Paradise Isle*) and *Target Earth*. His TV credits include episodes of *Ramar of the Jungle* and the *Twilight Zone*. Having failed to become a star, he retired in 1965 at the age of 50 and went into the real estate business in the San Fernando Valley.

Nick Reynolds, a founding member the Kingston Trio, died the same day, aged 75. The American folk rock group's first hit was "Tom Dooley" in 1958.

Japanese actor **Ken** (Akinobu) **Ogata** died of liver cancer on October 5, aged 71. He appeared in such movies as *Kichiku* (aka *The Demon*), *Vengeance is Mine*, *Virus*, *Samurai Reincarnation*, *The Peacock King*, the vampire comedy *My Soul is Slashed*, and *Izo*.

Prolific British film, television and stage character actor **Peter**

Copley died on October 7, aged 93. Often cast as stuffy authority figures, his numerous film credits include *The Hour of 13*, *The Man Without a Body*, The Beatles' *Help!*, Hammer's *Quatermass and the Pit* (aka *Five Million Years to Earth*) and *Frankenstein Must Be Destroyed*, *The Shoes of the Fisherman*, *Jane Eyre* (1970), *What Became of Jack and Jill?*, *Gawain and the Green Knight* and *The Colour of Magic*. He also appeared in episodes of TV's *Sherlock Holmes* (1954), *Dimensions of Fear*, *The Avengers*, *The Champions*, *Doomwatch*, *Out of the Unknown*, *Survivors* (1975), *Doctor Who* ("Pyramids of Mars"), *The New Avengers*, *Tales of the Unexpected* and *Strange*.

Scottish-born actress **Eileen Herlie** (Eileen Isobel Herlihy), who portrayed Myrtle Lum Fargate in ABC-TV's soap opera *All My Children* since 1976, died in New York of complications from pneumonia on October 8, aged 90. Earlier in her career she played Queen Gertrude opposite both Laurence Olivier and Richard Burton in two versions of *Hamlet* (1948 and 1964).

Sky News presenter **Bob Friend** MBE died of cancer the same day, aged 70. Following a twenty-year career with the BBC, he joined the fledgling satellite TV channel in 1989, and remained until his retirement in 2003. Friend appeared as himself in such films as *Independence Day* and *Mission Impossible*.

French actor **Guillaume Depardieu**, the son of actor Gérard Depardieu, died of complications from pneumonia on October 13, aged 37. He contributed voice work to the omnibus cartoon *Fear(s) of the Dark*.

American actress, Broadway musical star and TV celebrity **Edie Adams** (Elizabeth Edith Enke, aka "Edith Adams") died of complications from cancer and pneumonia on October 15, aged 81. She had been suffering from cancer for some years. Adams made her stage debut in a 1947 production of *Blithe Spirit*, and her film and TV credits include *Cinderella* (1957, opposite Julie Andrews), *The Spiral Staircase* (1961), *It's a Mad Mad Mad Mad World*, *The Oscar* (co-scripted by Harlan Ellison), *The Happy Hooker Goes to Hollywood*, *The Haunting of Harrington House*, and episodes of *Suspense* and *Fantasy Island*. Her first husband, comedian Ernie Kovacs, was killed in a car crash in Los Angeles in 1962, as was their daughter Mia exactly twenty years later.

TV announcer **Jack Narz** (John Lawrence Narz II) died of complications from a stroke the same day, aged 85. His credits include the 1950s series *Space Patrol* and *Adventures of Superman*. He subsequently hosted the popular CBS-TV quiz show *Dotto*

(1958) until it was cancelled when it was revealed results were rigged.

Levi Stubbs (Levi Stubbles), the lead singer with Motown group The Four Tops, died in his sleep on October 17, aged 72. He was diagnosed with cancer in 2000 and subsequently suffered a stroke. The Four Tops sold more than fifty million records worldwide, and Stubbs' deep baritone voice can be heard on such hits as "Reach Out, I'll Be There", "I Can't Help Myself (Sugar Pie, Honey Bunch)" and "Standing in the Shadows of Love". He also supplied the voice of the carnivorous plant Audrey II in the 1986 movie *Little Shop of Horrors* and that of Mother Brain in the *Captain N: The Game Master* animated TV series.

Burmese-born dancer, choreographer, singer and actor **Peter Gordeno** (Peter Godenho) died on October 18, aged 69. In the early 1970s he appeared as Captain Peter Carlin in seven episodes of Gerry and Sylvia Anderson's live-action TV series *UFO*. He was also in the movies *Secrets of a Windmill Girl*, *Urge to Kill* and *Carry on Columbus*. In 2005 he directed the stage production *The Baskerville Beast*, a two-hour musical version of Sir Arthur Conan Doyle's *The Hound of the Baskervilles*.

The 1960s soul and gospel singer **Dee Dee Warwick** (Delia Mae Warrick), the younger sister of Dionne, died the same day, aged 63. A former back-up singer with the Drifters, Ben E. King, Wilson Pickett, Nina Simone, Aretha Franklin and others, she made her debut as a solo singer in 1963 with the original version of "You're No Good". The record failed to chart, but Warwick went on to make several albums and have a few minor hits.

Comedian and singer **Rudy** (Rudolph) **Ray Moore**, the self-proclaimed "Godfather of Rap", died of complications from diabetes on October 19, aged 81. In the 1970s he made his name in such cult blaxploitation movies as *Dolemite*, *The Human Tornado* and *Disco Godfather*. He later returned in direct-to-video productions like *Violent New Breed*, *Vampire Assassin*, *It Came from Trafalgar* and even *The Return of Dolemite* (2002).

Eight-six-year-old former fashion designer **Mr Blackwell** (Richard Sylvan Selzer), whose annual "Best Dressed List" and "Worst Dressed List" spread fear through female celebrities from 1960 onwards, died from an intestinal infection the same day. He had collapsed at his Los Angeles home two months earlier. A former child actor and later talent agent, he became a designer in the 1950s. Mr Blackwell appeared as himself on the ABC-TV soap opera *Port Charles*.

Jamaican-born British character actor and restaurant and gym owner **Roy Stewart** died on October 27, aged 83. A former stunt-man, his many film credits include Hammer's *The Curse of the Mummy's Tomb*, *She* and *Twins of Evil*, the James Bond adventure *Live and Let Die*, and *Arabian Adventure*. He also appeared in episodes of *Out of the Unknown* (John Wyndham's "No Place Like Earth"), *Adam Adamant Lives!*, *The Avengers*, *Sherlock Holmes* (1968), *Doomwatch*, *Doctor Who* ("The Tomb of the Cybermen") and *Space: 1999*. Stewart retired from acting in the early 1980s.

Adult film-maker and actor **Buck Adams** (Charles S. Allen), the brother of hardcore actress Amber Lynn, died of heart failure on October 28, aged 52. He appeared in more than 450(!) films, including *Whore of the Worlds* (aka *Lust in Space II*), *2002: A Sex Odyssey*, *Amazing Sex Stories*, *Hunchback of the Notre Dame*, *Ground Zero L.A.*, *Genie in a Bikini*, *Edward Penishands 3*, *Whorelock*, *Princess Orgasma and the Magic Bed* and *Intercourse with the Vampire*, along with porno versions of *Frankenstein* (1994) and *Blade* (1996).

Reclusive "Peruvian Songbird" **Yma Sumac** (Zoila Augusta Emperatriz Chavarri del Castillo, aka "Imma Sumack"), an exotic soprano best remembered for her remarkable four-and-a-half octave vocal range, died of colon cancer on November 1, aged 86. Born in Cajamarca, Peru, she moved to the United States in 1940, where she appeared in a few films and TV shows, including *Secret of the Incas* and an episode of *Climax!*

Jimmy Carl Black (James Inkanish, Jr), the original drummer with Frank Zappa's 1960s band Mothers of Invention, died in Germany of cancer the same day, aged 70. He also appeared in Zappa's 1971 movie *200 Motels*.

German actor **Michael Hinz** died of a stroke on November 6, aged 68. His credits include *Lana Queen of the Amazons*, *Beyond the Darkness* and Mario Bava's 1972 sex-comedy *Four Times That Night*.

British drummer [John] **"Mitch" Mitchell**, the last surviving member of The Jimi Hendrix Experience, was found dead in a hotel room in Portland, Oregon, on November 12. He was 61. Mitchell played on such influential albums as *Are You Experienced?* and *Electric Ladyland*, and performed with Hendrix at the iconic 1969 Woodstock festival.

Cheeky British comedy actor **Reg** [Reginald Alfred] **Varney** died after a short illness on November 16, aged 92. He was best known for his role as Stan Butler in the later Hammer Film productions *On* *the Buses, Mutiny on the Buses* and *Holiday on the Buses*, based on the hit TV series *On the Buses* (1969–73). He also starred in the 1972 comedy *Go For a Take* (aka *Double Take*), which featured Dennis Price as an actor playing Dracula. In 1967 Varney became the first person to use an ATM machine in Britain.

American comedy actor **Paul Benedict**, best known for playing English neighbour Harry Bentley in the CBS-TV sitcom *The Jeffersons*, died on December 1, aged 70. Having suffered from acromegaly as a young man, which resulted in a slightly oversized lower jaw, he appeared in such movies as *They Might be Giants*, *The Electric Grandmother* (scripted by Ray Bradbury), *The Man with Two Brains*, *Arthur 2 On the Rocks*, *Attack of the 50ft Woman* (1993), and he had an uncredited role in *The Devil's Advocate*. Benedict was also in episodes of *Sesame Street* (as "The Mad Painter"), *The Twilight Zone* (1987), *Tales from the Crypt* and *The Addams Family* (1991).

American folk singer **Odetta** (Odetta Holmes), who was an influence on the civil rights movement as well as Harry Belafonte, Bob Dylan, Joan Baez and others, died of heart disease and pulmonary fibrosis on December 2, aged 77.

Dutch-born Hollywood leading lady **Nina Foch** (Nina Consuelo Maud Fock) died of long-term blood disorder myelodysplasia on December 5, aged 84. She was taken ill while teaching at USC. In 1944 she appeared in *The Return of the Vampire* (with Bela Lugosi) and played the queen of the lycanthropes in *Cry of the Werewolf*. Her other film credits include *Shadows in the Night* (with George Zucco), *I Love a Mystery* (1945), *A Thousand and One Nights*, *The Ten Commandments* (1956), TV versions of *Ten Little Indians* (1959) and *Rebecca* (1962), *Nomads*, *Sliver* and *Alien Nation: Dark Horizon*, along with episodes of *Lights Out*, *Tales of Tomorrow*, *Suspense*, *Climax!*, *The Thin Man* ("Lady Frankenstein"), *Shirley Temple's Storybook*, *The Outer Limits*, *The Wild Wild West*, *Kolchak: The Night Stalker* and *Shadow Chasers*.

"B" movie star **Beverly Garland** (Beverly Fessenden, aka "Beverly Campbell") died after a long cancer-related illness the same day, aged 82. Best remembered for her roles as feisty women in such Roger Corman cult movies as *Swamp Women*, *It Conquered the World* and *Not of This Earth* (1957), her other films include *The Neanderthal Man*, *Curucu Beast of the Amazon*, *The Alligator People* (with Lon Chaney, Jr), *Twice Told Tales* (with Vincent Price), *The Mad Room*, *Airport 1975* and *Hellfire* (aka *Blood Song*). On TV she played Lois Lane's mother Ellen in *Lois & Clark: The New*

Adventures of Superman (1995–97), was regular Estelle Reese on ABC-TV's daytime soap *Port Charles* (2000), and also appeared in episodes of *Science Fiction Theatre*, *The Twilight Zone*, *Thriller*, *The Wild Wild West*, *Planet of the Apes*, *Switch*, *The Hardy Boys/Nancy Drew Mysteries* and *Teen Angel*.

American character actor **Robert Prosky** (Robert Joseph Porzuczek), who played Sgt Stan Jablonski on NBC-TV's *Hill Street Blues* from 1984–87, died of complications from heart surgery on December 8, aged 77. His movie credits include *Christine* (based on the novel by Stephen King), *The Keep* (based on the novel by F. Paul Wilson), *The Natural*, *From the Dead of Night* (based on the novel by Gary Brander), *Gremlins 2 The New Batch*, *Last Action Hero*, *Miracle on 34th Street* (1994), *The Lake* and *D-Tox* (aka *Eye See You*), plus episodes of *Alfred Hitchcock Presents* (1986) and *Touched by an Angel*.

British character actress **Kathy Staff** died after a long illness on December 10, aged 80. Best known for playing Nora Batty in the BBC comedy series *Last of the Summer Wine* for twenty-five years, she also appeared in Stephen Frears' *Mary Reilly* (1996), a reworking of "Dr Jekyll and Mr Hyde".

Iconic 1950s pin-up **Bettie Page** (Betty Mae Page) died in Los Angeles on December 11, aged 85. She had suffered a heart attack nine days earlier following a short battle with pneumonia. Page was a *Playboy* "Playmate of the Month" for January 1955, and under the influence of photographer Irving Claw she became the "Queen of Bondage", appearing in more than fifty burlesque films, including *Striporama*, *Varietease* and *Teaserama*. After becoming a born-again Christian and working full-time for evangelist Billy Graham's ministry, she was diagnosed with acute schizophrenia and disappeared from public view for twenty years, eventually resurfacing in the early 1990s. She was portrayed by Paige Richards in *Bettie Page: Dark Angel* (2004) and Gretchen Mol in *The Notorious Bettie Page* (2005). Jennifer Connelly's heroine Jenny Blake in *The Rocketeer* (1991) was also inspired by Page.

Transgender voice actor **Maddie Blaustein** [Adam S. Blaustein], who provided the English voice of Meowth in the various *Pokémon* cartoons, died the same day, aged 48. After working at both Marvel Comics and DC Comics, she went on to create photos for *Weekly World News*. Blaustein also did voice work for various *Sonic the Hedgehog* video games and TV episodes.

Amiable Hollywood leading man [Charles] **Van Johnson** died on December 12, aged 92. His movie credits include *A Guy Named Joe*

(1943), *Brigadoon*, *The Pied Piper of Hamelin* (1957), *Murder in an Etruscan Cemetery*, *The Purple Rose of Cairo*, *Escape from Paradise* (aka *Flight from Paradise*) and *Killer Crocodile*. On TV he appeared as The Minstrel in *Batman*, and in episodes of *Alfred Hitchcock Presents* (1988), *Fantasy Island* and *Tales of the Unexpected*. In 1942, while on his way to a film screening, Johnson was involved in a road accident and sustained injuries that left him with a metal plate in his head. Following rumours about the actor's sexuality, MGM boss Louis B. Meyer arranged for Johnson to marry the wife of his best friend, actor Keenan Wynn, on the same day the couple's divorce came through.

West German character actor **Horst Tappert** died of complications from diabetes on December 13, aged 85. Often cast as a police inspector or doctor, his film credits include *The Horror of Blackwood Castle*, *Gorilla Gang*, *The Man with the Glass Eye* and *School of Fear*. For Jess Franco he starred in *The Devil Came from Akasava*, *She Killed in Ecstasy* and *Der Todesrächer von Soho*.

American film and TV actor **Sam**(uel) **Bottoms**, the brother of actors Timothy, Joseph and Ben, died of a brain tumour on December 16, aged 53. A former teen actor, his credits include *Apocalypse Now*, Charles B. Griffith's *Up from the Depths*, *Hunter's Blood*, *The Witching of Ben Wagner*, *Dolly Dearest*, *Project Shadowchaser III* (aka *Project Shadowchaser: Beyond the Edge of Darkness*) and an episode of *The X Files*.

Actress **Majel Barrett-Roddenberry** (Majel Lee Hudec), the widow of *Star Trek* creator Gene Roddenberry (who died in 1991), died of complications from leukaemia on December 18, aged 76. Although she appeared in a number of movies and TV shows in the early 1960s, she will be best remembered as semi-regular Nurse Christine Chapel in the original *Star Trek* series (1966–69). In fact, she had been cast in the show's pilot, "The Cage", as "Number One", but was subsequently demoted. She recreated the role (now a doctor) for *Star Trek: The Motion Picture* and *Star Trek IV: The Voyage Home*. Barrett also supplied the voice of Lt. M'Ress for the 1970s animated *Star Trek* series, and voiced various computers for *Star Trek: The Next Generation* (1987–94), *Star Trek: Deep Space Nine* (1993–99), *Star Trek: Voyager* (1995–2001), *Enterprise* (2005), *Star Trek Generations*, *Star Trek First Contact*, *Star Trek Nemesis* and J. J. Abrams' 2009 re-imagining of *Star Trek*. Her other credits include *Westworld*, *The Man in the Santa Claus Suit*, *Mommy*, *Hamlet A.D.D.* and episodes of *The Next Step Beyond*, *Babylon 5*, the animated *Spider-Man* (1996–98) and *Diagnosis Murder* ("Alienated"). She was also in Gene Roddenberry's TV movie pilots *Genesis II*, *The Questor Tapes*, *Planet Earth* and *Spectre*, as well as the posthumous Roddenberry series *Earth: Final Conflict* (1997), which she executive produced along with *Andromeda* (2000–02).

Singer and actress **Eartha Kitt** [Eartha Mae Keith] best known for her 1953 hit "Santa Baby", died of colon cancer on Christmas Day, aged 81. The second person to play Catwoman on ABC-TV's *Batman* (1966–68), her other credits include a 1958 adaptation of *Heart of Darkness* on CBS-TV's *Playhouse 90* (with Boris Karloff), and such movies as *The Serpent Warriors*, *Erik the Viking*, *Living Doll*, *Ernest Scared Stupid*, *The Jungle Book: Mowgli's Story*, *Holes* and *The Emperor's New Groove*, along with its sequel and spin-off TV series. Orson Welles once described Kitt as "The most exciting woman in the world".

Hollywood leading lady **Ann Savage** [Bernice Maxine Lyon] died of complications from a series of strokes the same day, aged 87. Best remembered for appearing as the *femme fatale* in the cult *noir* movie *Detour* (1945), she also appeared in such "B" thrillers as *One Dangerous Night*, *After Midnight with Bostom Blackie*, *Murder in Times Square*, *Scared Stiff* (aka *Treasure of Fear*, 1945), *Midnight Manhunt* (with George Zucco), *Apology for Murder*, *The Spider* (1945) and *Jungle Jim on Pygmy Island*. Although she semi-retired from the screen in the late 1950s, her last film credit was for Canadian director Guy Maddin in 2007.

American character actor and music producer **Bernie** (Bernard) **Hamilton**, best known for playing police captain Harold Dobey on ABC-TV's *Starsky & Hutch* (1975–79), died of cardiac arrest on December 30, aged 80. His other credits include the serial *Mysterious Island* (1951), *Jungle Man-Eaters*, *Captain Sinbad* and *Scream Blacula Scream*, plus episodes of TV's *Ramar of the Jungle*, *Jungle Jim*, *Alfred Hitchcock Presents*, *The Twilight Zone*, *The Alfred Hitchcock Hour*, *Tarzan* (1967–68) and *Galactica 1980*.

The body of 60-year-old American guitarist and songwriter **Ron Asheton** was found at his home on January 6, 2009. He had apparently died of a heart attack several days earlier. Asheton was an original member of Iggy Pop's late 1960s protopunk band The Stooges, playing on such hits as "I Wanna Be Your Dog" and "No Fun". One of his songs can be heard over the end credits of the movie *Mosquito* (1995).

FILM/TV TECHNICIANS

Brice Mack, who painted animation backgrounds for Walt Disney, died on January 2, aged 90. He worked on *Fantasia, Song of the South, The Adventures of Ichabod and Mr. Toad, Cinderella, Alice in Wonderland, Peter Pan* and *Lady and the Tramp.* He later produced Curtis Harrington's *Ruby* and directed the 1978 AIP horror film *Jennifer.*

British TV and film director **Claude Whatham** died on January 4, aged 80. A former artist and theatrical set designer, he directed episodes of BBC-TV's *Supernatural* and Anglia Television's *Tales of the Unexpected,* along with the 1985 Tyburn movie *Murder Elite.*

Costume designer **Bill Belew,** who created all Elvis Presley's stage costumes from the singer's 1968 TV comeback special until his death in 1977, died of complications from diabetes on January 7, aged 76.

American film producer **Jerry A. Baerwitz,** who also directed the 1962 US version of the Japanese monster movie *Varan the Unbelievable,* died on January 10, aged 82. His other credits include *Fright Night* (1985) and the Dean R. Koontz adaptation *Hideaway.*

Richard Knerr who, with his best friend Arthur "Spud" Melin, founded the Wham-O toy company, died from a stroke on January 14, aged 82. The US company was responsible for such innovative products as the Frisbee, the Superball, the Slip 'n' Slide, Silly String and, perhaps most famous of all, the Hula Hoop which, during its heyday in 1958, was being manufactured at the rate of 20,000 per day.

Reverend **Lynn Lemon,** the Baptist pastor who invested in Edward D. Wood, Jr's infamous *Plan 9 from Outer Space,* died of a heart attack on January 15, aged 90. He had bit parts in that film, *Invasion of the Bee Girls* and *Raising Dead,* and appeared in the documentary *The Haunted World of Edward D. Wood, Jr.*

Emmy Award-winning writer and producer **Robert Cunniff** died after a long illness on January 20. He was 81. From 1972–75 he produced TV's *Sesame Street* and created the long-running *Mouseterpiece Theater* for the Disney Channel in 1983.

Australian film distributor **Roc** (Roscoe) **Kirby,** who founded Village Roadshow in 1954, died on January 25, aged 89.

American TV director and producer **Dwight** [Arlington] **Hemion** died of renal failure on January 28, aged 81. Hemion was executive producer of CBS' infamous *Star Wars Holiday Special* in 1978, featuring Bea Arthur, Art Carney, Harvey Korman and The Jefferson

Starship. It was so bad, George Lucas later disowned it, and the show has never officially been released on video.

American TV producer and director **Herb**(ert) **Kenwith** died of prostate cancer on January 30, aged 90. He directed episodes of the original *Star Trek* ("The Lights of Zetar"), the Gothic soap opera *Strange Paradise*, and *Mr Merlin*, along with many other shows.

The body of 48-year-old **Diane Chenery-Wickens** was discovered in woodland in May after the British make-up designer disappeared in January. Her husband, a spiritualist minister, was subsequently found guilty of her murder and jailed for eighteen years. Chenery-Wickens won an Emmy for her work on the 2000 miniseries *Arabian Nights*, and her other credits include BBC-TV's *Gormenghast* and *The League of Gentlemen*.

British cinematographer **Bryan Langley** died on February 1, aged 99. He began working on films in the 1920s and his credits include a couple of early Alfred Hitchcock movies. His many other films include *The Limping Man*, *The Gables Mystery*, *The Dark Eyes of London* (aka *The Human Monster*, with Bela Lugosi), *Miranda* (uncredited) and the 1948 version of *The Monkey's Paw*. He also worked (uncredited) on *The Ghost Train* (1941), *1984* (1956) and *Night of the Demon* (aka *Curse of the Demon*).

Spanish film director and screenwriter **Carlos Aured** [Alonso] died of a heart attack on February 3, aged 71. His credits include *The Mummy's Revenge*, *Curse of the Devil*, *House of Psychotic Women* and *Horror Rises from the Tomb*, all made in the early 1970s and starring Paul Naschy. After the pair fell out, Aured went on to make films in other genres, returning to horror in the 1980s with *El Enigma del yate* and *Atrapados en el miedo*. He was assistant director on *Exorcism's Daughter* and *The Werewolf vs. Vampire Women* (also starring Naschy), and he produced *Monster Dog* and *Alien Predator*.

Japanese film director and screenwriter **Kon Ichikawa** (Giichi Ichikawa) died of pneumonia on February 13, aged 92. Acknowledging the influence of Walt Disney, his varied credits include the fantasies *The Firebird* and *Princess from the Moon*, plus an episode of the anthology film *Ten Nights of Dreams*.

Oscar-winning British cinematographer [Francis] **David Watkin** died of prostate cancer on February 19, aged 82. His credits include *The Beatles' Help!*, *Marat/Sade*, *How I Won the War*, *The Bed Sitting Room*, *Catch-22*, *The Devils*, Hammer's *To the Devil a Daughter*, *Return to Oz*, *Journey to the Center of the Earth* (1999), *Murder on the Moon* (aka *Murder by Moonlight*), *Hamlet*

(1990), *The Cabinet of Dr Ramirez* and *Jane Eyre* (1996). He also shot the uncredited title sequence for the 1964 James Bond film *Goldfinger*. Watkin invented the "Wendy Light", a suspended grid that has become standard equipment for lighting exterior night shoots, and he received a Lifetime Achievement Award from the British Society of Cinematographers in 2004.

Italian director, writer, cinematographer and producer **Osvaldo Civirani** died on February 20, aged 90. His credits include *The Most Prohibited Sex* (which featured a vampire and a Frankenstein Monster), *Kindar the Invulnerable* and *Hercules Against the Sons of the Sun*.

International film distributor **Sandy Cobe** died after a long illness the same day, aged 79. As chairman and CEO of Intercontinental Releasing Corporation he produced such films as *To All a Good Night*, *Terror on Tour* and *Access Code*.

British cinematographer **Larry Pizer**, who photographed *Morgan: A Suitable Case for Treatment*, died of cancer in New York on February 27. He was 82. Having started his film career at the Alexander Korda Studios in Denham, Pizer's later credits include *Phantom of the Paradise*, *Alice Cooper: Welcome to My Nightmare* (with the voice of Vincent Price), *The Clairvoyant* (1982), *Timerider*, *The Phantom of the Opera* (1983), *Svengali* (1983), *Mannequin: On the Move* and the Bruce Springsteen music video "Dancing in the Dark" directed by Brian De Palma.

Actor turned director **George Tyne** (Martin "Buddy" Yarus) died on March 7, aged 91. He began his career as an actor in the early 1940s, appearing (uncredited) in a number of war films. Later he was in *The Boston Strangler* and an episode of *Voyage to the Bottom of the Sea* before turning to directing with episodes of TV's *The Ghost and Mrs Muir*, *Tabitha* and *Space Academy*. Blacklisted during the 1950s, Tyne was also assistant director on Albert Band's 1965 TV pilot *Hercules and the Princess of Troy*.

Seventy-six-year-old British-born production designer and art director **Trevor Williams**, who began his career working on the 1960s TV series *Dark Shadows*, died of a heart attack on February 14 while on vacation in Devon, England. His many other credits include *The Strange Case of Dr Jekyll and Mr Hyde* (1968), *House of Dark Shadows*, *Night of Dark Shadows*, *To Kill a Clown*, *The Night Stalker*, *The Night Strangler*, *Dracula* (1973), *The Norliss Tapes*, *The Picture of Dorian Gray* (1973), *The Turn of the Screw* (1974), *Futureworld*, *The Changeling*, *Mazes and Monsters*, *Endangered Species*, *Murder in Space*, *Allan Quatermain and the Lost City of*

Gold, The Hunchback (1997) and the *Police Academy* films, along with episodes of *Out of the Unknown*, the *Dead of Night* pilot, and the 2000–01 series *The Immortal*, starring Lorenzo Lamas.

American film producer **William Hayward** (William Leland Hayward III) died from a self-inflicted gunshot wound to the heart on March 9. He was 66. The son of agent Leland Hayward and actress Margaret Sullavan, his mother and sister Bridget both died of barbiturate overdoses in 1960. Hayward, who in 1969 teamed up with Peter Fonda and Bert Schneider to produce the counter-culture classic *Easy Rider*, had a serious motorcycle accident in 2003 that left him severely disabled. His other film credits include the cult SF movie *Idaho Transfer* (1973), which was directed by Fonda.

Oscar-winning British director and scriptwriter **Anthony Minghella** CBE died on March 18, aged 54. He suffered a fatal haemorrhage in a London hospital after undergoing surgery for throat cancer. He began his career at the BBC in the early 1980s, and his credits include *Truly Madly Deeply* and *The Talented Mr Ripley*. He also scripted episodes of *Jim Henson's The Storyteller*, *The Storyteller: Greek Myths* and the children's TV drama *Living with Dinosaurs*. In 2000 he entered into a producing partnership with Sydney Pollack, who himself died two months after Minghella.

Welsh-born **Neil Aspinall**, often referred to as the "fifth Beatle", died of lung cancer in New York on March 24, aged 66. A boyhood friend of Paul McCartney, George Harrison and John Lennon, he rose from the band's roadie, personal assistant and confidant to running their London-based Apple Corporation. Aspinall had minor musical roles on such hits as "Yellow Submarine" (background vocals), "Within You Without You" (playing an Indian tamboura), "Being for the Benefit of Mr Kite" (harmonica) and "Magical Mystery Tour" (percussion). He was also an extra in the film *How I Won the War* starring Lennon.

American-born film director, screenwriter, producer and actor **Jules Dassin** (Julius Samuel Dassin) died of complications from flu in Athens, Greece, on March 31. He was 96. Starting out as an assistant to Alfred Hitchcock, his credits include the 1941 MGM short *The Tell-Tale Heart*, based on the story by Edgar Allan Poe, and *The Canterville Ghost* (1944), starring Charles Laughton. Blacklisted after refusing to testify before the House of Representatives Un-American Activities Committee, Dassin left the United States for France in 1953 and in 1966 he married the Greek actress and culture minister Melina Mercouri (who died in 1994).

Former talent agent turned studio executive **Guy McElwaine** died of pancreatic cancer on April 2, aged 71. He produced *Exorcist: The Beginning* and its original/variant version, *Dominion: Prequel to the Exorcist*. McElwaine was named president of Columbia Pictures in 1982, and later became president of Morgan Creek Productions from 2002 until his death.

American director and producer **Alex Grasshoff** (Alexander Grasshoff) died on April 5 of complications following leg surgery. He was 79. Grasshoff's credits include *Future Shock*, *The Last Dinosaur*, and three episodes of ABC-TV's *Kolchak: The Night Stalker*. He had to return the feature documentary Oscar he won in 1969 on a technicality.

American mathematician and meteorologist **Edward** [Norton] **Lorenz**, "the father of chaos theory", died of cancer on April 16, aged 90. Norton came up with the "butterfly effect", which postulated that small actions on one side of the Earth could cause major changes elsewhere. His hypothesis, widely regarded as the third scientific revolution of the twentieth century, following relativity and quantum physics, has been utilized in many Hollywood movies. He was awarded the Kyoto Prize for science in 1991.

Broadway music director and dance arranger **Peter Howard** died of complications from Parkinson's disease on April 18, aged 80. He arranged the opening dance sequence for *Indiana Jones and the Temple of Doom*.

Distribution executive **Stanley E. Dudelson**, who founded the television division of American International Pictures in the 1960s, died of lung disease on April 26, aged 83. After joining New Line Cinema in 1971, he was an executive producer on the first two *A Nightmare on Elm Street* movies. His other executive producer credits include *Morella*, *Horror 101* and *Museum of the Dead*.

Hollywood producer and director **Sandy Howard** died of complications from Alzheimer's disease on May 16, aged 80. He had suffered from the disease for ten years. After co-directing such films as *Tarzan and the Trappers* and the US version of *Gammera the Invicible*, he went on to produce *The Neptune Factor*, *The Devil's Rain*, *Embryo*, *The Island of Dr Moreau* (1977), *The Silent Flute* (aka *Circle of Iron*), *Meteor*, *What Waits Below* (aka *Secrets of the Phantom Caverns*), *Angel*, *Avenging Angel*, *Dark Tower* and *Blue Monkey* (aka *Invasion of the Bodysuckers*).

Scottish-born **David** [Nelson Godfrey] **Mitton**, who directed thirty-seven episodes of the BBC's *Thomas the Tank Engine & Friends* from 1984–95, died of a heart attack the same day, aged 69. A skilled model-maker, he had previously worked on the special effects for such Gerry Anderson TV shows as *Thunderbirds*, *Captain Scarlet*, *The Secret Service* and *U.F.O.*

Joseph Pevney, who directed fourteen episodes of the original *Star Trek* TV series (including "The City on the Edge of Forever", "Catspaw", "Wolf in the Fold" and "The Trouble with Tribbles"), died on May 18, aged 96. A former actor in the 1940s and early '50s, his other directing credits include the films *The Strange Door* (with Charles Laughton and Boris Karloff) and *Man of a Thousand Faces* (starring James Cagney as Lon Chaney, Sr), along with the TV pilot for *Destination Space* and episodes of *Bewitched*, *The Alfred Hitchcock Hour*, *The Munsters*, *Search*, *The Hardy Boys/Nancy Drew Mysteries* ("Hardy Boys and Nancy Drew Meet Dracula"), *Lucan*, *Fantasy Island*, *Cliffhangers: The Secret Empire* and *The Incredible Hulk*. He retired in 1985.

German-born NASA illustrator and designer **Harry Lange** (Hans-Kurt Lange), who created the look of *2001: A Space Odyssey* for Stanley Kubrick, died of complications from a stroke in Oxford, England, on May 22. He was 77. Lange went on to work on *Z.P.G.*, *Star Wars* (uncredited), *Moonraker*, *The Empire Strikes Back*, *Superman II*, *The Great Muppet Caper*, *The Dark Crystal*, *The Return of the Jedi*, *Monty Python's The Meaning of Life* and *Hyper Sapien: People from Another Star*. He was nominated for Oscars for his work on *2001* and *The Return of the Jedi*.

Seventy-three-year-old Oscar-winning Hollywood actor, producer and director **Sydney** (Irwin) **Pollack** died on May 26 following a nine-month battle with cancer. His directing credits include *Castle Keep* and two episodes of TV's *The Alfred Hitchcock Hour*. Pollack also executive produced Kenneth Branagh's *Dead Again* and produced Peter Howitt's *Sliding Doors*. In 2000 he began a producing partnership with Anthony Minghella, who himself died in March.

TV producer **Robert H.** (Harris) **Justman**, who produced fifty-six episodes of the original *Star Trek* series, died of complications from Parkinson's disease on May 28, aged 81. His father owned Hollywood's Motion Picture Center Studio, which later became part of Desilu Studios, and he worked as a production assistant (often uncredited) or assistant director on such movies as the remake of *M*, *Red Planet Mars*, *Kiss Me Deadly*, *The World the Flesh and the Devil*, and the TV shows *Adventures of Superman*, *One Step Beyond* and *The Outer Limits*. Justman's other credits include *Search*, *Star Trek: The Next Generation* and the TV movies *Planet Earth*, *The Man from Atlantis* and *Dark Mansions*.

TV and film director **Georg Fenady** (George J. Fenady) died on May 29, aged 77. The younger brother of screenwriter Andrew J. Fenady, he directed the 1973 horror movies *Terror in the Wax Museum* and *Arnold*. His other credits include a trio of TV disaster movies and episodes of *Manimal* and *Knight Rider*.

Oscar-winning special effects creator **Stan Winston** died of multiple myeloma on June 15, aged 62. Winston and his spfx studio set the standard for robotics/animatronics and prosthetic make-up effects, and his numerous credits in special make-up effects include *Gargoyles*, *The Bat People*, *Mr Black and Mr Hyde*, *Mansion of the Doomed*, *Dracula's Dog*, *The Wiz*, *The Entity*, *The Hand*, *Dead & Buried*, *Heartbeeps*, *The Thing*, *The Phantom of the Opera* (1983), *Chiller*, *Edward Scissorhands*, *Terminator 2: Judgment Day*, *Batman Returns*, *Interview with the Vampire: The Vampire Chronicles*, *The Island of Dr Moreau* (1996), *Galaxy Quest*, *Artificial Intelligence: A.I.*, *Terminator 3: Rise of the Machines* and *Constantine*. He also designed the special effects for TV's *Manimal*, *Invaders from Mars* (1986), *Aliens*, *Predator*, *The Monster Squad*, *Leviathan*, *Predator 2*, *Congo*, *The Relic*, *Small Soldiers*, *Lake Placid*, *Inspector Gadget*, *End of Days*, *Jurassic Park III*, *The Day the World Ended* (2001), *Darkness Falls*, *Big Fish*, *Iron Man* and *Terminator: Salvation*. Winston directed *Pumpkinhead*, *A Gnome Named Norm*, the Universal Studios theme park attraction *T2 3-D: Battle Across Time*, and the short film *Ghosts* starring Michael Jackson. He also worked on the infamous *Star Wars Holiday Special*. Actor turned California governor Arnold Schwarzenegger said, "The entertainment industry has lost a genius, and I lost one of my best friends". *The Winston Effect: The Art and History of Stan Winston Studio* was published by Titan Books in 2006.

French film director **Jean Delannoy** died on June 18, aged 100. His credits include the Jean Cocteau-scripted fantasy *Love Eternal* and the 1956 version of *The Hunchback of Notre Dame* starring Anthony Quinn and Gina Lollobrigida.

American costume designer **Kermit** [Ernest Hollinghead] **Love**, who helped puppeteer Jim Henson create Big Bird, Cookie Monster, Oscar the Grouch and other *Sesame Street* characters, died of congestive heart failure on June 21, aged 91. Love also appeared on the TV show as "Willy", the local hot dog vendor. Kermit the Frog was actually named after philosophy professor **Kermit Smith**, who died the previous month.

Oscar-winning film producer and manager **Charles H. Joffe**, best-known for his long association with Woody Allen since the early

1960s, died after a long battle with lung cancer on July 9, aged 78. Joffe's movies with Allen include *Everything You Always Wanted to Know About Sex* *But Were Afraid to Ask*, *Sleeper*, *Love and Death*, *A Midsummer Night's Sex Comedy*, *Zelig*, *The Purple Rose of Cairo*, *New York Stories*, *Alice*, *Shadows and Fog*, *Manhattan Murder Mystery* and *The Curse of the Jade Scorpion*, among many other titles. Joffe and his management partner Jack Rollins are also credited with fostering the careers of Billy Crystal, Mike Nicholls, Elaine May, David Letterman and Lenny Bruce.

Former actor turned journeyman TV director **Jud Taylor** (Judson Taylor), who directed five episodes of the original *Star Trek* series, died after a long illness on August 6, aged 76. His other credits include the TV movies *Revenge*, *The Disappearance of Flight 412*, *Search for the Gods*, *Future Cop*, *Doubletake*, *Kung Fu: The Legend Continues*, and episodes of *The Man from U.N.C.L.E.*, *The Girl from U.N.C.L.E.* and *Captain Nice*.

Seventy-seven-year-old **Bernie Brillstein**, a former agent turned Hollywood manager-producer, died of chronic pulmonary disease on August 7. He had undergone double-bypass heart surgery in February. Apart from being a major force behind the success of TV's *Saturday Night Live*, *The Muppets*, *Fraggle Rock* and *ALF*, Brillstein also received executive producer credits on such movies as *The Blues Brothers*, *Ghostbusters*, *Dragnet*, *Ghostbusters II*, *The Cable Guy* and *What Planet Are You From?*. He also directed the 1989 NBC-TV special *The Wickedest Witch*. While CEO at Lorimar Film Entertainment in the late 1980s, Brillstein famously feuded with CAA chief Michael Ovitz.

Legendary American music producer **Jerry Wexler** died on August 15, aged 91. He had been suffering from congenital heart disease for a couple of years. As a partner in Atlantic Records, he helped shape the careers of Ray Charles, Aretha Franklin, Wilson Pickett, Bob Dylan, Dusty Springfield and Willie Nelson. While a writer at *Billboard* magazine in the 1940s Wexler coined the term "rhythm & blues", and he was inducted into the Rock and Roll Hall of Fame in 1987.

American record producer **Jerry Finn** died on August 21, aged 39. He had suffered a brain haemorrhage in July and never regained consciousness. Finn worked with acts such as Blink-182, Green Day, Smoking Popes and Morrissey.

Morris F. (Francis) **Sullivan**, whose Sullivan Bluth Studios produced the animated films *The Land Before Time*, *An American Tail* and *All Dogs Go to Heaven*, died on August 24, aged 91.

French special effects make-up designer **Benoît Lestang** committed suicide on July 27, aged around 44. The films he worked on include *Baby Blood*, *The City of Lost Children*, *Wax Mask*, *Brotherhood of the Wolf*, *Satan* and many others.

Former radio producer and head of BBC TV comedy **Geoffrey Perkins** died when he fell into the path of an oncoming lorry in London on August 29. It is thought that the 55-year-old fainted while walking along the street. While working for BBC Radio Light Entertainment, Perkins produced *The Hitchhiker's Guide to the Galaxy*.

Mexican-born animator and director **José "Bill" Melendez** (José Cuauhtemoc Melendez, aka "J. C. Melendez"), best known as the voice of Snoopy in his numerous *Charlie Brown* TV specials since the mid-1960s, died on September 2, aged 91. Melendez began his career in the early 1940s working as an animator on *Looney Tunes* cartoons for Warner Bros., and his other credits include *Dick Deadeye or Duty Done*, *Frosty Returns*, and the 1979 TV version of *The Lion, the Witch & The Wardrobe*.

Mel Harris who, while an executive at Paramount, led the 1987 revival of *Star Trek* with *The Next Generation*, died of cancer on September 6, aged 65. A former radio announcer, during his fourteen years at the studio he was also responsible for helping to create the "sell-through" home video market and the USA Network.

British-born film, theatre and TV director **David Hugh Jones** died in Rockport, Maine, of emphysema on September 18. He was 74. Having begun his career with the BBC in the late 1950s, he moved to America in the late 1980s where he directed episodes of *Early Edition*, *Fantasy Island* (1998), *Now and Again*, *Ghost Whisperer* and the 1999 TV movie of *A Christmas Carol* starring Patrick Stewart.

Prolific Philippine producer and director **Cirio H. Santiago** (aka "Leonard Hermes") died of complications from lung cancer on September 26, aged 72. Santiago worked in all the exploitation genres, especially post-apocalyptic SF, and had a long-running production partnership in the 1980s with Roger Corman's New World Pictures. His many film credits as a director include *Vampire Hookers* (starring John Carradine), *Stryker*, *Wheels of Fire*, *Future Hunters*, *Equalizer 2000*, *Demon of Paradise*, *Dune Warriors*, *Raiders of the Sun*, *Vulcan*, *Bloodfist 2050* and *Road Raiders*. He also produced *The Blood Drinkers* (aka *The Vampire People*), *Up from the Depths*, *Terminal Virus* and *Robo Warriors*.

British film and television producer **Mark Shivas** died of lung cancer on October 11, aged 70. A former head of drama at the BBC and the first head of BBC Films, he produced such movies as *The Witches*, adapted from the book by Roald Dahl, Anthony Minghella's BAFTA-winning *Truly Madly Deeply*, and the TV film *The Cormorant*, based on the horror novel by Stephen Gregory.

Forty-one-year-old miniature effects model-maker **Mark "Buck" Bucksen** died in a road traffic accident on October 16. While at ILM he worked on *Starship Troopers, Star Wars Episode 1: The Phantom Menace, Star Wars Episode II: Attack of the Clones, Pirates of the Caribbean: The Curse of the Black Pearl* and *War of the Worlds*. After moving to Kerner Optical, his credits include *Transformers, Evan Almighty* and *Terminator: Salvation*.

American adult movie director **Gerard** [Gerardo Rocco] **Damiano**, best known for his ground-breaking porno film *Deep Throat* (1972), died of complications from a stroke on October 25, aged 80. Filmed in six days on a budget of just $25,000, *Deep Throat* grossed an estimated $600 million after it became the first hardcore movie released theatrically in America. His other films include *The Magical Ring, The Devil in Miss Jones*, and the non-porno horror film *Legacy of Satan*.

British-born film producer **John Daly** died of cancer in Los Angeles on Halloween, aged 71. In 1966 he co-founded the Hemdale Company with actor David Hemmings, and his many credits include *Strange Behavior* (aka *Dead Kids*), *Turkey Shoot* (aka *Escape 2000*), *The Terminator, The Return of the Living Dead, Vampire's Kiss* and *Miracle Mile*.

Executive vice-president of Def Jam, **Shakir Stewart**, died of a self-inflicted gunshot wound on November 1. The 34-year-old had only succeeded Jay-Z as the head of the recording label five months earlier.

Motown Records president (1988–95) **Jheryl Busby** was found dead in a hot tub at his home on November 4. He was 59. Busby brought Diana Ross back to the label after several years and, along with working with such stalwarts as Stevie Wonder and Lionel Richie, developed new acts like Boys II Men and Queen Latifah. After being forced out of the company by a legal dispute with MCA, he joined DreamWorks SKG as head of the company's urban music division.

Italian director, editor, scriptwriter and actor **Luigi Batzella** died after a long illness on November 18, aged 84. His many "B" movie credits as a film-maker include *The Devil's Wedding Night, Nude for Satan* and *SS Hell Camp*. Under the name "Paolo Solvay" Batzella starred in *Slaughter of the Vampires*, and he appeared uncredited in *The Bloodsucker Leads the Dance*.

Flamboyant British TV director **Robert Tronson** died on November 27, aged 84. He directed five *Edgar Wallace* second features in the early 1960s before moving to television, where his many credits include episodes of *The Avengers*, *Mystery and Imagination* (M. R. James' "Lost Hearts", plus two others), *Randall and Hopkirk (Deceased)*, *The Guardians* and Brian Clemens' *Thriller*.

American film and TV producer **Bill Finnegan**, a co-founder of Finnegan/Pinchuk Priductions, died of Parkinson's disease on November 28, aged 80. He began his career as an assistant director on *The Man from U.N.C.L.E.* (directing the 1967 episode "The Matterhorn Affair"), and went on to work as a producer on such TV films as *Maneaters Are Loose!*, Wes Craven's *Stranger in Our House* (aka *Summer of Fear*), *World War III* and *Babes in Toyland* (1986). He was an executive producer on the early 1990s TV series *She-Wolf of London*, and his movie credits include *Night of the Creeps*.

British writer, producer, director and voice artist **Oliver Postgate**, best remembered as the co-creator with puppeteer Peter Firmin of such children's TV shows as *Noggin the Nog* (1958) and *The Clangers* (1969–71), died on December 8, aged 83. Under their Smallfilms production company, the duo was also responsible for *Ivor the Engine*, *Pogles' Wood* and *Bagpuss*. He was a cousin of actress Angela Lansbury. Postgate's autobiography, *Seeing Things*, was published in 2000.

Dakota Culkin, the 29-year-old sister of actor Macaulay Culkin, died from a massive head trauma on December 10, after being hit by a car in West Los Angeles the day before. She had recently completed work as an art department assistant on the independent movie *Lost Soul* starring Nick Mancuso.

American film and TV director **Robert Mulligan** died of heart disease on December 20, aged 83. He began his career directing thirteen episodes of CBS-TV's *Suspense*, and went on to helm such movies as *To Kill a Mockingbird*, *The Stalking Moon* and *The Other* (based on the novel by Thomas Tryon).

Science fiction conventions would not be the same without 86-year-old **Alfred Shaheen**, who died in California of complications from diabetes on December 22. Shaheen was the man responsible for bringing Hawaiian shirts to the mass-market after Elvis Presley modelled one of his colourful creations on the cover of his 1961 soundtrack album *Blue Hawaii*.

USEFUL ADDRESSES

THE FOLLOWING LISTING of organizations, publications, dealers and individuals is designed to present readers and authors with further avenues to explore. Although I can personally recommend most of those listed on the following pages, neither the publisher nor myself can take any responsibility for the services they offer. Please also note that the information below is only a guide and is subject to change without notice.

—The Editor

ORGANIZATIONS

The Australian Horror Writers' Association (*www.australianhorror. com*) offers members mentoring, articles, competitions, markets, networking . . . and more! For details mail to: Post Office, Elphinstone, VIC 3448, Australia. E-mail: *ahwa@australianhorror.com*

The British Fantasy Society (*www.britishfantasysociety.org*) was founded in 1971 and publishes the bi-monthly newsletter *Prism* and the magazine *Dark Horizons*, featuring articles, interviews and fiction, along with occasional special booklets. The BFS also enjoys a lively online community – there is an e-mail news-feed, a discussion board with numerous links, and a CyberStore selling various publications. FantasyCon is one of the UK's friendliest conventions and there are social gatherings and meet-the-author events organized around Britain. For yearly membership details, e-mail: *secretary@ britishfantasysociety.org.uk*. You can also join online through the Cyberstore.

The Friends of Arthur Machen (*www.machensoc.demon.co.uk*) is a literary society whose objectives include encouraging a wider recognition of Machen's work and providing a focus for critical debate. Members get a hardbound journal, *Faunus*, twice a year, and also the informative newsletter *Machenalia*. For membership details, contact Jeremy Cantwell, FOAM Treasurer, Apt.5, 26 Hervey Road, Blackheath, London SE3 8BS, UK.

The Friends of the Merril Collection (*www.friendsofmerril.org/*) is a volunteer organisation that provides support and assistance to the largest public collection of science fiction, fantasy and horror books in North America. Details about annual membership and donations are available from the website or by contacting The Friends of the Merril Collection, c/o Lillian H. Smith Branch, Toronto Public Library, 239 College Street, 3rd Floor, Toronto, Ontario M5T 1R5, Canada. E-mail: *ltoolis@tpl.toronto.on.ca*

The Ghost Story Society (*www.ash-tree.bc.ca/GSS.html*) is organised by Barbara and Christopher Roden. They publish the excellent *All Hallows* three times a year. For more information contact PO Box 1360, Ashcroft, British Columbia, Canada V0K 1A0. E-mail: *nebuly@telus.net.*

The Horror Writers Association (*www.horror.org*) is a world-wide organisation of writers and publishing professionals dedicated to promoting the interests of writers of Horror and Dark Fantasy. It was formed in the early 1980s. Interested individuals may apply for Active, Affiliate or Associate membership. Active membership is limited to professional writers. HWA publishes a monthly online *Newsletter*, and sponsors the annual Bram Stoker Awards. Apply online or write to HWA Membership, PO Box 50577, Palo Alto, CA 94303, USA.

World Fantasy Convention (*www.worldfantasy.org*) is an annual convention held in a different (usually American) city each year, oriented particularly towards serious readers and genre professionals.

World Horror Convention (*www.worldhorrorsociety.org*) is a smaller, more relaxed, event. It is aimed specifically at horror fans and professionals, and held in a different city each year. For the first time in its history, the 2010 event will be held outside North America in Brighton, England.

SELECTED SMALL PRESS PUBLISHERS

Apex Publications LLC (*www.apexbookcompany.com*), PO Box 24323, Lexington, KY 40524, USA. E-mail: *jason@apexdigest.com*

Ash-Tree Press (*www.ash-tree.bc.ca*), PO Box 1360, Ashcroft, British Columbia, Canada V0K 1A0. E-mail: *ashtree@ash-tree.bc.ca*

Atomic Overmind Press (*www.atomicovermind.com*), 143 Wesmond Drive, Alexandria, VA 22305, USA. E-mail: *theovermind@atomicovermind.com*

Bad Moon Books (*www.badmoonbooks.com*), 1854 W. Chateau Avenue, Anaheim, CA 92804, USA.

Bloody Books (*www.bloodybooks.com*), Beautiful Books Ltd, 36–38 Glasshouse Street, London W1B 5DL, UK.

Cemetery Dance Publications (*www.cemeterydance.com*), 132-B Industry Lane, Unit #7, Forest Hill, MD 21050, USA. E-mail: *info@cemeterydance.com*

Comma Press (*www.commapress.co.uk*), 3rd Floor, 24 Lever Street, Manchester M1 1DW, UK.

Crowswing Books (*www.crowswingbooks.co.uk*), PO Box 301, King's Lynn, Norfolk PE33 0XW, UK.

Cutting Block Press (*www.cuttingblock.net*), 6911 Riverton Drive, Austin, Texas 78729, USA, E-mail: *info@cuttingblock.net*

Dark Regions Press (*www.darkregions.com*), PO Box 1264, Colusa, CA 95932, USA.

Earthling Publications (*www.earthlingpub.com*), PO Box 413, Northborough, MA 01532, USA. E-mail: *earthlingpub@yahoo.com*

Edge Science Fiction and Fantasy Publishing (*www.edgewebsite.com*), PO Box 1714, Calgary, Alberta T2P 2L7, Canada.

F&M Publications (*www.fandmpublications.co.uk*), PO Box 51243, London SE17 3WP, UK. E-mail: *penny@fandmpublications.co.uk*

Fantagraphics Books (*www.fantagraphics.com*), 7563 Lake City Way N.E., Seattle, WA 98115, USA.

Graveside Tales (*www.gravesidetales.com*), PO Box 487, Lakeside, AZ 85929, USA.

Gray Friar Press (*www.grayfriarpress.com*), 19 Ruffield Side, Delph Hill, Wyke, Bradford, West Yorkshire BD12 8DP, UK. E-mail: *g.fry@blueyonder.co.uk*

Hippocampus Press (*www.hippocampuspress.com*), PO Box 641, New York, NY 10156, USA.

Lachesis Publishing (*www.lachesispublishing.com*), 1787 Cartier Court, RR1, Kingston, Nova Scotia B0P 1R0, Canada.

McFarland & Company, Inc., Publishers (*www.mcfarlandpub.com*), Box 611, Jefferson, NC 28640, USA.

Medallion Press, Inc. (www.medallionpress.com), 1020 Cedar Avenue, Suite 2N, St. Charles, IL 60174, USA.

MonkeyBrain Books (*www.monkeybrainbooks.com*), 11204 Crossland Drive, Austin, TX 78726, USA. E-mail: *info@monkeybrainbooks.com.*

Mortbury Press (*www.freewebs.com/mortburypress*), Shiloh,

Nantglas, Llandrindod Wells, Powys LD1 6PG, UK. E-mail: *mortburypress@yahoo.com*

Mythos Books, LLC (*www.mythosbooks.com*), 351 Lake Ridge Road, Poplar Buff, MO 63901, USA.

Night Shade Books (*www.nightshadebooks.com*), 1423 33rd Avenue, San Francisco, CA 94122, USA. E-mail: *night@.nightshadebooks.com*

Pendragon Press (*www.pendragonpress.net*), PO Box 12, Maesteg, Mid Glamorgan, South Wales CF34 0XG, UK.

Pigasus Press (*www.pigasuspress.co.uk*), 13 Hazely Combe, Arreton, Isle of Wight PO30 3AJ, UK. E-mail: *mail@pigasuspress.co.uk*

PS Publishing (*www.pspublishing.co.uk*), Grosvenor House, 1 New Road, Hornsea, East Yorkshire HU18 1PG, UK. E-mail: *editor@pspublishing.co.uk*

Raw Dog Screaming Press (*www.rawdogscreaming.com*), 5103 72nd Place, Hyattsville, MD 20784, USA. E-mail: *books@rawdogscreaming.com*

Savoy Books (*www.savoy.abel.co.uk*), 446 Wilmslow Road, Withington, Manchester M20 3BW, UK. E-mail: *office@savoy.abel.co.uk*

Screaming Dreams (*www.screamingdreams.com*), 13 Warn's Terrace, Abertysswg, Rhymney, Gwent NP22 5AG, UK. E-mail: *steve@screamingdreams.com*

Strange Publications (*www.strangepublications.com*), 3038 West 7th Street, Lawrence, KS 66049, USA. E-mail: *strange.pubs@gmail.com*

Snowbooks Ltd. (*www.snowbooks.com*), 120 Pentonville Road, London N1 9JN, UK. E-mail: *info@snowbooks.com*

Space & Time (*www.cith.org/s&t_books.com*), 138 West 70th Street (4B), New York, NY 10023-4468, USA. E-mail: *glinzner@hotmail.com*

Subterranean Press (*www.subterraneanpress.com*), PO Box 190106, Burton, MI 48519, USA. E-mail: *subpress@earthlink.net*

Tachyon Publications (*www.tachyonpublications.com*), 1459 18th Street #139, San Francisco, CA 94107, USA.

Tartarus Press (*tartaruspress.com*), Coverley House, Carlton-in-Coverdale, Leyburn, North Yorkshire DL8 4AY, UK. E-mail: *tartarus@pavilion.co.uk*

Tasmaniac Publications (*www.tasmaniacpublications.com*), PO Box 45, Hagley. Tasmania 7292, Australia.

Telos Publishing Ltd (*www.telos.co.uk*), 61 Elgar Avenue, Tolworth, Surrey KT5 9JP, UK. E-mail: *feedback@telos.co.uk*

TTA Press (*www.ttapress.com*), 5 Martins Lane, Witcham, Ely, Cambs CB6 2LB, UK.

SELECTED MAGAZINES

Albedo One (*www.albedo1.com*) is a speculative fiction magazine from Ireland. The editorial address is Albedo One, 2 Post Road, Lusk, Co. Dublin, Ireland. E-mail: *bobn@yellowbrickroad.ie*

Alfred Hitchcock Mystery Magazine (*www.themysteryplace.com*) is a long-running digest magazine published monthly except for combined January/February and July/August issues. The editorial address is Dell Magazines, 475 Park Avenue South, New York, NY 10016, USA.

Black: Australian Dark Culture Magazine (*www.blackmag. com.au*) is a pop culture periodical covering books, movies, TV and music. Subscriptions and general information are available from: Brimstone Press, PO Box 4, Woodvale, WA 6026, Australia. E-mail: *mail@brimstonepress.com.au*

Black Gate: Adventures in Fantasy Literature (*www.blackgate. com*) is an attractive pulp-style publication that includes heroic fantasy and horror fiction. Four- and eight-issue subscriptions are available from: New Epoch Press, 815 Oak Street, St. Charles, IL 60174, USA. E-mail: *john@blackgate.com*

Black Static (*www.ttapress.com*) is a British magazine devoted to darker fiction. Published bi-monthly, six- and twelve-issue subscriptions are available from TTA Press, 5 Martins Lane, Witcham, Ely, Cambs CB6 2LB, UK, or from the secure TTA website.

Cemetery Dance Magazine (*www.cemeterydance.com*) is edited by Richard Chizmar and includes fiction up to 5,000 words, interviews, articles and columns by many of the biggest names in horror. For subscription information contact: Cemetery Dance Publications, PO Box 623, Forest Hill, MD 21050, USA. E-mail: *info@cemeterydance.com*

Dark Discoveries (*www.darkdiscoveries.com*) is a nicely produced quarterly magazine devoted to horror fiction and those who create it. For submission queries and subscription orders, contact: Dark Discoveries Publications, 142 Woodside Drive, Longview, WA 98632, USA. E-mail: *info@darkdiscoveries.com*

Dark Recesses Press (*www.darkrecesses.com*), nice-looking print issue of the Canadian web magazine featuring fiction, interviews and artwork. Dark Recesses Press, 18306 64th Avenue, Surrey BC, Canada V3S 8A7. E-mail: *letters@darkrecesses.com*

Locus (*www.locusmag.com*) is the monthly newspaper of the SF/ fantasy/horror field. Contact: Locus Publications, PO Box 13305, Oakland, CA 94661, USA. Subscription information with other rates and order forms are also available on the website. E-mail: *locus@ locusmag.com*

The Magazine of Fantasy & Science Fiction (*www.fsfmag.com*) has been publishing some of the best imaginative fiction for more than fifty years. Edited by Gordon Van Gelder, single copies or an annual subscription (which includes the double October/November anniversary issue) are available by US cheques or credit card from: Fantasy & Science Fiction, PO Box 3447, Hoboken, NJ 07030, USA, or you can subscribe online.

Midnight Street: Journeys Into Darkness (*www.midnightstreet. co.uk*) covers all the bases as a horror, dark fantasy, science fiction and slipstream magazine. Three-issue subscriptions are available from: Midnight Street, 7 Mount View, Church Lane West, Aldershot, Hampshire GU11 3LN, UK. E-mail: *tdenyer@ntlworld.com*

One Eye Grey (*www.fandmpublications.co.uk*) is described as "a penny dreadful for the 21st century" and contains fiction (up to 3,000 words) from another London based on old folktales or ghost stories. F&M Publications, PO Box 51243, London SE17 3WP, UK. E-mail: *penny@fandmpublications.co.uk*

The Paperback Fanatic (*www.thepaperbackfanatic.com*) fascinating magazine dedicated to old paperbacks and the people who produced and published them. With numerous interviews and many cover reproductions. E-mail: *justin@justincultprint.free-online.co.uk*

Paradox: The Magazine of Historical and Speculative Fiction (*www.paradoxmag.com*) is published twice a year by Paradox Publications, PO Box 22897, Brooklyn, NY 11202-2897, USA. E-mail: *editor@paradoxmag.com*

PostScripts: The A to Z of Fantastic Fiction (*www.pspublishing. co.uk*) is an excellent hardcover magazine from PS Publishing. Each issue features approximately 60,000 words of fiction (SF, fantasy, horror and crime/suspense), plus a guest editorial, interviews and occasional non-fiction. Issues are also available as signed, limited editions. For more information contact: PS Publishing Ltd., Grosvenor House, 1 New Road, Hornsea, East Yorkshire HU18 1PG, UK. E-mail: *editor@pspublishing.co*

Rabbit Hole is a semi-regular newsletter about Harlan Ellison. A subscription is $15.00 from The Harlan Ellison Recording Collection, PO Box 55548, Sherman Oaks, CA 91413-0548, USA.

Rue Morgue (*www.rue-morgue.com*), is a glossy bi-monthly magazine edited by Jovanka Vuckovic and subtitled "Horror in Culture & Entertainment". Each issue is packed with full colour features and reviews of new films, books, comics, music and game releases. Subscriptions are available from: Marrs Media Inc., 2926 Dundas Street West, Toronto, ON M6P 1Y8, Canada, or by credit card on the website. E-mail: *info@rue-morgue.com*. *Rue Morgue* also runs the Festival of Fear: Canadian National Horror Expo in Toronto. Every Friday you can log on to a new show at Rue Morgue Radio at *www.ruemorgueradio.com* and your horror shopping on-line source, The Rue Morgue Marketplace, is at *www.ruemorgue marketplace.com*

Something Wicked: Science Fiction & Horror Magazine (*www. somethingwicked.co.za*) South Africa's only horror fiction magazine features tales of darkness and suspense, along with book and media articles. Subscriptions available from Inkless Media, PO Box 15074, Vlaeberg, Cape Town 8018, South Africa. E-mail: *editor@ somethingwiscked.co.za*

Supernatural Tales is a twice-yearly fiction magazine edited by David Longhorn. Three-issue subscriptions are available via post (UK cheques only) or order through the British Fantasy Society Store (*www.britishfantasysociety.org/store*). Supernatural Tales, 291 East-bourne Avenue, Gateshead NE8 4NN, UK. E-mail: *davidlonghorn@ hotmail.com*

Talebones (*www.talebones.com*) is an attractive digest magazine of science fiction and dark fantasy edited and published two to three times a year by Patrick Swenson. For one and two year subscriptions or sample copies (US funds only) write to: 21528 104th Street Court East, Bonney Lake, WA 98391, USA. E-mail: *info@talebones.com*

Weird Tales (*www.weirdtales.net*) is a magazine of the unique, fantastic and bizarre, published by Wildside Press LLC. Single copies or a six-issue subscription are available from: Wildside Press, 9710 Traville Gateway Drive #234, Rockville, MD 20850-7408, USA. E-mail: *info@weirdtales.net*. For subscriptions in the UK contact: Cold Tonnage Books, 22 Kings Lane, Windlesham, Surrey, GU20 6JQ, UK (*andy@coldtonnage.co.uk*).

Writing Magazine (*www.writingmagazine.co.uk*) is the UK's bestselling magazine aimed at writers and poets and those who want to be. It is published by Warners Group Publications plc, 5th Floor, 31-32 Park Row, Leeds LS1 SJD, UK. E-mail: *writingmagazine@warnersgroup.co.uk*

DEALERS

Bookfellows/Mystery and Imagination Books (*www.mysteryand imagination.com*) is owned and operated by Malcolm and Christine Bell, who have been selling fine and rare books since 1975. This clean and neatly organized store includes SF/fantasy/horror/ mystery, along with all other areas of popular literature. Many editions are signed, and catalogues are issued regularly. Credit cards accepted. Open seven days a week at 238 N. Brand Blvd., Glendale, California 91203, USA. Tel: (818) 545-0206. Fax: (818) 545-0094. E-mail: *bookfellows@gowebway.com*

Borderlands Books (*www.borderlands-books.com*) is a nicely designed store with friendly staff and an impressive stock of new and used books from both sides of the Atlantic. 866 Valencia Street (at 19th), San Francisco, CA 94110, USA. Tel: (415) 824-8203 or (888) 893-4008 (toll free in the US). Credit cards accepted. Worldwide shipping. E-mail: *office@borderlands-books.com*

Cold Tonnage Books (*www.coldtonnage.com*) offers excellent mail order new and used SF/fantasy/horror, art, reference, limited editions etc. Write to: Andy & Angela Richards, Cold Tonnage Books, 22 Kings Lane, Windlesham, Surrey GU20 6JQ, UK. Credit cards accepted. Tel: +44 (0)1276-475388. E-mail: *andy@coldtonnage.com*

Dark Delicacies (*www.darkdel.com*) is a friendly Burbank, California, store specializing in horror books, toys, vampire merchandise and signings. They also do mail order and run money-saving book club and membership discount deals. 4213 West Burbank Blvd., Burbank, CA 91505, USA. Tel: (818) 556-6660. Credit cards accepted. E-mail: *darkdel@darkdel.com*

DreamHaven Books (*www.dreamhavenbooks.com*) store and mail order offers new and used SF/fantasy/horror/art and illustrated etc. with regular catalogues (both print and e-mail). Write to new location: 2301 E. 38th Street, Minneapolis, MN 55406, USA. Credit cards accepted. Tel: (612) 823-6070. E-mail: *dream@dreamhaven books.com*

Fantastic Literature (*www.fantasticliterature.com*) mail order offers the UK's biggest online out-of-print SF/fantasy/horror genre bookshop. Fanzines, pulps and vintage paperbacks as well. Write to: Simon and Laraine Gosden, Fantastic Literature, 35 The Ramparts, Rayleigh, Essex SS6 8PY, UK. Credit cards and Pay Pal accepted. Tel/Fax: +44 (0)1268-747564. E-mail: *sgosden@net comuk.co.uk*

Ferret Fantasy, 27 Beechcroft Road, Upper Tooting, London SW17 7BX, UK. George Locke's legendary mail-order business now shares retail premises at Greening Burland, 27 Cecil Court, London WC2N 4EZ, UK (10:00 am–6:00 pm weekdays; 10:00 am–5:00 pm Sundays). Used SF/fantasy/horror, antiquarian, modern first editions. Catalogues issued. Tel: +44 (0)20-8767-0029. E-mail: *george_locke@hotmail.com*

Ghost Stories run by Richard Dalby issues semi-regular mail order lists of used ghost and supernatural volumes at very reasonable prices. Write to: 4 Westbourne Park, Scarborough, North Yorkshire YO12 4AT, UK.

Horrorbles (*www.horribles.com*), 6731 West Roosevelt Road, Berwyn, IL 60402, USA. Small, friendly Chicago store selling horror and sci-fi toys, memorabilia and magazines that has monthly specials and in-store signings. Specializes in exclusive "Basil Gogos" and "Svengoolie" items. Tel: 1-708-484-7370. E-mail: *store@horrorbles.com*

Kayo Books (*www.kayobooks.com*) is a bright, clean treasure-trove of used SF/fantasy/horror/mystery/pulps spread over two floors. Titles are stacked alphabetically by subject, and there are many bargains to be had. Credit cards accepted. Visit the store (Wednesday–Saturday, 11:00 am to 6:00 pm) at 814 Post Street, San Francisco, CA 94109, USA or order off their website. Tel: (415) 749 0554. E-mail: *kayo@kayobooks.com*

Porcupine Books offers regular catalogues and extensive mail order lists of used fantasy/horror/SF titles via e-mail *brian@porcupine.demon.co.uk* or write to: 37 Coventry Road, Ilford, Essex IG1 4QR, UK. Tel: +44 (0)20 8554-3799.

Kirk Ruebotham (*www.abebooks.com/home/kirk61/*) is a mail-order only dealer, who sells out-of-print and used horror/SF/fantasy/crime and related non-fiction at very good prices, with regular catalogues. Write to: 16 Beaconsfield Road, Runcorn, Cheshire WA7 4BX, UK. Tel: +44 (0)1928-560540 (10:00 am–8:00 pm). E-mail: *kirk.ruebotham@ntlworld.com*

The Talking Dead is run by Bob and Julie Wardzinski and offers reasonably priced paperbacks, rare pulps and hardcovers, with catalogues issued occasionally. They accept wants lists and are also the exclusive supplier of back issues of *Interzone*. Credit cards accepted. Contact them at: 12 Rosamund Avenue, Merley, Wimborne, Dorset BH21 1TE, UK. Tel: +44 (0)1202-849212 (9:00 am–9:00 pm). E-mail: *books@thetalkingdead.fsnet.co.uk*

Ygor's Books specializes in out of print science fiction, fantasy and horror titles, including British, signed, speciality press and limited editions. They also buy books, letters and original art in these fields. E-mail: *ygorsbooks@earthlink.net*

ONLINE

All Things Horror (*www.allthingshorror.co.uk*) is a genre interview site run by Johnny Mains that mainly focuses on authors, editors, artists and movie stars of the 1960s, 1970s and 1980s. It also caters to reviews of both films and books, and features a short fiction section that is open to submissions.

Fantastic Fiction (*www.fantasticfiction.co.uk*) features more than 2,000 best-selling author biographies with all their latest books, covers and descriptions.

Pan Book of Horror Stories (*www.panbookofhorrorstories.co.uk*) is a tribute site dedicated to the best-known horror anthology series ever published in the UK. Comprehensive listings of all stories and authors can be found here, along with rare contractual and promotional material that has been gathered together for the first time, giving a unique insight into the series' publishing history.

Hellnotes (*www.hellnotes.com*) is now in its fourteenth year of publication, offering news and reviews of novels, collections, magazines, anthologies, non-fiction works, and chapbooks. Materials for review should be sent to editor and publisher David B. Silva, Hellnotes, 5135 Chapel View Court, North Las Vegas, NV 89031, USA. E-mail: *news@hellnotes.com* or *dbsilva13@gmail.com*

SF Site (*www.sfsite.com*) has been posted twice each month since 1997. Presently, it publishes around thirty to fifty reviews of SF, fantasy and horror from mass-market publishers and some small press. They also maintain link pages for Author and Fan Tribute Sites and other facets including pages for Interviews, Fiction, Science Fact, Bookstores, Small Press, Publishers, E-zines and Magazines, Artists, Audio, Art Galleries, Newsgroups and Writers' Resources. Periodically, they add features such as author and publisher reading lists.

Vault of Evil (*www.vaultofevil.wordpress.com*) is a site dedicated to celebrating the best in British horror with special emphasis on UK anthologies. There is also a lively forum devoted to many different themes at *www.vaultofevil.proboards.com*